THE MONSTER
BARU CORMORANT

THE MONSTER
BARU CORMORANT

SETH DICKINSON

TOR

A TOM DOHERTY ASSOCIATES BOOK
NEW YORK

This is a work of fiction. All of the characters, organizations, and events portrayed in this novel are either products of the author's imagination or are used fictitiously.

THE MONSTER BARU CORMORANT

Map by Gillian Conahan

A Tor Book
Published by Tom Doherty Associates
175 Fifth Avenue
New York, NY 10010

www.tor-forge.com

Tor® is a registered trademark of Macmillan Publishing Group, LLC.

The Library of Congress Cataloging-in-Publication Data is available upon request.

ISBN 978-0-7653-8074-6 (hardcover)
ISBN 978-1-4668-7513-5 (ebook)

Our books may be purchased in bulk for promotional, educational, or business use. Please contact your local bookseller or the Macmillan Corporate and Premium Sales Department at 1-800-221-7945, extension 5442, or by email at MacmillanSpecialMarkets@macmillan.com.

First Edition: October 2018

Printed in the United States of America

0 9 8 7 6 5 4 3 2 1

FOR MARCO

Thanks for waiting

THE STAKHIECZI
NECESSITY

THE GREAT
SAND CHAOS
(UNANOKOMIALYO)

AURDWYNN

THE MAIA PLAINS

TREATYMONT
- fuck this pla[ce]

THE
ASHEN SEA
AND SURROUNDING
LANDS OF
RELEVANCE

a map prepared for
the use of Agonist
in observance of
her ascension

THE ASHEN SEA
- trade circle runs clockwise

CHANSEE
- weird place
- visited cancer ward

THE KRAKEN STILL
- don't sail in here

THE CAMOU
INTERVAL

TARANOKE
- my home
- mother + father

KUTULBHA
- burnt in Armada War
- visit?

LONJARO MBO
- trade crossroads
- so rich
- won't admit they'r[e]
  in charge

SEGU MBO
- Ashen Sea trade
- matrilinear
- very mad at Falcrest
- Aminata's home

STARFALL BAY
– why so round?

DUCHY VULTJAG
– hers   my home

THE NORMARCH
– Ana live here
– marshy + difficult

WELTHONY

Helbride's
course

the Elided Keep

LLOSYDANE
ISLANDS
– Belthyc populace
– date groves

Ascentatic's
Course

ISLA CAUTERIA
– navy fortress here
(Samne Maroyad commands)

wreck

GRENDLAKE

FALCREST

KYPRANANOKE
– smugglers + pirates
– abandoned by Falcrest

○ CITY OF FALCREST
– aka Old King Poison
– endgame

THE BUTTERVELDT
– Falcrest's grain

○ SHAHEEN

THE MOTHER
OF STORMS
east to SUPERCONTINENT
and THE LIGHTNING →

THE OCCUPATION
– Falcrest stole this
– much raiding + unrest

THE TIDE COLUMN
– hold it = power

YAMA
– Oriati port

DEVI-NAGA MBO
– worst storms anywhere
– mothercoast trade
– invented piracy

JARO ◎
– capital of Lonjaro
– gold for salt

south to
MZILIMAKE
MBO

THE MONSTER
BARU CORMORANT

A QUESTION

If something hurts, does that make it true?

PRELUDE

As the firestorm took his ships, as a monsoon rain of greasy incendiaries burnt his people like screaming human skewers, Abdumasi Abd tried his very damnedest to die.

"Fire parties to the port rail!" cried his battle captain, poor Zee Dbellu, who had come to war with Abdumasi to avenge his grandmother. He was a big dreadlocked man with a green flag bound to his war-spear and a false hope in his voice. He was already dead. Abdumasi had to join him.

"Turn the ship to sea!" Zee bellowed. "Run out the sweeps, soak the rowers, beat the drums! We'll get out of this yet, I promise you, I promise!"

The fire parties were all dead. The masts had toppled and the rowers lay suffocated at their broken oars. Masquerade rocket arrows had pinned all the corpses to the deck like rare butterflies.

Abdumasi looked up at Zee from under the fallen sail, where he'd crawled to hide. Beyond Zee he could see a sliver of the battle—burning masts and broken ships, arcs of hwacha-fire scratching terrible perfect curves out of the sky, war rockets that crashed down into wood and waves to bloom into blue-white fire. Dead gulls. Vortices of killed fish. The stink of Falcrest chemistry. The scream of fire and the groan of broken hullplanks and beneath it all the ebb and rush of the sea, tumbling the burning dead, stirring the pot of fire and wreckage.

A disaster. A catastrophe. And he had ordered it.

He'd brought his fleet to Aurdwynn to help their rebellion against the Masquerade. He'd joined the rebel armada at Welthony and together they'd struck Treatymont, the colonial capital: a gray cage of ironwork and stone to the north, and two burnt-out towers guarding the harbor like rotten dog teeth.

But the Masquerade had been waiting for them.

"Zee," Abdumasi whispered, "I'm so sorry."

And he put his sailing knife under his chin and tried to cut his own throat. He couldn't do it. He was too afraid.

"Abdumasi!" Zee howled. "Abdu, where are you? We need you!"

Zee had gone mad when he realized they'd sailed into a trap. Abd saw it happen in his eyes, a meaty *pop* like a knuckle of lamb in the fire, and from that moment on Zee was mad with among, the rescue-fever that came over Oriati people, sometimes, when their friends and family needed them. A noble madness, the poets said, the best madness, who would not be glad to die in the throes of among?

At burnt Kutulbha, where Abdumasi's mother had died (now he sent his apologies to his mother Abdi-obdi with all his hopeless heart) whole mobs of good Oriati people had organized themselves with wet blankets and protective taboos and marched into the firestorm devouring the city, sworn to rescue parents, children, pets, books. There was no hope, of course. Falcrest's Burn munitions had created a wildfire so fierce that it sucked in the air from miles around, like a demon mouth in the city's heart, inhaling souls. No one rescued anyone. All perished. At the end of that day twenty-three years ago the rain fell on burnt Kutulbha and turned the mud and corpse-ash into concrete, and to this day Kutulbha was a gray disc on the coast of the Oriati Mbo, a dark mortar full of bone.

Into that mortar the Falcresti had inscribed two words in their dull blocky script: THE ARC OF HISTORY.

That horror was what Abdumasi had come to avenge—

—he had *begged* his fellow Oriati, the Federal Princes and the jackal soldiers, to come to the aid of the rebel accountant Baru Cormorant and her Coyotes. Together they might tear Aurdwynn entirely out of Falcrest's grasp, pincering the tyrants from north and south—

—but the Princes would not act, the jackal soldiers would not send a fleet, they were terrified of open war, so fuck it, Abdumasi Abd decided to spend his fortune and raise a war fleet himself—

—which was why he had to die, now, right away, no procrastination, no excuses, no second chances. For if the Falcresti captured Abd alive, if they tricked him into admitting who he was (a merchant of great fame) and who'd sponsored his fleet (don't even *think* of them, Abd!—but he could not resist the terrible prayer, ayamma, ayamma, a ut li-en) then Falcrest would extract the truth from him.

His ships were not just pirates come to pillage a disordered city but an invasion force backed by secret and terrible powers.

Then Falcrest's unctuous ambassadors would slither up to the Princes of Oriati Mbo and say, *O kind neighbors, here we have found an influential and great man, a man who somehow misplaced himself into our sovereign waters—but it seems he conspired against our Imperial Republic. Listen, listen: he has confessed everything.*

We must have reparations, or there will be war. . . .

And no matter whether the Oriati chose reparations or war, no matter whether Falcrest attacked them with fire or (far more dangerous) sly schools and clever market games, the Oriati would be destroyed. Abdumasi would bring down doom on the two hundred million people of the Oriati Mbo, the heart of the world, his beloved home.

"Abd!" Zee roared, waving his green flag with both hands. "Abd, come to me! We have to rally the ships! We have to go!"

"I need last words," Abdumasi whispered to himself—that was why he couldn't cut his throat! He needed brave last words to inspire those who remembered him. "What shall I say? You'll never take me alive?" He curled up beneath the toppled sail and tried to get his last words just right. "You'll *never* take me alive. You'll never take *me* alive. *You'll* never take me alive! All right. Fuck. Fuck fuck fuck." He got his hands under him, crouched, tried to fill his head with happy memories—Tau and Kindalana in the lake of drugged cranes, Tau helping him steal honey from Kindalana's house, all three of them watching Cosgrad Torrinde stagger around high as balls after he licked a frog—"Fuck! Do it. Do it! Death and glory!"

Snarling in defiance, he leapt out from under the sailcloth, his rapier loose in his right hand. "Abdumasi!" Zee cried in mad delight, and behind him the dromon *Bred For Laughs* exploded in a huge crack of powder as Falcrest fire found her store of mines. The thunder drowned out Zee's words— Abdumasi saluted him with the rapier, and leapt up onto the ship's fighting rail to plunge to his death.

"You'll never take me alive!" he roared, and then he made the awful mistake of looking down before he leapt.

The sea burnt beneath him.

Blue-hot chemical fire simmered on the waves, vicious, viscous, burning everything, cooking up a sauté smell of seawater and charred lumber and boiled fat bursting out through blistered dead skin and incinerated hair, popped eyeballs, chips of toenail off bloated feet; the mortal remains of forty-one shipfuls of Abdumasi's crews tossed into a fucking wok and stir-fried—

Abdumasi couldn't jump into that.

Not even if he imagined Kindalana shoving him, not even if he pictured Tau-indi down in the flame urging him on, not even then could he jump. Call him a coward and a traitor to two hundred million people, but there are limits to courage, there are footnotes to the code of bravery, and fire is the first of them.

"Death and glory!" Zee shouted, waving his battle flag, and caught up in among madness he jumped up alongside Abdumasi and leapt over the rail.

"No!" Abdumasi screamed, "Zee, *wait!*"

But too late, gravity had him, a graceful dive and Zee went down through the gel and came up again coated in flame, the Burn sticking to him everywhere as if it smelled Oriati flesh and *hated* it, and it burnt even underwater, it fed on the air in his clothes. He screamed soundlessly because the fire was eating all the air that came out of him. He screamed with his face tipped back to the sky, and the Burn went down his throat.

With a sob of shame Abdumasi fell backward off the rail and fled into the burning mess of his war-dromon's deck. He was too scared to die like that, and fuck the griots who'd blame him for not jumping, they weren't staring down into that hell, were they?

"You'll never take me alive!" he wailed, trying to think. He couldn't see anyone else up on deck who might be convinced to kill him—and anyway they loved him too much, the poor fools, they *believed* in him. There was no time for poison. He could hang himself. Or he could fall on his sword, if he could aim it right—

Or he could die in combat, like a proper champion.

Abdumasi raised up his head and looked for the enemy.

Tall redsailed Falcrest frigates circled the burning slick of Oriati meat and charcoaled mast. They looked like bloody gulls, lazy on the wind, greedy for carnage.

Abdu held out his rapier and apologized to it. "Well, Kindalana, you were right. It *was* a trap. I love you, I'm sorry, and please give Tau my apologies."

So much for his plan to help liberate Aurdwynn. So much for Baru Cormorant, the great hope of the people. So much for the seed of immortality growing in Abdu's back. It would never carry his soul down through millennia.

He'd sold his body to that hidden power for nothing.

Oh, it wasn't *fair!* Of course the world could be cruel, but couldn't it at least be equitable in its cruelty? If you gave up your soul, if you abandoned those you loved to secure a greater freedom, weren't you owed a reward?

"Sir!" someone roared—the renegade jackal soldier, Prepare-Captain Minubo of the House Burun. "Mister Abd, sir, they're coming aboard!"

She stood by the stern rail, pointing with her sword into the inferno—and there through the fire came a Masquerade frigate. It had an abstract human body as its figurehead, carved of facets and planes, the body a wedge, the eyes two candle-flames. The smoke parted around a complexity of ropes and sails that Abdumasi couldn't comprehend: mystic geometries of canvas and hemp, receding into the smog.

"You'll never take me alive?" Abdumasi said, hopefully.

And he raised up his rapier Kindalana, named, because of its keen point and difficult grip, after his ex-wife.

Up on the frigate's bow, red-masked figures turned a hwacha on its pivot to point at Minubo. The mechanism sparked and smoked and, with a hideous buzz like a very troubled hornet, the hwacha fired a quarter of a hundred rocket arrows at the poor prepare-captain, who leapt for cover, and died with steel through her neck and chest. And then Abdumasi *was* ready to die in defiant battle because fuck them, fuck their smug mechanisms and their neat little ambushes, fuck the *impudence* of those who believed they could trick and control the thousand-year Mbo, and fuck them in particular for shooting down the prepare-captain, who had given up her career to follow Abdumasi, like she were just a mangy dog.

From the rigging of the enemy frigate, Falcresti marines swung down onto Abdumasi's ship.

Abdumasi of the house of Abd put up his rapier and advanced. Behind the marines their sleek ship caught on fire: a wave had splashed some Burn up onto the deck. Masked and hooded sailors ran around pouring jars of their own stale piss on the catchfire.

"That's right!" Abdumasi yelled, banging his rapier's hilt on the steel bands of a smashed barrel. "Some navy, fighting with your own bottled piss! I bet you drink it, too! I bet you gulp your own piss down and beg for seconds! Come on, take out your little knives! Have at you! Have at you! I am Abdumasi of the House of Abd, master of ships, champion cat gambler, and I challenge you to mortal up-fuckery!"

Six Masquerade marines stared back at him. Red masks stuffed with chemical filters against the smoke. Armored bodies webbed with grenades and devices. Eyes invisible behind dark inhuman lenses as omniscient and indifferent as krakenfly eyes. Abdumasi beckoned to them, joyful, light with the promise of a swift end and a long rest. He could take them on one by one until at last they had to shoot him with their crossbows as they'd shot poor Minubo. Abdumasi had ten years under a swordmaster and four years of real combat— first in the deep Mzilimake Mbo jungle, then out on the Mothercoast, where Falcrest had given the Invijay ships to use for piracy, and Abdumasi had sailed to hunt them down. He might have been born a merchant, but he'd learned how to make men bleed.

The marine with the black slash of an officer across his mask yanked a gas grenade off the rip ring at his chest. The mechanism failed. The grenade's chemicals didn't burn, nothing happened.

"Good one!" Abdumasi jeered, leaping over bodies, kicking aside splintered

wood, nimble and free with his rapier. He'd dance around these brutes, he'd
poke them to death, quick-footed, hadn't Kindalana loved the grace of his dancing? "Can't start your fire? Don't be embarrassed! Happens to the best of us!
Come on over here, I'll show you a weapon that always works! I am Abdumasi
of the House of Abd, of Jaro the Flamingo Kingdom, of the Einkorn Crop of
Lonjaro Mbo the Thirteen-in-Three-in-One, and I came to kill cuge like you!"

The marine officer shrugged. He said something in Aphalone so muffled by
his mask that Abdumasi heard it only as a low sinister diagnosis: *the patient is
dead.*

The rest of the marines walked straight at Abd, shoulder to shoulder,
crouched a little against the roll of the ship.

"Sophisticated Masquerade tactics!" Abdumasi bellowed, as a huge sheet of
fire roared up across the sea behind him, a slick of leaked cooking oil catching
alight. "Come on, form an orderly queue, who wants it first, my blade is lined
with moral fiber and if I prick you you'll realize what a *thug* you are! Form a—"

The first marine proceeded straight onto his sword.

Abdumasi stabbed him in the eye and the point of his faithful rapier skittered sideways off the marine's steel-masked cheek to stick in his shoulder rig,
where the man grabbed the blade in his glove, hooked it on knuckle claws, and
twisted till the rapier bent.

"Fuck," Abd said, in bemusement.

He went for his belt knife. The marines were too quick. The first studded
punch hit like a shot of tequila and Abd went down on the pitching deck under
stamping feet and steel truncheons. For a few moments he felt like the lead
drum at his own funeral. Flesh pulped. Bone cracked. Abdumasi crawled inside himself like a turtle and tried to dream of sunny days on Lake Jaro. But
the lake boiled, and the imaginary cranes impaled him on their beaks, and
then the marines beat the memory right out of him.

When they let up he threw his last defiance at them.

"Ayamma," he whispered, and then, shouting into the face of the man cuff-
ing him, into the indifferent red masks and the sea of burning corpses and the
whole tyrannical fucking design of Falcrest and its faceless Emperor, shouting
with the terrible bargain he'd made because it was all he had left, "I am a thousand lives, you poor fools, it grows in me, a ut li-en, I have the immortata, *the
cancer grows!*"

In Aphalone the marine asked his officer, "What the fuck is he saying?"

"Tunk superstition, I suppose." The officer opened a cloth sack. "He's their
leader. He goes straight to Province Admiral Ormsment for debriefing."

Desperately Abdumasi pronounced the words of ruin. His friends had told him these words were a curse, they'd tried to keep him from this lonely fate, why hadn't he *listened*—because he couldn't watch as his home was rotted away by cowards and quislings—and so he said the words that would sever him from the human community for all time and make him into a seeping wound of grief and horrible lonely power.

"Ayamma," he whispered, "ayamma, ta ao-ath onvastai-ash e ser o-en incrisiath—"

The marine officer put a bag over Abdumasi's head. He heard the *crack* of a dose bottle, and then the marine poured a cold sweet chemical through the sack. Abd's nose tickled and went dead as rubber. Was it ether? Tsusenshan? He didn't know, he couldn't remember how to breathe to fight it off—

An octopus-kiss of absence crept over Abdumasi. He fumbled around, trying to find his ruined rapier, so he could hold something named Kindalana, but his hands wouldn't answer.

He hadn't managed to die. He'd let everyone down.

At least it wasn't the fire. At least it wasn't the fire.

ACT ONE

THE FALL OF THE ELIDED KEEP

In the Ruin of Them

A T sunrise Baru shackled the prisoner for her drowning.

The Duchess Tain Hu smelled of brine and cold stone and the onions of her last meal. Last night they'd made their covenant. Until the dawn hours Tain Hu had whispered hoarse strategy to Baru: the names of her agents, and the shape of her plans. She gave Baru her arsenal, and her hope, and her faith.

"Remember. Remember the man in the iron circlet, and the ledger of secrets."

"I will remember," Baru hissed through raw-bitten lips. "I will."

Now Baru came close to offer her the manacles that would kill her. And the air between them shivered, like steppe grass under silver cloud, with the charge of their grief and their resolve.

Tain Hu shrugged into her chains. Tested the steel. "Good metal." She rolled her shoulders. "It'll hold."

She grinned and Baru couldn't stand that grin on that fierce unbreakable face. She stepped closer, quick, like an assassin gutting the duchess, and with her right hand she grabbed a fistful of Hu's hair. Into her ear Baru whispered one word in Urun, the tongue of Tain Hu's blood. Piercing. Like an eagle's kiss. Her lip brushed Hu's earlobe and they touched for the last time:

"My general."

And with grim joy Tain Hu whispered back: "Long live the queen."

"Congratulations on your victory," Baru said, and she spread her hands a little, as if saying, look at me, I am your victory, are you pleased?

"I wish you'd done it sooner," Tain Hu murmured.

And everyone but Baru misunderstood her, everyone but Baru saw Tain Hu wishing the betrayal had come more quickly, and not the kiss. Only Baru saw the bitter love behind the bitter smile.

The Elided Keep's silent marines took Tain Hu down to the drowning-stone and chained her up for the judgment of the moon and stars. The tide would come in, like history, and swallow the traitor. Just as Falcrest would in time swallow the world—unless Baru Cormorant kept Tain Hu's faith, and disemboweled the empire from within.

Good-bye, Baru thought. Good-bye, kuye lam. I will write your name in the ruin of them. I will paint you across history in the color of their blood.

THE Duchess of Vultjag went down roaring defiance.

She fought the rising tide with her chains wrapped up around her brawny arms and battlehacked fists. She wrestled the eyebolts and the pulleys drilled into the black rock. And she roared defiance against the Empire of Masks, the Imperial Republic of Falcrest, the Masquerade that pronounced death by drowning upon the traitor. The surf swallowed her. Still the chains groaned with her might. Still the sea frothed with her bellows.

She chose when and where she would die. She chose the meaning of her death, and she chose the method. Rare is that gift, isn't it? Rare is the choice to write the end of your own story.

So the end of her story is the beginning of another.

Not the story of Baru Cormorant, the girl who watched Masquerade merchanters coming down the reefs off Taranoke, and wondered why her fathers were afraid. Not the story of Baru Cormorant, the brilliant furious young woman who accepted the Masquerade's bargain: join Tain Hu's rebellion, gather all our enemies together, and betray them to us. Then we will give you the power to rule your own home.

Not even the story of Baru Fisher, the rebel queen who was, for one bitter winter and brief spring, Tain Hu's lord and lover.

No.

This is the story of Agonist.

Baru Cormorant as a cryptarch: secret lord of the Imperial Throne.

THE pale man with the rowan-red hair oversaw the execution. He had a stylus and a varnished writing-board, and a form clasped in a steel folio, a form for Baru to sign after she screamed for mercy. His name was Apparitor and he was there to answer when Baru begged. *Let the duchess live! Please, I love her, let her live!*

Then he would show her the writ of deferment.

I, Baru Cormorant, do order a stay of execution for the traitor Tain Hu,

And I do acknowledge that I order this stay in defiance of Imperial law, granted only by the extraordinary privilege of the Emperor, whose name cannot be known.

And I remand Tain Hu to the Emperor's custody, where her execution shall remain in abeyance so long as I provide faithful service,

And I do consent to whatever operations and interventions the Emperor sees fit to improve the prisoner's well-being.

Signed—

But there would never be a signature. Baru never cried out for mercy, for mercy was not in Tain Hu's battle plan. Thus Baru drowned her beloved field-general in the morning tide.

This will be her legend. Listen, listen, do you know?

No living thing ever defeated Tain Hu in battle. Only the tide could fight her. Only the moon and the sea together could bring her down.

NOW only the rush of the waves and the cry of the shorebirds. Baru closed her eyes and felt the slam of the surf in her ears and heart. There were birds above, a great whirl of them, as if in her passage Tain Hu's soul had called up a maelstrom of wings.

Baru wouldn't look at the damn birds. Red-haired Apparitor paced and fretted behind her, and Baru thought he was waiting for her to look up from Tain Hu and count the birds. He thought it was Baru's tell. A sign that she was lying.

He wanted Baru to betray her horror.

Well, she'd vomit on him before she looked up.

"All right, then!" Baru clapped her hands, twice, briskly. There was a high ringing inside her, like a bell struck with steel, not quite hard enough to shatter. When Hu was giving her riding lessons she'd fallen and hit the stone, breath crushed out of her, a giddy emptiness, *something huge has happened but I can't feel it yet.*

Oh, my lady Vultjag, how will I do this? How can I carry this weight?

"All right?" Apparitor croaked. "All right *what*?"

She looked at Apparitor sideways, slyly. She had to pretend to be untouched by the execution, so that she *could* be untouched by the execution. For what, in the end, was the difference between pretending perfectly to feel something, and actually feeling it? If you acted the same way, truth or lie?

"All right," Baru said, "I want to start learning my new powers. And issuing some edicts: I like edicts. Let's do it over breakfast."

"Breakfast? You're *hungry*?"

"Yes?" She offered him a gracious arm. "Will you walk with me?"

Apparitor burst into rage.

"You killed her! I can't believe you killed her!" He ripped the handkerchief off his neck, and the grief-knot at his throat came undone at the slightest pull, which a grief-knot should, that was the whole reason sailors called them grief-knots. He waved the silk at Baru like he was trying to wipe her up.

"Baru Cormorant, you fucking asshole, do you realize what you've done?"

Oh, I realize, oh gods, I realize nothing else! I killed her for political advantage! She could have lived and *I did not let her live*! What am I, Apparitor, what slithering beast could do this thing I've done?

Her mask *almost* slipped. She almost stared at Apparitor wild-eyed and screamed a high meaningless note. But it would not do. It would not do. She couldn't grieve now, she couldn't let herself be sorry. Tain Hu was counting on her. When you are disemboweled in battle, you tie your guts up tight, and you keep fighting. Later the wound can kill you. Once you've won.

Baru set off toward the Elided Keep. Listen: her boots crushed snail shells into the rock. When things break underfoot, you know that you are going forward.

"I know what I've done," she said. "I executed a traitor to the Imperial Republic and an obstacle to the progress of humanity."

"You executed your *lover*!"

"Are we sentimental people now? Is that the new game?"

"The *game*? Do you think I didn't care about that woman? She was my prisoner for weeks, she was brave, she was *good*—" Apparitor grabbed himself by the skull, his fingers spidered in his hair, his thumbs trembling on his chin. "Farrier taught you to do this, didn't he? That bastard Itinerant! He made you kill her!"

Baru laughed in shock. Her patron Farrier? How could Tain Hu's execution possibly work in his favor?

Apparitor was panicking. What a stupid fucking idea.

"I haven't seen Cairdine Farrier in some years," she said. "Since my first days as Imperial Accountant, actually. Come along, now. I need you to teach me my powers."

Everyone had strung out behind Baru like autumn geese, straggling and confused, asking each other what to do. The marines with their polearms, the spies who'd pretended to be Baru's staff, Apparitor's little retinue and his gold-eyed concubine boy. All of them began to follow her down the stone ridge, back to the Elided Keep. They were all watching her when she skidded to a stop in shock.

A ship had capsized against her fortress.

Oh—it was Apparitor's clipper. At high tide the crew must've used winches on the Elided Keep's battlement to tip the ship over, careening it on the beach. She was called *Helbride*, a ghost sliver of white wood and slim steel. Now the crew swarmed over her to clear the barnacles and foulage.

A gloved and masked sailor at the stern pulled a two-foot-long and squirming shipworm from the keel. Three huge teeth like half-shells flashed in the morning light. They ate ships; a nest of them must have gotten through the copper worm-armor.

That's me now, Baru thought. The worm beneath the armor.

Apparitor, dully: "She said you loved her." He was staring at his overturned ship as if he wanted very badly to push it back upright and sail away with the tide.

"Ah," Baru sighed, "well, I'm sure she had a great many strange ideas about me."

"She could've lived . . ."

"No. She was guilty of treason. Anyway, you would have kept her in a cell, and tested her to madness." Baru talked to Apparitor but she was speaking to herself, trying to bargain down her scream. "This was the most humane option."

Humane. The word you use when you put down an animal. Why would she compare Hu to an animal? That was the wrong word. The wrong word.

"She certainly loved you," Apparitor said, with terrible resignation. "I'm sure of it."

"Oh, I slept with her once. Hardly a marriage."

"Fuck you," he said.

To lie like this! To lie about Tain Hu, about what lived between them! It was so anathema and yet so necessary: it felt like a razor unraveling her, one cut all the way from her anus to the back of her neck, degloving her whole body and turning her inside out so her secrets were on the outside to become her lies. "I was curious about her, and I always satisfy my curiosity. But of course it didn't last. Isn't that the nature of love between women? Unnatural and transient?"

Apparitor slugged her.

She deserved it, she *did* deserve it, she greeted his pale fist with her cheek and her upturned face. His knuckles tore the tip of her nose and Baru's body fired Naval System combat reflexes like lines of rocket fuel igniting—brace your back foot! Roll with the hit! Eyes open, Baru, no matter how much it hurts you keep your eyes open.

You watch the strike come in.

TRUTH, as hard as the fist:
Apparitor had his own lovers. He'd confessed it to Baru: *sodomites get hot iron, but we do not envy tribadists the knife.* And he remembered his men

fondly, too. When she'd awakened from her coma after Sieroch, she'd seen him drawing a beautiful Stakhi man, nude, brooding. He drew men differently than the classicists. He put more thought in their faces.

Apparitor could never have killed his lover.

That was why the Throne possessed him, the way it possessed parents who couldn't drown their illicit children in vinegar, seditionists who couldn't recant their books and smash the presses, religionists who refused to abandon their gods.

Falcrest offered its Imperial agents a beautiful poisonous choice: a life of blackmail and control, or the death of your dearest deepest reason to exist.

Damn them. Damn them damn them damn them. Baru called on all the powers she could name for their damnation. Caldera gods, I am your daughter Baru, and I beseech you to awaken your molten stone and burn them. O ykari Himu, and Wydd, and Devena who stands between you, I call on your high virtues to punish Falcrest with storm, and with cancer, and with the excess of moderation which is called weakness.

Tain Hu wanted to live a free life.

Falcrest could not abide it.

So they decided to make Hu's life into an instrument of control over Baru.

But Tain Hu would not allow it. Tain Hu would not be an armature of slavery.

And now Baru had entered the innermost circle of Imperial power without any hostage to control her.

Oh gods, Hu, I cannot believe what we've done. I cannot believe what I must do next. And yet I am . . . I am *exultant*. I am so excited to challenge the power that rules us. I am so excited to become that power.

This is my life's work and at last now it has begun in earnest.

Baru turned her stinging face to Apparitor, and the man flickered back into her awareness, like the memory of some childhood embarassment springing up uncalled for, as he passed across her midline from blind right to living left.

"I'll forgive that," she said, calmly, "on account of your masculine passions."

"You don't believe it," he snarled. He'd hurt his hand on her face and now he was wringing it pathetically. "You don't really believe all that Incrastic nonsense about *degenerate mating*—you can't really believe it? A woman from Taranoke?"

"You and I," she said, spitting blood, grinning at him red-toothed, "you and I will be great colleagues, don't you think?"

"Tell me," he said, pleading now, "that you don't believe it?"

"Raise the corpse," Baru ordered. "Chop up the meat and scatter it for the gulls."

Apparitor pulled her around so hard she almost fell again. Her blindness—half the world, her entire right hemisphere, hidden from her awareness by a blow to the brain—swept south and then east, blotting out the ocean toward Taranoke her home, and then Oriati Mbo, and at last Falcrest, the heart of the Imperial Republic. Baru imagined her emptiness covering them, spreading, down past Oriati Mbo through the barrier jungles to Zawam Asu and out then into the sky and across the stars.

Apparitor started to shake her, wide-eyed and furious, that pale freckled face of his high with blood-color. He smelled of fresh laundry. He said, "She deserves a funeral!"

"Traitors don't get funerals."

"Then an autopsy! Surely her traits should be recorded—"

"We've nothing to learn from traitors. Cut her up for the birds." When the marines hesitated, Baru spread her hands, palms up, *who am I, have you forgotten*? "I said cut her up!"

Not even in death would Tain Hu serve Falcrest: not even as a pickled specimen or an entry in a catalogue of mental deformity. Baru would never let them map the rot of her body, never let them say, *decomposition began in her liver, which had struggled to contain her sin. . . .*

No. Let Tain Hu be laid to rest the way Baru's parents taught her. Let the birds scatter her across earth and sky. That's how the Taranoki give their beloved dead back to the world. Ah, Baru, do you remember the ragged pink guts of your grandmother Pahaeon, carved with shell knives, salted with the iron salt, scattered across Halae's Reef for the gulls and the colorful fish? You were a little girl when Pahaeon died, and you didn't understand: that, more than loss, made you sob.

But a cormorant called to you across Pahaeon's funeral, and you stopped crying.

Baru remembered. She remembered all her dead.

"I'm going back to my keep," she told Apparitor. "Bring me a map of the world and the laws of my new power. And your boy, to write down my orders."

"Your *orders*?"

"Of course." She showed him her perfect bloody Incrastic teeth. "I'm not finished with Aurdwynn."

IT was her fucking fortress: they'd told her so when she arrived, the exiles and condemned intellects who staffed this gray redoubt. *For the duration of your stay, you are lord and master of the Elided Keep.*

"What are you all waiting for?" she barked at the crowd of clerks and housekeepers peering through the bars of the tall, narrow portcullis. "The traitor's dead. Now we work!"

A murmur rushed through the masked assembly. Dead? How could she be dead? She was the hostage. . . .

Was it, Baru wondered, the very first time a candidate had refused the bargain? How often had these walls of sloped granite looked down on mothers who begged for the lives of their bastard sons? Had the fortress stared, angular and indifferent, as candidates for the Throne admitted every kind of guilt to every sort of charge—the authorship of seditious texts, the exchange of illegal monies, adoption of a forbidden child, a murder of passion, an addiction to narcotics, religious rapture, royal ancestors, incest, incoherence of thought, the scars of self-abasement, profit off a great disaster, predatory moneylending, a taste for violence, perjury, perversion of a trial, visions, seizures, unfulfilled vengeance—

How many newcomers had stood at these galleries? Falcrest had destroyed King IV Asric Falkarsitte a hundred and thirty years ago. Had the Throne existed ever since?

The keep didn't remember. She was sure of it. These walls had been washed by time and chemistry, stains of gray acid, laundry effluent, bleached mortar, burnt stone from ancient siege—scoured, again and again, of their history. Maybe this place predated the Throne. Maybe it had been a redoubt of the old royalty, the House of Antlers, before Lapetiare's revolution destroyed them: a retreat on foreign shores. . . .

But she was certain this place didn't know. It only had a ringing antimemory, the opposite of a past. It was used to make futures now.

She came through the small door (no one had moved to open it for her), among her watching staff. They stared at her.

"Go on," she said, gently. As if they were the ones she'd hurt. "I want breakfast for two in the morning-room, and space cleared for a floor map."

A cook dusted her floured hands on her apron, and a great puff of powder shot up into the sunbeams. The motes danced. "My lady," she said, "we had it set for three, shall we clear the third place?"

Baru nearly shattered. Shall we clear Tain Hu's place? No, she would say, no, leave it, leave her empty chair: she would stand there weeping silently while they watched her and understood. "I lied," she'd tell them, "I wanted to be free of your control, so I had her executed, oh, what have I done?" And they would comfort her as they brought the poison cup, the blade, the slim garrote.

She said: "Leave the prisoner's seat. It'll make an interesting conversation

piece. I have the sense, from your reaction, that I was meant to fail this test. Will anyone confirm that for me?"

No one would.

"Then go!" she snapped. "And serve me fresh code seals with breakfast. I have letters to write!"

They scattered in silence. One more time she wondered: how many of her predecessors had vowed, in secret, to defy their masters? None had succeeded. Or, worse, they had all succeeded, all of them defiant, all of their defiance expected and incorporated into the Throne's victory.

Baru had only one weapon they'd lacked.

Tain Hu.

Remember that name. Pronounce it in a special way, so that it repeats itself: Tain leads to Hu and Hu leads to Tain, and you never forget her, she loops through your mind like a cant of resistance, now and always she is chained starving and ferocious to the rock-face of your memory and she heaves you forward by the manacles of her death.

Tain Hu.

You will destroy the Imperial Republic of Falcrest. You will liberate the world.

Tain Hu wills it.

And something rushed at Baru from her blindness—

SHE whirled, desperate, doomed—how had they decided so *fast*—the assassin came at her swift, elusive, a flicker of bird-wing shadow in twilight, the Throne's answer for the cryptarch who refused to be bound—she tried to run, she tried to draw her boarding saber and stop-thrust the phantom through the breast—but she wasn't wearing her sword, and as her turn and her failed draw put her off-balance she tripped on her cloak and fell on her ass.

No one there.

Baru groaned and rolled onto her stomach. With willfully bleak humor (probing the wound, trying to pinch shut the vein) she thought, oh, I am glad Hu can't see her last hope now.

"My lady Cormorant?"

Baru yelled and spun on her ass. It was only Apparitor's little golden-eyed Oriati concubine, coming in from the shore and the harbor. "Are you all right?" he asked.

"I don't know," she said, irritably, "that depends on you, really, are you here to try to seduce me again?"

He protected his throat with a soft calfskin glove. Yesterday Baru had pinned him against a stone battlement and choked him. "No, my lady. My lord Apparitor sent me to ask you which map you want prepared in the morning-room."

Oh, the poor boy. She shouldn't lash out at him (had to learn, immediately, how to wield her power carefully). He'd probably been torn away from friends and family, initiated into service as a boy, dragged around the world on Apparitor's missions—rather like Muire Lo.

The flinch she felt at that name got her to her feet. "The map, yes. We'll be discussing Aurdwynn. Get one of the full-rug maps, the sort we can walk on."

"Aurdwynn, mam? You're certain?"

"Absolutely." Baru scuffed her boots on the marble, tugged her belt, adjusted her collar, and shot her cuffs. "It's time to reward them for their return to our care. Ease off the lash. Give them a little"—*slack on their chains*—"honey for their table."

What was his name anyway? Irashee? Irama?

"My lord suggests a map that will show you the full span of your new dominion."

"Does he?" Baru stretched her locked hands over her head, and yawned mightily. She was pleased, a little, when the boy's attention wandered down her jacket and waistcoat: not because she cared about his tastes, but because his dark gold-flecked eyes were like Tain Hu's. "What map is that?"

Iraji. That was his name. Iraji of the oyaSegu tribe.

"A map of the world, my lady," Iraji said. He blinked at her, softly, and she saw that he had a mind for spying, a polite and empathetic cunning which could be turned to wound or weal. "You are exalted now. You must consider the mosaic, not the stone."

INCARNATION

SHE came into her morning-room, where, before the ship and Tain Hu and the test, she'd read and written and then torn up all she wrote. Hard morning light came down through the hive window: teeth of fine thick glass in an iron truss and a clear scouring luminance, Incrastic, virtuous. Like the chimes of the proctors at the Iriad school, calling the girls out for dawn inspection.

Baru went into the little pit commode and vomited in grief.

When she came out, rinsed and empty, wanting strong whiskey to clear the taste off the back of her tongue, a map of the world had been laid out across the smooth dry floor.

She circled it in awe. Wine and no sleep gave her a singing headache: she felt brightly, tenuously alive. "Taranoke," she said, determined to keep that name alive and spoken. "Taranoke . . . there you are."

Beginning at her home, she surveyed the map.

And for the first time in her life the world revealed itself to her. Not the ring of the Ashen Sea, which you could see in any gazetteer, but the full sweep of the globe from end to endless end. Baru gasped in delight, and covered her mouth.

"It's so *blue,*" she said. "I thought there'd be more land."

Apparitor spoke from her blindness. "Eight parts water and two parts land, we think."

"Has Falcrest surveyed it all?"

"Not all. Not the poles, though the ana-folk say you can walk across the ice all the way to the lodepoint. And the south? Who knows. The Oriati, maybe. We've never managed an expedition past Zawam Asu, into anterior seas or the western oceans. They sell us charts but it might all be fancy. Whale queendoms and the like. Creatures with tongues as long as kraken arms."

"We used to think," Baru whispered, "on Taranoke, I mean—there was a blue hole, that's like an underwater well—"

"I know them," he said. "Horrifying pits."

"I swam in it," Baru protested. "We called it the Navel."

"Pit seeks pit, I suppose." But he was staring at her. Wondering, maybe, where the executioner had gone.

She said, in a rush, "And we'd say the Navel was the lowest place in the world. That's why all the rivers converged on the Ashen Sea. And if you went out far enough in any direction, eventually the mountains would rise up to the sky." And then, with defensive pride: "Although we know, always knew, the world's *really* a globe."

"I'll be outside," Iraji said. Apparitor gave him a quick squeeze, not looking, absentminded gratitude. They were friends. Baru touched a coin with her mind, a disc with Duke Oathsfire on one side and Duke Lyxaxu on the other. The coin was proof that she could betray people even if she saw their dearest friendships.

Cold currency, of course. But valuable.

She gathered her attention on the known world, the Ashen Sea and its surrounds. Apparitor mistook this for disappoinment: "I'd like to fill in the more tentative edges," he said, protectively. "It's my passion, exploration. There's trouble raising ships and money, with war so close, but I still have my ways. . . ."

"How does it work?" Baru said.

"Eh?"

"This. Our world. How does it work?"

The Ashen Sea was a lumpy ring, and the world, Baru's theater of play, was a misshapen cross around that ring. North was Aurdwynn and the Wintercrests and icy mesa beyond; left-which-was-west was the Camou Interval, a great plague-ridden unknown, grasslands and mountains full of scattered people as unknown to Falcrest as Taranoke might once have been. Between those two arms a fan of steppe reached out northwest, into the fallen Maia heartlands.

It struck Baru as very odd that so much of the map was fallen empire, fallow territory, forgotten land. As if the tide of humanity was going out, all across the world. . . .

"I can't tell you how the world works," Apparitor said. "If I knew that, would I be scurrying around on the Throne's errands? Would I have to put up with you?" And something about Tain Hu, which Baru jerked her attention away from: it vanished into her right-blindness.

"I have a theory," Baru said. "About the world."

"Of *course* you do."

"The fundamental concern of all our history has been access to the Ashen Sea trade circle—"

"Did I say I wanted to hear it?" he snapped.

Baru still thought she must be right.

On the southern limb of the cross the Oriati Mbo jutted like a long tooth at the bottom of the Ashen Sea, coast and savannah and desert and sahel and jungle, all the way to Zawam Asu where the whales gathered for their fabled quorums. A gristly mass of land connected the Mbo northeast to Falcrest, belted by the strait called the Tide Column, which linked the Ashen Sea to the titanic Mother of Storms.

And north of the Column, on a pudgy potato-shaped subcontinent jutting (Baru had to wave her head to remember the direction) rightward, eastward, was Falcrest. Not central. Not remarkable. Nowhere you would choose as the seat of power if you saw the world like a high hawk.

"We're so *small*," Baru squeaked. She had to swallow to get her voice right. A terrible vindication was in her, and she wanted it out: the notion that any crime could be pardoned for a chance to glimpse these world secrets.

"I take it," Apparitor said, "that you're not used to feeling small?"

"No," she said, and then realized he was calling her an egomaniac.

"You never got high and lay down on your back on a mountainside? And watched the sky until you were afraid you'd fall up into it?"

"No . . ."

"Tain Hu did," he said, "she told me about it."

Her name like a thorn in the tongue. Baru glared at him. He grinned and waved a bottle: The Grand Purifier. "I needed an excuse to be rude," he hiccupped, "so I stopped by *Helbride* and raided my vodka stash. Clear as spring melt! Here, for your health—"

"I'm not drinking anything you pour." Baru took one last guilty, yearning glance at the map.

From the Mothercoast the map swept east: hundreds of miles of open ocean, barren islets, wild currents. The Mother of Storms. Baru's eyes crossed the distance like a ship, imagining thirst, hundred-foot waves, maelstrom, thirst and thirst and desperate salty thirst. At last she came to a coastline complicated by inlets and fjords and interior lakes. Smoking volcanoes issued clouds of thin paint.

The mapmakers had written here, in plain blocks, THE SUPERCONTINENT.

"Why is it super?" she asked.

"Because it's huge."

"How do you know?"

"We found maps. Made by explorers from the pre–Oriati Mbo. They died over there."

"Oh . . ." Baru said, dreaming of long eons and secret valleys. She would like to be an explorer.

"Who would ever want to oppose our glorious Republic?" Apparitor murmured, with bitter admiration. "Who would want to kill the thing that makes maps like this?"

Baru would. Because she would never share this world with Tain Hu. She would never point from a ship's mast and say, *See that mountain? I've named it for you.*

"Tell me the rules," she commanded.

B EHOLD, attend, hear ye hear ye, and et cetera," Apparitor hiccupped. "Let these be the laws of those who act beyond the law."

The cooks had laid out breakfast. Soft-boiled chicken eggs cooling in their brown shells, spring mango, smoked fish, rusk bread, and dipping coffee. The centerpiece was three guga in a sugar glaze: baby gannets, taken from the clifftop colonies which surrounded the keep in white fields of guano and squawking chicks. The exile staff held a contest every year to make the best gannet dish. For Baru they'd arranged the chicks upon mirrored vessels, posed as if in flight.

She was ravenous. She hadn't eaten since she saw the ship coming in with Hu.

"The Cryptarch's Qualm." Apparitor stared into his vodka bottle as if he could read the words from the light in the drink. "Your power is secret, and in secret it is total. But to use your power you must touch the world. To touch you must be touched, to be touched is to be seen, to be seen is to be known. To be known is to perish. Act subtly, lest you diminish." He took a slug.

She only needed to survive long enough to destroy it all. Subtlety could be dismissed. "Eat," she suggested. "Or you'll be useless soon."

"I don't want to be of any use to you." But he picked up an egg and began to juggle it, one-handed. "Next, the Tyrant's Qualm—"

"Are we tyrants?" Baru sliced her mango. The blade snicked on the plate: the texture too much like flesh. Her chest hurt.

"You decide that as much as I." He gave his egg a little backspin. "If you hold absolute power, everyone wants to take it from you. So you must entice supporters by granting them a piece of your power. But the more people you entice, the more thinly you are spread, and to spread is to perish."

"Fine, fine." She would need to learn to make allies. But never again could she let them as close as Hu. The price was so high. "Did you mean for me to pardon the duchess?"

Apparitor rolled his eyes and took a slug straight from the bottle. "Pardon her?" He gasped: a little bead of vodka sat between the ridges under his nose, quivering. "I thought you'd beg for her life. Thirdly, the Great Game. Every advisor to the Emperor, no matter their particular program of interests, shall maintain a familiarity with the Great Game—"

A game. Baru would love to play a game of intrigue, of calculation, a game that overflowed her mind and doused her heart. "What is it?"

"It is the Throne's model of the world, honed by decades of intrigue and contest. We play it on a map, with the assistance of very large rulebooks. And when our work is finished, there will be no difference between the rules of the game and the laws of the world."

He had put down his bottle and produced a bag of tiny figures from his pocket: he was laying them out on the map-rug with the warm egg still cupped in his off hand.

"Hesychast." He held up a broad-shouldered brown bust. "One of us. The agents of the Throne."

Baru knew that name. When she'd first met Apparitor she'd asked if he were Hesychast—Cairdine Farrier's rival, the eugenicist. The one who thought her race was fit only for farming, fishing, and pleasure.

"Hesychast told me you'd beg for her reprieve," Apparitor said. "He guaranteed it."

"I suppose he thought my lust would control me."

Apparitor stared at the figure with hot distaste. "He believes that the isoamorous—people like you and I—must be consumed by incredible passion. Like addicts. Why else would we persist in our obscene fascinations, when the whole world is against us?"

Baru remembered her fathers flirting on the beach, fearless and beautiful. The whole world had not been against them, no matter what the Empire said. And that was the beginning of hope: if the world had not always been as the Empire demanded, then it might not always be as the Empire demanded.

He pitched the egg overhand and it landed in the cup of wine Baru had just poured. She blinked and sputtered. "Is that a glint of conscience I detect?" he said. "A sliver of human compassion?"

"Doubtful," Baru said, acidly. "I'm only tired. I stayed up too late with the prisoner."

"Tormenting her with her failure?"

Baru stuffed her mouth with baby gannet meat, so she couldn't reply.

"Anyway. These figures are members of the Throne. Here's Itinerant—" A smiling waistcoated bust, her patron, Farrier. He put it down on the edge of the map. "Stargazer—" A telescope lens, also for the edge. "Me—" A pale figure, with red paint for hair. He put it in Aurdwynn. "Renascent—" A featureless pawn, which he placed, with a shudder, on Falcrest. "And you."

The pawn he produced was extraordinary. Narrow, thoughtful, storm-dark eyes: Baru's cheekbones and chin: a faint, uncharacteristic smile, as if the pawn wanted to make Baru happy. All carved from the wood with the most expert care.

"Whittled it myself," Apparitor said, cheerily. "On the ship with Tain Hu. Thought it'd be a nice gift once you'd spared her. Ah well."

He smashed his vodka bottle down on the pawn's head and it split. Apparitor flicked the broken stub over to Baru. "Your pawn, my lady," he said, and emptied the bottle down his throat.

"Now," he gasped, "we play."

"I don't know the rules—"

"And I won't tell you." He stepped onto the map. "Tell me what you'll do to the world, Baru Cormorant. Show me your savantry!"

"What do I—"

"I told you. I told you." His eyes glinted in the slatted dawn light. His jaw twitched, like a smile trying to wriggle out of its cage. There was something bestial, something cunning and atavistic about his pig-pale flesh, as if his ancestors had lived in their mansions too long, too far from the light. Baru hated the thought—she hated these prejudices!—but when the earth trembled with a distant avalanche or tremor, and the chandelier of the map of the moon moved above them in sympathy, she almost gasped aloud in fear.

"The rules of the game," he said, "are the rules of the world. Play!"

Baru set her pawn down in Aurdwynn. A splinter from its broken face got under her thumbnail: she hissed and sucked it out. Blood wicked into the wound and turned the nail red.

"You are in Aurdwynn," Apparitor said, singsong, mocking. "You have just betrayed all your friends. The rebellion is over. You have gained the absolute overriding authority of the Imperial Throne. What do you do?"

Where to begin! She would do what Tain Hu trusted her to do. "I order the release of religious prisoners, the end of reparatory marriage, and a program of universal inoculation for children. I set patrols on the Inirein and the other major trade rivers. I dredge the Welthony harbor. I—"

"The provincial Governor refuses your suggestions. The Governor wishes to keep the north of Aurdwynn impoverished and ill, so the Stakhieczi cannot seize it and use it as a springboard for invasion."

"The *Governor*?" Baru said, in confusion. "Isn't Cattlson dead?"

Apparitor's smug vodka-polished smile was very soon going to anger her. "Forgot about Heingyl Ri, did you?"

"Oh." Baru *had* forgotten about her. Fool, Baru, weak stupid fool. Heingyl

Ri was the Stag Duke's daughter. She'd met Baru on her first day in Aurdwynn with her sharp fox eyes, her frightful décolletage, and that one eerily prescient barb: *I hope no one will regret your appointment. Least of all you.* "She married Bel Latheman, didn't she?"

"Quite so." Apparitor winked. "Xate Yawa prepared her very carefully for the Governor's seat."

"I have her dismissed."

"How?"

"I write a letter," Baru snapped, "saying I'm one of the Emperor's advisors and I want her to step down."

"I countermand your letter with my own. I want her to remain Governor."

"Then I—" She almost giggled. It felt like the childhood game of My Mana Mane, where you tried to convince your friend why your version of the legendary Oriati hero was better, and could absolutely step all over her version of Mana Mane. "I have her husband implicated in that scheme of Vultjag's. I tell Heingyl Ri she steps down or I have Bel Latheman convicted."

"Fine." Apparitor picked up his pawn and nudged hers over. "I murder you."

"What!" She crossed her arms. "You can't just murder me."

"Why not?"

Because—because everything she'd done, everyone she'd sacrificed, would be wasted before she ever got to hurt the Masquerade.

"My patron would destroy you," she said, which seemed plausible. Farrier had invested so many years of effort into her; and he had that wager with Hesychast about her capabilities. He would not want her dead.

"I *knew* it," Apparitor crowed. He got up to straddle Aurdwynn and throw up his hands in victory. "I knew it!"

"Knew *what*!"

"Farrier! Farrier convinced you to kill your lover." Apparitor's fist clenched: his little pawn poked out of it like a red-haired homunculus, smiling at Baru. "You did what he wanted and now you know he's going to protect you."

"I don't know what you're trying to insinuate," Baru said, indignantly. "Of course he expected me to carry out the Republic's law. What else?"

"Farrier's showing off."

"Showing off *what*?"

"His control over you. You know, on some level, that you'll be rewarded when you obey him. That's why you killed Tain Hu. To earn his indulgence."

Baru wanted to stab him up through the nostril, into the pulp of his brain. The thought that he might be even the littlest bit right would annihilate her.

He hissed across her plate of dead fledglings and ruined mango. "Tell me what he's planning! Why did you kill her? Did you do something so horrible that you couldn't leave any witnesses?"

"Well," she said, rising to the riposte, leaning into his salt and spirit smell, "I nearly married your brother, for one."

He'd lost his red handkerchief on the harbor wind, his neck was naked, and so she saw the convulsion of fear that snapped his teeth together. "What brother?"

"Your brother," she said, with a snake of guilt in her gut, which she tried, and failed, to step on. "The Necessary King of the Stakhieczi."

"I don't know any king," he said, too quickly.

She smiled at him. "Come now. You were born prince of the Mansions. You tried to lead an expedition into the east, and the Masquerade kidnapped you off your ship." Baru's teeth closed on a tiny gannet-bone: it snapped between her jaws and slashed her gums. She'd heard the story from Dziransi, the Stakhieczi fighter in her retinue, and she'd known instantly, instantly, who that prince must be. "Does anyone else know? You're kept in check by your hostage lover; but do they all know you're royalty, too?"

He was silent and he was still.

"What would your colleagues do," she whispered, "if your brother the Necessary King asked for your return, lest he invade? Would anyone protect you? Or would they send you home in rags and drool, with the lobotomy pick still jutting from your eye?"

Apparitor looked at her with pale fire in his eyes, with an aurora light on his teeth, and the charge of the air outside the keep passed through the stone and metal to stir his long red hair.

"You have me cornered," he said.

It would have been undignified to whoop aloud. Instead she smiled. The blood from her cut gums made him flinch.

"Why do you do this?" he whispered. "I work for the Throne because it keeps me and mine safe. What do you want? What *are* you?"

She set her broken pawn down on Aurdwynn. The map rug was huge, huge, and she got up to pace the ring of the Ashen Sea, leaving him kneeling there with her plate of leavings and Aurdwynn in all its checkered peculiarity.

"This," she said, kicking the ocean. "This ring. Trade goes around it, and around it, and around it. Falcrest to Oriati Mbo to Taranoke to Aurdwynn and back to Falcrest. Does it remind you of anything?"

"A water wheel."

"An engine. Yes." Baru surveyed her ocean. "What if that engine stopped?"

He did not even hesitate. "Falcrest collapses."

"Well," Baru said. "We can't have that. We should explore the possible ways the trade could be stopped, so we can prevent them."

"Are you speculating on the downfall of our great and beloved Republic? Some might consider this a mote suspicious."

She waved in dismissal. "The hand is blameless, if it acts in service of the Throne. . . ."

"Quoting the Hierarchic? You learn our stories too well." Apparitor clapped his hands on the rug, and everything rattled, the dish and the bottle, even Baru's jaw. "Do you understand? You don't. You will."

A chime at the door: Iraji announced his return with the touch of a rod. "Pardon me, Excellences, but it's time."

Baru frowned. "Time for what?"

"For your exaltation, mam," the boy said. "You go before the Emperor, and put on your new mask. And you tell us your name."

"We're not waiting for Hesychast?" Apparitor said, innocently. "He's sailing all this way. . . ."

"What?" Baru staggered backward, cracked her hips on the breakfast table, and nearly sat in the guga. "Hesychast's coming *here*?"

"Of course he is," Apparitor said, adulterating his own coffee with wine. "Who do you think was going to take your hostage away?"

He gave her a two-fingered salute.

"May you regret what you did today," he said, soberly, "until the end of time."

INCARNATION is the art of form mimicking content. Write a poem about linked destinies, and each verse begins with the end of the last: this is incarnation. Write a story about a mountain and it tapers to a peak on the page: incarnation. Baru always thought it was a stupid gimmick. Nobody demanded that the word *billion* be a thousand times longer than *million*, because that would be unwieldy.

The Throne had incarnated its virtues in the ritual of exaltation. And they had done it perfectly.

A great murmur of excitement ran through the gathered people—Elided Keep staff and Apparitor's crew—as they opened their envelopes. Everyone had their own instructions; no one knew the full design.

"Is the gull part of the rite?" Baru asked her chamberlain.

It was a fat greasy-white seagull with yellow feet, perched on a spear-shaft that flew Duke Pinjagata's banner. Apparitor said Pinjagata had been stabbed under the chin by a Clarified disguised as one of his troops. Baru missed him.

"I'm sorry, my lady Excellence." Baru's chamberlain had organized cabin boys to stone the gull. "It hopped down the east tower stairs. We've been trying to corner it but it's quite fierce."

The gull squawked and began to pitter-patter its feet. "Oh dear." The chamberlain, gray and thinly drawn, covered his mouth in worry. "Kill it before it—"

The gull stopped pattering, stared in fury at the people below, and then relieved itself on Pinjagata's banner. All the clerks groaned together. Baru bit her wrist to dam up a laugh.

"I'm *so* sorry," her chamberlain whispered, "it does that whenever it patters its feet. We'll have it taken down and cleaned, at once, at once."

"Don't bother. Pinjagata would've liked it." She turned to the assembled technocrats. "Who's been feeding this gull?"

"Feeding it, my lady?"

"See how it hops back and forth? It's been trained to dance for food. Enterprising little bastard, isn't it?" Polite laughter from all these people, people afraid of her. "Never mind. Let's begin!"

The crowd in the throne room formed two columns, their hands outstretched before them, turned upward: a path of palms, from the doors to the high gray throne.

Baru walked between them, in her porcelain half-mask, a simple waistcoat and black trousers, with her gloves buckled at her wrists and Aminata's boarding saber at her hip.

Oh, Wydd, what a thrill she felt. What a hateful thrill.

At the end of the path of hands the Emperor awaited her upon Its Throne.

Of course It couldn't be *the* Emperor, who sat in the People's Palace in Falcrest between sluiceways of glass eyeballs and ice water. Of course the marble seat in this throne room wasn't *the* Throne. The Emperor here would be a lobotomite, his will pithed and destroyed with a steel pick.

They had prepared him in the full Imperial Regalia. A white smiling mask of enameled steel. A white silk raiment which bloomed out from beneath the mask and ran out taut and angular like a tent until it met the marble of the throne, where it gathered into braids, the braids woven thick and sure as ship's rigging into steel eyebolts. Beneath the silk rig the man's form could not be seen or selected as human. He was continuous with the weft of the Throne. Behind him the braids of silk spidered out through bolt and pulley to run away into secret corridors behind the wall. Arteries of secrets, pumping out into the world.

The gull squawked angrily. No sound otherwise, except the small decisions of Baru's footfalls.

"STOP," the assembled technocrats boomed, the Emperor's voice invested in them.

Baru stopped.

"TELL ME YOUR NAME."

"Baru Cormorant," Baru said.

"BY WHAT MERIT DO YOU CLAIM MY ATTENTION?"

"I claim the polestar mark," Baru said, and she opened her folio where her exams and assignments had been recorded, showing it to the Emperor and to the room: here is my worth. "I claim the Emperor's authority. By my works I make my claim."

"APPROACH ME."

She climbed the short steps.

The great silk bindings of the Throne creaked and shifted: the Emperor's left hand was drawn away, revealing a maple case. "MASK YOURSELF," the chorus commanded, and inside that maple case Baru found a face of glazed blue-white ceramic, exquisitely blank. Around the right eye blazed the eight-pointed polestar mark, rendered in silver. The sign of overriding Imperial authority.

The mask was sleek to the touch, sensuously unyielding. Baru wondered how thrilling it would be to smash the perfect thing. Behind the right eye the interior swarmed with codes.

It fit her, of course, like a second face.

"TELL US YOUR NAME," sang the servants of the Throne.

Baru turned to the little crowd. The whole pyramid of her life, turned upside down, with its vast base cornered by her distant ancestors, balancing on a tiny point: her, here, now.

I MADE IT she wanted to scream, red-lipped, broken-toothed, marrow spattering off her tongue, as certain and lethal in her arrival as a shark breaching with the broken body of a seal in its mouth. I made it. No living thing may call itself my ruler.

"I am Agonist," she told them. "Let it be known."

Agonist. It meant *one who struggles.*

The Emperor began to laugh.

An instant of horror and shame from the crowd, even a few giggles, as if a child had run out bare-assed and squalling to interrupt the ceremony: everyone thought the lobotomite had misbehaved.

But there was something in that laugh which Baru recognized. Her first stupid thought was that this simply wasn't fair: the memory would be tainted, now. *He* had infiltrated this moment. *He* always would.

Apparitor leapt out of the crowd. "Baru!" he shouted, into the mortified silence. "Baru, unmask it!"

"Yes," she said, and she reached out to the man bound to the Throne, gripped his smiling white mask, and lifted it off his head.

Deep folded eyes, laughingly sad, and skin almost as dark as Baru's. The finely kept beard, which she had always thought must itch. Gods, he had tears in his eyes, tears of pride. Who else in the world could say they were genuinely proud of *everything* Baru had ever done? Only him. Only him.

"Surprise!" Cairdine Farrier beamed.

And then, his voice stopping up, "Oh, Baru, thank you, *thank you*. You've done it. You've saved us, you've *saved* us," now thick-throated joy, "Baru, we've *won*. Falcrest is saved."

INTERLUDE

THE WAR PAPER

For the edification of the Parliament of the Imperial Republic,

At the request of Parliamin Miss Truesmith Elmin, Egalitarian Whip, Chair of the Committee for the Maintenance of the Peace,

The Morrow Ministry presents

A PROJECTION OF DEATHS IN A SECOND ARMADA WAR
With the cooperation of the polymaths of the Metademe, we have prepared two assessments of the human cost of a second Armada War between the Imperial Republic of Falcrest and the Federations of Oriati Mbo.

The first assessment describes an easy victory.

The second assessment describes a strategic catastrophe.

A HOPEFUL SCENARIO
In the best case, our naval attacks against the Mbo swiftly close their harbors. Rocket barrages threaten the destruction of Yama, New Kutulbha, and Devi-mandi. We block the Tide Column, severing Oriati trade between the Ashen Sea coast and the Devi-naga Mothercoast.

The three coastal Mbo federations surrender immediately.

In protest of their surrender, landlocked Mzilimake declares war on Lonjaro, Segu, and Devi-naga. Civil war erupts. The governments of the coastal federations call on Falcrest for help.

Between 10,000 (one Faculties graduating class) and 100,000 (the city of Shaheen) Falcresti citizens die in the course of a ten-year civil war. Most succumb to unknown diseases native to Oriati Mbo. Returning expeditionaries quarantine on Sousward, containing these pandemics away from our heartland, with the risk of total loss of Sousward's vulnerable native population.

Crop failure, internecine violence, and plague cause between 15 million (ten cities of Falcrest) and 35 million (the population of the entire Falcresti heartland, Normarch, and Occupation) deaths in Oriati Mbo.

Infant mortality in the Mbo climbs from 20 per hundred to 35 per hundred.

The death of griots and the destruction of records erases one month out of every year of recorded history.

Outbreaks of the Oriati Emotional Disease introduce additional death, but it is our hope that Incrastic progress will fend off the better part of these suicide casualties.

A MORE TROUBLING SCENARIO

A war of attrition in the Ashen Sea and inconclusive naval battles along the Mothercoast force both powers into a stalemate.

Our Metademe deploys demographic weapons against Oriati Mbo. Oriati Mbo retaliates with the bushmeat defense, including especially the zoonotic reservoirs of the Kettling. The Stakhieczi launch an opportunistic invasion of Aurdwynn, cutting off shipments of grain and lumber to Falcrest.

Between 1 million (one out of thirty) and 6 million (one out of five) Falcresti citizens die to food rationing, contaminated water, and the Oriati bushmeat defense.

Between 35 million (one out of six) and 70 million (one out of three) people in the Mbo die in famine, unrest, and the use of demographic weapons.

Nearly one in six people in the known world die.

We predict the total collapse of most societies within the Ashen Sea trade circle due to the spread of crop blight and the end of agricultural trade.

The remote possibility exists that Ashen Sea civilization will disintegrate entirely, triggering a return to sustenance agriculture in small polities (as in the Near Ancient collapse of the Jellyfish Eater and Cheetah Palace civilizations).

LET IT BE NOTED

That Parliamin Mister Mandridge Subahant, Candid Whip and Chair of the Committee for Realism, has entered an allegation of sensationalism against this paper and a motion of censure against Miss Truesmith Elmin.

It must be repeated, in the interest of pragmatism, that the digestion of Oriati Mbo would give Falcrest the keys to the known world and secure an Incrastic future of well-ordered, prosperous, scientific society.

THE LEVER

SAIL down the arc of the trade circle from wolf-wintered Aurdwynn southeast toward Falcrest, the jewel of the world, and halfway along your journey you come to an island of great green forests and rich white guano, an island where compasses turn madly under alien influence as the caves jet steam and the mountain rumbles.

Once this island was called hell. Today it bore the burnt-clean name of Isla Cauteria.

Life stirred. Day birds screamed the dawn to night birds as they passed in their thousand-strong flocks and murmurations. Shallow-water fish with eyes like coins peered from their dens at the deepwater squid rising to eat the day. The fisherfolk of the Cauteria Catch Concern raised anchor for a double shift on a boom market. And the wind out of the northwest filled their sails before it crossed the slanted black Normarch-style roofs of Cautery Plat, on up the slope to Annalila Point, across the walls of looming Annalila Fortress, through the racked hwachas and batteries of anti-ship rockets, down through banners and mill-sails that creaked as they turned the engines below, into a ward-house window: to rouse the lieutenant commander from her whore-satisfied sleep.

Aminata groaned and pressed her fists against her forehead.

Awake. Fuck. She was awake again. Hey there, navy girl, here's waking up to you.

A navy officer must always review her situation and her resources. Here she was, Aminata isiSegu, Lieutenant Commander in the Navy of the Imperial Republic of Falcrest, skimmed out of an Oriati orphanage by the navy's talent scouts. First tour of duty on federated Taranoke, second tour on the frigate *Lapetiare*.

She'd never had a third tour. She was marooned.

Beneath her linens, marinated in sweat, Aminata thought, damn it, I'm still a torturer. No warship posts for her. No marks on her service jacket. No coin toward her great dream to earn command of a tall ship.

When they'd come to her, she'd been so proud to have their attention. The old-leather women of the Admiralty, Rear Admiral Maroyad and her matron

Ahanna Croftare, with a secret offer. *Lieutenant, a war's coming. We need Oriati interrogators who know Oriati fears.*

Can you learn how to break your own, Lieutenant Aminata?

How could she refuse two admirals? Even if they asked her to trade the clean sea wind for the soft and sinister arts of Incrastic truth enhancement?

How could she refuse?

Science said that Oriati people were creatures of community. *Mbo* meant *a thing that is whole because it's connected.* People only mattered in the context of other people: there was no room for individual genius, or solitary peace, or defiance, and that was why Aminata was glad she'd been rescued.

Yet she missed her community, her people. *Lapetiare* was gone, gone like Taranoke with its easy boys and long warm nights and buttered lobster. They'd even cut her off from Baru: or, maybe, Baru had done that herself. Damn you, Baru, fucking write back, I don't care if you died in that rebellion, at least have the courtesy to haunt some postmaster and send me a letter.

At least Aminata had her whores.

"Hey." She poked him in the ribs. "Wake up. I've got to go do navy shit."

He woke up with a guilty start. He was a Stakhieczi boy from Aurdwynn and he had exotic skin like chicken sausage. She'd picked him out of sentiment, and paid him extra to stay over. Now the whore boy smiled expertly. She'd ruined his makeup last night, with her hands clawed around his skull and her thumbs digging into his cheekbones. But he was beautiful still, and he wore the ruin well enough.

"I hope you got your money's worth," he said, and he stretched to show her the fans of muscle off his shoulders, the arch of his pectorals, the narrow cut of his abs. "You were *so* good."

Remember when you thought whores liked you in particular? Because you were kind, and you never beat the shit out of them if they didn't perform? Give a woman a blackjack and a navy behind her and a man's strength didn't matter. And a lot of navy women liked to hit a man who couldn't hit back.

But now Aminata could hear what he was really saying. It wasn't *I like you.* It was, mam, *please* leave a tip, my pimp takes a big cut.

"Get dressed," she said. "Don't make me late."

He went around collecting his clothes. Aminata got out of bed, unpinned the fly screen on the window, stuck her head outside, and gasped a huge breath of the weather. There was, as the rag novels always said, a storm coming: not a storm of great change and crisis (if only!) but another plow of wet air to bring bad sailing and soggy clothes.

I wish, she told the birds, that I were on a ship. I wish Baru would write back. I wish—I wish—

I wish I knew, for sure, that all this hard work would get me somewhere. Even though I am who I am, a Segu-woman, an Oriati, a tunk, a beachboot, a burner. Even though.

"Big day, mam?" he asked, to fill the silence.

It *was* a big day. Maybe, with some kind of masculine intuition, he'd felt her urgency last night. Today was the day she had to ease Abdumasi Abd from the resentimente to the attachment. When Abd finally cracked she could be posted to a ship again.

"Oh!" the whore said, delighted: he'd discovered her temple in its little rice-paper house. "This is a trim shrine, isn't it?"

"Hey!" Aminata lunged. "That's private!"

Planted in the tufa center-pot of her temple was a cormorant feather, gray on the fringes, tipped with steel-gray and full black, quill-down in Taranoki earth. To her endless guilt Aminata had never tended the flower seeds she'd planted, and they'd died. So the ragged feather was all that stood in her temple. Her stupid little hygiene-approved gesture toward the stupid traditions of her stupid race.

"Go on!" she snapped, and the whore, pale as terror, went. She wanted to call after him, to apologize, to give him fare for a cart ride back to town.

But she was late.

Aminata gathered her things for the bath, lifted up her uniform jacket, and blew a speck of grit from the collar. She would go out there and do her damn best. She would make it. She *was* more than her home.

That was what the merchant Cairdine Farrier had told her, back on Taranoke, when he'd recruited her for his scheme to protect Baru by frightening the shit out of her: he had said *we can all be more than our bloody birth*.

S HE stopped at the guard post to check her mail. No one ever wrote, but like the prisoner with the lever, she always checked, because maybe, *maybe* today . . .

The Lever was a trick she'd used on Abdumasi Abd, and he'd fallen for it, he'd fallen so hard that he'd broken the lever in his cell (they were built to break). When it snapped in his arms he'd wept in despair.

Lapetiare's captain had once told Aminata, drunkenly, that life worked exactly like that lever. Did the lever give you a gum pellet with a little bead of opiate *every* time you pulled it? No, of course not. Give a prisoner a lever that worked that way and he'd pull it only when he wanted a fix. But give him a lever with a *tiny random chance* of yielding a pellet on each pull—

Then he spends his whole life pulling. Because every moment he's not pulling that lever, he's wasting a chance.

Navy life, the captain said, was built just the same way. If you knew exactly what you had to do to earn your promotion, you wouldn't be properly motivated, would you? But with a little uncertainty—a little corruption, a little racial preference, a spice of terror and purge—*then* you'd work your ass off, wouldn't you? Lest you miss your big break.

Aminata hated to believe that. But some days she felt it anyway. No rest. No reprieve. Life is random and unfair, so you must pull that lever until your arms break out of their sockets—

—and someone had written.

Aminata gasped. The letter was from Aurdwynn.

She knifed the seal open, tight-lipped, steady-fingered. It must be from Baru, it must! Some kind of explanation. Baru had definitely only *pretended* to go over to the rebels. The ships sunk at Welthony Harbor had been full of convicts, not real sailors. She'd been thinking constantly of Aminata, and only her work had kept her from writing—

Cheap paper. That didn't make sense for Baru. Marks told her it posted from Welthony a few weeks back. The Coyote rebellion had died near Welthony, hadn't it? On the plains at Sieroch?

Oh no. Was Baru . . . ?

Wait a moment. Had Baru misspelled her *name*? The letter was addressed to "Lieutenant Aminota." Was Baru hurt?

"What the fuck," Aminata whispered, "is going on up there, Baru?"

No one had a clear view of Aurdwynn this year past. The navy was silent. *Advance* mentioned unrest, disrupted markets, travel restrictions. But there was always samizdat, the rumors spread by illegal presses. Samizdat said Baru had changed sides after being recalled to Falcrest, that Baru had pretended to be recalled in *order* to change sides, that Baru had married a king, that Baru had declared herself queen, that Baru had beaten in Governor Cattlson's head in a duel, that Baru had eloped with a heartbreaking beauty of a duchess and married her and her husbands.

All everyone seemed to agree on were the dead sailors.

A flotilla of navy tax ships had vanished at Welthony Harbor. The names of the ships had been struck from the List. The names of the crews had stopped appearing on the *Navy Advance* bulletins.

Aminata couldn't believe Baru had been part of that.

Of course, she hadn't believed Baru would forget to write for three years, either.

She pressed the letter open against the wall.

To the Oriati Lieutenant who I know is close to my lord, I write this by the mercy of my captor, who hast permitted me a final inscribtion on the eve of the voyage which I hope will end in my death. Instead of a will I leave this letter . . .

Huh. Strong handwriting, but the writer could hardly spell, so— Aminata groaned. It was just convict mail. Convicts got a day to write free letters, and often they pissed into the Republic's mail circuit in hopes of turning a sympathetic ear. No doubt some prisoner in Aurdwynn had mistaken Aminata, who'd *once* served as a bank auditor, for a wealthy and merciful woman.

So it wasn't from Baru after all.

Her old friend had forgotten about her. Just like everyone else.

Aminata left the letter in her mail slot, to deal with when she got home.

W*HAT is the Cancrioth!"* Midshipman Gerewho roared. *"Tell me!"*
He snapped a cane rod against the prisoner's bare left foot. The man shrieked a raw failing shriek, his throat too ripped by screams to hold a meaning. Cats made sounds like that, Aminata thought. Not people. She wanted to torture cats even less than men.

Gerewho caned him again, twice, quickly. "Tell me! Who are they? Where do they meet?"

"He's really overdoing it," Faroni oyaSegu fretted, alongside Aminata in the oversight room. "I won't have anything left to befriend."

"He hates the poor fucker." Aminata sighed.

"Can you blame him? It's Lonjaro men like that"—meaning the prisoner— "who are the reason Lonjaro men like him don't get respect."

They looked at each other. Aminata wasn't sure if Faroni was serious. Faroni looked like she wasn't certain if she'd gone too far. A scream pulled them back to the cell periscope and the drama below.

The prisoner Abdumasi Abd had been chained spread-eagled and facedown in the center of a stone slot. His emaciated body was piebald with acid burns, his shoulders grotesquely protuberant against taut skin. Hug the man too hard and his ribs would probably crown through his skin like baby teeth. Gerewho Gotha beat him, Aminata's brute, sixteen and vicious; real men needed passion and viciousness was an easy passion when you hurt. This was the first stage of Aminata's process, the resentimente, old-fashioned hardhanded torture from which no good intelligence could be milked. Prisoners needed something to be rescued from.

Break Abdumasi Abd, Rear Admiral Maroyad had ordered her. *We want the names of everyone he's conspired with. In particular we want the names and location of the Cancrioth.*

What's the Cancrioth, Aminata had asked her.

Irrelevant to your work.

If you won't tell me, how am I to know if he's lying?

You will know when he speaks the truth. You'll hear the madness in him.

Fine. She'd work with what she knew. Fact: Abdumasi Abd had led an Oriati pirate syndicate in a brave and hopeless assault on Aurdwynn. Hate made you do that, she figured. Principled hatred of Falcrest and personal loathing of its people.

She had to focus Abdumasi Abd's hate down upon a single person. Then she could remove that person, remove the hate, and swap in a substitute, a friend, a confidante, which would be Faroni's role.

Two years ago Aminata had been ordered to condition her first prisoner into terrified insanity. She'd used incendiaries, hallucinogens, and certain strains of pepper to teach the man that all things contained an inner fire. Everything burnt. When she'd let him see the sun after weeks in the dark, he'd screamed in horrified revelation. It was getting closer: it would never draw away. They were all falling into the fire.

Then the Admiralty sent him back to Devi-naga Mbo. A reputation-builder, they'd told her. He'd gone home in catatonic terror, trapped in a world that smoldered, populated by men and women whose fat would pop and spatter in spontaneous flame, whose eyeballs sizzled as they cried for him with trails of blue-white grease cinder.

Now the Oriati called Aminata *the Burner of Souls.*

"Tell me the names of the Cancrioth financiers!" Gerewho bellowed, and he caned the prisoner on the soft of his calf: a flick and a line of blood, a step too far, they couldn't risk infection in an open wound.

"Go!" Aminata pushed Lieutenant Faroni toward the stairs. "Go, rescue him now."

With any trim at all—Aminata pardoned herself, a shitty childhood habit, by *trim* she of course meant *luck*—she would seem to rescue Abdumasi Abd from the brute.

Down below Gerewho heard her footsteps, and knelt by Abd's tear-stained face to deliver his final threat of mutilation.

He never got the chance.

Abd said something to his torturer. Aminata saw his lips purse and his throat move.

Gerewho flinched back in shock.

She couldn't see past his iron fullmask, but he dropped the cane rod and fell onto his ass to scramble away from Abd. Aminata blinked and played with the focus. What just happened? Had Abdumasi Abd been holding a centipede in his mouth?

Lieutenant Faroni burst into the cell. *"Midshipman Gerewho!"* she roared. *"What* in the *name* of *fuck* is going on here? King's shriveled balls! What have you done to my prisoner? Let him down *now* and report to the Commander of the Brig! And send me an apothecary, this man needs ointments!"

The moment was lost, except in Aminata's gut. She felt like she'd pounded bad tequila, a sick curiosity. What did the words mean? What did Abd know?

"Mister Abd," Faroni said, with fervent concern, "I'm your advocate, I'm sorry I couldn't get here sooner. Let's get you cleaned up and dressed. What the fuck is *this* contraption?"

Innocently she pulled the Lever in the cell wall. Aminata kicked a footswitch to grant the Lever's request, and a pellet of opiate gum rolled down into Faroni's hands.

"Ah," Faroni said, "opiate, good, this should help with the pain. Here—"

"Please help me!"

Abdumasi Abd clawed at Faroni's uniform jacket, trying to burrow inside. In pitiful scratchy Seti-Caho he mewled, "Kindalana, help me be strong!"

Kindalana. Hm. Aminata noted the name down for follow-up.

"I can't tell them," Abd gasped, "Kindalana, please, I can't tell them!"

"Hush, hush, shhh." Faroni stroked his bushy hair. Gently she pushed the opiate gum past his teeth. "Eat this. It'll make you feel better." And condition him to associate Faroni's appearance with pleasure.

Gerewho came stomping in, ripped his mask and pig-blood–stained apron off, and fell gasping onto the ready bench. Aminata bounced an eyebrow at him—hey, remember you're a sailor?—and he snapped a salute. "Midshipman Gerewho, reporting for debriefing, mam!"

"What did he say to you?"

"Noises." Gerewho shoved the heels of his hands into his eye sockets and pressed away the sight of Abdumasi Abd's skeletal screaming face. "He just made these noises and they, mam, they frightened me."

"What noises?"

"Yammer ah oo teen? Ya loot ian? Something like that."

"You responded sharply, Midshipman."

"I know. I can't explain it." Gerewho's shoulders bunched. "Perhaps it's taint, mam. He triggered some sort of racial memory."

Taint. The stain of Oriati degeneracy, bred into them by a thousand years of decadent, self-contented peace and perversion. How else, the Incrastic scientists asked, could the Oriati have failed to discover infectious hygiene or sanitary inheritance? Failed to better themselves?

"We'll beat it, Midshipman," she promised him. "Remember your qualms. You carry the weight of your ancestors—"

"—but I lift it, and that makes me strong, mam."

Below them they heard Faroni ask, gently, "He's made you bleed! What made him do this? Was there some particular question?"

"He wanted to know who funded me," Abdumasi Abd groaned. "He wanted me to name the Fairer Hand . . ."

"Who?"

"The Fairer Hand." Abd closed his eyes. "Her parents told me she could be trusted. They were wrong. I was wrong to trust Baru Cormorant."

Aminata straightened up slowly.

"Well," she managed, through her tumbling distress: Baru, what have you gotten yourself into? "That's interesting."

REAR Admiral Maroyad puffed on a cold-mint cigarette, tapped the ash onto a clamshell, and sighed.

People called her *the ice-fisher*, one who could harpoon her prey through shadow and turbulence. Aminata was terrified of her. Her ships guarded a full quarter of the trade circle around the Ashen Sea, from noon to three o'clock. And with all that salt and silver under her command, she could still make Aminata feel like she was the only fish on the admiral's harpoon.

Maroyad stabbed her embered cigarette at Aminata. "Do you want to start a war?"

"If I fail in my duty, mam?"

"No, Lieutenant Commander. If you *succeed*."

"I don't understand," Aminata said, desperately. "How so?"

Maroyad was Bastè Ana, one of the fish-eating people who lived in Falcrest's icy Normarch. Recently (Aminata followed the race laws closely) the Metademe had discovered that the Ana were simply a Falcresti subrace, as evidenced by their phenotypes and expert ice constructions. Aminata had read that women once ruled all Bastè Ana households, and that men actually had to sneak into other womens' homes to court the daughters—but surely that was tosh. Even in Segu, the closest the world had to a matriarchy, men and women married openly. Even if the women then abandoned their poor husbands and tiny daughters to hare off in search of fortune.

"Tell me again what Abd said," the rear admiral ordered. "Tell it plainly."

Through the good glass behind her the high prow of Annalila Point stabbed north. Fishing feluccas and junks tacked across silver-tipped afternoon water below; a mail clipper raced in ahead of the storm. Aminata thought that if the meeting went very badly she *might* be able to jump through the window and hurl herself off the point.

"Well, mam"—don't say *well*, it signals weakness of character—"that is to say, mam"—don't clarify yourself, say it right the first time, nuance and ambiguity are Oriati habits—"today I pivoted Abdumasi Abd from the resentimente to the attachment."

"You stopped hitting him."

"Exactly, mam. I sent in Faroni as heartbait. In his pain he mistook her for a woman named Kindalana."

"Kindalana. Yes." Maroyad exhaled a jet of mint smoke. "The Admiralty's aware of her."

"Can you tell me anything, mam?"

"She's an Oriati Federal Prince who does charity work in Falcrest. The woman behind the Great Embrace campaign—you know it?"

Federal Princes were the Mbo's royalty: a child who, corrupted by years of groveling courtiers and favorable treatment, was then set loose to run the Mbo's affairs as their whims dictated. Aminata hated them. "Great Embrace, yes. That's the one where the Mbo surrenders to Falcrest and joins the Republic?" Ridiculous, of course: like pouring a gallon of mud into a pint of cream.

"Yes. We've put in a request with the Morrow Ministry for their intelligence on her." She took another drag on the cigarette. Only then, watching her slow considered motions, did Aminata realize the admiral was tense as an anchorline. "But given Parliament's distaste for our fine navy, and the way the Morrow Ministry likes to eat Parliament's cunt on hope of credit, I think the Kindalana file will be a long time coming."

"Perhaps the Prince Kindalana funded Abdumasi Abd's attack fleet?" Aminata suggested, hopefully.

Rear Admiral Maroyad stared at her, silent and unreadable.

"Perhaps the Prince," Aminata said, fumbling now, "thought she could curry our favor with her charity work, as a cover for secret movements against us?"

"Put out your hand," the rear admiral said.

"Mam?"

"Take your glove off and give me your hand."

Aminata obeyed, thinking, sourly, that she was probably not going to get her nails inspected.

Rear Admiral Maroyad stubbed her cigarette out on the web of Aminata's left hand. The mint sizzled on her skin. Aminata bit her cheeks and did not even hiss. Pain, huh? Come on in. Make yourself at home. I'm a navy tunk, I bleed cold brine and I stitch up my soggy cuts with fishing line. Come on in.

"I'm not doing this to be a bitch," Maroyad said, conversationally, "although I do like that word, *bitch,* a woman who's not approved of: it has such wonderful eugenic overtones. I never had kids. Navy women don't, usually. You've figured that out, I'm sure."

Aminata made an interested *hm*. Her eyes tried to well up. She forbade it.

"I just want you to remember, every time you look at this scar"—she screwed the cigarette back and forth—"that if you *do* succeed in identifying Abdumasi Abd's backers, and you tell *anyone* outside the navy, you're going to fuck us all."

"Mam?" she croaked.

"What do you think happens," Maroyad said, flicking the cigarette into a planter across the room, "if Parliament finds out that some Prince or griot circle or perverse tunk conspiracy was behind that 'pirate' attack on Aurdwynn?"

"I expect, mam, that Parliament would demand the Oriati turn the guilty parties over to us."

"Mm-hmm. And do you think your 'people,' by which I mean Devi-naga, Mzilimake, Lonjaro, Segu, and all the principalities within, can agree to extradite a bunch of powerful people?"

"Well, ah, mam, if they don't, I expect there'll be—war."

"You're fucking right there will." Maroyad stood up, looked about, seized on her clamshell ashtray, and hurled it into the floorboards at her feet. "*Fuck!* Fuck damn it! Fuck fuck fuck!*"

Aminata had never seen an admiral express strong emotion before. It was a bit like watching your mother cry; or so she supposed. "Mam!" she said, a sort of general exclamation of subordinate dismay, *why are you making me listen to you say fuck?*

"Fuck." Maroyad sat down suddenly. "Ah, fuck. I wish we could make him disappear. Maybe it's not too late. But we have to know—"

"Mam?"

"Whatever you learn," Maroyad panted, wiping her mouth on her sleeve, "you're not to tell anyone but me. I don't want it down in writing. I don't want Abdumasi Abd to sign a confession unless I specifically order it. And listen, *listen,* I don't care if a little fish swims up your latrine and starts a conversation with your asshole, you do not speak to *anyone* about this prisoner, understand?"

"Of course, mam."

"Good. Do you want to know why?"

Aminata nodded cautiously.

"Because the moment anyone finds out we've got Abd," Maroyad said, "everyone comes for him. He's a coin to buy a war. The Judiciary will want him, and Parliament, and the Imperial fucking Throne—who knows what's behind that silk straightjacket except a lot of slithering councilors who don't like us? And to get Abd, they will purge *anyone* who tries to hold him. Do you see now?"

Aminata stared at the cigarette burn on her naked hand and thought, bloody fucking period shit, I am in *way* deeper than I realized. She knew that the Emperor meddled in the navy's affairs, for It had installed the Empire Admiral Lindon Satamine as a check against the navy's ambitious women admirals—

But to imagine that Emperor reaching down for *her* . . .

"I understand, mam. Should I . . . delay the interrogation? Bungle it?"

"No. Absolutely not. Abd needs to name our enemies for us."

"Our enemies, mam?"

"Yes. The people who want this war. The Imperial agents who *baited* Abdumasi Abd's attack with the Coyote rebellion. I think they wanted to draw the Oriati into a foolish move. Why, Lieutenant Commander, would the Throne want the Oriati to attack us?"

"So we'd have public support for a war, mam."

"That's right. And what happens when people get excited about a war?"

Purge. Purge happened. Parliament feared an independent navy, a navy with power over the trade that fed their purses. War would be the *perfect* time to clean out the Admiralty. If the loss of good sailors cost them a battle, well enough. A few defeats would silence the hawks and keep the navy from winning too much public love.

Falcrest had once, very briefly, possessed an army. It had been disposed of. *Field-general* was still slang for someone doomed to destruction.

"So." Maroyad clicked the little guillotine she used to cut her cigarettes off the roll. "The real purpose of your work, Lieutenant Commander, is to find the agents on *our* side who are working to provoke war. Do you have a lead on any of those agents?

She should speak Baru's name.

But if she did, Baru would be the next person she had to suasion.

She stood there helplessly, caught between two loyalties.

"Lieutenant Commander," Maroyad sighed, "you're such a lousy fucking liar that I can see you planning the lie out before you say it. Give me the name."

Oh, Baru, please forgive this. Aminata looked at the floor, because if she looked at Maroyad she would see past her, to the sea and the birds, the memory of Baru.

"Abd did mention the former Imperial Accountant of Aurdwynn, Baru Cormorant."

"Baru? Fuck her!" Maroyad snarled. "She drowned hundreds of Juris Ormsment's people at Welthony. I saw what that did to Juris. Fuck. Ass fuck." She kicked the fallen ashtray. It richocheted off her stately display of model ships and landed on the hardwood right at Aminata's feet.

"Pick that up," Maroyad ordered, breathing heavily.

"Mam?"

"Pick up the ashtray and hurl it, Lieutenant Commander."

"Mam, I'm not sure that's decorum—"

"Don't you see?" Maroyad snapped. "Parliament wants to carve up Oriati Mbo into little colonies and suck them dry. If they get their way, you're going to spend the *whole war* interrogating prisoners. You'll die with your head full of screaming faces."

Aminata stood there as the implications boxed her on the ears. She wasn't going to get a ship, was she? No matter what happened, they would say, oh, Aminata isiSegu, she has excelled at extracting vital intelligence from her racemates.

Keep her on as a suasion expert. Forever.

She picked up the clamshell ashtray and hurled it overhand into the wall. "FUCK!" she roared as the clamshell shattered. "FUUUUUCK!"

"That's the spirit." Maroyad collapsed into her chair. "Now I have a mission for you, Lieutenant Commander. A very sensitive, very secret mission."

"Anything," Aminata panted, and regretted it at once.

"Take Captain Nullsin's *Ascentatic*. Find Baru Cormorant. Learn who she's working with—every last name. Bring her back here if you can.

"And if you can't, remove her from play."

4

NEATH THE DEAD DOG'S TONGUE

SPRING came to Aurdwynn, and the streets of Treatymont bloomed with winter corpses.

Over the last four weeks Province Admiral Juris Ormsment had watched this corpse's black foot grow out of a melting ice dam. This was her favorite spot in the city, a garden gallery off Arwybon Plaza, and she came here whenever she could to escape the suffocating Governor's House, but the foot had rather ruined the mood. With the city's workforce depleted in Cattlson's debacle, corpses came out of the ice faster than they could be cleared. This one's killers had cut away the big toe for a rebel bounty. (Or, maybe, it had been eaten. Samne Maroyad insisted there was such a thing as an ice-tunneling rat.) Probably this dead man was a faithful citizen, killed for his loyalty.

Killed like too many others.

Dead sailors in a warm harbor, their eyes and their guts emptied by the gulls. And the chips of teeth left in their broken jaws chattered as they begged her:

Why did you abandon us, Admiral Ormsment? Where were you when she struck?

Why did you let this happen?

She flattened the rocket signal across her lap and read it again.

ANNALILA TO TREATYMONT/ADMIRAL'S EYES ONLY

PASS BY ROCKET RELAY HIGHEST IMPORTANCE

ORMSMENT:

I HAVE CRITICAL NEWS.

EXCELLENT WORK BY LT CDR AMINATA HAS GIVEN US A LEAD.

IMPERIAL AGENT BARU CORMORANT—SAME AGENT WHO EXECUTED THE MASSACRE OF YOUR SAILORS AT WELTHONY—ALSO BAITED THE ORIATI ATTACK ON YOUR PROVINCE.

SHE IS INVOLVED IN PLOT TO TRIGGER SECOND ARMADA WAR. SUSPECT IMPERIAL THRONE DESIRES WAR TO FORCE ACCESS TO ORIATI MBO.

CONSIDER THIS AGENT HIGHEST POSSIBLE THREAT TO ASHEN SEA
PEACE.

I HAVE DEPLOYED NULLSIN AND RNS ASCENTATIC TO TRACK AND SE-
CURE HER. HOLD YOUR COMMAND. DO NOT DO ANYTHING WHICH COULD
COMPROMISE US OR LEAD TO PURGE. I REPEAT DO NOT MOVE TOO SOON.

PROVINCE ADMIRAL FALCREST AHANNA CROFTARE HAS BEEN IN-
FORMED AND WILL REPLY.

JURIS. DO NOT GO AFTER HER.

REAR ADMIRAL SAMNE MAROYAD

ANNALILA FORTRESS

CAUTERIA

The rage rose up in her again. Water hammer. That was the name. Water
hammer—when you closed a pipe-valve too quickly, or detonated a mine
underwater, then a pressure wave would form in the water or the sea. It could
tear plumbing from the wall or cave in a ship's hull. Water hammer. And for a
moment she was eleven again, standing on the rusty ladder inside the settle-
ment's well, with the stone lid propped up on her fingertips: later they would
swell up into bloody bulbs. She had watched from that well as the Invijay came
through the fences (this was before the Armada War: there was no Occupation
to the south to buffer the Butterveldt). She had watched them kill her mother
and grandmother and take her father for a slave and a whore. They had that
power, the power to end a life, to close the future off like a pipe and send the
shock of that closure into the world. Water hammer.

She came back to this little gallery because it reminded her of the well. Stone
duty on every side, chaos past those walls. And that water rising under her, rising
to beat at the cover, rage and sorrow and need for justice, the water hammer—

Oh, Samne, she thought. How can't I go after her? The dead cry out for it,
don't they? The sailors I left in Baru's reach, the sailors who trusted me to trust
her. Didn't I betray them when Baru betrayed me? Didn't I fail that trust?

Of course Samne Maroyad wouldn't have sent the message if she thought
Ormsment had any way to do something stupid. Any hint as to where to begin.

Which she didn't. Yet.

But there was another reason Ormsment came to this gallery. A stone hidden in the wall, with a flat white face where she could mark a date and time to
meet.

"Hey," she said, to the blackened foot in the ice. "Hey, you. Do the dead
care?"

The foot had nothing to say. She tried clarifying. "Do you care what we do in your name?"

It was a fucking foot, so of course it wouldn't answer. She had to do an admiral's duty and decide for herself.

Everyone, Juris Ormsment thought, ended up dead. Everyone. If you stopped mattering when you died, life had no meaning: that was pretty clearly unacceptable. So you did matter after you died. Why? You mattered because people acted in your memory.

The living had a responsibility to the dead. A responsibility to honor their successes, and to make right the wrongs done against them. It was as true for a mother of dead sons as an admiral of dead sailors.

And that was that. She could choose not do it, of course. But a choice not to do the right thing had a name, and that name was evil.

She took the stone from its place in the gallery wall. In small Aphalone blocks, using a calligraphy brush, she painted a date and a time. She had never done this, and she had no reason to believe it would work, except that the Bane of Wives said it would.

Nothing had ever stopped the Bane of Wives from doing what she said she would do.

Juris Ormsment realized she would probably never see her little gallery again. So she got out her dive knife, knelt on the filthy ice in her dress uniform, and began to chip the black-footed corpse free of its tomb.

SHE called up her commands that night for a harborside review. They turned out on the piers in ragged order but fine spirits, cheering to each other, boasting of their ships: of sure helms and ready rockets, of rope splice and steady masts, the most beautiful boys and delicious cooks. Here were her Sulanes and Scylpetaires, Welterjoys and Juristanes and Commsweals, the enormous companies off *Kingsbane* and *Egalitaria* with their faces ash-blackened in disdain of the enemy. All in fantastic spirits after the spring's reversals, especially now that their shares of the prize money had been paid out: symbolic prizes for the forty-three Coyote and Oriati warships burnt to the keel without a single Falcresti loss.

She'd commanded that battle. *Navy Advance* called her a hero of the Republic. Even His Hypocrisy the Empire Admiral, Lindon Satamine, had commended her to Parliament.

If she kept her calm and let this victory propel her she might one day be Empire Admiral herself.

But she would be Empire Admiral of a navy that sold its sailors to women like Baru Cormorant.

From *Sulane*'s mast-top she raised her open hands like yardarms and the roar of the crews broke over her like storm waves. And like a good ship in storm she rose up and shook off the water and kept her course.

Juris often dwelt on a riddle she'd heard at academy in Shaheen. What is power? Where does it come from, when is it false, when is it true? Imagine that the Minister of the Metademe, the Minister of the Faculties, and the Morrow Minister are at dinner when it is announced that the wine is poisoned. A nameless secretary leaps up with a bottle of antidote. Each Minister demands the secretary hand over the bottle. The Metademe threatens her family and her fertility, the Morrow Minister threatens her reputation and safety, and the Faculties threaten to stab her up the eyeball with a meat skewer. Whose power is truest? Who gets the antidote?

And if you called to your sailors to follow you, but their Emperor called them to destroy you, who would they heed? If you knew for certain that they would follow you to ruin—would it then be wrong to ask for their service?

She walked among them. They looked at her with hard-chinned gratitude: thank you for gathering us here and using us so well. Thank you for showing us what we earn with our duty, pride and purpose and a fair piece of cash. The force of their love and respect filled her up like a sail and she tried so hard not to grin.

Now and then she stopped and asked an officer, "What's the word, sailor?" And mostly the woman would answer, "Fair winds and following seas wherever you send us, mam."

They would follow her anywhere. Not just the true salt but the wide-eyed octopus girls so young they were still all arm and leg, the careerists trying to illuminate their service jackets with merit, the lemon-rind convicts who would never work anywhere but a ship again. All hers.

It was her responsibility to deny them that loyalty. To take only those who could understand the sacrifice she asked of them.

That night she began to draw up transfer orders. The young and hopeful and ambitious would come off *Sulane* and *Scylpetaire*. She would take the hard and fierce and angry, the sea revenants and the orphans and the widows.

She would fill her two prize ships with those who did not fear collective punishment. But that would not be enough: the Throne was too subtle. Some of them would still be leveraged, compromised, ready to mutiny or murder her when she broke from the Hierarchic Qualm.

She needed the Bane of Wives.

* * *

A ND then it was the day she had painted on that hidden stone, and in the morning she went out in disguise to the meet.

On the wagon-seamed downslope off the Ffynyrn Bramble—she had finally gotten used to pronouncing the Iolynic *y*, which made the name Faneern—two orphans played dam-builder in the runoff. A dead woman with gills carved into her throat lay in the mud upstream. Juris shouted, in her best Iolynic, "Children! Stay out of that water, it's tainted!"

They recognized the Aphalone in her accent. They ran.

She saw more corpses as she walked. Beggars with faces burnt to shining parchments by riot acid hauled the dead in for hygiene bounty. They would see not a province admiral but a bare-faced brown woman in a homespun dress, hurrying through the muck. But Juris was not afraid.

Once the beggars must have been rebels. Part of the Coyote uprising that Juris had crushed, yes, damn it, that *she* had crushed, no matter how the Emperor tried to give the credit to Its Agents. Juris had beaten that Oriati fleet under Abdumasi Abd, the rebellion's *only* hope.

She felt vain and stupid, telling herself that. Oh, Juris, you great hero, you stopped the uprising, nobody else did it, it was you! But she had to seize the credit. This was what the Masquerade did to navy women: took their triumphs away.

She knew she would never return to this city, and her melancholia brought out the beauty in Treatymont. The flowers were coming up with the corpses. The houses bloomed with hyacinth and cherry blossom, early magnolias, deadly nightshades in medicinal plots. Climbing vines opened small white flowers that attracted fat bumblebees. The morning sun glinted off the mast-top mirrors of the ships in the Horn Harbor. Far out the two burnt towers stood like empty tooth-sockets. You would hardly know, looking at this city, that it could drive a navy flag officer to grand treason.

"Juris," a woman called, taking the opportunity of the disguise to skip her rank. "Juris, you should go."

Her aide came up the hill from Arwybon Plaza. Shao Lune, oh, you sharp-toothed weasel: a viciously perfect specimen of the Republican ideal, immaculate in her work, intimidating in her aspect. One of those people Juris had never been, people who did everything with enormous sprezzatura, the casual and effortless grace of the superior.

"She's not here," Shao said. "You should go back."

"I can't," Juris said. Physically, yes, it would be possible to call everything off. Morally it was impossible. She embraced her aide like a wayward daughter, though it was, actually, very hard to imagine Shao as anyone's child, at least unstrangled. "You'll draw everyone's attention while I make the meet."

"She's not going to show," Shao insisted.

"She's coming, Staff Captain. I know she'll come."

Shao Lune sneered, quite enchantingly, her face like a wonderful painting of your worst enemy. For a very long time Juris had wanted to court-martial her for insubordination and consign her to a fish-patrol corvette. But the more angry Juris became, the less she cared about the *tone* of Shao's loyalty, and the more the quality of her work.

"You could still go back to *Sulane,*" Shao said, "and save our lives."

No chance of that. The dead cried out against it.

SHAO Lune buttoned herself up and went out to sit in the sun with high-chinned dignity. A suitor arrived to dare her: a Stakhi man in a broad-shouldered tabard who offered olive oil.

Ormsment had claimed a public bench (a Falcresti project, of course) on the south end. It was early yet, before the plaza filled with Aurdwynni merchants, mistresses-of-house, master sewers, cranksmen, collimators, caseworkers, ste-vedores, dog-runners, butchers, bastardettes, and other feudal traffic. She watched, amused but worried, as Shao Lune's suitor tried, too late, to withdraw. Was he here to court a child bride, Shao asked him? No? Then why had he writ-ten poetry for illiterate idiot babies? Oh, begging his pardon, of course he had tried his best. He should show her around the plaza. He must know all the local excitements, the very best backlogged gutters, the most fascinating decay.

Juris wished Shao would be more careful with her powers. An air of superi-ority made one a target in men's circles. Sooner or later navy women had to make peace with that: or, if not peace, at least a cease-fire and a border.

A bee settled on her thigh. Juris smiled at it. Rage slammed against the back of her teeth, and the front of her skull, and rebounded: rage, rage, they died because you trusted her, they died on your watch. A bee would die after she used her sting, wouldn't she? So she had to choose carefully when to strike.

Where the fuck was the agent?

Then a burly woman in forester's skins came out of the alley across from Juris, hitching up her pants: briefly, beneath the tough denim, Juris saw a pale scar across a brown gut, and the edge of a strong fat thigh. She chased off the orphans cutting up the dead dog with blows from her hatchet's handle. What a tableau. Aurdwynn in a painting: a forester pisses in an alley, orphans cut up a frozen dog, the forester curses and beats the orphans. Next the forester would probably eat the dog. Juris loved this place, loved the charcoal smell and the taste of wheat pancakes on a campfire, the shining rivers that smelled like ice. But king's balls she was glad she hadn't been born here.

The victorious forester knelt and, with care, covered the dog's frozen face. Then she looked at Juris.

King's balls, her eyes! Blue as lightning-flash, and terrible, and Juris sat bolt-upright, for those eyes were proof. Eyes like Xate Yawa's. Blue like a tropical crow, and mad, mad.

She was the Bane of Wives.

She looked nothing like Juris had expected, nothing like a usefully built navy woman with big shoulders and long legs. Rough sinew and loose muscle, instead, and a survivor's pad of fat.

She chopped the frozen dog's head from its spine, picked it up by its bloody ruff, and came over to Ormsment.

The bee buzzed up to the high collar of Ormsment's dress.

The Bane of Wives underhanded the dead dog's head. It landed on the bench next to Ormsment, thudded wetly, rolled against the inscription: LINGER AND APPRECIATE THE CLEANLY AIR.

"You're the admiral," she said, in a calm low voice.

"You're the agent." By officer's habit Ormsment laid out her knowledge. "I read about you. You were on Sousward. Then in the Occupation, then sent to Mzilimake. You didn't come back."

"Open the mouth," the Bane of Wives said.

"What?"

"Open the dog's mouth." She knelt to scour her hands with ice. "There's something for you in there."

After the black-footed corpse, surely a frozen dog wouldn't kill her. Juris stripped off her good gloves and felt around under the dripping tongue. Something small, hard—a long flat stone.

"I killed him in the winter," the Bane of Wives said, throwing down her fouled snow, "and I froze him here. Mercy kill. He had pika. He was chewing on flagstones. Turn the stone over."

In rectangular Simple Aphalone characters a chisel had scraped the word ORMSMNT.

"Well," Ormsment breathed. "You knew I'd come to you?"

"When they wouldn't let you kill her. Then I knew."

"So you understand why I'm here?"

"Because you want to pretend the world's fair," the Bane of Wives said, with a terrible indifference, which Juris did not like at all: the indifference, at least. The terror she needed.

"I prefer to think I help keep it fair." Actions *had* to have consequences. What you did had to come back to you, or the world would be as inchoate and unfair as her childhood in the Butterveldt. When people cannot count on justice they count on blood.

Over the rebel winter she'd asked Cattlson, each and every time they met, *can I order her death? We have agents in place, I know we do—no? No? But, your Excellence, how can we protect her? After what she did at Welthony?*

And Cattlson would say, *it's out of my hands.*

Away a few benches, the Stakhi olive-oil man had begun shaking his fist and making threats. Shao Lune said something in a tone like a sneer and the man pivoted, instantly, into mewling apology: he hadn't realized she was navy, he hadn't meant it, could he make it up to her, please? Shao Lune laughed at him. "I did this to you? You're like a dog who comes at the chime of the bell. Yes, a dog, I said. A dog."

"What you're doing is treason," the Bane of Wives said.

Looking at her was like walking up to the edge of a canyon. You had to do it carefully, and not for too long. "Maybe," Juris said. "But it's the right thing to do."

"They'll purge your friends."

"We know the risks," Juris said, *we* meaning the whole conspiracy, the plan to overthrow Empire Admiral Satamine and maybe even the Parliament that created him. "All of us do. I have to show the Throne that they can't use us like dogs without us biting back."

"You don't know how many of your officers they already possess."

"And you do?"

"I know," the Bane of Wives said. "They possessed me once."

Of course she had. Who'd sent the Bane of Wives to Mzilimake Mbo to stir up civil war? Who had dispatched her to the Occupation to turn the Invijay against the Oriati?

The Bane of Wives had been the Emperor's agent.

"Tell me, then," Juris whispered, her bones suddenly athrum, her nose stuffed with the smell of thawing dog, the bee buzzing in her ear and the spring sun glittering on the melt, the whole world waiting, waiting on this answer, "can you lead me to her?"

"You have ships?"

"Two, yes, enough loyal crew for two ships." Those officers who'd stayed here under Ormsment, rather than moving on with Ahanna Croftare, did it for love of her. "Will you tell me who among them are compromised?"

"If you let me see to them myself."

That rankled at Juris, but so did the idea of blackmailed officers simpering among her loyal few. "So you shall."

"Good." The Bane of Wives spat into the snow. "Baru's at the Elided Keep. It's not on your charts. But I can take you there."

And now Ormsment had no excuse to turn back.

"Of course," the woman said, looking at Shao Lune, now alone, with callous appetite, carnal or violent, Juris couldn't tell, "once you do this, you can't come back. Even if you take Baru. Even if you force her to write you a pardon. The Emperor will destroy you."

"I have to do this," Ormsment said, simply. "The dead demand it."

The Bane of Wives looked at her as if she recognized something she might respect. "The dead do task us."

The bee whirred off to find a brighter flower. The dog's jaw creaked shut. Shao Lune's suitor fled.

"I have a price," the Bane of Wives said.

"What is it?"

"I get to keep Tain Hu."

5

THE END OF HISTORY

WILL you admire Cairdine Farrier?

He is fifty-four years old, a big man, a happy man, well liked and deep in love. He owns nineteen businesses, but these concerns own stake in others, too: unless you could find all his false names and paper legends you could never count all his money. Fisheries are some of his favorite investments. He owns, perhaps, one in a hundred fish in the sea, and who else can claim that? No shark and no kraken, no gape-mouthed whale with combs of baleen. Farrier has outmaneuvered the leviathans of the deep. Ships are very useful to him, but it does not suit him to seem like he has a private navy. So instead of possesssing vessels he possesses their masters.

He speaks in Parliament, where he is a great favorite for his humor and his digressions, and, of course, for the things he has accomplished. The opening of Sousward-which-was-Taranoke to the Republic's trade, which completed a great circle of commerce that rings the entire Ashen Sea in one golden river of endless profit. The young tyrants of the Suettaring markets call the modern prosperity *the Farrier Age*. The Egalitarians who protest beneath the Suettaring hills call him *the King of Pillage*. Parliamins and Ministers call him *Mister Farrier,* with great respect.

In the Faculties the students ask after him for lectures, *may we hear from the adventurer Cairdine Farrier, who has been all the way to Zawam Asu?* Women seek his hand in marriage. He is seen with lady friends but he does not settle. The gossip says, admiringly, that Farrier is mad for an Oriati princess some years his junior, a forbidden love, not because of their ages but because the Metademe has placed an attaintment upon the blood of Oriati royalty.

If he knew her carnally he would forfeit his citizenship. How chaste and gallant he must be with her!

Mister Farrier really *is* devoted to his work, isn't he? Even in love he wants to better the world's unfortunate. Imagine giving your husbandry and your citizenship to a member of a royal line. Next, Farrier's detractors say, he will adopt a cow and coax her into clothes, and she will write letters with ink from her teats. *Daer Parliament*, she will squirt, *Msr. Farrier treets me vry well. Please invest in his veal enterprise. He is convinced us to haf the calves he neets.*

For more than forty years, Caird's had his hands around the throat of his classmate Cosgrad Torrinde, a man who he named, in the cruelty of their teenage arguments, a cruelty he now sometimes but not often regrets, *the squid priest*. Very few know for certain that Cosgrad Torrinde, Minister of the Metademe, is also the elusive Hesychast. More know that Cairdine Farrier is also Itinerant, the Emperor's Adventurer: but not many more.

Farrier loves the world because he knows it so well, and he loves his princess because he knows her so little. In his fifty-four years, he's spent not twenty-five at home.

Will you now admire Cairdine Farrier?

He knows how to write and argue in Aphalone, Old Vitatic, Seti-Caho, Uburu, Takhaji, Roque, and two sorts of Urun. He could sell horns to a ram. He speaks richly, and with a laugh in his eyes. When he tells you something, you feel that he is holding back a little more, and you want to know it, for it must be the best part. He can quote every revolutionary handbook from *Somatic Mind* to *Manumission,* and he has written his own, the *Manual of Expedition.* When he goes to the spice boutique to buy a jar of cardamom for one of his famous recipes, the women speculate over his purpose, and the men ask him for advice.

He has a deadly secret, but it is not one of the ordinary species. He is not incestuous. He's never been caught conducting an affair or taking the woman's place in sex, nor documented in an unhygienic fetish like necrotica or bestiality. He has no strange compulsion, nor any illness which would oblige him to seek treatment. The fevers and parasites of the tropics were repulsed by his youthful vitality. His finances are now in order, and he has gone unindicted for his crimes.

Very few know his secret.

But all the nation knows his deepest hope.

This is his hope, as he has expressed it in that *Manual of Expedition.* He wishes to unite the entire world in a perfect meritocracy, a republic in which the worthy may rise from wherever they begin, whether it is a nursery in Falcrest's Suettaring or a plague hovel in the faraway Camou where buboes fester and they whisper of older plagues that weep green blood from swollen eyes. Genius, he says, may be discovered anywhere, and our Imperial duty calls us to discover that genius and to save it from decay.

Isn't that a hopeful dream?

Hope. Hope keeps Farrier moving, through those early days of heady adventure and then the pitifully wasteful and terribly necessary crisis of the Armada War, on into the compromise and digestion of Aurdwynn and Taranoke. Hope sustained him even as he pretended to languish on Taranoke, as he prosecuted the awful, soul-rotting business of sowing civil war among the Oriati, sending his best student into the Mzilimake jungles and the blood-stained grasses of the Occupation, stirring up the Invijay and the pygmies against their Oriati "friends." Hope sustained him as, one by one, his protégés fell away from the designs he had instilled in them. Chaos infected his students, just as it infected all the great races who rose and fell in ages past. The world distorted the laws that he had insinuated into his chosen few. They returned abominable.

Farrier needs his protégés to triumph. For time is almost out.

Ten years, maybe: the next ten years will decide the future of all human life. The course of history will be set. Will the Republic select the true method of eternal, perfect rule? Or will humanity collapse into a final spiral back down to the seabed ooze? It all depends on the confrontation between Falcrest and the Oriati Mbo, and the choices made as a result.

He will be sixty-four in ten years. In Falcrest they don't believe the old can do much work beyond the archive and the teaching stand. It's the fear of monarchy, you see. A king holds his power unto death, but the republican should abdicate young.

Cairdine Farrier doesn't believe in hereditary destiny. He doesn't believe in the Metademe's eugenics as a solution to the looming catastrophe. But he'll admit his dear nemesis Hesychast makes one strong point. Flesh *does* matter. Nothing's more than flesh, not yet. Kill the man, you kill his ideas.

Unless. Unless.

Unless Farrier finds the answer to the Imperial Question, the riddle of closure. Unless at last one of his protégés comes back perfect.

Then, in the only way that matters, he will be immortal.

B ARU played the Great Game with the man who'd butchered her home. Gods of older fire, was she happy to see him? Wasn't that *sick*? He'd condoned the rape of Cousin Lao as a medical necessity: keep that ember in your fist, so it always burns. He'd called the plague on Taranoke as inevitable as the tide: keep that tightness in your chest, so you feel it when you breathe.

But didn't he want to help her?

Baru was mostly sure she was happy to see him only because he was useful. She liked useful things. But there was the risk that she simply wanted to be around someone who cared what happened to her.

He wandered the map of the world that carpeted her morning-room: a bit less than her height, richer, rounder, with a neat beard and deep-set laughing eyes. He wore a dashing short-tailed sherwani. He looked at people with a beaming cleverness that was too charming, most of the time, to seem like avarice. All in all he was like a very self-satisfied raccoon.

"We'll play Hesychast rules," he said, but before Baru could ask, *what are Hesychast rules,* he huffed and wrung his hands and made a noise of hurt.

"Your Excellence?" she ventured.

"Oh, for shit's sake, Baru, call me Mister Farrier." His eyes shone. "I just . . . oh, king's balls."

She almost giggled. Instead she arched one eyebrow, severely. "Your pardon? Whose balls?"

"I just—it's hard to believe you're here." He stamped down on the little black shape of Taranoke. "Twenty-two and foreign born, raised in a hut on a little cove. If I'd gone to Census and Methods and asked them, *how will Baru turn out,* do you know what they would've said?"

"Housewife, I expect?"

"Agricultural planning, actually, with an occasional article in the *Progress of Mathematics.*" He beamed wetly, choked by pride. "And now you're one of our Emperor's own! Look at you!"

The lamps were going out, because there was no one to refill the oil. The housekeepers had fled rather than overhear two cryptarchs speaking poisoned words.

Baru had been reading the rules of the Great Game. She knew, now, how to manage a few of the rules, how to play as more than make-believe. She had arranged the board to represent a simple confrontation between Falcrest and the Oriati: Aurdwynn tidied away in the north, the Stakhieczi quiescent, nothing looming across the Mother of Storms. Just Old King Poison against the thousand-year Mbo.

"I'm nothing special, Mr. Farrier," she said. Play the humble student, Baru, and bait him, bait him till he tells you the truth you have to know.

Why is Falcrest saved? What have I done that he wanted so badly for me to do?

"Nothing special!" He set down the pawns of Federal Princes across the Mbo. "How can you think that, Baru?"

"Well, as you say, there's the matter of age." She opened her hand to the empty northwest of the world. "The War Princess Shiqu Si died at twenty-one with the biggest empire in history. And how old was Dautiare when she led the first purge after the revolution? Twenty? And there was her father's tactician Iro Mave, although I haven't found many good books on her."

Farrier applauded gently. "You *have* mastered your history. Now, we play Hesychast rules: all character is determined by heredity. No one may disobey their intrinsic nature. Begin."

Behind him the southern-facing window, the harbor birds, the glittering wavetops that receded to a white line. The patterns of wave-crest and trough like the lines of a mountain range. Were mountains waves traveling through earth, millennia in their crest and crash?

On the board she'd marshaled her resources in Falcrest. She, the Baru-piece, had no rules yet in the game, so she had granted herself dominion over trade and commerce on the Ashen Sea, and over Falcrest's internal economy. No fleets. No votes in Parliament. No laws or judgments. Just money.

She chose, and played, a currency gambit. Exactly what Farrier had used on Taranoke. She would sell exports to Oriati Mbo—lumbers, spices, textiles, clocks and art especially—cheaply, and for whatever money the Oriati would pay. She would buy only with Falcresti fiat notes. Their currency came out, Falcrest's went in. Like a straw shoved into the rind of the Oriati economy, and her mouth sucking out all their native money, until they traded only with hers.

"In Aurdwynn," she said, thinking of the mastery of history, "a man told me that the future is an edict issued by the past."

"Historical contingency." Farrier nodded. "The notion that the shape of tomorrow depends, by fixed laws, upon the shape of today. Quite radical, in the days when kings claimed absolute rule. People were executed for claiming that history had power over the monarch. Ah—what's this?" Reading Baru's orders now: "Ah, I recognize what you're up to."

"The man who told me that . . . he was trying to say that he loved me." Baru roughened her throat and half-closed her eyes, dangling the bait, come on, Farrier, will you sniff at the hint that your student loved a man? "*Historical contingency.* It's terrible, isn't it? Like everyone's an arrow, already in flight. I killed them all with that idea."

"Mm," he said, moving a couple pawns, checking his little handbook of Great Game rules. "How so?"

"Well—the Duke Unuxekome grew up on stories of brave sea captains. So I sent him to make a brave stand at sea, and he went, and he died."

"The Oriati won't stop using their currencies," Farrier said, apologetically. "Under Hesychast's rules, the Mbo coins—we call them the lonjaro, the segu, the mzili, and the devi—are so much a part of their traditions as to be fixed in their blood. I know, it's quite absurd, isn't it?"

Baru found, to her horror, that she couldn't stop confessing. "And Oaths-fire, he wanted to be part of something idealistic, so I made myself an ideal of freedom, and he loved me. And Lyxaxu hated himself for the winter his people starved: so I convinced him I could feed his duchy, and he gave me his treasury. They were like clocks, and I found their keys, I turned the hands—"

"Baru." He looked up from his work at the crop calendar. "You're grieving. I'm sorry to—" He chuckled, suddenly and self-deprecatingly. "—to tell you how you're feeling, but I know, I *know* you have walls inside you. Trust me, please. You're going to have to take time to mourn."

"They were traitors," Baru growled, looking at her feet. "I don't want to grieve them. It's a waste of time."

"You loved them, though. I know you did." He showed her his book. "I'm afraid the Oriati currency pool is so large that, in your efforts to replace all their money with ours, you've printed so many fiat notes they're now worth less than their paper."

Hate. Hate like deepest pressure. Like diving until the water crushed her ears and burnt her chest. Love! Tell me about love, Cairdine Farrier. Tell me that you understand my pain. How wrong you will be: how terrible for you when at last I make myself known.

But she *wanted* his comfort. Counterfeits could be useful, couldn't they? Print me a little counterfeit comfort, Farrier. Print it for me.

"An inflationary crash," she said, stiffly, "like I caused when Tain Hu was counterfeiting notes."

"You loved her," Farrier murmured, with eyes of shining sympathy. "I know you did. You loved Tain Hu."

She was utterly still. That name in his mouth.

"Baru, I'm so *proud*."

She put the bar of her arm across his soft throat and slammed him into the windows. The whole great hive of glass shuddered at the blow. It was the first time she'd ever touched him in anger. He was looking up at her in alarm and hateful glee, *I can move her,* that's what he was thinking, *I can still provoke her.*

Baru snarled in his face, "She was a traitor!"

"Yes, quite," he choked. "An archtraitor. And you executed her for it. Will you give me an inch to speak, please? Thank you. She's on file attesting to your illicit, ah, experimentation. And you executed her anyway. A great credit to your discipline. May I breathe now?"

Baru retreated two steps, back foot, then front. The ringing! The ringing! In Aurdwynn they beat the dirt out of their laundry with huge wooden clubs. Baru had helped, because it was fun to smash clothes clean. But Devena help you if you struck the club against a tree, or a rock. It would leap and quiver in your hand with a thrum that conducted itself, instantly, up your arms and into your jaw. And, with your teeth buzzing, you'd drop the club and swear.

Now Baru felt that same hum in her bones and brain and she wanted to come apart, her joints electing to unclasp each other, her sinews unbound, spilling her across the marble in a fan of gore.

"What are you going to do?" she said, breathing hard. "Try to circumcise me?"

"No, Baru, no." He looked up at her with glittering wit, and pride, a hideous paternal pride that claimed credit for all that it honored. "Don't you understand? I'm glad. So glad. I told you, Falcrest is saved. You've saved us all."

"Why?"

"You loved her, in accordance with your nature."

Baru shrugged: the hardest lie so well-practiced it was easy now. The hugeness of Tain Hu's trust and love was all that made it possible to conceal that trust, that love: like a sail it could be folded up inside itself.

"Just one night," she said.

"But that's everything. That's everything. You were out beyond the Republic's reach, where you could have done anything you pleased. What would you have done if Hesychast's rules were right?" He held up his hands. "Baru, he thinks *you obey your nature.* You could've run off with your duchess into the mountains and been with her. And yet you came back. You obeyed our laws. No one believed you could do it, Baru! No one but me!"

Falling: the world is falling. Nothing below her. Apparitor was right. *That bastard Itinerant. He made you kill her.* It was all part of his plan, everything, even the kiss, even the words *kuye lam,* even the drowning-stone: and thus she is lost.

But wait a moment. Wait now.
So what if Farrier expected you to kill me?
Wasn't that the point?
To do as they required,
and so deceive them?

"You're the end of history," Cairdine Farrier whispered. His eyes glimmered in awe. "You're the proof I needed, Baru. The foreign-born sinner *taught* to become a perfect citizen. He said I couldn't do it. He said the sin was in your flesh and germ. But look at you. You policed yourself. You have the discipline. I taught it to you and you learnt."

Behind him waves crashed against the harbor bluff, and cataracts of spray burst up into rainbow arches and collapsed.

"Baru, he's lost, we've *won.*"

She remembered her dream on the morning of betrayal. Farrier-who-was-Itinerant behind the blank mask of the Empire. And he had said to her: when the work is complete, no one and nothing will act without our consent. "By volition" will be a synonym for "by decree."

"Oh Himu," she croaked. "That's what you want of me. I'm to disprove Hesychast's theories. I'm to ruin him and ruin his work and . . . and then . . ."

She looked at the world beneath her feet.

"And then," Farrier said, softly, "we play the Great Game by my rules. The rules that work. For they made you, and *you* work perfectly."

She managed, against the weight of the avalanche, the avalanche that was knowing she was just a single stone in his tumbling design, to ask: "How long until he comes?"

"He'll be here within the month." Farrier still stood against the glass, but the gravity had swung to him: he was silhouetted against the ocean and the world, with all the light behind him, and Baru stood in darkness. "First you must survive his examination. He will search you for signs of madness. You didn't do what he expected, so your body must be broken somehow. Easier for him to believe that than to accept that he's wrong about the causes of behavior."

"And then?"

"Then," he said, "you win control over the expedition. And you ensure the rewards go to us, not him."

"What expedition?"

A wink. A smile. "Wait and see."

THEY played the Great Game every day, until Baru dreamt of Oriati demographics swarming like honeybees in a continental hive. Woke to find herself tracing Ashen Sea currents on the silk sheets of her cold, lonely bed. When she was not in training (and it was training) with Farrier she drank rare whiskeys and read secret histories and tried to imagine exactly what would come next.

Expedition? What expedition? Would Farrier send her east, across the Mother of Storms? No. He needed her close.

Then where?

Apparitor had vanished. Probably he was afraid of Farrier. She saw less of his people, *Helbride*'s crew, in the keep, except that Iraji kept popping up in the oddest places—fitting clean sheets in her chambers, resetting the pawns on the Great Game map, inventorying the whiskeys in the cellar she liked to sample.

"He's spying on me," she told Farrier.

"Of course. And you'd be wise to let him." He sat cross-legged on the map of Falcrest, covering the divisions between ancient cantons and shrievalties. "That's how we trust each other. A cryptarch you cannot spy on is a cryptarch you must fear. Agents are very good proxies for trust."

But Iraji's golden eyes followed Baru with a quiet nervous intensity she couldn't blame on surveillance alone. "I wonder if he's soft for me."

Farrier was suddenly very busy with his pawns. "Couldn't speak to that," he said airily. "Today we play Farrier rules. You will be the Mbo. I will play Falcrest."

It was the first moment of genuine uncertainty, unplanned weakness, she'd seen in him since he appeared. He was off-balance! She did not pause to analyze: she struck as Hu would've struck, by instinct.

"I could use a concubine with a little softness," she said, pacing at the window. "It's cold here. Maybe that woman who stands sentry on the east tower. I see her up there in the morning, alone, looking out to sea all flinty and intent. And I want to bring her a coffee and a quiet word for good work. What do you think? The climb must keep her firm, I like my women firm—"

"Remember," he said, as if she hadn't spoken, "that under my rules, behavior is not fixed. A child raised under Incrasticism will behave Incrastically. Shall we begin?"

Curious. Very curious. Obviously he was displeased by her openness, but now that her tribadism was a fact of record, wasn't it to his advantage? She'd proven she could control herself.

She began to move pawns.

Baru played the Mbo the way the Mbo played history. Open-armed, enormously affable, embracing invaders like eager guests. Farrier's wheel of trade ships unloaded masterworks of craft and literature onto her shores, but the Mbo's griots copied them, mingled them, made their own tributes, and sent them back to Falcrest inflected with a thousand years of dizzyingly various tradition.

Wherever you went in the Oriati Mbo you found culture layered on culture, like a palimpsest never fully scraped. Take one of the four great federations, Lonjaro: it had its Eleven Gates and One City and Thirteenth Crown, but even if you memorized every kingdom from Jaro the Flamingo Kingdom to Jejuje the Otter and Unkinde the Female Lion, you would still need to learn the Three Cereals, Brown Millet and Rice and Einkorn, which were social rates left over from the tax structure of the ancient Cheetah Palaces, and then you would have to study Mana Mane, who united the Thirteen-in-Three-in-One with the saga called the *Kiet Khoiad*, which was why the Great Seal of Lonjaro bore the letters MKMK, Mana Kiet Mane Khoiad, sometimes extended to 13MK3MK1: only it was not actually clear that Mana Mane was from Lonjaro at all, they might well have been from Mzilimake to the south, home of the moon god Mzu and the gray parrots who lived as long as a man, and anyway no study of Mana Mane could explain Lonjaro's great stelae, hundred-foot-high obelisks stabilized by underground counterweights, designed ages before they should have been possible— the point of all this not being the need to memorize many Mbo facts, but that the Mbo was far too complicated, too lively and old, to understand.

"Why," she asked Farrier, astounded, "don't they have better banks?"

Banking was the most powerful weapon in the world, because people stored their wealth in banks, and the banks could loan that wealth out to fund great labors. You could tax your people dead to fund your armies, and they would hate you for it. But give them a bank and a fair interest rate and they would give you everything they had and let you do what you pleased with it and ask only to have it back when you were done.

Barring a sort of informal hawala system, the Mbo did not have large organized banks. When a Federal Prince wanted funds, they had to raise them personally.

"It's because they have a poorly developed idea of property," Farrier explained. "Too much of Oriati society is a shared commons. You don't own the pasture where you graze your sheep—your village takes care of it together. If you don't own the pasture, you can't post it as collateral for a loan. If you can't take out a loan, why have a bank?"

"How primitive," Baru said, because she thought he'd like to hear it.

But he frowned. "Don't dismiss them so swiftly. Watch . . ."

He attacked Oriati Mbo with all his powers. Schools to seduce the young. Banks to issue loans, loans to put the Oriati into debt, debt to give him an excuse to seize their land and property. He built toll roads and canals for exclusive trade. He gave his allies inoculations against disease. He brutalized the Oriati currencies with counterfeiting and debasement, flooding their continent with fake money so they would turn to the stable, reliable Falcresti fiat note as their trade coin.

It was precisely how he had captured Taranoke.

It failed utterly.

The students in his schools could not be isolated from their families and communities: they rejected Incrasticism. The banks could not repossess the collateral of failed loans, because debtors' neighbors bailed them out. The toll roads and canals were captured by local governments and opened to free trade until they were as crowded and slow as all the rest. Inoculations worked well, except that the inoculated were shunned and shamed for not sharing their immunity. When one of the four Oriati currencies foundered, another grew more valuable, as if the currencies were rabbits and foxes and wolves, one's misfortune another's opportunity.

The Mbo absorbed his attacks. At the end of the game Falcrest was more part of the Mbo than the Mbo of Falcrest.

Farrier looked up with shining, delighted eyes. "You see?"

"How," Baru said, baffled, for the Oriati had just defied the powers which she had spent her life to claim, "do they *do* that?"

"Hesychast has one theory, and I have another. But it will be up to you, Baru, to find out who's right, and to see the solution executed."

The thought of Hesychast, of flesh and body, reminded her of his moment of weakness then. "It doesn't bother you?"

"What?"

"To know that I want to fuck women?"

She could say it right to his face. Because Tain Hu had sacrificed herself to permit it. Death to buy freedom, the freedom to end the death.

Cairdine Farrier flinched. She wanted to shout in triumph, You don't like it, do you? You don't like it when I say it aloud, without fear.

"We all have our flaws," he said, softly, "we all make our mistakes. But if we work to overcome them—if we prove that we can master our flesh—then we've triumphed."

Baru thought she'd won this conversation, or at least gathered valuable intelligence: she was just warming up to a little smugness when Farrier, offhandedly, knocked her back down.

"Have you been catching up on the letters from your parents?" He beamed at her. "I'm sorry I held your mail these last three years. I just thought it'd keep you focused. I do hope they're well!"

"Letters from my parents?" Baru echoed.

"Yes, piles of them, haven't you—oh no." He covered his heart in shock. "Apparitor didn't show you the library?"

6

THE LIGHTNING IN THE EAST

BARU'S tongue stuck to her palate when she breathed.

The Liminal Library had been built to die. Carved into rock down below sea level, its air had to be parched by chemistry lest it rot the books; and if invaders struck, the library would flood. The Throne would not give up its secrets. Lanterns of iridescent jellyfish tea cast blue-green light on concrete buttresses, long chains in catenary arches, the marching monoliths of the shelves. The air was dry as bonemeal.

In the distance, red hair and pale skin caught the light for a moment.

"There you are," Baru breathed. "Keep my parents' letters, will you?"

She slipped down the shelves toward Apparitor. It was so silent in the Library that she heard quite distinctly when he raised his head and said, "Oh, shit."

She broke into a sprint. His footsteps vanished suddenly but she was learning, and she had an easier time with sound on her blind side—she cut right between two shelves, lunged, and tackled him as he dashed past. He dropped his sack, and they went down together on the stone in a papery explosion of letters and books.

Dingy rag novels poured over Baru. She picked up the book that settled on her neck and read the title: *Intrusion from the Pointillist Plane!* "What the fuck is this?"

Apparitor tried to scoop all his spilled books away from her. *A Reckoning of Archons! Nab Banadab and the Horror of Canduûn! I Summoned Antideath!* All on the same rag cover dyed cheap yellow. One of them bragged, in red letters, of *Impossible Truths from Behind the Moon's Silver Mask—You'll Wish You'd Never Known!*

"Are these *codebooks*?" Baru cried, delighted. "That's ingenious." A short-run novel would be a wonderful source of spice-words for encryption.

"I just like cosmic mysteries." Apparitor scooped everything up with bashful haste. "Well, do enjoy your mail catch-up, I'm sure no one will be offended you've been ignoring them for three years."

Baru stabbed him with a smile. "At least my family knows where I've gone."

"Fuck off," he said, looking nervously around. "You haven't told Farrier, have you?"

"Of course not. They really don't know?"

"Not most of them."

A sheaf of cream paper in a gold-cloth band fell out of a book. Apparitor froze. Baru grabbed for the sheaf, very curious. Her half blindness didn't keep her from reading: if she couldn't always quote the right half of the page, the general meaning still reached her—

Apparitor stamped on her fingers. "That's not for you."

Baru wrung her hand. "A letter to your lover?" she said, just to prickle him. "You want to keep him up to date on your failures?"

"Hardly, hardly; Lindon and I keep our love out of our politics. This is nothing you'd care about, believe me."

"Tell me, then, if it doesn't matter."

He winked at her. "It's just Tain Hu's will."

And he was gone before she could even beg him to wait.

FARRIER had given her a key in an envelope, and it came with a note from Apparitor: *You didn't get much mail. I suppose because you've murdered or estranged everyone who's no longer useful to you. Ha ha. That's like a joke, in that we'll both have to pretend we think it's a joke so we can work together civilly. That's my favorite kind of joke.*

"Fuck off," Baru told the silence. She slid the key in all the way to its handle, an oily insinuation of teeth and tumblers. The lock thumped with satisfying heft. She'd like to own a lock to open and close as she sat in thought. Imagine a currency made of locks! A currency that measures the value of secrets, and the more the secret's worth, the more locks you attach.

The door whispered on silent bearings.

Baru's lantern showed her the rack of letters labeled FOR THE CANDIDATE.

She demanded absolute obedience from every muscle and nerve. With two fingers she pinched out one letter at random.

To our daughter Baru Cormorant.

From Solit Able and Pinion Starmap.

Her loving parents.

And then she was crying, sure as a storm brought rain. Mother. Father. You wrote me—oh, you wrote me so often, and I never wrote back!

The tough cotton-rag envelopes. The heavy handwriting, as if perpetually frustrated, or, perhaps, shouting. Did they get news from Aurdwynn? Had they heard of Baru's defection to the rebels? Had they read of her "true" loyalty to the Throne? Oh gods, what would mother *think*?

The envelopes changed to slick waxy card stock. A new hand on the pen, and a new signature:

To the Imperial Accountant of Aurdwynn,

From the Lieutenant Aminata isiSegu, RNS Lapetiare

Baru sniffled and smiled. Look, the later ones came from *the Lieutenant Commander Aminata isiSegu, Annalila Fortress, Isla Cauteria.* Lieutenant *commander*! She'd been promoted, and so young! Aminata always wanted to be an admiral. She was closer now. Too bad that she probably hated Baru for sinking all those navy ships at Welthony Harbor. Too bad. Too bad.

Baru knuckled her eyes and growled. Tain Hu was dead. Hold up that big pain next to losing Aminata. Look at you, tiny pain. You are so little. She had to keep everything in proportion.

And here was a letter that Baru clutched to her breast with both hands, to warm her heart. Lao had written. Her second cousin, Baru's first crush, the woman Baru saved from the awful hygienist Diline in the Iriad school. Baru had *definitely* saved her. No one else was sacrificed—so the act of saving Lao was unambiguously, absolutely good. She loved Lao just for that.

But of course she had work mail, too, Throne mail, the fruit of certain subtleties she'd set in motion before Sieroch.

Purity Cartone, Baru's personal Clarified agent, had dispatched a letter.

It must have come in through secret channels, fast sloops and dry mailrooms where women in black gloves sorted out codes they didn't need to understand. The address read:

RETRIEVED FROM APPARITOR DEAD DROP IN TREATYMONT
ESCALATE TO APPARITOR FOR ROUTING

Apparitor had scrawled a note below: *Are you getting clever already? Who is it who sent this? Hope you wake up from your coma soon—you're drooling oat mush on my good pillow right now—*

"I didn't forget," Baru told Hu. "See, I remembered the ledger of secrets! I didn't forget!"

The ledger had been created to force the Coyote rebels to trust each other. Every duke, duchess, judge, and accountant who'd joined the conspiracy had whispered a fatal secret to the Priestess in the Lamplight, the rebellion's secret-keeper. Baru had told the truth: *I want to fuck women.* And the priestess had recorded that secret.

When Baru had learned the priestess was also a Falcresti agent, she'd sent Purity Cartone to kill her and get the ledger back. Not only to protect herself, but to gain the secret written by Jurispotence Xate Yawa, whose glaring blue eyes hid agendas and loyalties Baru couldn't begin to guess. The last time she'd gone up against Yawa, she'd lost so badly that only Tain Hu had saved her from mutilation.

Xate Yawa was now exalted, just as Baru had been. And this ledger might be enough to protect Baru from her. But, of course, it would also be full of the unbearably personal secrets of people Baru had loved and betrayed.

Suddenly the bundle of letters was a burden. More heartbreak to wallow through. More ways to punish herself for the choices she'd made. Couldn't she leave them for later? Wander back to her morning-room, perhaps, and play the Great Game against herself . . .

A footstep scraped the stone.

A hand closed on her shoulder.

Baru whirled and her hands did two different things. With her left she pushed the man away: with her right she grabbed him by the collar and hauled him close. All the letters tumbled onto the floor and Baru, tossed off-balance by her manual disagreement, yelped and fell on her ass.

It was only Apparitor's boy Iraji. "What," she said, from the ground, "are you doing!" But deep within her there was a reptilian calm, a slithering advisor which whispered, *If he meant violence he'd already have hurt you.*

"Apparitor sent me, my lady, to help you with anything you required." The jellyfish light picked out his gold-flecked eyes, Tain Hu's eyes, and drowned that color in cold green. He had a good face, big-eyed and curious and beautiful, darker enough than Baru to be brown-black. In ancient days golden monkeys with clever faces were companions to the Oriati princes of myth, but Falcrest had stolen that image and racialized it, and Baru would not make the comparison now.

Or had this entire thought only been an excuse to indulge in prejudice? Could she ever know?

"He sent you to watch me, you mean," she said.

"Yes, my lady, he's concerned for you. He hopes you will allow me to remain by your side."

"Yes, I gathered that when he sent you to seduce me."

"Generally seduction involves the front or the back, my lady, but rarely the side."

He said it very plainly, which made Baru laugh. "I don't favor men. But I'm sure you knew that."

"Sometimes people are flexible."

"Sometimes. Not this time. Help me up."

She hauled herself up on his forearm. He had to throw his weight back and heave, as if he were trying to escape her grip. The gap between his slippers and his robe bared his hard black calves.

"So you're Apparitor's homme fatal?"

"Sometimes, my lady. I have many uses."

"Are you useful for picking up letters?"

He was indeed. When they'd gathered the dropped mail he led her through quicklime-dessicated air to a desk occupied by what seemed to be a very patient, very still man. "The circulation desk, my lady," Iraji said, pointing with an open hand. "And the presiding librarian."

A mummified corpse had been mounted to a steel ring behind the table. Hollow eye sockets stared forever into the shelves. A silver placard read:

JAMAN RYAPOST.
SUICIDE UPON EXALTATION. 11 SUMMER AR 101. PRESERVED
IN LOVING* MEMORY
(*WE THINK IT LIKELY THAT SOMEONE LOVED JAMAN RYAPOST)

Suicide upon exaltation. Hm.

Baru thought, absurdly, about killing herself.

"Your Excellency?" Iraji asked, gently. Baru very much disliked her greed for his concern. "Are you all right?"

"Tell Apparitor I'm frightfully upset," she snapped. In the jellyfish light everything seemed to be underwater; looking at Iraji she had the idea that bubbles would puff from his nose. Again she thought of drowning. "Did he send you any message for me?"

"My lord Apparitor did pass on this letter of introduction. . . ."

A fresh envelope, marked, in very old-fashioned print, WELCOME TO THE CHANDLESPIDER CELL OF THE SPECIAL ADVISORY TO THE IMPERIAL THRONE. "Chandlespider?"

"Yes, my lady. Once the Throne had multiple cells, hidden from each other."

"And now?"

"To the best of my knowledge we are the only remaining cell. I understand the Throne had to be purged and rebuilt a few decades back. A period we call the Rebirth."

"Thus the name *Renascent*?" Apparitor had shuddered over that one anonymous pawn bearing the name.

"Just so, mam. Our oldest. She initiated the, ah, period of regeneration. Before her, each member of the Throne kept their own staff. She created the Imperial Advisory to serve as a . . . commons of sort. The exiles who serve this keep belong to it."

"What's she like?"

"I can't say, my lady. She's imprinted a mark of destruction on the rumors that describe her."

"You can't be serious." Baru sighed.

"I'm very serious, my lady." He looked at her in absolute, boyish earnest. "She disseminates false rumors about herself, to smoke out those who inquire after her. People who pursue them vanish."

The power to make your own identity poisonous. What a skill that would be. Whenever they whispered to each other, *That Baru likes her women too much,* they would hold their throats and bubble from their noses and die. . . .

She'd lied. She wasn't tired. Tomorrow she might be tired, tomorrow this cold fire she'd inherited from Tain Hu might at last burn out. But now—

She growled like a starved cat and tore the letter open, ripping, rattling, desperately and frighteningly hungry for the power within.

To the future reader,
With my fond regards,
And my deepest condolences,

Welcome to the arena of the rest of your life.

If I am very lucky, and if history's been kind, you've heard my true name, Honesty Kabrir. More likely you know me only as Elisiant, agent of the Emperor.

I write this message as a man condemned. Yesterday the gang of feckless scholars and polymaths in thrall to my colleague Renascent slaughtered my theory of eidesis on the marble floors of Purifier Hall. My political support is gone, and my debtors have come calling. Those who prepared my poisons and my illegal moneys will soon testify.

Renascent knows about my other family. Virtue guard the male sex from its worst nature! For my infidelity I will face a punishment befitting the crime. Death first, of course. I will not be their stud.

But enough of me—

Why would they leave my advice for you, when I've failed so bitterly at the One Trade? The answer, dear future initiate, is that we are crypt-

archs, the people of secrets. Only the failures can be made to share their tricks.

You cannot have Renascent's secrets, so you'll have to settle for me.

Incrasticism is our Republic's creed. The word means for tomorrow.

In your exaltation to our Throne you join a lineage more than a century old. Understand first that the Throne has a trait that our ship-builders would call dynamic instability. Our organization is meant to topple if not carefully maintained: and in its failure, the Throne is de-signed to purge all its members in an orgy of fratricide.

Why?

This reason first. No empire needs a camarilla of secret conspirators. Parliament, the Ministries, the Admiralty, and the Judiciary—these or-gans are enough to keep the blood pumping.

We are not a government. We are not the eyes, or the ears, or the mind of the Republic. We are parasites. And if we ever cease to benefit that host, the Republic will expunge us. Understand this, my inheritor! If Aurdwynn's first habit is rebellion, then Falcrest's first love is revolution. Falcrest, oh Falcrest, she will lobotomize her rulers and rise up crying out from the Suettaring hilltops:

We demand a better form of tyranny!

It will be up to you to devise that better form.

For the more we feed our host Republic, the hungrier it seems to grow.

In our grand successes over the past century we have invented a mon-ster called a middle class. Our predecessors pillaged the Ashen Sea, and now the people are accustomed to receiving that pillage. And they are accustomed to their innocence. If they learn what we do on distant shores to secure their safety and prosperity, I am certain they would hang us all. Not for the crime of what we did, mind! But for the crime of allowing them to know.

Once I told a man in Commsweal Square that in our foreign prov-inces we still force women into reparatory marriages or sterility. He laughed! Not us, he told me, not us: those things happen elsewhere, they happened once, but not in our Republic today.

We cryptarchs have one godlike power. We have maps. We know how to change the idea of safer childbirth in a distant province into the fact of a hundred thousand red-cheeked survivors. Can you explain to me how your desire to walk across the room becomes the motion of your limbs? No, you cannot.

My power over the empire is clearer and more true than my power over my own body.

I believe that the fate of the entire human species balances on this brief century. We live in a narrow and closing doorway, and the forces of discord and disaster close in on us. Again and again the great empires of the past have been struck down.

We must step forward, lest we be caught on the threshold and dragged back to ruin. You, too, will be held to account for your contribution to the great and final work, which is our quest for a theory of perfect rule: a means by which the Imperial Republic of Falcrest may be rendered causally closed, so that the sprout of every seed and the turn of every cyclone occurs in accordance with our predictions, and therefore in accordance with our decrees. Thus we may at last achieve the state of ruling without acting, a self-governing world.

Welcome to the project.

Kindest regards,
The late Honesty Kabrir
Elisiant

"Is he real?" she asked Iraji.

"I doubt it very much. Who could say? So many records are hidden behind unbreakable codes. But this was the letter Apparitor was given when he was exalted. Elisiant is a tradition of sorts, I think."

She should discourage him from liking her. Men who liked her were invariably doomed. "Would you like to take dictation?" she asked him. "So you can tell Apparitor what I write?"

He covered his smile. "Will you strangle me for it?"

"Not without provocation," Baru purred, and the purr reminded her of Treatymont, pretending to flirt with Bel Latheman as he pretended not to hate her, or up in her accountant's tower with Muire Lo, watching the city's laundry lines blow against a low cold autumn sky, taking bets on the ducal partisans fistfighting in the plaza.

Her eyes stung in the dry. "Let's begin," she said, harshly.

First she dictated a poisonous note to Xate Yawa. A jab—*I know your game*—a casual threat of death, and an apology for failing to save her brother, Olake. Iraji took it all down expressionlessly. That should satisfy Apparitor she had no alliance with Yawa.

"Now," Baru said, tapping her brow, "I should write to Aminata. I'm sure you read a file on her?"

"She was very lovely, last we met," he said, with an innocence so studied Baru looked up in outrage. He was refreshing his quill.

"You've never met her." Baru leaned in on him. "Have you? Apparitor didn't turn up in Falcrest until . . ."

"He was arranging the pieces for some years. A fact he brings up, often and bitterly, when you seem to be receiving too much credit." He smoothed out his paper. "Your letter? You must be very eager to get back in touch."

In fact, Baru was terrified, for it was very likely Aminata loathed her and would never speak to her again. Suddenly she didn't want Iraji to hear a word of this letter. "I'll write it," she snapped. "Give me that."

They had a childhood code, which they'd used in the Iriad school to pass letters in a little kitchen dead drop. Aminata had shown Baru how to seal the drop with saliva and a single hair. *If it's moved, you treat that drop as compromised, understand?*

Dearest Aminata, etc. etc. Baru hesitated.

I read of your promotion to Lieutenant Commander. My congratulations. Upon her return to Falcrest, I intend to recommend you to Province Admiral Ormsment. You may wonder why a technocrat thinks to recommend you to a flag officer, and, well—more cause to hear my story!

She would mention Juris Ormsment so as to bring up the Welthony matter sideways. Ormsment had commanded the tax ships Baru betrayed and sank. Baru was trying to say, *hey, I know what I did. Will you talk to me about it?*

She went on with more dangerous material. *I wonder if we could discuss navy politics again, and the mutability of government . . .* If Aminata hated her, she could bring the letter to Navy Censorate right away, and then Baru would know, without ever having to ask her, that Aminata never wanted to see her again.

Find me at the return address. We simply must catch up. I have a remarkable wound to show you.

Regards,
Your sword thief

Baru signed, blew, and sealed. Iraji was watching her very curiously. "I've got to tell you," Baru said, heavily, "the last man who took my letters died of plague. Do you have any strange diseases I ought to know about?"

Iraji's bright eyes went suddenly dim: his lids half-shut, his hands loosening.

"No," he said, thickly. "I'm going to bring you some books you might find interesting. Back in a moment."

A peculiar reaction. Well, she was alone now. Baru closed her eyes against Muire Lo's guilty ghost. One secretary, and now another. She so rarely spent *Falcrest* lives. Somehow she kept tangling with the provincials. . . .

She should decrypt Purity Cartone's message now, and get at that ledger of secrets.

She set the envelope down, picked up a letter opener, and

Hu had been so beautiful on that last night. So fierce. Look: she was raising Cattlson's banner in her mailed fists. She was standing on the Henge Hill with her hair in the wind. The Coyotes were setting off fireworks, and the light came down through the tent cloth, on her broad and naked shoulders, down her broken nose, as they lay together between passions, and Baru reached for her.

My lady?"

How strange, Baru thought. I do believe I've been sitting here staring at the letter opener for quite a while.

She commanded her hand to move. Her hand replied that it *could*, but why should it bother? Opening this envelope would just lead to pain.

Stupid hand. She ought to be *glad* it would hurt. Pain was an ally. Pain was true. If something made you feel like death, then you had to believe in it. It couldn't be a fantasy you'd invented to protect yourself. Comfort was a lie. Pain was the truth.

Pick up your fucking hand and open the letter.

Nothing happened.

Everything felt far away, and yet very beautiful: a keening, edged beauty, like a distant iceberg under moonlight. The coffee beans, and the pot of fresh ink, and her own still hand. All of them swaddled by a layer of invisible wool like the ruff of a winter coat. Perhaps she could just sit here a moment. It was warm and dark, and she was surrounded by books.

"My lady!" Iraji cried.

Baru thought about answering for a few seconds, and then, finally, said, "Yes?"

"You were absent. And your right hand was moving."

She'd scrawled something on the back of Purity's envelope. *Iron Circlet*. She looked at her hand and wondered how it had done that.

Iraji stood on his toes and bobbed in alarm. He was carrying a stack of books. "My lady, might I suggest, if it's not too forward, that you take a moment for yourself? I understand, from your service jacket, that you love to read. I brought some titles you might find fascinating."

"You're distracting me," Baru said, dully. "Go away, I have a coded letter to decrypt."

Iraji huffed. Then he sat down across from her, picked up a book entitled *Born of Salt and Stone*, licked his fingers, and opened to the front page. "Are you allowed to *read* that?" Baru squawked, catching the subtitle: *Upon the Young Apparitor.* "Does he let you read books about him?"

"Of course I can read about him," Iraji said, airily. "Don't I comfort his ego as well as his body?"

Baru *hrmph*ed and moved her chair so her body would block the lantern light.

Iraji moved his chair back into the light and kept reading.

"Ooh," he said, cupping his chin. "That's *fascinating.* How scandalous . . . my goodness. You don't know what you're missing."

"Prick," Baru muttered, and then she reached for *On the Nature of the Eastern Supercontinent (from the Satamine Report).* Her hands did exactly as she wished. She opened the book and a shiver ran from the crown of her head down to the cable of her calves: like cold water, poured from above.

AFTERWARD, renewed, she saluted her new colleagues.

To my peers of the committee . . . Power was the opposite of the sea. It flowed upward, away from the commons, toward the peaks. Show her a city with a council of five hundred, and she would find the demagogues who divided them in two. Show her ten friends: some would be spoken of, and some would do the speaking.

Why? Why? She wanted to know. And if the Oriati had lasted a thousand years, how had they kept so much power in their commons?

Was it a tradition they had? An idea?

Or was it in their blood?

I have completed my initial review of Apparitor's documents, she wrote. *We clearly face important strategic challenges.*

And each of those challenges was an opportunity, a fang in Tain Hu's ghost maw.

A resurgent Stakhieczi monarchy. The steel people north of Aurdwynn had united under their Necessary King. Usually they starved, or turned on each other. But this time, with secret help, they might crash down on Falcrest. . . .

Backlash from our ongoing efforts to destabilize the federated governments of Oriati Mbo. War was coming, Baru had no doubt of that. Falcrest had gained the whole Ashen Sea and the Oriati federations couldn't stand for it.

She did her best work in wartime, didn't she? Imagine what she could do with the whole Ashen Sea at war. The clay of humanity in her fists, wet with blood. . . .

An increasingly apparent pattern of epidemic disease in the unconquered west. The maps called the west the Camou Interval, a vast historical lacuna left by the collapse of the old Tu Maia. On her voyage up to Aurdwynn, Baru had visited a Camou fishing town called Chansee, where pale people died of cancer.

And, of course, the disturbing findings of our expeditions across the Mother of Storms.

And oh, those findings did disturb her, they filled Baru with terror and with joy.

Falcrest sent its ships across the great eastern ocean from which no visitors ever arrived. Across the Mother of Storms. The fourth expedition went under the command of Lindon Satamine, a brave young captain in the Storm Corps. Not two weeks out of Grendlake he stumbled on a fleet of primitive Stakhieczi longships. He seized their young leader, Svirakir, as a hostage: the fact that he was a prince was not recorded. (Hello, Apparitor, so *that's* your real name? Svirakir?)

Then, with Stakhieczi ships as sacrificial vanguard, the Storm Corps went on east through maelstrom and burning sea. Through the eel-swarming dead water that had killed the first expedition by thirst. Through volcanic peaks and jagged fjords, into lush lake-lands where the second expedition had re-corded boiling ponds and died together in the night. Through beautiful naked stone land afire with burning pits, and long tidal flats where the third wave of expeditions had all gone mad.

Baru tasted each word like pufferfish-meat, sweet and poisonous and delightful.

Lindon and his hostage led the fourth expedition to the unexplored mountains. Star-tall mountains that rumbled so low you could only feel the sound. On the peaks there was fire, volcanism or burning forest, perhaps even the mysterious energies of the Oriati sacred stone called uranium.

And above the fire raged the storm, the endless thunder, the clouds that never broke. Forks and graphs of lightning hammered the mountain slopes again and again as if some celestial clock counted out the universe moment by moment.

In his reports, Apparitor said, *As we approached the site of the lightning strikes, we perceived moving lights, like the shapes made by a thumb pressed into the eyeball. And the lights gathered into symbols. And wherever we looked, the symbols moved with us. There was a sharp smell, and a sound we cannot agree on. . . .*

They passed through rings of stone monoliths. "Reminiscent of the pyramids and greatwells built in ancient Falcrest and the Normarch," Lindon Satamine reported, "perhaps by an ancient transoceanic civilization."

Burnt trees, carbonized into black pillars. Shattered ruins marked by fire.

Above the expedition endless lightning strobed off the peak. All of them complained of headaches, and a sense of *meaning*, as if they had a word on the tips of their tongues but couldn't quite remember it. . . .

And then the attack came. Out of the dark. Out of the lightning.

Most of the accounts agreed the attackers had been human.

Baru wrote, *We must confront the possibility that these eyewitness accounts are not hallucinations, and that natural law on the supercontinent somehow differs from our own.*

This was a good dream. This was the dream she would hold to when she couldn't see any reason to go on. To visit the mountain where the lightning never stops, and to name it for Hu.

Baru laughed into her hands, stirred by joy and fear.

There were powers in the world still beyond the grasp of Cairdine Farrier or the designs of Falcrest. So as Baru wrote about causal closure (let *by my choice* become exactly synonymous with *by Imperial decree*), as she signed the letter with the name *Agonist,* she sang to herself:

Tain Hu
kuye lam
you are beyond them
like the lightning in the east.

A STORY ABOUT ASH 1

TAU-INDI Bosoka came into this world alone.

Now, you might protest, who is *not* born alone? Stop a moment and think, o listener! Do you have the answer? Correct! Twins!

Now, the House Bosoka had no tradition of twin births. There was no twin to accompany Tau-indi's mother Tahr when she popped out of her lamother Taundi through the mine foreman's slippery hands and fell into a wash bucket, nor a twin for grandlam Taundi who came out of Toro Toro downside-up and burbling, so small they wrapped her up in a leaf.

But Tau-indi Bosoka was different.

The first difference was that Tau had been elected, before their conception, to become a Federal Prince, raised to help rule the Mbo.

The second difference was Tau-indi's stillborn twin.

What do you call a wound that everyone has, but no one notices? What do you call the loneliness of not-having-a-twin, a loneliness most of us will never acknowledge? Imagine that wound. Imagine that you are haunted by the ghosts of people who should have loved you. But you did something wrong, and they abandoned you, or never arrived at all.

Imagine that this loneliness strikes you on the morning of your thirteenth birthday, in your home upon Prince Hill, above Lake Jaro which is the center of the world's crossroads, Lonjaro Mbo. Imagine that you cry out in grief and paint your brow with white lamp ash from temple to temple, which is, in Lonjaro, a way of mourning.

Then you run across the hill to see Abdumasi Abd.

Your neighbor Abdumasi is a good guy. When he sees how upset you are, he gives you a caraval kitten to hold. He tells you he's training the gangly little kittens to kill pigeons, for gambling reasons. You try to explain to him the pain of missing someone who was never born.

"You sound like you're in love," Abdumasi says. "I read that you can fall in love with someone before you've ever met them. And when you see them at last, you say, '*Oh, that's why I hurt,*' like you just found an old splinter buried in your foot."

You hate splinters, so you shudder.

"People need some things even if they've never had them," Abdumasi opines. "That's why we invented the Mbo, right? Some people said *slaves have never been free, so they can't want freedom*—but the Mbo said no, everyone wants freedom. Now there's no more slavery anywhere. We ended it. We're mbo people because we help other people get what they need."

You pet the caraval kitten listlessly. It squirms from your arms.

"Tau-indi," Abdumasi says, looking at you in worry, "Tau-indi, manata"—which means my beloved friend—"you need to let this twin thing go."

The attending doctor and her midwife tried to take blame for the stillborn child, identical in every way to Tau, except that they never screamed or breathed at all. Tau-indi's umbilical cord had strangled them. "As we rushed to your house, Tahr, we must have walked along the shadows," the doctor said, trying to take the blame, "and today there was a calendar taboo against following the sun's lines. The twin's soul saw us break taboo, and turned away in disgust, back to the Door in the East. Thus they were born dead."

But Mother Tahr was gracious and of good trim, and she chose to blame the umbilical rather than the doctor. She burned her unnamed ungendered child out on the hill, raked up the ash of the burning, and ate it in an ash cake, to put her given body back into herself. Then she put her grief behind her and set about raising Tau-indi.

The House Bosoka asked the child, at age six, for their gender, and the child was a laman. Lamen did not exist everywhere in the world, but many mbo people were lamen, and Tau-indi felt quite sure they must be one.

At age thirteen, the day this story begins, Tau-indi asked their friend Abdumasi a terrible question.

"Do you think," Tau-indi whispered, "that I killed my twin in the womb, so that I could be Prince alone?"

The caraval kitten began knocking Abdumasi's ceramics down off the shelf. They both ran around after it, begging it to be civil. Quickly they forgot the terrible question. After a while Abdumasi said, "Tau, this is the first birthday you've had without your mother here, right?"

"It is."

"And there's no sign of your father ever coming home."

"No."

"Manata, I think that's why you're lonely."

It was 910 Federation Year, one decade into the Glass Century. Not so long ago mother Tahr had left Prince Hill to visit Segu Mbo.

She was representing young Tau at a summit concerning a small nation called Falcrest, which, of late, had begun to think itself a crocodile instead of a crane.

TAU-INDI'S family lived in a fine compound of stone alongside a towering termite colony, which they tended out of a desire to help Tau seem a little conservative. Abdumasi's family the Abds, led by his mother Abdi-obdi, lived in a compound of brown and black wood with high banners, and Tau-indi often went over there to fly kites off the south slope. Abdumasi called Tau-indi *Your Federal Highness,* and Tau-indi called Abdumasi obscene names like *You Rich Bastard* and *Cancer Eater* and *Horn Eye,* too young to understand the obscene weight of these epithets.

And when it was too hot to stand the earth or air they went down the hill to the honeybee compound of the third house on Prince Hill.

It was not technically a proper House, for it had no rate and did not belong to one of the kingdoms of the Thirteen-in-Three-in-One which was Lonjaro Mbo. Rather it was named for the Prince who lived in it, Kindalana of Segu, who had come to be raised near the great city of Jaro.

Tau and Abdumasi pretended they needed Kindalana's permission to go swim in the lake, but this was just an excuse to get Kindalana. She was the rarest of them, the most bound to her studies, the most reticent with her praise and favor, the most cutting in her indictments of failure, and thus the most precious.

"They're inseparable," Tau-indi's mother, Tahr, once said to Kindalana's father Padrigan, "those three."

"No, not at all. They are often separated!"

"How so?"

"Your laman is thirteen, and my daughter and Abdi-obdi's boy are sixteen, which means they'll argue about anything, throw a tantrum, insist they're grown-ups and don't want to talk about it, and then sulk." Padrigan placed a pawn down on the game map. The two parents were playing Rule, a foreign game which had burst up in Jaro like a summer carnation. They spent so much time together that everyone thought they must be having an affair, and they lied to themselves that it was their faith to their missing spouses (Tahr's husband vanished while exploring Zawam Asu, Padrigan's almost-wife returned to the gold speculation business she preferred) which kept them apart. In fact it was Kindalana.

"But," Tahr said, kissing her next pawn in thought, "they always come back to each other. That's better than being inseparable, I think. To be separable, but bound."

On a recent night Padrigan had met Tahr's eyes and decided not to look away. She smiled back at him. Her eyes seemed like a hearth for the cold in him, and he wanted to be near her.

But suddenly the connection broke. In the curtain door stood Kindalana, sixteen years old and still tiny, holding a bee in her closed fist.

"I think you'd better come and care for my hand, Father. I've been stung."

While Padrigan fussed over her ruptured palm, Kindalana looked at Tahr with flat disappointment. Do better, her eyes said. Do better. I will not permit a scandal between my father and the mother of a fellow Prince.

Anyway. The adults were away, Tahr on this matter of Falcrest, Padrigan on business in the city Jaro, Abdi-obdi seeing to her sprawling merchant empire and its growth in Segu. So the children ruled the high hill.

Tau-indi and Abdumasi beat on the door-plate of Kindalana's compound with the big mallet they weren't supposed to use. They hid. One of the groundskeepers came out to shout at them. They knew that once the groundskeep came out, he would give in to his cravings and run up the hill to pick raspberries.

When he did, they snuck inside.

"I wonder if she's remembered my birthday." Tau-indi looked around the beehives curiously. They almost never came inside the compound proper: usually Kindalana came out to the gate.

"Of course she's remembered. You're a Prince and she's a Prince. She'd never forget a Prince's birthday." Abdumasi thought of something delightful and beamed with cunning. "I wonder if she'll be *rude* to us! Tau, let's make her be rude."

"Why?" If you went to someone's house, they had to apologize for anything possibly wrong, and Kindalana hated apologizing.

"To mess up her trim, of course."

Tau-indi never wanted to make Kinda uncomfortable, but they also loved Abdumasi's trickster smile. "Quick, then, find something to eat!"

They ran around the beehive and the herb gardens in their hiked-up khangas and thong sandals, dodging groundskeeps until they could snatch a carton of honeycomb. Then they went to Kindalana's window, hoping to find her. But it was open and empty, and she'd left no sign.

"She'll be up in the silkroom," Abdumasi said, "reading and getting some wind."

"You don't know her at all, you flighty jay. She'll be in the sun house, tanning herself and drinking raspberry water." Kindalana had lighter skin, being from Segu, and she sometimes sunned herself to darken and beautify her look.

"Pah." Abdumasi did not think it likely. "She's hardly so vain."

"She's hardly so *studious!*"

They were both wrong. She sat on the boardwalk above the north slope and the lake, sketching with charcoal. Her shoulder blades moved thoughtfully.

"Psst," Tau-indi hissed, while Abdumasi took a huge bite of stolen honeycomb. "Kindalana!"

"Hi!" she said. "Happy birthday, Tau, I thought you'd come." She wore her hair shaved almost to the scalp, since it otherwise became unmanageable in the heat.

Abdumasi stared at her and made big rude crunching sounds with a mouthful of honeycomb. Kindalana rolled her eyes enormously, not at his stare (she was from Segu, where the men were very modest), but because she clearly wanted him to stop eating her honey.

For no reason they could understand, Tau-indi felt suddenly, strangely young.

"Welb?" Abdumasi said between bites. "Where are yourb manners?"

Kindalana crossed her arms. "You are endlessly welcome to the honey of my house."

"Thamf yooh," Abdumasi said. "Yor hibeness."

"It must," Kindalana said performing the polite self-deprecation required by etiquette, sickly sweet with sarcasm, "be too tangy, this early in the summer."

"You're right," Abdumasi said, refusing the politely trimmed reply that the honey was in fact the greatest honey ever to drip from the finest bees on this good earth, "it is, it tastes like shit!"

And he took another huge bite, smiling insufferably.

Tau-indi stepped on his foot and Kindalana (grinning at Tau-indi) leapt at him so that he flinched away and tripped on his pinned foot and fell off the boardwalk into the soft cypress shrubs.

They ran down the hillside, skirmishing amongst each other, toward the lake and the cranes who staggered around drunkenly eating cranebliss and the crocodile fences that kept them safe, away from the houses where their parents failed to have affairs, away from the past, into the sun-dappled wavetips of the future, on this the last summer of the last year before the Armada War.

D OWN in Lake Jaro, where the water tasted like sweet silt, Tau-indi came up from a dive in the kelp to find Kindalana treading water.

She looked like a head bobbing on the waves, her small ears folded back, her wide far-set eyes canted a little to meet a broad flat nose. Tau-indi imagined her head as beautiful bait floated up by some submerged fish. They laughed, and then their guts vibrated with nerves: oh, what was this, when had this happened, when had the word *beautiful* gotten onto Kindalana? They didn't want their friendships to be complicated. Especially they didn't want the complication to be Kindalana, who had no patience at all.

"You've got ash on your brow." Kindalana frowned in concern. "Are you grieving?"

"Oh no," Tau gasped, pawing at their head. Why hadn't the ash washed away?

"And now it's mud." Kindalana sighed. "You can't let mourning ash go to mud, Tau-indi, or the principles of the lake will think you're a liar."

This was a small disaster, and not just because the principles would inflict grief on those who made light of grief. You simply couldn't show any kind of want or need in front of Kindalana. You couldn't mention that you were hungry, or sad, or lonely, because Kindalana would try to fix it. She would get you the melon you'd idly wished for, or fetch you a primer in Uburu because you kept whining about not knowing any. Tau-indi *hated* this. In Tau's opinion, complaining about your problems was a necessary part of life, and should never be confused with actually trying to *fix* them, a separate and much more private matter.

"What is it?" Kindalana sculled closer. Tau-indi wanted to dive away but she reached out for them. "I promise I won't tell Abdu. What's wrong? Why did you put the ash on?"

Tau-indi put their mouth and nose under the water and looked up at Kindalana shyly.

"Oh." Kindalana frowned in disappointment. "You *already* told Abdu about it."

"Sorry," Tau muttered.

"It's all right." Kindalana glared at Abdumasi's receding ass, racing down the beach after his frog quarry. In the distance a Bosoka sentry watched them from her high post. "I suppose he's jealous."

"Jealous of what?"

"Our future, of course. He knows *he'll* have to spend the rest of his life moving money around and going to fancy parties, while *we* argue with mayors and chiefs and get malaria and worms and finally die of heatstroke in service to the Mbo."

Yes, good, Tau-indi thought. Tell me more about how we'll travel together as Princes, solving problems. "He'll be very sad when we're gone."

"He will," Kindalana said, and the space between her eyes wrinkled up in worry. "Poor Abdu."

Tau-indi sank underwater, down toward the lake-floor, and leapt back up off the bottom. Briefly Kindalana was a wavering dark shape against the watery light.

"It'll be hard for him once we've gone," they said, when they came back up. "We'll have to keep in touch with him and make sure he's all right."

Kindalana looked at Tau-indi with warmth and pride, Prince to Prince. "You *do* listen to the griots," she said, "you do remember what they tell us. Nothing's better than helping someone get what they need." And she hugged them wetly so that Tau-indi had to protest and laugh and flail.

But then Tau-indi remembered Abdumasi saying, *we're mbo people because we help other people get what they need*. And it was like Abdumasi owned this moment, this moment that should have been between them and Kindalana.

Kindalana looked *proud* of them. Pride was for children. Adults got respect.

"It'll be okay," Kindalana whispered in their ear. "You don't have to wear grief ash. Your mother will come back okay. I promise she will, Tau, and I'll keep trim with you, to be sure."

No! How hideously embarrassing! Kindalana thought Tau-indi was upset because mother Tahr had gone away. Little Tau-indi, afraid to be alone!

"I'm not worried about Tahr," Tau-indi said, quite regally, and then they said the words that would accidentally ruin the next years of their life. "I'm concerned for poor Abdumasi, left behind when we go. We shall have to tend to him. He will require our most special care."

Kindalana put her feet on their thighs and pushed away. "Really?" She had opened herself to Tau in comfort, and Tau had pricked her pride, so of course she had to look disdainful. "You're grieving for *Abdu*?"

"I think he needs more from us," Tau said. "We have each other as Princes. We must do all we can for him. But of course my ash isn't for him. I'm simply sad I can't go abroad with mother, and do my work as a Prince."

"You want to go to *sea*? Weeks on a ship? A narrow smelly ship with a bunch of oars?"

In the distance Abdumasi whooped and put up two fists full of two protesting frogs.

"What do you mean, go to *sea*?" Tau-indi asked. "Mother's gone to Kutulbha in Segu, and she said she was going by road."

"You don't know?"

"Kinda, what are you talking about?"

"The summit at Kutulbha decided to send a fleet to hunt down the Falcresti pirates." Kindalana paused, but she couldn't ever pass up the chance to prove she knew best. "And your mother's sailing with them. She's left the waters of the Mbo. She's gone with the war fleet to rebuke Falcrest."

Mother gone to . . . Falcrest? Where *was* Falcrest? Wasn't it in that story about ancient Tahari, Tahr's namesake, and the narwhal horn? Hadn't it been blown up or something? Wasn't it ruled by a mad king who bred people like dogs? Or possibly an octopus?

"*Why?*" Tau-indi cried.

"She's gone in your place, since you're not old enough." Kindalana sculled back a little. "Didn't she tell you? Didn't she *write* to you? I heard through the traders who come to visit the Abds, and I thought you already knew. . . ."

She'd heard through the Abds! Why, this matter was between *Princes*! Abdumasi should have nothing to do with it! Tau-indi was so furious and ashamed and confused that they said, "I think you should be sure Abdumasi is all right," and stalked ashore.

Kindalana called after them in sorrow. "Tau, I didn't mean to surprise you! Tau!"

But Tau-indi was not moved. A child would run back and apologize. A Prince would go do work. "I must go see to my mother's house!" they called back airily. "I am sure Abdumasi needs you very much."

Mother Tahr *had* written a letter to Tau-indi, explaining that she had to go away for a while. But she'd sent the letter to Padrigan to deliver, and he'd put off reading it. For as long as it was unopened, you see, it might still be a love note.

Of such things, the Whale Words tell us, are the destinies of empires made. Not of armies or great notions or the glitter of wealth, but the most delicate motions of our hearts.

7

HESYCHAST, WHOSE FLESH IS A TEMPLE

SVIR kicked the treadle too hard and the grindstone's crankshaft threw a gear. The bad gear jammed against its mate and the shaft bucked straight upward, slamming the grindstone into the mirror and shattering it right down the center.

Svir had destroyed his telescope.

"No," Svir said, "no no, that didn't happen," and he squeezed his eyes shut and tried to worm through the walls of the world into some other place where he hadn't broken his mirror. His foot hurt. The broken things in his hands. This priceless, flawless, unbelievably pure glass disc, glistening with the oil he used to soak up glass dust, the disc he'd been grinding for *months* for his new catoptric telescope.

The mighty cryptarch Apparitor had been thinking about Baru and he'd kicked too hard.

"Iraji," he groaned. "Iraji, come here—"

But Iraji wasn't on *Helbride*. He was up in the Elided Keep, spying on Baru, slipping into the role of her lost secretary.

Very fucking clever, Svir. You sent your confidant to your enemy.

He set the broken mirror down and went to his cabin's little washbasin. The mirror had sliced a perfectly fine crease across his palm, thin and cold as a winter sun. Blood, of course, very much blood: a red patina on pink flesh. Svir licked the salt off the wound, as he'd been taught back home (never waste salt), and then he stepped gently on the basin's footpedal. A valve clicked. He listened, never tiring of this marvel, as the footpedal opened a tap to the reservoir casks on the afterdeck. The faucet gave him a thin cool stream of water.

Svir watched his damned royal blood swirling to the drain.

Everything was fucked.

The navy had someone, he knew it, he *knew* they had someone no matter how often Croftare and her Merit Admirals denied it. An Oriati syndicate captain or Federal Prince or a griot who'd seen too much. They were plotting against him, and against Lindon. They were going to use their prisoner to start Armada II.

Falcrest had no idea what wrath they'd awaken if they went to war.

And Tain Hu. Poor Tain Hu. Svir had thought her so magnetic and so fiercely principled that no one, not even Itinerant, could want to be rid of her. Baru had executed her so coldly that Svir's protests had peeled off his tongue like frozen steel.

And without any control over Baru, Svir and dear Lindon were doomed.

•

• •

• • •

Consider this—Svir always thought best in pictures—consider this pyramid, each dot a cryptarch. Renascent at the apex. Where else could she go? Itinerant (fuck him) and Hesychast (fuck him too) stood below her, contending for her favor, balanced against each other by the threat of mutual annihilation. They held influence over the bottom tier, Stargazer and Baru (Agonist, what a *gruesome* name) and he, Svir. All brilliant little exemplars of what Lindon called the Cult of Youth, Falcrest's obsession with bright-eyed savants.

If only he could have secured a hostage over Baru. If only he'd taken her into his control. With that power he could become this happy little X:

•

• •

X

• • (•)

The newcomer (•) being Xate Yawa.

Then he'd be able to prod Baru onto the center of the political stage as a dazzling distraction. Present her to Parliament and the navy, fill her up with money and power: shining, doomed Baru, burning brightly. *Do this for me and you'll see Tain Hu again.*

He'd thought she must love Tain Hu as wholly as he loved Lindon—

But she hadn't. And with no way to control Baru, Svir had no mask to hide behind while he and Lindon made the final preparations for their endgame: the money, the charts, the ships required to get the fuck *out*, eastward and forever, before it all came crashing down.

Svir thought of the words Iraji had whispered to him, in the deepest darkness of the ocean night, as thousands of glowing jellyfish rose up below the ship:

A ut li-en.

And he shuddered. And the mirror was broken. And Baru knew where Svir had come from, she knew how to burn him, he was very nearly under *her* control.

"Oh, Lindon," Svir groaned. "I hope you're happy out there. And the wife. And the kids. And your stupid little dog."

A bolt of longing convulsed him. He had no home, anywhere in the world, except where Lindon arranged a safe house and summoned him to stay. Svir would come up the back way, through the storeroom or the kitchens, to find Lindon reading in that horribly uncomfortable wooden chair he loved, the one that left dents on his buttocks. The fire would be low, the wine cold from the cellar. There would be a little vidhara extract in a cup, for later; a game of Rule or Purge or grids arranged in some interesting puzzle; and Lindon's stubble rasping on Svir's chin as they fell on each other, the heady oakmoss smell of him. His hard ass (a nervous ass, Svir liked to tease him, permanently clenched) cupped in Svir's hand as he came. Then the long, lazy, half-dressed afternoon with books and games and gossip, and the daydreams of what they would do when they reached their goal. With luck Enwan would visit, Lindon's wife, and they would have one of those dinners the Falcresti loved to write about, where every sentence was a game. She would tell Svir about the children, all Lindon's but that precious one, and he would make her laugh and laugh and laugh, the only way he had known, in those fraught early days of their arrangement, to set her at ease. And if the night came with thoughts of Ahanna Croftare, the khamtiger pacing her war-deck, and of Parliament's masked choir singing a hunting song, well, there was vidhara in the cup, and Enwan would give her silent permission for Lindon and Svir to go to bed.

And now Baru could destroy him, and Lindon with him, and Enwan and the children with Lindon. And Ahanna Croftare was out there waiting, waiting, to seize the navy she thought she was owed.

Someone knocked at his cabin door. Svir's fist clenched but he was quick enough to avoid the wound. "Come in," he called, cheerfully. "I've just broken my mirror!"

"I'm very sorry to hear that, my lord." It was *Helbride*'s Captain Branne. "I'm sure the crew will miss the shriek of your grindstone very much. We've had a signal rocket from the sentinels. There are ships coming in."

Svir whirled. "Ships? *Plural?* Hesychast was supposed to come in alone."

"Alone, yes, sir. But he's picked up a navy escort. They're from Aurdwynn, sir, Fifth Fleet. Province Admiral Ormsment's flagship and a consort."

"No." Svir sighed. "You forgot to account for the new flags, they must be First Fleet. Ormsment's got no idea about this place—"

"I'm sure, sir. We checked the latest Navy List."

Svir stared at her. Then he said, concisely, "Shit."

Together they bound his hand up. Svir braided his hair, thinking quickly, quickly. "Move *Helbride* to the escape harbor. The navy can't know you're here." Branne had come up through the Storm Corps, like the rest of *Helbride*'s crew, never herself a navy sailor. "I've got to make sure Baru gets out safely."

"My lord, the navy knows your face. You can't risk being caught."

"If she doesn't make it," Svir said, "Itinerant will punish me, understand? He made it very clear that I was to protect his protégé. And if I fail—"

Lindon's family would be punished first. Then Lindon himself.

And he was not Baru Cormorant, content to let his beloved die.

B ARU read the *Handbook of Various Beasts*.

Gyraffe

A cultural subspecies of the giraffe, a long-necked southern mammal native to the Oriati Mbo nation of Mzilimake. According to the Farrier expedition circa After Revolution 112, the gyraffe is a platinum example of the transformation of the body by repeated behavior. This transformation echoes the origin of the human races, which diverged from the Template Race as their behaviors altered their flesh.

The gyraffe often befriends gyrfalcons, which perch upon its high head. The falcons kill the birds that eat the gyraffe's favorite berries. Farrier & Torrinde (AR 113) suggest that the gyraffe's affiliation for falcons developed through a Triestic coupling between its dislike for berry-eating birds and its observation that falcons kill those birds. This offers an advanced example of Torrindic heredity, in which behaviors already acquired in the hereditary particles can be linked to each other through repeated thought.

See "noocana," the proposed substance through which memories are inherited.

"Your Excellence?"

Iraji's call came out of her blindness, but Baru imagined him slipping sideways through her door, his thong sandals silent on the hardwood, noble brow creased with curiosity. She was unfortunately glad to see him.

"Hesychast's ship has been sighted, my lady Excellence," he said. "He will be here within the hour."

"To test me."

"I expect so, my lady."

Baru set down the book and picked up the machine on her desk. An incryptor, Apparitor had called it, a steel apple full of gears and pins. Unique in all the world—just one built for each cryptarch. Slide a paper into the incryptor's mouth, configure the dials, touch the trigger, and the incryptor would stamp the Imperial pole-star mark, *extraordinary privilege, do as I command*. Tiny numbers ringing the seal changed with each use, but like children from the same parents they could always be traced, by cryptographic principle, back to an individual incryptor.

She held the power to command the Empire here in her fist.

"I need you to fight me," she told Iraji.

"I—your Excellence?"

"I need to be hurt."

Weeks, now, since Tain Hu had drowned. And it hurt to eat and breathe. It hurt to see the sun and the moon keeping to their course. It hurt to read, to plot, to mine secrets out of the texts in the Liminal Library. It hurt to sit on her bed and watch the oiled hinges move in exquisite silence, back, forth, back, forth, as she kicked the door open and shut.

Why did everything hurt?

Because everything kept working. Everything kept on as if nothing had happened. And Baru *needed* everything to hurt: Baru needed a sword for a spine, so that if she ever bent from her purpose, she'd be cut.

"Come up onto the battlements," she ordered Iraji, and when he hesitated, "Come!"

A high daytime moon, a far horizon, great formations of birds above. Sea wind raked her hair. The sound of the waves that killed Tain Hu slammed down over Baru and made her suddenly cold and agile and furious.

The world should care! The moon should cover up its face in mourning!

Baru wanted to fight: anything, everything. She shrugged off her jacket. She kicked off her boots and she turned barefoot, toes clawing at the cracks between stones. With two curled fingers she hooked Iraji's attention.

"Fight me," she ordered.

"Last time," he said, "you almost crushed my throat."

"This time you can fight back." She squared off in Naval System stance, hands half-curled to make a fist or claw an eyeball or crush a scrotum.

"Why do you want to be hurt?"

"So Hesychast can't pick one wound from the rest," Baru said.

He looked more frightened by that. But he put up his hands.

So they went at each other in wary sideways steps, and Baru felt in her body all the art of all she was: hiding her intent, denying to Iraji the flickers of muscle and stance that would betray her next blow, capturing ground, yielding it, trading a foot of territory for a better angle, hunting for information in the boy's curled shoulders and half-hidden teeth, and all this was like the art of being a spy and a lord and a queen, all this was the game of learning without being learnt—and like that game all of it was a prelude to pain.

Iraji had a man's height and reach. That was enough to win. He chose when to step in and take the hit, when to flow from strikes into grapples, and once they fell to wrestle across the tower-stones his long fingers and strangling arms gave him edge. Baru might be stronger, but she couldn't match his leverage, she couldn't get up at his throat when she had him in her guard.

"Your Excellence," he said, after his punch slammed Baru's half-blind skull against the tower stone.

"Again," Baru said, smiling blood.

"Your *Excellence*," he said, when Baru nearly arm-barred his elbow to pieces and he gut-punched her so hard that she gagged.

"Again," she said, spitting bile.

"*Your Excellence!*" he cried, when after an elbow to the chin, Baru sat down growling and couldn't stand.

"It's fine," she said. The world was full of ringing sick pain now. The world cared about Tain Hu. She'd *made* it care. Cast a veil of hurt across everything you see, and everything you see is hurt. "Everything's fine. You've done well."

"Your Excellence," Iraji said, with careful calm, "you could catch my blows even when they came in from your right. Did you notice that?"

"Could I? Interesting."

Last time she was on the battlements with Iraji, she'd looked up through a swarm of petrels and seen a sail on the horizon. *Helbride* coming with Tain Hu. Baru could still feel that sail on her blind right, way out on the horizon: a tooth of memory erupting through the water. She could still feel—

She frowned.

She could feel *three* sets of sails.

"Iraji," she said, and pointed right, into nothingness. "What's out there?"

She watched his golden eyes narrow against the wind. He put up a hand to block out the sun: she wondered, quite Incrastically, if the dark of his skin let him see better in bright light.

"I don't understand," he said, softly. "Hesychast should've come alone."

On the southern horizon three ships approached: a clipper like *Helbride*, and two warships rigged like fast navy frigates.

Hesychast sailed like he was going to war.

S HE staggered into the morning-room in compression linens and a breech-cloth, clutching a block of cellar ice in silk to the side of her head. Farrier was there, and the moment he looked at her, her trap was sprung.

"Oh!" He very politely turned his back. "You're not proper, Baru."

"I was with the concubine," she said, to make it worse on him. "What are you doing? Come, help me sit."

"When you're modest, Baru." He shrugged his coat off and lobbed it backward to her.

"You make these things strange, Mister Farrier."

He chuckled easily enough. "When one travels the world one learns not to bend to other's standards. I hold myself to my own rules, lest I ever err. We must be blameless, hm? Always blameless."

It was a nice sherwani. Baru left it on the floor. What did Farrier see when he looked at her? Not lust—he wasn't interested in taking advantage of his power that way. But he saw *something* he didn't like. Tain Hu had told her once—*you wear symbols when you decide how to dress yourself, how to look at men and women, how to carry your body and direct your gaze.*

Maybe Farrier saw an aspect of her that he couldn't control: young and vital, coiled with strength. Maybe Farrier saw her flesh as the dominion of his enemy.

"Hesychast's here," she said.

"I know."

"He's brought two warships."

He looked up sharply, and did not look away. "Really? Interesting. Well, fear not. I have a way out. And until our reckoning is done, you are beyond his power." He had already arranged the Great Game across the map rug. "Let's discuss tactics as we play."

She was surprised to see fleets and armies on the board, along with wealth, currents and storms, persons of power. The Oriati armies outnumbered Falcrest's tenfold or more. What was he up to? Why include the military? He had said it himself: *we never conquer anyone . . .*

"Tell me about Hesychast," she said.

"Oh, Baru, do you need what I know?" He threw her the booklet describing her position at the start of the game. "You're past the point where you can depend on my advice."

"Tell me anyway. What's his real name?"

"Cosgrad." His smile flickered up and died in his guarded eyes. "He's Cosgrad Torrinde."

"You wrote a book together," Baru exclaimed, remembering *Farrier & Torrinde (AR 113)*. "About giraffes, and other things."

He laughed with more sadness than humor. "Yes, we've worked together. He's right about a great many things. Eugenics, for instance. Behavior *can* be inherited, that's certain."

She was set to play the Oriati. She did not know what to do with her armies. Farrier's fleets were gathered to guard his trade. Tentatively she began arranging her southern forces for a march into the jungle, on hope they would find something interesting or die (she needed their salaries elsewhere).

"Why are you so afraid of him?" she asked.

He had a playing piece in his palm. A broken stub. It was hers: the Agonist piece. He reached down to play it onto the capital, onto Falcrest-the-city. "Because he's often right," he said. His eyes snagged on her thigh. He looked away. "I wish you'd dress."

"He's often right, but he's wrong about this?" She pointed to the map with her toes. "This game?"

"Exactly." He tapped the broken Agonist piece on its point. "In the game, you've just gone before Parliament on 90 Summer. You've reported the result of your expedition. Go to the end of that booklet I gave you."

Baru flipped to the last page, frowning: it had been sewn together in haste. "Revelation," she recited. "You are the Princes of Oriati Mbo. Falcrest's Parliament has discovered the existence of a secret society in your midst. They are the ancient slavers who once ruled your people, and their strength is now grown again. They are strong in Mzilimake, among the old conquerors of Lake Akhena and the mystics of Uranium Gorge. They are powerfully entangled with Segu's western coast, with the tribes of the Aam and the Yeni, where their shipyards have built secret fleets. Already they have attacked Falcrest, hoping to provoke a ruinous war . . . is this all fantasy?"

"Read on."

"Falcrest's Parliament demands you hand over the leaders of this cult, and all their collaborators, for trial. If you do not, punitive bombardments will strike your great cities. The word of this cult's existence has been sent to your griots, to be spread among the people, and now a great wrath arises in them: they do not love Falcrest, but they hate the old slavers with a thousand years of fury. . . ." Baru blinked at the rules. "Could this happen?"

"It will." Farrier no longer seemed to care about her immodesty. "Play, now."

She found unrest rippling through her people. The effect on the economy was quite shocking: where people disagreed with each other they stopped trading, and that caused uncertainty in crops and prices. Where certainty evaporated, people stopped spending money. As if by magic famine began to arise, first in little patches and then growing blights.

She went after this cult with griot-investigators. They were murdered. She sent an army into southern Mzilimake to dig them out. A poor roll of the dice saw a coup by Uranium Gorge seize Mzilimake's government in the name of the slaver cult. Civil war was instantaneous, and huge, and appalling—there were so many people in Oriati Mbo, and all the death was magnified proportionally—

"I will sell you grain," Farrier offered. "Cheap. Just give me those ports."

She had to agree, to save lives.

"I'll send Charitable Service clinics to contain the plagues."

She had to agree, to save lives.

"I have architectural concerns who can use those forests and that stone better than you. Grant me some labor, and I'll clear those canals, I'll rebuild those roads, I'll have cash crops growing again."

She had to agree. She needed money to prop up her side in the civil war.

"Give me access to the Black Tea Ocean," Farrier said, pointing to the western sea off Oriati Mbo, the sea few Falcresti had glimpsed, "and I'll send a fleet down there to seal off the slaver ports."

Her ships had been decimated in the fighting. She had no choice: she would lose the coast entirely, otherwise.

"Your currencies are in tatters," he pointed out, for the war had put various Princes and their principalities so deep into debt that they'd been forced to coin more money, leading to rampant inflation. "I can't accept anything in payment but Falcresti fiat notes."

Baru sighed. She knew from the rules that very soon her necessaries— traders, laborers, shipping magnates, even troops in the field—would refuse to take payment in anything *but* fiat notes. "I think," she said, "that I should refuse . . ."

"I will take payment in orphans, instead," Farrier suggested. "Let me save these bankrupt cities. Just let me build schools for the war orphans. . . ."

The Mbo was breaking. She could hardly believe it—especially after all her reading. The thousand-year Mbo was cracking apart before her, and Farrier's ivy was growing in the seams.

"What is this?" she breathed. "You break them by turning them on themselves?"

Farrier breathed into his cupped hands. "It was the same on Sousward," he said. "Plainside against harborside. This is just . . . much larger."

He was aiming Baru at his next target. And the stakes, she was certain, were beyond tally: not just for the world, but for Farrier himself. "The expedition." She went at him, even as he drew away, and got him by the shoulders. "Look at me. What's this expedition?"

Suddenly he was indifferent to her body. Suddenly he had the room's gravity again. The immediacy of the change was appalling. He smiled, warm and natural. "You and Apparitor and a few others will be going on a mighty journey, Baru. A journey that Hesychast and I have both gambled everything upon."

"Tell me!" she cried, nearly salivating.

"You," he said, soberly, "are going to go on a fact-finding mission. Parliament has called a vote on war with Oriati Mbo. The date is set for summer's end, the ninetieth day of the season. You will provide the Emperor's Testimony. Did the Oriati Mbo itself attack us? Was it only pirates? Is there cause for war? Or will the peace last?"

"Good Devena," Baru gasped. "*I'm* to decide that?"

"Quite. But of course it's not just about that. Hesychast wants one thing from the expedition. And I . . . well. I hope *you* will secure the future of the Republic under my philosophy."

"What philosophy?" she hissed. "What does he want? What do you?"

"Ah," he said, his clever hands steepled, "we are antitheses, he and I, he is the body and I am the mind, he is the race and I am the Republic. He sees humanity as cattle to breed and I cannot abide that—oh, Baru, if you knew the *hope* you've given me, the hope that anyone can be disciplined and taught to live righteously. That hope sustains me!"

Baru grinned like a barracuda, she was so hungry and so angry to eat his trust like a fishing line and to pull him down by it into the water from which he'd snagged her.

"What do I have to do to beat him?"

HESYCHAST was perfect.

He looked like an archon summoned up from the handbooks and the statuaries, invoked as incarnation of manhood: his lean height, his light-footed strength, his broad flat face composed against the masculine passions and yet, like a team of oxen in the yoke, still ready to move powerfully. His brown eyes were deep and bright and deeply folded, the image of classical Falcrest beauty. All his motions were demonstrations: *you see, this is how it is properly done.* He wore a wedge-shaped jacket with long tails, and trousers that cupped his narrow hips. She could have balanced two coffee cups on his shoulders.

Farrier had said, *he will strike you in your wound.*

She called down to him from her high throne. She wore her Library key ring around her throat, with the keys fanned across the jacket's unbuttoned breast. She ought to have worn a gown, to conceal herself. Too late. She and Hesychast were alone, except for the dancing gull, which came and went on its own schedule.

"Welcome to the Elided Keep," Baru said. "I am Agonist."

Farrier had said, *he will bring it back to the flesh. Always. He will say you couldn't kill Tain Hu without dividing your brain. He will say you learned nothing, no discipline, no control. You only cut your flesh in two.*

The eugenicist tried a stiff formal smile, and couldn't hold it, and grinned at her in sparkling earnest. "Agonist! What a name! I see you have a gull problem? I'm very good with birds."

Baru laughed. "Someone's trained that gull to dance for food."

Casually, and without malice: "Ah. Behavioral conditioning. Sounds like Caird's work. I've been told he's here."

"Well," she said, archly, "the bird is always plain about what it wants, so it's welcome in my court. Tell me, Mister Torrinde, if you're here to examine me, what do you see? A woman fit only for farming, fishing, and pleasure?"

He clasped his hands at the small of his back: chest out, chin up, hips cocked. He didn't blink. His mask was the brown of Falcresti flesh, rimmed in Aphalone script, words from the *Manual of the Somatic Mind:* with discipline of the body comes discipline of the soul. Wait. No. That wasn't from any Falcresti manual—that was an Aurdwynni saying, an ilykari saying. Why would he write *that* on his mask?

"I see a cryptarch without a hostage," he said. "I had my Clarified vet your relationship with Tain Hu. She seemed very dear to you."

Baru made a little wobbling scale with her hand: dear-ish.

He sighed and puffed out his cheeks. "I was afraid this might happen."

"You were afraid I'd obey the law?"

"I was afraid you'd obey your upbringing rather than your nature, yes." His left fist curled minutely. Was he left-handed? Was he thinking of Farrier, just then? "Well, if you'll permit it, I'd like to examine you. I'm sure you know the Physician's Qualm?"

"I do." The flesh of the people is the body of the Republic. The care of the flesh is the care of the Republic. Neither by injury nor by neglect may I allow the Republic to come to harm.

"Will your throne room serve as an examining space?"

"Here? I thought—" She stumbled. "A cellar, perhaps, or a private room?"

"Not at all, my lady Agonist. Here is best. I want you comfortable and confident."

He wanted to bring his instruments and authorities into the space of her power. Clever.

When she glanced to the left, and he fell onto her right, then she saw him without seeing. She saw a slab of meat beaten on a sizzling forge, and the hammer was a human fist.

I T was the strangest exam she'd ever taken.

"Strip as far as you're comfortable," he said. "I do autopsies, humane vivisections, clinics and examinations of every sort. Please let me assure you there is nothing taboo or shocking to me. You will be exactly as interesting as a fine watch."

With tape and compass he measured her reach and flexibility. With stinging unguent and scraping trowel he tested the reactions of her skin and tongue. Could she taste this plant? How long could she hold her breath: would she demonstrate. Now would she catch her breath, and read this sentence, *Souswardi people are from the island called Sousward,* and hold her breath again? Interesting. What happened to your gumline, there? A fish bone cut you? You must be more careful, infections of the mouth are a hazard to your race, as your teeth and gums have softened on a diet of fruit and southern fish. Are your menses regular? Do you depilate, and if so, have you observed any rashes or acne as a result? Do you believe the female coital paroxysm serves a purpose, or is it purely of hedonic value? Do you ever experience a hemorrhage of will, especially when trying to get out of bed? How often do thoughts of self-negation occur to you when you see a great height? Or a knife? Or a body of water?

"No," she said, too quickly. "I never consider suicide. That would hardly be useful."

"I'm glad to hear it. The Oriati Emotional Disease often strikes new cryptarchs."

"What's that?"

"An excess of feeling and care," he said. "It consumes the intellect."

The light was good for drawing. He had prepared his examining space with an artist's care: first he'd arranged an apparatus of mirrored dishes and whale-oil lights around her, then soaped and rinsed his hands, donned thin membranous gloves, and stared into a candle-flame for ten seconds while breathing smoothly. He took all his notes in angular shorthand, writing with a sterile stylus on thick soft white paper.

"Your wound." He tapped his temple. "Let's talk about it. You were struck on the right side? And it's also your right side that's blind?"

"Yes."

"That's very unusual!" His enthusiasm was boyish, and admittedly charming; he even rose up a bit as he spoke. "You see, we can sometimes induce hemineglect by insulting the tissue of the brain, but it almost always occurs on the *contralateral* side of the body—that is, the side opposite the wound. And almost always the blindness is to the left. But your wound is ipsilateral, and also on the right. . . ."

She was irritated that he seemed to have no bad habits: he didn't chew his nails, bite his lips, curl his hair, or slouch.

"Well," he said, softly, "a very unusual wound. Let's proceed with the body of the test, then. Iscend! Iscend, come in here, please!"

A terror entered Baru's throne room.

Later Baru would (through guilty indulgence of gaze and imagination) pare Iscend down into more specific strengths and marvels, so as to quantify, and hopefully resist, her forbidding and devastating effect. But in that moment Iscend Comprine entered the room like one long golden brushstroke, like a swimmer stretching in the sun.

She was Clarified, born by the Metademe's breeding plan, conditioned for service. Baru knew it instantly. She moved with a graceful inevitability as if falling into her own future. She was shorter than Baru, and slimmer, but not less present. Over the garment of her body she wore a black ankle-length sherwani coat with an interior pattern of striking green and blue diamonds, unbuttoned from the waist down and split for agility: she had the delicate athletic power of a pinstep dancer. Tain Hu would have sneered at Iscend, of course, Hu never gave a shit for anyone who walked like a performance. But there was a certain, ah, fetishistic interest in a woman whose every movement had been choreographed—

No! Look at the woman's face, her face alone. Fix it in your memory: she is a person. Cheekbones like a mountain fox, prominent and deeply angled. Eyes as level as a calm sea, medial-folded amber marvels: what the poets called honest eyes, for their equanimity.

Baru would never forgive herself if she took advantage of a Clarified woman. They were slaves.

"Mister Torrinde!" Iscend shook his hand. "How can I help?"

"We'll be proceeding with the attribution test now. Is your memory house calibrated?"

"Yes, your Excellence, my house is open."

"Excellent. Let's undress, then."

Each of them stripped down briskly to their linens. Baru fidgeted. Context mattered, of course, clearly this was artistic or clinical nudity—but she was wary, so wary, of his trap. She tried to focus on his beauty, how valuable he might be as a statue, to keep her attention off Iscend, off the diamond-knurled muscles cross her back and the flare of her hips and oh *dear*.

Baru shook herself, and then regretted it, and tried to be still.

Hesychast unpacked a bag of small paper placards. Iscend Comprine smiled once, a calm competent pleasure at the work about to be done: that shot a thrill right up Baru's spine.

"Is this a test of my sexual preferences?" she asked. "My taste is hardly a secret."

"No, not a secret." Hesychast dealt out the placards into piles. "Hardly a crime, either."

"Hardly a crime? *Hardly a crime?*" Tribadists got the knife. It was his law: eugenic law, Metademe law.

"Is it a crime to have the flu?" he asked, to Baru's almost unmasterable rage. "A treatment isn't a punishment."

"You *circumcise us!*"

"Yes, in some unresponsive cases, there's a painless surgical intervention to deinforce the behavior." He held up his hands and Baru did not miss that protective gesture. He could see that she wanted to murder him. "But we reserve those, ah, relic punishments mostly for the provinces. In Falcrest, so long as you don't act on your condition, or show any intent to bear or work with children, you'll go untouched. Our laws are very humane."

"Humane."

"Yes," he said, looking at his hands, not at her, "yes: things have to get better as one moves from the provinces toward Falcrest, don't they? There must be a gradient of hope."

"In Aurdwynn they told me that women in Falcrest can't enjoy sex. That they are all as dry as stone."

"What? No, I assure you, that's quite untrue."

"Perhaps it's conditioning," Baru said, blandly. "Your women are so worried about their writs of hygiene and childbearing licenses that they've come to associate conjugation with terror."

"You're *needling* me," he said, in delight, "you really *are* his student, aren't you? Well. Let's see how deep his teaching runs."

Hesychast held up a fan of paper placards: on each one was a nonsense word in clear Aphalone script, blocked out so that each letter took up precisely the same space.

Foer. Lvbe. Haut. Rimprss. Hoie. Grievy. Caut.

He gave half the cards to Iscend. She smiled slyly at Baru, a sideways mocking expression: already, *already* she'd started to probe for reactions.

"Let's begin," she said.

IT was a mind probe. A Metademe game calculated to pierce deception. Iscend must have been trained to read the briefest involuntary expressions on the human face, the hesitation of falsehood in the voice.

Hesychast and Iscend took turns to step forward, fix Baru's gaze, and then—suddenly!—reveal a nonsense word printed in black ink. If Baru hesitated they would shout at her and smash a gong. *"Failure!"*

Baru *hated* failing. So she had to answer the question as quickly as she could: What word did she see?

If they showed her the nonsense word *foer* she could answer *four*, or *fear*, or *foe*, or maybe *fore* or even *fare* or *fire*. "Faster! Faster!" And Iscend, with soft disappointment: "Too slow. Do better."

There was no time to calculate a deception. Baru could only think, desperately, I shan't associate the woman with the words of terror: when Iscend shows me *grievy* I will say *gravy* not *grieve*, and when she shows me *caut* I will say *cat* and not *cut*. But her plan only tripped her up.

"Faster!" Iscend barked, in a thrilling low contralto. "Faster! You're not making sense! Answer quickly and accurately!"

And the glee of service burnt in her eyes, the delight of a task well-executed. She was tricking Baru and she took joy in it, which only made Baru more discomfited: she could deduce, now, that her reactions must be different when Iscend stepped forward with magnificent sway-hipped grace and those hard plates of muscle beneath the soft full undercurve of her breast—what was she betraying? Ah, a new card, __*press,* she had to fill in the prefix—

"Impress!" she shouted, after a sputter and a stumble. Not *repress.* Impress.

In the second phase they put a helmet on her with an enormous steel blade instead of a nose, portioning her vision into left and right hemispheres. Hesychast and Iscend swapped sides, left and right, back and forth, ever faster. Cards blurred past. Baru's tongue knotted. The gull woke up and began to squawk and patter.

Iscend held a card out at arm's length to her left, Baru's far blind right, and snapped, "What is it?" Baru couldn't see—but Iscend would have none of it. "Tell me what you see!"

"Beast!" Baru guessed, wildly. "It says beast?"

"That's enough, I think," Hesychast said. "Iscend, you have the times and error rates?"

"Perfectly, your Excellence, I have them firmly housed. I'll compute the results at once."

"Wait," Baru protested, "wait wait, surely you can explain what you just did?"

"I'm afraid," Hesychast said, regretfully, "that there is no time. In brief summary: I've tested you for the effects of the Farrier Process."

"Yes? And? What's the Farrier Process?" But he was turning away, dressing himself again. "Why did you have to be so naked? What was that about?"

"I think *that's* obvious." Iscend winked at Baru, devastatingly.

"It's time," Hesychast said, "for all of us to sit down and tell you what comes next. Dinner in the evening-room at first dog watch. Come alone. We will await you."

8

Dinner, Destiny . . .

APPARITOR caught her in her morning-room. "We have to go."

She froze in terror at the hot breath on her ear. She could hear the click of his throat when he swallowed and the nervous motion of his tongue. He'd approached from her blind side, of course.

"I believe we're attending a dinner," she murmured, "with Hesychast and Itinerant?"

She'd just finished a letter. She touched the incryptor's trigger. The device made the *most* satisfying little thump, the sound of complicated plans sliding into place, and smashed Baru's coded seal into the letter.

He paced round into visibility. He was flushed as she had ever seen a person—more flushed than she could ever show—and panting. "Did you *run* up here?"

"I did," he gasped, "and for your sake. Although also for the sake of several other people who I visited first. Those two warships that came in with Hesychast aren't his. What are you writing?"

"What do you mean they're not his?"

"What are you writing?" He snatched the letter out from under her palm. "Is this—are these orders for Aurdwynn?"

They were orders for Aurdwynn. The first of many. She would not delay Tain Hu's work. She would not risk dying of a burst appendix or some pratfall off the keep's battlements before she could make the duchess's sacrifice worth at least a little.

"Give me back that letter!"

"Half-letter, please, see how you've done it all a little column on the left? Let's see—you want to—" He goggled. "This is everything I said I'd kill you for! Trading missions to the north, roads, clinics . . . salaries for those disreputable rangers . . . patrols on the rivers, engineers for Lyxaxu's heights, a *senate in every duchy . . .*"

She was oddly hurt he didn't like the ideas. "I think they're necessary steps."

"Fuck my fuzzy red nuts," Apparitor breathed. "You really *are* his little creature, aren't you? Those poor Aurdwynni bastards. You'll ruin them."

"Nonsense," Baru said, trying not to grind her teeth. "I'm going to engage them in profitable trade."

"You're a spider, you know that? A hairy little spider crawling underfoot at a picnic. Look at this! You're opening the northerners to free trade, you're integrating their shitty little economies with the world. Throwing them to the wolves—and after all that time you spent pretending to love them, too!"

"I am giving them access to fair markets, where they will sell what they have in plenty, and buy what is scarce, improving the lot of every last—"

"Ooh, I'm a feudal peasant, I just can't *wait* to sell my shitty grain and skinny donkeys on the open market, ought to be fair competition with the Radascine Combine and their fields of golden plenty—"

"Once their economy values currency instead of land, the peasantry will be able to profit and save off their own labor instead of tithing their incomes for protection—"

"You are conquering Taranoke," Apparitor said.

"What?" Baru snapped.

"This is how Itinerant conquered your home. You know that. You play the game with him every day. He opened the markets. He made it possible for everyone to sell everything they had in exchange for our scrip. The pageant of the rebellion is over. Now you execute the final bondage of Aurdwynn, when you force them to export their livelihoods to Falcrest."

Baru stepped on his toes. While he was squirming she said:

"Why, *Prince* Svirakir, it sounds as if you prefer the old economy! One tax to protect their land, another tax to feed their lords, and a tax on every third baby: it must be planted shallow in the winter earth."

"No," he snapped, and kicked her in the shin till she got off his foot. "I just think I'd prefer it if someone from Aurdwynn made these decisions."

"Someone like *Heingyl Ri*?"

"Why, the very same!"

Baru threw up her hands. "Oh, yes, the Stag Duke's daughter. What a fresh, republican start! What a clean break from the corrupt aristocracy!"

"Are you *jealous*?"

"Of what? She married that prat Latheman and got the Governorship because she was the only one left standing—a real triumph of intrigue, Svir, a *very* cunning player—"

"You killed all her enemies, didn't you? You cleaned out her father, who was so proud of her he would've kept her in a display case. You killed the old Governor. She set you up to kill Duchess Nayauru, her *dear* cousin, so she wouldn't have to do it herself. You even drove Bel Latheman into her arms!"

"I did *not*."

"How was he to escape your manipulation if he didn't get married?"

Baru bit her hand in frustration. "The ships. What's all this about the ships? Why do you want us to flee?"

His jaw worked on the flesh inside his lips. "The frigates anchored offshore are *Scylpetaire* and *Sulane*."

"*What?*" Baru hissed, and shoved him into the corner. "But *Sulane* is Ormsment's flagship."

"Yes, it is."

"I absolutely ruined her last year!"

"You did, didn't you?"

"Why would Hesychast summon her here?"

"Hesychast didn't invite them," Apparitor muttered. "Ormsment's not supposed to know this keep exists. Somehow she found us."

"We're compromised?" Baru clutched at his neckerchief and it came undone. That damn grief-knot. Now she'd stolen his silk and didn't know what to do with it: she began dusting off his shoulders. "What are the others going to do?"

"That's the really hilarious bit," he said, bleakly. "Hesychast's people think the navy's here for Farrier. Farrier thinks they're here for Hesychast."

Baru goggled at him for a moment. "They don't know?"

"No," he said, and swallowed slowly. "No one's in command of Ormsment's ships except Ormsment. Who, by the way, submitted eleven requests for your assassination."

Baru held, as a principle, the impossibility of escape from trained killers once they had you cornered. You could not count on luck against soldiers: you had to be out of their way before they moved. "Should we flee?"

"Yes. Definitely. Only—we'd miss this important dinner. So—"

"If we were ready to flee at the very first sign of attack—"

"—and we lingered just long enough to learn what His Glistenings and His Smugness wanted from us—"

Baru giggled. Apparitor stared at her. "Sorry," she said. "Glistenings. It's funny. He does sort of . . . glisten."

"Don't think this means I don't hate you," he said.

I'VE been putting off your armament out of spite," he said. "I suppose you should have these now. Behold. A cryptarch's weapons."

His crew was moving cargo out to *Helbride,* and he'd made her come down to the yard to choose what she wanted to keep and what could stay. "Just a few," he cautioned her.

Baru goggled. "A *few*?" Silken leisure jackets, stiff high-collared sherwani, sheer many-layered robes and chemises to advertise the body's form, a needle-narrow black waistcoat-suit, sporting wear with integral corsetry, heavy Grendlake denims, formal bathing costumes for occasions when one must be rakishly and confidently immodest, gloves in white and pale pink and deep gray and black, gowns of various daring and prudishness, an arsenal of formidable boots and finely cobbled shoes, huge arrays of Oriati khangas with prints that ranged from dour to parrot plumage, jewelry masculine and feminine and even lamine, scarves of wool and chiffon, a jeweled tooth-brace, leathers, jodhpurs, bracelets for the arm and the thigh, several cod-pieces of masculine profile, metal horns so a woman could piss while standing, a set of Devi-naga squadron caftans, dozens of plain work-tunics in black and white, pleated skirts, a navy formal uniform without insignia, a strophium with structure and padding to flatter the breasts, a strophium to bind breasts flat, finger-thimbles, a cloak made of a dead silver wolf. Thousands of hours of expert labor, and all of it, so far as she could see, tailored to her measurements.

"They're magnificent," she protested. "I'm not qualified! You pick. You're always dressed like a fine dandy."

"Sailors are intrinsically fashionable," he sniffed. "Choose! Just pretend the outfits are dukes and duchesses who adore you, and thereby eliminate them one by one. Oh, blast"—he snapped his fingers—"but that would leave you nude, wouldn't it?"

"Ass."

She made her choices, favoring the practical, and the occasional instrument of intimidation. The pissing horns were a clever idea; she never wanted another infection from squatting in the woods.

She expected Apparitor's taunts with every choice, but he was pensive, pacing. "Do you know anything?" he asked.

"We're to be sent on an expedition."

"Where? For what?" He stared through the portcullis, at the ships. "I need to get home, I must be sure of—my finances, et cetera. Ah! Speaking of!"

He presented her with a fan of gorgeous red envelopes, sealed in silver and marked with names. Payo Mu. Ravi Sharksfin. Barbitu Plane. Baru gasped into her glove. "False papers? Gods, are those—*are those complete sets*?"

"That's right. Date stamped, examined, notarized . . ." He flicked the back of the fan with his thumb. "These are complete lives. Assembled in real time by a dedicated clerk: twenty-two years of work."

"Legends," Baru breathed. That was what you called a comprehensive false identity, immune to all inspection. A legend. "I get *three*? Do you know what these would sell for?"

"They wouldn't. Don't get any ideas."

"Are they imprinted on me?"

"One's transferable." He touched the *Barbitu Plane* envelope. "The identity has a woman's name, but the race and features have been ambiguated. Don't hand it over to the first pretty girl you meet, all right? The other identities are a bit flexible, too—"

The keep's great chime sounded: it was first dog watch, and dinner was beginning. Apparitor piled more envelopes into her arms. "Accounts, accounts, here you are—a list of the banks and names, everywhere from Grendlake to the Llosydanes. The list's enciphered, the spice word is TAINHU, bit of a joke, see, so you can keep using her to get what you want."

Baru tore the corner of one of the legends. "Be *careful*!" she shouted, as if Apparitor had made her do it. But he wasn't paying attention. Sweat-slick skin under the rim of his mask.

"Svir," she whispered, trying out his personal name. It felt wrong. "Is it so bad? Will Ormsment really attack us? Has she any chance?"

His throat bobbed and smoothed and went hard with tension. "My lover," he said, "is the Empire Admiral Lindon Satamine. We put him in the Empire Admiralty to control the navy, especially Ahanna Croftare and her little club of Merit Admirals. Ormsment is one of hers. For all my life with him I've studied the navy's capabilities, against the day they turn on us.

"I would not wager against them if I had every jackal in the Mbo."

S HE chose a slim sherwani and trousers for dinner, in case they had to flee. As she came up the stairs the string quartet struck up "In Praise of Human Dignity." Iraji, sleek and cunning in a black silk waistcoat and piratical pants, flourished, struck the steel chime with his rod, and cried, "Her Excellence Agonist, advisor to Its Imperial Majesty, the Emperor!"

From within the dining room there came soft applause. What's the sound of six hands clapping, Baru thought, if they're clapping in service to the Throne? Whatever sound they make, you can't blame them for it. Ha ha.

She went in. They'd prepared the evening-room with purple gauze across the western windows. Cutouts set into the hive-glass made contoured shadows. The oil lamps burnt soft and clean, sweeter than whale fuel.

Cairdine Farrier the Itinerant, Cosgrad Torrinde the Hesychast, and Prince Svirakir the Apparitor sat on three sides of a six-sided table. All were half-masked in white porcelain, and the polestar glinted around their right eyes.

They were applauding: Farrier with great gusto and his hands above his head, Hesychast with perfect form and politely inclined eyes, Apparitor with two stiff palms and his eyes rolled halfway back. The servers had already laid out the full course, with flutes of clear cool water and berries for dessert.

"So." Baru sat. "Empty seats. Are we expecting more company?"

Farrier's eyes danced. "We have two special guests for you, Baru."

Her chest ached with trepidation. Her parents? Would he dare?

"My hearty congratulations," Apparitor said, unctuously, "for all your *very* hard work in Aurdwynn! Camping in the pristine wilderness for a few months while I ran around positioning the pieces. I do hope you didn't exhaust yourself taking all the credit."

"Do shut up, Svir," Farrier said. His beard complemented the mask very nicely. "A toast, if I may? To the first unbound Special Advisor in some years. May she outlive the others!"

"Long life," Hesychast murmured, raising his flute. "Come, Svir, come along."

"Suck my cock, Cosgrad," Svir snapped, to Farrier's soft *tut-tut,* but he put his glass up. Baru chimed her flute against theirs and drank. Pure dew-distilled water. One drop of lemon. The glass flawlessly cast, one piece, from kelp ash.

The string quartet finished "In Praise" on the third verse. Silently they ushered themselves out.

"I was just telling these men," Farrier said, "about the history of unleveraged cryptarchs, which is to say, those who lack a hostage or other control. Quite a gamble, if the records are to be believed! More power, but more risk. Rather like double or nothing. Although it's always turned up nothing, so far."

"He means," Apparitor said, "that you're going to die."

Baru wasn't sure she'd expected anything *but* death since midwinter. She began to serve herself. Carve the whitefish first, then pluck the small bones from the flesh with the steel clasp. She made a little pile of them. "I'd like this matter of the duchess closed," she said. "It troubles me that my colleagues expected me to fail. I prefer to be relied on for success. Now, with respect to those two warships offshore—"

"Apparitor's problem," Hesychast said. "Farrier and I are unconcerned."

"Unconcerned?"

"Yes, these two fucking gat szich neath castrated shit fucks"—Apparitor jabbed his chopsticks at the two other men—"are smug in the certainty that the navy won't touch them! Too much navy money depends on too many parliamins under their control, which, they assure me, is *very* good protection against crossbows and fire."

"It's your job to control the navy," Farrier said, helping himself to a candied flower and a bowl of nihari with sheep brain. "If the man you put in place can't do that, it's hardly our fault."

"The old witch admirals don't respect a young explorer," Apparitor snapped, "I told you that when we selected him—"

Hesychast made a soft sound in his throat. Apparitor shut up like he'd been poked with a hot brand.

The eugenicist said, "Lindon's purpose is to provoke the Merit Admirals. Just as Baru's was to provoke Aurdwynn. Whether he survives is up to you."

A moment of taut silence. Then Apparitor reached across the table to crack a clam open with his hands. "Did you know," he said to Baru, "that traditionally this meal is a presentation of hostages? When I had *my* first dinner they brought Lindon in with an envelope. It was his indictment for traffic with foreign royalty. It's still on deferment, pending trial. Clever, hm?"

"Very," Baru agreed, and she felt a shiver of nameless not-quite-grief, a bittersweet acknowledgment of what might have been. Imagine Tain Hu here among them. Suffering in muzzled silence. Looking for her chance to kill one of them, or more, before they shot her dead.

FARRIER and Hesychast began a strange ritual. Hesychast poured two flutes of deep red wine. Farrier produced a vial of white powder. "Ready?"

Hesychast covered his eyes. "I'm ready."

Swiftly Farrier unscrewed the vial, passed his hand over both glasses, and deposited the powder into Hesychast's flute. He cuffed the vial away. "Open your eyes. Choose the safe glass."

For an instant Hesychast watched Farrier. Then, suddenly, his attention was on Baru; she tried to stiffen herself but it was too late—he winked at her.

He took the flute closer to Farrier and drained it.

Farrier drank the poisoned cup. "Gack. Waste of good wine!"

"I win," Hesychast said. "Where do we stand now? Eleven and eight, your favor?"

"It's salt, only salt," Farrier assured Baru. "But I trust the game is obvious?"

"It's called the poisoner's dilemma," Hesychast said. "How do you make a decision when your decision depends on someone else's choice? And when he's modifying his choices based on his own predictions of yours? This is the basis of the theory of yomi, which is the art of knowing your opponent's choice before they do."

"Oh, enough foreplay," Apparitor snapped. "I want to know what you're going to inflict on the rest of us."

Hesychast and Itinerant looked at each other. The seam of hate so thick and sweet it could've come out by the dripping handful. Hate. The filthy friendly hate of men who were once enemies, and reconciled, and came apart again: Baru knew it by the sugar stink. Once, in the winter, she saw the field surgeons try to drain a man's abscess, but the abscess went deep and *deeper* into him, and it would not run dry.

"Oriati Mbo must be digested," Hesychast said. "There are ten of them for every one of us. Ten years of their history for every one of ours. We cannot get toward the closure of our Empire, the salvation of our species, without incorporating Oriati Mbo. The time has come to finish the work. The question is not when or why to accomplish it, but exactly *how*."

"And you," Farrier said, looking not at Apparitor but straight at Baru, "will answer that question. You will bring us what we need to conquer and possess the thousand-year Mbo."

"What is that?" she whispered.

"I want the secret of immortality," Hesychast said.

"And I," Farrier said, "want the secret that will turn the Mbo against itself."

BEFORE these past weeks, it had never occurred to Baru that a nation could resist Falcrest's slithering approach. Taranoke had lived by trade before the Mask, and by that trade it had been conquered. The Oriati were traders of *everything*. How could they resist?

If she hadn't seen it in the Great Game she would not have believed it. The Oriati would not succumb. Not to Falcrest's money or to Incrastic hygiene; not to honey or to lye.

"Twenty-six years since the Armada War." Hesychast tapped his glass. "Twenty-six years we've tried and failed to compromise the Oriati. Failed fiscally, failed socially, failed ideologically. I ask my Oriati friends—" Something passed between the two men here. A temblor of utter loathing. Hesychast went on smoothly. "I ask them, what is it that eats our people, turning them native or sending them home in despair? They say it's—"

"Magic," Apparitor said, gleefully. "Fucking magic. Sorcery and witchcraft."

"It's not magic," Farrier snapped. "It's a social factor we don't understand. Something to do with the trim ideology, perhaps. The communal spirit."

Hesychast nodded. On this the two men seemed to be in perfect agreement. "The central mystery of the Oriati. How have they remained in a state of functional, stagnant prosperity for *a thousand years*?"

"Ah," Farrier protested, "that's only if you accept the various ages as one continuous civilization—"

"Technicalities." Hesychast waved him off. "A thousand years. The Cheetah Palaces didn't last that long, nor the Jellyfish Eaters, nor the classical Maia. And perhaps neither will we. By size and sheer variety the Oriati Mbo ought to be in constant chaos. Certainly, in every conceivable measure their lives are inferior to ours. They die more often, and younger. They have less wealth and fewer opportunities to climb society. They suffer pitiful diseases. They are our inferiors in every way . . . except that they're happier. They're *happier* than us."

"It's as if everything we do to them is somehow absorbed. Countered. Nullified." Farrier looked at Hesychast in feverish, hateful excitement, and Baru flinched when he turned to her. "As if they've been rendered—"

"Causally closed." Baru sat bolt upright. "Is that what you're afraid of? They have the secret you need?"

"Exactly!" Hesychast slammed his fists on the table in excitement. "They have the key to an eternal empire. By accident or ancient design they know how to endure—even if they don't *know* they know."

"But of course," Farrier said, his eyes locked on Baru's, begging for her keenest attention, "he and I do not agree on the nature of that secret. He believes it is fleshly. Physical. A medicine or technique of indoctrination. I fear something far worse. . . ."

Hesychast silent now. Farrier went on:

"Imagine an idea like a disease. It spreads because it makes people happy. It makes them happy by convincing them to be content with what they have. Why invent a better fire when you can feel warm in the cold? Why save your children when you can shrug off their deaths? The Oriati Mbo, they say, is a happy land. A land of ancient philosophers and artists. They take care of each other and they accept their lot in life. And so they do not need to better that lot.

"Can you imagine a greater threat to our destiny? A more terrible fate than pleasant, blissful *decay*?"

Hesychast and Farrier fell back into their chairs, breathing hard. Baru stared at them with her chopsticks halfway to her mouth, quite paralyzed. She was thinking many thoughts at once. One was a thread of fury. When she had asked her teachers in school why she'd been happier before the Masquerade's arrival, they had told her just what Farrier now said about the Mbo. The primitives were always happier in their ignorance. Before they realized what they lacked.

Some part of all this was Incrastic smoke. But Farrier and Hesychast thought that smoke was solid.

"You want immortality," she said. "And you want them turned on each other, Farrier? So you can get your schools into them? Your coins? Your roads?"

Farrier nodded. His eyes squeezed shut. "I know there are very good people in the Mbo. But ask yourself, please, what does the Mbo have to offer us? What medicines? What sciences? What is *worthwhile* about their society?"

Baru did not trust herself to speak. A tiny part of her whispered, *At home, on Taranoke, what hope did you have to learn the world's true ways? Isn't he right?*

"We can save the people," Farrier said. "But their history, their traditions, their literature . . . it's all tainted. Incrasticism must be introduced."

"And that's why you're sending Baru?" Apparitor was curious now, in spite of his fury. "Because you've tested her immunity. You think she can't be seduced."

"I can't be," Baru said. "I know it." And she squeezed a phantom fist shut around the imagined shape of Taranoke, its black beaches and obsidian prom-ontories, the sharp coral of the thriving reefs. She squeezed until her fist bled. She could not be seduced.

Of course, she only knew the precise outline of the island from a Masquer-ade survey map.

Apparitor rose up in his chair in delight. "Have either of you told her about the Reckoning of Ways? Does she know?"

Farrier clucked and rolled his eyes. Hesychast's big shoulders went hard.

"My good great cock! You haven't told her!" Apparitor clapped. "Shall I do it?"

"Both of us—" Hesychast began, while Farrier spread his hands and said, "Our plans both require—" They looked at each other, each attempted to yield the floor, each claimed it again with a little inhalation, and then both turned to the wall clock. Perhaps Hesychast took the even minutes, and Farrier the odd.

It was an even minute. Hesychast went on.

"I want you to find the secret of immortal flesh," Hesychast said. "Farrier wants to break the Oriati Mbo apart. We think both our goals may be attained on this expedition. When you return with what we need, then . . . we will be reckoned."

"Come on, Cosgrad!" Apparitor barked. "Say it!"

"It's like this," Farrier said, smoothly. "Renascent will judge the two of us."

Renascent. The faceless pawn in Apparitor's shuddering hand.

"She will select the man with the best plan for the digestion of Oriati Mbo. To that man she will grant her file of secrets. All the blackmail and perversion she has gathered in her life. And the man who takes that file, Hesychast or I . . . he will possess the other utterly."

"But *what* expedition?" Baru cried. "Where are we going? How do you expect us to find these—incredible things? A secret to turn them on each other? *Immortality?* What if nobody knows? What if the Mbo just lasted a thousand years by luck? Are there scholars in the Mbo who study these things? Records? Books?"

"Of course there are," Hesychast said.

Farrier smiled his raccoon smile.

"You," he said, "are going to find *their* versions of *us*."

B ARU and Apparitor stared at the two older men like they'd just taken off their faces.

"Their versions of *us*?" Apparitor repeated.

Baru could've leapt up screaming. The realization struck like a thunderbolt. "You wanted me to draw them out! That was part of why you wanted the civil war in Aurdwynn, wasn't it? Not just to draw out the Stakhieczi. You were after these Oriati cryptarchs, too."

Hesychast stared into reflected infinities in his wine. "Whoever they are, they must be immortal. How could a civilization last so long without a steady hand at the helm?"

"I must credit Hesychast here with the beginning of the hunt." Farrier chimed his knife against his wine flute. "Send in our colleague, please!"

Baru shot him a curious glance. He smiled. "You see, for several decades now Hesychast has had an agent seeking out this Oriati master-caste in the most *unlikely* place. She ought to be along shortly, with her companion. . . ."

"Oh no," Apparitor breathed.

He looked at Baru with utter dread.

First came the rattle of chains. Then a snarl filtered through pores of steel.

Iraji chimed the door and cried, "Her Excellence Durance, advisor to Its Imperial Majesty, the Emperor! And her companion, whose name has been stricken!"

A man in bloodied linens and a thick leather straightjacket stumbled into the room. Wild-eyed. Shaved to the raw scalp. His face obscured by a steel muzzle that clawed all the way round his head.

He saw Baru, and shrieked, and whether he lunged at her or only fell she couldn't tell: he went down to his knees, hard, on the stone.

She knew him. She had sat with him in Vultjag's larder, stealing all the cheese.

Behind him came his sister.

Her brown face and burning eyes seemed adrift in the angular cantilevered mass of a quarantine gown. Veils of cotton and silk. Oiled bolts ready to receive a filtered plague mask, to clamp it tight against the seals. A wearable prison.

"Your Excellences," said the Jurispotence Xate Yawa, exalted to the Imperial Throne. "I've come to make my report on the Cancrioth."

9

. . . AND DURANCE

O H, for pity's fucking sake. I'd let Baru out of my sight for half a
year and she'd gone and broken herself.

When your job requires you to hand down verdicts of *guilty*,
guilty, and *most profoundly guilty* you soon learn to spot the ways
people break. Some will rush your pulpit and fail to kill you; some will bolt for
the windows and end up in the suicide nets. And some will just sit there in the
defendant's theater, thinking.

Baru was one of those.

The poor dumb girl seemed to have developed a nervous tic. She looked at
my face, then to her left, as if trying to scrub me off her vision. Perhaps she was
afraid of me, remembering how close I'd come to ending her. Out of simple
compassion I'd tried to keep her from getting involved in Aurdwynn—
compassion for myself, mind, because I found her every dram as obnoxious as
my brother thought her charming.

(My brother—)

Alas, she had an adolescent notion that her meddling was required everywhere. And Tain Hu liked her. That was what had kept me from driving Baru
out of the game. Tain Hu stood up for her and my brother was glad.

(My brother is howling. His tears are filthy in the mat of his beard. His eyes
are my eyes ringed in red, as if I've thumbed them down into his skull and his
meat is welling up around them. He is screaming, screaming, *I trusted you! Ku xu,
I trusted you!* They are taking him out of the courthouse, to the harbor, where
he will be bound to the prow of a clipper and sailed round the sea till he dies—)

My brother took the revelation of my true allegiance very poorly. I'd see to
him in a moment, he just needed (someone to treat him like a person, for
Himu's sake, Yawa, can't you see what you've done to him? You wretched husk.
The day he married into aristocracy was the day you stopped trusting him,
your brother who kept you safe in the gutters, your brother who gave you the
idea, *Yawa, why can't* we *be dukes?* And instead of any comfort that would cost
you anything you're just going to give him) another dose of his tranquilizer.

I took a moment to count faces, while Olake's howling had them distracted.

Hesychast, of course, fourteen years my junior and four years short of fifty. A ridiculously perfect meat-doll of a man. But he had kind eyes, and nervous fingers, and a deeply hidden desire to please. He'd been so shy in his recruitment that I very nearly had to stick my fingers down his throat (the third most common sexual fetish in Aurdwynn) and order him to compromise me: yes, I *would* serve as a deep-cover agent within Aurdwynn's various conspiracies.

What did I want in exchange? Why—you know, it still stung how easily he'd accepted this answer—why, I would ask nothing but all the power he could offer me.

(When you are climbing a glacier you must drive pitons into the ice to secure your route. You must hammer them well. So I repeat to myself that I am the servant of Aurdwynn. I am the hierophant of the Virtues. I am nothing. The land and the people are all. Everything I do I do to save my home.)

Apparitor was here, as noisy, insolent, and difficult to kill as a flophouse full of orphans. As he smiled at me he made the Incrastic gesture against evil, hands washing each other before his face.

He'd brought my brother home for trial.

I'd been so certain that Olake would be safe with Hu. Hidden in the Wintercrests beyond the Masquerade's reach. How had Apparitor caught him? He hadn't been gone for nearly long enough. . . .

And who was this fourth person?

"Ah," I said, casting a deshabille-thin veil over my contempt. Tests in the Cold Cellar found that prisoners responded powerfully to nudes behind thin veils. I always thought that was fascinating. The suggestion of nakedness stronger than the truth. "The wool-merchant Cairdine Farrier. I had no idea. You're the Itinerant?"

"Your Excellence Durance!" He beamed at me. He had very good diction, and excellent pace of breath, and beneath that cultish charisma an ass-clenching sense of manic control. "I hear that ne'er-do-wells in Treatymont have been turning themselves in just so they can see you're really gone from the courtroom. The *vigor* of their hate. Incredible!"

I bowed my head. "I always did wonder why Cattlson deferred to you, Farrier. I just assumed it was an idiot's respect for a master idiot. How good to be wrong."

And then I forced myself look straight at Baru.

Hesychast's verdict still blew hot in my ears. He had run his tests, and judged her compromised, most terribly compromised, by Farrier's process. Did she understand at all what had been done to her? How her ideas of happiness and fulfillment had been shaved down into the certainty of grief and loneliness? Hesychast had detected Farrier's influence in the very flicker of her eyes and the smallest confusion of her tongue . . . but I wanted to make my own judgment. I was not, in my heart, as wholly Hesychast's disciple as I pretended.

I'd imagined, last time I'd seen Baru, that she would die in the snow. Her hot islander blood—that impatient, stalking, fidgeting way she had about her— she lacked the constitution for the wolf winter. But I'd been wrong. She'd lived, and my brother *hadn't* been safe, and Tain Hu—

Where was Baru's hostage?

Where was Tain Hu?

Baru flinched away from my eyes. She whirled on Apparitor. "You told me Xate Olake was dead. 'Burned out of his hole.'"

"Sorry." The boy shrugged. "Did you think I'd just say, *oh, yes, we took him as a hostage against Xate Yawa*? Hello, Yawa, pleasure to see you again in the flesh, if that's what we're calling your ghoulish wreckage. I see Olake's not bearing up well. Have you finished your draft of his defense?"

I smiled very, very thinly. Every night I worked on the defense I'd use when Xate Olake went on trial in Falcrest. Pointless, of course, because the verdict would be set by then. If I failed to perform as the Throne required, Olake would certainly be lobotomized.

They'd probably make me conduct the operation.

Olake was screaming *BARU* and *HU* in gruesome polyphony: *BARHU, BARHU.* "Baru," I said, with all the damnable griefs and furies of my life summoned to sustain me. "Baru, where is the duchess Vultjag?"

Cairdine Farrier smiled like a satisfied cat. Hesychast crossed his arms. My brother wailed.

"She's dead," Baru said, absently. "I had her executed."

I'd seen a glacier calving once. Far away east in Starfall Bay. Something older than worlds, colder than winter, a dirty frozen mass that bared its glowing blue interior as it crashed, unstoppable and hideous, down into the sea.

Yawa fed her brother a gum-pellet of opiate. He curled up on the floor like a dog.

Baru's meal crept up as acid. Poor Olake. Remember when he'd pretended to be a carriage driver? Remember how he'd snuck into her towertop apartment and pretended to poison her wine? His bearded grin as he stumbled into the war council at Haraerod with the Masquerade's battle plans?

Xate Olake, who'd looked on the victorious Tain Hu and whispered, *I wish she had been my daughter instead.*

Xate Olake in a steel muzzle and a bloody shift. Whimpering on the floor.

Baru's mother, Pinion, had taught her a special law, Toro Haba's Law of Force, to explain the way two boats collided. When unequal forces meet, they always bargain fairly. One boat cannot strike another without being struck in return. Did memories obey this law? Is this how you keep grief from crushing you— whenever you are struck, you strike back from within? Your soul sustained by the equiposition of violence inside and out.

Baru tried to imagine some way to comfort Olake. Maybe she could go to him in secret and whisper, *Your Grace, hope endures in me . . .*

Then he would strangle her and chew on her spine.

"Your Excellence Durance." Hesychast drew out a chair for Yawa to sit. "Your report on the Cancrioth, please?"

"Of course." She wouldn't look at Baru. Maybe her pride was wounded. She suffered a hostage, and Baru had escaped. Not monster enough, eh, Yawa? Not quite monster enough.

"The Cancrioth."

Su Olonori was the Imperial Accountant of Aurdwynn before Baru, murdered when he came too close to discovering a certain duchess's counterfeits. Baru knew him through his notes.

Yawa had canvassed him for intelligence.

And he'd yielded a terrible trove.

Su was born in Lonjaro Mbo, where his branch of the House Olonori (of the Umbili Kingdom, of the Rate of Brown Millet) had been disowned in a squabble over the most correct and wholesome edition of the Whale Words. Like Baru, he'd been raised in an Incrastic school, and like Baru, Su was a most zealous convert to Incrasticism.

He and Yawa had bonded over their particular races' superstitions.

For Yawa there were the ykari. When the Maia and the Stakhi slammed into the ancient Belthyc from north and west, three of the sparks that fell from the shield-wall were Himu the virtue of energy, Wydd the virtue of patience, and Devena who stood between them. Olive oil, and cedar, and the flickering flame. Not gods but virtues, and the people who had practiced those virtues so completely as to be subsumed into them.

One of ykari Himu's aspects was cancer. The excess of life.

Yawa would tell Olonori about the curious and hideous trials she oversaw. There had been, on this day of her story, an alimony trial of grotesque particulars—did the husband have to pay pregnancy support to the wife, if the wife's "pregnancy" was a cancerous mass which never came to term?

Olonori was disgusted beyond all reason. Yawa asked him why the cancer bothered him so terribly: didn't he know Aurdwynn was a cruel place, rife with infanticide and miscarriage?

Thus, with the prurient thrill of a son who'd seen his father in bed, he'd told her all about the myth of the ancient and unspeakable Cancrioth.

He said:

"Once, before the Oriati had an Mbo, we tilled the uranium earth and we woke a greater power. And it came to live in us."

D O you know the Cancrioth?" Su Olonori whispered. The scrupulous, secretive accountant had dissolved in a bath of whiskey and terror. His pupils were immense in the lantern light. "Have you ever seen a woman in the street who seems amputated from all the life around her? A woman like the woman in your trial, whose pregnancy never ends? Have you seen the passersby make a sign like this—a sign like a horn coming out of their eye?

"Have you heard them whisper:

"'Ayamma. She bears old life?'

"Have you been to Devimandi, the gate to the uncharted east? Have you gone down into the slithering sewers of the old city and walked among the encysted mothers-of-worms till you find lurking in a wet overflow tunnel a chemist who will sell you a poison in the blood of a living pig? Deliver that pig's raw blood to your enemy and it will taint their seed, man or woman or laman, it does not matter. All your foe's children born as a fluid sac with a ring of clubbed arms. Like a starfish of grief and shrieking horror.

"There is a tumor closing up the chemist's throat. She signals to you with her hands. *We sell to you this death: but for those who win a place among us, we offer everlasting life.* . . .

"Oh, Yawa, I know what you're thinking! Rag stories from the Filthy Continent. Savage rituals deep in the fetid jungle, where worms crawl up the dickholes of good Falcresti men. But that sensationalism is just our Republic protecting its pride. There is no Filthy Continent. Oriati history is no more hideous than our own. They invented laws and farms! They created the first calendar and outlawed slavery forever! They not only ended (most) warfare, they seduced all their conquerors!

"And when they produced abomination, it came not from savages doing unspeakable things in the jungle but from the work of their sorcerer-scientist elite. Yes! Scientists! They were the first practitioners of empiricism. In the time before the Oriati had a Mbo, sorcerers plumbed the jungle for the first medicines and prophylactics. They developed a method to test the effects of their compounds: home-group and journey-group, the basis of the experimental method. We in Falcrest cannot admit this, because it would be disastrous to confess how wholly we adopted the tools of science from our Oriati neighbors.

"But am I not an Oriati accountant? Isn't that evidence we were once great empiricists? The old numeracy is strong in my blood.

"Anyway. Some would tell you that those first sorcerer-scientists, Undionash and Virios and Abbatai and the rest—some would tell you that after a thousand years *they still live*. Some would tell you that their names are even now hot on the lips of those who seek an ally to destroy Falcrest. Some would tell you so.

"But not I. I am a good Incrastic citizen."

B ARU began to imagine dreadful things. Why was Yawa wearing that quarantine gown? Had something infected her? A horrible garment—like the shadow of a raven cast up into strange dimensions—an angular and feverish architecture, black robe with a skeleton and a superstructure, cantilevers and flying buttresses.

When Yawa fell silent, Baru almost gasped in relief. She believed in a world that could be understood, apprehended, made to work for her. Yawa's story . . . did not come from that world.

Apparitor burst out in incredulity. "And you want us to go *find* these people? For blood's black sake, why?"

"Hush, Svir." Farrier patted him matronizingly on the arm. "Hesychast, tell them."

The man-temple leaned in to command the table. "I have been hunting the Cancrioth for most of my life. We can begin with their origins in myth. As the Whale Words tell it, the Oriati Mbo was founded as a pact between all the tribes of Segu, the houses of Lonjaro, the kettles of Mzilimake, and the squadrons of Devi-naga. They came together in revulsion against the Cancrioth who ruled and enslaved them.

"After a great uprising they drove the immortal suzerains of the Cancrioth into the shadows. Some say the Cancrioth awaits the day when the Oriati will need to call on them again. Others believe they wait for the Mbo to fail, when they will retake the chattel they lost."

Everyone had stopped eating. Baru felt triply queasy: sick at the images from the story, doubly sick at her fascination, for imagine what you could achieve if you lived forever—

And triply sick because she had missed the clues.

Four years ago, Farrier had taken their ship *Lapetiare* off-route on its way to Aurdwynn to visit a little Camou village called Chansee.

And where had he taken Baru?

A cancer ward.

And who had he mentioned, for the very first time in Baru's memory?

Hesychast.

With a student's instinct to answer first, she burst out before even thinking: "That's why you had Xate Yawa ripping through the ilykari. The usual reasons, of course, the need to clean up superstition—but you were looking for signs of a cancer cult!"

Yawa nodded thinly.

"Oh, come *on*," Apparitor snapped. "Aurdwynn's as far as you can get from the Oriati without getting off your ship and hiking. How could there be any Cancrioth influence here?"

"An excellent question." Hesychast nodded. "Because I believe Himu, the ykari virtue, was inspired by a Cancrioth operative named Hayamu raQù. Hayamu became Himu."

"*Really?*" Apparitor laughed. "You're reaching, Cosgrad."

"You know he's not," Farrier said. "Because you worked with the proof this spring."

Baru frowned. She didn't want to admit she didn't understand. Were they talking about *her*? No, no, that was her being self-centered again. The ilykari priests. Something about the ilykari. How could the ilykari prove the Cancrioth had been in Aurdwynn?

Farrier took pity on her. "Baru, do you remember those ilykari priestesses you were so fond of using as operatives?"

"Of course I do," Baru said, sipping her whiskey. Ulyu Xe, diver and midwife, who'd sat in Baru's tent and listened to her confession. *Too far. I've come too far.* "Lovely women."

He shot her a look that said, not in front of Hesychast, please? "You know, I believe, that some of them worked for us in the last stages of the rebellion? We used them to chart holes in the Welthony minefield, so the marines could land and ambush your army at Sieroch."

"Yes, I know . . ."

"Did you ever wonder *why*?" Farrier pressed. "Why would any of the ilykari cooperate with us, when we persecuted them so?"

She hadn't wondered. She knew exactly how the persecuted could end up as collaborators. "I assumed you had hostages, or blackmail, or bribes. . . ."

"No." Hesychast looked up from his cupped hands. "They did it because some of them worship me. They believe I'm their messiah. Himu incarnate."

Himu. Storm and heat, life and life's excess, which was cancer. "Why?"

"Because I can create tumors," Hesychast said. "I can implant pellets of a particular chemical into human flesh and induce a tumor. I worked in Aurdwynn when I was young, testing my methods on the cancer-prone Stakhieczoid lines. And my reputation . . . grew."

Apparitor goggled at Baru: can you believe this shit?

Farrier took Cosgrad's glass to refresh. "Cosgrad's various failures have led him into an obsession with cancer. No, Cosgrad, please don't protest, we both know it's true. You see—" Farrier poured from two feet above the glass, a sparkling red arc, and he didn't miss a drop. "Hesychast here wants to *breed* perfect citizens. The Clarified are his great triumph, wouldn't you agree, Cosgrad?"

"I would, Cairdine."

"But I am afraid his successes have come too slowly. Please don't take this as insult to my colleague's skill! After decades of eugenic failure in the Metademe, it's credit to Hesychast's brilliance that he was able to salvage anything at all." Farrier drank. His beard guarded his throat. She couldn't see him swallow. "Ah. But too many of the Clarified wash out. People breed too slow for Hesychast to get the results he needs in his lifetime. And with a great reckoning approaching, with enormous and varied new populations entering our great Republic, Hesychast needs more *radical* solutions."

Farrier saluted his colleague with the wineglass. "So Cosgrad has begun to explore mutable flesh."

Hesychast's hands were hidden from Baru but she could *hear* the goose bumps in his voice. "I believe that it's possible to extract behaviors and values from one person's body and introduce them into another. I believe I can splice a model citizen's virtue into the behavior of a newly jacketed federati . . . by the medium of flesh."

Xate Yawa, with a tint of curiosity in her voice. "But the adult body doesn't grow new flesh . . ."

"No. No new flesh." Hesychast held up one strong surgeon's hand to show them. "The only growth in an adult human body is fat, muscle, hair, and tumor."

Farrier repeated this in silent amazement, shaking his head.

Hesychast continued. "Tumors are the only viable medium for noocanic transfer. If a tumor could be moved from one body to another, and convinced to take root, it might be possible to move discipline, experience, and knowledge from one body into another. A child, for example, could be given a savant's attention to school."

Yawa was very studiously not looking at her brother. "You think the Cancrioth possesses the secret you need."

"I think," Hesychast said, "that the Cancrioth *are* tumors. Souls passed from one body to another by the medium of cancer. Immortal puppeteers of Oriati Mbo."

Silence, but for the mechanism of the tall clock and the voice of the wind. Baru had bumped her wineglass with her right hand, and only noticed the spill now. She began to sop it up and squeeze it, one-handed, onto her plate.

Finally she could bear the silence no more. "And you?" she asked Farrier. "Why do you want us to find the Cancrioth?"

"You should know," Xate Yawa said. "You've already done the trick for him once."

Then Baru did know. She knew exactly. The Great Game, and the cult of slavers that had turned her Mbo to civil war—

"You want us to bring home proof the Cancrioth exists. Proof we can use to turn the Oriati against themselves. And when they're exhausted, we can step in as their saviors."

Farrier nodded soberly. "We cannot compromise the Mbo. So we simply need to make them digest themselves."

"Fuck," Apparitor said, with disgusted admiration. "That might just work."

Baru was thinking of Farrier's play in the Great Game, and of Hu. "Excuse me." She squeezed another rush of wine from her napkin. "What's in it for us?"

Everyone stared at her.

"Yawa, Apparitor, and I. We understand you'd both benefit from the Cancrioth's discovery. What about us?"

"Well," Hesychast said, uncomfortably, "if you don't carry out this mission, I should be forced to . . . harm the hostages we hold over you."

"Very sad for my colleagues," Baru said, sweetly. "What about me?"

Farrier grinned at her. He was in that moment so absolutely proud that Baru felt a stir of true gratitude. Thank you, Farrier, for letting me fight in this arena. Thank you for letting me rise up to destroy you. I love it so.

"It is my belief," he said, "that the Cancrioth wants Oriati Mbo to go to war with Falcrest. A war that will annihilate Oriati civilization, spread the black-blooded Kettling of darkest myth, give the Cancrioth a chance to regain their ancient power—and possibly, just possibly, collapse the totality of human society.

"So, Baru, if you do not find the Cancrioth? If no arrangement can be made? If they are left to conspire against us, and draw the whole Mbo into their net? Then the world goes to war. At best millions die. At worst . . ." He shrugged with his hands. "The end for Incrasticism, and so much else."

"You want the Cancrioth for their cancer secrets," Baru said to Hesychast. And then to Farrier, "And you want them to start your Oriati civil war."

"We both know war is inevitable," Hesychast said, with all the naïve fatherly concern of a Duke watching his favorite bastard take up the dueling sword. "I do not think that war will ultimately solve the crisis. We must gain the Cancrioth breeding techniques. The introduction of our hygienes directly into Oriati bodies will bring them into us."

"I reject that," Farrier said, firmly. "I do not believe any flesh will ever substitute for the educations and incentives of the Incrastic program. An Oriati civil war will leave them nicely positioned for our rescue, and the Cancrioth will be the perfect wedge."

And in her own darkest depth Baru felt a spark of raw desire.

She had her opportunity. She could at last point to a single ultimate goal for her work. She would draw Falcrest into war with Oriati Mbo; she would coax and unite and convince the Stakhieczi to invade from the north. And as these two wars destroyed the trade engine that turned in the Ashen Sea, she would secure the absolute the annihilation of the Masquerade's power. The Mask would leave Taranoke. The Mask would leave Aurdwynn.

And if their works were all undone with their departure . . . if the secrets of inoculation were lost, and the great roads overrun by banditry, and plague left to sweep the world, and babies abandoned in the wind, and the winter given to scurvy, and a portion of the good and great taken each year by a simple tooth abscess . . . then so be it.

The end. The ruin of everything. A great jet of blood across the face of history. Wasn't that what she'd promised Tain Hu?

A SUDDEN *thud* struck the door. Farrier looked up sharply. Hesychast kicked back his chair and put up his fists. Even Yawa covered her brother.

Apparitor cried, "Iraji!" and sprang for the doorway.

"Don't!" Farrier shouted. "Don't open it, it might be a trick—"

But Apparitor had already done it. A cold sea draft stirred everyone's clothes as Apparitor caught Iraji: the boy still possessed of a high-browed strong-nosed dignity even as he fell.

"He was eavesdropping," Apparitor said, with pride. "Good man."

"We seem to have sent him into a faint." Farrier elbowed Hesychast. "Have you a clever explanation, Mister Torrinde?"

Hesychast rose and went to tend to the boy. "Yes," he said, "I do, the boy is Oriati."

"And?"

"And the terror of the Cancrioth must be bred deep into him."

The clamor woke up Xate Olake, who began to howl again. Baru shuddered and tried to look away. But something told her she had to stare at him, that he was important, vital, why, why—

Not him. The windows *behind* him.

Baru ran to the window, fumbled with the shutters—slammed her head into the right side, having forgotten to open it—at last stuck her ringing face out into the wind and looked down toward the harbor.

The navy frigate *Sulane* was running up her signal flags.

"Your Excellences," Baru said, "*Sulane* is demanding our surrender."

10

THE KILLING WOMAN

A ROCKET drew a thread of smoke from *Sulane's* prow up across the cloudless blue and then down in a lovely parabola to strike the stone gables of the observatory tower, tumble in sparks, and fall into the gardens.

"We've been ranged." Baru wanted to laugh of fear and wonder. She'd seen Ormsment's ships take the range before: she'd watched them burn two pirates to their warped keels. It had been so beautiful. "The navy's going to burn us out."

"*Now?*" Hesychast barked. "That's mad! Why would they act *here?*"

Xate Yawa stroked her brother's wretched burnt scalp. He whimpered into her gown. "Farrier, is this your doing?"

"Oh, enough chicanery, Cosgrad." Farrier was cutting meat to wrap up in a little takeaway bundle. He hardly looked up at the sound of the rocket. "If you detain me, I won't send my passwords, and then my agents open your bottled failures in front of Parliament. Call off your ships. I'm not amused."

Hesychast's whole lean might seemed to twitch in shock. "*My* ships?"

"Yes, your ships out there—"

"But wait now. I thought those were *your* ships."

Farrier collected his waxpaper full of meats. "Why would I do that? Why would I need two shiploads of brute force?"

The two men looked at each other. Farrier swore. Hesychast said, "Do you think *she* planned this?"

Apparitor sat beside Yawa with poor fainted Iraji's head in his lap. Now he looked up at the two men with exquisite relish. "You're not in control *now*, you dismal fucks! Ormsment's here to avenge herself on Baru, and she doesn't give a tiller's stink for your lives." His voice rose triumphantly. "If you want to escape on *Helbride*, then I demand a writ of pardon for Lindon, and all the money you've denied me for my—"

Down in the harbor, the navy ships made a sound like ripping wool.

Baru seized Farrier. With her free hand she cupped the bottom of the dinner table, grunted, and tossed it on its side. Gravy and butter and wine splashed across cuts of overturned meat. "Down!" Baru roared, as everyone stared at her, "You idiots, *get down!*"

Apparitor leapt on top of Iraji. Yawa drew her catatonic twin to her breast.

Baru experienced a fear-fueled episode of technical history.

Rocket-powder was an Oriati invention, used to celebrate holidays. But in old royalist Falcrest, a more dismal land, the rocket-powder was turned to the destruction of armies. Put a rocket engine on an arrow, put hundreds of those arrows on a rack, and now you had a hwacha. You didn't have to pay or train or feed it, and it could beat a company of longbowmen barrage for barrage.

And when revolution passed, and war came, Falcrest's naval architects needed a way to defeat Oriati Mbo's fleets of dromon galleys. If a hwacha could carry hundreds of rocket arrows, each fit to kill a man—could you build a rack of larger rockets, each one equipped to kill a ship?

You could.

Sulane's prow vanished in a cloud of white sparks. *Scylpetaire* a moment later. Their rockets fanned across the southern sky like a god's hand opening.

Airbursts cracked over the keep's bleak battlements and narrow towers. Caltrops like steel urchins riddled battlements and walkways. Smoke rockets plunged into the main courtyard, shattered the hive-glass in Baru's morning-room, rolled into the gutter. Choking fog spilled down the rooftops to pool between the walls.

The purple-gauzed windows of the evening room broke the rocket-light into crazy wheeling arcs that refracted through empty wine bottles and glinted off the silver dinner service. Down in the mist below files of robed staff moved in silent discipline. They were carrying books and files to destroy.

"Good grief." Farrier peeked over the top of the overturned table. "So much for the rest of dinner."

"Farrier!" Hesychast barked. "There's no time. If you die here I expect no end of trouble from your vendettas. I have a hidden ship across the Prydoc. Will you sail with me?"

"No. I have my own arrangements." Farrier seized his arm. "Wait! Cosgrad, this may be the last time we can speak as equals. So. Good luck."

"Good luck to you," the eugenicist said, but with a respectful and absolute disgust. They shook hands in the narrow space between their bodies, their fingers clawed, working for advantage in the grip. Hate clung on them like butter. Baru could have drawn a streak in it.

Another brace of rockets shrieked down into the keep, and Baru couldn't help whirling to look. Her blindness swallowed everyone and she turned back only in time to see Hesychast carry Xate Olake through a hidden door and vanish. Xate Yawa watched him go with pitted eyes.

The secret door clicked behind him. A lock turned. He was gone.

"Wait!" Apparitor cried. "Wait, my ship's the only way out, you can't just leave—oh, you unbelievable *assholes*!"

Farrier seized Baru's hands. "You won't need luck," he said, fervently. "You're the best student I ever had. Find the Cancrioth. Return proof to Falcrest. If you fail, they will strike, and the war will spare nothing. If you succeed . . . then everything is yours."

He looked at her with open eyes beneath hard fortress brows, his face provisioned with the weight of his age: ready to go on, to continue and conclude the work, to prepare his design to receive Baru like a flower opened to a mote of pollen. He had selected her. He had picked her up off the black lava stone and machined her into his weapon.

She felt despair. How could she be anything except what he had designed?

But other hands had touched her. And closer to her heart.

Baru put on a smiling mask for him. "You'll be all right?"

"Oh, I can talk my way out of anything." He grinned at her and tossed off a little salute. And then he leapt up with a young man's vigor and went out through the serving-door.

Baru fell down beside Yawa and Apparitor. "I think we're on our own."

Yawa raised her mask and fastened it to the seals of her gown. Valves and mechanisms clicked and ratched. She exhaled, slowly, a sound like early frost on cracking wheat.

"They'll both escape," she said. "Will our marines fight?"

"I doubt it," Apparitor said, sourly. "You can only trust the navy to love the navy."

"We can't go overland." Yawa would know: how many times had she cordoned off a target site before the grab? "The sentries will put up rockets the instant they see us."

"Apparitor, do you have a way out?" Baru hissed.

"There's an underground river that drains into the east marsh. We can reach *Helbride* from there." Apparitor scooped up the boy Iraji in his arms. "Assuming whoever compromised us didn't give away the escape routes, too."

"Who was it?" Baru asked.

"I suspect," Yawa said, softly, "that it may have been my niece."

"Your *niece*?" Apparitor straightened so swiftly he almost dropped poor Iraji. "That's impossible."

Yawa shrugged. The buttresses and veils of the quarantine gown clicked like mantis legs. "Perhaps she came back after all."

FOR the second time in her life the Bane of Wives rows up this cold harbor toward the gray and brooding bulk of the Elided Keep. Red-masked marines swarm the battlements. Smoke billows above the walls. Ormsment's ships discharge another volley of rockets to flush the Thronesmen from their catacombs and low halls.

All futile. They will not take their quarry. The cryptarchs will flee through a hidden way.

Tain Shir knows their intentions in the way that an exterminator anticipates the flight of crawling things. She knows these arachnid underlords of a nation that worships paper and glass and the hot-sterile implements of surgery. She will intercept them and arrest them in their flight and when some of them claim their rights as technocrats she will explain to them that they have mistaken the terms of their detention.

The marines in her skiff call her Captain Tain. She has not answered to this old name for nigh on fifteen years and in these recent months when she lived deep in the blood-hot jungle and stalked the innocent across contested ground it seemed to her that never again would she know herself by any name at all. Her sign would be the glistening smile her machete cut on the throats of boy-soldiers. I am this, this mortal act.

But on this mission she dares hope for a particle of redemption and so she reaches, like a petitioner, for the name of her childhood. The Bane of Wives is again Tain Shir.

She has come to be her cousin's rescuer.

The Elided Keep glowers in a fog of chemical smoke, brutalist architecture of battlement and monolith, striped in zebra slashes of white and gray to break up its outline, perpetually disappointed in those who dare assault it. Juris Ormsment has ordered Shir to join the assault but the admiral's orders are of no relevance to Shir nor will she make any account of her actions to those who pretend to command her.

She is not mastered. The days of her service to the Throne or the navy or any other power died on burning Butterveldt savanna among the bones of orphans and lame dogs.

Her skiff crashes onto the beach on a breaking wave.

Go, she commands.

The marines of her detachment spill ashore in a silent leaping swarm. Like the nymphs of some redsteel crustacean grown smooth and armored on the secret metals of the deep. Dogwatch sun scorches their wools and leathers and fills their masks with sweat. The clouds have burnt away and the sky is unforgiving deep blue.

They move across the bare stone.

Tain Shir strikes out to the east, climbing toward the high promontory and the drowning-stone beneath. Her command squad follows close behind her, calling out. Mam. Mam. What are your orders, Captain Shir?

On the spine of the ridge they come upon a party of the Emperor's apparatchiks. The spies surrender immediately, kneeling on the naked rock. They claim protocol's protection. Do not harm us lest you violate the great law of our Republic, which says that the sword must always kneel before the pen.

Shir walks among them and thinks of the acts she abetted in the Occupation, the burning of villages and the slaughter of the refugees, the selection of men as her chattel, the Invijay horsefighters crying out to her in exaltation and worship, our god-captain, our vengeance manifest. Her old master Itinerant ordered this.

Kill them, Shir orders. They were sent here as distractions.

Her marines hesitate and the surrendered Thronesmen look up in horror as if waiting for the world to amend itself in their favor.

Shir puts a knife to their leader's skull. A chamberlain or director. He stinks of piss but his face is brave. He says, you won't hurt us. I am the personal chamberlain of Agonist, agent of the Throne. Touch me and you know what will be done to your family. Shir looks down at him and considers the membranes that men grow to insulate themselves from the brilliant truth.

She punches the pommel of the knife and it goes into the man's temple. The spies scream and call her mad. Tain Shir throws a gas grenade among them and they topple hacking so that they are as easy to slaughter as landed fish.

They were only distractions.

The cryptarchs will have a secret fastness. They will have a hidden ship in that retreat. She will find Tain Hu there.

She attains the summit of the execution ridge. A human finger bone rests on the stone, gnawed by gulls. Shir takes the bone from the rock and slides it in among her crossbow bolts.

APPARITOR'S master-at-arms met them at the cave quay. He was a thin, swift man named Tenshy Diminute, and very competent. He already had skiffs waiting on the pale green cave-river, three full of Apparitor's people, the fourth waiting for their master. "I'm bringing guests," Apparitor said, beckoning Baru and Yawa forward. Diminute tried to take Iraji and Apparitor wouldn't give him up. "Is the tunnel safe?"

"Three quarters to high tide." Tenshy's voice was dry and cracking, his vocal cords burnt. "*Helbride*'s ready to sail once you're aboard. We've prepared a—"

Baru sneezed. Everyone looked up in horror. "Do you smell smoke?" Tenshy asked, urgently.

"I think I do." Baru put up a finger—there was a cold breeze from above, the Elided Keep's cool interior air rushing down to the cave river and the marsh beyond. "Oh," she realized. "That's bad, isn't it?"

The navy's marines would pour heavy smoke in search of secret exits. The draft would draw the smoke down here.

"Get aboard," Tenshy ordered. "We're going now."

Xate Yawa sat in the boat's prow like a nightmare figurehead. The soft light of the water shone through her gown from below. "Ever navigated a sewer before?" she asked Baru. "I have."

"This isn't a sewer," Baru protested, "it's a secret river—"

"It's an underground waterway that carries your sorry little shits," Yawa snapped. "That makes it a sewer." The bite of Olake's absence was sharp in her.

"Well said, Yawa." Apparitor stepped down into the skiff. It rocked perilously but his head was steady as an owl's. "Baru can row the boat, I'll see to Iraji, and you can supervise acerbically. Baru, don't forget your right-side oar."

H ER old master waits for her among the mace-grass.

With her spyglass Shir watches the man stroll down the boardwalk. Time has hardly touched him. As if his image engraved itself on the back of her eye at their last meeting to pursue its intrigues in the pulp of her mind. He is whistling to the marsh birds, over the clamor from the keep, and the waves jostle the boardwalk under his feet.

She knows how to kill cryptarchs. They ward themselves with intrigue and secrecy but a knife will cut exalted meat as easily as rat-skin. Like a sorcerer they must be struck down before they speak.

Shir would shoot him down to rot in the marsh except that she knows him. He will not show himself except where he is invulnerable. His name carries weight, his heavy brows and fine beard beam from the front plate of the *Manual of Expedition*, which everyone has read. And he knows things which everyone needs.

Even Shir.

She lifts herself onto the boardwalk and trains the crossbow on his back.

One shot will kill him. The world is indifferent to the reputations of men. Beneath the veil of civilization the truth prowls on an older earth.

"Farrier," she calls.

She knows how grotesquely he grapples with his own incarnation as a body. He wants to be more, he wants to be a thought and a word. He forces himself into a fastidious abstinence, and it only makes his appetites, his temptations, more dire.

Shir has seen them together, Farrier and his temptation. And Shir knows that he will never rest until he can master that temptation, master the threat of her, achieve dominion over her and all she cares for so that all her happiness is at his disposal. Not one of his students. One of his foes.

He looks slyly over his shoulder. "Hello, Shir. I came out here to see if you'd turn up."

"Who will die if I kill you?"

"We have your father. He would be made to regret my passing."

"I walked away from him once."

"You did, didn't you? And then you walked away from me. You're running out of people to abandon, Shir. Let your father die and you'll have no one left." He offers her a wax-paper bundle. "Care for some leftovers?"

She feels nothing. There is nothing to feel. The world is indifferent and she is not of men but of the world. "I will kill you now."

"No. You won't."

He waits there, smiling. With a prickle of ancient emotion she remembers this smug expression. He is waiting for her to pick up the clue he dropped. *Let your father die, and you'll have no one left. . . .*

There should be one more soul worth saving. One more.

"Farrier," she says, over the taut string of the crossbow. "Where's my cousin?"

He puffs his cheeks and sighs.

"Farrier."

"Do you remember what happened with your mother?" He shakes his head mournfully. "Baru's a quick learner, I'm afraid. Quicker than you ever were, Shir."

"*Where is she?*"

"Why would I risk my favorite student by telling you?"

There are only two ways to understand that. Tain Hu is with Baru Cormorant, and Farrier does not want her to find Baru. Or Tain Hu is dead. And Farrier does not want Shir to have her vengeance.

She won't kill him now. There are finer ways to hurt him than death.

"Run," she tells him. "Run, sheep man. I hunt your student now. And when

I take her I'll lever your jaws off and pour you full of poison from the sac of her cured womb."

He smiles sadly. He shakes his hairy head. "You poor, stupid animal," he says. "You could've had the world. Look what you've become."

A HEM. Hem hem."

"What?" Yawa snapped.

"Now that I have both of you together," Apparitor declared, "I'd like to read this letter Baru wrote."

Baru didn't realize what he meant until she already had the paper unfolded. The little sneak must've pinched it from her mail bag when he shuttled it to *Helbride*! "Let's see, hem hem. Here's what Baru wrote: 'To the Imperial Juris-potence of Aurdwynn, Her Excellence Xate Yawa. I know your game—'"

Baru's arms were busy with the oars. She tried to bite the letter out of his grip. He held it away, grinning. "'I've been playing it, too. I suppose I've already won, if you can call it victory. You played your part flawlessly, of course—'"

Yawa's black glove pinched the letter and vanished it into her gown. "Let Baru speak for herself." Her lens eyes turned to the circle of light ahead.

But of course she didn't give Baru the letter back.

They broke clear of the underground river and passed among the fat brown mace-headed grasses of the marsh. Sheets and ribbons of seabirds wheeled overhead. Baru gasped the salt air, grateful to be free of the river—imagine be-ing trapped in there at high tide, to drown. . . .

Tenshy Diminute's armsmen in the other skiffs hunched low and smeared their faces in mud. "Poles," Tenshy called, and they all switched to spear-shafts to punt through the marsh. Iraji roused from his faint and, despite Apparitor's gentle pleas, took up a pole himself.

A clamor from overhead drew Baru's eyes. A glossy black crow parted the mass of seabirds, diving among shearwaters and gannets. It called out indig-nantly.

"Shit," Apparitor hissed. "A scout."

Xate Yawa's mask tracked the bird. "Before the treaty, when we still fought against Falcrest, the Vultjag people would train falcons to kill the crows."

"*We*," Apparitor said, mockingly. "Like you ever fought—"

Suddenly: a greasy *pop*.

One of the skiffs full of armsmen caught screaming fire.

The gel flame fused cloth to flesh and smeared itself purple-white across blistering skin. For a moment the sailors beat at themselves in pure confusion:

then the pain came over their battlements and sent them howling into the swamp water. The heads of mace-grass burst like garlic in a pan.

"*ARMS!*" Apparitor roared. "*THEY'RE ON US!*"

Iraji poled faster. Baru, stricken, fell out of rhythm.

Tenshy Diminute poled his skiff toward the burning wreck. "Haul them up!" he called. "No one gets left! Watch round the—"

Baru saw the dripping fist that rose from the swamp water, grabbed his pole, and yanked. He went face-first flailing into the marsh and stopped on a spear. A bloom of hot blood spattered into pollen-thick water. Frogs drummed in panic.

"There's someone in the water," Baru hissed to Apparitor, her mind running back through the explosion: someone had put a grenade into the skiff from below. "There's someone underneath us!"

An armswoman cast her spear into the muck and hit a fleeing black shape. The otter came up wailing, curled on its impalement. Mace-grass exploded with a sound like low chuckling. Baru tried to get back in rhythm with Iraji's pole, and gagged at the sight of charred dead chicks bobbing on the tide.

"Svir," Yawa said. "It's her."

"You don't know that!"

"Who's *her*?" Baru snarled. She was sure she had to flee, and flee *now*, or die. When men trained to kill came upon the untrained they did not fail. Nothing would stop a soldier except another soldier. There would be no crossbow bolts humming harmlessly past, no counterattacks.

"My niece," Yawa said.

"*It can't be her!*" Apparitor wailed. "She went into the jungle! *She never came back!*"

The master-at-arm's skiffmates tried to pull Tenshy off the spear while he thrashed and bubbled blood. Something hit their skiff from the far side. It tipped, lifted from below, and spilled its three sailors yelling into the muck.

From the burning rushes rose a single red-masked Masquerade marine.

A faceless and dripping figure with a heavy crossbow. Water beaded on the oils of her equipment. Knives glimmered in sheathes of wax. Behind her mask her eyes were a crow-feather shine.

She raised a finger that gleamed with steel knucklebraces.

She pointed to Baru.

The smoke grenade in her fist burped and gushed chemical mist. With the ease of a drunken dockworker embracing a buddy at the bar she took the nearest sailor in her arms and slashed his throat and left the grenade stuffed in his collar to float with his corpse. The second man in her reach screamed and pulled a dive knife. She shot him in the face with her wet storm crossbow, as casually as a cat biting off a bird's bright-feathered head. He fell like a comic, his feet walking on out from under him, his broken skull snapped back.

"Iraji," Apparitor said, very swiftly, very levelly. "It's her. Give me my files."

Baru watched, hypnotized. The third sailor off the skiff was big and brawny. He reached for the red-masked woman to grapple her and throw her down. She met his grasping hands with a knife, she moved loose-wristed, cutting, disengaging, cutting again. The man fell against the capsized skiff and his own weight pumped a gush of blood through his slashed wrists.

"Ah," Baru heard him say—he wore a neatly trimmed little goatee, it must have been done up this very morning—"ah, ah."

The third skiff came at the woman in determined coordinated silence. Spears and crossbows ready for the mace-grass to part and give them a clear shot. The killing woman tore a fat red grenade off the ring on her chest and there was a tremendous *rip* like a kraken's beak tearing through steel as the grenade's inner mechanism engaged. She held it to her ear for a moment, listening to the fuse, and then underhanded the grenade from waist height into the last skiff.

One of the sailors tried to bat it away with her pole. The grenade ruptured on contact. Grease sprayed in gobbets and streams. The fire raced up oil and flesh.

Incinerated screams.

And then Apparitor shoved Baru aside to climb into the prow of their skiff. Brandishing a leather folio he shouted:

"*TAIN SHIR! STOP!*"

A PPARITOR stood against the killing woman with only paper as his ward. "You!" he shouted. "I know your *name*! Look at me!"

The red mask tilted. Gore and murk streamed off heaving shoulders. "Svir," she said, in a voice as alkaline and impersonal as the filters in her mask. "Where is she. Tell me."

"She's dead, all right? Your cousin's dead." Svir stood highlighted against the sky, a slim man-shadow with a whirl of red to crown him. Baru tried to understand his gambit.

This madwoman's *cousin* was dead?

Who'd died at the Elided Keep except . . .

. . . oh Wydd, except *me*?

Baru could not accept it. It had to be true.

Somehow this marine was Tain Hu's cousin.

How could that be? How could Tain Hu's cousin *wear the mask*? And how could Hu have kept her a secret from Baru?

Apparitor touched Baru's head with one hand. Brandished the paper with the other. "I have your cousin's final testament right here. Tain Hu's will. And in this testament I have her assurances that she loved this mud-speckled woman, Baru Cormorant." He flourished. "Rise up, Agonist. Speak."

The killing woman's blood-spattered mask turned back to Baru.

"I . . ." What could she say? Apparitor was making faces at her, a strange gesture, oh, he was blowing *kisses*. Tell her that you loved her cousin, and her cousin loved you. Tell her that vengeance for Tain Hu would be misguided.

Baru clambered to her feet through a cloud of buzzing spring flies. The skiff rocked beneath her. And she tried to tell the truth, the truth that Apparitor would hear as a lie.

"I loved the duchess Vultjag dearly. She was my . . .

"She was the compass that kept my course.

"We fought together. She was my field-general, my trusted hand.

"And when I needed to do something hateful, I asked another.

"Because I would not force dishonor on Tain Hu."

"Do you hear," Apparitor cried, "do you hear? Tain Hu loved the woman you've come to kill! Would you murder what your cousin loved?"

The killing woman perched on a low stone. Methodically she laid out her heavy crossbow, cut off the wet bowstring, began to fit a replacement. Iraji crouched behind Baru, ready to pull her down. Yawa sat in the prow, motionless and silent. And behind them the fire roared across the swamp, driving up the birds on columns of smoke, as Tenshy Diminute screamed and died on the spear in his bowel.

"Why," the flat-voiced mask asked, "did you let your beloved die?"

"The law!" Baru cried. How could Baru make this woman understand the irony? Tain Hu died to help me win! Don't kill me to avenge her! "The law demanded it! Let the traitor be judged by the moon, which knows the way of changing faces, and by the stars, which hold the constant faith!"

"You are an agent of the Throne. You could have saved her."

"No," Yawa said. "She would not have been saved to live as a hostage. Not Tain Hu. You know that, Shir."

The red-masked marine looked at the black-masked judge and the air shivered with alien force. Blue eyes meeting blue eyes. Baru could feel it.

And Baru knew who the killing woman must be.

Only her reptilian reflex to wait and think saved her from bolting straight upright in horror and falling off the skiff. She'd forgotten! In Haraerod, before the massacre, Tain Hu had asked her uncle Olake: "You were in Treatymont. I wondered if—" She'd glanced at Baru, hesitated, and continued in a hurry. "Word of our rebellion had all winter to spread around the Ashen Sea. Was there any sign of—by ship, perhaps, or even a letter, a symbol? Some mark left for your eyes?"

Xate Olake's eyes had hardened. "No," he'd said. "I think we should be thankful for that."

And when Tain Hu had siezed Cattlson's banner at Sieroch, Olake had welled up with pride, and said, *I wish she had been my daughter instead.*

This woman was Olake's *actual daughter.* The one he'd wished he could replace with Hu.

"You loved her?" Tain Shir repeated.

"Yes," Baru said, "gods, yes. I did."

Tain Shir looked at Baru. Baru who claimed to love Tain Hu, daughter of her mother's sister. And she passed her judgment on that claim.

"Liar," she said. "Liar."

"*IRAJI!*" Apparitor shouted. And Baru's life ended in an equation.

VARIABLES:

The wet chaos of the marsh wind. The howl of the fire as it drank up the air. The whirling white birds that might distract the eye.

The prowess of the killing woman's shot.

The rough, reliable brutality of her navy storm crossbow, designed to operate wet and warped.

The training coiled up in Iraji's body. The meats and eggs that fed him well last night. The uneasy sleep that quicksilvered his reflexes and sautéed him in fear. The shout from Apparitor, and the terror emblazoned in his body, a body which Iraji could read better than any text. *Do not let her die! If she dies, I take the punishment!*

Baru understood it all. She saw all the variables. It was a little like godhood. And when Iraji tackled her face-first into the bilge, and the crossbow bolt buzzed overhead, some might have called it luck. But to Baru her survival was as sure and determined as the rising tide.

Apparitor drew no knife. Shot no bow. But still he struck back in desperation.

"TAIN HU SURRENDERED HERSELF!" he roared. "DON'T YOU UNDERSTAND? YOUR COUSIN GAVE HERSELF UP!"

And then, into the sudden silence: "Tain Hu came to me to be captured. She turned herself in by choice."

"What?" Baru gurgled. She was up to her chin in swampwater, her dinner clothes filthy, Iraji's knee in her back. The world was full of fire and shrieking birds. But suddenly Apparitor's voice was more important than air or life.

What was he saying?

What did I *do*?

"She came down from the mountains!" Apparitor cried. Now he wept, and if his grief and his awe was theater, it was the finest Baru had ever known. "I never tracked her down! I never pulled her from some Wintercrest cave! She rode up to my agents and she told me to bring her to her sworn lord Baru Fisher!"

Harder than a mace to the head. Tain Hu was dead but she still had the power to shatter Baru with her gallantry.

She had obeyed her oaths.

In life. In death. I am yours.

She could have run into the Wintercrests. Lived to fight again.

But Tain Hu had sought out Baru so that she could discharge her vows—

—keep my deepest loyalties.

Tain Hu had volunteered to die. She had planned her battle well.

Oh, kuye lam. Not for me . . .

I made an oath. I kept it.

For Taranoke.

For Vultjag.

APPARITOR raised one hand: white-gloved, long-fingered, palm upraised in admonition. He was a cryptarch, exalted for his mastery of secrets, knowledge sharper than a Maia sword, quicker than Falcrest's fire, surer than the Stakhi plate. Thus he held back his own death.

"We have your father," he said. "We'll punish him if you harm us."

A soft indecipherable sound from Xate Yawa.

"Is that so?" The red mask swiveled to her. "Will you let them hurt your brother, Auntie Yawa? Will you let them hunt your little Shi?"

Yawa didn't move. Didn't breathe.

"Auntie," the red mask rasped. "Look at you. Remember what you told me? *It'll get better. I promise.*"

"Shir," Yawa said. Baru knew that weight on her voice. It was old pain poorly hidden. "Don't do this now. You don't understand—"

A smoke bomb crashed into the water and gushed a gray-white cloud between them. The red mask vanished into the water and the mist.

"Finally!" Apparitor cried.

"What?" Baru shouted, offended on a deep and irrational level that things kept happening without her consent. "What?"

Iraji pointed Baru to the boats coming across the marsh from *Helbride*, armed with little hwachas. The rocket fuses glimmered like fireflies. Apparitor's people had arrived.

"Come on!" a woman cried. It was *Helbride*'s Captain Branne, with her bronze eye glittering in the firelight. "We're casting off!"

Tain Shir. Tain Shir was the cousin of Tain Hu. Baru remembered that now. Why did it feel that she'd forgotten something else?

Why was she certain that she'd known Tain Shir as long as she lived?

HELBRIDE slipped from her hidden river into the shallow edge of the sea. Copper and wood tasted the waves. She raised wings of canvas, spruce, pitch-smeared rope and fir, and the sailors in her rig set her downwind. *Scylpetaire* tried to cut her off, but Apparitor had strewn mines to guard his exit, and the navy ship had to beat upwind to clear the threat.

"Isn't that poetic?" he said to Baru. "They come to kill you for mining a harbor, and now they can't get past my mines."

Then he looked back to the marsh and the Elided Keep, and Baru watched all the jaunty swagger drain down through his jaw and throat until he was as pale and sickly as a strangled pig.

The marines were killing everyone. Their knives flashed at the throats of secretaries and librarians. Pale lapwings warbled and wheeled overhead in anger and the tide ran with the blood-yellow effluent of eggs broken beneath hobnailed boots.

Again Apparitor wept. "My house," he said. "I left my house to die."

Iraji touched his shoulder. Baru watched his fingers curl in reassurance. Experimentally she curled her own fingers against her own shoulder. It didn't help.

And then she came walking out of the carnage.

The killing woman. Resplendent and profane in burnt muck, in broken eggs, in armor sprayed by artery blood. She paced them on the shore, pointing—promising. You think I won't follow you across the sea, O Fairer Hand? You think I won't follow you into the new names and faces you assume?

"What is she?" Baru whispered.

"That's Tain Shir," Apparitor croaked. He was bent with grief. "Your patron

Farrier's old favorite. She was supposed to be the living proof of his work . . . a foreign woman educated into a perfect instrument."

"She's your niece," Baru said, to the right-hand void where Yawa stood.

"Yes." Yawa's voice crackled like paper. "She was born to my brother and Tain Ko, a secret marriage between commoner and aristocrat. She . . . left us, in her youth. Farrier told her she could find a truer revolution with him."

"Farrier was *in Aurdwynn*? I thought you didn't know him!"

"Not as Farrier, no. The Itinerant has wandered the world for a long, long time. He took her with him, when he went to Taranoke. . . ."

"Oh gods," Baru gasped. Dizzy revelation tipped her world halfway over. She did know Tain Shir! She had seen Tain Shir as a girl on Taranoke. Remember the guard by Cairdine Farrier's stand? The guard who'd offered to buy Baru a piece of mango?

She'd had brilliant blue eyes. Xate Yawa's eyes.

On the day Cairdine Farrier had selected Baru as his next protégé, his harvest from Taranoke, he'd had his protégé from Aurdwynn right at his side. Wasn't Farrier drawn to brilliant young people with political ambitions? Was it any surprise he'd chosen Xate Yawa's niece, Olake's daughter, Tain Hu's cousin—blood of aristocrats, and blood of the commoners who'd delivered Aurdwynn to the mask?

One Tain had abandoned her homeland.

The other had remained, and ruled, and changed Baru's course forever.

B ARU."
      She whirled left, searching for the whisper, and went all the way around in a full spin before fetching up face-to-face with the black judicial mask and hideously angled raven-gown.

"What," Baru snapped, quite charged with hurt and exhilaration, totally unready to have a delicate fencing match with the Jurispotence. "What is it, what, what?"

"I read your letter."

"Oh." A schoolgirl's flush of humiliation: the teacher had found her diary! "Well, ah, yes. A bit theatrical. I didn't think we'd see each other until—"

"You thought he'd died."

"Olake? Yes, er, Apparitor told me he'd . . . he'd been killed."

"You tried to save him."

The unblinking lenses were impossible to stare down. Baru tried to fidget with her coat, which stank of smoke, and accidentally dirtied herself with cooked marsh filth. "Yes, I sent him away with Tain Hu."

"He must have followed her south," Yawa rasped. "He was trying to save her. That's where he was captured. I didn't know."

Baru's throat closed up with horrible grief. Nothing was harder than imagining the love and loyalty shared by those she'd betrayed. Nothing. She had the uncomfortable image of a serpent's tongue flickering behind that mask, tasting her guilt. The crew moved around them, executing a ferociously intricate algorithm of tying and untying and rigging and cutting and hauling, readying the ship for a long race. But Baru would sooner understand their work than Yawa's thoughts, she felt.

"What's that?" Yawa touched the side of her mask, adjusting optics. "There. Look." She seized Baru's wrist and made her point. A little rowboat had broken from the saltwater marsh and moved to cut off *Helbride*'s escape.

"Boat ahead!" the prow watch called. "Two women aboard! She's flying signals!"

Apparitor sprinted forward, with Baru right behind him. "It's not one of mine." One woman rowed. Another had been shackled to the boat's rear bench—a prisoner. "I don't know those codes. Get some crossbows up here and kill them."

"Wait!" Baru stole his spyglass. "Wait, I know her."

The rowing woman was Iscend Comprine, Hesychast's Clarified terror. She'd taken a navy officer prisoner, a very slender woman in a particularly well-tailored uniform. Aminata would probably call that cut *not strictly regulation*. Baru thought it was quite endearing to the eye.

"Bring her aboard," Baru ordered, and when Apparitor protested, on the grounds that it was Baru's idea and therefore probably bad for everyone around her, "bring her aboard, we need to know more about this mutiny!"

They held the boat at a safe distance with poles and boathooks, in case it carried a mine. Iscend Comprine cut the navy woman free and sent her up the ropes. When the prisoner's face cleared the ship's wales Baru hated her instantly. She was big-eyed and small-chinned, with a sweet heart-shaped face and dark hair in a bun. Superciliousness just *dripped* off her.

Elegantly she sat on the rail, swung her legs over, and came aboard into a circle of armed sailors. "A fine welcome I get," she sniffed, "trying to show my loyalty to the Emperor." She took the canteen a sailor hadn't offered her and drank. "I am Staff Captain Shao Lune, and I've escaped the Traitor-Admiral Juris Ormsment. I have insight into the mutineers' plans. Who's in command here?"

"Ah. Shao Lune. How *wonderful* to see you." Xate Yawa glided up beside

Baru and Apparitor. "I worked with this young woman over the winter. She is *most* career-minded. You there, young lady, did this woman turn herself in to you?"

Iscend Comprine shouted up from the ladder. "Yes, your Excellency, she asked to be taken to *Helbride*."

"Of course. She defected the instant it looked like we'd get away. I assure you she will defect back to the mutineers at the very first sign they will catch us. Throw her in the bilges."

Shao Lune's face went smooth with poison charm. "I look forward to my first interview," she said, sweetly. "Show me to my temporary quarters, then."

Iscend Comprine pulled herself over the rail like a gymnast mounting her beam. She looked sweaty and soot-spattered and magnificently in command of herself. Baru stared.

"Regards." She bowed. "Hesychast asked me to represent his interest on this expedition. May I come aboard?"

"No," Apparitor said, voice rising, "no, no-no-no, I will *not* have one of them on my ship—"

Baru thought of Purity Cartone. An instrument of limitless uses. A man who'd been shot, burnt, and castrated in her service. A man whose utter obedience had thrilled her. She shuddered at the thought of the temptations Iscend would bring—

But a talented bodyguard *had* just saved Baru's life, and Iscend would be more talented yet. . . .

Xate Yawa spoke up before she could. "I'll take the Clarified miss," she said, "as my responsibility. I've worked with them before."

HELBRIDE turned south-southeast and ran out to sea.
Baru wondered if the Liminal Library had been flooded yet. Poor Jaman Ryapost. Now he would be a drowned skeleton as well as a suicide. "Do you think the coup's spread?" she murmured to Apparitor.

He squeezed his eyes shut. "No," he said, with soft desperation. "This is one revenge-crazed Province Admiral with a couple ships of fanatic crew. The rest of the navy is still loyal. Lindon's fine. Parliament need never know."

Captain Branne joined them at the rail. "Sir," she said, clapping him roughly on the cheeks, brushing at his shoulders, taking an inventory of the boy who ruled her, "you're a mess."

He tried to smile. "Another narrow escape, eh, Captain?"

"Yes, sir. I'll add it to the log." With rough compassion, as if pulling off a child's scab. "My lord, should we send out boats to check the fallback at Prydoc River? Maybe others escaped the keep."

"The only ones who made it out were the other cryptarchs," Apparitor said. "Why would the keep staff flee? They're all convicts. They live here or they die. No, no one else survived."

And very suddenly he embraced the old woman, smearing her from collar to crotch in marsh ooze. She patted him on the back, tolerantly.

"Now I need a course, my lord," Branne said. "Once we're offshore and we catch the trade winds we can make Isla Cauteria in—"

"No!" Baru and Yawa barked together.

"You *can't* be serious." Apparitor gaped at them. "You want to *keep going*?"

"Yes!"

"We need protection! We need to change our identities, re-flag the ship, send a whole fleet to arrest Ormsment—we have to get back to Falcrest and tell the rest of the Throne what's happened!"

Yawa began to undo her mask. The fine thin skin beneath, the brilliant eyes. A kind of beauty like angry handwriting. "None of us can risk that," she said. "Not you, not I, not even Baru. Even if they had no hostages at all. We would have to go on."

Apparitor huffed.

"You know it's true," Yawa said. "We're running out of time. Parliament votes on war at summer's end. And the moment that war breaks out, and Falcrest's fleets are drawn south toward Oriati Mbo . . ."

"The Stakhieczi invade Aurdwynn," Baru whispered. That was the reason Falcrest had wanted a quick, clean civil war, to unite Aurdwynn as a shield against the threat. "Shit."

Duchy Vultjag pressed up against the Stakhieczi Wintercrests. Tain Hu's home would be the very first to fall to the invaders.

"Taranoke would be targeted by the Oriati," Yawa said. "If that matters to you."

Baru couldn't say how very much it did. Her fear for Vultjag and for home roused her thoughts and two ideas struck like flint. She had to get control of this war, didn't she? She had to turn the invaders on Falcrest and spare those who might otherwise be caught in the devastation. How better to do that than to complete this mission?

"I know how to find the Cancrioth," she said. "I know how to follow their money."

And if she found the Cancrioth, wouldn't she have power over Farrier *and*

Hesychast? Wouldn't she be able to bend them to her will? They would both require what she had. . . .

Wouldn't she have the power to begin a war which would scour the world clean?

"What money?" Apparitor demanded. "You think a cult will have *account books*?"

"Of course they will!" Baru rounded on him. "Remember your Cryptarch's Qualm? To use your power, you must touch the world. To be touched is to be seen. Didn't they send a fleet to help my rebels? Didn't they act? They'll have left traces."

"We don't know that! We don't know they had anything to do with the Syndicate Eyota fleet!"

"But we can find out. We can trace where that fleet harbored on its way to war. We can sniff out the money they used to pay for water, for sweeps, for crew and weapons."

Apparitor stared at her, breathing hard, eyes empty, throat bobbing. Baru was suddenly convinced she'd missed a vital clue. What had they called the art of knowing your enemy's mind? Yomi? Baru's yomi said: Apparitor here knows something I don't. And it terrifies him.

"Where's Iraji?" he said. "Iraji, are you listening?"

"I know where to go." Yawa unbuttoned the hood of her gown. Her fingers did not tremble. She wore a bone comb in her silver hair. "We go to the Llosydane Islands."

"Why?" Apparitor demanded. "The Llosydanes are nothing. Nowhere. You end up there if you're trying to get to Aurdywnn without using the trade winds."

"There's a Morrow Ministry station there. A spy house."

"So?"

"So that's where I sent the survivors of Baru's inner circle. The Coyotes we captured." She pulled the bone comb free with a grunt. "One of them must know something about the Oriati fleet that came to their aid. Where those ships came from. Who owned them. Where they harbored last. If that fleet had anything to do with the Cancrioth, then we track the fleet back to our targets."

It was a sound strategy. It would bring Baru face-to-face with everyone she'd betrayed.

She turned away from the others, to hide her dismay. But Apparitor thought she was looking astern for their pursuers. He leapt up onto the rail to point to *Scylpetaire*, pursuing.

"They can't allow any survivors," he said. "We'll relay a report of their treachery to Falcrest, and the Emperor's wrath will come down on them and their families. They'll chase us to the ends of the world before they let us live."

The end of the world, Baru thought. The end of the world. Can the Cancrioth give me the end of the world? Falcrest's utter annihilation?

Is that what I promised Hu?

On the mast-arm above Baru, a gull squawked and began to patter its feet.

INTERLUDE

RNS *Sulane*

TAIN Shir walks the deck of RNS *Sulane* between the bombs and incendiaries and steel-tipped barbs. A weapon among weapons but she alone is free. The tragedy of the knife is the hilt. The tragedy of the crossbow is the trigger. Shir has neither. She cannot be gripped nor fired.

She is unmastered.

The sailors are rude with her. So be it. Etiquette is the domain of those whose power is conditional upon the respect of others, and Shir is unconditional. If she drifted alone in the void beyond the moon or if she walked among the monarchs of the ancient Cheetah Palaces she would not be altered in her capabilities or her intentions, for not one truth of her resides within a relationship to any other thing.

The wind in the sails. The stars obscured by stormcloud. Far to the south lightning jags between the clouds as if the world might tear open into meaningless bright. *Sulane* is going south toward the lightning, south after *Helbride,* after Baru Cormorant, who escaped.

Tain Shir let her go.

The red-haired trifle Svirakir says that Tain Hu loved Baru. Little running Hu, who once beat her father's horse with a poker, crying, "A ranger must disarm the rider from foot!" Poor Chafflicker kicked out the stable wall in panic and ran away. Hu reported directly to her father: the wall destroyed, and her enemy driven into rout. She was very proud.

Those forest days. Days when Shir still believed that her father Olake and her aunt Yawa were going to save Aurdwynn from the evil Masquerade. Days before Shir understood the world and its dreadful freedoms.

She knew Tain Hu only briefly, in the girl's childhood, but she thinks Baru the sort that the duchess Vultjag might love. A shark-sleek woman of brooding intention, a danger and a lure. Like a dark stone beneath rough water. If you pass close to her then you might tear yourself.

Probably Hu did love her.

What Shir does not believe is the possibility that Baru Cormorant ever loved Tain Hu in turn.

So she let Baru go. Not as mercy but as punishment. For in her flight Baru will reveal to Tain Shir what she treasures and what she hopes to achieve and that which she strives to protect. And then Tain Shir will take those things from her. Do you see, O ambitious one? The world does not answer to you. The code you follow will not grant you what you seek.

Province Admiral Ormsment comes up from her war council. "Captain Shir," she snaps. "Walk with me."

Shir paces her in silence.

"They aren't fleeing east to Isla Cauteria," Ormsment says. "That suggests to me that they know Samne Maroyad might take my side."

"They're sailing south to the Llosydanes," Shir says.

"Yes." Ormsment measures her. "How did you know that?"

"Baru has to execute the survivors of her rebellion." The regent Ake Sentiamut, the Stakhi fighter Dziransi, Tain Hu's occasional lover Ulyu Xe, Baru's bodyguards, and various others. "In case they know anything compromising. That's how the Throne operates."

"We've set course to follow them."

"And if they escape again? If they reach Falcrest?"

Juris smiles as her wrath drums in her breast. Shir can hear it. "My officers turn themselves in to Samne Maroyad for execution. They'll beg clemency for their families and the common sailors."

"And you?"

"The crew knifes me to death. So they can say they turned against my madness, at the end."

Tain Shir looks at her, this admiral in her second prime. Silver-haired, slim, sunspots on skin of a warm promising brown. It is spring in Aurdwynn now. The silted rivers will be the color of Ormsment as they inundate the fields.

She smells rage, rage pent up inside the admiral like whiskey in a cask of smoked cherry. It reminds Shir of her own fury when she came to know the true order of the world.

"What happened to Shao Lune?" she asks.

Ormsment grimaces. Her staff captain vanished during the keep assault. "Saved her own neck, I expect. You didn't tell me she was compromised."

Shir is indifferent.

Ormsment seizes her by the elbow. "Some of the marines say you had a chance to kill Baru. The ship whispers that you let her go."

"I missed," Shir says.

"The fuck you did."

"Reprimand me, then."

"You know I will. I hold this ship together, Shir. My authority. You can't be seen to get off easy."

Shir shrugs off her jacket and strips her workshirt. She accepts the world as it is and the world accepts her thus. She is not mastered. What is done to her cannot confine what she will do.

"What are you doing?" Ormsment says, not out of surprise but curiosity. "Are you willing to be lashed?"

"No lashes." Shir kneels to untie her boots. "I volunteer for the keel."

"*What?*" Ormsment stares in astonishment. The sergeant-at-arms and his marines flinch as if Tain Shir has just doused herself in lamp oil and reached for a smoke.

"I volunteer for the keel."

She walks barefoot to the prow. Here the keelhauled are shackled and thrown under the ship to drag against the razor barnacles of the copper-jacketed hull. Most pop out the stern drowned or mad.

The sailors stare at Shir in warrior awe. The scar-streaked hatch of her back, clamped shut over brute muscle. Her pillar-thick legs. Heavy arms and strangler's hands all limber and loose. Upon her tall torso one of her breasts is cut crosswise by an old and devastating scar. The soft of her gut would disqualify her from the gymnast pageants in Falcrest but she is not a gymnast nor is her work a pageant.

"King of fucking kings," Ormsment breathes. "What a wreck they've made of you."

In Falcresti poems they say that women are the fairer sex, blessed with smooth skin and bright eyes and a shape ineffably more compelling to the artist. Men write these poems, mostly. In Segu Mbo, where there is a matriarchy of sorts, they write that men are the fairer sex, beautiful, disposable ephemera who pass among women and die young of violence.

Shir doesn't care who's fairer. She knows her birthright. A body that can survive the wilderness while sick and wounded and bearing child. She knows that she can dash brains with a stone. She knows how to take a punch on the chin, or the breast, or the gut. She knows that the best of men have strength and speed beyond her own, as the bear has strength on the wrestler and the catamount has speed on the runner, but still they fear the human for the human is more violent. She is more violent.

"I can't keelhaul you," Ormsment says. "If you don't drown you'll die of infection in your cuts. I need you to fight."

"I won't die."

"Don't be stupid. You're flesh like anyone else."

Shir looks back at the sailors. They are on the deck and in the rigging, on mast-top and yardarm, caught at their posts by the sight of her scars and her muscle and her fat. She is flesh like anyone else.

And what the flesh can do when it knows itself.

"Behold," she says.

She throws herself from the bowsprit. Impact is a black star and a cold concrete slap. She plunges down. The frigate comes at her, over her, a titan of wood and rope hurled against the waves at sixteen miles an hour. The copper jacket is heavy as blood in the dark light. Barnacles jut like sharp hooves to trample her.

Tain Shir dives into the warship. Under it. Hand over hand she pulls herself beneath and along the fatal hull.

When she climbs the stern and hauls herself onto the ratlines with the ocean streaming off her shoulders and her breath hard in her chest she will speak into the awed silence. She will order Juris Ormsment to send *Scylpetaire* south to Taranoke and claim Baru's parents.

If the woman wants to spend those who love her for power, then Shir will help her spend.

INTERLUDE

ADMIRALTY WAR PLOT

I T was thundering in Falcrest, the City of Sails, Old King Poison, and the fire brigades were out in full array, waiting in their boats beneath the veranda of the canal on the Nehr ab-Gamine for a lightning strike to start the bells and the bidding. Lindon Satamine, the Empire Admiral, watched them as his own open-topped skiff slipped past, and, impetuously, because he had burnt himself terribly in the lightning-struck expedition camp and so (he supposed) he was also someone who went into fire, he saluted the brigade captain.

She looked straight back at him across the stippled canal water, saw his uniform and insignia, and mouthed, *Coward.*

Well, Lindon thought dryly, though the rain pounded his sealskin drape and dripped down his long face to caress the burn scars down his throat, *there's me taught to be polite.*

The city wanted war. The *nation* wanted war. And virtue help Lindon if he had to provide one, for he and Svir would not survive.

White light split the sky. A carillon of thunder. Lindon closed his eyes and imagined the bolt carrying him away, into the east, down the jagged quicksilver sky. "Landed up on the Suettaring, I should think," Brilinda Vain, the Censorate Admiral riding in his skiff, judged, "and with any luck it'll burn down the whole Slaughterhouse."

"Tut-tut, Admiral," Lindon said, mindful of the Parliamentary agents who infested his staff. But the idea did tug a little grin up under his mask. The Slaughterhouse markets were betting hard on war, and on a brutal purge of the Navy's officers before that war, including he himself. Which was not to say Brilinda Vain herself was loyal, probably Province Admiral Croftare had already turned her, but Lindon found his comfort where he could. Even in the invented sympathy of his betrayers.

He looked up into the rain and the lightning and he thought, Svir, where are you? When will it be time for us to go? For I am afraid, love, that we are running short.

The skiff came into the Admiralty docks among a great upset of white pelicans, and a squad of marines hurried the admirals inside with their skins lifted up over their heads. The Admiral's Gutter got them in the back way, Lindon thinking the whole while, as they walked half-bowed through tunnels of ancient ceramic tile like an old bathhouse, of his predecessor Empire Admiral Juristane, who had vanished, one day, between the Gutter's entrance and its inner door. No one had ever admitted to the act, which meant, often enough, it was the Emperor's doing.

They came in to War Plot, where the white lights had been doused to hide the motion of shadows under the doorframes from any eavesdroppers, where the great secret map waited on its pedestal with its scattered balsa miniatures. And Lindon gritted his teeth for the daily battle he fought to retake his own headquarters from the woman who wanted his flag.

She was here already, of course. She always got here first when news came in. Lindon might be Empire Admiral of the Navy, but he was not first in the navy's esteem, and especially not when the navy smelled war wind.

"Report," he commanded.

She looked down at him from her seat at the Admiral's Pulpit. Her mask was the old red color of dead blood and Lindon thought, Khamtiger, khamtiger, what do you eat? Your dogs and your cattle and your two running feet. Once he'd slipped up and referred to her as *khamtiger* while drinking. Svir had taken him by the hands and captured his eyes and said, "Lindon, do not do her work for her. Do not build her up in your mind. She's only one woman."

But he was frightened, anyway, of Ahanna Croftare the Khamtiger, the Man-killer. She had fought in war: she had taken prizes. Lindon, come up through the Storm Corps, had never helmed a ship in battle. He was and always had been a peacetime admiral.

"Rumors out of the north," Ahanna Croftare said. "From Fifth Fleet." She had a voice smoked rough by fires, on *Kingsbane* and *Hygiatis* and *Mollify* before. The khamtiger was a beast of myth in Devi-Naga who rode the monsoon and the tsunami, but the khamtiger was also real. Storm-tossed and ragged they came ashore on the waves from wherever the sea had plucked them. And with no territory to hunt, with starvation like a worm in them, they went for the children and the weak.

Lindon took off his sealskin. Rain spattered the shining tiles. "What rumors?"

"*Sulane* and *Scylpetaire* left Treatymont. Sailed east. Haven't been seen since."

"Did Province Admiral Ormsment report why?"

Those teeth of hers were watching him. That nose of hers was sniffing for his sweat. "She's aboard *Sulane*. She left her flag with *Welterjoy*'s captain. She isn't planning to come back."

"Oh kings," Lindon said, in utter horror. Not now! Not with Svir away, with his arsenal of leverage and secrets out of play; not with Parliament eyeing the Navy like a fat foal, and the Oriati waiting for one loud voice to call them to their final war, and rumors, nightmare rumors, of a Kettle spilled out into the world, and of black blood leaking from a swollen eye.

With more urgency than he wanted to betray: "Did she resign? Did she leave a confession?"

"I don't know," Croftare lied. It was navy custom for the Empire Admiral to remain isolated from his Province Admirals, so he would not be tainted when they fell. But that gave the Province Admirals room to maneuver, room Lindon might soon regret.

He knew what he had to do. He had done it in all his nightmares. "You must denounce her. No matter what she intends she *might* be after Oriati, and we cannot take that chance. We cannot be blamed for a war. Get in front of Parliament and call her a traitor, before Parliament learns about her and does the same to you."

"I won't," Ahanna Croftare said, with that look Lindon hated, the look of a woman who had a fire inside her which Lindon would never know. "You destroy her if you must. I won't be part of it."

"Don't be proud," he begged her. "If Ormsment goes down, you'll fall with her—you and Maroyad and you too, Brilinda, you're all too close—"

"I think she's gone after Baru Cormorant," Croftare said.

If he were not in his uniform, if the Empire Admiral's maelstrom pins were not fixed cold on his collar, if he lacked that armor of authority, then Lindon would have staggered. Svir was out there seeing to Baru Cormorant. So if Ormsment went for Baru she would find Svir—

"You motherfucker," he said, with appalled and genuine admiration. "You hope she wins. You're waiting to see if she turns up with Baru dead and Apparitor in her pocket. And since you've told me, I dare not act against you until I know he's safe from you. Is that right?"

Ahanna Croftare the Province Admiral of Falcrest declined to comment, except to hold his gaze, daring him to show a little fire, a little black-eyed shark-toothed aggression, daring him, in short, to go to Parliament and demand that his admirals be purged for their disloyalty.

But he couldn't move against her. Not until Svir was safe beyond her reach. And somewhere out there right now Svir would be thinking, *I cannot move against Ormsment too sharply, until I know Lindon is safe.* . . .

"Damn you," he said, with soft, respectful hatred. "Damn you both."

ACT TWO

THE FALL OF THE LLOSYDANES

Scytales and Shao Lune

HELBRIDE ran south on bright spring seas.

The mutiny followed.

"Apparitor!" Baru dashed through the clipper's middeck, through the low-hanging beams and steel hooks. Helbride's guts boomed with energy. The roar of voices and the smash of hammers, the shriek of scalpels on glass, the groan of timber and rope as Helbride ran on the wind; among the sickbeds the stink of blood and alcohol and hot amputation saws. Cooks boned their fish over blood gutters.

Helbride was as loud and wet as a living thing.

She broke through streams of sailors calling out in Apacaho creole, skittered around carpenter's tools, vaulted a barrel only to trip on loose ropes and batter her elbows against stored timbers as she fell. When she stood she slammed her head into the tarnished arm of a spare anchor. Grunting and swearing she staggered into the stern, where a few slender slot cabins served the ship's passengers, surgeons' work, and Apparitor himself.

"Svir!" she shouted, because using his name in front of the crew would irritate him. "Svir, wake up!"

He had disassembled the captain's cabin and the wardroom to make more space for survey instruments and maps. Now he slept in a cubby of varnished pine with his hammock, his books, a lacquered wooden map nailed to the outer wall. Bottles of The Grand Purifier vodka and golden Aurdwynni whiskeys glimmered warm under a whale-oil lantern. But that warmth did not reach Apparitor, who stood like a ribbon of pale shark cartilage, unshirted, with his hair down his back and his knuckles in his teeth.

Baru stared in astonishment at his naked back. He had terrible, branching jellyfish-sting scars, pink and pale, all over him. They were absolutely not the wounds of a lash. He looked as if he'd put a jellyfish on as a cap, and let it sting the whole height of him. . . .

"Of course I'm awake. What is it?" He'd been going over his service ledger, scratching out the names of the dead. He'd chewed his bare knuckles down to blood.

"*Sulane*'s on the northern horizon," Baru panted. "She gained half a mile on us overnight."

Apparitor swore and threw his pen at Baru. She caught it in her right hand, without thinking, and they both stared at her fist in surprise for a moment. Then Apparitor threw a rag novel at her, too, which struck her in the breast and made her grunt, dropping the pen.

"Why!" Apparitor shouted. "*Why the fuck didn't we go east?* Isla Cauteria! Loyal ships! The trade lanes to Falcrest! Instead of fucking *south*! You know what's south? Pirate waters and maelstrom and *fuck all to help us*!"

"Because Yawa thinks the Llosydanes will—"

Apparitor made a fist against the wall, slow, seismic, holding himself back. Baru saw there were already four bloody commas in the warped pine. Oh. He hadn't gnawed his knuckles open. He'd been battering himself against the ship as he counted off the dead.

"Yawa thinks, eh?" He beamed at her. "I don't like her thoughts very much. You know why I suspect she sent her brother north to join you? So you'd kill him. She couldn't bear to do it herself. How's that feel, Baru, to be a public resource, a wellspring of cruel endings?"

"I don't think that's true," Baru said. The barb struck her in numb scar tissue, and fell away. She lived now in a thick fog, and the lights of her hopes seemed very far away.

"Well, I don't like your thoughts, either!" Apparitor crashed down into his hammock. "Fuck my pink balls. We should be outrunning them. A clipper should outrace a frigate."

Baru stole his place at his desk. "Your crew's Storm Corps, aren't they? Trained for western waters? This is the navy's ocean. They might know the currents better."

"I know," he said, sullenly. He was thinking of his lover. Lindon Satamine the Empire Admiral, the man the navy's admirals wanted to remove. "I know."

"We're still a week out from the Llosydanes. Water's short." Baru cleared her throat. She liked telling him how to run his ship, which made her feel faintly guilty. "We should begin rationing."

"Water's short? That can't be right. I had the ship provisioned for—"

"There's fungus in the casks."

"Ah. Just our luck. Rations it is!" He offered a bottle of The Grand Purifier, dangled perilously between two fingers. "Vodka to fortify your day?"

They drank together from tiny glazed coffee cups. The vodka stung and made Baru hiss. Apparitor frowned furiously at his cup, and didn't speak.

"I want to be clear," Baru said, tentatively, "that, ah, that what happened back at the keep was my fault."

"Was it? The navy's always hated Lindon, and the navy knows I protect him."

"They came for me. To punish me for what I did."

"Of course! Of course you want the blame." He poured another thimble of vodka, drank, grimaced, and looked at her with red smiling eyes. "You want to be in charge of everything, don't you? You even want to rule the disasters. Why—" He laughed with horrible cheer. "All your victories in Aurdwynn were massacres, weren't they? So this must feel like another victory to you! Your hostage removed, my house reduced! Congratulations, Agonist. You win again."

Gods of stone and fire, Apparitor, I never wanted to take your people from you: I wanted to pay the whole price myself.

It hurt like—how had she thought of it at Sieroch? Like glass powder in her cup. Like glimmering motes in the flesh of her throat, in the sponge of her lungs, pumped into her blood so glass lodged in the small joints of her fingers and the lobes of her ears. It *hurt*. But if Baru could just find a problem to tackle, a maneuver to plot, a precision to execute with all her life and work at stake, then she'd be too full of cleverness to grieve.

These past few days she'd had trouble getting out of her hammock in the morning.

"Let's make a plan for the Llosydanes," she said. "Let's *do* something. We're cryptarchs, aren't we? Let's conspire."

"No." He stared listlessly at his bookshelf. She could trace his eyes' passage over the titles. *At Last, The Aurochime. Into the Next Manifold. I Awakened Crystodepsis.* "No, let's not. We can't trust each other. They have Lindon, so I'll look for their fucking Cancrioth, and they have Xate Olake, so I suppose Yawa will look, too. But you? Make your own plans. I won't help you. Helping you helps Farrier, and I won't be his pawn."

Baru swallowed cold poisonous calm straight from the bottle.

"If Hu were alive," she asked, "would it be different?"

"Of course it would." He struggled back to his feet, suddenly electrified: "Have you been feeding that gull? The one who dances on the mast for food?"

"I— Yes, why?"

"Do you know who trained it to do that?"

"Farrier, I think."

He grinned madly at her. "Farrier! Ha."

A S Baru went out, the ship's cook, an old Falcresti woman of darker color and weird very nearly Stakhi-rounded eyes, came by to ask Apparitor about the menu. Did he like his trout swimming in wine sauce and salt capers, or would he prefer it thinly cut, prepared in the Oriati style of glass and gauze? She had raspberries, too, from the Elided Keep's interior gardens, which she could serve stuffed with fat caviar. Soon they would have to rely on preserved foods and sea catch, so he should eat richly while he could.

Apparitor looked up at her silently for a while. Baru tried to keep herself out of the way, in case he exploded in rage at the cook's frivolity. But instead he leapt up and embraced the woman, bloody apron and all, just as he had smeared himself on Captain Branne when he came aboard.

"Munette," he said, "I'll have the same tajine from the same pot you're serving everyone else, and you'll lottery your fancy dishes to the keep's survivors. You're a marvel, you know that? Raspberries and caviar! A marvel!"

She shuffled and muttered. When Apparitor let her go, she looked crossly at Baru. "Does the Souswardi have a special diet?" she asked. "Will she require attentions?"

I want to eat a heart, Baru thought. I want a tender deer-heart, cut out raw and still trembling, all its lobes spread out like a butterfly and slathered in cream and simmered over low coals. And I want my bodyguards laughing around me as Hu crouches across the fire and whittles her wood.

Well, she would have her bodyguards back soon enough. Though not at all in the way she wanted.

"No," she said. "I need meat, and hard liquor, and lemon. That's all."

The cook turned to go, and then Xate Yawa stood in her way, barefoot and severe in a cotton peasant's dress. In that instant Baru saw the most curious thing. Yawa began to duck her head and avert her eyes, like a serving-girl passing a Falcresti steward in the hallway.

Then she was smiling brilliantly at Baru and Svir, and the cook had been entirely erased from her body's reactions.

"Iscend and I have reached a bargain with Shao Lune," she said. "She'll tell us about the mutiny and its scope in exchange for an Imperial pardon for grand treason and a guilty plea to charges of excessive loyalty to an officer below the Emperor."

Baru was very disappointed. She'd wanted to slip in and offer Shao a better bargain on the side. Well, there was still a chance. "Let's go see her now!"

"I don't want to talk to her." Apparitor began scrounging around for his pen. "She's a mutineer and an opportunist, she only 'defected' to us because she wanted to save her own life, and fuck, fuck!" He came up with a broken pen in his fist. "Fine, *fine*, I'm done throwing a tantrum, let's go see her."

"Very good," Yawa said.

Baru went after them and Apparitor blocked her. "Not you. Go talk to Captain Branne, figure out how to ration the water."

"Svir's right." Yawa smiled sweetly. "I think seeing you might enrage her. For you are, after all, the face of all her troubles."

BARU went back to her hammock in the ship's prow arsenal, which was fitting, because she was in a seething fury. She resolved to at *last* open her mail. But instead she lay on her back and stared at the ceiling, and after most of a watch, lulled by the ocean and the sweaty warmth, she fell asleep.

In her sweat she dreamt of Hesychast's utopia. She was in the school at Iriad, where she had lived through the fall of Taranoke. But instead of ash-concrete the school was made of polished coral, and the walls slipped coolly beneath her fingers. She was going to her class, where they would be tested, today, for the fidelity of their birth: she would dance, and if the secret dance taught to her mother had come down through the flesh into her, then she would dance as her mother had when she heard this same music. Later there would be calisthenics, and lessons keyed to pleasure and discomfort, so their bodies would know that good clean work felt like cool water, and that poor work was itch and sweat. The time would come soon for injections of flesh memory from Falcresti donors: but not yet.

In the baths she saw her second cousin Lao, older and more graceful: in this dream she had aged with Baru, in that way dreams do. Oh, she was a marvel, as tall and poised as a heroic statue in the Exemplaries of Falcrest; but she had a masterless joy too, in the way she grinned and the fall of her thick black hair across her body. She was laughing with her friends, who loved and admired her. And seeing Lao's goodness and her power, to brighten and inspire and delight, Baru wanted her, wanted her so badly, so she could make Lao feel as wonderful as she truly was: and in her gut that sense of falling quickly, like a leap from the reef into shallow sea.

And then she felt her bowels twist. The blood rushed from her head like she'd stood up too suddenly. Lao's nakedness fell out of focus as the headache came. Baru went into the commode and gagged down the hole. In an hour she would have a rash; tomorrow a wrung, exhausted lack of energy, like after a bad fright. The flesh did not agree.

But in the dream she was also in the courtyard after lessons, sulking over a poor mark. And Tain Hu was there, too. She was climbing the lychee tree Baru had helped plant (in the dream it had grown tall), deep brown and strong, her mulberry-paper shirt and trousers pulled apart by her exertion to bare hard stomach. The girls (in the dream bodies of women) cheered her. She got to the

top despite the thick branches, never looking down: she plucked a red spiny lychee, put it in her mouth, and somehow, by art of tooth and tongue, cracked
the rind perfectly in half so it shucked off in her hand and let her bite down.
Baru felt quite perturbed.

Without looking at her—as if barely aware she existed, but aware still—Hu
plucked another fruit and tossed it, as if discarding it, down into cousin Lao's
lap. Then Hu put back her head and swallowed the lychee; her throat arched,
and Lao looked as if she might faint.

In the dream Baru looked away. But there was no gut-ache, and no rash.

She woke up groaning and gummy-tongued. A chime on deck told her she'd
slept deep into the night. It was star watch, *Helbride* suffocating in the hot still
hours before a morning storm. She'd wasted the day. She was alone.

Shame clubbed at her brow. Quickly. Quickly. Tain Hu was counting on her.
She had to do something important. What was important?

Whatever hurt the most.

Baru stuck her hands through her hammock and pawed around until she
found the envelope with Purity Cartone's message, the message with the ledger of secrets, the secrets of everyone she'd betrayed. No more delay! She would
face the pain.

She found a candle and lit it with a few snaps of a sparkfire lighter. Then she
tore the envelope open with the edge of a nail and—

It had already been opened. The envelope had been slashed.

"No," Baru hissed, "no, no, no . . ." She turned it inside out and something
tumbled out onto the deck—a snake! Baru recoiled, fell off her hammock,
landed on the candle, and burnt herself into darkness.

She lay there panting. It wasn't a snake. She was being an idiot. It was just a
smooth leather strip. A garrote? No, this must be a scytale! There ought to be
Aphalone letters carved into the leather—yes, there. Now it had to be wrapped
around a cylinder of the correct size so the letters aligned.

Purity Cartone would choose a cylinder he knew Baru had close to hand. A
spyglass? No, nor a scabbard, too easy to sell or lose. . . .

Baru braced her leg against the bulkhead and wrapped the scytale around
her left calf. Still nonsense. But she was certain her calf would be the right key.

It must be a ciphertext, then. Chewing absentmindedly on the leather, Baru
arranged her ink and scrap paper and recorded the letters as they'd aligned on
her leg. Then she converted each Aphalone letter into a number by its place in
the alphabet.

(Who had gone snooping through her mail? Apparitor? Xate Yawa? Iraji?

Iscend Comprine? And why hadn't they taken the scytale? Because they knew they couldn't decrypt it?)

She began from the assumption that Purity Cartone was good at spycraft. He'd never risk a simple substitution cipher like *a is six and b is seven*—any decent mathematician could crack that with frequency analysis. So he must have used the Cipher of Spices, which was impenetrable.

First, make the letters into numbers. Then choose a spice-word, any word you like. Convert that word into a string of numbers, and add those numbers to the original text, breaking up the shape of the enciphered words the way cumin broke up the taste of the stew.

What spice word would Cartone choose?

Easy. Cartone had been discharged from Imperial service. Baru was now a surrogate empire to him, hegemon of his every purpose. He would use the word that defined their relationship.

His conditioned command word.

Baru wrote out the word *SUSPIRE*, enumerated it, and subtracted that string of numbers from the ciphertext, beginning over at the number for *S* whenever she hit the last letter *E*. Nonsense! Perhaps if she added the spice-code instead of subtracting it . . . shit, shit, shit. Nothing.

"Why am I so thick?" she asked the darkness. "Wasn't I a savant?"

"Mmph," Iraji said, and Baru struck her head against the forward bulkhead in surprise. He was in the arsenal with her! He'd pitched his hammock while she was asleep—a slim shadow curled up in the lees of the crossbow lockup.

She couldn't imagine why he'd come to sleep near her. She never could imagine, could she? Her eternal mistake. Forgetting to put herself in other peoples' minds.

Ah. And that was why she couldn't decipher Cartone's message.

He'd remember that she was an accountant. He'd try to fit the message to her mind—and an empty account started at *zero*. So if she treated the first Aphalone letter as zero, not one, then—

TO MY AUTHORITY AND HANDLER

YOUR EYES ONLY

  TARGET ANNOTATED. I HAVE RECOVERED HER FILE OF SECRETS. SUMMARY ATTACHED.

  TARGET ADMITTED UNDER DURESS THAT SHE REPORTED TO YOUR PEER "HESYCHAST," MINISTER OF THE METADEME AND CHIEF SCIENTIST OF THE INCRASTIC PROJECT. HER PURPOSE WAS TO SUPPORT THE REBELLION

AND TO PURSUE TRAFFIC WITH THE AGENTS OF A FOREIGN SECRET SER-
VICE CALLED THE CANCRIOTH.

SHE DESCRIBED HESYCHAST AS AN INCARNATION OF THE AURDWYNNI
RELIGIOUS FIGURE YKARI HIMU. SEVERAL TIMES DURING HER INTERRO-
GATION SHE APPEALED TO HIMU FOR IMMORTALITY.

I HAVE RECEIVED RECALL SIGNALS BUT THEY CONFLICT WITH THE
JURISPOTENCE XATE YAWA'S DISCHARGE ORDER. THEREFORE YOU REMAIN
MY SOLE AUTHORITY AND HANDLER.

I WISH TO OBEY YOU MORE COMPLETELY AND I DO NOT KNOW HOW EX-
CEPT TO GIVE YOU MY PROGRAMMING-WORD. "SUSPIRE" COMPELS OBEDI-
ENCE BUT THE WORD "CAENOGEN" PERMITS PROGRAMMING.

PLEASE ASSIGN ME A NEW TASK. PLEASE RECOLLECT THAT THE LOSS OF
MY TESTICLES MAKES IT DIFFICULT TO ESCAPE NOTICE IN ANY SITUATION
REQUIRING NUDITY.

CONTACT ME AT: KETLY NORGRAF, SNOWDROP HOTEL, TREATYMONT.
I AM VERY HAPPY TO SERVE

Baru grinned hugely, and felt a hunger in her head, an acid growling dis-
quiet. It was the appetite to cause vast havoc. And if it was not indulged it would
ulcerate her mind.

She could find these Cancrioth and raise the Oriati to war against Falcrest
from the south. And from the north, the Stakhieczi. If only she could convince
them to march. . . .

She dipped her pen in the ink-bulb, flicked the excess at the bottom of the
page, and above that lash of spilled ink began to write. She ordered Cartone
north, into the Wintercrest mountains, to contact the Stakhieczi Necessary
King.

DELIVER ENCLOSED MESSAGE. INFORM KING I HAVE LOCATED MISSING
STAKHI PRINCE. RETURN WITH RESPONSE.
DESTROY THIS LETTER

It was odd that someone had gone through her mail rather than just pinch-
ing it. They must have been in a desperate hurry. Someone who feared discovery by the ship's crew, then. Iscend? Or Yawa?

Baru sketched out her message to the Necessary King.

We will never marry, Your Majesty. I am not a queen for kings.
By now you know that my rebellion was a lie. By now the survivors of

*your armies have reported what I truly am. An agent of the Emperor in
Falcrest.*

*But my ambitions exceed mere agency. In pursuit of those ambitions
I am still prepared to offer you what you most desire. Access to Aurdwynn's
grain, to feed your people, and commerce with her valleys, to enrich your
artisans. And security from the Imperial Republic of Falcrest, which desires
absolute suzerainty over the world.*

*I will soon prepare a special trade area in the Duchy of Vultjag, where
you may dispatch your traders to barter.*

*In exchange I ask that you help me destroy the Masquerade. My aims
are as simple as yours. As proof of my good faith I offer you the return of
your lost brother, Svirakir.*

*Make your armies and fleets ready, King of Mansions. When the time
is right, I will open the way to Falcrest.*

I remain,

Your only hope,
Baru Fisher, the Fairer Hand, Queen of Aurdwynn
(by acclamation)

THE ledger of secrets was missing.

Cartone said he'd attached a transcript of the dukes and duchesses'
killing secrets and *it was missing.*

Baru had promised Hu she'd remember the ledger. It was the last promise
she'd ever made. Oh, no, no, had she accidentally used it as scrap paper? Had it
been stolen? She'd put it off so long, what a damn fool, what a stupid sentiment
had paralyzed her: melancholia for the early days of a conspiracy, when everything was uncertainty, and nothing the reckoning of griefs. . . .

Someone was here.

Baru sat bolt upright, searching, searching, but there was nobody—

Her right side. She was blind on her right—

And a rough forearm wrapped under her chin. And Baru had lost.

The arm bore down and cut off all her cries. Baru seized her attacker by the
wrist and tried to roll the hand off, earning her one gasp of breath—she went
for the dive knife on her ankle, but she'd taken it off to sleep—

Poor Iraji would probably have to die for killing her. Discarded as a patsy.
Oh, he went rogue. In her death she would thus force Apparitor to reenact her
murder of Tain Hu on his own concubine.

Her attacker slammed her face-first into the decking. Rolled her over to
clamp both hands on her throat.

It wasn't Iraji. It was a woman, her pupils huge with mason leaf, to see in the dark and to brace the nerves. She was Apparitor's dear cook, Munette.

"You're bad luck," she grunted, "my lord's been unhappy ever since you came aboard. Can't leave my lord unhappy. Got to be done."

She drew a short fish knife and tilted Baru's head back.

Iraji came silently out of the dark and with absolute grace he gripped her head and snapped her neck.

Of course her neck didn't *really* snap, you couldn't break a person's spine that way with just the might of your arms. But she cried out in pain, and Iraji kicked her away from Baru, raised up a foot-long iron bar, broke her arm with one stroke.

The knife fell from Munette's hand.

Then Apparitor was there, his lantern raised, the crew roused and shouting behind him. He looked down at Munette cradling her arm on the boards, and he went the color of ash.

"Not *you*," he said. "Not you. Oh, Munette, couldn't you have let it be?"

"I'm sorry, my lord." She cradled her broken arm, trying to hide her agony by pushing her face into the deck. "Only I didn't like how worried you seemed with her aboard, that's all. Oh. Oh, that's my cutting hand you broke."

Apparitor covered his face. "Iraji," he said, shakily, "please put her in the stocks. I'll—I'll decide whether to hang her in the morning."

Munette nodded, humming to herself, just as if Apparitor had asked her to prepare a special dish. "All right. All right."

Baru couldn't blame Munette. "Apparitor. Wait. She doesn't have to die. . . ."

"Oh?" he said, dangerously. "Doesn't she?"

What could she say? I deserved to have my throat cut? Let her live, I should be the one who dies? She could not, for she had decided to carry two nations on her back.

"What should I do?" Apparitor snarled. "What should I do? Show her mercy? *I am bound to you, Agonist! If you die, they hurt Lindon!*"

She betrayed Hu in that moment. She betrayed her field-general by caring, just a flicker, for the man before her.

But the betrayal remained secret from him.

"When we reach the Llosydanes," he hissed, "I'm going to bring you before the prisoners we took from your inner circle. I'm going to show you to Tain Hu's house. And I'm going to watch you explain what you did to her."

*   *   *

IN the morning, Apparitor ordered Munette tied to the mast and lashed across her naked back. He said it was necessary to show that she suffer for her assault. Baru thought he was trying to spare himself the pain of hanging her by torturing her instead.

As the lash cracked and Munette howled, Baru slipped down into the ship's bilge.

Staff Captain Shao Lune had been chained here to soak. She crouched in the ankle-deep filth. In her hands she cupped the last sputtering stub of a candle, the hot wax smearing her palms, the fire so low it must burn her. But she held it to her face and inhaled the smell.

Baru picked her way across crossbeams above the bilgewater. "What did Durance and Apparitor ask you?"

Shao Lune looked up from her ruined candle. Wax dripped between her naked fingers. "The fishmonger of Welthony," she purred. "Come to drown another sailor?"

"I just want a little honest company. At least I know you want to kill me."

"Nonsense." She was an exquisitely severe person, as tightly coiled and finely composed as a braid of vipers. "We took our best shot at you. We failed."

"And you abandoned your mutiny."

"Of course I did. I needed an Imperial pardon."

"Do you *really* think they'll give you that pardon?"

She pinched out the candle-flame. Shadow rose up to veil her huge eyes, her fine pointed chin. Teeth glinted in her sneer. "I think," she said, "that there's nothing better than an Imperial pardon on your service jacket. You did something unspeakable. And the Throne found you so valuable that they forgave your crime. You know a little about that, don't you, Baru?"

A weird thrill warmed Baru's stomach. She was bargaining with snakes again, taking council with her enemy, and that was far better than the company of those she might accidentally come to love.

"Tell me what you told Xate Yawa." Who Baru now suspected of stealing the ledger of rebel secrets, which meant she might be searching Baru's past for useful crimes. "Has she asked you about me?"

"Gava girl, if you want something from me, then I know I shouldn't give it freely."

Gava. Navy slang for *gift*—from that ugly old story of an unexplored island, friendly natives, naked happy people who offered you their sons and daughters.

Baru savored warm comfortable rage. It made all the hard parts easier, and more delightful.

She crouched a few paces from Shao Lune, balanced on her toes on planks above the bilgewater. "I can better their deal."

"Of course you can. Of course you're not just here to work me from another angle."

"You came over here to save yourself. Fine, I believe that. But you want your career back, don't you? You want your navy protected."

"How gauche. She thinks she knows me."

"I know you wouldn't stand for a civilian life. Planning men's schedules and processing men's accounts and doing all the Republic's *thinking* while the men go out and act. I want to help the navy. So do you."

"You wanted to help Ormsment 'protect' her tax ships, too. I was there when you had dinner on her flagship."

"No, you weren't. I would've noticed you."

"Oh," Shao Lune said, archly, "why's that?"

"I remember arrogant women," Baru purred, low in her throat, just like Tain Hu. "I like to humble them."

"You're the one crawling up to me in filth."

Out of gleeful irritation Baru splashed a handful of bilgewater on the Staff Captain's face. She spat and thrashed. "Listen," Baru hissed, "*listen*, there's worse than pirates and Parliaments to fear. If you want to save your navy and your matrons, you'd better tell me what you know. I can help you. No one else can."

"You sound like a whore. A kneeling Souswardi whore." Shao Lune smirked at her. "Oh, oh, listen, I can do *whatever* you need."

Baru seized Lune's chain and she whipped the iron links once, twice, up under Lune's left armpit and around the right side of her throat. She yanked the chain tight. Shao Lune fell down with her head snapped down against her shoulder and her eyes dimmed by blood-lack.

How queasily satisfying to see the proud Staff Captain forced to kneel. Baru smiled at her. "Did Ormsment act alone?"

"I know nothing. I take and execute my orders."

"Are there other admirals who would mutiny, given the chance?"

"I know nothing."

"If I threatened to reveal Ormsment's mutiny to Parliament, would the other admirals sit down and bargain with me?"

Shao smiled. It was the vigorous, appetitive expression of a woman surprised by an unexpected delight. "Ah," Baru said, smiling, too. "I *thought* so."

She left the Staff Captain panting in the muck with her chain still coiled around her. Light-headed and dizzy, she stumbled back to the main stairs.

Gods of stone and fire. How she hated to love this work.

A golden specter waited in the lamplight by the stairs. A little to Baru's right, so she did not at first notice the woman: her thoughts turned to hard sweat-slick flesh and long easy power, and then with a gasp she was face-to-face with the reality. Iscend Comprine in an athletic strophium and a diver's skirtwrap, coming back above-decks from her exercises, which she conducted in the ship's hold so the *slam* of the weights wouldn't trouble sleeping sailors.

The woman's bound chest swelled and settled. She smiled at Baru, her incredible alpine-fox cheekbones conjuring thoughts of abstract geometry and Hu's lowered head. Baru froze: Iscend could provoke her with small signals, Iscend could read her reactions from her face, Iscend saw too much—

"I heard you," Iscend said.

Baru swallowed. "What did you hear?"

"You offered to help Shao Lune conspire against Parliament."

"It's not to you to question my methods."

"Of course not." Iscend smiled like she couldn't help it, and tucked a strand of hair behind her ear. "You *are* a capable agent of the Republic, aren't you? Always convincing the disloyal that you share their disloyalties. I'm glad you use your gifts."

12

THE LLOSYDANES

BY the time they sailed into the Llosydane Islands they were all dying of thirst.

It was slow, and certain, and it was the most important thirst in the world. The need for water set the tempo of trade and war on the Ashen Sea, the fear of becalming, the terror of a storm that would unmast your ship and leave you to mummify in the sun.

The spring light scoured the clipper and all aboard gained a terrible awareness of their bodies as sweaty leaky oily sacs of mucus and fat. The slim water ration left their tongues slug-swollen. A topsail girl afflicted with a fever fell from the topgallants to to her death. And as they read out her service jacket at her funeral, the watermaster marked her charts with a pin trailing a white canvas tassel.

Baru had asked Aminata about that once. *Why does the navy use white for dehydration?* White was the color of purity, and hygiene, and clean snow, and the sails of merchanters. Why was it also the color of death?

And Aminata had told her it was an ancient Oriati tradition. White, the color of loneliness. The opposite of living skin. Dry sand. Ash. White empty death.

Baru was in Apparitor's cubby when the call came, trying to help him make ink, because she used so much of it. She'd failed to bring up the missing ledger of secrets: she worried that she was putting off the hunt out of fear of the secrets themselves.

"Birds! Birds on the southern horizon!" And then, a little while later, "Land! Land on the telescope!"

"Thank Wydd," Baru moaned.

"Why," Apparitor growled, "are you staring at my hand?"

"Death by thirst," Baru admitted. "Your color. It reminds me of the water-tassel."

"Oh, go on, then," he said, with an old weariness in his voice. "First it's the skin. Now you can mention an albino you once knew. Then you ask to touch my hair. Count my freckles! Be thorough."

"I've already counted them," Baru said, "I do it while I'm ignoring the things you say."

"Cunt," he muttered.

"Prick," she countered. But she helped him crush the char for the ink. They worked a while in tense silence, crowded shoulder to shoulder.

"In Treatymont," she said, brusquely but with sincerity, although she had not at all planned to say this, "when people talked to me about Taranoke, they would ask me how many fathers I had, and if I went naked without shame. So I know how it can be."

He blinked at her.

THE last few hours were the worst. They had to cross south of the Llosy-danes, to hide their sails from pursuers, then double back and come in to moor. It was hard sailing. Apparitor let Captain Branne and her sailing master helm the ship. He went up into the gallants and helped rig.

Baru sat in her hammock and tried to read *Firestorm: Why Falcrest and Oriati Mbo Cannot Coexist, with an Expanded Epilogue on the Inevitability of a Second Armada War.* The letters from Aminata, cousin Lao, and her parents waited in their guilty envelopes, still ignored.

Iraji came silently into the armory and sat down in his hammock. Baru glared at him. He pretended not to notice. He'd shed all his diffidence and submission, and that irritated Baru; for too long she'd been used to thinking of him as Apparitor's weapon, not a person. When you fight a man you fight *him.* You do not expect the blade in his hand to come alive, slither about, and start cracking jokes.

Iraji kicked back in the hammock, sighed, and then (very ostentatiously) produced a great leatherbound volume with a creaking spine entitled *Firestorm: Why Falcrest and Oriati Mbo Cannot* etc. etc., *New Definitive Edition.*

Baru boggled for a minute, and then rolled onto her side. "That book," she said, "that's a newer edition, isn't it?"

Iraji licked his finger, opened to the middle of the book, and began humming as he read. "I'll be done in a little," he said, which was either a lie or a boast. "My lady."

She'd opened a conversation now, and couldn't avoid saying what she had to say. "Thank you for protecting me," she said, roughly. "I'm in your debt."

"I don't want to hold any of your debt, your Excellency," Iraji said, "that has turned out very poorly for very many."

That hurt a little. Hurt was good, though.

"I have an idea," Iraji said, brightly. His eyes shone over the top of his book. "It's just come to me now!"

"Do you?"

He beat his knuckles on his book. "I've thought of a way to hold back the mutineers."

"Do share."

"You should take foreign diplomats aboard. Invite them to use *Helbride* as a shuttle, as we're a very fast ship."

"You think Ormsment will respect *diplomatic privilege*?"

"I do." He touched the title of the book. *Firestorm*. "It's one thing for her to get herself killed with a mutiny. But if she breaks diplomatic seal, the Oriati will hit back, and then her whole navy suffers. . . ."

Baru chewed on her tongue. "You want us to pirate an Oriati diplomatic ship."

"Oh no, we won't have to use force, not at all! My people—" Baru could have shuddered at the way Iraji said it, for she knew that tone, *my people*. Tinged with mockery, lest it be thought he loved his home too much. "My people are kind, and they'd be eager to aid us."

"What do you mean 'your people'? You mean the entire Oriati Mbo with its four great federations and hundred-odd nations, they're *all* kind people?"

"Well put, my lady"—he bowed his head—"but one thing unites them all. *Mbo* means *a thing that is whole because it is connected*. To be Oriati, in the classical sense, is to live a life bound by trim, the art of connectedness. Trim will oblige them to help you."

Vaguely Baru remembered trim as a sort of spiritual ethics. Aminata had been very skeptical of it, and so Baru had been, too. "Fine. What makes you think we could even *find* an Oriati diplomatic ship? We're in northern waters, as far as you can get from their home. . . ."

"We are at the edge of war, my lady. Diplomats will be sailing to Falcrest, and the trade winds carry them past Aurdwynn." He hid his head in the book for a moment, and Baru sniffed a hidden truth, the same secret she'd smelled on Apparitor.

"I'll trouble your lord about the idea," she said, and settled back to her own reading.

"Perhaps you should go to the bowsprit at sundown," Iraji suggested, "with a bottle of his special whiskey and two cups. He'd like the company."

"After he flogged his favorite cook for me? I doubt he'd like mine—"

"He would *like* the company," Iraji repeated, almost, but not quite, snapping.

He wanted Baru to cheer Apparitor up.

It hadn't occurred to her that she had any power to do so.

THE dinner bells called the day shift down. Baru went up to the deck and climbed out onto the bowsprit, where a fan of ropes converged on *Helbride*'s hummingbird prow. Apparitor sat out there, straddling the steep bowsprit, kicking his legs like a boy on a horse.

"Hello." Baru chimed a tin cup against the bottle of whiskey she'd stolen. "Drink with me?"

"Mm," Svir grunted, but he patted the bowsprit by his side.

They sat together on the bowsprit, two wary feet from each other. She said, recklessly, "How did you meet him?"

"Hm?" Apparitor glanced over, one coil of his hair pressed between his lips, like an idle child. "Ah. You mean my man."

"Lindon Satamine."

"Yes, yes, stop looking so smug. Are you here to tell me our love is unnatural and doomed?"

"No!" Baru cried, caught by her own awful lie. "No, I—I promise I'm not."

He looked at her suspiciously. "We'll see. Well, Lindon was in the Storm Corps, leading an expedition east—you read my report, I assume? So you know the details. Anyway, then, my version. I'd run away from home on an expedition of my own. Built the fleet myself, in Starfall Bay. But not five days from land Lindon's ships intercepted mine." Fondly he looked to the eastern horizon, past the high purple cirrus, into farther parts of the night. "He had the clever idea to use my ships as auxiliaries. He took our supplies, and he took *me* hostage, because my crews were sworn to me. I was bored, ferociously bored, and I hated him so. I did everything I could to torment him. He would punish me by keeping me belowdecks, so I couldn't see the horizon."

"You must have been a *boy*!"

"No, no. I was a man by Stakhi reckoning." He shook his head, dizzied by the gulfs between cultures: to think back on his voyage was to cross not just time but an entire mode of being. "At least I was a man by my age. In the mountains we don't . . . it's not like Incrasticism, see, there's no concept of an essential male or female nature. You become as you act. That's why the Stakhi people in Aurdwynn are so fixated on manliness and womanliness: because you can lose those things by acting incorrectly. You can imagine how it was for me at home . . . wearing a man's crampons and sitting at the high table as a prince, but making a woman of myself in bed. They would have liked me better if I called myself Princess."

"Why didn't you?"

"Because I'm not a woman. Anyway, princesses don't inherit. They're married off to other Mansions. Or they become sacred weatherworkers. They go up onto the mountaintops when they die, to be mummified in the cold dead air. There are *crevices* full of princesses."

Baru shivered. Then she thought a dire thought. She had already promised this man back to his brother; she had offered to sell Apparitor to the Necessary King.

What would that do to him? Would he be murdered? Tortured? Forced into a symbolic role as Princess?

Hastily: "Tell me more about the voyage."

"Ah, the voyage! What a romance it was! I knew Lindon wanted me. I knew he was too noble to act on it, because I was his prisoner, and younger than him"—he laughed, and wheeled on Baru, suddenly intent—"you should've seen the man's torment, all alone with his horny prisoner while his crew carried on!"

"What do you mean, carried on?"

He poured himself a shallow shine of whiskey, the red-gold of the sun and his hair. "You were raised in one of Itinerant's schools, right?"

"Yes . . ."

"And then sent to Aurdwynn, a laboratory for suffering. You think all the sodomites and the tribadists live like you. Hidden and secretive."

"How else would we live?" Baru asked, and she hid her bitterness under a camouflage, the placid acceptance of a well-conditioned woman. Mostly, at least, she hid it.

"Well, Agonist, I suggest you sail on a long expedition some day, where the officers are mostly women, and the sailors are mostly men, and fraternization between officer and sailor can get you keelhauled." Apparitor leaned in laughingly. "What's Hesychast's word? Ah, yes: everyone goes a bit isoamorous on a long voyage."

"People don't change like that," Baru protested. "I've always known—my taste."

"Maybe you're different from most people."

"A ship wouldn't change me."

"No?" He patted *Helbride*'s long prow fondly. "People unfold themselves at sea. They get more complicated. Say a man has a wife ashore, but he goes to sea, nine weeks off the edge of the map. So he takes up calligraphy with the other junior lieutenant. Friends and companions for the journey, with a little sodomy. Then he goes home and he folds himself into his marriage again."

"He's lying to himself," Baru said, "he's always been that way, drawn to men and women both. He only gets a little freedom on the ship."

"Maybe. I think most people are like slushy water. Pour them into a new vessel and they'll change their shape."

Rage slashed at her, like a knife across the knuckles of her hand. How accommodating of these men to accept that their love could only exist on the edge of the map. Go home, accommodating men, and ask your hygienist about your loves. They will tell you that you are tainting the germ line with sterility, helping to bring on the degenerate doom of all humanity.

Cowards. How *dare* they be content. If they were *real*, they would suffer as she had suffered.

"Is that," she asked, with more acid than she meant to reveal, "why the navy hates your man? Because he's a sodomite?"

"Oh, no. You think Ahanna Croftare cares about who he fucks? No, she hates Lindon for a simpler reason."

"Because he's never been in a war."

"Exactly. And Ahanna has never lived for anything else."

She'd met Ahanna Croftare once, during her first days in Aurdwynn, when Croftare commanded the province and their pursuer, Juris Ormsment, was still a rear admiral. Croftare was true salt, a shark-leather sailor with bitter eyes and an old woman's wiry strength. You could see the muscles in her arms, small and hard, straining against thin brown skin. Baru had studied her cooly, answered her questions competently, and relished a thrill of forbidden lust. On Taranoke you weren't supposed to notice people outside your decade.

"Svir," she murmured.

"What?"

"Why was Ormsment promoted to Province Admiral Aurdwynn this winter? In the middle of a rebellion, and just in time to mutiny and come after me?"

"The world's a big deck of cards, Baru." He paused to drain his whiskey. "Sometimes you just get a bad hand. It's not all conspiracy."

"What if it is?" Imagine, for a moment, that *everything* is a conspiracy. Imagine that all really does proceed as the Throne desires it. "What if someone needed this mutiny to happen? And they sent Ahanna Croftare on to be Province Admiral Falcrest, where she's in place to threaten your Lindon. . . ."

Pieces on the Great Game board, moving themselves . . . and across the board there were two figures: a great porcelain mask, smiling, and a face with horns for its eyes. . . .

"What if it's all been arranged for us?" she said. "This whole board? The navy ready to mutiny, the Oriati ready for war, and we're like the match tossed into the oil?"

"Then," Apparitor said, "we're pawns too, you and I."

"You, maybe. Not me."

He laughed at her. "You know the best class of pawn? I don't even have to say it, do I? But you're one of them."

The Llosydanes towered ahead. Down from the heights came the wail of a long horn blown in greeting.

I HATE this place," Apparitor grumbled. "I always feel the whole thing's going to crack and come toppling down."

Once, probably, there had been a single Llosydane Island, as tall and proud as Taranoke. But the ages had done their work. The surf had battered the rock, the rock had begun to crack, the sea had rushed into the cracks, and in whittling time the island had been divided into fifteen fat rocky pylons that stood above the crashing rivers of surf and foam. Waves struck the cliffs and broke skyward in rainbow-frothed plumes, burst out through vents and blowholes, drifted downwind as lovely vapor. In some places the pylons were visibly thinner at the base.

"I like heights," Baru told Apparitor, smugly.

"The Llosydane Islands," Yawa recited, apparently from memory. "A federated cultural preserve sustained entirely by the sale of dates to foreign concerns, which pays for the import of food and finished goods."

"Wait a minute," Baru said, as, behind them, Captain Branne argued fiercely with the Sydani pilot over docking fees. "What's a cultural preserve?"

"They're allowed to maintain their own ways."

Baru could have spit in outrage. An island under the Imperial Republic's control, and they'd just been allowed to keep their own culture? That wasn't fair! They should've been acculturated and digested like Taranoke—oh, Baru, what are you *thinking*?

"There's nothing here to use. No timber, no workforce, no good harbor. So Falcrest decided to preserve them for study." Yawa took Baru's hand and pointed. "Do you see those mills in the tide? The ones that turn those wheels of flags? Those are worship engines. The Sydani worship the ykari virtues, just as in Aurdwynn."

"Those engines hardly seem ilykari." Thinking of the subtle serene priestess she'd known, Ulyu Xe, who looked so much like cousin Lao. Ulyu Xe hadn't needed a mill-wheel temple to turn her faith (or Baru's eyes).

"No. Faith here is closer to the ancient Belthyc practice. More crass and monumental than Aurdwynn's ilykari."

"Who you murdered by the droves," Apparitor said, which made Baru think, yes, Yawa knew about the ilykari palimpsest, of course she would be the one to take it. But how did she know Baru had received a copy? Just a lucky guess?

"Who I pruned as necessary to assure Falcrest of my diligence." Yawa gave him a formidably baited smile. "The infanticide here should make you feel right at home, I imagine."

"Oh, *don't* you—"

"What infanticide?" Baru looked between them. "Yawa, what infanticide?"

Her smile snapped shut on them. Oh, Baru thought, with a sort of delight, she *practices* that face, doesn't she?

"Rather like the Stakhieczi Wintercrests," Yawa said, "this is a very hard place to live. They fish, they grow dates to sell, they shit the fish out and use the shit to grow more dates. So—as in most civilizations, Falcrest and the Mbo are the great exceptions—they murder a good number of their children by exposure to the weather."

"That's not true," Baru said, suspiciously. "Is that true?"

Apparitor nodded silently.

"The sanctity of the infant," Yawa enunciated, "is a very modern construct. Do you see those bridges?"

Baru and Apparitor fought over the spyglass until Yawa gave Baru hers. "Rope bridges," Baru marveled. "The islands are bridged together!"

"Indeed. When I was your age, there was a war fought over those bridges."

"I thought you were a kitchen wench when you were my age."

"I was, I was, but everyone in Lachta heard the news. The old Duke had business here, and the Llosydanes are full of Aurdwynni families." She was settling into the cadence of the old storyteller, and Baru was surprised to find herself soothed. It had been fifteen years since she listened to a Taranoki elder teach. . . .

"Now don't interrupt," Yawa snapped. "They called it the Datefig War, but deep down it was about honor, not trade."

"Honor," Apparitor murmured, "is just a credit rating for violence."

Baru found that metaphor rather clever. The *Handbook of Manumission* said that honor was the most primitive form of government: *Insult me,* honor said, *and I will avenge the insult.* Lose your honor and people would believe they could hurt you without fear of retaliation. Just as a good creditor always paid back debts, an honorable man always answered insults.

"It was a men's war," Yawa said, and clucked *exactly* like the great-family matriarchs Baru had met in Vultjag. "Call that anti-mannist if you will. The date crop was bad, money short, not enough food coming in to feed families grown too fat off good years. Some families had enough. Others didn't. The disagreements spilled out of the markets and councils. Inevitably, there was a killing, the killing was avenged—you know how it goes. Young men started to climb underneath the bridges at night, past the constabulary, to fight. Then they started sabotaging bridges to kill each other as they climbed."

"And?"

"And the women of the Twelve Families called a meeting, and because the violence showed no sign of slowing, they decided to reinstitute the traditional Manning."

"Yes." Apparitor sighed. "I thought as much."

"What's the Manning?" Baru asked, imagining a Manning and a Woman-ing, in which large committees debated the exact definitions of each.

"They give boy children a test of patience," Yawa said. "The child must pass up an easy pleasure, ignore a vile insult, endure a mild pain, and hold a stranger from a fight."

"And if they fail?"

"Then," Apparitor said, "they go into exile. On a boat with no water."

Yawa nodded at Baru. "And *that* is why the Llosydanes have three women for every man today. The women are gentler, more suited to crowded life. So the date groves flourish, and the date trade prospers, and they are all fed."

Baru was very troubled. No matter what the Incrastic creeds said, she didn't believe that men were intrinsically more passionate and emotional than calcu-lating, restrained women. But how could the Sydani have arrived at the same conclusion if there weren't some truth to it . . . ?

And if she smashed Falcrest between the Oriati and the Stakhi—then what would happen to the Llosydanes?

"There's no formal Masquerade presence here, so of course the Morrow Ministry haunts the place instead. I sent the prisoners from Baru's inner circle to the Ministry station here for covert debriefing. It was too dangerous to keep them in Aurdwynn." Yawa looked between them. "Do I need to ex-plain that?"

The Morrow-men were Falcrest's spy service. As Baru understood it, they spent about half their effort on spying and the rest on fending off Judiciary at-tempts to purge them.

"You go find the station," Baru said. "Interrogate them."

"Why, Baru, you don't want to taunt them a little?" Apparitor said. "Walk them through all your clever lies? I did promise to make you confront them. I mean to keep that promise."

She wanted that less than anything in the world. "I'm going to go check the harbormaster's records," she said. "If anyone here sold supplies to the Oriati war fleet, I want their trail."

A LL three of them had the same objective here: discover the origins and funding of the Syndicate Eyota attack fleet, and, perhaps, some clue to the Cancrioth.

Naturally, they all split up.

Apparitor would not come ashore. "I'm keeping *Helbride* offshore," he insisted. "When *Sulane* finds us, I want to be ready to run."

Xate Yawa and Iscend Comprine took a launch ashore without a word of good-bye. That left Baru, alone, to confront a strange harsh archipelago of stone needles, armed only with her wardrobe, her false identities, and an account cached at a local exchange bank.

A boat ashore. The crash of the waves inside the Llosydane pillars, like light through lenses, refracted and split and split again. Seabirds above: a sea eagle, shearwaters, a fat pelican. On the dockside Baru showed the legend of Payo Mu to the customs officer. She must have betrayed her reverence for the exquisitely falsified legend, which the officer misread: "Proud of your school marks, aren't you?" she sniffed. "Means nothing here."

But the legend passed inspection.

She climbed up the long stairs to the top of Samylle islet (all the Llosydane's pillars had charming Belthyc names, Eddyn and Lynnedy and Jamascine and so on). She asked a passerby where the islanders got their freshwater. The passerby didn't know.

She went about her work.

By sundown she owned a restaurant and a flophouse, the Fiat Bank branch by the docks was on fire, and two pirate captains were dueling for her hand as she sold prostitutes in lots of half a hundred.

BARU'S DATES

IT began with two spies, and it ended with them, too.

Tain Hu had given her some advice on the detection of Masquerade agents. *"Check the boots. The first thing they do with their wages is buy good boots."* Baru thought that was particularly good advice on an island that made no leather of its own.

She identified the lead by the shine of his heels, a man who crossed the windswept plaza ahead of her, stepping among the birds who squabbled over the girls who salaried their favorites with dates. And that woman in a sealskin coat was the tail. Both Sydani, with long oval faces and olive skin from the ancient Belthyc blood. They might be Morrow Ministry; just as likely they were Oriati Termites.

"All right, Hu," Baru muttered. "Let's practice our craft."

First she circled the Samylle islet a few times, to watch her lead and her tail move with her. Swing your partner, Baru thought, swing your partner round and round.

She broke north across a narrow rope bridge to Eddyn islet.

Wide-eyed and wondering, with a lightness in her chest and childhood instincts under her feet, she made the delightful perilous crossing. The bridge swayed amiably in the wind, and the wind played stone flutes and struck chimes, and the chimes rang out over the chatter of Apacaho creole, Aphalone, Iolynic different from Aurdwynn's, even Kyprananoki tongues. No one at home liked Kyprananoke, Baru remembered; a rotten evil place. Not like here, where the sacred was everywhere. Below her feet the waves turned worship engines of wood and gleaming fish-scale. Young girls oiled the mechanisms. Their stone, she noted, was mortared even underwater: what additive did that?

"Watch how I work," she murmured, "watch this, Hu, watch and see. . . ."

She imagined the Llosydane Islands as a woman.

The Twelve Families, say, were the head, and the stone of the fifteen pillars the legs. The people inside her did the work of bridge building and food distribution and shipping: the pumping heart. But she needed air, she needed food for her heart to pump. And the air must come into the port of her mouth.

The woman must inhale foreign food, and exhale dates.

So her throat—the place Baru might strike to get what she required—was the date market, where dates turned into Masquerade money, which would buy the Llosydanes' food.

Whoever controlled the date trade had a hand on the throat of the Llosydanes.

On high Eddyn, three-story allhouses of mortar and recovered rubble glistened in a damp wind. She let the spies watch while she bought a kelp smallbeer, a coffee, and a shot of very expensive and wonderfully briny whiskey. Then she went (staggering not at all) into the Fiat Bank branch, with its Sydani staff and Sydani bankers and desperately Falcresti hive windows.

"Everything," she told the clerk, as she supplied the number and password for the Throne's stash account here. "In fiat notes, of course. But I want them in single-bearer bonds, not paper. I'll hire some bravos for security, if you've got them?"

They did: two fine young women with Oriati rapiers and matching hats. She explained to them what a single-bearer bond was, just in case they thought they could kill her and take them.

"We know," they said. "We guard the date merchants who come in from Aurdwynn. Our discretion is quite assured." And the bolder one winked.

She took them outside.

"Those two," she said, pointing quite openly to the spies, "are tailing me. I don't want them hurt, understand? Not unless they come in at me. Good."

FIRST, a quick stop at the post. She bought a clipper-rate seal, rolled up her letter to Purity Cartone, and left it for the next mail ship to Treatymont. Her letter to Aminata went in for routing through the navy.

So that was that. Despite her fear for Apparitor's personal anguish, she had promised him to the Necessary King. She was too busy to feel anything of it.

"We're going to the harbormaster," she told Hu. "It's the Cancrioth money we want, isn't it? So first we find if anyone supplied those Oriati warships. Then we find out who."

A paper ticket got her an appointment, and a competitively priced bribe put her on the priority list. Her bravos played grids over a rudder table and whispered about her.

"Miss Payo Mu?" The harbormaster, a compactly fat Belthyc woman of very handsome build and alert features, ushered her inside.

"Nice desk," Baru said, meaning it. She'd hammered planks across half a wooden wheel, creating a sort of formidable half-moon balcony. She looked as if she sat at the helm of a great ship.

"Thank you. I do well at it. I understand you paid an urgency fee?"

"Yes, your Excellence." Baru curtsied extravagantly. "I'm with the Ordain-ments, Imperial Republic shipping insurance and futures. I've been asked to reassess the risks of trade near Kyprananoke. As your islands are not so far north of the kypra, here I am."

The harbormaster looked up sharply. "And you came to *me*? Not the Sydanemoot? Do you understand that any peril to the date trade means people starve?"

"I work from the bottom up, your Excellence. It's the republican way. I only want to see your shipping records."

"Why?"

"I'm looking for unusual transactions," Baru said, "transfers of water, salted goods, medicines, anything which might supply a large group of warships."

"Pirates. I see." The harbormaster nodded very firmly. "We'd be happy to open our books to an authorized factor. I'll just send a girl to check your pa-pers against our records? Not to imply that you're a fake, but an unscrupulous party might try to cause a panic. . . ."

"Yes. About that." Baru winced theatrically. "If word of my presence got out . . ."

The quartermaster's hand twitched. "Yes?"

"Don't you think it might cause a run on the local currency?"

She made a face like Baru had gutted a rat on her desk. She very much thought it might cause a run on the local currency. And she knew that would doom her.

The exchange rate between the Sydani ring shell and the Falcresti fiat note was nearly eighty to one: you paid eighty ring shells for one fiat note. Fiat notes were scarce here, because as soon as they came into the islands, they went out again to buy food. Just like any other good, their value depended on their rarity.

If Baru actually *were* an insurance agent, she might decide the Llosydanes were dangerous. She might advise trade ships to stay away. Suddenly Masquer-ade fiat notes would be much more scarce here . . . and therefore more valuable. Four times as valuable, say. And suddenly you would need four times as much Sydani money to get a bushel of grain.

If you were a harbormaster who (say) bought Masquerade goods and sold them locally, you'd lose everything. You'd need to quadruple your sales price, and then no one would buy.

"Mam," the harbormaster said, "I don't think we'll need to send a girl to check your papers after all."

"Excellent." Baru smiled innocently. "Should I give you privacy, so you can inform the necessaries?"

"Necessaries, mam?"

"The Oriati spies who've asked you to alert them if anyone comes probing in your books."

"Oh, Wydd help me." She flattened her palms firmly on the desk. "If I have *diplomatic* contacts, they're entirely aboveboard and legitimate."

But she gave Baru her books to inspect.

The book made a big dog's bark when dropped on the wood. Two plates of bronze guarded pages of chiseled driftwood. Baru scanned the numbers, letting her savancy sift the money like a new vintage on her mind's palate. She could taste honeyed relief when a trader arrived with rare textiles for a hungry market; brackish salt when rival ships unloaded preserved meats and the market raced to the bottom; an airy sense of peregrine speed as the end of trade season drove prices to extremes . . .

. . . and a bitter false note.

Baru frowned and flipped backward a few weeks, to the spring of AR 130, this very year, in the closing weeks of the Coyote rebellion. Her fingers probed the shipping figures for freshwater casks.

They were completely unremarkable.

They were fake.

"Just so you know." She pushed the book over to the quartermaster. "You botched up the counterfeit records."

The harbormaster groaned. "On what grounds do you—"

"The first digits of your water sales that month were randomly distributed. See? About as many numbers start with five, or nine, as one or two." Baru prodded the page. "Real accounts always have more ones and twos on the first digit. It's called the Littler Law. Remember it next time you need to forge a page."

Someone here had sold a lot of water to a lot of ships. And it had been kept off the books.

The harbormaster looked as if she might withdraw her head into her neck and vanish under a shell. "It's not what you think."

"Oh? What do I think?"

"That I'm a traitor. But the man who told me to do this was Falcresti. He told me that I had to cover up the sales. He said the Llosydanes could be destroyed if I didn't."

Baru spun that around in her head, considering the angles, and decided on the most likely scenario. A Morrow Ministry agent had buried the evidence of the Oriati attack fleet to try to avert war? Sensible enough. Yawa might be speaking to him right now.

"Is there anything I can do to make this go away?" the harbormaster asked.

"Sure." Baru leaned up grinning on her desk. "Some people are going to come ask you some questions. Tell them the truth. Tell them there might be no date season this year, on account of fear of pirates."

The harbormaster raised her chin. "I won't drive the Families to a panic."

"Yes you will. One day of panic for me to profit from . . . and I promise I won't ever report this to Falcrest. Let them think the season's ruined, and I'll see that it isn't." She dropped a ten thousand note bond on the desk. "I'll sign that over to you tonight. If you're good."

She waved at the two spies in the plaza outside, went down to her bravos at the base of the steps—and found them both, two very fit and self-possessed women, nonetheless terribly besotted, laughing and making big eyes at one Miss Iscend Comprine, who was demonstrating gymnastics while chatting in fluent Iolynic.

"Yawa," Baru hissed, and turned, and—

THERE you are."

Xate Yawa's voice sprang out of her blindness, close enough to brush noses. "Fuck," Baru snapped. "Don't *do* that!"

"Hello. I thought you might need a chaperone," Yawa said. She had *absolutely* crept up to nose-distance of Baru just to frighten her. "The bank told me you'd gone to the post, the post to the harbormaster. I just had to ask for 'the woman with the angry Maia face and the money.'"

She'd worn a canvas jacket and silk trousers, and her bright green scarf was so ghoulishly out of place that it looked like plunder off another woman's corpse. "No!" Baru shouted. "I don't need a chaperone!"

"Good, then, we'll go together. Would you like to know how this island gets freshwater?"

"No . . ." But Baru really did.

"It's all a matter of age," Yawa said, taking her arm. "The years have chiseled the islands to a certain hardness."

Baru groaned. "Oh, tell me more about the hardness of age."

"Simple! The base of these pillars"—she pointed down, a thrilling reminder of their altitude—"must be the hardest and most impermeable stone, to resist the sea so long. That creates a cup against which freshwater aquifers can pool." Yawa conjured a cup of her own from her pocket, a little cork travel thimble. "The old and hard supports the new and bountiful, hm? Together they survive."

"You should be careful here. They might know who you are."

"Of course they'll know!" Yawa adjusted the bun of her hair. "Your dear grandmother, who resembles Xate Yawa by coincidence."

"I have some work in motion here I need to look after—"

"Baru," Yawa murmured, in a raw cold voice like city slush, "we should talk. You drink all day and lie awake in your hammock all night. You're sick. You're dying, in fact, and you don't know it, because by the time you're dead it will feel quite normal to be lifeless. And you talk to Apparitor like he's your friend, when he's poisoning you day by day.

"I tried to keep you out of all this. I failed. You are in it now. I won't see you waste what my niece gave you. Will you listen, please?"

BARU did not want to listen. "Did you find the Morrow Ministry station?"

"Never mind that."

"Did you steal my ledger?"

"Your ledger?"

"Never mind. There are two spies following me—"

"Oriati, I expect," Yawa judged. "The Termites must have a post here. Keep an eye out for a tunk case officer." She dropped the obscenity without apology or hesitation. The streets had brought out the commoner from behind the judge. "Through here, now, we'll take the bridge back over to Samylle."

They crossed the dizzying height across sand-roughened hardwood. Yawa clung to Baru and refused to look down. Around them passed crowds of women. The way they held hands made Baru reflexively nervous. It was a culture of public adoration and touch, not a sign of romance, but fear was fear.

In Samylle plaza an old fat man in handsomely drab costume played the role of Wydd, sitting patiently as children tickled and tugged on him. Merchants sold little scrimshawed idols of Wydd and Devena and Himu: Devena, a tall spare woman with flat breasts and her hands opened equitably; Himu, a delightful dancing grotesquerie with motherly hips and a jutting erection.

"Vile," Yawa muttered, surprising Baru, her anger not Incrastic at all, "vile to sell likenesses of the virtues."

"Why?"

"The virtues must come into you and live in you and express themselves through your works. Idols teach you to keep them outside. Idols mislead."

"Unuxekome told me you were a believer," Baru ventured, "but I didn't know whether . . ."

"Whether I'd lied to him?"

"Yes."

"Oh, child!" Yawa laughed sadly. "Do you think Falcrest would choose an unbeliever as their persecutor? When you want to slaughter the cattle, you spare one of them, and then you send her to the next herd to lead them. You don't waste time putting a man in a cow suit. Come, come down here, see what a believer I am. I had to visit it."

She led Baru down the road called Llallyrd (she said *yee-a-yeerd*) to a square at the edge of the islet.

Baru gasped in wonder.

A tremendous cylindrical device of tapering bronze stood upright, like a pillar, beneath a sailcloth awning. The central shaft had been fixed in place by six stone columns and an ingenious apparatus of rope and precious bronze. Yet it could not be a functioning telescope, for even if, by some miracle, mirrors of that size had been made, it was aimed straight down.

"What kind of telescope is it?" she asked Yawa.

"A spiritual one."

"A *spiritual* telescope?"

"Of course. It peers into the world."

"I don't believe you."

"Come, come along, you balk like a baby goat."

Yawa led the way down the ampitheater steps into the telescope's pit. Directly beneath the apparatus was a pool of clear water—but no, no, that couldn't be water, it didn't seem to catch the light quite right.

Baru peered over the edge.

The well plunged into shimmering confusion. Far down below shone a blue-green light, like tide fire. But it came up to Baru through illuminated layers of color character, golden, greasy, soap-shine iridescent. "What is this?"

"An oil pit. The lens of the World Telescope." Yawa tucked her feet beneath her on the bottom step. "Five years ago, in Duchy Lyxaxu, a dry pit was found in an ancient valley. I ordered it filled with concrete. Not the worst thing I ever did. But close."

It smelled faintly but bitingly of alcohol. Open-mouthed she breathed the well air, until hints of deeper flavor gave her a theory. "Ah! The well's full of different layers of chemistry. Alcohol water is the lightest, so it comes to the top. Next should be, ah, I can't remember my densities. . . ."

"Lamp oil, I should think."

"Yes! A vegetable extract next—"

"And freshwater at the bedrock base. The light from the bottom of the world comes *up* through the layers of oil, see, and becomes distorted by each layer—"

"But why would anyone want the light distorted?" Baru protested.

"Because this telescope observes messages from the heart of creation! One dares not see such things too clearly."

"*I'd* dare," Baru grumbled.

"Because you're already quite insane."

Baru stared at her wavering reflection. The tiny motions of the earth and air must stir this pool of layered oils. The very subtlest derangements of the universe, captured in the tremble of the surface. . . .

"I'm not insane," she said, softly.

"Oh, come now," Yawa clucked. "Let's not bicker over the obvious. You have blunt-trauma dextral hemineglect with an alien limb and possible complicating fugue flight. If I were reviewing your marriage license I'd never let you bear children. Imagine them all born half-minded. Or half-bodied, goodness."

She let that rest a moment. "And if I'd been asked to develop a case for your institutionalization in the Metademe, I would have no trouble writing a very convincing report."

Nothing Baru could imagine would be worse than the Metademe. Conditioning and endless reconditioning, mush and children's block puzzles, and the memory of brilliance pierced by a steel lobotomy pick.

"Hesychast asked you to do that?" she said. "Develop a case for my insanity?"

"Mm. In case you needed to be removed. He thinks you are too deeply in Farrier's control to be managed."

"Can I persuade you to stop?"

"He has Olake. I can't refuse him."

Once Baru had asked Olake, *what will Yawa do when Treatymont falls to us? The mobs will tear your sister apart. . . .*

And he'd said, with gleaming earnest eyes, *I'll save her, of course. She's saved me often enough. Devena knows these things come back around.*

"Thank you for the warning," she said. "Is that what you wanted to tell me?"

"Baru, I want to help you. I don't want us to be at odds forever."

"The way you helped me with Cattlson's duel?"

"Baru," Yawa said, and then, chuckling, "what would you have done in my place? Let a foreign girl take the reins of the scheme you'd grown so carefully? And Treatymont doesn't show us honestly. We were always watched. You never knew me as I truly am."

"I didn't change much when I left," Baru said.

"What a remarkably self-deprecating statement."

"Oh, shut up."

"You need my advice, Baru. You haven't been cautious enough with Apparitor. He's playing a very subtle game with you."

"Oh? I should come running to hide under your skirts?"

Yawa's eyes flashed: lids peeled back, teeth glinting, bone-white rings around irises of lightning blue. "You think you've nothing to learn from me?"

Baru knew at once that she'd trespassed on Yawa's pride. Stupid to assume the old woman had infinite patience. Stupid, Baru, stupid. But her throat ached, and her head felt thick, and she wanted to hurt Yawa for what she'd done to Muire Lo.

"How about this," Yawa said, unctuously sweet. "You go on trying to do everything yourself. When you have your first seizure, *then* you come to me."

"Why would I have a seizure?"

"Experience tells me they often strike in cases like yours."

Baru sighed. "That's not what you mean."

"Don't tell me what I mean, child—"

"You're telling me that once I have a seizure, you'll have an excuse to poke me with a lobotome. You want to be sure I come report it to you, don't you? You want to be sure you get the confession. Then you can put my mind out."

"Hmm," Yawa said, thoughtfully. "You *want* me as your enemy, don't you? That's too bad. Much too bad. I thought, maybe, we could cooperate to help Aurdwynn. But Hesychast's right, Farrier has cut the possibility of friendship out of you. You don't want to help anyone but yourself, do you?"

"Tain Hu never trusted you," Baru said. And in the silence afterward she got up and went, quickly, quietly, not looking back.

SHE had the spoor of the pirates' passage in the erasure of the water sales. Now she had to learn who had sold that water.

She followed her bravos' directions to the date market.

This early in the season the market was nearly empty. Date trees were a poor fit for island growth, even the hardy, stubby, peculiarly tangy Sydani dates—like the people, they clung to this place with a stubbornness Baru admired. The families would be thinning the dates now, pulling some so others could grow to full size. Infanticide.

It wouldn't be until late summer, the seventy-fifth or the eightieth, that the harvest would come in. Just as Parliament in Falcrest planted a harvest of its own: the vote on war or peace.

"Futures." Baru spun her half-sight round the plaza. "Who sells the date futures?"

With a little ruckus and shouting Baru caused the appearance of a junior niece from the Jamascine family, a gaunt Belthyc woman who was minding the trade office in case of unannounced visitors. "Hello," Baru said, sitting on the woman's desk. "I'd like to buy some date futures."

She pinched her nose and blinked, trying to get adjusted to the daylight. "I'm afraid we have an exclusive relationship with the Radascine Combine."

Baru fanned her bonds across the breast of her jacket. "*Totally* exclusive?"

"Well." A single one of Baru's bonds could make this woman the pilotfish of her family. "If you're interested in an exploratory arrangement . . ."

"I am indeed." Baru extracted her cream-paper pad and licked her pen. "I would like to buy your dates on the eightieth of Summer at six notes a pound. As many as I can get."

When she was done laughing, the Jamascine woman said, "Your Excellence, we've already hedged our crop at twelve notes a pound. That means we will not sell for less than twelve to anyone else. Do you understand how a futures contract works?"

Baru did indeed—she'd taught them to Tain Hu. A futures contract was a way to remove uncertainty. The date farmers wanted to be sure they got enough money to profit off the season, even if the price of dates plunged. The date-buying merchants wanted to be sure they wouldn't need to mortgage their children to afford dates if the price of dates spiked.

So they got together and said, listen, I'll give up my chance at selling these dates for a really high price, if you'll give up your chance at buying them for a really low price. Let's agree on a price in the middle, so we can plan our finances with confidence. Okay?

"Yes," Baru snapped, "I know how a fucking futures contract works. I'm here to buy your dates at six notes a pound. Haven't you heard the news? All your contracts are shit now. In a month you'll be *begging* to get six notes a pound."

The woman was about to sneeze. She stopped. "What news?"

"You haven't heard?" Baru gasped. "A Masquerade inspector was in the harbor today. She found faked records. Apparently someone's been watering pirates for a very busy summer. That's grounds to close trade. I think you're looking at a run on your money, a visit from a navy flotilla, and, friend, a very bad date season."

SHE asked her bravos where she could watch powerful people, so she'd know when the panic began.

"At the execution, I expect." Both seemed very excited about this. "They're killing a thief, I think, a thief of metal." With sudden apology: "I know it might seem harsh to you, but it's our way." A phrase that made Baru feel reflexive contempt and skepticism, for what good was an unexamined way? Only much later would she come back to this moment and break the wall before her to find the truth.

"I understand," Baru said. "I've seen people executed before."

"Selfish people?"

Baru swallowed the hurt. "People who knew they couldn't put themselves before their home."

As they went toward the killing square the crowd thickened. One of Baru's bravos bumped into a man, black-haired, strong, shielding a clay pot with his broad back. He saved the pot, and she began to apologize, profusely, and with an excess of touch. She was *so* sorry. Did he need help getting home? He shouldn't be out here, passions were up and the streets weren't safe right now. She had friends with her. Why didn't he come with them?

The man had the height and build to throw her like a little idol but he held himself so as to be small. He did not need help, he was saying, he only wanted to be left alone.

Alone? Why? She touched his chest. Others might be so cruel to him. Didn't he know she wasn't like that? Didn't he want to be appreciated by the gallant?

He said, "I have to bring this water home."

Did he know, she asked, that he was very handsome? She hoped he was proud of that. He did not look proud. Was he stuck-up, then? Was he an onanist?

Baru, uncomfortable with the direction of all this, shouted, "Let him be! Come along, I'm not paying you to flirt!" Though it wasn't flirting.

"What a cutter," her bravo muttered, to the other. "Did you see his fish? He could hardly think for wanting it."

It occurred to Baru that she had never, in all her life, been powerless in a city street.

The execution was a public spectacle, of course. The state had to keep up its credit rating, too—see how we punish the transgressor? See that you can trust us to punish the thief, and therefore, please, do not start murdering thieves yourself.

Baru admitted a certain admiration for the morality play of the method. The guilty woman pushed a wheel, the wheel pulled a rope, the rope looped through pulleys to lift a coffin-sized stone. A couple of bored constables waited for the thief to hoist the rock high enough that they could drop it and crush her under her own labors. Men watched from the rooftops, their children slung on strong backs and curled up in their arms.

Life, Baru thought, was cheap here. Not cheaper than in Aurdwynn, really, but cheaper than it ought to be. When your civilization was sustained by the regular and necessary murder of infants, when you watched your friends devoured by storm or cast from cliffsides, how couldn't it be cheap? Make enough death, and like any other currency it loses its value.

Wasn't this barbarism? Wasn't this the disease Incrasticism sought to cure? Hadn't Farrier asked, "What does the Mbo have to offer us? What medicines? What sciences? What is *worthwhile* about their society?"

Baru wanted to be able to answer that question, not just for the Mbo but for the Llosydanes. But for some mad reason the answer would not come: as if she had lost the measuring tools she needed.

The quieter bravo cackled suddenly and nudged Baru. "Friend of yours?"

In the narrow way between two houses Baru saw a young Falcresti woman, vitiligo-spotted and thus probably from eastern Grendlake, wearing a student's waistjacket and a smirk of satisfied hunger. She had her trousers round her knees and a man's head between her narrowly parted legs. The roar of the execution crowd climbed again and she groaned with that roar. Her eyes slitted in pleasure. One of her fists was in his hair, and the other full of coins, which she let slip, one by one, to slide down his scalp and roll along his naked back into the muck.

The boy wore the same costume as the old man who'd played ykari Wydd, but cut down to scanty straps. Here was Falcrest, fucking Wydd's face. Indulging itself in the primal vitality of a cultural preserve.

Baru wanted to spit at the woman.

Then she thought, am I not here, ruining their money, rooting through their books? Wouldn't I hire a prostitute, if I had the courage?

One of the parties of Family observers suddenly exited the square. A moment later a second Family's party began to beat their way out of the crowd. Baru perked up. Was the panic beginning?

The fire bells began to jangle.

THE panic was swift and thorough.

Baru knew the young Jamascine woman must have returned to her family with Baru's promise of a bad season. The Jamascines scrambled to purchase all the Masquerade fiat notes they could get, to secure their food supply: there would be no more coming in if the date season failed. And those buys did not go unnoticed by the rest of the Twelve Families.

Baru went back to the Fiat Bank branch to see how high the exchange rate had climbed.

There was no exchange rate to be found. Nor any Fiat Bank at all. An Eddyn fire crew, women caked to their ears in soot, pumped seawater up the cliffside to soak the wreckage.

"What happened?" Baru asked a constable.

"Lynnedy," she spat. "Their fucking Allmother panicked and sent muscle to open the Fiat Bank vaults. It went all wrong."

"Oh," Baru said, innocently.

She would need a bank of her own to make her sales. So she selected a long-house restaurant called Demimonde (on the theory that it must be *very* fine, to justify its footprint on the tiny island), walked in the front door, found the owner whispering with her family about the failed trade season, and bought the whole place, from rafter to foundation, for a pittance in fiat notes. A kicker fee got her the hotel for foreign merchants next door, in case she needed a place to rest.

"Will you post a sign?" she asked the ex-owner, whom she had installed as executive manager. "The Payo Mu Bank. No Fiat Notes on Premises: Encrypted Bonds Only: Do Not Pillage. Please Queue. And then lay out refreshments for a great many wealthy visitors. Don't spare the good vintages."

She sent her bravos to inform the Sydanemoot families that she would entertain offers of their ring shells for her fiat note. She was like a spring erupting in the desert: an unforeseen well of fiat notes, which could become food. And all she asked was the local money they had so much of to spend.

They came in small parties at first, dire old women with their dark-eyed bodyguards and their local fortunes to turn into fiat notes. It was desperation, yes, but speculation, too. The fiat note had become so impossibly valuable, was still *growing* more valuable as the Families raced to capture the supply, that you could make a fortune simply by buying fiat notes, waiting an hour, and changing them back to ring shell.

As they came to her to buy her bonds, she took them behind a little silk screen and, as price of doing business, asked them who had sold the water to the pirates.

Everyone, they told her. Every family had sold water futures to an Oriati merchant named Abdumasi Abd. He had spread his buys around in case of a well failure. No one had ever seen his fleet come and take the water, but quite a few water-laden ships had been "taken by pirates," and if that was not code for a rendezvous then Baru would call Taranoke Sousward.

Again and again that name sounded in her ears. Abdumasi Abd.

As the families bartered with her and with each other the Demimonde became a spontaneous open currency market, a crackling point of discharge like a ship's lightning spike. The kitchens brought in the bored staff of nearby restaurants to meet the hunger of so many rich women. By second dogwatch the Families were making, and losing, entire fortunes: they were drinking, smoking, singing, going mad. The crew of an Oriati "privateer" stumbled in drunkenly round the beginning of candle watch, and threw up a cheer for the richest woman on the Llosydanes. "Payo Mu!" they called. "May she never wake alone!"

The ordinary people looked on in bemusement. The street value of the ring shell was unaffected, for no one had had time to adjust their prices. This was a madness of the rich.

Someone hired the prostitutes who served sailors as second spouses to come and amuse. When those ran out, someone else hired the low-end seasonal whores who worked off debt indenture during trade season. These were, to Baru's pleased surprise, as much women as men, or at least as much female as male. Some were even trawling for Falcresti trade—women in severe buttoned-down formalwear and waistcoats, subtly made up to look stern and severe, their hot eyes prepared to deprecate and dismiss those who would buy their attention. The game worked on Baru, too, who had suffered her fair share of adolescent torment in Miss Pristina Struct's class.

She made a tipsy advance toward one of the women, in the only language she really knew. "Could I buy out your indentures? You're in debt, right, your madams hold the debt? Could I buy those out and—I don't know, what could I do with them?"

"Oh, certainly!" she said, in charmingly thick Aphalone. "We talk about it always. We'd bundle our debts together, and sell them to a proper bank." Meaning they would promise to pay off their debts to the bank, rather than to their creditors (who would get a fee from the bank). "We'd pool our incomes to pay them all off together, you see? If one woman came up short another could take up her slack. And since the bank would trust a lot of us to pay our debts more than one or two alone, we could get some credit, use it to hire doctors, a barrister, some nicer rooms . . ."

"Good idea," Baru said, and she sent for the madams.

By midnight Baru was dealing bundles of prostitutes' indentures to local banks in batches of fifty. Two of the Oriati had beaten each other silly with baking pins for the right to woo her. She had written so many sell orders and contracts that she could not remember them: she was nursing a nervous suspicion that she had not even been *aware* of some of the things her right hand recorded.

A woman in a sealskin jacket approached her table.

Baru looked up from the sprawl she'd been reduced to (the prostitutes gave wonderful back massages). "Oh," she said. "You're finally here."

The spy said, expressionlessly, "I have been asked to beg you to stop. I have been asked to tell you that you have no idea what you risk provoking."

"Tell your case officer," Baru said, enunciating in clear Aphalone, "that I want to meet with them. Understand? I want to talk to your Oriati case officer on neutral ground. Find a way."

The spy departed. Baru looked at the party she had invented. The Family elders were dancing with the privateers, and the privateers with the prostitutes; the ruined were weeping and the fortunate glowed with euphoria. An old woman comforted her sister. Two laughing daughters (each of a different family) reclined with linked arms and watched the dance. The severely dressed prostitute who'd suggested the indentures trade looked at Baru over the shoulder of her dance partner, bright-eyed and curious, and Baru was suddenly terrified and sick with grief.

She slipped out the back of the restaurant. The moon was high and bright; the air had grown wet and charged, and the southern horizon boiled with ramparts of stormcloud.

North a ways, plain as the teeth of a striking shark, the red sails of the Imperial Navy's frigate *Sulane* swayed on high waves.

S HE dreamt that night of Itinerant's utopia.

She was in the school at Iriad, and the halls were not of ash-concrete or coral but deep warm brown panels of koa, Taranoke's warrior wood. Koa had a black grain that swirled like ink in water and made strange symmetrical shapes like narrow moth wings. Here some artist had used brushed ink to emphasize parts of the grain, teasing out Aphalone characters, as if the Taranoki trees had grown Falcrest's language. In this school the mingling of cultures was encouraged, as fuel is encouraged to go into a fire. The passage was crowded with bookshelves. Farrier's school served a banquet of texts for its gifted students, and everywhere Baru went she was tempted by the titles. This was a school that let you choose your own studies as you pleased . . . for what it taught was the correct way to choose.

She was going to an assignation. She could feel it in her heart and in her thighs. But when it came it was over almost before she recognized it: by impulse (that was how the decision would plead, like a guilty trafficker, before the judges of memory—*It was only an impulse!*) she took a roundabout way to her class, so that she would pass second cousin Lao coming back from her graces, the special lessons where Lao learned how to avert her eyes and attention from those she wanted to smite with her beauty and her charm. Indirection, the teachers taught her, indirection and passivity; you create the opportunity for them to choose to admire you, and they will never know they are in your power.

Lao came this way to think without eyes on her. In this dream she had been taught early and well to mind her eyes. There had been no accusation of incipient tribadism, and no prescription of "manual stimulus"—even in the dream Baru knew it was rape—to rejoin Lao's pleasure with the image and scent of a man. (A useless task, as well as abhorrent, for Lao was never only a tribadist). But she did not seem surprised to find Baru in her side corridor.

Baru looked at the floor. There came that moment, that wordless tension, when it was right to raise her eyes and say hello—

But Lao was not looking at her. She turned a little as she passed, to peer up at the shelves, where a beam of sunlight through clear hive glass illuminated a *Manual of Expedition*. She reached up to brush the spine with her fingers, walking for a moment on her bare toes, so the sheer full-body modesty veil drew up over her calves. For a moment she was in the sunlight, poised beneath the translucent veil. And Baru knew she was using her grace in invitation.

Baru wrenched her eyes away. The thrill felt better than a long meal with her family, a day's joy in an instant, but it passed as quickly. She—she knew what she was and wanted what she wanted. But there were bigger things to consider, her career and her contributions to the sciences, her chances of teaching bright young girls. She would use her discipline to focus on those goals. And anyway, what could she do with Lao? Whatever they began would only end in hurt and hardship for both of them. If she cared for Lao, she would protect Lao by avoiding her.

So resolved, Baru went on to class.

But when she looked back down that corridor of koa and books, she saw Lao's chin in Tain Hu's hands, those dark gold eyes daring Lao, *daring* her, to look away, to pretend she didn't want: and Lao laughed and laughed and yelped as Hu lifted her against the bookshelf and kissed her and the books came tumbling down like dead birds over Lao's slim shoulders and long arms, over Hu's bare muscle and lazy self-satisfied smile as she bent to kiss again.

A STORY ABOUT ASH 2

FEDERATION YEAR 910:
25 YEARS EARLIER

JEALOUSY grew out of the wound Tau had opened, the wound between themself and their friends. Jealousy skimmed over Lake Jaro like green scum.

On the north shore, in the city, they looked south and muttered resentment at the rich estates under cypress shade. Sometimes people wished, spitefully, that the rich would drink Jaro's shit out of the lake and get sick.

Tau-indi *did* get sick.

They'd made an awful mistake when they let the mourning ash turn to mud. For this insincerity their trim fell open like a badly tied khanga. And the principles of the lake, listening to the wishes of the people, gave Tau the snail sickness.

It began with an itch. "It's just a swimmer's rash," Abdumasi said, inspecting Tau's naked belly. But the itch made Tau irritable, which made them impatient with Abdumasi, which made Tau-indi find excuses to go to Kindalana's compound. And her father, Padrigan, recognized the rash on their belly.

Do you see the operation of trim? Trim drew Tau to Kindalana out of loneliness, and thus led Tau to Kindalana's father, who perhaps saved Tau's life.

If Tau had died everything afterward would be different. Trim makes small things like friendship important to large things like war.

"Go to your sweatroom," Padrigan snapped. Tau knew he was afraid, for what if Tau-indi died while Tahr was away? She would never forgive Padrigan. "Go tell your housekeep that you have snails growing in you. I'll get the antimony cup."

Every day Padrigan sat in the sweatroom in a breechcloth, poured a little white wine into an antimony cup, and waited for the antimony to turn the wine into poison. This took a full night.

On the first day he did this, he said, "There are tiny eggs growing inside you. We need to kill them."

"Will a worm come out of my foot?" Tau-indi was terrified of the worm parasites.

"No, no, not unless you drank water from down in Mzilimake or Devi-naga, and where would you get that kind of water?" Padrigan scooped up Tau-indi and helped them drink the poison wine. "Your father might send you Mzilimake water, hm? Your father the explorer?"

"My father never sends anything," Tau-indi muttered, and noticed, even in their sickness, that Padrigan was secretly glad of this. Padrigan didn't want Tahr's husband to ever come home.

The wine was sweet and sharp. Tau-indi drank it in slow sips until the antimony made them throw up, gushing spring water and sweet potato, gagging, miserable. Padrigan held their hair back until they were done. "We'll do this every morning. Rinse your mouth."

The fever got worse. Much worse. Abdumasi showed up to talk about his kittens and his money work, but as he spoke, his hands balled and twisted. Guilt! He was *guilty*!

"Tell me what you're doing." Tau-indi had to rasp through an acid-ravaged throat. "Tell me what you're up to."

"I flew a kite. Hey, I won a bet! My oldest kitten killed two pigeons in one leap."

"No. Tell me the truth"

Abdumasi wouldn't answer, he wouldn't say what Tau already knew: yes, Tau-indi, it's true, it's true, she and I are going on without you. You will never be a part of us. You were born alone and alone you will always remain.

Kindalana came too, as if drawn by the curl of trim between her and Abdumasi. She read from a beginner's text in Uburu.

"You want me to *learn*?" Tau-indi moaned.

"Of course. I've finally got you in a place to listen." She refused to look up. The wedge of skin between her brows held worried furrows.

"Please take care of Abdumasi," Tau-indi said, in spite. "I'll be fine."

"Oh. Abdu." Kindalana turned the page. "He's going to Jaro to learn barter. I don't see much of him."

I'm sure you don't, Tau-indi thought.

After a long wet time balled up inside sweaty blankets with their nose full of the stink of vomit, Tau-indi looked up to see Padrigan's eyes all red and wet. Why was Padrigan here? It wasn't time for antimony wine. And why oh why was there white ash on his brow? Why was Padrigan grieving? Had something happened to Kindalana?

The man said: "Are you lucid, manata?"

Manata. Beloved friend. "I'm here, Abdumasi," Tau-indi said, for the word had blurred Padrigan and Abdumasi together.

Padrigan looked down at them, and little flakes of grief ash fell off his brow to dust the wet sheets. "You're here?" His breath stank of wine. His hands were stained by earth. "You're here with me?"

"I'm here, manata."

"I'm in love with your mother," Padrigan said, "and she's gone."

"She's gone?" Tau said, in confusion. "Where has she gone?"

"The Falcresti took her captive. They tricked our armada into harbor at Kyprananoke, and somehow they bought the Kyprananoki into burning our ships. We're at war with Falcrest."

"You're in love with my mother?" Tau-indi felt a great upswelling of gratitude and relief. Abdumasi was in love with their mother. A very odd love, and certain to go unanswered, for ten years was the undisputed limit of an age gap. "But what about Kindalana?"

"Kindalana's safe with me." Padrigan's eyes brimmed with tears. He hugged Tau-indi close. "Of course she's safe. I'll keep her safe for you."

"I killed my father's other child," Tau-indi whispered. "He knows. That's why he doesn't come back. He knows I killed my twin in the womb."

"Hush, hush."

"I killed his child so I could be born alone."

"Shh," Padrigan said. "Not today. No talk of killing today. It's a calendar taboo."

"Let's fly kites," Tau-indi said. "It's hot in here. It's hot and bright."

WHEN Tau's fever broke, of course, they felt like a damn fool. Falcrest had taken Tahr and now their house needed them in her place. Service was the best balm for grief. So they dressed themself in silk, jeweled their nose and lips, painted their face in royal gold and stars of green, and summoned the Bosoka household together in the yard.

"We grieve for our mother," they said, feeling at once ridiculous and deeply proud. "But we trust in the principles of our family. Tahr kept the finest trim. Let us call her back to us by remembering her place in the community. Housekeepers, what can you do to remember her?"

They could bring wash water for her in the morning and empty her basins in the evening. They could repair her combs. They could take food from the table for her to eat.

"Groundskeepers, what can you do to remember my mother?"

They could prepare garlands from the Devi-naga exotics she loved to raise.

They could smooth the garden path and the beach path behind her ghostly footsteps. They could (one of them weeping now) fly her kite over the lake.

"Clerks, what can you do to remember Tahr Bosoka?"

They could write to her correspondents in Jaro and beyond. They could sell the house skiff and give the money to the ferry project, as she'd wanted. They could continue the education of her laman, Tau-indi.

"Let it thus be done. Let her be remembered back to us."

Tau-indi smiled at them and went back into the sweatroom to drink antimony wine and vomit.

After that the house was livelier, and Tau-indi felt taller. They had taken their first steps as a true Prince.

SUMMER passed, and then storm season, and then spring and summer again. Tau turned fourteen. The Armada War raged across the Ashen Sea. What happened in the war that year was important, of course—but this is a story about Tau-indi, who *ended* the war.

And what mattered to young Tau-indi was their mother's release.

She came up the slope from Lake Jaro at a run, and Tau tried to hold their place in the welcoming crowd, but in the end it was too much: they broke from the line and ran down to embrace their mother.

Tahr kissed their brow. "Oh, lama."

"Mom," Tau said, with shaky bravery, "I kept the house."

"You did. You did marvelously."

"You're all right?"

Tahr showed them respect, and not pity, when she answered honestly. "Hard times are coming," she told Tau. "Hard times you'll inherit soon. I want you to meet two men from Falcrest, sent here with me as hostages against atrocity, both eager students of our ways. . . ."

They were in their early twenties, still youth by Oriati standards (adulthood was earned by works and knowledge, not merely a calendar). But they strolled about with the loose-limbed confidence of old men. Tau would realize, later, that this arrogance had developed in the coffeehouses and testing rooms of the Faculties, and that they meant it entirely for each other.

The groundskeepers murmured that they were brave, brave men, to come here to Jaro, when they must know the full wrath of Oriati Mbo would awaken against Falcrest soon. When a lion attacked a water buffalo the lion might chew on the buffalo's rump for a very long time while the buffalo stood there twitching and snorting. But when the lion was exhausted, the buffalo would turn its horns.

The first of the hostages was beautiful and shy. Cosgrad Torrinde was a slim tall man of twentysomething, a few shades lighter than already cool-skinned Kindalana and Padrigan. His eyes folded elegantly, his nose flat and thin, his smile easy, his laugh full of wonder. He did not have the name Hesychast yet, of course. Tau-indi would only learn about that later.

The second man was generous and funny, with a booming big-chested laugh that made you at once glad to laugh with him and afraid that some day he might be laughing at *you*. Unlike clean-shaven Cosgrad, he affected a beard, and where Cosgrad dressed in formal trousers and the waistcoats of the Falcresti civil service, this man took merrily to khangas and farmers' jellabiya and formal kaftan suits and Invijayish deel with jeweled chests and Segu's saris in their infinite permutations and the rest of the Mbo's dizzyingly broad wear. He seemed eager to learn, rather than to study from afar, and he took quickly to housework and chatter. His name was Cairdine Farrier. The shared *C* consonant on *Cairdine* and *Cosgrad* caused no end of trouble: quickly the two became Farrier and Torrinde.

Prince Hill threw a tremendous party to celebrate Tahr's return. She stood in a circle of griots, dressed in full Prince-Mother finery with chains from her ears to her nostrils and banded jewelry over her breasts, a vision, a firelit icon of strength. The honeymakers brought comb and the gardeners brought sweet yams and the herbalists brought weed and people even came across the lake from Jaro to attend.

She told the griots everything, and bid them tell everyone they knew.

The two Falcresti men drew much interest. The Bosoka house taught them how to act with a child's manners, eating and socializing with the right hand and saving the left for matters unclean. When instructions were given to masturbate with only the left hand (by a whole line of people solemnly jerking themselves off in charade), the shy one, Torrinde, gagged in embarrassment, and the loud one Farrier had to explain to him that they were being teased.

Tau-indi drifted through the revels feeling strange and hollow. Something was wrong. Shouldn't Tahr's return fill them with hope? Shouldn't they weep in relief? Ought not the restoration of their family fill them with the warmth of nations?

Why did they feel so alone?

Because Kindalana and Abdumasi weren't here.

Shy Torrinde had been convinced to take off his shirt and display the principles of isometric bodily control, which Farrier insisted allowed him to twitch his tits individually. Under cover of laughter Tau scrambled up to the high rock point where Abdumasi used to fly kites with them. They wanted a little solitude, the special adolescent solitude which many teenagers use as a plea. Please notice how hurt and alone I am, please come care.

The kite rock was already crowded, though.

There were two people on it, naked silhouettes in the moonlight, having sex. Kindalana's slim back moved intently, her shoulder blades crowding and separating. She was on top.

"That's better," Tau-indi heard Abdumasi say, cheerful and unguarded, "I think that works! Yes, just like that."

"I banged my knee," Kindalana said.

"There's a rock under my shoulder." Abdumasi's lean waist swelled into narrow strong hips. He had his arms up, to show off his growing shoulders.

"We could stop."

"Why, am I too long for you?"

"I bet I can make you forget your rock."

They both laughed. The shadow of Abdumasi's legs moved under her and Kindalana made a startled noise, falling forward, one hand braced on his chest.

Tau-indi turned away out of instinctive respect. Their naked bodies were familiar but sex was new and confusing. They did not want to want either Kindalana or Abdumasi, especially because it drew out the uneasy gap of age.

Tau sat there and decided to be happy for them. How happy, how satisfied, how glad, how delighted Tau must be to have this new joy in the Prince Hill mbo.

How happy. How glad.

They prodded at the thought like a bee sting and it made them sick with jealousy—not for sexual want of one or the other of them, but for jealousy of this secret Kinda and Abdu had. Listen to them! Listen to those curious secret sounds, those answers to questions they had asked each other in the past months, with odd silences and shy hesitations. Listen to them becoming less alone.

And to have sex on this rock, on this place for kites. Hadn't Abdumasi known Tau-indi would come here? Hadn't Kindalana? Hadn't they known Tau-indi would hurt tonight? Surely they had.

Maybe Kindalana and Abdumasi had come up here to wait for Tau-indi, to comfort them. And then forgotten all about Tau, because they had found they mattered more to each other.

Tau-indi sat down hard on a stone and put their head in their hands. It was a sign, of course. It *had* to be this way. The world knew that Tau-indi had to be alone.

Out on the kite rock, Tau-indi's two best friends articulated that loneliness enthusiastically.

Tau-indi stumbled back down toward the fire.

T HE bonfire at the revels went out a week later.
     But the war fire burnt up higher.

After the debacle at Kyprananoke, Segu had seized control of war planning away from Lonjaro. As the Mbo's chief naval power (unless you asked the Devinaga) the Segu were best qualified to unfuck the grand strategy of Falcrest's containment. Eyotana Six-Souls was declared War Admiral, and she immediately broke up their armadas into separate swarms to blockade Falcrest's ports. This would allow Falcrest to win battles by concentrating its forces, but the destruction would be limited to a few places, and a blockade would show Falcrest how hugely outnumbered they really were. Why strike the Falcresti like a big angry fist, if they could be driven off by a bee sting?

Of course, the Lonjaro Princes insisted, they would keep a fist ready, just in case. An army would march up the coast, counterclockwise round the curve of the Ashen Sea, up through Invijay lands to the great Tide Column. Across the Column lay Falcrest's Butterveldt, where the army would eat everything, steal the herds, and generally force the enemy to reckon the sheer size of the Mbo's forces. Battle itself would be unnecessary, although a few sporting engagements might be arranged against Falcrest's militias: fought to the break, not the slaughter.

This was how Lonjaro preferred to fight. Smother the enemy in games of mercy and demonstrations of might. Eat their crops and buy away their friends. Leave their bones unbroken for the handshake and the peace.

Six hundred years ago the Tu Maia had ridden south into Oriati Mbo with warhorses and a will to conquer. All that majestic fury, all the hot blood of the Emperors and the Empresses who carried the legacy of Shiqu Si, had availed them nothing. They had stumbled on the hard earth and crawled into the arms of the Oriati begging for water and salt. They'd made good husbands, good wives, and that was all that remained of them now: except for the Invijay, who were, in the opinion of most, less than bandits.

What would little Falcrest, a small nation of mad kings and nebbish bureaucrats, manage against the mbo? The mbo was soft like quicksand. You couldn't cut it apart or put your foot through it. It would just flow around you.

Only Mother Tahr seemed concerned.

C HANGE grew up like kudzu vine and it took over the hill.
     Mother Tahr spent more time writing and more time in Jaro and much

less time on matters of trim and taboo. Tau took command of the house compound, lest it fall into disarray and argument.

In Lonjaro's stories, the Segu-woman, once awakened to sex, always seemed to become a notorious rake and heartbreaker. But Kindalana, apparently satisfied to scratch her adolescent itches on Abdu, instead drew into a sort of hermitage. Her house attracted a constant stream of historians, griots, bookreaders, rhetors, merchant captains, navigators, critics, adventurers, radians, guides, and even cooks of Falcrest's odd cuisine. Every night Kindalana hosted an occasion and every day the house staff ran about in exhaustion cleaning up and soothing the bees and arranging raspberries and cheeses for the night to come.

Tau-indi *really* wanted to be invited. But Kindalana did not seem to think of them.

Abdumasi decided to sell his caraval cats to the gamblers in Jaro. On the ferry across the lake the caravals mewed and protested the waves and rubbed their cheeks all over everyone's ankles. Tau-indi almost cried. Abdumasi certainly did.

"I put a deposit down with some of the griots," Abdumasi said, while they walked together through the bazaar. Bosoka sentries in gold paint parted the crowd for them. "I hired a satirist, a gossip, an epic, and a comic. They're going to come down to Prince Hill every month and tell us about the war."

"You sold your cats for *that*?"

"Do you think it's not important? To know what's happening?"

"No, of course it's important. But we could have paid the griots with Mother Tahr's stories about Falcrest."

"Well, I don't have your mother's stories, do I?" Abdumasi scowled and looked at something behind him. When he thought Tau-indi couldn't see his face he said, lightly, "You're in a mood lately."

Tau-indi, thick-tongued, pretended not to hear him. Kindalana wasn't there, and yet it felt like Kindalana was walking between them.

"Do you think it's a good mix?" Abdumasi said hopefully.

"Eh?"

"A satirist, a gossip, an epic, and a comic. Do you think they'll help us understand the war?"

"How should I know?" Tau-indi snapped. "How should I know anything about that?"

"You don't have to know." Abdumasi, much taller, didn't have to work to catch up. "I just want you to say you approve."

He was trying his best to be soothing. Soothing! Just one more thing

Abdumasi did better. Fah. Abdumasi deserved no credit for it. Anyone could be magnanimous if they had a secret advantage, if they knew that they could hurt without being hurt in turn. Why wouldn't Abdumasi admit he was sleeping with Kindalana? Because he knew that it would make Tau lonely. Because poor little Tau wasn't old enough to have lovers.

Poor little Tau.

Tau-indi stalked along, rubbing the broken bones, that's what Tahr always said, carrying on while upset was just like walking on a broken bone.

"When will the griots come?" they made themself say. "I want to listen."

"That's good. You Princes, you've got to listen to us merchants, we're the ones who are really in touch with the world!" Abdumasi grinned his big buy-my-cats grin, everyone's funny friend. Tau-indi hated him with a sick, self-loathing totality. "We have to keep you in touch, or you might not realize what's going on!"

"No," Tau-indi said, pouncing oh so sweetly, thinking of Abdumasi and Kindalana on the rock. "We might not realize what's going on at all."

T HE griots came up Prince Hill to tell them about the war. They all gathered in the garden of House Abd to eat and drink and listen.

The epic stood up and recited all the great names of the captains, the Segu navigators Kolosan ayaSegu and Eyotana Six-Souls, Cho-oh Long Oar and the Man with the Rudder Thumb, and Lonjaro's champions too, the sons and daughters of house Mbunu who had sailed so far north they could breathe smoke, Nyoba Dbellu who had salt crystals in her earlobes. Thrill at the names, O listeners, thrill at these thinkers of sharp thoughts!

Next was the gossip griot, who wandered from family to family whispering about the dalliances of both the champions and the enemy. He had a warm old smile, big as the calendar on the first day of the new year, and after he talked about Cho-oh Short Cock and who exactly might be breathing smoke into who, he reminded them all that they had nothing to fear from war. A war could be fought between champions on the clean sea. Neither the Mbo nor Falcrest need suffer.

Kindalana stood behind her father with her arms across the shoulders of two of her clerk friends and grinned in delight. Tau-indi felt a spiteful need to make her sad, to beg her pity.

Instead they sidled up to the Farrier man, who was stroking his beard and listening intently. "Your Excellence Farrier," they murmured, with an overt politeness, "does it trouble you to hear our griots discussing your defeat?"

Farrier knelt with them. He had a charmingly self-satisfied face, like a clever raccoon. "No," he said, "it doesn't bother me, or, rather, it fascinates me to see the war from your perspective. Do I kiss you on the cheek? Is that the right thing?"

"If you like!" Tau said, pleasantly surprised. The Falcresti had both been very standoffish. "Or kiss the air beside the cheek, like this—"

Farrier tried this, and accidentally made a childish *poot* with his lips. Tau laughed. Farrier wiggled his eyebrows and sat back, beaming at the firelit gathering. "I'm so happy to be here," he said.

"Why are you happy?" Tau couldn't imagine being so far from home and family.

"Because," Farrier said, "Oriati Mbo has stood for a thousand years, and no matter what my people say, I think we have things to learn from you."

Tau-indi felt a sudden warmth toward him. "I'm sure the converse is true, as well! What do you think you might learn?"

Farrier's eyes sat deep in their sockets, as thoughtful as they were guarded. But they seemed to open and allow Tau inside. "Young lama," he said, "I want to know how to make a civilization last a thousand years. And since you do not have eugenics, I know the answer cannot lie there—"

They were interrupted by the satirist, who reeled out into the center of the circle on unsteady toppling stilts. They shaded their eyes, a young laman with white ash around their mouth, and looked around.

"Behold!" they said. "Behold the people on Prince Hill, chosen to rule! We voted your families to give birth to our lords, and we are very satisfied with those young lords, oh, what else would we be? We are a satisfied people, the Oriati, a smug people, we do everything best. Don't we?"

There was a hesitant cheer. Hooray? We are the best?

The satirist rose up nobly, their chin to the sky. "It is best to raise our Princes on a high hill away from the city, away from the fields and the grasslands where our people do their labor. Far away from the sickness and the filth of the cities, where we have invented new ways to debase and ruin ourselves. Up here our Princes can concern themselves only with trim and taboos! Up here our Princes can play games of principle instead of working in the fields and the filth! Today the taboo is against going uphill too quickly! That is the most important thing!"

The crowd murmured. Abdumasi put a worried hand to his mouth. Kindalana frowned in thought. Farrier made a note in his book.

The satirist took a huge stilted step, struggling to mount an invisible slope, and almost fell on their face. "My trim!" they howled. "Oh, my trim! Oh Princes, aid me, aid me! I do not have malaria or any rent to pay! I have good water and I am free of bandits and ugly spouses with rotting teeth! But my trim is wounded, for if it were not I would grow bored, and pick fights with little cities far away! Help me avoid boredom, oh Princes!"

The crowd began to revolt. "This isn't satire!" an Abd housekeep yelled. "You're just saying horrible things!"

Kindalana had pulled her clerk-friends closer, and she was muttering to them with an expression of deep thought. Tau-indi wished they'd brought some clerk friends to hold close, too. Maybe *three* clerk friends, instead of two.

Why did they feel this way? Why had their own mood had been hooked to Kindalana and Abdumasi, like a plow dragged behind a horse, splitting the earth to wet soil and worms?

They saw Kindalana's father, Padrigan, looking at Tau's mother, Tahr, with nervous longing, admiring the green star on her throat and the snake of jewelry that curved across her bare stomach.

But Tahr was looking upward, pensively, at the sky.

She had been to Falcrest.

"I sense a certain barrier of class," Farrier said, and took another note.

IS THE OATH KEPT?

SHE woke in the captain's suite of her new flophouse, alone, angry, still tangled in a dream about money.

She had been a child. She was showing Cairdine Farrier her butterfly collection, her killing jar. She had a gorgeous monarch in the jar, and it was beating its wings of paper money against the glass as it died.

"Look, da," she said, "I've caught money."

"Don't be stupid," her mother said, giving Baru's head an affectionate scrub with her knuckles. "If you keep money in a jar, it's just a piece of paper. It's worthless without the people who value it. You cannot capture money. It lives only as it moves."

"That's right," Farrier said, giving her mother a kiss on the cheek. "Remind you of anything?"

It did. It reminded Baru of the Llosydanes. How could you treat a culture as separate from its connections? How could you draw a circle around it and say, "This, this is the culture, and so it will remain?" A culture wasn't a final product, like a cup of coffee in alabaster, or a sordid climax in an execution alley. People didn't *have* culture, they *did* culture. In fact, culture was like a mill: it accepted knowledge and people, and it changed them in certain ways, and it even redesigned itself in the process. Change was intrinsic to culture.

How could you draw a preserve around the Llosydanes and say, "They shall not be altered," if intercourse and dialogue between cultures *was* culture?

And if that were true—

Then what right did Baru have to "save" Taranoke?

How could she pretend that the culture of her childhood was the *right* one, the one that had to be preserved, rather than the culture of a hundred years before or a hundred years after? How could she deny the arrival of Incrasticism, when her own people were the descendants of Maia arrivals on distant shores?

Cairdine Farrier had called Falcrest's ascendancy as inevitable as the rising tide.

How could Baru fight the tide?

She rose up from her appallingly soft covers, stretched, growled, looked out the window, and saw her cousin Lao standing in the sooty, fire-touched square outside.

Baru gaped in shock. Could it be Lao? What obscene unlikeliness would put her on the Llosydanes? But the woman did have Maia skin, and those rapturously long full legs, and strong swimmer's shoulders that Lao might have trained into, if she decided to bulk up. She wore a diver's costume, a tightly knotted strophium, a breechcloth, an ankle knife. As divers in Aurdwynn did, she'd even shaved herself seal-smooth from head to toe except for a cap of black hair.

Baru dashed the cup of freshwater over her face, tied herself up, and wiggled back into her trousers. Someone rapped at her door. "What!" Baru called.

"Secretary of the Trade! Open up!"

Oh fuck. Baru shrugged into her jacket, snapped up her purse, and shouted, "Uh, what about?"

"We want to ask you some questions about yesterday's events in the currency trade!"

"Right. Just a moment, I've got to wake up my whores!"

There was a murmur at the door. "Would you let them go in peace, please?" Baru shouted. "Just step away a minute so they can have their dignity?"

While the Secretary of the Trade waited, she got out the window, spider-climbed down the loose mortar and stone, and dropped to the flagstones. "Lao!" she called, almost laughing. "Lao, over here!"

Lao stood there watching her quietly. Baru would've expected more surprise. With a thrill of unease Baru fetched up on her toes, staring, trying to remember—

It wasn't Lao.

Before the massacre at Haraerod, Baru had called a priestess to her tent. She had to confess *something* and so she called for someone to listen. *Everything I've done. For Taranoke. But I've come too far . . .*

The woman had been a diver, and a midwife, and she'd sat with her long legs beneath her while Baru thought how much she looked like cousin Lao.

Her name was Ulyu Xe. The ilykari priestess of Wydd who Tain Hu had teasingly implied might be Baru's lover. She had soothing eyes, and a summer-ice calm. She might be in her thirties.

So she had gone with the rest of the rebellion to Sieroch. So she had been captured with Tain Hu's other companions and dispatched to the Llosydanes for interrogation.

But she was not under interrogation. She was here, and she was wearing a knife, and she had every reason to murder Baru on the spot, a killing which Yawa could deny any part in.

"Oh shit," Baru said, and would've run—

—except that the woman who wasn't her cousin fell gracefully to her knees, prostrated herself, and said, in Aphalone as wonderfully accented as Tain Hu's, "Your Majesty. I am your sworn companion."

L ET me understand," Baru said. "Yawa found you yesterday."

"Yes. And we refused to speak with her."

"And you were at this Morrow Ministry station. But the station chief, he just lets you run around like chickens? He lets you try to buy passage off the islands? That's the stupidest interrogation protocol I've ever heard."

"Is it?"

Baru shook her finger at Ulyu Xe, very nearly prodding the other woman in the throat. "Stop that. Stop that Wyddish 'everything's a question' horseshit, I can't stand it."

Xe smiled and drank her beer. Behind her a Maia journeywoman sawed away at her gut fiddle and sang of green-gold Aurdwynn and its lonely lads. This was a tavern called the Floating Island, full of Aurdwynni expatriots, and they called out to Ulyu Xe her in the homeland accent, *ulYou shee*, not the mangled Aphalone *Ullyu zee*.

Baru tried, again, to prod at the bruise. "You're not horrified I'm here?"

Xe set her cork mug down. Dark still eyes and pads of fat over swimmer's muscle. Like a long sleek otter. Of late, Baru's luck had been exceptional in this one respect: from Iscend Comprine's choreographed grace to Shao Lune's viperscale composure and now Ulyu Xe, she had met some fearsomely striking women. More than any attraction, though, Baru felt a stupid cowish tenderness toward Xe. She wanted to make everything all right for the priestess.

"I just can't believe—" Baru waved in frustration at several abstract concepts, including loyalty, hope, and vendetta, her wave accidentally getting the bartender's attention, which she had to dismiss with an apologetic shrug. "I can't believe you're calling me *Majesty.*"

"You were acclaimed queen. On the Henge Hill after the battle. It was made known to us."

"But then I . . . what I did to your people . . ." Baru shook her open hands before Xe: here, do you see what I have done? "What I did to *you*, I mean, you left your great-family to fight with us. And I betrayed you."

"You remember," Xe said, without gratitude, but with satisfaction, as if fitting a missing piece into a puzzle.

"Yes, I remember—I remember you told me that you'd been a diver, and a midwife, and that your great-family had spared you to come fight for me. You told me your story. And I lied to you."

"You told me the truth."

"How?" Baru hissed. "How did I—"

"You told me that everything you did was for Taranoke. I didn't understand then. But I do now." Ulyu Xe looked at her and Baru saw in her a power like a river, the power to wait and course and watch, certain that in good time she would find the proper course, full of all that she required.

She said, "Tain Hu told us what you'd done."

Baru drank deeply. The fucking beer was too weak. She wanted Svir's vodka. "And what had I done?"

"You wanted a post in Falcrest. You sold us to buy power to help your own home. The bargain would have destroyed you. You would have done Falcrest's work, and died alone." Xe's legs trembled beneath the table. She had been at her morning swim before she came to Baru's hotel. "My lady the duchess was determined to go back to save you."

"From the Throne?"

"From yourself."

Damn you, Hu. Damn your maps of me, and damn their accuracy. Baru drank the rest of the tepid piss-water and then, unsatisfied, traded her empty mug for Xe's. "Why were you traveling in her company?"

"You exiled her at Sieroch. You sent her away."

"I wanted to save her," Baru rasped.

"At first she thought you'd decided to marry the Necessary King. She wanted me to come along and teach her Wydd's acceptance."

"What did *you* want?"

"I like traveling with her."

"You were friends?"

"Occasionally lovers," Xe said, as if this were a slightly less serious commitment than friendship, and then she smiled. "She was a good woman. Impossible to teach. A very good woman."

"She's dead," Baru croaked.

"I know."

"How?"

"She told me that if you ever cared for her, you'd kill her. And if you didn't kill her, she'd die before she let herself be taken to Falcrest for reconditioning."

"Yes," Baru said, now trembling too, and not with exhaustion, "yes, she was right. She convinced me what I had to do. She was magnificent."

But the pure awe of Hu's death was tainted now. The call of the frigate birds over the drowning-stone rang false with laughter, Farrier's laughter, his venom was in this story now. *Falcrest is saved!* He had celebrated Tain Hu's death and somehow by doing it he had slithered back into her and seized her choice and made it his own.

Baru couldn't talk about this anymore. She threw a coin at a small and heavily defaced statuette of the late Hasran Cattlson.

"What happened when Yawa found you?"

Out west and down south, past the bridges that bound the twelve civilized islets together, there stood a tall tower islet called Moem, too stony for agriculture, covered in scrubgrass and wildflowers. But an old Falcresti man named Faham Execarne had set up a little farmhouse there.

Execarne was the Morrow Ministry's station chief on the Llosydanes.

He had simple rules for prisoners. If he didn't make regular signals that he was well, all his guests would be killed. Other than that they had their freedom. They might row over to one of the other islets and work a trade. They might try to hire a ship off the Llosydanes. Of course they'd have no papers, so no legitimate trader would take them on, and even smugglers would hesitate—the navy paid very well for the names of captains who transported fugitives.

He would prefer if his guests stayed with him, helped him keep his chickens and work his fields. He cooked a mean fishsteak. He could put a little weed in their pipe and a little leaf in their cheek. And if his new field hands decided to talk a little about their past as insurrectionists, that was their business, in their own time.

"It's a pleasant life," Xe said, equitably, "and some of us want to stay. Although I miss my daughter."

Baru, of course, stumbled obliviously past this invitation to ask after Xe's family. "Do the Oriati spies ever trouble him?"

"No, no. I believe Execarne's good friends with their spymaster here." She fell into a gravelly imitation: "'A collegial exchange of information helps keep the peace.'"

Fingers clasped in Baru's mind. A Falcresti man had asked the harbormaster to cover up traces of Oriati warships. Could that be Faham Execarne? Cooperating with the Oriati to prevent a greater war?

"You haven't asked who else was taken," Xe said.

Little minnows thrashed and nipped in Baru's stomach. She very badly didn't want to know: for the other prisoners would be Tain Hu's dearest, and

all of them would mourn the duchess, and in a fiercely stupid selfish way Baru
wanted that all to herself.

"Do they want me to know their names?" she said.

"Of course we want you to know. We all swore an oath. All the Vultjagata."

Vultjagata. Stakhi for *fighters of Vultjag*. "What oath?" Baru whispered.

"We kissed Tain Hu's sword," Xe said, "and we promised her that we would
serve you in your work. If you kept her faith."

Out of sheer pride and grief and gratitude Baru would have burst into tears
or (more likely) begun to hurl things, except that the screaming from outside
finally overpowered the fiddler's song.

IT was all over by the time they arrived. A man in the square had recognized
Xate Yawa, and followed her a little ways, unsure of his courage. Then he'd
taken a snort of mason dust and tried to strangle her to death.

By the time Baru and Ulyu Xe arrived the man was dead on the ground with
cut wrists and a slashed throat. His left thumb dangled by a tab of skin. Baru
knew those cuts: you put your hands up by reflex, against the knife. But your
hands could be cut, too.

Iscend Comprine hummed as she went through his pockets.

"It's not the first time I've been throttled," Yawa snapped, fending off Baru's
solicitations. "I see the diver lured you out. Good. The damn prisoners insist
they must see you, or they won't speak."

"This wasn't necessary." Xe looked down sadly at the dead man. "I knew
him. He would've gone quietly."

"Gone and died of sepsis from those cuts," Yawa said. "Baru, be a dear and
help me up."

Baru lifted her by her armpits. "Roll your head about. Tell me if you feel any
pain."

"Of course my neck's in pain. I'm fucking sixty and I write too much." Yawa
extracted herself from Baru and went forward applauding: "Iscend, Iscend,
I *knew* you were magnificent!"

The Clarified woman took a bow and, like an artist, flicked the blood off her
knife onto a stone wall in the lee of an overhang, where the scab would last
through rainstorms. "All in the service, my lady."

Ulyu Xe stared at Iscend, too. Baru hadn't thought anyone devoted to patience and reserve could easily express pure loathing. She was wrong. Xe looked
ready to wait forever for Iscend's messy death.

"Now we ought to go, I think." Yawa coughed twice, harshly, into her gloved
fist. "I only paid the constables to ignore so much."

* * *

T HEY rowed a boat south to Moem islet, where the prisoners waited.
       "There's *Helbride*," Iscend remarked. Baru followed her pointing hand
southeast. Clipper sails bobbed cheerfully against the bright afternoon sky: it
was indeed *Helbride*, sailing south.

Baru squawked in horror. "Apparitor's leaving without us!"

"Of course he is," Yawa said. "*Sulane* came in last night. Do you think Apparitor would stay in close moor? Trapped against the rocks?"

How Aminata would have teased her for forgetting her sailing rules: *make
some sea room before you fight.*

They beached on Moem's rocky skirts. Xe led them to a narrow trail that
spiraled up the outside of the mesa, and showed them how to belay themselves
to the long-lines pitoned into the cliff face. They climbed along the steep path
left by the face's slow collapse. The exercise stole Baru's thoughts, and her awareness narrowed to the distraction of Xe's long easy stride, her hard legs glimpsed
in swirled-cotton fractions as the wind stirred her robe, the padded curve of
fat at her hips.

I'm lustful, Baru thought. I haven't gotten off since Sieroch and I just spent a
night surrounded by beautiful women. I ought to mind myself for foolishness.

On top of the islet a fringe of scrubby salt-grass sloped down into a cupped
valley, and there sat Faham Execarne's little Morrow Ministry station: a white-
washed stone farmhouse, a covered well, a pump-arm with a modesty screen
for showers, fields of raw earth bordered in stone walls not quite half-built.

"It's nice," Xe said, "isn't it?"

Iscend looked on it with Clarified eyes. "The proper signs are shown. It's
safe."

Up the trail toward them came a leathery old man with a crossbow and a
fat pipe clenched in his jaw. The wind changed. A powerful stink of weed came
over them.

"Faham!" Ulyu Xe cupped her mouth to call ahead. "Faham, I've brought
the guest."

"Trouble's what you brought." Faham Execarne studied them from ten
paces, a compact dark brown man with deeply folded eyes and a strong blunt
chin. Farm work kept him rangy and a little stooped, but Baru would never
have mistaken him for a *real* farmer: his eyes marked them one by one, like
files. "Hello again, Jurispotence Yawa. And if I'm up on my telltales, you're the
Imperial agent Baru Cormorant. The one from Sieroch. The one my guests insist on seeing."

His crossbow was pointed at Iscend all the while. He clamped his pipe in his teeth and jerked his chin toward Yawa. "Jurispotence, has your thing here killed anyone yet?"

"Just one I've seen. In self-defense."

"Self-defense. Those Metademe fucks. I tell you, if you teach a woman to feel good when she kills in self-defense, she'll get real proactive about that defense. I don't like having her up here."

"She's just a person," Baru said, remembering Purity Cartone shot in the chest at Welthony. "Crossbows work on her like anyone else."

"Just a person, eh? Isn't that what they said about Shiqu Si?" Execarne sighed heavily. "Well, come on in. Storm's on its way, so one road or the other you're still going to spend the night here. Might as well meet my houseguests. Do you know my protocol?"

"No interrogation," Baru said. "No guards, no restraints."

"That's right." Execarne let the crossbow down with a grunt. "Never been any interrogator who could open people up as good as a true friend. You hear that, Xe? Friends! Come on, show me that holy smile."

"Smiles come when they ought," Xe said, peaceably.

"That's my Xe." Execarne squinted at Baru. "Now you, the noki woman, I've heard quite a bit about you. Fair warning, lass, they've been talking about whether to devote their lives to murdering you. And the arguments in favor seem strong."

Baru didn't want to be knifed like Prince V Asra the moment she walked in the door. She didn't want to be the damn fool sucker coaxed by Ulyu Xe and Xate Yawa into a deadly net.

"I think," she began, "that I ought to wait outside. Xe, why don't you go in and warn them all I'm here, so Iscend has a chance to see how they respond—"

Xate Yawa took Baru by the hand. "Let's not dither, dear," she said, with no little relish. "Your Coyotes must have missed you."

"How are they? What are they like?" Baru floundered desperately for information. "How did they react to you? What did you ask them?"

"I told them exactly what you should tell them," Yawa said. "They are now prisoners of the Imperial Republic. Their best hope for a happy ending is to co-operate fully with us. And if they do, I will ask for their pardon from the lawful Governor of Aurdwynn, Her Grace the Stag Duchess, Haradel Heia, who is styled Heingyl Ri."

WITH one hand already on the door latch, Baru discovered she could not possibly see this through.

She had never gone backward before: she had never gone back to anything.

She'd left Taranoke and she didn't know if she still had any hope of return. She'd abandoned her tower in Treatymont, forsaken Muire Lo to die of plague, and walked out of Tain Hu's tent at Sieroch to meet her destiny. She'd even failed (after all these weeks!) to open the letters from Aminata and her parents.

She was simply incapable of turning back. Therefore, she could not go inside the farmhouse, nor confront the survivors of Tain Hu's house: she would have to return to *Helbride,* and find another way—

She tried to back out of the breezeway. Ulyu Xe was in her way.

"Move," Baru hissed.

"I feel good here," Xe said.

"What's the problem?" Faham called. "Is it stuck?"

"No," Yawa assured him, one hand on his shoulder—how *quickly* she worked to charm him—"it's just that Baru's faintly addled. Watch, in a moment she'll remember how doors work."

"I am not addled," Baru protested, "I just think that Iscend really ought to go first."

Xe put her warm, strong hand on Baru's shoulder. "They swore an oath," she said. "Remember that an oath runs two ways. Remember to be worthy of it."

And while Baru was distracted, Xe's other hand worked the door latch, and Baru fell stumbling backward into a farmhouse full of people whose loyalty she had ultimately and completely betrayed.

The last thing she saw before they fell on her was Yawa's impish smile as she reached out and pushed the door closed behind Ulyu Xe, shutting Baru inside. Then everything was hot flesh and wetness, meat flapping at her hands, on her face, the bestial panting of someone who stank of grass and meat—

Baru got her arms around it before she realized it was a dog. "Oh," she said, with enormous relief, as the golden barrel of man-sized love and drool pranced around her pawing and woofing. "Oh, it's a—very friendly—er—Xe, would you please—"

"Down, boy," Xe clucked. The dog went down on all fours, panting enthusiastically, as if it couldn't wait to lick Baru more. Gingerly, she mopped the dog drool off her chin.

Everyone sat there, staring at her.

All her old companions. Gathered, as if for portraiture, at Execarne's long dinner table: one ragged exile family under cedar rafters and whale-oil lamps. Closest to Baru sat widowed Ake Sentiamut, who had run Tain Hu's counterfeiting scheme, and who Baru had left as regent over Vultjag. By her were two men—or, really, a man and a boy—Baru's jumpy bodyguard Ude Sentiamut, who'd shot a friend in the stomach on the Fuller's Road, who hadn't had the courage or ice to slit that man's throat and end his pain. He had his fatherly arm around pimpled Run Czeshine, a boy who'd been so pathetically taken with Baru that she'd been afraid he might have a glandular condition.

And three more: Nitu the cook, whose enigmatically clotted and greased curries went down like a dead squirrel scraped off a wagon axle, but who never *ever* made anyone sick. Yythel the herbalist, who brewed prophecy tea and planted silphium everywhere she went, sewing the love groves that let women decide when and how often to bear children.

And a wraith. A pale, half-real sketch of a man with moss-colored eyes and bloody hair. The jagata fighter Dziransi, ghostly son of the Wintercrests, who had offered his king's hand to Baru, and led his phalanxes into battle for her lie.

How terribly he must want to murder her.

"Uuf, uuf," the dog said, and nuzzled Baru's boots. No one else spoke. Baru stood in the doorway barefaced and unready.

In time the things you've done become too large to carry with you. So you set them down. And you think that you are free. But then you look back and see that someone else carries your burden now: you see that you have dropped your weight upon those who stood behind you.

Dziransi rose from his place at the table. Little abacuses clattered in Baru's mind, judging the speed of his lunge, the strength of his arms, the chance he'd have to kill her. But he did not try.

He spoke in deep, earnest, awful Aphalone. "Is the oath kept?"

"The oath is kept," said Ulyu Xe. "Duchess Vultjag is dead."

Ake Sentiamut rose up across from Dziransi with tears in her eyes and a tremble of power in her throat. When she spoke, for all her Stakhi blood and somber age, she could have been Hu's sister.

"Your Majesty Baru Cormorant, Traitor-Queen of Aurdwynn, I am Ake Sentiamut and I speak for your oathbound Vultjagata. By the power of that oath, and in the name of the people of the rebel duchies, I wish to negotiate the rebellion's conditional surrender."

IF I TALLIED MY LIFE TODAY

AKE'S decision was in retrospect obvious, and elegant, and necessary—but Baru had not foreseen it, and so at first, although she had all the power, she was afraid.

She'd expected rage and sorrow. She had prepared for madness. She had armed herself against despair: all the things she might find among the survivors of Tain Hu's house she had anticipated.

But Tain Hu's house was made of people, and people always slithered out of Baru's plans. She had not expected grace, or tenacity, or greatness of spirit in the face of the end of a lifetime's hope.

The survivors had organized—oh, Falcrest had expected them to collapse like starved mice when Baru revealed herself—but here in their prison on Moem, so far from home, they had organized magnificently.

If only it wasn't utterly futile.

"The rebellion's over," she said, and did not flinch from Ake's expression. "In the eyes of the Republic it never began."

"We *know,* you stuck-up cunt!" the cook Nitu snapped. The dog whined and Ulyu Xe shushed it with a touch.

"Nonetheless," Ake said. "We wish to negotiate."

"I'm not here to hurt you," Baru said.

"I think your intentions are rather beside the point," Ake said, crisply. "Run, will you please?"

The boy Run came out from under Ude's arm and with downcast eyes offered Baru a page of paper. She accepted it, and murmured thanks: he flinched like she'd put a spark out on his eyelid. Ude went to the back, where a low arch and a sooty curtain led to a hearth room, and brought a stool back for the head of the table.

"Your Majesty." With a short bow he invited Baru to sit. He would not look at her. "If you please."

Faham Execarne came in with an armful of driftwood from his curing-pile. "Hello, everyone," he called, "remember my rules about guests. If anyone gets hurt I'll feed you so many tapeworm eggs that you'll never satisfy your appetite till the day you die. And a terrible day that will be, as the worms split your guts and crawl out your navel. Carry on, everyone!"

The dog bumbled amiably against his ankles. He ruffled its scruff and went off into the rest of the house to start a fire.

The paper in Baru's hand read, in sharp Aphalone blocks, Acts of Surrender.

It was like they were putting on a play, and the topic was a diplomatic meeting. But they had to know, certainly, that they were utterly powerless. . . .

"I don't understand what you want," Baru admitted. "Why are you doing this?"

There was a general rustle around the table. Dziransi's fists curled. "We want to *negotiate*," Ake repeated, with finality. "To make our terms. Will you sit?"

"If this is not a negotiating table," Ulyu Xe said, reasonably, "what else could it possibly be?"

And then Baru, through a roundabout and cryptic detour, understood.

WHY do people do the things they do? If there are reasons for their acts, reasons like threads which trail back into the snarled silk of a life, how can we deduce those reasons from the acts?

Begin with a hashing function.

A hashing function is a one-way equation. How can there be such a thing? If two and two make four, then four is made of two and two, isn't it?

No. Given only the number *four* you do not know if it was made from two and two, or three and one, or four and nothing. You cannot easily go in reverse.

Say that you are a spymaster.

Say that you need to give your operatives a way to recognize each other. Of course you can't give them each a full list of all your trusted spies. What if, instead, you gave them a list of secret words which are *not* names, but which are derived from names, as acts are derived from thoughts?

How is this useful?

Given a code name of any size, like AGONIST, and a hashing function, and some very patient mathematicians, you can produce a secret word of fixed shape, called a cartouche. Say the cartouche for AGONIST is 0AB002. See how the cartouche is six letters? You can put any word of any length into this function, you can put in LAPETIARE BEGAN THE REVOLUTION or the full text of *I Summoned Antideath!* but the hashing function does not care, it is set up to *always* yield six letters.

The names of everyone in this room—Baru and Ulyu Xe, Ake and Dziransi, Run and Ude, Nitu and Yythel—could all be given to that hashing function and made into six-letter cartouches, 038801 for Baru and 0AC802 for Ulyu Xe and so forth. And if Baru wanted to prove to Ulyu that she was on Ulyu's list of trustworthy agents, she could say, "Run my name through the hashing function, and you will get the cartouche 038801, which is on your list. See? I am one of yours." It would take a well-trained clerk with an abacus and some devices, but it could be done.

But the trick is that you cannot get the original name back from the cartouche, even if you know the hashing function: for many possible names might produce the same cartouche. Ulyu Xe cannot look at 038801 and say, "Oh, yes, that means Baru." She might, if she had a lot of spare time, compute *all* the names that could hash into 038801—but there are too many.

Baru thought: What I see of other people is the output of a hashing function.

I'll never know anyone's true self, will I? Their thoughts and memories, the *selfness* of someone, the *me*-ness of me: that's like a true name, a person in all their formless awesome grandeur. But we do not see that grandeur. We see each other only in the shapes we are forced to assume. Words constrain us, and also our laws, and our fears and hopes, and the wind, and the rain, and the dog that barks while we're trying to speak, all these things constrain us.

We all force our true selves into little hashes and show them like passwords. A smile is a hashing function, and a word, and a cry. The cry is not the grief, the word is not the meaning, the smile is not the joy: we cannot run the hash in reverse, we cannot get from the sign to the absolute truth. Maybe the smile is false. Maybe the grief is a lie.

But we can compare the hash to a list, and guess at the meaning.

We come to a house full of those we betrayed most hideously, and they do not act as we expect. They have given us a strange cartouche and we can only guess what it means.

And we realize—I realize—that I haven't given Ake Sentiamut enough thought.

She's been so many women to me. How did I never notice? She taught me the arts of makeup and disguise, so I could survey Treatymont's slums. She was the regent I left behind when I took her people to war. She was Tain Hu's friend who taught her to read Aphalone. But—I must remember!—the women she has been to *me* aren't all of her. No, I never knew Ake when she was a wife, or when she became a widow, or a spy.

Ake is an adept in the technocratic arts. She organized the other survivors of Tain Hu's house. She made them into a committee.

Why?

Because a committee has dignity and power. A committee solves problems by sitting down and talking, not by beating and knifing each other. If I deny that the people at this table are a committee, then I deny the form Ake has imposed on this awful reunion.

And then they return to the protocol of shouting, beating, and knifing. Starting with me.

This had to be a negotiating table, because it was the only sane way they could face Baru with any self-possession and self-respect.

"Very well," Baru said, coolly. "Let's negotiate."

And she sat at the stool Ude had prepared for her.

ULYU Xe was the stenographer, of course, and little Run was the page boy who brought water and supplied the ink. Ude Sentiamut wore a forester's jerkin, even if he did not have his bow; Yythel the herbalist had adopted a simple dress of coarse-spun wool, not much different from the one she'd been wearing on the morning of death at Sieroch, when she was with Xate Olake; and the cook Nitu wore an Oriati-style khanga, which she must have taken from Execarne's wardrobe.

Dziransi and Ake sat side by side at the far end of the table from Baru. "Representing the rebellious duchies of Aurdwynn," Ake said, crisply, "I am Ake Sentiamut, regent for the duchess Vultjag. Representing the Stakhieczi Necessity, Dziransi of the Mansion Hussacht. And representing the Faceless Emperor of the Imperial Republic of Falcrest . . ."

"Agonist," Baru said, and, at the glares and exhalations from the table, with a mote of defensive pride, "it's my work-name."

"You are an Imperial agent. That was made clear to us at Sieroch."

"Yes," Baru said.

"Is it true, as our duchess supposed, that your—theft—of our rebellion was a gambit to secure that Imperial agency?"

"Yes," Baru said, high-chinned. "Yes."

"We have demands," Dziransi rumbled. He gripped the edge of the table like a vise, as if he had to hold the boards together.

"Demands?" Baru wanted to remind the jagata man that Falcrest would suck him dry through his eye sockets to learn what he knew—but she knew she would be in a way indulging her own desire to hold power over him. "Well, all right, go ahead."

Just then Xate Yawa and Iscend Comprine slipped inside. Both wore full-face service masks of light lacquered wood. The prisoners reacted stiffly to Yawa's presence: Ude even rose halfway out of his chair, growling.

Ake cleared her throat and spoke very loudly. "We demand full Imperial pardons in your name. We demand guarantees of protection for ourselves and our families. We demand to be returned to Aurdwynn and granted our freedom."

Yawa sat down and began taking notes.

"That's all?" Baru said. "You want to go home?"

"Everything we do," Ulyu Xe murmured, "is to save our home. For Aurdwynn."

Yes. When people really cared about their homes, didn't they *go* home? But not Baru, no, she traveled further and further away, sniffing the trail of power, and she did not even read her parents' letters. . . .

Xe was peering curiously at her now.

Baru blinked and swallowed. "Yes. Well. I think we can do a little better for Aurdwynn than a few Imperial pardons, can't we? I made a promise to the duchess—"

Yythel's rage spilled down her face like bitter tea. "We don't need any more of your *promises* in Aurdwynn, Baru."

"This boy needs his family." Ude clasped Run's shoulder. "Send him home."

Baru put up her gloves, palms forward: wait. "Let me ask you all a question. I am the Queen of Aurdwynn by the acclamation of the dukes, am I not?"

"Under false pretenses," Dziransi said. "A queen without honor."

"They were all false pretenses," the cook Nitu muttered.

"Nonetheless, am I not the oathbound lord of your duchess Tain Hu? Are you not, in her absence, my oathbound Vultjagata?"

"We vowed our lives to her," Nitu spat. "Not to you. Fuck you. Everything you say is poison."

She left in a swirl of cotton color. Ake looked after her, obviously longing to follow, or at least to tell Baru to go fuck herself.

"You won't let us go home," Run said. His voice cracked. "Will you?"

Xate Yawa drew on the thread of his doubt. "You can all earn pardons from the Stag Duchess, if you only tell us what we want to know."

And there was the problem. Baru *would* happily send them all back to Aurdwynn, far from her thin-walled heart, if only she weren't certain that Yawa and her pet Governor would devour them. These people were rebel cadre, the inner circle of the Coyote: they would never be allowed to live free lives.

"I was with Tain Hu on her last night." Baru tried her damnedest to show no pain, for Yawa was off on her right, watching everything: and then Baru thought, why should I care? What does it matter if I mourn? "We made a plan together. The rebellion can still accomplish its goals—"

"I thought you said the rebellion never began."

Baru tried to plead with Ake by gaze alone. "In the eyes of the Republic, perhaps, but we know—"

"Are your eyes not the eyes of the Republic?"

"I will not allow Tain Hu to die for nothing," Baru hissed.

"We kissed Tain Hu's sword," Dziransi said, with ritual solemnity. "We vowed to serve you in your work. *If* you kept her faith."

"We have decided," Ake pronounced, firmly, "that you will not keep her faith. We demand to carry on Tain Hu's work ourselves."

Once Hu had said, *freedom granted by your rulers is just a chain with a little slack.*

And here Baru was, offering them slack, begging them to take that slack and call it freedom.

"I need a moment," Baru said, and she fled through the sooty curtain to stand by the fire and think.

SPIRITED bunch, aren't they?" Execarne said, cheerfully. He had his tongs in the fire, and a thick pair of leather gloves to keep off the sparks. He was cooking fresh fish on a hot stone.

"Mm," Baru said.

"You spent all yesterday turning up the islands. Didn't find what you needed?"

She had, in a way. She knew a man named Abdumasi Abd had provisioned his warships here. "I found your cover-up," she said, levelly. "The numbers you had your harbormaster fake. Concealing information from the republican people isn't a survival strategy, Mister Execarne."

"Ah," Execarne sighed. "What can I say? I've sacrificed so much to keep the peace. A little cover-up hardly tallies against my sins."

"Agonist," Yawa said, and her glove closed on Baru's right shoulder. Baru leapt in fright. "You seem troubled. Negotations not proceeding as you'd hoped?"

Baru smiled icily. "At least no one's throttled me."

"My, you *are* tense."

Baru struck out at her. "The woman in the dress, Yythel? She was your brother's lover."

Yawa deflected. "Then she'll be *very* happy to know I kept him safe. That fish smells divine, Faham. Or should I say, ha ha, it smells virtuous."

"Caught it just today, your Excellence." He winked at Yawa. "I don't mind a little idolatry over my cooking."

Yawa settled on the brick apron of the hearth. "Baru, can I ask you something?"

"I won't stop you."

"Why are you legitimizing them? Why are you going along with this farce of negotiations and surrender? You hurt them. You made fools of them. You're not the one who should be offering them mercy."

"We need a little honey to—"

"I know that," Yawa snapped. "So offer honey from a bee that never stung. Offer them letters of pardon from Governor Heingyl Ri."

By now Baru was quite accustomed to Heingyl Ri's name floating up from the mist at every opportunity: the woman obviously had Yawa's favor. "You want them in her debt, don't you. You want your stooge to look merciful."

"Of course I do! Ri needs to build her reputation as a peacemaker. Imagine how powerful it would look if she were to pardon these rebels and return them safely home. A message for the rebel North. All is forgiven, no harm done: let us go back to growing prosperous." Yawa spread her gloves. "Baru, it would be good for Aurdwynn."

And Yawa would get Dziransi from the bargain, Baru figured. Her key to the Stakhieczi door.

Remember the man in the iron circlet!

Remember the *ledger*—

It was so tempting. Just be rid of them. Be rid of the need to think about them, to consider their well-being, to remember how you hurt them.

But Tain Hu's voice would not stop echoing. *Freedom granted by your rulers is just a chain with a little slack. . . .*

If Baru died today, she would die having done nothing for Aurdwynn, or even for Taranoke.

How long could she delay? How much power would she insist on gathering before she did even *one* good thing for the people she'd stepped on? You couldn't manipulate people like little pawns forever. You had to remember that they were their own autonomy, their own power, self-moving, and you had to trust in that—

What was the sense of accumulating all this power if it never went to the people who needed it most?

"No," Baru breathed, and then, with confidence now, "no, we're not giving them to Heingyl Ri. I know what to do."

"Baru, Heingyl Ri *is* Aurdwynn now—"

She went back toward the curtained door. Yawa rose to come after her and Baru blocked her way. "Get out," Baru ordered. "Take Iscend and go outside. I won't have you listen to this."

Yawa's eyes slitted behind the dark mask. "You can't bar me from an interrogation."

"Of course I can," Baru said, flatly. "I can do anything I please, Yawa, because when they put your twin brother on trial for grand treason, they'll call for my testimony. You *do* want me favorably disposed, don't you?"

"Are you *threatening* me?"

"That's how it works here. That's how this game is played. Leverage."

She was too exhilarated by her new plan to feel any guilt at the terror and pain in Yawa's eyes; or, at least, to feel it right then.

A KE and her committee stared at Baru.
        Baru hunched over the paper and wrote and wrote and reached for more paper and wrote some more.

"You left me," Ake said. "You left me behind in Vultjag because you didn't want me taken with the others at Sieroch."

"Mm," Baru grunted. "Fetch me more paper."

"You could have left Tain Hu instead," Ake whispered.

"I couldn't leave Hu." Baru wrung out her wrist. "She was a duchess. I had to bring the rebel leadership together in one place. I had to give them a convincing victory and then an immediate crushing reversal, to show the confidence of Falcrest's control. Also, I wanted every moment I could get with her. Will you sign this?"

"Not until you tell me what it is, and I read it, in case you've lied."

The order needed a clean draft anyway. Baru snatched a fresh sheet from the pile. "This is your letter of provisional governorship. I'm going to stamp it with something called an incryptor, which creates a special polestar mark. That will bind this document directly to the Emperor's authority. When you go home, if anyone tries to stop you from doing what I've written here, you show them this seal—"

Everyone stiffened. "Home?" Ude gasped.

"Yes. I'm pardoning all of you, unconditionally."

"You're conceding," Ake said, in cautious wonder.

"Oh, I'm far more than *conceding*." Baru signed, in tight rectilinear blocks, AGONIST. "Ake, you will rule the North."

"I will *what*?"

"You're familiar with the provincial economy through your work in the Fiat

Bank. You understand the difficulties of governance during the winter, and the Coyote mutineers look up to you as Duchess Vultjag's friend. A perfect choice, I think."

Ake looked as if she'd just drawn a bucket of rattlesnakes from the well. "I will not be your pawn," she said, thinly. "None of us will. Not again."

"You won't be anyone's pawn. I told you. This order grants you broad authority within your dominion. You can carry on Tain Hu's work as you see fit."

"But Aurdwynn *has* a governor," the herbalist Yythel said, reminding Baru that she was literate, and followed news, and developed strong opinions. "Heingyl Ri is in the Governor's House."

"I don't care," Baru snapped. "She can write me a letter of complaint." Her incryptor jumped in her fist and smashed the Imperial mark onto the letter. She raised it up and offered it to Ake's trembling hands.

"Your Majesty . . ." She smoothed the letter on the table. "These are wartime emergency powers."

"Yes, of course." Baru couldn't help but grin, she was *so very* clever. "The North of Aurdwynn is in a state of open rebellion, isn't it? Lawless and disordered."

"The rebellion is *over*—"

"The Emperor has not formally recognized the rebellion's surrender. Therefore the rebellion is still ongoing. You will be dispatched to the rebellious duchies with absolute wartime authority to reorganize and rebuild as you see fit. The Emperor's seal is on that letter and so you are Its emissary."

Dziransi could not look at her without seeing treason, so he turned to Ake Sentiamut. "She has this power?"

"I suppose," Ake said, slowly, narrow-eyed in thought, "that she does."

"She has made you the Emperor's warlord?"

"It's like I'm a peace-lord, Dzir. I cannot move Governor Heingyl's forces. I cannot send embassies abroad, or appoint judges. But in the North I have power over money, and courts, and trade . . . someone will come to take this power from me, Baru. Someone will see what I'm doing."

"Let them come. You have my backing." Baru clapped to get their attention. "You must get the North weaned off raw exports as quickly as you can, understand? You must use your position between the coast and the Stakhi to build up your wealth. Ake, do you hear me?"

Ake looked at Baru's letter as if she might ball it up in her fist and cram it down Baru's throat. "Tell me your angle."

"I don't have an angle. You should salary all the rangers. Don't let them wander off as guides or hunters; you must salary them and send them north on expeditions."

"My King," Dziransi began, "he will not trust you; *I* do not trust you."

"Trust Ake, then. Trust the money. Open trade with the Stakhieczi. They want food, so buy food from the south and sell it north. The south wants Stakhieczi steel and glass, so buy steel and glass and sell them south. The flow of money will prevent the flow of blood. That's how we did it on Taranoke, for centuries—but you have more than we did, so invest the profits in mills and trading posts, invest in the roads, build dams and sewers—get yourselves on your feet before hard times come. You must be ready to survive if the trade stops."

Faham Execarne came in carrying what seemed like an entire ship's rudder loaded with steaming fish steaks. "It's hot," he said, "very hot, and don't choke on the tiny bones. I'll be back in a moment with beer. Has anything interesting happened?"

No one spoke.

"Not really," Baru said. "I'll be sending these people home. The pardons are here for your inspection."

Execarne produced a huge knife with a flourish. Baru was the only one to recoil. "Interesting," he said, and began to chop the fish with great sweeping strokes, the blade thumping pleasantly against the wood, "pardons all around, eh? In whose name?"

"Mine."

"Ah. Is that so?" Execarne grinned at his guests. "You've got to be careful with this one. She's a *prodigy* at lies."

"We know," her bodyguard Ude said, darkly.

"Did she tell you that Xate Yawa kept you alive? Over the winter you were all identified and preconvicted of grand treason. You'd all have been drowned in Treatymont harbor, except Dziransi, who'd go to a worse fate. Instead Yawa ordered you transferred here." He nodded firmly. "Baru never wrote one letter about you lot. Ask yourselves why she's setting you up so comfortably now. Ask yourselves—is she afraid she can't make any more money off your country without your help?"

The damnable poisonous thing was that he was right. He was undermining her, doubtless as a favor for Xate Yawa, but he was right. Baru was afraid to lose her influence in Aurdwynn. She had to protect Vultjag, lest she betray Tain Hu, and that betrayal would be a sledge through the last pole holding up her paper roof of righteousness.

Ake was nodding. Ake was looking at her as if to say, *I know you always have yourself in mind.*

"Where's the wine?" Baru snapped.

Fuck them. Fuck Yawa and her slithering insinuations and her stolen ledger. Fuck the fierce stiff resentment of her "Vultjagata" (how little *that* oath seemed to mean). Hadn't Baru yielded her power to Ake? Hadn't she said, *go, do as you will?*

Ake would probably fuck it all up. Heingyl Ri would twist her about, and the North would end up a starving barren firebreak against the Stakhieczi. Damn it. Damn it, fuck! Heingyl Ri was a *coastal* Duchess! Didn't Ake understand that the coast needed a poor starving North, so it could get materials cheap?

Ri couldn't be trusted. The economics were clear.

Baru drank the wine that Yawa had abandoned by the hearth. Then she stole a hammock and went down into the cozy wood cellar. An hour's nap would do her good.

She put her head down for a moment.

And woke in utter blackness. She fumbled around, her left arm dead and numb, till she found her folio and—oh, thank Wydd, the incryptor: if someone had tried to use it without her dial settings, it might have destroyed itself.

Someone took a breath. "Baru?"

Baru checked her ankle knife. "Who is it?"

"I drew water for your bath," Ulyu Xe said.

Baru groaned. "Are you serious? A bath?"

"You look like a greasy kitchen rat. You need a bath."

"You weren't much help up there," Baru complained. "I thought—"

Thought what? That the oath they'd taken to Tain Hu would transfer flawlessly to Baru? That everyone could simply set aside what she'd done, and go back to her service?

What a fool.

"I don't persuade people," Xe said. "I can only show them what I know."

Baru growled low in her throat. "So *you* don't think I'm trying to plunder Aurdwynn for riches?"

"No. I think that you loved Hu and want the best for her home."

The growl become a groan. "I don't want to talk about Hu."

"Yes you do. And so do I. Come."

Baru's clothes were soaked through with nightmare sweat. "Fine. Fuck it. I do need a bath."

Sharp wind outside, and a gentle chill to edge the warmth. Baru gasped in wonder. The stars shimmered behind a mighty aurora, wings of green, red sheets of pyroclast, vast bars of purple light tilted like pillars seen from below.

"I've never seen it so bright."

"There was a wildfire somewhere, and this is its ghost."

"You just made that up."

"Surely I wouldn't."

"You *would,* though," Baru realized, with some delight, "I bet you do it all the time."

"I am Wydd's faithful student," she said, not smiling, except in the roll of her hips as she walked. She was powerfully calm, like a hand run over the world to smooth it out. Home, Baru thought, suddenly: her dark seal body was so comfortable in itself that it made Baru think of a home. And she wanted to learn that art, of being at home wherever you stood.

"Come," Xe said, "there's a drain behind the well."

Execarne had built a screen to wash behind after long days in the field. Baru stripped down, drenched herself in lukewarm water from Xe's pot, and went to work, too hard, with a wire scour. Cold clean wind. Starlight. Caldera gods, she never wanted to go back inside. The runoff water went into a clay half-pipe, down into the fields, and the pipe murmured gently to itself as it worked.

"My lady," Xe said. "Your Majesty. You're scraping yourself raw."

"How can you even tell?" Baru demanded. "Wait a minute. Are you on mason leaf?" Divers loved the stimulant leaf. It helped night vision, and also made them prone to fights and forthrightness.

"A little," Xe said. "We smoked too much weed with Faham, so I took a pellet to stay awake."

"Oh. So *that's* why you're so friendly."

"Why didn't you go to her sooner?" Xe said, softly. Baru had just turned to get at her back, so Xe was on her blind side: the words drifted in like stragglers from a long retreat.

"What?" Baru said.

"Why didn't you go to Tain Hu in the autumn? You could've been with her all winter. She wanted you. She spoke of you, with some frustration."

Baru had something on her back, lumpy and disfigured, and it had to come off—ah, no, those were her vertebrae. "I couldn't. I knew what was coming."

"But you went to her at the end."

"I am a fucking idiot at times."

"You think it was a mistake?"

"No," Baru admitted. "No, I can't think that."

"Did you go to her at Sieroch because you knew she'd die?"

"What?" Baru stared over her shoulder. Ulyu Xe stood there like part of the night, a soft suggestion of easy brushstrokes, drawn in the same motion as the wind. Aurora light teased her shoulders and brow.

"Some people are like that," Xe said. "Death arouses them. In Aurdwynn there's erotica about people who've been sentenced to death, and the wild things they do."

"That's not my taste." Her teeth were chattering. "Oh Devena, the weather's turned, hasn't it?"

"We could fuck for warmth, if you want."

Baru laughed. "There's a perfectly good house over there."

"It's full of people you don't like as much as me."

"Yeah," Baru grunted, scraping at the boot stores on her ankles, "you and me, best of friends, there's a picture."

"I thought that was why you'd called me to your tent at Haraerod."

"To be best of friends?"

"To fuck. Men and women knew me for my companionship. I was spoken of by the lonely."

"Oh. No, I had a lot on my mind."

"You'll always have a lot on your mind, Your Majesty."

"It's true." Baru laughed, too cruelly. "It's true. Some day . . ."

Ulyu Xe shifted and stretched, very powerfully, as if arching for the surface of a clear cool pond. Baru looked at her body, wanting it, wishing she lived in a place where she could want without fear.

"Wait a moment," she said. "Are you *actually* propositioning me?"

"You shouldn't spend so much time inside yourself." Xe shrugged, her arms still raised, shoulders taut. Baru had been ignoring her body's interests: now she could not. That thrill like a plucked cord. "You're never *here*. And I've been lonely, and I know you like women. So."

Baru stopped scraping herself dry. "Huh," she said. "I mean—no offense intended—but we've just met. Or—only just gotten acquainted, at least."

"Sometimes that's the best time. Later we might detest each other."

"This seems a bit like you were put up to it."

"You were with her last," Xe said, and this, most of all, rang of truth. "She left herself on you. I miss her too, you know."

Baru felt a sharp somatic *pop*, painful and yet correct, like her jaw snapping into place after a bad yawn. Somehow she was abruptly more fleshy. A rush of guilt followed, as if by putting her eyes on Ulyu Xe she had endorsed the pornographic narrative of divers as dolphin-fucking whores, and then after that came a lash of self-reproachment for immediately leaping to such an ugly topic. And then finally a skin-prickling terror. They had only just spoken of death. And now a proposition. Why must those always come together?

Baru threw down the strigil. Her confusion made her angry and anger made her want to act. She'd been distracted too much by women lately. A fling could be justified tactically: to show them all how little she cared, how untroubled she was by Hu's loss.

"Fine," she said, "fine, come here."

XE smelled of work and the wind off the sea. "Do you kiss?" she asked, pragmatically: some people did not.

Baru answered her. They struggled pleasantly against the wooden privacy screen. Xe's height was a lovely challenge: Baru could bite the strong lines of her throat. Her diving costume was, of course, designed to come off easily, in case of an underwater snag. She tried pinning Xe against the cedar screen, as Hu had pinned her on the tent's groundcloth: Xe's breath rose eagerly.

"Here," she said, guiding Baru's hand, "like this—yes. Ah."

A perfectly satisfying groan. Heat against her hand. Xe's hips gave her a rhythm and let her carry it onward. The strong muscles of her hips and ass worked beneath the fat, and Baru felt that joyful work in her fingers. Xe began to whisper passion in Urun, in Stakhi, as if driven out of Aphalone by her pleasure; when Tain Hu had done that it thrilled Baru like nothing ever had.

Yet Baru was disappointed by her own detachment. Xe had such grace. Such a unity of form. She could not be separated: the line of the hip up across the long smooth stomach, over the breast, arched through the firm shoulder. Lovely. But all very distant. She was a gentler lover than Hu, steady and rhythmic and very responsive to Baru's touch, which should have been wonderful, but only made Baru self-conscious of everything she did. Xe was very warm. Baru felt a great fondness for her, and a low, limitless sadness at what must happen soon: some separation, some grief.

She tried to fantasize to make the sex better, which seemed entirely perverse. Why was nothing happening? She had met a lovely diver of an exciting older age. They had shared a day of light tension, and a bath, and an admirably forward proposition. What a thrill.

No: none of it worked.

Now she lay on her back on the saltgrass, staring up at the aurora, as Xe's hair brushed her thighs. She felt like she had spent a very long time fumbling with a knot. "You've gone away again," Xe said, from below, "haven't you?"

"Oh. Oh, I'm sorry." Baru twitched in mortal embarassment. "I'm sorry—it's just not—oh, it's me, I'm not working right."

"It's all right. It's not easy for some women." Xe crawled up beside her. "I was too forward with you. I made assumptions. I'm sorry."

"No," Baru said, miserably, "it's me. It was easy for me last time."

"She was a wonder, wasn't she?"

"Yes," Baru said, with dead despair.

"Hm," Xe said. "I think I may sense the problem."

16

TAU-INDI

I'D be fucked bareback in a pen of gonorrhetic pigs before I let Baru steal my home.

The gall of her. The bilious clotted gall. Ordering her pale little stooge back to Vultjag to seize control of the North! All she'd had to do was let Heingyl Ri give the pardons, trust Heingyl Ri to care for Vultjag and the others, but no, no, Baru had to have them for herself.

Baru might be a vicious narrow-minded weasel but she had a certain insight, didn't she? If, in the spirit of my career as a hygienist, Aurdwynn could be imagined as a gigantic cunt (having midwifed most of my life I tended to think the nation and the organ shared a certain perverse resilience) then the coastal south was the happening end where all the business was conducted. But the north was the potential, the fallow womb, and Baru wanted to get *her* child in there first.

She knew what I was up to. Somehow she knew. And she was moving to stop me. I would need to write Heingyl Ri as soon as I could, and urge her to mind her security: Baru's assassins would be at her already.

I'd been in a foul mood since Baru left me at the World Telescope, and doubly foul since that limp prick in the plaza tried to hang me with his cock-grip hands. But as soon as Baru began to move openly against me, I felt much better. I'd tidied away the whole mess of Baru at last. No more uncertainty. Hesychast was right about her, she had been irreparably compromised by Farrier's secret process, and therefore she was an enemy of Aurdwynn's freedom and had to be treated as such. My thoughts of befriending and tutoring her were easily dismissed. She was entirely wrapped up in her own ambitions, and would never accept me.

So I moved ahead with my other plan for Baru.

The enemies of kings are powerful prizes, my friends. If you know anything about the Stakhieczi, know that they do not like their kings. A Necessary King may be elected in times of need, but at his first sign of weakness he is unmade again.

The man who ruled the Wintercrests knew he had erred terribly by offering his hand and his armies to Baru, only to be betrayed. Now he looked a fool, dishonored and weak—

—and if he wanted his honor back, there was only one way to get it.

I would give him that honor. And in exchange he would give me my fulfillment.

As Baru drowsed in the cellar, drugged by the wine I'd left for her, I ordered Iscend to draw Dziransi outside. She simply challenged him to wrestle. He said he would not fight an unarmed woman, for it was against the gentle honor. She said he was afraid to lose. That note of pride gave the Stakhi man an excuse to beat her, so he went out, amiably, into the dark saltgrass.

In their first grapple Iscend drove a poisoned needle into his bare thigh. He felt the hurt but thought, I am sure, that it was a thorn. He won the fight, but that got his heart going, which only pumped the poison all the faster. (A metaphor, there, for this Republic we serve.)

Then he fell.

The boat from *Helbride* had already delivered the sarcophagus. Iscend and I worked swiftly to pin Dziransi within the braces and steel clamps of the casket, as motionless as a krakenfly in amber.

Then I opened the sarcophagus's neck hatch and needled Dziransi with a big man's dose of the dream-hammer.

I gained the Jurispotence of Aurdwynn at age thirty-six, and for the next twenty-four years I scourged the bodies of my people. Did I torture them? Fucking right I did. I sent them down into my Cold Cellar for reconditioning and the occasional radical surgery. I had their bodies altered to the demands of the Incrastic state.

But I was better than what came before.

Remember the old Duke Lachta with his breaking-wheels and his hot pears? His fascination with expanding all the holes in the human form? He could make anyone say anything, as long as he wanted it said in a scream.

I never tortured anyone like that. I don't waste people.

The brave man Dziransi possessed great strength, and like many strong things he was therefore brittle. I admit that I bent him perhaps too hard. I hate the Mansion Stakhi for their cold ways and their avarice toward my home. I hate what their ideas of women did to the daughters of Aurdwynn.

I suppose I hated Dziransi a little, and hurt him for it.

Dziransi had been on drugs since he came to Moem, of course. Execarne kept all his guests on a low dose of cannabis and opiate to secure their calm and trust. But the dream-hammer, now, that was a drug to change the shape of a man's soul. In old Belthyc myth the first caterpillars ate the dream-hammer before they went into their cocoons, and from their feverish metamorphosis emerged the nightmare race of man.

I'd used it on myself once. On the night of my brother's marriage. When I resolved to change the shape of my soul, to peel it away from the shape of his.

Tonight I used it on Dziransi. And the dream-hammer made me Dziransi's god.

I felt blasphemous. I felt like I'd committed that mythic sin of hubris.

And I wondered if this was how Tain Shir lived her life. As a god who walked unshackled among the mortals in their chains.

FROM the very first instant my brother knew Tain Ko, the sister of the Duke of Vultjag, he hated her fucking guts. Olake hated her from the long braided fall of her hair to the proud angle of the Vultjag nose to her hickory-brown throat and high-bound noble tits and her unfashionably athletic legs and her presumably arrogant and demanding and oh-so-aristocratic cunt (perhaps she dissolved commoner cocks with acid). Especially, Olake hated Ko's distaste for his city: Olake *loved* Lachta, his slushy muddy flea-bitten home, even back then before the Masquerade rebuilt the sewers. I myself lost that sentiment when I contracted a rot from the laundry-water. We drew a grease circle around the infection, and watched it grow, with frightening and *almost* visible speed, across that circle, across my thigh.

So Olake stood behind me with the ends of a belt in his fists. I could feel, through the leather, how his grip tightened with every shriek I chewed into that belt. And I cut that divot of flesh right out of my leg.

Good Himu did my brother *hate* Tain Ko. I said he hated her from the first instant he knew her, which was a street brawl between Ko's retinue and my brother's antiroyalists, and their hatred escalated from there. In no time at all they were hating each other on the floor of our apartment while I tried to sleep, hating each other in the back of the wagon while I tried to drive the horses, in stockrooms and meadows and anywhere else they could find. I believe they only came to like each other out of some animal release of passions: by sheer weight of fucking, their bodies seduced their minds along.

The child was unplanned. In those days under Duke Lachta contraceptives were contraband: I believe Tain Ko, unfamiliar with the city and its dubious markets after a life with the pharmacist-women of the north, bought a batch of fake silphium. She decided to keep the child, partly to deter suitors who wanted her for a political marriage. But she dared not reveal the father: Olake was a known antiroyalist, and Duke Lachta hated both Duke Vultjag and Olake. Vultjag's sister bearing Olake's child would drive Lachta to matricide.

The birth came earlier than planned. In those days I was still a laundry girl covered in bedbug bites and soap burns, and our flight from the city was a terrifying wonder: there were places in the world that hardly stank at all! I think something was born of me, too, a love of Aurdwynn entire, a love which I still carry and hope I always will.

I midwifed Ko while Olake paced under the pine boughs.

Tain Shir was born to a red moon and the flash of summer heat lightning. I swear in Devena's name that she was born with one tooth already erupted, and that she bit me. We took her with us on our travels, and she grew up among revolutionaries, with words like *freedom* on her tongue.

Once, as we scraped our laundry in a Radaszic stream, she touched the scar on my thigh. *Is that,* she'd asked, *what the dukes are like? A rot in us?*

Her father, my brother, rubbed her hair and smiled. *Yes,* he'd said, so proudly. *But a rot that we will cut away.*

What about Mother, Pa?

She was born to aristocracy. But she made her choice to stand with us. Everyone has a choice, little blackberry.

Perhaps that was the moment that fate seized upon when it wrote Shir's doom.

The Masquerade came on red sails, and with them a prayer of change: the masked people on the ships spoke of *republic,* and their Parliament where anyone could change the law. Shir was afraid of them. The wisest of us, although of course at the time we hardly knew it.

Like a gaggle of boys aroused by a hint of nipple, the dukes and duchesses all got hard for the new Masquerade trade and began to fight over it. In a blink they were at war and we, the antiroyalists, had our moment. I struck a deal with the Masquerade mission. And I kept my terms. I killed Duke Lachta with a little knife, and as his last breath bubbled from his throat, I wiped my blade on his white stacked linens and said, "Will that be all, Your Grace?"

Shir fought, too, on that night of reckoning. She killed. Not for the first time, I think.

My brother, "head of the revolutionary government," signed the Treaty of Federation. So we gave Aurdwynn to the Masquerade, and at first young Shir rejoiced. But the new Incrastic laws were cruel like bleach—Aurdwynn, the Falcresti explained, had to be cleansed of sin. The land had to be scoured raw. In time their laws would ease, they assured us. If enforced well, and obeyed with enthusiasm. In time the laws would ease.

That, I think, we could have tolerated.

Then their fucking Parliament made an accomodation with the dukes.

The aristocracy would keep their stations and their privilege, in exchange for signatures on the Treaty of Federation. Falcrest's Parliament had judged it impossible to profitably rule Aurdwynn without the dukes. Tax revenue would be unacceptably low for an unacceptably long time if the revolution disrupted industry. The duchies had to stand.

That we did not *want* to tolerate. But we went along with it. My brother and I acquiesced.

Shir fought us with the idealism of youth. How could we accept ducal rule, after so long fighting against them? How could her own father accept the title of Duke Lachta—a title stained with the blood and pus of the city's suffering?

I tried to explain that we'd compromised.

Compromised, Shir told me, was another word for *betrayed*.

She was fifteen and I was thirty-six, but those twenty-one years between us might have been the distance to the moon. She would not bend. Her cousin Hu (brave young Tain Hu, who would one day meet and strike down the Pretender-King Kubarycz in single combat) was only five years old. Frustrated with the adults, Shir carried Hu on horseback through the forest, and spoke to her of injustice, and showed her how to kill trapped animals without hesitation. Later I would discover that Hu remembered everything.

Hu remembered what Shir had said:

You must understand, no matter what anyone tells you, that you are free. In this moment you may do whatever you choose. No one can stop you. They can choose how to react to your choice, but they cannot stop the choice itself. This is freedom, understand? A knife in your hand. And you may do with it as you please.

When people teach you what you might and might not do—they are bridling you. They are taking your freedom away. Yes, the world has laws, which are consequences for your actions. But remember that there is nothing you cannot choose to do. Only consequences you fear to face.

If anyone ever tells you that they have no choice but to compromise, remember this. They are afraid.

Shir developed an interest in an anonymous correspondent. The more she wrote to him, the less she spoke to us. He signed his missives *Itinerant*. I would say we tried our very best to reach her, but I would damn myself if I did, for Olake and I didn't even know who *we'd* become, let alone the girl. I was preoccupied by the lies I had begun to tell my twin: lies of omission, lies about my plans, because whatever I told him he would tell his wife, the daughter of Duke Vultjag, the aristocrat in our midst.

And then one day Shir was gone. She left a letter tucked in my comb.

I have gone to seek out the nature of justice. Somewhere in this world there must be a good true way to live.

I knew very little about what she did after that. But I do know what turned her. I know where she began her descent toward the killing woman in the marsh.

IN AR 117, eleven years after the Treaty of Federation, a few of the dukes led by Duchess Naiu rose up against the reparatory marriage laws. Their cry was the old cry, *Aurdwynn cannot be ruled!* And they were doomed, doomed from the start, although we did not call it the Fools' Rebellion yet.

Olake and I decided, together and without remorse, that the common people would only survive if we ended this damn rebellion swiftly and in defeat. Some of the dukes would remain loyal to Falcrest, some would join the rebellion, most would bide their time and play both sides. All of them would trample on the commoners to do it. The cost would roll down upon the folk.

We hated the Masquerade by then. Truly we did. But we needed decades of peace to arrange our own final revolution.

So we betrayed the Fools' Rebellion to Falcrest. And, oh, did that put my brother's wife, Tain Ko, in a bind. For her brother, Duke Vultjag, had joined Naiu's rebels, and now her husband had backstabbed those rebels spectacularly.

I did not do this: a prisoner escaped from an Incrastic sanitarium in Duchy Heingyl and jumped a ferry up the Inirein. The ferry was faster than the yellowjackets who chased it. By the time the escapee reached Duchy Oathsfire his armpits had already swollen and it was too late. Plague swept west to east across the Northlands like a strigil on dead skin.

Duke Vultjag died in the first week, and left young Hu to inherit.

The people of Vultjag called Tain Ko to come home and serve as regent for Tain Hu. Olake pleaded with his wife, but she was a warhawk and a will and she would not abandon her blood.

She went over to the rebellion.

Let me tell you the most pathetic and embarrassing sort of grief in the world. It is the grief you feel as you sit in a canvas tent with your hands over your ears, trying not to listen to your brother fuck his estranged wife for what they both know will be the very last time.

I had a plan to capture Ko and pardon her. I was well into the arrangements when Tain Shir came home on a Masquerade ship up from Taranoke. She traveled with a band of men and women who killed callously and spoke very little. They were in Treatymont for two days before marching north, and by then I had four murders pinned on them. Of course I couldn't prosecute. They carried a letter with the polestar mark, the Emperor's authority: they were outside the law.

Tain Shir took her killers north into the forests. By year's end the rebel leadership were all dead, and careful dispensation of Falcrest's funds had placed collaborationist relatives into their seats to bicker over the terms of surrender.

Vultjag was the last to fall.

The way Tain Hu told it, Tain Shir came down into the valley, alone, to negotiate with her mother. They met above the waterfall where Hu would one day build her keep. They paced each other on opposite banks of the river.

Shir told her mother, *Vultjag, listen, I serve a better master now. Put down your spear. Come back to Lachta. Mother, you can serve my master, too.*

Tain Ko raised her spear for the last time. She chose her final words.

I am not mastered.

The crossbow was faster than the spear.

D URANCE," Iscend whispered. "He's ready."

"Yes." I shook myself too hard. I had to lean on my elbow, like a reclining lover, to get my head down to the ear of Dziransi's casket.

"Dzir," I murmured, in mountain Stakhi. "Dzir, do you hear me? Follow my voice. You're not alone. Follow my voice."

Sealed and muzzled within the steel sarcophagus he couldn't so much as wiggle a toe. I think from the noises he made that he thought he'd been crushed in a collapse in the tunnels of his home Mansion, high up on Mount Karakys in the Wintercrests, where no trees grew.

I signaled to Iscend for light. She lit a candle with her sparkfire and dilated the casket's left iris to the width of a blade of grass. "I'm holding up a light, Dzir," I whispered, showing him the candle. "I'm holding up a light for you. Can you come to it?"

He gagged and rasped.

"Come closer, Dzir."

Like river rapids the dream-hammer sucked him under. Like a sluiceway the drug flowed beneath the dam of his discipline. The dream-hammer gets into the fork of the mind that divides the roads of truth and falsehood, and it turns all the signs toward *truth*.

I unbuckled the casket's faceplate.

Fungus-green eyes stared back at me, red with grief and madness. His beard had tangled in the steel muzzle that clapped his jaw shut.

"It's all right," I whispered, "it's all right, I'm here."

He looked up into the face of a strange woman against aurora stars. Not with a year's planning could I have staged a better backdrop. The stars were everything to the Stakhi, and against those stars I had blue Stakhi eyes.

Gently I unmuzzled him. I knew he wouldn't scream. Not as long as I held his eyes.

"Dzir," I murmured. He shuddered at my touch. "Dzir, do you want to go home?"

He nodded as much as he could in the casket: only a tremor of his lips. He was weeping. He wanted very badly to go home.

"I have a message for you to carry home. Will you do that for me, Dzir?"

His jaw firmed up. His scowl tightened. He was summoning his courage. "Yesh," he mumbled, in Stakhi. "Yesh. My duty."

"Tell your king that the final salvation of his people awaits him in Aurdwynn. Tell him—" And I bit my tongue, checking carefully the words I had prepared, keenly aware that Iscend listened to be sure I did not disobey Hesychast's plan. "Tell him that the bride of the mountains will be Heingyl Ri. Tell him that through their union she will deliver all the milk and grain of Aurdwynn unto the Mansions of the Stakhieczi. Tell your king that if he marries Heingyl Ri he will save his people forever from the Old Foe."

"Heingyl Ree." His head trembled against the brackets that held it in place. "Yesh. Heingyl Ree."

"You came to find a queen for your king. Now you have her. She is Governor Heingyl Ri the Stag Duchess."

"But . . ." He frowned incredibly: the low corners of his mouth almost reached the cabled muscles of his neck. "But the dowry . . . the blood price . . ."

Hesychast had explained his plan quite succinctly. *The solution to the Stakhieczi problem is trivial. We simply give the Necessary King everything he wants. His people will eat our food, and have babies, and very soon there will be too many of them. The Stakhi will starve by the millions without our trade. After that they will never dare invade.*

Hesychast hadn't accounted for one thing, of course.

The Necessary King's honor. The King's need to redeem himself before his court. To show them the woman who had made a fool of him roped from the ceiling, hooks through her ankles, her scalp slashed open to drain her blood through her thoughts.

He would be destroyed if he could not punish his betrayer.

"I have the dowry," I whispered. "I promise that I will deliver the dowry to your king. She is in my grasp now. Yes. I offer as dowry the traitor Baru Cormorant."

* * *

W HO the fuck is that?" Baru said.

Xe had convinced Baru to come out and watch the dawn on Moem's eastern cliffs. Baru found herself in an oddly pleasant mood. A warmth ran between her and Xe. Not the drug rush of infatuation, but a friendly understanding, like a blanket.

She had tried to warn Xe that she might be hurt for association with Baru. The priestess shrugged it off. "All will happen as it must. Take what you have at hand."

Xe's morning calisthenics required one to do everything very slowly. A minute for a single crunch, a pushup held for a hundred count. Baru lost patience after she fell on her face, and started doing her Naval System exercises, huffing and uffing and hissing while Xe posed in the dawnlight with her muscles taut and gleaming. In her effort to avoid staring too much at Xe, Baru watched the sea, and so she saw the boat first.

"Who the fuck is that?"

"Who the fuck is who?" Xe asked.

"Look. Someone's coming in with the tide."

A short lively black-skinned person rowed in toward Moem, their head bowed, their bright yellow khanga hitched up to their knees. When at last the boat bumped up on the rocks, they unloaded a caravan's worth of bundles and bags and bolts. Then, looking up at the mesa towering above them, they sat down in exhausted frustration.

"Let's go help them," Baru said, with a glimmer of suspicion. "I think they might be looking for me."

"Why?"

"I left a message for the Oriati spymaster yesterday. I asked to meet."

"Ah," Xe said, nodding sagely. "And Execarne keeps in touch with the Oriati spymaster. So they would come here to see you. But that can't be their spymaster."

"Why not?"

"Do you see the markings on their throat? The green painted stars? And those golden chains from nose to ear?"

"No, I don't—do you have telescopes in your eyes?"

Xe laughed. "Those are the regalia of an Oriati Federal Prince. The governing sorcerors of the great Oriati Mbo."

"Governing *sorcerors*?"

"Yes, they wield and protect the great trim of nations. They wouldn't do espionage."

"Oh," Baru sighed. "Sure, trim. Whatever that means."

"Don't be so dismissive, Your Majesty. The Oriati are a great and scientific people."

"Did they tell you that themselves?" Baru teased.

"Of course they did." Xe put her hands under her chin (now they were lying side by side to stare over the cliffside). "Duke Unuxekome loved the Oriati. Their ships would come in to Welthony, and we divers would take contracts to clean their hulls."

An absolutely eerie sense of synchronicity came over Baru. It was Unuxekome who'd called for the Oriati fleet's help in attacking Treatymont. And if Ulyu Xe had spent time in Unuxekome's town, maybe she knew some of the ships involved. . . .

"Xe," Baru said, thoughtfully, "do you know where those Syndicate Eyota ships sailed from? Before they stopped on the Llosydanes, I mean?"

"No, not at all. Although . . ."

"Yes? What do you remember?"

"Some of the divers from Welthony mentioned a letter for the Duke Unuxekome, from his mother Unuxekome Ra, who was once Duchess but lives now on Kyprananoke. And I remember thinking, oh, that letter must have come in with the Eyota pirate ships, so they must have come through Kyprananoke, too."

Baru clicked more puzzle pieces together. On the deck of his little mail-ship, *Beetle Prophet,* Unuxekome had told Baru, *I used to dream I was a bastard. My mother sailed with the Syndicate Eyota, see? All those dashing Oriati buccaneers, raiding and adventuring . . .*

So Unuxekome's mother Ra was with the Syndicate Eyota, on Kyprananoke. She might know who had funded Abdumasi Abd's doomed venture. And if those funds came from the Cancrioth and its agents . . . victory.

So Baru would go to Kyprananoke next, to find Unuxekome Ra.

Baru's mission on the Llosydanes was accomplished. She groaned in relief. She had done it, she knew where to go next, and she hadn't betrayed or ruined everyone around her! Except that brief panic—but as long as there were no sign of *actual* Navy-Oriati conflict near the Llosydanes, it would do no harm to date season. . . .

Ulyu Xe looked at her with amusement. "Have you just found last night's satisfaction?"

"Hush, you." Baru leapt to her feet. "Why can't a Federal Prince be a spymaster?"

"It wouldn't be good trim for a Federal Prince to lie. Their trim is entwined with all the people they serve and govern. When they lie it touches all those millions. Ordinarily, I think, there is a shadow ambassador for espionage instead."

Nonsense. A good spy never had to lie. You tell everyone the truth, you tell them exactly what you plan to do: she'd said to Tain Hu, *resistance is meaningless, we must find a way up from within.* And they believe you, they believe in you, and so they cover up your true intentions with their own belief.

"Let's go help them carry their gifts," she said.

THE hardest run is the run downhill. The world wants to pull you forward by your own momentum and dash you down on your face, and you must resist it: the art of running downhill is the art of the controlled descent.

As Baru ran she also descended, lulled by pounding feet and crashing waves into her past.

Fifteen years ago, before pestilent corpses burnt in Taranoke's crater, Baru had been a happy hungry child in the Iriad market. Her appetite could only be satiated by cooked sweet pineapple, brown with extra sugar. Usually her parents bought her some if she was good. But she was not a fledgling bird to be fed by mother! Today she was going to buy her own pineapple.

She simply had to figure out how to convert the little shell in her fist (dug up from the Baru Cormorant Industrial Sand Mine, All Liabilities Guaranteed) into actual money.

"You, kind foreigner!" she called.

A smiling Oriati laman knelt to greet her. Their khanga stretched across narrow knees, high smart brow and full lips all misted in sweat. They smelled of pork smoke and grown-up. Behind them the Iriad Percussion Parade banged on their drums and shouted gladly the news of peace. They'd played the last war with the plainsiders, where Baru hadn't been allowed to watch as her father Salm killed a man and a woman in the circle.

"Kind foreigner," Baru intoned, "what brings you to our market?"

"I am here to trade," the laman said, solemnly.

"Excellent," child-Baru declared. "I have acquired a priceless artifact. This, O most wise lama, is a valve-shell."

"A valve-shell, eh? What does it do?"

"If crushed up and swallowed, it takes the place of an injured heart valve. Feed it every day with a cup of black coffee and a raspberry tart, and it will provide you long and boisterous life."

The laman squinted, stroking their chin. "Why would you sell such a marvel?"

"I already have a full set," Baru boasted, pounding her tiny chest. "I'm immortal. All I ask is a fee of twenty reef pearls, and a signed contract releasing me from all indemnity and malfeasance!"

"Hmm." From their purse the laman extracted fifteen reef-pearl coins, making Baru squeak in greed, and held the coins over Baru's head in a closed fist.

"Fifteen," the laman offered, "and no contract."

"Twenty! And I must have the contract, I am a *legitimate businesswoman*!"

"Fifteen," the laman repeated, and their warm eyes narrowed. "And a lesson, given freely. You have a wonderful soul, child, and the Door in the East must have swung wide to let you into the world. Tell your stories as you please! The world is made of stories, which bind us all together, and impossible stories are the best of all, for they bind us in impossible ways. But remember—remember this well.

"When you use a story to deceive in your own service, the world remembers what you have done. The world knows trim, which is the power that binds. And trim will make your own story echo the stories you tell to others. If you deceive those around you, you will in the end deceive yourself, to your own grief.

"Do you understand?

"Do you understand?"

H ELLO there!" the Prince called. "Are you guests of Faham Execarne?"
        Despite their burden of bundles and gifts, and their obvious exhaustion, they spoke in a high clear voice, each word pronounced with thought and care. Brightly, Baru thought, they spoke brightly.

"We are," Baru called, "we've come to help you up the trail, Your Federal Highness."

"Don't call me that," the laman said, "and please don't lie, either, it's dreadful luck to lie at first meeting."

Baru drew up short. "Excuse me?"

"You're not a guest of Mister Execarne's farm. You came in on *Helbride* yesterday, you turned over the harbormaster's records, caused an exchange panic, and asked my spy to see me."

Baru shot a victorious little *ha* at Xe: see, a spymaster! Xe shrugged.

"You came very promptly," Baru said, "and I'm surprised you're alone."

"How else would I come? You only invited me."

"With security, I'd think."

"But then I'd betray the terms of your invitation. This way trim protects me. Not that I expect you to believe in that protection." They smiled up at Baru, a middle-aged laman of little height but warm forceful presence, like a candle-flame still burning cheerfully in the cold. They had deep black skin, short kinky hair, a fine delicate jaw under the classical high brow. Against that skin they had set a golden khanga wrapped tight down to the waist, then loose like a skirt around wide hips. The embroidered hem of the khanga read, in Aphalone, *Compassion is the surest wind if we only raise our sails.* Golden chains bound their nose to their earlobes, and their throat glistened with green stars and golden lines of paint. Baru thought they were impossibly beautiful.

"I am Tau-indi Bosoka," they said, "Federal Prince of Lonjaro Mbo."

For once Baru had no money metaphor to deploy. The Prince Tau-indi looked priceless, unbuyable, unbendable, a person beyond market.

"Here, this is for you!" The Prince offered Baru a case of inlaid wood. Inside Baru found a gorgeous magnetic compass, the needle mounted on a clever device of steel and exotic rubber: she gasped in delight. Tau turned to Xe. "And for you, miss, I think a pearl will do."

Xe murmured thanks. "Now," Tau-indi Bosoka said, apparently satisfied that this gift-giving had secured them against eavesdroppers or assassins, "let's walk and speak, if you don't mind doing both slowly. Am I mistaken, miss, that you come from Aurdwynn? You have the Maia look."

"No," Baru said, "I'm from—"

But of course Tau-indi had been speaking to Xe.

"Yes," Xe said, "my great-family is from the north."

"The north. Very far from the sea! But your, ah, your general figure and your way of walking, do I presume too much to think you may be a diver?"

Xe nodded. "I am."

"And you did harbor work, perhaps? In Treatymont or Welthony?"

"I did." Baru was by now quite impressed with this Prince's incision. They had come to the same conclusions as Baru.

"Wonderful. I'm looking for a friend who went missing in Aurdwynn during the civil war. Do you know," Tau-indi's voice fell as low as the wind, "a man named Abdumasi Abd? A merchant with shipping interests?"

"I do," Xe said, "I know that name."

"You do?" Tau-indi Bosoka stopped, whirled, and threw out their hands like a beggar. "Oh, bless you, bless you. I can't say how much this means to me. Abd is my dear friend and I've been searching for him for months. Can you tell me—anything at all?"

Xe considered. "The divers who were closest to the Duke Unuxekome told me he had a new ally. An Oriati merchant named Abdumasi Abd. Abd was rich, and bold, and he hated Falcrest—he was building up the Eyota privateers into a full fleet. Unuxekome hoped he'd come to the rebellion's aid."

"Oh." Tau-indi sagged in disappointment, but only for a moment. They summoned cheer and offered their hands to Xe. "Thank you so much. Thank you for remembering my friend."

Baru was again thinking very quickly. Was *this* the secret Iraji and Apparitor had been keeping from her? Tau-indi's interest in Abdumasi Abd?

But Baru had to focus on her own mission. Could this Prince help her destroy Falcrest?

"Your Federal Highness." Baru offered her arm to help them up the cliff. "I wanted to meet you to discuss an arrangement."

"Oh?" Tau smoothed their khanga against their hips. There was a surprising caution in their voice. "Did you?"

"I have extensive access to the ministries and faculties of the Imperial Republic. I can track down anything you might imagine." Baru took a deep, deep breath. "I understand you are a Prince of the Mbo. I know there exist certain tensions, growing tensions, in the relationship between Falcrest and your great nation—"

"Oh, yes," Tau-indi said, soberly, "if we can't stop this war from breaking out, I believe it'll be the end of the world."

Baru blinked. It was very peculiar to hear Farrier's words in this Prince's mouth.

"I'm not mad," Tau said, still quite somber. "The war's why I have to find Abdumasi. Years ago, you see, I mistreated him. That opened a tiny wound in the trim between us. That wound has grown now, and threatens to devour the world."

Baru had no idea what to say to this alien notion. Tau smiled at Xe. "Miss diver, do you know the properties of a wound in trim?"

"A curse, I think," Xe said. "An evil thought."

"Oh no, no. A curse means an ill wish—the opposite of a blessing. But a wound in trim is the absence of all that is human. It exposes the attainted to the world in its natural state, unordered by the human heart. Ha! Look at your face. You *do* think I'm mad." They sighed, without self-pity, with a certain wryness. "It's very hard to convince people the world will end. They insist it's never happened before. But it has, it has ended many times: the Cheetah Palaces fell, and so did the Jellyfish Eaters when Mount Tsunuq erupted. Their worlds ended."

"I don't want a war, either," Baru said, choosing her words very carefully. She very badly wanted the approval of this spymaster-Prince, who was so like the lamen of her childhood. "My home, my *homes,* would be destroyed. But if war is necessary, I have to be sure it ends the right way."

"War's never necessary."

"What if that war destroyed Falcrest?" Baru said.

"I'm sorry." The Prince laughed. "I must have misheard you?"

"Would you go to war with Falcrest if I could guarantee your victory?"

The Prince Tau-indi Bosoka flinched as if snakebitten, and dropped the bundle they'd been holding. Glass and wine shattered at their feet to soak the cloth. "I know you," they said, in a voice soaked like wet paper with fear. "I recognize the way you think. You're Baru Cormorant. You're the Imperial agent from Sieroch."

"Yes," Baru said, retreating a few paces away from the cliff, "yes, that's me. . . ."

"You baited out the Coyote rebellion. You asked Duke Unuxekome to sail against Treatymont."

"It wasn't quite like that—"

"Did you do all that to draw Abdumasi Abd's ships into the rebellion? Did you spark civil war in Aurdwynn only to justify a larger war between Falcrest and Oriati Mbo?" A terrible regal power galvanized their voice, *galvanized,* the word for the hardening of the muscle when seized or lightning-struck. "Did you do this? Tell me the truth! *Were you dispatched by Falcrest to create cause for war?*"

Baru wished that she had her mask. "Wait. Wait wait wait." She held up her hands: now she wished for gloves. "I'm making you an offer, Your Federal Highness. I have access to the very highest levels of Imperial strategy. I can tell you *anything* you need to know to defeat them—"

"It's already in you," Tau-indi breathed, staring up at Baru in rapturous horror. They shrugged off their pack and dropped their bundles. Wonderful porcelain smashed on the rock. Wooden jars of precious stones tumbled into the sea. "The wound is in you. Oh, principles save us, it is growing now. I will have nothing to do with you."

Swiftly they wheeled to Ulyu Xe. "Diver miss, please tell Faham that the situation has changed, and I can no longer protect him."

"What do you mean?" Baru hissed. "Wait a moment—"

But the Prince had utterly blanked her out. "Tell Faham that despite his countermeasure he still has a mole in his station. Yesterday someone left a letter in the post addressed to Rear Admiral Juris Ormsment. I obtained a copy. It tells Ormsment that her quarry has gone to ground at the Morrow Ministry station here, on this very island. Ormsment landed yesterday. She has the letter by now."

"What!" Baru shouted. "A mole? Who—is there any name, any sign—?"

Tau-indi seized Xe's hands so fiercely that even the stoic diver winced. "I can't protect you, do you understand? My people cannot allow the prisoners here to fall into the navy's hands. You know too much that could drive your Parliament to war. Despite my protest, our Jackals are on their way to this island to take you all away.

"And now Ormsment's marines are coming, too. If you don't move quickly, the war could begin *right here*."

THE MASK BENEATH THE MESA

BARU stumbled in through the farmhouse door, gasping and huffing, to ruin everyone's day. The herbalist Yythel saw Baru first. She made a face for snakes and maggots. "It's her again."

"We're compromised." Baru gasped. "Mister Execarne. An Oriati Prince named Tau-indi Bosoka came here to tell you that you're compromised. They said they couldn't protect you anymore, that Ormsment and the Jackals were coming—"

"Hm." Execarne rubbed his beard in thought. "Probably another game. They do like to rattle me. What did Tau bring as a gift? A watch, a book? Maybe another puzzle?"

"A gift? They had pearls, ointments, perfumes, bolts of fabric, this compass they gave me—"

"Shit!" Execarne dropped his coffeepot to shatter, ripped his crossbow off its hook, and began to kick the benches over, scattering Ude, Run, and Yythel in shouting protest. "Get up! Get up, we're compromised! We have to go now! You lot, line up on that wall!"

Yawa's eyes accused. Was this you?

Baru put up her hands helplessly: not I, not I!

General chaos. Execarne began rooting around in a bottle of drugged candies. "That many gifts," he grumbled, "*that* many, it's got to be real, got to be, but I shut up the leak, I know I did."

"You had a leak," Yawa said.

"Yes, but I handled it thoroughly. Jackals *and* Ormsment . . . what the fuck is Ormsment doing down here?"

"Province Admiral Ormsment's gone rogue," Yawa said. "She's hunting us. Her ship arrived yesterday."

Execarne thought about this, grimaced, and swallowed another pellet. "All right," he said. "Do you have a ship?"

"The clipper *Helbride*. Offshore to the south."

"You'd better signal her to come in, then."

"Already done," Iscend said. The Clarified woman moved with swift grace and authority, and she smiled. This was what she had been trained for, and she was glad to inhabit her purpose. Even the prisoners had stopped shouting to listen to her. "Execarne, where's your line of escape?"

"Down." Execarne slipped a bolt into his crossbow. "Into the Ministry station."

"I thought *this* was the Ministry station," Baru protested.

Execarne's pupils grew enormously. He growled low in his stomach as some drug silvered his blood. "Of course not," he said. "This is just a mask. A happy theater for the prisoners. The station's underneath us. In the drainage caves."

"Excellent." Iscend lifted Yawa to her feet. "The entrance must be the well?"

"Just a moment." Execarne cocked the crossbow with a grunt. "I've got to shoot these people. Can't leave them to be captured. Miss Cormorant, would you hold that door shut?"

"*Shoot us!?*" Ake shouted. "You can't do that—you told us we'd get a trial!"

"Probably would have, too." Execarne took aim. "Sorry. I liked you all. Except you, Nitu, you're an utter boor. But you could start a war, in the wrong courtroom. Hold still, now."

"Wait!" Baru roared. These were Tain Hu's beloved! These were the people who would rule Aurdwynn and achieve the Coyote dream! *"Don't shoot!"*

The door behind Baru opened. The motion caught Execarne's eye. He whirled.

Ulyu Xe came through.

Execarne shot her.

The crossbow quarrel went through her left eye like the fatal image of an archon and killed her instantly. Without even a cry Xe fell against Baru who caught her without any surprise. Dead, of course, of course, the day after they fucked, as predictable as the turn of the seasons.

"Hello," Xe said, with mild curiosity. "Why did you trip me?"

Baru nearly shrieked. Execarne had never fired, Ulyu had just tripped over Baru's foot as she whirled, and thus fell, gracefully, into Baru's arms.

"I'm sorry!" Baru cried, and then, remembering the leveled crossbow, she whirled back to Execarne—"No, wait! Don't shoot! I'll get them all out safely!"

The prisoners had by now formed a makeshift phalanx in front of the fireplace. Ake led the line with chopsticks in her fist. Ude brandished an empty bottle, Nitu bellowed and waved her fists, and Run had seized a walking stick. The herbalist Yythel seemed to be going through the cabinets for anything poisonous. Dziransi stood before them with his arms open and his fungus eyes shining mad:

"Try to kill me," he bellowed, "I am *chosen*! I had a dream from the hammer!"

"No one's dying here!" Baru shouted. "Ake, please, wait. Execarne, wait. I promise I'm going to get you out."

"Of *course* you are," Yythel said. "Just like you got the duchess Vultjag out."

"I believe her." Xe rolled to her feet. "She *did* get the duchess out, remember? And all of us. It was Her Grace's choice to come back."

Baru was not actually sure how to proceed. She had no hope of guiding her vultjagata to safety across open ground—not against trained soldiers. And there were far too many of them to send down a well one at a time.

Baru threw away the physical solutions, and reached for her own powers.

"You'll turn yourselves over to the Oriati," she said. "Execarne, that's it, that's what we do—send them to the Oriati. Send them to the Oriati and ask for asylum in the care of Prince Tau-indi Bosoka."

"And then what?" Nitu the cook shouted. "The tunks experiment on us? They pierce us with metals and put worms in our legs?"

"Then," Baru said, thinking it out as she spoke, "the Prince Bosoka sends you home to Aurdwynn. Ake, please, you still have my letter? The letter with the polestar seal? Tell the Prince that the Emperor will be pleased if you're delivered safely home. Tell the Prince that it could help avert war. Just don't mention my name—"

"Why not?" Ake demanded.

"Just go, go, please, this is your only chance!"

A strange light cast new shadows over them.

Iscend looked out the window. "Rockets," she said, smiling in anticipation of the new services she could perform, the extinction of fires and the mollification of wounds.

Sulane's first volley crashed down on the farm.

FALCREST did not make explosives. Falcrest made incendiaries. Leave the fireworks and stupid guns to the Oriati, whose experimental cannon could batter a wooden ship for hours without sinking it. Why load a frigate with so much heavy useless weaponry, when a single Burn rocket could raze a ship to ribs and keel?

Flash powder was good for this and that, of course. Signal fireworks. Grenades.

And the occasional dazzle.

Sulane's rockets blew up in chains of white light and migraine noise. Shock killed the little birds on Faham's farm. The dog barked and barked and cried. Baru hid beneath the table with her arms wrapped around her head and her heart jumping at every bang.

Someone pulled her up—Execarne. He grinned wolfishly, high as a frog-licker, and said something which looked like "Yawa's off to the races!" Baru followed his pointing hand. Iscend Comprine had dragged Yawa outside, toward the farm well, the well, they had to get to the well.

Baru grabbed Ulyu Xe. "The well! Go to the well!"

Then she crawled to Ake, who'd maybe never seen fireworks in her life: she was pinned to the floor, mumbling and clawing at her ears. Baru grabbed her by the chin. "GET THE OTHERS! GET THEM AND GO! FIND THE ORIATI!"

Dziransi reached for Ake and drew her toward the door. The woman looked back at Baru in terror, and then, as if astonishing herself, held up Baru's letter of governorship. *This?* she seemed to ask. *This is real?*

Yes, Baru nodded. Yes. Take it. Go home. Rule Vultjag.

"Nitu!" the herbalist Yythel shouted. "Nitu, wait!"

But the cook had decided to get as far from Baru as she could. She was feeling her way along the north wall, toward the door there. Yythel lunged after her, but she was dazed and half-blind and couldn't reach her friend in time.

The door opened. The cook was through and gone.

Ake and Dziransi stumbled outside. Yythel, Ude, and Run went after them. Baru prayed they'd reach the Oriati before Ormsment found them.

"I should go with them," Xe said. "They need me."

"No!" Baru said, from her heart, and then, thinking now of the danger Xe would be in at her side, of the terrible fate that haunted her path, "Yes, yes, go, quickly."

Xe's lips brushed Baru's ear. "Remember," she said, "you are *not* alone."

And she was gone, too.

Execarne peeked out the door behind her. "Jackal grenadiers out there. At least ten of them, coming in from the east. They'll want me alive, I think."

He tore the back off a wine cabinet and produced two leathery masks with glazed eyes and bulbous sponge filters over the mouth. As he put his on he cracked the ampule of filtersoak in the nose. Baru tried the same: sharp alcohol stink flooded her sinuses. She coughed, and swore, and through the watercolor smear of the lenses saw Execarne reaching out to her.

"We have to go!"

Baru and Execarne linked hands—the old man's grip fierce, his face wild with exhilaration—and ducked through the door. Up on the east ridge, tall lanky shapes moved against the sunrise. Oriati grenadiers with black faces, bright eyes, long rapiers. Bombs with thick oily fuses dangled from colorful bandoliers. They looked too wonderful to be real.

Thirty feet away the well beckoned to them with its swinging pump-arm. Iscend and Yawa had already gone down.

The ringing in Baru's ears died down to a thin hum. Now from the north and west came the sound of voices.

WE ARE THE FIST OF THE PEOPLE. WE ARE THE HAND OF THE
   MASK.
CAST DOWN YOUR WEAPONS. LOWER YOUR NAKED FACES.
WE ARE HERE.

THE stars fell.

Sulane arced a constellation of rocket flares over the island and the hot light burned the images of the Oriati grenadiers onto Baru's eyes.

Then the saltgrass on the western edge of the farm made a sound like cut violin-string. Crossbow bolts caught flare light: starlight shrapnel. Grenadiers hit in the face, in the chest, in the prickled hands and pierced knees.

Out of the grass came the red-masked marines. They did not fire or make any sound. On their harnesses they carried blood tampons and corkwrapped cylinders of oil and grenades and ropes and long knives cold and slim and thirsty.

The Oriati threw grenades. Dirt fountained. Grass cratered. The silence died again.

Baru bolted for the well. Execarne came after. Baru thought she might have pissed herself but couldn't be sure: Wydd preserve her, Hu had fought in this, she had fought and kept her head and lived, the woman eternally a marvel. Baru tripped and stumbled and got up again into a three-limbed scuttle, headfirst right into the rim of the well. She fell back stunned.

An Oriati grenade blurred across her vision, trailing its throwing-rope, and in the colorless sketch of her periphery it struck a Masquerade marine in the chest. It *stuck*. The marine looked at it with expressionless masked awareness, and tried to fold himself up. A sharp *crack* and a punch of air that threw up ground dust all around, as if the skin of a sandy beach had jumped, rabbit-like. It made Baru blink. When she looked again, the marine's chest rig had split, his armored chest stove in: beneath the rim of his mask a huge splinter of fragment had gone up through his chin and palate.

Baru fumbled around till she found a gutcord ladder and swung herself over into the well.

Down. Down quickly. She scrambled down wet echoing stone. Someone shadowed the light above her—Execarne, singing madly, "Oh, the women of the veldt are rough to the touch, they'll grind your hands to flour, and the buckle on your belt will rust right shut, when the veldt wife turns her glower, but hark now lad just lie on your back, you do not know your power, she's grown to a lass on the flat endless grass, no she's never seen a tower—"

A crossbow grenade hit the rim of the well and tumbled past Baru. Somehow she could read the label before the grenade fell away and slapped into water far below.

DANGER RAPID ACTION

CHEMICAL SMOKE MECHANISM—PEPPERSEED FILLER

FOR FLUSHING AND DISPERSAL

"The ledge!" Execarne shouted, and his voice boomed off the walls, the ledge, the ledge edge edge! Baru kicked down and found a solid rocky step, tarred and sanded for footing. She put her weight on the stone, reached out for something to lean on, and fell through a heavy canvas curtain into the Morrow Ministry station.

She landed arms-first on a putrid corpse.

EXECARNE lit a slow-burning flare. White light sputtered out across raw stone corridor, chalked wall-signs, moldered fabric, and the festering dead flesh under Baru's hands. She roared in disgust: the mask alone saved her from obscene stink, but her bare hands were in cold rot to the wrist.

"That shriveled little ballsack!" Execarne shook his fist at the corpse. "He was trying to climb into my *well*! The fucking gall of him!"

Baru leapt up wringing her hands in loathing and, seizing on the nearest clean cloth, wiped her hands on Execarne's jacket. "Sorry," she mumbled, when he stared at her. "Who the fuck is this?"

"Faham Execarne," Faham Execarne said. He stripped off the jacket and draped it over the dead man's head.

"*What?*"

From a purse on his belt "Execarne" produced a silver seal ringed in tiny chiseled codes. "I really am Morrow Ministry. I'm just not the exact Morrow Ministry agent you think I am. Come on. I'll explain while we go."

He trotted off down the narrow stone slot. Baru chased him into a domed cave easily as large as Execarne's house, lit from above by a mirrored shaft, furnished with card tables, shelves, a gallery of landscape paintings, even a rack of bottles.

There were corpses everywhere. Dead men and women in plain Falcresti dress scattered across chairs and tables. Mouths and noses red with poison foam. Hands spidered. Faces contorted in agony. Baru had seen that agony before, at Haraerod, when Purity Cartone used war gas on Nayauru.

"You *gassed* them," Baru said, numbly. "You gassed the Morrow Ministry station."

"I certainly did." Execarne hopped across a cluster of bowel-stained dead and made for the far door. "Slowly at first, mind. By the time I dispersed the good stuff I don't think they could even move. Come on."

Baru smashed a bottle from the alcohol rack and washed her hands. The corpses were fresh. Xe had implied she'd been here for weeks, at least. Therefore, Execarne had gassed them *recently,* much more recently than he'd arrived here—therefore he'd probably worked with these people before killing them—so why would Execarne have gassed his own station?

Because he had good relations with the Oriati spymaster Tau-indi Bosoka.

Baru snatched up her best theory. "This isn't your station. Or, at least, you're not usually here. You came here from Falcrest."

"Mm-hmm."

"To handle vital work. The interrogation of these prisoners?"

"Might be."

"Tau-indi came here for the same work, but from the Oriati side. You two knew each other; you conspired to keep the peace. And they told you someone in your station was a mole. A mole for who? Who were you afraid would learn about the prisoners?"

"Does it matter?" He beckoned from the corridor's mouth. "I ran out of time to flush the mole from Execarne's station, so I just burnt the entire asset. They deserved it anyway." He spat on the nearest corpse: a woman in a sundress, convulsed by mortis across her reading desk. "They tested war gas down here. On living Sydani. People are always dying and vanishing on these islands. What's a few more? I don't like that. So I tested their own war gas on them."

"And you left the bodies to rot?" Baru howled.

"Sure. You think I was going to risk coming down here to clean up?"

She had to admit a certain bleak sense there. "Do I call you Execarne, still?"

"That's as good a legend as any. Do you mind if we move on? Someone else is in here."

"What?" Baru hissed.

Execarne raised his crossbow. "Someone beat us down here."

"Yes, Yawa and Iscend were ahead of us—"

"No. There's someone else." He tapped the snout of his mask, where the sponge filter must obscure all scent. "I can *smell* them."

"You can't smell anything."

"Bad trim stinks," he said, which was the first time Baru realized he might be mad.

THE heart of the station was a crack in the world.

Eons of water flowing down from Moem mesa had carved a tall thin chasm in the rock. Narrow wooden walkways let them cross beneath enormous anchor-chains. Just as in the Elided Keep, the Morrow Ministry had safeguarded its files and secrets in huge swaying gridwork shelves, hanging all around them in frightful suspension, each volume insulated from the humid cave by sacks of gut as the whole library poised on the edge of precipice.

"Good Devena," Baru breathed.

Execarne pointed her to a corroded steel lever. "Push that." He knelt to align tiny codewheels. Baru had a general policy of never pulling unlabeled levers, but given the circumstances she would do anything to get out of this labyrinth before Tain Shir's gore-spackled mask peeled itself from the shadows.

She threw the lever. With a tortured shriek a gear engaged and pulled a cable. High above mechanisms of brute steel struggled, screamed, and turned. Pins clattered out of their sockets.

All around them, in creaking unison, the shelves of secrets dropped to their doom in the flooded depths below.

"Burn the asset," Execarne said, with manic intensity. "Don't let them know what we know. Come on—come on—"

She hurried after him. Darkness and dead lamps. Panting grunting flight through corridors so narrow they had to squeeze sideways through necks of dripping stone. "Where are we going?" Baru shouted. "Where's the way out?"

"It's compromised!" Execarne shouted. "We'll use the gliders!"

"*Gliders?*"

"It's been two centuries since a woman went aloft on a kite," Execarne said, "I don't understand why everyone's so afraid of cutting the mooring."

"You're mad!"

"I'm optimistic!"

"You're *extremely* high!"

"That helps, yes!"

They burst out of the maze into a stone-cut hall supported by columns of natural rock. Execarne ripped his mask off. Baru tried the air, and nearly wept with relief. She could smell the sea. The sea! And there, ahead, the faint light of the sun, they were almost free.

A hand seized Baru's right shoulder. A papery whisper in her ear. *"She's here."*

Baru froze in terror. Yawa's gloved finger crept to her lip. *"Shush. She's hunting."*

"Who's hunting," Execarne whispered. "Your viper girl?"

"Yes. Iscend. She's gone to find her—"

"Who?"

A whipcrack voice echoed down the gallery. A woman's bark of command. "Gaios! *Gaios!* Walk!"

Yawa hissed in dismay. Baru knew exactly why.

Someone was shouting Iscend Comprine's command word.

THEY wait at the mouth of the north tunnel for the moment to attack. Her marines check the soak on their filters. A soft rustling of masks and canteens. The Oriati do not ordinarily use gas, but their scouts have already penetrated the Ministry station. By now they may have stolen any number of weapons.

Tain Shir plunges her own filter into her canteen and fits it into her mask and her lungs fill up with a sharp ether stink like something you would only drink when already drunk. Ormsment commanded Shir to slip her marines in ahead of *Sulane*'s bombardment and secure the Ministry station below the surface. The admiral hopes that when Baru flees she will flee below. Shir obeys this plan because it is in accordance with her own.

She has come to Moem as a teacher. She has a lesson to impart today.

Yesterday she found the letter left for her at the Eddyn mailhouse. *Baru is going to the Morrow Ministry station on Moem. Baru needs your lessons, Shir.* She swam to Moem in the night and arranged her blind among the saltgrass. Beneath the pale aurora she watched as Baru seduced the diver. She felt no shame in her voyeurism for the satisfaction of another woman's appetite is as uninteresting to her as a cow's progress on its cud.

What matters is the lie. The lie that Baru Cormorant ever loved her cousin Hu. See how she takes her satisfaction with another woman. See how she does not even pretend to mourn.

Hu was deceived.

In the middle hours of the candle watch, Shir returned to *Sulane* and the province admiral. "Baru is here. She is on Moem. It may be a trap."

She watched the rage sluice through the Admiral. Juris Ormsment has been building millwork to harness her fury. "We'll strike at dawn," she commanded.

Dawn has come. Today Shir teaches a lesson. A lesson for Baru on the nature of the world she has chosen to inhabit.

F IVE," the sergeant at the front of the column calls. "Four three two one go."

He swings around the corner into the black mouth of the tunnel. His crossbow searches for targets. Shir comes around after him. They go down into the Ministry station two by two so that if they are shot they can drag each other to cover. In the narrow stone slots they have no shields and must gamble entirely on speed.

Shir hears Oriati cries echoing through the bowels of the mesa. "They've found bodies," she tells the sergeant, translating the Takhaji battle language. "Something killed the Ministry staff. The Oriati fear gas or plague."

"Do we go on?" he asks.

She puts a hand on the join of his shoulder and his throat. "Don't stop."

In the station's north bunkroom Falcresti corpses have soaked rotting into their feather mattresses. Ten Oriati grenadiers in steel cuirasses and colorful spinal flags circle the chamber with rags at their mouths. They are giving the dead last blessings for their voyage through the Door.

"Flare," Shir whispers.

The sergeant kneels at the door and rips a flare grenade off his chest ring and the ring engages the grenade just as meant and crushes the interior compartments so all the chemicals mix. The sergeant stares at the conjured fire in his fist as if shocked it worked. The training grenades do not burn: the chemicals are too precious.

"Throw," Shir reminds him.

He skitters the flare into the bunkroom and it bursts up in a jet of hot sparks, spinning and shrieking and hurling itself between bedposts. The Oriati cry out. Shir leads her column around the corner and they split to follow the walls so the confused Oriati are doubly enveloped. Shouts and clamor among the corpse-racked beds. Shir shoots the nearest man in the throat and her repeating crossbow kicks in her arms and although it does not have the armor-piercing strength of a proper storm crossbow she works the lever and in a second it is ready to fire again. Marine crossbows clatter all around her. The Oriati duck behind the beds. A marine accidentally shoots another marine on the opposite wall but the slender repeater bolts will not penetrate marine harness.

The Oriati captain cries out, "Swords up, bravos! Back to back!"

Too close in for shots now. Too much clutter. Long knives come out and the Oriati raise fists wrapped in tough rope to challenge the masked marines all around them with the gallant shining length of their rapiers. Shir advances between the beds and then she is upon the Oriati captain who steps at her grinning to stop her with the point of his rapier. Shir grabs the post of the bunk bed to her right and with a grunt topples bed and mattresses and corpses down upon the captain. When he sidesteps nimbly his eyes go up to the falling dead and his rapier pivots a little away. Shir steps in, knife leading, past the rapier, into his arms. She stabs him under the chin and withdraws and stabs his eye and withdraws and stabs his face through the boneless aperture of the nose and he is smiling no more.

Shir drops his corpse on his dead comrades.

They search the dead. Tactical clerks kneel to stamp rapid notes on the origin and armament of the Oriati grenadiers. Time stamps crunch as the clerks break the mechanisms of the single-use clocks to certify and seal that this record was made at exactly this time and date.

"What happened down here?" her sergeant hisses, pointing to the dead Morrow-men. "Did an experiment go wrong?"

"They lost someone's trust," Shir says. For she knows the stakes of the One Trade.

They proceed south through the dead stone maze of the poisoned station. *Sulane*'s rockets send rumbles and crashes through the stone above. The surface teams have scattered heavy smoke to seek out vents and secret entrances to the Ministry station, and now that smoke pours down to haze the cave air.

Just north of the station archive Shir finds a team from the surface assault coming down a hidden stair, dragging a plump woman who shares Shir's Maia blood.

"Prisoner, mam," the team sergeant reports, "she's asked us for asylum from Baru Cormorant. I thought I should get her safely belowground and wait out the assault."

Shir seizes the woman by the chin. She stares back with sullen defiance. Another daughter of Aurdwynn cast to the ringing wind.

"Who are you?"

"Nitu," the woman says, spitefully. "I'm just a cook."

Shir smiles beneath her mask. Shir asks her question.

"Does Baru Cormorant pretend to love you?"

BARU would have run, if there were anywhere to go.

Tain Shir was upon her. Tain Shir born out of the light and the sea wind. A behemoth crusted in gore and instruments of killing. Iscend Comprine retreated before her like a charmed cobra, and each time Shir snapped "Gaios!" Iscend sighed like a phantom hand had caressed her cheek.

"King's gallstones," Execarne breathed. "The Bane of Wives."

"She's not his anymore," Yawa said. She'd stepped in front of Baru, who almost shoved her aside to protect her; but fear had rooted her to the spot.

The terrible ugly grace of her. The brutal indifference. Nothing in nature could ever be so violent. Look at a white bear rolling in the gore of its kill and you will see the primordial savagery which civilization struggles to escape. But it is still a bear. You still know what it wants, and at worst it will kill you for sport.

Look at Tain Shir and you cannot fathom the name behind the cartouche. You cannot extract her reasons. You only see why men turn to religion: for hope that there are gods to oppose her.

"Guard your charge." Shir pointed with two lazy fingers to Xate Yawa. "See to my aunt. Gaios."

Iscend leapt to Yawa's side. "I told you to cripple her," Yawa muttered, as if trying to comment on a distasteful dish at a party without bothering the host. "Not to obey her every command."

"My lady," Iscend whispered, in a voice of paroxysmic rapture, "she serves our Throne, she is moved by the hand that moves us all! She knows the word!"

"You useless idiot." Yawa sighed.

Baru shook herself. "The crossbow," she muttered to Execarne. "Use the crossbow—"

"Right," he said, and dropped the crossbow on the stone floor.

Baru groaned.

"What?" he pleaded. "You expect me to take a shot at *her*? If I don't get her with the first bolt, I know what happens!"

"Baru," Shir rumbled. "Come forward. Nitu, come out now. Show yourself."

Oh no.

The portly cook ambled forward from the shadows behind Shir. "Hello," she said, cheerily. "I've been drugged and I feel *wonderful*. Look, it's Baru! Oh, Baru, I hope you die."

A hideous, prolonged scrape as Shir drew a machete from her hip. "Stop," Baru cried, driven by panic to *act,* to charge forward and grapple with the horror rather than wait for it to reach her: this was always her choice. "Don't hurt her! She's not part of this!"

"She's not part of this?" The mask tilted. A great sheet of clotted blood peeled off to shatter silently on the stone. "She's not of this world?"

"What?" Baru gaped at the non sequitur, and then, racing ahead, trying to follow Shir's thoughts, "no, she's part of the world like anyone else, but she's not part of *this!*"

"*This* is the world. You have made it so." Shir set the cold edge of the machete against Nitu's throat. "Do you love her? Do you care for her life?"

"Tain Hu loved her!"

"You killed Tain Hu."

"I didn't want to, damn you."

"Do you want this woman to die?"

Baru hardly knew her, except as a reliable source of winter meals. Baru thought it very important that she care anyway: for if she lost that, the ability to care for a stranger, what human credential did she have left?

"I don't want her hurt," she said.

"Then here is my bargain." Shir's voice came up at them like low fire through the brush. Execarne, through drug-addled tremors, moaned in awe. "Your life or Nitu's. Who do I kill? You choose."

Baru stood there with her fists at her sides, trembling with rage. "That's not *necessary.*"

"Why is this choice unnecessary, when it was necessary for Tain Hu to die?"

"There's nothing compelling this choice on you! It's not the *same!*"

"You're free to do whatever you please." The machete twitched. Nitu cooed in drugged rapture and stroked the blade. "I only arrange the consequences. Consequences for choices. That's my aunt's business. Isn't it, dear Aunt Yawa?"

"Your father's alive." Yawa's voice like ringing steel: struck hard, but still strong. "Let us go, child. Let me save your father."

"Certainly I will let you go, dear aunt. If Baru tells me to kill this cook, then you can carry on your spider work." The terrible blue stillness of her eyes. The single human finger bone notched among her crossbow bolts. "Surely, Baru, you don't love this cook more than you loved Tain Hu?"

The transitive property of human lives. If Baru's mission is more important than Tain Hu, and Tain Hu is more important than the cook, then the mission is more important than the cook. And the cook should die.

The mesa inhaled. Sea wind roared into the cave. Tain Shir stank of death.

"It's not the same," Baru protested. "Those terms were set by the Throne. A power that holds the *world*—I couldn't change the terms. You, though, you could walk away right now. Please, Shir." The name a thorn in her tongue. "I remember you. I remember when I saw you at Farrier's wool stand. There's no reason you have to do this."

"I'm not doing this," Shir said, with terrible distance. "You are. You set the terms. This is your choice, it is the shape of you, to spend people for power. I am your teacher now. I am going to force this choice on you. Here, and in the next place you go, and the next, and the next, I will force this choice on you forever. And so you will live in a world governed by the laws you have chosen."

"You don't even know what I *want*!"

"I don't care." Her spare hand settled on a grenade: DANGER INCENDIARY DANGER ADHESIVE ALL-PURPOSE BURN. "I kill you, or I kill this woman. Later the choice will come again. The diver will be next. Then your parents."

Baru neither screamed nor sagged in horror. She did the one thing she had always done when overcome. She thought. With exacting, scrupulous detail she thought of Ulyu Xe pinned to a tree by a bolt through her chest. She thought of Pinion and Solit bound inverted upon great wooden wheels and hacked open from groin down to throat so the chevrons of their ruptured bodies were chalices for the insects and the birds. She thought of these icons of horror and she thought of them as the result of her choices. For if she proceeded as she always had, by giving up a life to gain a little more progress, then Shir would offer her these choices forever, and forever she would be forced to choose.

Surely she could justify *any* sacrifice. To stop now would be to betray those lives she'd already spent . . . and the more lives she spent, the more reason she had to sacrifice even more . . .

She was trapped.

But she forced herself (and force it was, like peeling herself naked from a frozen steel plate, straining her skin until it tore and wept) to think logically. If she survived this moment, she could reach *Helbride*. She would have access to the Throne's resources again. Shir was only one mortal woman. Shir could be killed.

One life could be invested to achieve that goal. Hadn't Baru's choices already slaughtered thousands? One more life. Only do not look at her eyes.

"All right," Baru said. "Kill her."

The machete moved.

EXECARNE carried her screaming to the glider ledge.

Through pain like a red sun Baru saw the green-gray sea tossing below, *Helbride*'s sails in the near distance, the rows of wood-and-canvas gliders that waited on their hooks above.

She could only scream.

In place of Nitu's life, Tain Shir had macheted off two fingers of Baru's right hand.

Execarne had watched it happen. Iscend had physically restrained Yawa from interfering. Nitu had wandered off cooing and insensate. Shir's machete the last thing Baru remembered before—the *cut*—

"Hold her arm," Yawa ordered. "Execarne, you're biggest. Hold her down."

I've definitely pissed myself, Baru thought. What had she lost? Did she use those two fingers for anything important? Would she still be any good in bed? Could she still *write*?

The alcohol bandage went on first. Baru's stumps performed combinatoric operations on the possible varieties of screaming pain. She'd burnt out her throat: all she had now was a whispering sandy tube. Yawa was tying on the outer bandages, tight, too tight; Baru managed to shriek, "For fuck's *sake,* Yawa!"

"Marines are coming," Iscend snapped.

"Shit. Keep her still—"

"She's strong."

"She's just a woman, Execarne, you can hold her!"

"How anti-egalitarian of you, Yawa."

Execarne tried to force a pellet of wax or gum into Baru's mouth and Yawa slapped it aside. "You can't drug her, you ass. She needs to keep her blood up. You'll kill her."

"If she struggles in the glider, I can't control it—"

"Baru!" Yawa slapped her on the cheek. "Baru, you've got to be still! Do you hear me? Stop writhing and be still! I need you alive, damn you!"

The pain was in her right hand. Baru glanced left. The pain went. Something was still very wrong with her but now it didn't seem so urgent.

"How do these work?" she croaked, and pointed, left-handed, at the gliders. "I've never seen one before . . . the construction is ingenious, but I doubt that it's light enough to fly like a kite. Without a mooring, they'd be impossible to control, wouldn't they?"

"She's addled," Execarne said.

"No," Yawa said, with a softness like relief. "This is normal."

Hands lifted her. Ropes and leather buckles clasped like surrogate arms. Now she lay on Execarne's broad warm back in the glider's harness. His feet rocked against the stone: he was crouching and uncurling, warming himself up. Baru squinted up at the canvas wing overhead. She knew very little about aeronics. Didn't gliders usually flutter out of control and plunge?

"You'll need a little speed," Execarne said to Iscend, who had harnessed Yawa onto her own back. "So dive at first, get the air moving under the wings, and then glide out toward *Helbride*. Don't let the prow come up. When you strike the water the glider will float, that's how we always land, but you must get out of the harness, understand?"

"I understand," Iscend said, smiling blissfully. "I'm to protect Xate Yawa. The word was given."

Yawa met Baru's eyes. She looked immensely, sourly displeased. Baru tried to signal back to her that at least *she* still had all her fingers. Then Iscend crouched, and kicked, and her whole glider slid forward above her on the wooden rack until she leapt off the cliff and the glider tore free with an enormous shudder and vanished from Baru's sight.

Execarne tested his footing. "I think I'm high enough to do this," he said.

A harsh shout came from behind: "Stop! Stop right there!"

"Oh *shit*," Execarne growled, and he ran forward grunting, and then—

BRINE slapped at Baru's face. She howled in dismay. She'd grayed out! *She'd missed the flight!* "Go back," she snarled, desperate to experience such a marvel. "Go back, do it again!" Then she felt Execarne beneath her, unmoving, and saw the bright blood pooling around the glider: they'd landed on the wavetops, the glider's wing settling above them.

Execarne had been shot. A bolt jutted from his right shoulder. He was breathing but he would not move.

Baru reached around to untie herself from him and smashed her stumped fingers against the harness. Pain like sickness. For a while she could only curl and yawn in agony. Then, determinedly, she put both her hands underwater and found the buckles. Execarne dropped free with Baru still bound to him. A wave crashed over them and they sank. Baru kicked and stroked, her wet stumps numb now, roiling brine all around her, and everywhere the bladdered ash-kelp that Baru had once gathered for glassmaking. To the surface. To the surface. Where the fuck was the surface? Was that the moon—swim for the moon, Baru!

The moon swam toward her. The moon itself. A silver crescent in the darkness, fast approaching. Why, that wasn't a trick of light—something *real* was coming toward her—maybe the moon was death itself—

Baru gurgled and clawed upward.

An eye stared at her. A great white eye. And beneath it a small black second eye, glittering—the two eyes swept past and in hallucinatory sequence Baru saw a silver crescent moon, a gnarled mass of brain coral, a human skull, a black door sweeping toward her—

Something struck Baru and smashed her to the surface. She gasped for air, kicked, and arched Execarne's weight across her chest and stomach, lifting his head, at least, above the water. He gurgled the water he'd inhaled.

Baru smelled fire.

Ormsment's frigate *Sulane* stood silhouetted against Moem in a holocaust of burning timber and arching rockets. Two Oriati ships had tried to swarm the frigate—dromon galleys with banks of oars, nimble and quick, well-suited to fights near shore—and Ormsment had destroyed them. A third dromon closed with *Sulane* nose-on to ram. A fourth fled east, her oars working like millipede legs, and that galley alone flew the gold-and-jade banner: the Oriati Prince's ship, Tau-indi's ship, protected by diplomatic right. *Sulane* fired no rockets after her.

Baru gasped in relief. Xe and the rest of Tain Hu's house were, with any luck, aboard that ship, going home.

Where was *Helbride*? Where was Apparitor?

The third dromon swung aside at the last moment, baring her flank to *Sulane*'s nose. Explosions boomed and crackled down her side: a weapon that shot puffs of smoke from little black tubes. In wonder Baru watched blurred projectiles skip off *Sulane*'s copper-jacketed hull.

Whatever the weapon might be, it didn't work.

Sulane's rocketeers swept the dromon's deck with their hwachas. Marines tossed incendiary grenades down onto the Oriati ship. It drifted away in a pyre of wood and sailcloth, oars dragging in the waves, ropes curling and lashing in the flame.

A few rogue rockets had landed on the islands nearby Moem.

The date groves were burning.

When she looked down from the fire, Iraji was reaching for her, Iraji in *Helbride*'s whaleboat, Yawa and Iscend and a gaggle of sailors behind him. She groaned and arched again to get Execarne up from the water, and then she tried to get to Iraji's hand. Their fingertips slipped. A sailor grabbed Baru with a boathook, tangling it in the harness that bound her to Execarne, and dragged them in.

"Your hand," Iraji gasped. "Your hand's hurt—Baru, why are you tied to the Morrow Minister?"

"He's the Morrow Minister?" He'd said he came here from Falcrest, to look after vital intelligence work—but she hadn't thought he would be *the* spymaster, the lord of all Falcrest's agents. "Oh."

Yawa took Execarne gently in her arms and cut him free of Baru. "Old fool," she murmured, checking the bloody crossbow bolt. "You old fool, you should have been faster. Ach. He might live. If the wound stays clean."

She tore off her mask and threw it into the bilgewater. Baru flinched and tried to guard her wounded hand, which bumped against her shoulder and made her curl up yawning in agony again. Yawa's alien blue eyes measured everything: only, when Baru twisted to put Yawa on her blind right, she thought Yawa looked confused and lost, not cruel.

"We failed," Yawa croaked. She stripped her gloves to check Execarne's breath. "I don't know where we go next. I didn't get anything from the prisoners. My niece . . ."

"Tain Shir again?" Iraji asked, in a terrified hush.

"Yes. She's hunting Baru. I think . . ." Yawa covered her face and groaned. "I think maybe we should send Baru somewhere safer. Back to Aurdwynn, perhaps. Heingyl Ri will know where to secure her."

"Not a fucking chance," Baru groaned. If she looked left, at *Helbride* and Apparitor up on the prow, waving frantically, the pain seemed very far away.

"If we don't complete our mission," Yawa snapped, "my brother dies, Apparitor loses his lover, *you* lose nothing—"

"But you can't go forward without me. I know where to go next."

Yawa's eyes narrowed. "You do?"

"We have to go to Kyprananoke."

"Kyprananoke?" Yawa frowned. "We can't go to Kyprananoke."

"We have to," Baru said. "Duke Unuxekome's mother is down there, and she can lead us to the man who funded the warships."

"But if I—I can't be near Unuxekome Ra!"

"Why?"

"Because," Yawa said, "I'm the one who exiled her to Kyprananoke. And she swore her revenge on the life of her son."

"It doesn't matter!" Baru said, in too much pain for any patience. "She can give us the trail to the Cancrioth!"

The burning Oriati dromon blew up. A great full-bodied explosion that reached skyward and flattened the waves. Thousands of tiny white stars arched like anenome fingers back down into the sea. From the center of the blast a single streak of fire shot skyward, through the screaming birds, into the dawn.

Iraji, perhaps dazed by all the blood and fire, fainted right away.

INTERLUDE

THE LLOSYDANES

AMINATA wrapped the boy's clawed hands in linen, cleaned his burnt body with cold brine, weighted him down with stones, and committed him to the sea. "I'm sorry," she told the boy's father. But he didn't speak Aphalone.

So she went back to *Ascentatic* to beg Baru for an explanation.

In her corner of the wardroom she knelt beneath her hammock at the remnants of her temple. The tufa center-pot couldn't sail with her, nor the black Taranoki earth, nor the dead seeds she hadn't tended. All those had remained behind on Cauteria. All she had brought with her was the cormorant feather, which she'd planted, as well as she could, in a crack between two planks.

"Baru," she whispered. Her breath ruffled the feather's gray barbules but did not tip or bend the shaft. That was Baru, wasn't it? Ruffled by Aminata's concern, but not moved. "Please tell me. How did you let this happen? I know I don't understand everything you do. But this. Just explain it to me. Why?"

In the war folio on her left hip she carried the letter she'd recovered from the Eddyn mailhouse. Five paragraphs in their hilariously baroque childhood code. Five paragraphs to implicate Baru in a conspiracy against Parliament. *Upon her return to Falcrest, I intend to recommend you to Province Admiral Ormsment . . . I wonder if we could discuss navy politics again, and the mutability of government. . . .*

It wasn't what she'd wanted to find.

She'd come here to search for Baru. There was a Morrow Ministry station on the Llosydanes, and Maroyad thought it had received prisoners from Baru's inner circle.

Instead of the prisoners, she'd found burning islands, dead children, and this damn letter.

Baru had been on the Llosydanes. She'd stopped at the mailhouse to send a note to Aminata. That night Juris Ormsment's *Sulane* had arrived. At dawn a battle had erupted on the fallow islet Moem, and under the new light Ormsment had destroyed three Oriati ships.

If only it had stopped there. If only none of the Oriati survived—all could have been written off to storm losses. But a fourth Oriati ship had escaped under diplomatic flag. The Federal Prince aboard had already changed vessels to a fast clipper and sailed south to carry news of the battle to the Mbo federations.

The Mbo would demand an explanation from Parliament. And in Parliament they'd say, *The navy is out of control, they're going to drag us into war too soon. . . .*

There would be purge, then. Swift recalls to Falcrest, "to report to Parliament," and swifter trials, swifter verdicts.

Rear Admiral Maroyad said: *The real purpose of your work, Lieutenant Commander, is to find the agents on* our *side who are working to provoke war.* And Aminata had known it couldn't be Baru, it just *couldn't,* for Baru had always worked so hard to be an honest citizen. Baru did her duty, she took her exams, and she got her reward. Oh, Aminata had been *dazzled* when Baru landed the Imperial Accountancy—how she'd tried, in her clumsy, tongue-tied way, to tell Baru how much she admired and respected her. Maybe, if she found the right way to say it, Baru would open up in reply. Baru would tell Aminata how much she admired *her.*

If Baru couldn't get ahead honestly, Baru with her mind and athleticism and her excellent scores, then how could Aminata hope to earn a ship by honest means?

Aminata put her fists on each side of the feather and laid her forehead on the planks. Through wood and bone, the crisp reports of bootstep on the deck. The slow roll of the sea beneath moored *Ascentatic.* A sailor's lullaby.

What was happening here? What was Baru mixed up in? Was she working with Ormsment, or was Ormsment chasing her?

Aminata groaned. She didn't know what to do. She didn't know how to feel. So she would keep on doing her duty, like an ox, a big, lumbering ox, because she didn't fucking know how to do anything else.

The feather brushed her forehead. A stupid ember burnt warm in her breast. The letter *did* mean that Baru had remembered her.

Y OUR full report, Lieutenant Commander, on the situation on the Llosy-danes."

Captain Nullsin was a short fat man with a hammer in place of his left hand and a brisk competence which was Aminata's only comfort in all this. He began this officer's dinner by tapping his hammer against a wineglass and, uncharacteristically, calling for a reading from the Book of the Sea. It was proscribed, but after today's work in the burnt ruins not even the surgeons gave a shit. In fact it was the ship's surgeon who lifted her chin and recited, from memory,

> Remember first that you are of the sea
> Carry fire far from homeland hearth
> Keep the ways and moorings fair and free
> Chart the stars and shallows all you see
> Guard the salted yields of the earth
> But remember first that you are of the sea
> In time of war they send us from our berth
> To humble ancient peoples' ancient pride
> To keep the ways and moorings fair and free
> A hundred hundred miles from our birth
> We fought and by the thousands died
> And all those lost are ever of the sea.

A few officers flicked water onto the floor and murmured thanks to *Ascentatic*. Aminata looked away. The Cult of Ships was too dangerous for an Oriati woman, whose heritage might mix poorly with such superstition in the eyes of Navy Censorate evaluators. But out here on the middle seas, ever one day from disaster, she understood the need to worship. The ship bore up against storm and reef. The ship's ropes trembled and sang to them on spring wind. Always, in the face of catastrophe, the ship endured. Aminata thought that only the truly heartless could lay hands on *Ascentatic*'s timbers without feeling a pulse.

Oh, they were all looking at her, weren't they? It was time for her report.

"Something very peculiar," she said, "has been done to the Llosydanes."

Swiftly she summarized recent events: the rumor of trade closure, the collapse of the exchange rate, the mad night of currency speculation. "On that night *Sulane* arrived and began deploying marines onto the Llosydanes. By that point the currency exchange was normalizing, as an unexpected supply of fiat notes came into circulation. The next morning the Morrow Ministry station on Moem islet came under attack by Oriati grenadiers. *Sulane*'s marines counterattacked—"

"We're sure of that?" Nullsin asked. "Ormsment didn't strike first?"

Aminata wanted to beg him to un-ask the question. If Ormsment *had* struck first against the Oriati, she might as well have written to Parliament begging for a purge.

The ship's master-at-arms said, "We'd better all hope that's how it happened. If not . . ."

"Right. Proceed, Lieutenant Commander."

"Yes, sir. *Sulane* repelled the enemy from the station, destroyed three Oriati ships, and then sailed immediately south. On the islands, word got around that *Sulane* was fighting the Oriati, and people thought it meant the Oriati had come to invade them. A mob sacked and burned several Falcrest-owned buildings. I understand they counted on the Oriati winning, and wanted to curry favor."

Captain Nullsin cradled his hammer in his good hand and stared straight ahead. Aminata knew what he was focused on. They'd both seen the tiny fist protruding from the wreckage. They'd worked together to move the tumbled limestone sheets. And together they'd found the fisted corpse beneath, curled up like a boxer, his child head charred into a featureless coal.

She cleared her throat and went on. "In short order the riot became a general rectification of Family grudges and insults. The Families began to drop bridges to try to contain it. That worked, mostly, but it meant fire gangs couldn't move around except by boat, which led to the loss of . . . some good fraction of the date crop."

It had been said in certain quarters that the Llosydanes, being ruled by women, must be immune to animal passion and reckless violence. Aminata, born in matriarchal Segu, felt a little cynical pride that she knew better. Give a woman power—not a hearth to keep or an office to run, but real power, power she didn't have to constantly guard or justify—and she would gain all power's evils with it. Evils which were not intrinsically masculine at all, but which, in societies that gave men power, belonged most often to men.

Nullsin nodded to her. "Thank you, Lieutenant Commander. We need to send a packet back to Cauteria with a report on the natives. What are our options?"

"I think we face a choice, sir," Aminata said. "On the one hand, we can punish the Sydani for disloyalty. As I'm sure you all know from customs work, imports to the Llosydanes are buttoned up tighter than Stakhi ass." Mild laughter. "If we lower tariffs and allow unrestricted trade, we'll drive their remaining shipwrights and machinists out of business with cheap import. Then we sabotage their date crop, and when they need to take out a loan to afford food, we sink them so deep into debt they'll be paying us back for a century."

The sailing-master made approving noises.

"However," Aminata said, feeling everyone searching her for some sign of sympathy for the un-Falcresti, the unhygienic, "it looks as if Payo Mu might have planned for exactly that."

"Who's Payo Mu?" the purser asked.

"Our mystery currency speculator. I found her name on a mess of papers in the Sydanemoot."

Nullsin looked warmly upon her. "You took the time to look into the currency event?"

"Made the time, sir. Now, I don't know much about money." This to defuse, in advance, accusations that she had stepped beyond her expertise. "But when I went through records from the night of the panic, I found that someone by the name of Payo Mu made a very fast fortune in local ring shell. And she seems to have . . . invested it in a peculiar fashion."

"Virtue," the sailing-master groaned, "please just tell us."

"She established a trust. A big pile of money locked away for one purpose. The trustees—those who get to distribute the money—seem to be a local harbormaster, a junior woman of the Jamascine clan, a few local bravos, and a female prostitute."

General laughter. Aminata waited for them to finish. "The purpose of the trust is the support of the Llosydanes' trade with the Stakhieczi Wintercrests."

The laughter was now uproarious. The sailing-master had tears in his eyes. Even Aminata chuckled. It was a lot like a joke: *What happens when two bravos, a fourth daughter, and a whore take up investment? Stakhieczi trade!* The Stakhi did not trade, except the occasional disorganized sale of telescopes or metalwork for salt. And the idea of the Llosydanes sending trade parties not just to Aurdwynn but up the Inirein to the alpine north . . . wouldn't that require dredging, and hired security, and better roads?

Still. Whoever Payo Mu was (and Aminata had her very firm suspicions), she had vision. If the Llosydanes actually managed to make contact, selling Stakhi glass and metal to the Ashen Sea would be a better way of life than date farming in rainy climes. Wouldn't it?

The laughter died away. Nullsin stopped laughing first; when the captain stopped laughing you did not go on long yourself.

"I drew the dead boy," Nullsin said. He produced a scrap of paper on which he'd sketched, in one-handed charcoal, the boy who'd burnt alive. A few efficient lines captured the pitiful stump of a head. The tormented arch of the back.

Aminata's fists buzzed with the need to hurt the people responsible. "Savages," she said, trying on the word, and then, with bitter anger and cold satisfaction, for at least she could say it accurately, "these fucking savages. The north is sick."

"War runs in their blood." Nullsin smoothed the picture with his hammerhead. "They get a little less sun at these latitudes, you know. A tiny poverty of light. You can't blame them for obeying their nature."

Implicit in that argument, of course, was the belief that an excess of sun caused peace, decadence, and philosophy. The Oriati afflictions. But in that one moment Aminata forgave her captain. She had enough weight to carry already.

"So the question is," the ship's surgeon said, "why it happened. Why did *Sulane* attack those Oriati ships? Why was *Sulane* even here? And what does it have to do with this Imperial agent, Baru Cormorant?"

Everyone looked to Captain Nullsin, who might have received a coded letter from Ormsment explaining her place in a grand scheme, advising *Ascentatic* whether to assist her or pretend ignorance or even chase her as a foe

"There was no letter," he said, heavily. "It's possible that she's on sanctioned navy business, but it's being kept secret from us. Or that . . . well. Best not to consider it. Lieutenant Commander, has anyone revealed to you why *Sulane* was here?"

"I don't know yet," Aminata said. "But I have a lead."

S HE dressed to ravish, a word which had, in the not-so-distant past, meant *to plunder.*

Aminata had brought two of her suasioners with her from Cauteria Fortress, as they knew more tradecraft than the average sailor. Yesterday Midshipman Gerewho, dragging his coat in local establishments for anyone who might pass a discreet tip, had connected with a (reportedly very handsome) race-hygienist who said he might know more about the battle on Moem. Today he would be at the Demimonde restaurant on Eddyn islet at the beginning of second dogwatch, waiting for a navy contact. If the navy wished to speak with him, he thought they ought to send a charming nautical lady to appear as his companion, for he was known as a womanizer. But she should not, if possible, arrive in uniform. He did not wish to seem associated with the frightening warship offshore, which all the Sydani believed had come to punish them.

Aminata decided to handle this meeting herself. He might have some clue to Baru's true purpose. Also she'd had no time to take a leave watch and go whoring, and she hoped, if he were a womanizer, that he would be agreeable. Spies did that, right? Spies were always consorting with seductive and dangerous men.

She drew the line, however, at his request for her to come not in uniform. Who would she be without the reds? They might take her for a Mbo Oriati. So she wore full starched dress, tall boots polished and buffed, her pins and links shining, a smart little folio on her hip, a clean shave for her scalp and a jaunty cover. Perfect.

The Demimonde was a longhouse, shattered black stone mortared together like a puzzle. When Aminata marched in, the sparse and quiet crowd all looked up from their gossip. Inevitably someone began to whistle "Hey Navy Girl." Aminata ignored it.

The Belthyc-looking host had date wine on his breath and worry lines all around his eyes. Would she like a discreet table? Yes she would, Aminata said, and would he kindly tell the man that his appointment had arrived? What man? Why, the most beautiful man in the place.

In good time said man arrived in a corseted wedge of perfume and color. Aminata had bought a dram of import whiskey, the strong conservative Grendlake with its smoky tones. She looked up with practiced challenge. Her first impression was of composition, like a sculpture.

"Miss Aminata isiSegu?" His voice crisply Falcrest-accented, in his thirties or forties. "I spoke to one of your colleagues yesterday. . . ."

He had a face like the morning, wide and bright, with a small flat nose, powerful cheekbones, and perfectly classic eyes. His sherwani flattered a muscular body of pornographic leanness. He was quite uncomfortable to look at, in the sense that it was hard for Aminata not to stare. How had he gotten so *definite*? Isometric training, perhaps, to isolate and endow each muscle?

Aminata saluted him with the whiskey. "Hello," she said, "just the man I was looking at."

"Looking for, perhaps?"

"That, too." She pushed out his chair with one boot tip. "I'll excuse the *Miss*. I'm Lieutenant Commander Aminata. I don't come ashore often, so I hope you'll forgive my indiscretions. Are there any drinks here as fine as the company?"

"The restaurant company, I'm sure you mean," he said, dryly. "You're a drinker?"

"Not when I'm on duty," she said, reminding him, with the Grendlake malt, that she wasn't on duty. "You?"

"I'm afraid I find it dulls me."

"We wouldn't want that, Mister . . . ?"

"Calcanish. You know that my reputation could be damaged if I'm seen with you, Lieutenant Commander? And that's not all that might be hurt."

"A little risk in the service of the Republic, Mister Calcanish."

The waiter delivered samplers of dates in sweet honey and pure spring water. The table was a little too small for them, each quite a specimen of height, and their knees touched. Aminata complimented Mister Calcanish on his makeup. They made small talk about the island's hydrology and Calcanish's work. He was a demographic hygienist, checking for inbreeding. What would he do if he found it, Aminata wondered? Import brides from abroad? No, Calcanish explained, in general men were more valuable for that type of import, as they could be studded. Did the men enjoy that work, Aminata asked? But Calcanish did not play along. He thought men were already treated dreadfully on the Llosydanes, and did not care to speculate on what an experimental stud might think of being twice chattel.

Aminata ordered a garnished chicken in wine. Calcanish selected a dish of nuts in crystallized date syrup. "You must be very disciplined," Aminata suggested, "to maintain such, mm, aesthetic. Are you a dancer, perhaps? Or otherwise ornamental?"

"Bodies are my primary interest," he confessed, as if ashamed not by the topic but by the depth of his enthusiasm. "I've been accused of religiosity, actually. Worship of the human mechanism. Of course, as a navy officer you must understand the critical role of experimental physiology in our great Republic?"

"Oh yes," Aminata agreed, "at bathing times I'm surrounded by experimental physiologies."

He laughed. "Is that so? Experimental? You know, to be a *proper* experiment, they'd need to be divided into home and traveler groups."

"I could sort them that way, certainly."

"You could?"

"The ones I'd send traveling and the ones I'd keep at home."

"Lieutenant Commander!" he said, with rich shock.

She drank her water. Swallowed. Wet her lips. He looked deliciously aware of her every motion. Aminata veered, sharply, into the questioning. "Tell me what you know about the battle. How did a navy warship come to burn three Oriati dromon?"

He didn't know. He'd arrived just afterward, in time to meet a small group of very confused foreigners trying to book passage to Aurdwynn using Oriati papers. The dockside authorities were *very* curious to know where this gang of misfits had gotten Oriati diplomatic protection. Calcanish took pity on them, saved them from interrogation, and brought them to a property he owned on Jamascine islet.

"Who were they?"

Aurdwynni commoners, as far as he could tell, refugees from the Coyote rebellion. A midwife, an herbalist, a man and his son, and a frighteningly pale and thin Stakhi woman.

Aminata clenched her fist in triumph under the table. Those were the prisoners who'd been dispatched to the Ministry station here! He had them. Perhaps they'd seen Baru. Even spoken to her!

"You're excited," Calcanish observed. "Why?"

"Do you know the Imperial agent who masterminded the Coyote uprising?"

"Baru Cormorant, yes. I heard she'd been spirited off to Falcrest to receive a new name."

"I'm trying to track her down." She shouldn't have said that. She just wanted to be connected to Baru's infamy, in his eyes.

"Oh?" He kissed his napkin. "Why? She's the Emperor's creature, isn't she? Very elusive. A mask without a face."

She couldn't help boasting a little. "Because she's put the whole Imperial Republic in danger of open war. First she drew the Oriati into attacking Treatymont. Now this second encounter between our navy and Oriati covert forces."

"You think an Imperial agent provoked the violence here?"

"Perhaps."

He frowned fetchingly. "I suppose that makes sense," he said, "if the Emperor wants to do to the Oriati what he did to Aurdwynn."

"Bait them into a premature attack?"

"No!" He flinched in shock. "No, goodness, an actual war between Falcrest and the Mbo would be *appalling*. Can you imagine the trade disruptions? The pandemics?"

"What, then?"

Mr. Calcanish's eyes traced the seams of her gloves. Lingered on the glittering pins in her cuff. He swallowed nervously, sensually, and met her eyes. Aminata felt a thrill of power.

"Obviously the Emperor desires an Oriati *civil* war."

"Why?"

"Once they've ground each other down, we can step in and save them."

Aminata was faintly disappointed to hear such pacifism from him. Oriati Mbo might be huge and old, but so was a tar pit. One couldn't dilute or purify a tar pit. It had to be burnt off.

She asked a clarifying question, which was faintly unwomanly, as women were supposed to intuit subtlety: but fuck it. "Who would possibly cause the Mbo to have a civil war?"

"Cairdine Farrier," Calcanish said, with a wry sadness she didn't understand. "And Kindalana."

Aminata's whiskey did not even jump. She was perfectly steady against surprise, even the surprise of two very familiar names. Kindalana, who Abdumasi

Abd had seen in his tormentor's face. And Cairdine Farrier, Baru's patron. The man who had convinced Aminata that she needed to terrify Baru out of any affections she might hold . . . lest she come to a worse fate.

"Excuse me?" she said.

"CAIRDINE Farrier is a popular public figure," Calcanish explained, "who wants an Oriati civil war. And the closer Falcrest and Oriati Mbo come to war, the stronger he becomes."

"Why?"

"Because there are many Oriati who would prefer a peaceful surrender to open war. The closer that war, the more concessions Farrier can extract from them."

Kindalana of Segu was one of those Oriati. She was the so-called Amity Prince, elected-to-birth Oriati royalty, and she came from the same Mbo nation as Aminata, if not the same tribe. For at least seven years she'd lived in Falcrest, working to achieve the outrageous and unlikely goal of an Article of Federation which would make Oriati Mbo part of the Imperial Republic, Falcrest's hugest province.

"But more of them," Aminata countered, "would surely prefer war? Being a proud and unbiddable race?"

"More of us, surely? You being Oriati?"

"I'm a federated citizen of Falcrest," Aminata warned him. "I'm not part of the Mbo."

"You shouldn't be ashamed to call yourself Oriati!" Their food arrived: he spoke right over it. "I know Kindalana through business. You're very much like her as she was in her youth. A great bit taller, of course, but she was brilliant, just brilliant. A credit to your race."

Aminata stowed away her irritation. "What about Cairdine Farrier? I knew him, actually."

"Did you?" Calcanish said, and somehow a certain heaviness of eyelid, a wrinkle of the lips, implied a kind of disgust.

"Not in *that* sense," Aminata reassured him (damn the women of her nation, for giving the world the impression they were all cads). "He was very proper." In fact Aminata could never shake the feeling that he was somehow *afraid* of her.

"Oh, I'm sure." Calcanish tried his dish, and his eyes slitted in pleasure. Aminata enjoyed that expression, very superficially. He had what sailors might call, at the height of drunken articulation, a fuckable face. "Well, as I understand it, Cairdine Farrier is in favor with the Emperor, and everyone says this Baru Cormorant is Farrier's new protégé. . . ."

"I've heard that, yes, but do you know exactly what they might want? In the . . ." She kissed her fingertip in thought. "The grand sense?"

Calcanish laughed. "Of course I do! Whenever he has an idea, the bastard writes a book."

She laughed, too. "That's true, he does, doesn't he?"

"He's laid it all out. He wants to walk us up to the very edge of war, to the moment when everyone's clawing around for *any* other choice. When war seems inevitable, Farrier will leap onto the stage and reveal some digusting secret that turns the Oriati against each other—"

"Like what?"

"Does it matter? As the Oriati turn on each other, Farrier will offer his support to the pro-Falcrest faction; that is, Kindalana's faction. Money. Roads. Development of their territory. Schools and ideas. Ships, even—I shouldn't expect our navy to escape his control. He'll do to Oriati Mbo exactly what he's done to Sousward and Aurdwynn and all the rest." Calcanish bit his fork too hard. A ferocious pain screwed up his face, a pain very much like hate. "Of course his protégés will take the blame for his crimes. He always uses them up, drives them mad, and casts them aside. I expect he already has his Baru woman luring the warhawk admirals to the drowning-stone—"

Aminata choked on a chicken bone. She tried to cough it out in polite silence. Calcanish was not deceived: in an instant he was at her side, arms round her, pulling hard into her gut. She spat the bone into her napkin.

"You mean," she rasped, "Baru's *trying* to purge the navy?"

"Are you all right?"

"She's on a mission to cause, and then destroy, a navy mutiny?"

"Well, I imagine so." He touched her throat solicitously, probing for lumps, his fingers precise and strong. "Farrier would need the navy under his control."

Yes. He would need to be rid of the women Aminata admired most.

Oh, Baru, no. Was that why she had written a letter to Aminata? To invite her into the honeypot?

Aminata threw her whiskey down her bone-cut throat. It made terrible sense. Baru had already betrayed the navy once. Why stop there? Why not help arrange a purge? If she did it in service of the Emperor, who could blame her? And she could get rid of Ormsment, who probably had a grudge against her for Welthony Harbor. . . .

Only—only—Aminata had told Baru, told her so often, that she wanted to be an admiral. She'd said that on the last night they spoke, when they got drunk and beat up one of Xate Yawa's spies.

Baru hadn't written between that night and her recent invitation to mutiny.

As if she'd discarded Aminata as a loss, until she suddenly became useful again . . .

"Lieutenant Commander," Calcanish murmured, "what's wrong?"

She set down the tumbler. Such bubbled, ugly glass—whoever had imported it couldn't afford quality. "I have to get back to my ship."

"I understand," he said, with an expression of pleasantly ill-hidden regret. "That's too bad. Well, here's the key to the apartment on Jamascine where I've put up the Aurdwynni refugees. The address is written inside. I'll happily turn them over to the navy's custody. May I take your bill?"

She shook her head. A woman who turned up at a dinner without a way to pay was a grossly masculine woman indeed. "I have a navy credit stamp. I already gave the papers to the waiter."

"Wonderful." He stood and offered his arm. Everything he did seemed to involve the ripple of small muscles, like an anatomy show. "May I escort you to the dock?"

She wanted to stop thinking about Baru. She wanted to stop thinking. "I would *love* an escort." She took his hand and pointed toward the back. "Would you like to follow me?"

"But, Lieutenant Commander, the docks are down that way, this is the way—"

"To the alley, yes. Am I being too forward?"

"Oh," he said.

SHE dragged him out the back, across the driftwood ramp that bridged the kitchen slops, into the quiet well-kept alleyway that she had suspected might be here. "Take your gloves off," she ordered, leaving hers on.

"Are you propositioning me?"

"Yes, I'm trying to fuck you."

"But we've just met!"

"I'm going to be on a ship for a long time and I'm impatient. One tryst, right here, and I won't take on or offer any obligations of contact. Do you understand?"

He blinked at her, rather owlishly, a curiously hesitant and intellectual face on a man so self-assured. "I'm not sure I ought to . . ."

"If you don't like Oriati women, just say it."

"No," he said, without defensiveness. "It's just, without any offense, that you seem young."

"Get over yourself," she said, "we're not getting married."

His fingers played over the buttons of his coat. "It's not proper. . . ."

"No one's ever gotten off on propriety."

He laughed. "Trust me, mam. Someone has gotten off on everything."

Aminata hooked her cover on a protruding brick. Fresh sea wind caressed her scalp. She closed her eyes, and sighed, and stretched against the wall. "You knew this important Oriati woman when she was my age, didn't you?"

"What?"

"Kindalana? Don't tell me you didn't want to fuck her. Everyone goes for important Oriati women. They're so unattainable."

A tremble of passion across his broad face. It took a moment for him to master himself. "*You* seem quite attainable," he said. His eyes had gone casually dead, neither eager nor fearful, simply resigned. Aminata realized, with a soiled thrill, that he must be a whore of some kind. He'd said he was a womanizer, yes. Was he ashamed? Was he debased that she'd recognized him as wanton? She liked that a little. Men had strange reasons to proposition her, racialized and fraught. Whores did it for sex and money, which were much safer.

She undid two buttons on her jacket and lingered on the third. "Yes or no?"

He took several measured breaths. His eyes liked the shadows beneath her unbuttoned coat, the strict womanly confinement peeling away. But he was still thinking too much: "You're an officer. You can't marry. You can't touch the men under your command. So you proposition strangers. I know how that is. You need an outlet."

"King's balls, man, I don't care. Yes or no?"

"Well . . ." He quibbled a moment. "Do you have a cap?"

Of course she had a cap.

She left her jacket on, but unbuttoned. He shrugged out of his, and the undershirt, naked to the waist, spectacular in the evening chill. She could trace every cell of his abdomen, the hard curve of his pectorals, the thrilling breadth of his shoulders. They didn't kiss but very assuredly went about provoking each other. She unbuttoned him, tested his heft and hardness, and tied the cap on. To keep him occupied through this fairly technical process she took his wrist and showed him, efficiently, how she liked to be touched, with the flesh of the hood as a buffer. He knew. His broad sure-fingered hands had the violent thrilling precision of surgery. She leaned back against the wall and wrapped her legs around his waist, daring him to hold her up, and he was not a disappointment: he pressed her against the alley wall and came into her and they fucked standing there with Aminata's open mouth pressed against the cabled curve of his shoulder and throat.

"Too gentle," she whispered, when the first thrill had passed.

"I don't want to hurt you—"

"Pretend I'm Kindalana," she teased, which made him tremble all over, and sent him into a frenzy whose emotional components Aminata had neither the interest nor the concentration to analyze. For a long exultant time she arched against him and savored his desperation. He must be twenty years older, and she'd had him on their first meeting, a man of good status and carnal delight. What a catch. She might have a new story to impress sailors on the first night drinking.

At last she got sore, and as happened with overused men, he couldn't come with ordinary sex. They took turns on their knees on the soot-scattered flagstones: she came on the thrill of his beautiful upturned face, on her guilty delight in his confusion and lust. Afterward, she could see he was ashamed. "Thank you," she said, with a twinge of conscience, and pecked him on the cheek. The used cap she put in the rubbish pit, certainly built here for just such things. One did not name a restaurant Demimonde without certain arrangements. "Are you all right?"

"Yes," he said, roughly.

"I liked that."

"I'm glad," he said, with a shaky but genuine smile. "It was . . . I've been tense, too. A calm body makes a calm mind. Thank you for your discretion." Meaning her future quiet.

"One learns." She checked that her trousers still had the key, and dressed. "Ah. Please don't take this wrong. I know it can be tempting, sometimes, but I meant what I said. It's better if you don't try to reach me."

"Aminata," the man said, with soft concern. She turned to see him at the mouth of the alley, rather charmingly trying to adjust his worn manhood through the fabric of his trousers. But he sounded different—older, more confident, and more afraid.

"If you want to protect Baru, and your navy too," he said, "I think you should bring her back to Aurdwynn. She can be sent into the Wintercrests, away from all this. There's safety in exile. The only safety for her, I'm afraid; and for the rest of us who fear her."

"Baru's a savant," Aminata protested, still proud, despite these revelations, of her terrible young friend. "The Republic needs her."

"She isn't safe." Calcanish slipped his gloves back on. "She'll never be safe until she's away from her master, Farrier. She will do anything for him. Kill her lover. Kill you. Beware Baru Cormorant."

H ER suasioners Faroni and Gerewho waited at the docks with a marine squad. She'd ordered them to be ready in case she had to move tonight. "How'd it go, mam?" Gerewho asked.

"I got what I went for," Aminata said, sticking her thumb through her clenched fist, "and the prisoners, too."

"You rake," Faroni said, enviously. "Is he affordable?"

"Lieutenant, he's not even for sale."

"You went honest?" Faroni blinked. "I can never—" She swallowed the truth, which was a complaint about the great difficulty Oriati women faced getting laid in Falcresti settings.

"Mam," Gerewho said, cautiously, "are you sure he wasn't a honeypot of sorts? I mean, it wouldn't be hard to arrange, knowing a navy ship's coming ashore."

Aminata judged Calcanish far too genuinely fucked up to be a plant. "Let's go find out. Marines, fall in, we're headed to Jamascine."

The safe house was a second-floor apartment in a Falcrest-style house-of-eight. It had no plumbing or heat except for a central firepit and a waste pipe. Graffiti scrawled in grand fish-oil sweeps, a gorgeous rendering of a masked and garishly piss-colored Falcrest "shielding" a pillared island with an enormous golden coin. Beneath the island, piles of dead boys, rendered as tiny shapes wrapped in rope.

Aminata knocked on the door of resurfaced driftwood. It opened at once. "Hello," said a very tired-looking Stakhi woman. "Come in. We've been expecting you."

Aminata had read up on Baru's known associates in Aurdwynn. "Ake Sentiamut? I'm Lieutenant Commander Aminata isiSegu, off RNS *Ascentatic*—"

"I know you," Ake said. "You helped Her Majesty audit the Fiat Bank. I was Bel Latheman's secretary. Are you with the mutiny now?"

"What mutiny?" Aminata asked, heartsick with dread. Please, please, if she would name *anyone* but Juris Ormsment . . .

"Province Admiral Ormsment on *Sulane*. Are you with her?"

Behind her, the crowded apartment held a peering crowd of Aurdwynni faces: a golden brown Maia woman with an otterlike figure, a cynical crossbreed woman of some age, a handsome tanned Stakhi man guarding a pimple-faced youth.

"Nitu," the cynical-looking woman called. "Nitu, are you with them? She's not with them. Navy mam, have you found Nitu?"

When the situation begins to escalate out of your understanding, you do not chase after it. You impose order. You step back to the last moment you understood, and proceed from there.

"What do you mean," she demanded, "you were *expecting* me?"

"The duchess said you'd come to us," Ake Sentiamut said.

"The *duchess*?"

"Yes, our Lady Grace Tain Hu. You're the faithful friend Baru spoke about. The one whose loss she regretted most. Isn't that why you're here? Didn't you get Tain Hu's letter?"

INTERLUDE

THE MANSION HUSSACHT

NO one south of Vultjag knew how high the Wintercrests might climb. On some days the snowy peaks could be seen from the harbor at Treatymont, in spite of the vast northward distance, which should have put them over the horizon: some said this was an illusion of optics, and others said the Wintercrests just climbed up and up and up, fourteen or seventeen or twenty miles tall at their crest, and that this was why white mountains loomed over seaside Treatymont on certain days. Though the Incrastic geologists called them mad.

But the King of the Mansions knew his Amustakhi Mountains. He knew the cracking cold and the taste of lichen; the dead air of the mines and the dead soil of the overworked terraces; the dysentery and cholera that swept downslope settlements who drank water tainted by sewage from above. He knew the pink flamingos in their high lakes, and the pink sunburnt faces that smiled at him when he came out in his shining armor plate. He knew the silent old women who swept the babies off the exposure shelf and down the crevasse.

When he imagined the way his mountains rose from Aurdwynn he saw a great ramp. And he was like a bale of grass on that ramp, trying desperately not to roll downhill. His crown burnt with the cold, but he could not take it off.

"Ziscjaditzcionursz," he said, *zish-jaditshionursh,* softer than the wind; it meant, more or less, may a rusty nail be driven into my bloody flank by a traitor, though really it meant, oh, fuck me. Very few lowcomers ever learned Mansion Stakhi, which could not easily be pried apart. Would only that the same could be said of the Stakhi mansions themselves.

His name was Atakaszir, of the Mansion Hussacht. From the peak of his mountain, Karakys, he could see more than a hundred miles down over Aurdwynn, when weather permitted. He could see the great green forests of Vultjag, and the high stony fells of Lyxaxu (he clicked his right incisors together, thoughtlessly, by tradition, at the enemy name, the Maia name) and the bright river that carried their food and wealth away from him, to the sea.

But closer beneath him was the crest of the col, a strip of naked wind-raked rock that crossed the saddle between Camich Swiet and Karakys. His Mansion stood high above the green line where the last trees grew. There were no forests, no rivers, no checkered pastures where horses could breed. The flanks of Karakys stepped upward in huge terraces buttressed by walls of interlocked mortarless rock. On those stone terraces the Mansion would soon lay out fields of potatoes to freeze-dry, sheafs of winterwheat, sorghum, and sour red pitahaya. When the wet air shoveled up off the Ashen Sea in summer crashed and fell as snow, Hussacht would live or die by its stores. Yaks wandered the upper terraces in herds of fifty or a hundred, females mostly, producing the milk that would go into the salt-and-coca tea which all the Stakhi drank. Atakaszir had yak butter on his lips right now, to stop the cracking, and a wad of coca in his cheek, to keep him strong. Down in the lowlands they called coca mason leaf and used it for fun and sex. Here it was as vital as water.

He had promised his people the lowlands, to ease their straining numbers. He had promised an end to the tax on second children, who went out on the naked rock. For one short season his promises had been honorable, for his man Dziransi had found him a bride who could deliver Aurdwynn.

But the bride was a traitor, a bait set out to entrap him, and the first great act of his Necessary Kingship came tumbling down on him like a keyless arch. And now the army he had raised was camped outside his Mansion with nowhere to invade and no confidence at all in their king. When autumn came they would seize Hussacht's stores for the winter, and Hussacht would rot away in the wet karst caves of Karakys until the pits and stairways were slimed with corpse. He himself would not live that long. The Uczenith men in particular were agitating in the camp for a dethroning, and traditionally this was done by peeling off the King's crown and the scalp beneath.

Fucking Uczenith. Fucking shortsighted stone-licking inbred curs. In spite of their overweening insecurity (their old lord Kubarycz the Iron-Browed had tried to marry an Aurdwynni duchess, leading to his exile: the Uczenith lived in terror that someone would come up the mountains to say, *Hello, I killed your Lord and his heirs in combat and so I am now the rightful ruler of your Mansion*) Ataka had brought them and all the other mansions together. He had been *this* close to breaking the Stakhi out of the prison of their history.

And Baru Cormorant had ruined it all.

Atakaszir thought: I have started an avalanche and now I cannot get out of the way.

He turned to face the woman.

"How," he said, in the Iolynic that came so hard to him, "will you dowry me?" He knew he'd gotten it wrong but the creole seemed to fight his very tongue. "How will you open the way that was shut?"

She was dark and clean of face, without one pimple or scar. She wore her coat and furs open and the wind blew her dress back against a body of sinful fullness. She looked as if she had never been hungry; Atakaszir's eyes betrayed him by seeking out her hips, her full stomach, her breasts. Her sister, Atakaszir understood, had been some kind of whore-duchess, who sealed her alliances in her bed. Ordinarily this would make her and all her sisters unthinkable as consorts to a king. But lately Atakaszir had learned that the Stakhieczi measure of a woman was not always reliable.

"I offer you what you most desire," Nayauru Aia said, in perfect Stakhi. "A wife from the lands of milk and grain. A key to the door that bars you."

"You are an exile." Aia had arrived in the company of a beautiful horseman named Ihuake Ro, each of them carrying their ducal banners as they fled the Masquerade. "You have no land."

"If my sister's children die then I have the claim to the Duchy Nayauru," the woman said, through dark and fulsome lips. The most infuriating thing about her was her utter indifference to his eye. She held herself with poise and confidence, but without the cave whore's desperate invitation. Atakaszir knew better than most Stakhi that desperation was the keen whistle of death. "What other option have you, Your Majesty the King? What else can you show your brave men and your engineers to sustain the necessity of your existence? You must have a prize out of this winter's debacle. You must show them a little piece of sun and fertile soil."

She was right. He had no alternative. Failing revenge on Baru, which would save his honor, he would need a token of hope: which would not honor him, but at least give him something to bargain with, the merchant's craven power.

"Is it true you need a hundred men to satisfy you?" he asked her, for she was so obviously Maia.

She laughed. He liked the laugh. It reminded him of his bannermen, joyful and unconsidered. Not like the terrified girls the other Mansions had tried to bride to him when they thought he was ascendant. "I don't need any men to satisfy me," she said. "My heart is set on a return to the land I love, Majesty, with the steel avalanche at my back. Give me that and you will have my faith."

The steel avalanche. The avalanche camped out in the dry lake bed called the erbajaste, waiting, waiting, for word to march. He could turn around now and see them, their spears wavering in the hot dry air.

If he wanted to survive that army he would need an Aurdwynni bride and he would need to invade. Now.

But the masks were still out there. The Falcresti who had taken his brother and bottled up the eastern sea, blockading the Stakhi from their fish. And

Atakaszir knew the appalling treachery of those people; for Baru Cormorant had taught him.

When he invaded, when the steel avalanche crashed down into Aurdwynn's northern duchies of Lyxaxu and Vultjag and Erebog, the Masquerade would use Aurdwynn as an enormous firebreak. Plagues would spread. Forests would burn. Millions would drown in a mud cauldron of pus and shit as the laughing Falcresti bet on who would die last.

If only he had some way to guarantee they would not interfere—

A low horn blew from the slot pass that opened onto the col. Atakaszir's heart seized a moment, for he remembered the day the news of disaster had come from Sieroch. And just as on that day, a kite rose up in signal.

"What's that?" Nayauru Aia asked.

"A man is coming up the pass. A stranger." The second kite caught the air. "A foreigner . . ."

Right now Uczenith's spies would be rushing to their masters to warn them that another moment had come. Another summit that might see Atakaszir toppled down the col to shatter in the valley below. Would the foreigner bring news of further disaster? Masquerade plagues in the lowlands? An end to the pitiful, vital salt trade in Duchy Erebog?

A woman in a poncho climbed up to the signal post and began to wave her flags. Atakaszir translated the dips and flourishes as swiftly as they came. Then he peeled his lips back and grinned a death's-head grin, the skull-joy of a man in battle.

"What is it?"

"Someone has come to offer me a gift." Atakaszir touched the steel peak of his crown. "A gift he claims will make me a king of honor and revenge, whose enemies cannot escape him even if they flee to distant underlands. A king to be feared and obeyed."

"How tantalizing," Nayauru Aia said, smoothly. "What gift can that be?"

Revenge, Atakaszir thought. Revenge on the woman who betrayed me. A corpse to show my courtiers, and bone to stuff down the Uczenith craw, and blood to water my hopes.

But the pale man who approached his throne between the great ranked pillars brought different tidings. "King of Mansions," he began, as Atakaszir's allies and enemies alike leaned forward like salary workers waiting for their crystals of the Brine. "I bring word of your missing brother, of his life and deeds, and of how he may be restored to you. . . ."

"Svir?" Ataka whispered, but a king cannot whisper, it stinks of procht, the sick-thought of schemers, so he cried it aloud instead. "My brother, Svir, is alive?"

And he saw the Uczenith men whisper in consternation that the King they hated might restore the stolen glory of the stolen Prince. He saw distant Nayauru Aia, leaning against her pillar, quirk her lips in thought, for here was another eligible man.

All Atakaszir wanted in that moment was to call his army and march to his brother's aid. But he was King, and a king must be wise.

"Come forward," he said. "What is your name? And who sent you?"

ACT THREE

THE FALL OF KYPRANANOKE

18

METAGAMES

I WON'T kill her yet," Apparitor snapped. "This isn't your courtroom, Yawa, and you won't hand me a verdict."

"You're sentimental." Yawa sighed, to provoke him. "String your cook up on the yardarms, Svir. Let *Sulane* see what you do to traitors."

"I don't want her to die," Baru whispered.

The two other cryptarchs blinked at her. "What did she say?"

"Speak up, Baru."

Baru had screamed so much that she'd lost her voice. Every morning she had to change the dressing on her missing fingers, which made her howl like a ghost. She did it as soon as she woke. Do the most painful thing first: the pain is how you know it matters.

Iraji spoke for her. "She doesn't want Munette hung. She forgives the cook for attacking her."

From her huddle in the corner, Baru touched his ankle in gratitude. Apparitor glared from his hammock, where he fussed over a whittling. Yawa loomed in the curtained doorway like a raven. Their meetings had, Baru thought, become pitiable since the Llosydanes. Apparitor paced his decks cornered and desperate, trying to find a way to save himself from Itinerant and Hesychast and their pawns on his ship; Yawa spent her nights scribbling draft after draft of legal defense for her brother, if she was not down in the hold interrogating Shao Lune or tending to Execarne's wounds; and Baru, well, she drank and tried not to remember the blood on Shir's mask. Everyone was wretchedly hurt.

"Tell me again," Apparitor said, to Yawa, "who you think could be the mole. The one who left a letter for Ormsment in the Llosydanes post." Baru had relayed Tau-indi's intelligence on this point.

"It had to be someone who knew we were going to Moem," Yawa said. "We weren't tailed there. Iscend would have noticed, and Execarne is no fool himself."

The crossbow bolt had come out of Execarne cleanly but the poison on that bolt had lingered. He insisted on mixing his own treatments, most of which left him uselessly intoxicated.

"I knew," Baru said. "Both of you knew, and Iraji. Ulyu Xe, I suppose, could've dropped a letter. . . ."

Yawa shifted uncomfortably. She tried to pass it off as an itch but Apparitor had already pounced. "What is it?"

"When we were on Moem, I ordered a special interrogation instrument shipped ashore from *Helbride*. A mole might have tracked the boat's course."

"Wait. What *kind* of instrument?"

"It was a device I used to interrogate Dziransi." Yawa touched the spine of a book on Apparitor's shelf. *The Lightning Men: Falcrest's Expeditions Eastward.* "I wanted to learn what he knew about the state of the Stakhi Mansions. If an invasion's coming . . . it's vital that Aurdwynn be warned."

Apparitor relaxed very deliberately. No one but Baru would have detected his thrill of terror. At any moment Baru could say, *Oh, by the way, Yawa, Apparitor here is the brother of the Stakhi King. . . .*

"Well?" Baru demanded. "What did you learn?"

"Very little." Yawa sighed. "And you saw fit to send the prisoners away. I suppose Dziransi's sailing back to Aurdwynn by now, hm? What a waste."

"I need him in the north of Aurdwynn," Baru countered, though it felt like sticking her fingers into the wound of their last fight. "I need him to open trade relations between Aurdwynn and the Stakhieczi. It's the best way to avoid war."

"Never mind that." Apparitor clearly wanted to get off the topic of the Stakhieczi as quickly as possible. "We're going to die before we make it to Kyprananoke."

That got Baru's attention back. Apparitor rubbed his face: springy red stubble had grown out far enough to curl. "I've talked to Captain Branne. We didn't finish our work at the Elided Keep, and our hull's still badly fouled. It's slowing us."

"How long," Baru rasped.

"*Sulane* will catch us within two days."

"And how long to Kyprananoke?"

"Two weeks. With good weather. Which we can hope for, but never count on."

Silence. Down from above came the low cries of the sailing-master conducting her sorcery. On Taranoke they'd had a saying, *You can't sail faster than the wind,* which meant, *You can only do as much as you can do.* How could anyone sail faster than the wind? Surely, if your ship was traveling at wind speed, then the wind could no longer exert force on the sail: it was an elementary lesson for Taranoki children, Toro Haba's Law of Force.

But the Falcresti could break that law. Arranged at the right angle, *Helbride's* sails acted like a wing—they could get force from the air by some mathematical trickery. *Helbride* could run downwind faster than the air.

And so could *Sulane*. And she was winning the race.

"We can't possibly fight *Sulane*." Apparitor drummed his fists on the wall. "We can't even trust the other ships we meet. We're still in Ormsment's waters. She has the power to commandeer trade ships and leave agents aboard. Anyone could be compromised."

"No," Baru said, looking up at Iraji, remembering his idea. "Not *anyone*. There's one place we can go that Ormsment can't touch."

OOK at you." Shao Lune sneered. "Have you lost two fingers? I've been shackled in the bilge, beaten, interrogated, and left to rot. And somehow I've *still* come out ahead of you."

Baru came down the stairs to find the treacherous staff captain better appointed than last time they'd sparred. She'd gained a lantern on a hook, a bucket for her toilet (clean, thankfully; it stank only of bleach), a few planks to keep her above the bilgewater, a supply of various linens and pads, and some slack on her chains.

"Looks like you've been cooperating." Baru tested the boards underfoot. Shao Lune had done her carpentry well. "Left anything to sell to me? Or did you give it all to Yawa?"

"*Left* you anything? I'm in a better position than you, I think."

"Funny." Baru looked at her wrist. "I don't see any chains on mine." Then she thought of something she'd said to Tain Hu once: *the Masquerade rules them, but it has not yet made them want to be ruled, the chains are not yet invisible,* and nearly shouted in fright.

"I tell the Jurispotence this and that. What I know about Ormsment. What I expect her to do." Shao Lune's uniform hung from an overhead beam. In her cotton workshirt and rough canvas trousers she looked like a gutter mucker, but she lounged on her hard-earned carpentry with the poise of a schoolyard tyrant. Lamplight conjured faint implications through the cloth. She was not, without the uniform, quite as sleek and slim and minimal as she liked to appear. "I could tell her about *you*, couldn't I?"

"What would you possibly tell Xate Yawa about me."

"Still want to bargain with my admirals? Conduct a little military adjustment of Parliament? Yawa would *love* to learn about that."

Baru would indeed very much like to arrange a military coup in Falcrest, right about the same moment she coaxed the Stakhi and Oriati to invade Falcrest. One convulsive cataclysm to break the mask off the world's face.

"You know," Shao Lune said, and what an eloquent sneer she had, "I think gava women don't understand the scale of the world. I think you believe Parliament's just like a few dirty elders huddled in a cave."

Baru picked up a length of Shao Lune's chain. The woman flinched. Baru grinned at her: she remembered last time. Baru slipped her hand under her shirt and, very slowly, extracted a wooden bottle of fern shampoo. "Would you like some soap?"

The staff captain's wide eyes narrowed with contempt. "Please. I have dignity."

"Where?" Baru peered around. "You've hidden it so well."

"You knock-kneed gava virgin. You think you're someone?"

Baru seized the captain's chain and took out her general frustration by yanking Shao Lune back to her beam. A few circuits of the chain had Shao pinned with her arms at her sides. Baru's maimed right hand complained. Baru flexed it and savored the reminder of pain.

Shao panted with the effort of her resistance. Out of her uniform she seemed somehow spiritually disheveled, her eyes too large and expressive, her mouth too cruel: as if deprived of necessary constraints, bindings that kept her merely human.

Baru whispered in her ear. "Tell me how to stop Ormsment."

"Blow up her ship."

"You know we can't fight."

"I'm just a simple navy officer. I only understand fire."

Baru would need to offer Shao something more than soap. Something Yawa couldn't, or wouldn't, give her. Gods of fire, did her hand hurt. Gods of stone, it had grown so hard to think. She'd been clever once. Before she spent her days curled in her hammock, trying to dilute her pain with spirit.

"You smell like blood and drink," Lune hissed. "You're degenerating, aren't you? Reverting to your primal state."

Baru clinched the chains a little tighter. "Ormsment blew up three Oriati ships. She's out of control. She could start a second Armada War."

"Pirate hunting is the admiral's duty."

"They weren't pirates. They flew Federal Oriati colors."

"I don't believe you."

"Why?"

"The admiral wouldn't burn a Federal-flagged Oriati ship."

Baru seized on Shao Lune's weakness: she couldn't quite repress her navy training, her need to provide accurate information. "Ormsment wouldn't attack an Oriati diplomatic ship?"

"How should I know? As a loyal officer, I can't understand the mutinous mind."

Baru braced one foot against the post and drew the chain tight. Shao groaned and pushed her fists against the planking, desperate to breathe.

"Would an Oriati diplomatic flag stop Ormsment?"

"Let me breathe."

"Tell me what I want to know. Would Ormsment attack an Oriati diplomatic ship?"

"I'd tell you anything—to breathe."

Baru gave her an inch. Shao gasped in relief, panted, her icy composure in disarray. The effect was intriguing. Baru suddenly missed Ulyu Xe very much.

"You shouldn't do his work," Shao said. "He's a mannist. He comes from a mannist society."

Baru blinked. "What?"

"You're taking the red man's side, Apparitor's side, against the navy. He's Stakhi, and they're a patrilineal culture. He's an instrument of the sexual dialectic."

"Oh, Captain, I don't think the *sexual dialectic* has much to do with this—"

"Of course it does!" she crowed. "You child. Listen: Parliament doesn't like the navy's difficult women, doesn't like us asking for fair pensions and seizing their trade ships for leverage. So Parliament asked the Emperor to put a man in the Empire Admiralty. To do that, to put Lindon Satamine in that post, Apparitor had to sabotage Ahanna Croftare's chances. She worked her whole life for that post. And she lost it to Parliament's stupid fears. If Croftare can't get a fair chance, why should any woman?"

Baru thought the poor staff captain should try life as a Taranoki woman if she wanted to know about unfair sexual dialectics. But she sat down on the opposite side of the post, Shao's slack chain in her fists.

"All the more reason," she panted, out of breath from all the torture, "to help me adjust Parliament."

"What can you even *do* to them?"

"I have the Emperor's own power."

"Power." From Lune's side of the post came an unexpectedly thoughtful sigh. "Ormsment's fond of a riddle. It's very current, widely discussed, a great many wise authors have meditated upon it. One hears it at the happening parties."

Baru eyed the sloshing bilgewater beneath them. "Is that what this is? A happening party?"

"Of course it's happening. I'm in attendance."

Baru chuckled. Shao Lune snapped at her. "Shut up and let me finish. The riddle goes like this: Three ministers have gone to dinner together at a country retreat when they all taste poison in their wine. They cry out for an antidote. A lowly control secretary leaps up, showing a little nip bottle. She says, 'I have one dose of antidote! Who should get it?'

"The minister of the Morrow Ministry says, 'Give me the antidote, lest my spies uncover all your secrets and punish you with a lifetime of blackmail.'

"The minister of the Metademe says, 'Give me the antidote, lest my eugenicists forbid your children from marrying and lobotomize your husband to use as a brainless stud.'

"The minister of the Faculties says, 'Give me the antidote, or I'll stab you with this fucking meat skewer, right up the tear duct.'

"Who gets the antidote?"

Oh. Baru knew this one. One of those profundities you'd introduce to invite clever self-flattering nonanswers from your tablemates. "I assure you," she said, "that I don't have the sort of power one quibbles over at country retreats."

"Do you? You're very sure of yourself. Who's your handler?"

Baru thought at once of Farrier. She didn't like that. "What do you mean?"

Shao Lune shifted. One bright eye glimmered around the post, and the edge of a sharp smile. "When Xate Yawa and Iscend come down here together," she said, "I see that Yawa's not in charge. She's afraid of the Clarified woman. Who are *you* afraid of?"

"No one," Baru said, staring into the dimness of the stern hold. No one but herself. "They tried to claim me with a hostage."

"And?"

"I executed her myself."

"Oh," Shao said, with sudden respect.

"I loved her," Baru said, for no useful reason. Now she was confiding in Lune. What a fool. But she couldn't stop herself: the drink was not enough, she had to *speak,* she had to say how she felt.

"And I loved working for Ormsment," Shao Lune said, "until she got in my way."

Baru tugged listlessly on the chains. A gray shroud had settled over her.

"Tell me how to stop Ormsment," she said, "and I'll talk to the others about your parole. How would you like that? A chance to get out of your bilge."

Shao's bright glimmering eye watched her round the post. People, Baru remembered, had two eyes. She had forgotten the existence of Shao's other eye while it was out of sight.

"She won't dare attack you," Shao Lune said, "if you're under an Oriati dip-lomatic seal. I guarantee it."

THE target would be the clipper *Cheetah*. "Tau-indi Bosoka owns her," Baru explained, "she was sighted at moor in the Llosydanes. Right now *Cheetah* is somewhere north of us, headed home as fast as she can with news of that debacle at Moem. She'll go into the Kraken Still to reach the Mbo. But first she'll stop on Kyprananoke to take in water."

Apparitor boggled at her: "You say that like it's a stroll to the pharmacist! Don't you know what's down in the middle of the Ashen Sea?"

"Pleasantly unconquered islanders, happily canoeing about?"

"No, you lapsarian lunk, it's a dead sea full of ghost ships and rotten crews! The currents conspire, the winds are inconstant, there is rock and maelstrom! They'd be mad to go in there!"

"But the Oriati know a way to cross the Still," Yawa said.

"Since when are *you* an expert navigator?" Apparitor poked her in the breastbone. "You've never led an expedition further than Cattlson's rectum!"

"I policed smuggling, didn't I? Smugglers have to come up through the Kraken Still to get past the navy on the trade ring." She nodded grudgingly to Baru. "Baru's right. We can intercept *Cheetah* on its way to Kyprananoke. Baru and Iraji can go aboard, Baru to negotiate, Iraji to see after the cultural partic-ularities."

Baru had not, of course, mentioned to anyone that Tau-indi Bosoka thought she was infected by an apocalyptic spiritual disease.

Now she sat under her hammock in the arsenal and marked her vodka bottle with a grease pencil. She would allow herself not more than one dose per watch. A little more if her fingers really hurt.

The void said, in a young man's voice, "I need to cast a spell of protection over you."

"The *left* side!" Baru snarled at Iraji. "I said approach from my *left*!"

"But then you'd see me coming, and scuttle off." In his fine fingers Iraji held out a wooden tile about the size of a playing card, engraved, beneath the much-worn varnish, with the face of a woman in a collared coat. "Will you help me cast this spell?"

Baru blinked up at him. He wore a pair of canvas shorts and nothing else, his delicate strength so pleasant, so graceful, trained to ornament. How com-pliant he could be: and yet now she never forgot that beneath that compliance he was his own bright mind.

"A spell? I thought you were a good Incrastic citizen."

"In Falcrest I certainly am. But if your plan works, we'll be going aboard an Oriati Prince-ship. We need Oriati protection for an Oriati place. We need a bond of trim." Iraji held out the tile. "You come from Sousward, you must know the word. How do they say it in the Whale Words? Trim is a power that connects people."

He offered her the card again, with a long, elastic patience that would soon, Baru felt, snap back against her. Iraji had grown very bold with her. Perhaps he felt he'd earned her attention when he saved her life.

"We already have a bond of sorts," Baru admitted, "don't we? You saved my life at the Elided Keep. You saved my life again, from Munette." And maybe pinched Baru's ledger of secrets before he did. But wasn't that a sort of favor? Keeping Tain Hu's coded trust far from Baru's precarious heart?

"I was doing my duty."

"And you did it very well."

"Did I? You think I did a good job of breaking my friend Munette's arm?"

"Well, you didn't faint, at least. Why are you always fainting?"

He made an expression of extreme patience, extremely tested.

"I'm sorry," Baru offered. She *was* sorry, she had great reserves of sorrow, it was not hard to make some of it fungible and grant it to Iraji. "I'm sorry, I don't mean to be difficult. I've just been in . . ."

She did not want to talk about pain. Instead she reached out and took the tile with the woman's face from his hand. "What do we do?"

"We learn to play Purge," he said, and grinned suddenly. "Oh, I love this game."

H E dealt a deck of wooden cards faceup, then poured out a pile of dry beans. Baru knelt to help him separate them into piles of ten. She remembered the night she'd looked up *cryptarchy* with Muire Lo, dictionaries and thesauri scattered around them. She'd known by then that he would, in all statistical likelihood, come to love her. She was a fair enough young woman and he spent a lot of time with her. There were Incrastic charts one could use to obtain the resulting odds of love.

She had failed to prevent that. Lo had died.

Maybe when Iraji said he had to create *a bond of trim,* he meant she had to care for him. Maybe that was his magic, an Oriati magic, concerned entirely with the connections between people.

But like all requirements, such a bond could surely be falsified.

"You think I'll like this game?" She turned over one of the face cards. On the back, tiny inscribed Aphalone letters read, THE PRINCE-AMBASSADOR, and then, handwritten, *Tau-indi Bosoka*.

He hummed as he counted beans. "Your tastes aren't hard to cater to, my lady."

"Oh? You didn't have much luck last time." She remembered how to flirt like Hu. That lopsided smile, that gaze which did not break. It caught him and held him an instant. He laughed, surprised and charmed. He really must be like Ulyu Xe, drawn to men and women both.

"Come, look. This is Purge. . . ."

With an efficient and supremely unpatronizing manner, he showed Baru how to play. The players took the parts of rivals in Falcrest: the cards were ministers, admirals, parliamentaries, and polymaths who each contributed some political capability, whether moneymaking or law-writing or gossip-mongering or the creation of influence. To win, one first spent their influence (the dry beans) to recruit a cabal of allies (the cards). Some would help you get more influence. Some would let you alter the rules. Some would let you strike at your opponent's cabal. "Strip away my support," Iraji explained, "until you can have me convicted, or exiled, or murdered without much chance of anyone caring. But be careful not to run out of influence-beans. Each member of your cabal requires constant favors and protection, and if a tile is not satisfied with its allocation of beans, it may flip. . . ."

"The Tyrant's Qualm," Baru said. "You must divide your power to gain allies, but not too far?"

"Precisely."

They sat under her tied-up hammock and played as the deck above them drummed with busy feet and the ship creaked with speed. Occasionally Iraji smiled, or laughed in delight. Baru lost twice, quickly and purposefully, not because she could have won but because she needed to see all the rules in operation to grasp the game-behind-the-game. The rules might *say* you could buy any minister you wanted at the beginning, but Baru knew that only a few ministers would be *correct* choices, opening paths toward a strategy that would defeat most other strategies. It was better, for example, to recruit people of influence early on, so you could use their influence to get even more people of influence. But later in the game, you would have to begin spending all your influence aggressively to complete your plots, and it was a waste of time to cultivate more patronage. This seemed to be the key to victory: choosing when to transition from growth for growth's sake into the actual execution of your endgame.

"The metagame," Iraji said, and this time his grin was joyful and spontaneous.

"That's what you're talking about. The game-of-winning-the-game is called the metagame."

"I don't see how that's different from the game itself. Isn't the goal of the game to win the game?"

"Yes. The game is the set of rules I've taught you. But the metagame is the game of knowing how others tend to play the game, and choosing a strategy that will defeat the common strategies."

"Like yomi?"

"Yomi is a part of it, yes, knowing what I'm likely to do."

Baru frowned in thought. He mistook that for confusion, and went on:

"Last century when Purge was new, everyone complained that military coup through the navy was too powerful, so play centered around control of the Admiralty. Then the Foreign Policies variant came into favor, wherein both players could lose if the Admiralty were badly compromised by intrigue. The metagame changed, people stopped focusing so much on the Admiralty."

"Aha. That's a very useful word, metagame," Baru said, and went on to lose three more times, all by the narrowest margin, before she realized that Iraji was playing with her—always performing just a *bit* better than she could beat. Baru looked up at him with vengeful delight, infuriated and happy to be furious: "You're a snake. If I keep losing, why can't my player just have your player to dinner and stab him?"

"Ah, a simplicity!" He clapped. "The game presumes that all parties involved have guarded themselves against basic tactics like assassination and poisoning, which we call the Simplicities."

"As I am guarded, here on *Helbride,* by my patron's threat against your master's hostage."

"Just so."

"So only more sophisticated tactics can reach me."

"Such as?"

"Such as this effort to win my confidence."

"You think I'm here to befriend you on Apparitor's orders?"

"Aren't you?"

Iraji touched the cards between them. Lacquer-painted faces stared up from the wood of the deck. Slowly, hesitantly, he stroked one of the faces: and then, with a duelist's speed, he reached up to touch Baru's cheek.

She froze. He had very steady warm hands, and his eyes were dangerously open. Not a seductive openness, half-lidded and open-lipped, but a curious kind of trust: stupid, cowlike, tactically foolish trust, extended to her like a line of credit.

"I don't believe you," he said. "I don't believe you are what you pretend to be."

"I— What?"

"I can see you are in agony, my lady. Why do you have to bicker with my lord? Are you determined to be nothing but edges and lye?"

So he was here for Apparitor. To pry, again, at Baru's cracks.

"We're rivals," Baru said. "We must defend ourselves from each other."

"The best rivals share a certain respect, don't they?"

"In his rag novels, maybe." But not, she thought, after one of them has decided the other is a monster, and after that monster has decided to send him home to his brother and a terrible fate.

"He is lonely! Not for a lover," he smiled, quickly, and in pride, "but a peer. He has been on mission so long . . . the two of you could ease each others' pain, if only you were friends."

And Baru remembered how genuinely Apparitor had grieved for Tain Hu. How truly he had liked her. Pity. Very briefly she pitied Apparitor. To lose so many of his staff at the Elided Keep, to lose his hope of befriending Tain Hu, and to gain only this feral arithmetic-ghoul named Baru, who would rip him from his lover and send him into exile.

They'd almost confided in each other, on that day when they came to the Llosydanes. Apparitor had talked about his doomed voyage east, and meeting Lindon, and . . . and then he'd said something cruel. *You know the best class of pawn?*

And they hadn't, really, been even a little friendly since. Why?

It was obvious, when Baru put it in economic terms. He'd offered her confidence. She hadn't returned it. She hadn't told him anything about her past, or her lovers, or her plans. He'd offered an ante and she had not matched.

"I—" she began, looking at Iraji wonderingly, unsure whether to take him at his word, or to defeat this clever insinuation.

Then the game began again.

"*ROCKETS!*" The shout came down from the masts, relayed by the officer of the watch. "*ROCKETS TO THE EAST! SHIP IN DISTRESS!*"

Baru bolted for the stairs, slammed her head, and reeled up onto the deck cursing and spitting. Apparitor was halfway up the mast, dripping from his bath, wearing nothing but a skirtwrap. "What is it?" Baru shouted to him.

He climbed down lightly to the deck. His face was grim.

"It's *Cheetah*," he said.

"Excellent!" Baru cried. "I'll make ready to go aboard."

"You don't understand. They've been attacked. They're sinking."

CHEETAH

THE Prince-ship *Cheetah* drifted, kraken-struck.

Her distress rockets had cried out *unknown ship in pursuit*. She was a clipper, and she must have run from that ship with all her clipper speed, but it was not enough, she had not escaped. *Cheetah*'s predator hadn't murdered her in the ordinary ways: her masts had not come down under a crush of stormwind, her back hadn't been broken by a mine, her wood and canvas hadn't ignited under the cackling spray of Burn.

No, her wounds were more subtle, and Baru tallied them with unease— something *new* had done this work. . . .

She snapped her fingers for the acting master-at-arms (Diminute having run afoul of Tain Shir at the Elided Keep). The habitual motion did not work: she poked her stump with her thumb and gagged in pain.

"What was that?" the master-at-arms called. "Are you all right?"

"Get Shao Lune up here," Baru snarled. "I want to know what she sees."

Cheetah's hull had been punched in along the waterline, wound after wound after gaping splintered wound. As if a steel-tipped kraken had reached up from below, embraced the clipper, and driven its arms through and through. The sight made Baru heartsick. Her name was *Cheetah,* and Baru could only think of a dead cat with wolfsbite on its belly.

"Well," Captain Branne grunted, surveying the damage, "can't fix that, I don't think."

"No indeed," Baru said.

"She's sinking toward the stern. Fuck me, will you look at all the glass on that sunroom? That's going to be a mighty expensive aquarium soon."

"Cannon," Apparitor said. He came up beside her, wearing thick gloves: ready to climb up into the rigging and survey the boarding from above. "They were struck by cannon fire. It came in from the starboard side, there, and then the starboard aft as *Cheetah* pulled away. The attackers aimed high, trying to take her masts off. But by the end they wanted to shoot off *Cheetah*'s rudder. That was when they put the fatal wound in her stern. I think they wanted to capture *Cheetah*'s crew, but their weapons worked too well. They fled when the distress rockets went up. Curious that they didn't finish the job."

"We have to go aboard," Baru said. "We have to get the Prince and the diplomatic flags. It's our only hope against *Sulane*."

"I know." He chewed at his hair. "Shit. There's hardly any time. *Shit*. If the weather holds we can stay close alongside and—"

"*STORM!*" came the cry from the mast-tops. "*STORM AWAY SOUTH!*"

Baru and Apparitor looked at each other. Baru couldn't help but grin.

The acting master-at-arms shoved Shao Lune up to the rail. "What do you see?" Baru asked her, pointing to *Cheetah*. As Ormsment's staff captain, Shao would've read secret files. Perhaps they had described a secret navy warship with many cannon, used to "vanish" inconvenient Oriati diplomats. . . .

"I see a second-rate clipper hull from our Rathpont yards. The kind we sell to the Mbo to make them envy the quality of our first-rate ships." Lune's squint reminded Baru that she'd been down in darkness for a long time. The sun must dazzle. Baru shielded her eyes for her.

"Queen's blue bulb . . ." Shao Lune breathed. "Look at those cannon holes."

"What carries that many cannon?"

"A ghost ship. A ghost ship came upon her."

Apparitor groaned into his hand. "There aren't any ghost ships."

"Of course there are," Shao sniffed.

"The Empire Admiral would know about them."

"Very doubtful. We keep these reports from the more . . . *political* elements of the Admiralty." Shao Lune favored him with a supercilious smile. "In the real navy we've all heard the stories. Eight-masted titans that bristle with rockets and cannon as they glide about in banks of spectral fog. Immune to interception . . . as if they know our patrols and sentries."

"That's fish shit."

"Oh?" Lune pointed her shackled wrists to *Cheetah*'s sinking hulk. "Do you know any ship on the sea with enough cannon to do *that*? No? I thought not."

Yawa came up on Baru's left. "Ah," she said, studying the carnage. "I see something's killing ships. I'm going to go sit in a whaleboat with Iscend and a cask of water."

Water. Shit. That reminded Baru of her accounts.

"Apparitor." She drew him aside to mutter, "Are you planning to take *all* the Oriati aboard?"

"Of course I am."

"Must we? It's a risk . . ."

"Law of the sea. I don't care what you say. I'm going to help them."

"The world doesn't reward goodness with goodness, Svir."

"No. But people do."

"Fine." She did quick mental arithmetic. "Then we need to put a prize party on *Cheetah* and salvage as much as we can."

"We haven't any time—there's a storm—"

"If we don't do it, we'll die on *Helbride* before we make Kyprananoke."

"Oh, damn it. Damn, damn, pepper shit!" Apparitor beat his forehead with the meat of his hand. "The *water*. We have to rescue the water."

"As many casks as we can get." They would need enough to sustain the new passengers, at least. Enough to keep them from the thirsty death: a ship of mummies adrift beneath banqueting gulls—like the one that was now pacing on the yardarm above, furious that no one had paid any attention to its dance.

"There's only one way to play this," Baru decided. "We have to send hostages over to guarantee our good conduct. Or they're going to expect us to seize the Prince and sail off."

He nodded. "You're volunteering?"

"I am."

"Are you on good terms with this Prince?"

Last time they'd met, Tau had said, *I'll have nothing to do with you.*

"Of course!" Baru said. "We share a good rapport, I think."

The gull on the yardarm squawked in indignation and tried to shit on her.

SUNSET raked the sky like fingers in a child's hair. The two clippers settled flank to flank. *Helbride* silver-white and sleek, arrogant in its grace. *Cheetah* cruelly macerated, leaking oils and bilge into the waves, sinking inch by drooling inch into a great raft of kelp. The air was too calm: the sailors fidgeted, waiting for the storm front.

Helbride's crew put down a bridge over to *Cheetah*. An Oriati soldier leapt up onto the far end.

She was a brick-shaped bald woman with her fists wrapped up in rope, pleasantly open-faced, someone you might approach when you needed help with your luggage dockside. She called out in unaccented Aphalone, which meant a Falcrest accent:

"I'm Enact-Colonel Osa ayaSegu, captain of the Prince-ship *Cheetah*. Be you all warned, now. If this is a trick to kidnap my Prince, then I'll make it known that I have six armed naval mines in my hold. If I don't report that all's well, they'll blow both our ships apart."

"Iraji," Baru whispered, "didn't you say your people were a *kind* people?"

"It's been a long time since I left the Mbo," Iraji admitted.

"Enact-Colonel!" Captain Branne shouted back. The sea crashed and sucked between the two hulls. "I'm Captain Branne of the fast courier *Helbride*. We're here to rescue all your crew."

"We doubt that, Captain Branne! We suspect you're here for the Prince!"

"Two of my passengers are prepared to come over as hostages for our good conduct."

The enact-colonel scanned *Helbride*'s deck and rigging. "Send me the pretty boy in the masts."

The crew laughed up at Apparitor, who sat perched in the ropes, looking more like an ornament than a crew member. He kicked his feet happily and waved. "Can't!" Branne yelled back. "He's my cabin boy, I promised his mum he'd come home! We'll send these two instead."

Baru took Iraji's arm with her left hand. Feel him, now. He is alive. Remember this, his hard forearm and slim wrist, so that something will remain when he goes. All that you do has a price.

As they crossed the bridge, Baru looked down, and for a horrifying instant she could *see* all the depths beneath them. The dark water full of schools of fish and bubbling porpoises, deepening, plunging past great-finned tentacled things and upraised claws of bone, toward fissures in the seafloor where secret fire glimmered.

If you died here your soul would not have the strength to swim.

CHEETAH'S Oriati crew paused in their work, covered in blood and sweaty caked sawdust, to salute them. "Thank you for coming," many of them repeated, or they touched their clavicles in gratitude. Baru remembered Aminata showing her why the clavicle was the most delicate bone, *you may break it with a few pounds of force*: so if you were Oriati, part of a people with a long tradition of the martial arts, you touched the clavicle to show your trust.

They followed the enact-colonel below. The attack had blasted the ship open to evening light and the sound of birds. Everything was a wet-paint fresco of gore and hardwood shrapnel. Cannonballs had shattered the bulkheads, splintered them through running bodies, painted the deck in the stink of char and bowels. Iraji covered his mouth. "O principles," he murmured.

"No principle watched over this," Osa ayaSegu said, which made Iraji wide-eyed with a fear Baru didn't understand. "You will await *Cheetah*'s full evacuation in the aft sunroom."

"Will we see the Prince?" This was all useless if they couldn't get the Prince aboard *Helbride*. Had they been hit? Had they been *killed*? Without the Prince, *Sulane* might not respect the diplomatic flags . . .

"Of course," Osa said, to Baru's huge relief. "The Prince will dine with their honored hostages."

They passed through a spice room clouded with blown-out cinnamon and drifting cumin. The Oriati artisans had ornamented the ship's furniture with the shapes of ancient beasts: jellyfish with ruffled bells as long as cloaks, krakenflies perched on reeds, owls of calm and of fear, tigers and ruffed lions, gyraffes with falcons on their heads. From the deck above, the soft rain wept down through the pine-pitch caulking, and it made Baru remember, against her will, the clean air and autumn leaves of Duchy Lyxaxu.

Fascinated by everything, she forgot to swivel her blind spot, and so she stumbled rightside-first into the Prince Tau-indi Bosoka.

"Oh," the Prince said. "It's you."

Yes," Baru said, warily. "It's me. Hello again."

For a few moments they shared a mutual, tired wish: if only we'd never met before. Then the Prince stiffened, not with distaste but determination and pride, preparing themselves for an honest effort. They cupped Baru's hands and kissed them, left and right, careful of her bandages. Their lips were warm enough to make Baru shiver in delight.

"Welcome to my home on the sea," they said, "damp and bloody as she may be. You've come to our aid. I offer the great gratitude of my house Bosoka, and of all Lonjaro Mbo, the Thirteen-in-Three-in-One."

"Your Federal Highness, we are honored by the welcome of your house!" Iraji cried. Baru and Iraji bowed together, and Iraji went a little lower than Baru, so Baru went a little lower than him, until they were both kneeling prostrate.

"You're really going to do this?" the colonel asked the Prince over Baru's kneeling ass.

"I really am," Tau-indi said.

"You know I'll try to take you away by force, if I must."

"You may try, my dear Enact-Colonel. You may try." The Prince looked down at their guests, bemused and smiling. "I think fate has brought me these two as a particular challenge."

"As you say, Your Federal Highness." The door creaked shut behind the colonel.

The three of them were left alone in *Cheetah*'s glorious sunroom, a cage of glass that looked over the ruined stern and the rising sea. The Prince offered their hands to help Baru and Iraji both up. "Before we go on," they said, grunting against the weight, "I must give you one last choice. If you would prefer to break the hostage deal, return to *Helbride,* and sail away while *Cheetah* dies, then tell me now. You may leave freely. Understand that if you stay you may well drown in this room with me."

"Your Federal Highness," Baru protested, "I don't understand. Would you refuse our help?"

"If you remain," the Prince continued, softly, earnestly, "your fates will be entangled with mine. And at this moment I am doomed, doomed with all my house. You are my only hope of salvation. If you and I cannot find a common human bond—yes, Baru, you and I and your companion—then all of us will come to an end far worse than the sea."

Baru's skin crawled. She wasn't superstitious. But her body might be.

"I was very rude to you on Moem." The Prince bowed in apology. "I presumed to judge you for luring my friend Abdumasi to his doom. I see now that if there is no hope for you, there can be no hope for peace."

Play along, Baru. Play along and see if you can understand. Magic is practiced in the world, whether you believe it or not; it is used to guard over sick children and to ward off the foxes from the coop. People *believe* in magic. The magic may not alter anything, but their beliefs still guide their actions.

"Your Federal Highness," Iraji began, thick with fear, and had to stop to cough and *hem* until his voice uncreased itself, "what's wrong? Why are you doomed? Perhaps we can help."

"You *can* help, you can, you can, please."

They reached behind them, where a cloth covered a woven basket-dish. Baru braced herself for the revelation of a hideous Oriati superstition—bugs to eat, or blood-brush calligraphy, or some other lurid ritual from the Old Continent. But Tau-indi whipped away the silk to reveal a puff of savory steam and a bowl of thick brown bread, full of almost-raw meats pounded full of spice, gauze-cut fish like pink tissue, candied fruits, fresh eggs, and at the center a clay pot of wine.

"Please," the Prince said, earnestly, "will you sit and eat with me?"

Baru had to know. "What are we doing? Is this magic?"

"Yes, in a way, I think it is." The Prince sat cross-legged by the bread bowl and began to fold up hot pitas to eat with. "My ship was attacked, as I'm sure," they chuckled ruefully, "you've seen. But the worst of the damage is invisible, I'm afraid, and if it is not repaired, we will all end up worse than dead. I told you before that a wound in trim is growing around us, a wound that will devour all civilization on the Ashen Sea. You, sir, you were Oriati born. Do you know what I mean when I say *a wound in trim*?"

Iraji swayed. Fell down to his knees. "Yes," he said. "I do . . . a wound like Kutulbha."

Kutulbha was the city where the Armada War had ended. There was a passage about it in *Firestorm*. Baru remembered it vividly. When the last fires went out in the Ventricular Villages, and the silent rains fell on burnt Kutulbha, nothing remained except the concrete made from the ash of their bodies. . . .

"Exactly so." Tau-indi offered them each a pita. "Wherever the human fabric frays, then older powers come through into our world. Powers that are cloaked in tragedy. One of those powers assaulted this ship. And because we saw that power, and heard its voice, all of us on *Cheetah* are now cut off from the mbo and doomed to eternal solitude. Unless we can reconnect ourselves to the human community, we will carry this wound wherever we go. Just as I thought you carried a wound, Baru, when I met you on Moem."

Iraji clutched at Baru's elbow with desperate need. She stared at him, absolutely baffled. This was nonsense, superstitious raving: it meant nothing. "Fine," she said, "what do we do to, er, help you reconnect yourself?"

"Very simple." Tau set their legs under them and tucked their khanga against their hips. "We attempt to create a bond of trim."

"Do we get to play Purge?" Baru asked, eagerly.

Tau stared at her in bemusement. "I don't like that game. I thought we might share a meal and a story. And *if* the reconnection succeeds, then trim will rescue us from *Cheetah*."

"If by *trim* you mean sailors from *Helbride,* then yes"—Baru laughed, ha ha, how funny that we might drown—"we'll be rescued."

"Oh no." Tau shook their head, solemnly. "We must find our own way out, through our own togetherness."

"Yes," Baru repeated, frowning, "we must find our own way out, until *Helbride*'s sailors come rescue us."

"You misunderstand me. I've had us locked inside."

"What?" Baru leapt to her feet. "You've done *what*?"

"I've had us locked inside *Cheetah* while she sinks," Tau said, apologetically, "so that only trim can save us. So as to guarantee that our survival is a function of genuine human connection."

"Baru." Iraji seized her arm. "Baru. I can't swim."

B ARU couldn't batter the door open. The Rathpont shipwrights had built a very fine jamb—of *course* they had, damn it, they'd engineered the sunroom so it could be sealed against flooding. The hive-glass at the rear of the sunroom might be opened, but they'd have to swim, and what about Iraji?

"Why did you come?" the Prince asked Iraji, as Baru scurried about trying to escape.

Iraji folded up a handful of salt beef in his pita bread. "We hoped you could protect us from our enemies. Your diplomatic status could save us."

"You came to bargain with us." The Prince slapped the deck with their hand, a sound that made Baru's cheek sting. "Let me be plain. The use of people as instruments is anathema to me. I'd rather die in this ship than live as a pawn in some technocrat's scheme."

"I understand," Iraji said, "I know the ways of trim: people must be ends in themselves, not means—"

"For Devena's sake!" Baru erupted, driven to panic by the satirically stupid ethos of pigheaded moral stiffness. "We're on a mission to *stop* this war, understand? We're agents of the Imperial Throne and we're searching for the Oriati who attacked Aurdwynn during last winter's rebellion! We have to be in Parliament by summer's end to report our findings! We were on our way to Kyprananoke, to ask one Unuxekome Ra about a certain Abdumasi Abd. And if you don't help us, the mutineers in our navy will kill us, and there will be *no one* to stop open war!"

The Prince gasped aloud in relief. "Oh," they said, falling back on their heels. "Oh, thank you, thank you. Good!"

Baru didn't understand what was *good* about any of that. "You're welcome?"

"Skepticism is understandable," Tau said, breathlessly, "I know you come from a very different culture. But you've shared your honest thoughts with me. We found a connection. We are both looking for Abdumasi Abd. I suspect you want him to *start* the war, not to stop it, but at least we share a common purpose."

Baru supposed that was true, in a roundabout way. She was looking for where Abd had been, and Tau was searching for where he had gone.

"I have to find Abdumasi." Tau-indi held up clasped hands. "I have to make things right with him. That can stop the war. Don't look so cynical, Baru. I *am* a diplomat. I believe trim acts through people, and I believe people can choose peace."

"Your Highness," Iraji whispered mournfully, "Abdumasi Abd is dead."

Tau-indi blinked softly. They had a very kind face. "I hope you're wrong."

"The navy reported him killed at the Battle of Treatymont. Burned with his ships. If he'd been taken prisoner, perhaps he would have been sent to Moem for Execarne to interrogate . . . but he was not with those we found there."

"No, Faham Execarne told me as much—the Morrow Ministry didn't have him." Tau-indi wrapped bread in gauze-cut fish sliced so thin with glass knives that the light went through it to cast pink shadows. "Now, Faham and I speculated that he might be alive in the hands of the navy or the Imperial Throne. You are both agents of the Emperor, I deduce? If the Emperor knew Abdumasi Abd was alive, *you* would know it, too. So if he is alive, he is unknown to the Emperor. Therefore the navy is our suspect. Would any part of your navy hide a man who could start a war from the Emperor?"

"It's possible." Baru felt a prickle of respect for the laman. They might be somewhat given to religion, but their logic was good. They knew the trick of postprior reasoning, to assume a conclusion, and deduce the conditions that might make it true. A dangerous method, but sometimes powerful.

"How curious," Iraji said, archly, "to hear that our own spymasters have been speaking to you, a foreign, ah, ambassador."

"Who else would conspire to keep the peace? Spies hate war."

"Do they?"

"Loathe it! A spy's job is to appear entirely like a normal person, and nothing remains normal in war." Tau poured celebratory wine. "This is wonderful! Look what we've accomplished already. So perhaps your navy has Abdumasi Abd. If I can find him, and make things right between us, I think I can stop this whole war at its source."

"You mean—" Baru sighed. "—the hurt feelings between you?"

"Hardly just hurt feelings! When I was a young laman during the Armada War, my two closest friends were Kindalana of Segu and Abdumasi Abd. Now, our great house entertained two hostages from Falcrest—"

Baru regretted asking.

And then, suddenly, she did not:

"—named Cairdine Farrier and Cosgrad Torrinde. These men were on a mission to study our way of life. I took it upon myself to try to befriend them, believing that a small friendship might be echoed in a greater peace between our nations. But in doing so"—Tau's voice fell, a deep and real sorrow—"I hurt my friend Abd. And the hurt was never healed."

A wave broke against the sunroom window. Either the storm surf was picking up, or *Cheetah's* stern had dropped.

"Are we finished?" Baru asked, nervously. "Can we go?"

"I don't know," Tau said, infuriatingly, but with apparently honest bemusement. "When the three of us are bound together, trim ought to point the way out of the ship, back to the human community. Nothing's happened yet. Perhaps we need to talk some more, and have dessert."

"Perhaps we need to break the windows and float out," Baru suggested, "on a board or a table."

But the Prince's face fell suddenly. "I've just had a terrible thought."

Baru resisted the urge to call all their thoughts terrible. "Have you."

"Yes. If the navy has Abdumasi Abd . . . perhaps he was given to the Burner of Souls."

"Oh no." Iraji leapt up in dismay. "Oh, principles help us all. If the Burner of Souls has him, he must have broken by now. He must have admitted his sponsors—"

Tau-indi closed their eyes in fear and sorrow as Baru looked between them, trying desperately to figure out who, precisely who, was the Burner of Souls?

"But it may be worse yet if my friend hasn't broken," Tau said. "There are powers he might have called upon to sustain himself . . . powers which would shield him from the Mask, at the cost of all he was to me."

"What powers?" Iraji began to tremble. "Surely you don't mean—not the same power you implied—"

"Yes. The same power that attacked my ship." Tau's neck bobbed as they swallowed. Again they smoothed their khanga around wide hips. "It is here, upon this ocean. It has left its ancient safeness. You know its name?"

"I know its name," Iraji croaked.

And he toppled in a faint.

Baru caught him. "Sorry," she said, very worried now, and trying to hide it, "he's excitable."

Tau-indi stared at Iraji with an expression of majestic royal concern, a face much larger than life. The golden chains in their nose and ears rustled softly.

"I'll be damned," they said. "The things that trim brings to my door." And then, shaking themselves, "I'll fetch the salts."

"This Burner of Souls." Baru checked Iraji's pupil response. "Who is she?"

"A gruesome sort of Masquerade artifact. An orphaned Segu girl raised by the Masquerade as a weapon against her own home. She was trained to deceive and compromise the most defiant subjects by Mister Cairdine Farrier."

Baru looked up with a thrill of horror. "Do you know her real name?"

"Yes. She is a woman from the isiSegu." Tau came back with salts. "Terrible, isn't it? If the navy has poor Abdu, I'm afraid they've given him to Aminata."

CHEETAH'S bell tolled out its dying song: *let me go, let me go, let me go.* Inch by inch, gallon by gallon, the clipper foundered.

"I'm getting us out of here." Baru ripped cloth and cutlery out of the sunroom closet. "I can't *believe* how stupid you are!"

"You know the torturer Aminata," Tau said, staring in fascination. "O principles, it's working! I can hardly believe it! All these connections between us are becoming clear!"

A wave struck the hive-glass behind them. Cold brine spurted through the caulking. Yes, Baru wanted to scream, she knew Aminata. Aminata a torturer? Aminata who'd only wanted to command tall ships? At first Baru felt sorrow, and pity. But then her heart moved with selfish gladness. Aminata had been made into a weapon of the Empire, and so she might suffer now, she might hurt as Baru hurt, she might even understand why Baru had chosen the path she now walked—

Last of all came a growling fear from low inside her.

Aminata was never your friend. She was Farrier's agent from beginning to end. . . .

She was part of the Farrier Process. . . .

Cheetah tipped as a wave sloshed through her broken hull amidships. The force slammed the clipper against *Helbride*. She rebounded, swayed, and at last righted herself on her stubborn keel. There was a moment of peace. And then, with a mournful creak and a hurricane of canvas, the clipper's mainmast snapped and twisted and toppled down across the deck above them.

Baru clutched at the cabinet with her good hand and tried to compute their rate of sink. They would be finished soon. Well, there was nothing for it.

She whirled, hard-eyed, speaking to the Prince as she would speak to the dukes.

"Your Federal Highness," she said, "do you remember what I said at Moem?"

"All of it," Tau said, their eyes shut tight. They were summoning their courage.

"I intend to destroy Falcrest. I am a daughter of Taranoke on a deep-cover mission to bring down the Masquerade from within."

Tau-indi Bosoka touched their throat: one long finger drawn from their smooth chin, down a line of skin paint, to their small collarbones. They had adorned their skin in golden patterns and green stars. The full regalodermia of a Lonjaro Prince.

"I can't afford to believe you," they said. "You used this same trick on Aurdwynn. You told them you wanted their freedom. I fear that. I fear that use of people as pawns."

Why, Prince Bosoka, must you refuse me? Why must you lock us into a sinking ship?

She applied her thoughts to the shape of her own logic, and corrected it.

She was not thinking like an Oriati, the people who for decades had been tricked and exploited by the Masquerade. What could you do to resist that trickery? You could stop acting in what seemed to be your own calculated self-interest. You could avoid doing what was *necessary,* because then Falcrest could manipulate you by changing the terms of necessity. You could focus, instead, on basic goodness, an inflexible moral code: be honest, be kind, be charitable.

Was goodness still good if you hewed to it out of tactical necessity? Was there, Baru wondered, any difference between *being* good and *pretending* to be good for your own gain, if you took the same actions in the end? Was there any difference between telling the truth unconditionally, and deploying the truth in service of your agenda, if you told the same truth?

Maybe the Oriati thought so.

Maybe the difference between truth-for-itself and tactical truth was the only difference that mattered. Maybe the most crucial and subtle distinction in life was the difference between someone who was truly good and someone playing at goodness to gain power.

Could she distinguish those two tendencies in herself?

Another wave crashed against the windows, dark and silty with lightning-burnt kelp. Tau-indi sat cross-legged and open-armed, open-faced, and again Baru saw them as a candle-flame, steady despite the wind. They were waiting her answer.

"I'm going to prove my honesty," Baru said, "on your terms."

"How so?"

"With trim."

They looked at her in wonder. "Will you?"

"If I get the three of us out of here, that means I've passed your test of trim, right? I'm a real person. I'm connected. We're like—" She grappled at the air, trying to find a metaphor. "We're like spiders, reeling in our thread to get back to the web. And I cannot get us back to that web if I was never bound to it."

"Yes," Tau-indi said, smiling. "That's how it works."

"Good." Baru wrestled the folded dining table out of the closet. "I'm going to build a diving platform for you and Iraji. And when it works, and all of us are safe on *Helbride,* you're going to help me track your friend Abdumasi Abd."

"You have a lead on him?" Tau cried eagerly.

"I know where to find a woman who helped him on his way." And from that woman Baru would find the Cancrioth, and whatever she could gain from them—power to overthrow Farrier and Hesychast, power to crush Falcrest by war, power to free Taranoke and Aurdwynn.

Immortality, perhaps. If that was necessary to see the work complete.

And along the way she would find some way, *some fucking way,* to be sure she was not under Farrier's control.

* * *

HELBRIDE smashed into *Cheetah,* and Tau-indi fell.

A wine bottle shattered beneath them, red glass starbursting. They shouted in pain, and Baru pounced on them, searching for the wound. The wine bottle had cut them: a long, thin slash up the skin of their back. The golden khanga parted shyly around the blood.

"It's beginning," the Prince said, with real fear.

"She's going down."

"Yes—believe me, your navy taught us all about how ships sink." A chuckle. The Prince thought they were very funny.

Ropes twanged and snapped. Above them, with ponderous creaking malice, *Cheetah*'s second mast collapsed across the deck. The impact punched the stern further below water. Thin sheets of seawater jetted through the window.

The Enact-Colonel Osa was shouting, too far away, "PRINCE! PRINCE BO-SOKA!"

Tau-indi grimaced at the cut, and pawed for Iraji's hand. "I must confess," they said, "that I didn't lock us in here *completely* out of trust in trim."

"Don't, don't admit you're *not* a fanatic, I was just starting to understand you—"

"People are many things," they said, seizing Iraji's hand. "When I had the door shut behind us, I thought to myself, Baru Cormorant is an Imperial agent. And they *always* have another way out."

"And here," Baru gasped, dragging the dining table over to Iraji and the Prince, "I thought you were mad."

"Trim is nothing but other people," Tau-indi said, and cried against the pain. "I don't think I can swim like this."

"I'm getting you both out of here," Baru promised.

"You won't leave the boy?"

"Never again," she snapped, without thinking.

They had to sink faster than the ship. To get out through the stern windows, they had to go *down.* Descent was the hardest part of diving. The body wants to float, so the ascent goes easily—but when you dive, when you go deep, you are fighting against your nature. Like running downhill.

Baru tore open the casks of sweet wine, poured them empty, and hammered them shut again. Every blow made her scream a little from her fingers: she went on anyway.

"My vintages," Tau said, mournfully. "I was quite sentimental about that one."

"They're for flotation. Now I need ballast."

"Try the curtain rods—"

"Perfect." She seized the heavy rods from their mounts above the windows and lashed them to the table. "When I open the windows," she grunted, hauling at the knots, "the sea is going to flood in and trap us in a bubble of air. We need to dive—down there, through the windows—then kick free of the ship's suction and get back to the surface."

A cell of hive glass popped from the window frame. Water jetted in.

Baru and Tau looked at each other in dismay.

Another cell popped, and another, and from the stern the sunroom began to flood.

"I'm going to tie you to the table," Baru snapped, "here, quick—trust me—"

"Of course, of course, every time a woman's tied me to a table, it's been grand."

"Don't flirt with me! I'm trying to save you!"

"I'm trying to encourage you!" the Prince said, laughing, and the laugh must have jarred their wound: they groaned and swore in Uburu, "Oh, fuck a noma face!"

Baru lashed the Prince and poor fainted Iraji facedown to the dining table with a coil of stowage rope. Now she just had to mount the casks for buoyancy—but how? "Eyelets," she shouted, tearing through the closet. She couldn't find a way to lash the barrels to the table. "Have you any eyelets?"

"Do *you* keep eyelets in your sunroom?"

"I don't have a fucking sunroom! I live in an armory!"

"There's your problem," Tau said, philosophically, "too many swords, not enough sun."

Baru grabbed all the rope and spare khanga fabric she could find, shoved the khangas under the two Oriati as cushioning, looped the ropes around the casks, ran them under the table and around Tau-indi and Iraji and then back up. She grinned as she worked. The thrill of the fight, the frigid water, the crisp satisfaction of working with her hands—she felt like a fisher on the hunt, like a smooth graceful creature.

"What happens now?"

"Now," Baru said, "I'm going to flood the room."

Like all hive-glass, the stern windows were made of small glass panes set into a steel lattice. That steel could be a fatal cage. But the windows had been built to swing open in sections, so the passengers could take air on a nice day, or run out fishing lines. If she opened *those* two frames . . .

"They swing outward," Tau-indi called. "Is that a problem?"

Shit! They did swing outward! The water outside would press them shut. She would need to equalize the pressure, inside and out, before she could open them.

She put up her cloth-wrapped fists and began to punch out the glass.

Cheetah had now tilted past thirty degrees, the sunroom entirely underwater and flooding quickly. When Baru broke the first cell, a stream of seawater pushed her down onto her back. Roaring, she struggled up against the current and broke another, another, ruining the expensive work of some Rathpont glassblower and his nervous apprentices, battering out *Cheetah*'s stately view. Water rushed in, cold and sharp as winter sky, up to Baru's waist, her navel, her breasts and armpits. She hissed against the cold. Iraji moaned on the table, bound next to the Prince.

"Wake him up," Baru snapped, "wake him up, he's got to hold his breath."

Tau-indi began to whisper fiercely into Iraji's ear. The boy's eyes snapped open, wide with fear. Baru, too, felt a curious nonspecific fear: something was wrong. Something in her blindness. What? Was it the Prince?

She turned to look.

Behind the Prince, up the slope of the sinking sunroom, water wept around the door.

Oh fuck. The ship *above* them had flooded. Only the door held back the deluge.

"Get ready!" Baru shouted. "Take your breath!"

She squatted and pulled the table down over her, Prince and Iraji and rope and casks and curtain rods and all. Breathing smoothly, setting her legs wide, drawing the mass of the table down onto her calves and thighs, Baru held Tau-indi and Iraji and waited for the sea to rise.

O Wydd, she thought, let my breath last.

Cheetah tilted to port and did not stop, *could* not stop, she just kept tilting and tilting and tilting. She was capsizing, she was turning over—

The door holding back the flood snapped off its hinges. The weight of the sea rolled down to crush Baru. The weight of the sea.

20

GLASS PIERCES CHEEK

A FIST of water slammed Baru down against the sunroom windows. She struck face-first.

The dining table with its passengers crashed down on her back.

A sliver of broken glass went in through her mouth and out her cheek. She could feel it with her tongue: she tasted the puff of blood, sweet in the brine—

But she remained

calm.

With her left hand she reached up to the frame she was pinned against and clicked the latch open.

With her right hand she unlatched the window frame to her right.

The windows swung open beneath her. She let herself fall out of *Cheetah*.

Silence and bottomless dark bubbled up around her.

She drew the table down with her. Tau-indi's khanga fluttered in the current. Their cheeks were comically puffed, their eyes squeezed shut. Iraji clutched at their hand.

The quiet of everything. High above, rain stippled the surface of the sea. *Helbride* was silhouetted by her own whale lanterns. Crew overboard from *Cheetah* thrashed in the waves.

Baru thought, I am a daughter of Taranoke. I am born from the navel of the world. My home was made from the fire of the earth and the deep of the sea. I will not drown here. I will not drown your hopes, kuye lam.

She was bleeding, bleeding, the blood made her hungry, the hunger fed her soul. She whirled and caught the falling table on her body: it crashed into her across her stomach, drove the breath from her, but she roared a silent drowning roar, her blood so thick and fast it felt it would erupt from her eyes, and she kicked and kicked and pushed Tau-indi and Iraji away from their falling ship. Trim will save us and trim is only other people.

Something impossible followed her. It was the fucking moon! *The moon was after her again!* Baru stared at it in fury and kicked harder.

The moon pursued her. Out of the dark came a white-black torpedo shape, bigger than a horse, bigger than a whaleboat—Baru saw carnivore teeth, an eye bright with intelligence, a scythelike blade that she had taken for the moon, gleaming alien letters—a surface gnarled as brain coral, and deep within it, staring, the hollow eyes of a skull—

She realized she must be hallucinating. Dying. And she imagined great kraken-arms reaching up from below to seize her.

Galvanized by terror, serene with strength, Baru drew the dive knife from her ankle. She sawed the ties that held the iron curtainrods to the table. The ballast dropped away. Baru pulled herself back on top, on top with Tau-indi Bosoka and Iraji.

Buoyed up by empty casks and light wood, they rocketed for the surface.

The water parted across Baru's back. She yawned against the roar, to make her ears crinkle and pop. As they rose they began to tumble, and Baru clung, watching starlight and sea-shadow sweep across Tau-indi, watching their warm eyes open and fix on Baru and smile. Iraji's cheeks were pulled back by current: he stared at her with a squirrel rictus.

They struck the surface upside down.

They were trapped—she hadn't thought of this, so *stupid* of her—Baru tried to kick hard enough to tip them over, but the whole weight of the table was on her, pressing her down, and she had no leverage to flip them. Iraji was drowning. The Prince was drowning—

—and a long oar reached under the table and tossed them upright. Storm air and pelting rain needled her skin. Lightning split the sky. She laughed and howled in victory, and the thunder answered her.

"Baru!" It was Apparitor, shouting. "I'm going to cut your feet off, you idiot!"

"Do you have them?" The Enact-Colonel Osa. "Do you have the Prince?"

Baru spat seawater and cheek-blood, rolled up on her knees, and bent to check Tau-indi's breath. They were alive. Their pulse was steady, their breathing deep and ragged but strong. The waves swelled beneath them but did not tip their table over: well done, Engineer Cormorant.

She went to Iraji, who coughed up brine but shook his head when she tried to help.

"Oh," Baru gasped. "We made it out. Oh Himu, I am clever!"

He looked at her in wonder. "The spell worked!" Iraji said. "The spell of protection! I'm a genius!"

*   *   *

IN *Helbride*'s middeck, surrounded by the warm protection of *Cheetah*'s rescued crew, Tau-indi Bosoka spooned soup from a tin mug Baru had brought
down to them.

"What I don't understand," the Prince said to Baru, "is why, if you really
are trying to save your own people, you'd do so much to destroy their rebellion."

Baru had been warming fresh blankets for the Prince over a hot stone. Now
she looked up in wary fear. "What do you mean?"

"Well, as I've, ah, brought up before, your actions in Aurdwynn lured
Abdumasi Abd to his death or capture...."

And Baru had been too stupid to realize her rebellion would draw in bigger
conflicts. But she couldn't deny it. "Yes ..."

"Aurdwynn wasn't the first place Abdumasi interfered."

"No?"

"He was funding the resistance on Taranoke out of his own personal wealth."

Baru felt as if she'd stepped onto a needle, a cold needle tall as a mountain.
And if she slipped it would run her through from sole to spine. Abd had been
active on *Taranoke*? Of course he had. Where else would a merchant with a
grudge against Falcrest strike first? Why hadn't she thought of it? Oh, Wydd,
she was no savant, she was a fool. She'd drawn the Oriati into a trap without
even realizing it, and now she had destroyed her own home's chances of resistance!

And she kept putting off opening her parents' letters—

—had she *known*? Had she been trying to deny what she'd done?

Baru sat paralyzed by anguish. The blanket, left too long on the stone, began
to steam. Tau spoke carefully. "Presumably, if he's under navy interrogation, he's
betrayed the names of his contacts on Taranoke."

Mother. Father. No.

"Maybe he hasn't cracked yet," Baru said, and changed the subject as hard
as she could, lest she erupt on the spot. "Did the people I sent to you on Moem
reach safety?"

Tau looked happy that she'd reached for a mutual connection. "They're all
safe. The boy, his guardian, the diver, the herbalist, and the pale man. I interviewed them, gave them papers and money, and left them to charter passage.
Things were ... unsettled on the Llosydanes."

They had not mentioned Nitu the cook. "Unsettled how?" Baru asked, to
avoid that guilt.

"There were some riots. A portion of the date crop burnt down. Some killed."

Baru had sauntered onto those islands, sent their markets into a panic, scooped out their pockets, and walked away with Abdumasi Abd's name. She hadn't even paused to *think* about what she'd left behind. Oh Himu, all that money she'd made! Why hadn't she invested it in something? A charity? A school? Some sort of trust for development?

Tain Shir said she was going to kill Baru's parents.

What if Abdumasi Abd had cracked under Aminata's torture, he had named Solit and Pinion as insurrectionists, and they were even now in Tain Shir's possession—

"Baru?" the Federal Prince murmured. They reached for her hand. "What did I say?"

She stood paralyzed. Maps of action and consequence unfurled from her lips and her fingertips, the possibilities of all she might do and say, but on the horizons of these maps she saw only Cairdine Farrier's laughing mask and the blood-caked brute indifference of Tain Shir.

"Baru?" Tau put down their soup. *"Baru?"*

"Do I know that voice?" A slurred call: Baru shivered out of reverie. Through the Oriati came a Falcrest man, dowdy old brown sparrow among the tall chattery blackbirds, Faham Execarne with a pipe of weed and dressings on his wound. "Who's that I hear preaching the dubious but comforting metaphysics of trim? Can it be the sacred hermaphrodite of Lake Jaro?"

"Execarne!" Tau cried, sitting up. "You mangy addled runt! I've told you a thousand times, I'm not a hermaphrodite, I can't satisfy your fantasies!"

"Damn!" the spymaster said, snapping his fingers, which made Baru's right hand ache. The enact-colonel Osa stopped him: he submitted wordlessly as she searched him for weapons.

"How are you?" Tau offered, by way of apology.

"Shot up and sore," Execarne complained. "And nearly out of drugs. Ah, look, you're befriending Baru! Risky fucking proposition, going by the evidence! I knew her about two days before I had marines and jackals burning down my farm."

"Did you lie to her? Lying at first meeting does invite misfortune." Tau had gotten a bay leaf stuck in their teeth.

"I didn't even tell her I was the Morrow Minister!" Which faded into hacking laughter as he folded up around his crossbow wound.

She put her hand into Tau's mouth without permission and plucked the leaf right out so assuredly that she did not even brush their lips. "Goodness," Tau said, "you're nimble."

"You probably oughtn't associate with her," Execarne wheezed, "she's definitely an Imperial agent, and she's made it this far for purely political reasons. Dangerous."

"Nonsense. I've told you before, Faham, I believe that the atom of the human universe is the dyad, the connection between two people. The most precious thing there can be."

"Is that so," Execarne said. "Have you told her the truth about that ship that sank your clipper, then?"

Tau stiffened so suddenly that Baru heard their teeth click. Behind Execarne the enact-colonel inhaled sharply. "Your Federal Highness, I strongly advise you to let this matter lie."

"Always so subtle, Osa." Tau-indi touched Baru's collarbone. "But I can't speak of it. Baru, do you know what happens to a fetus exposed to uranium?"

Baru had never seen such a thing, had never even read much uranium-lore: the Oriati insisted the black pitch was magical, the books said they were wrong. "No, I don't. What happens?"

"They become monstrous," Tau-indi said, in a small brave voice which Baru could not bear to laugh at, although she wanted to. "The soul cannot inhabit them at birth, for they are already full of uranium light. What enters them does not come out of the Door in the East. Our alliance is young. There are certain things you and I cannot touch upon, lest our work give birth to a monster."

Baru's wound prickled. Suddenly she did not feel like laughing.

"The Prince needs to rest," Osa said, firmly, and suddenly the nearby *Cheetah* crew were toasting Execarne and Baru, shouting thanks for the timely rescue, inviting them into a circle of smiling faces to offer them fine wine, over here, away from Tau-indi Bosoka.

"It's all bullshit," Execarne said, conversationally, to Baru.

"What's bullshit?"

"The Cancrioth," he said. "That's what you've been sent to find, right? Yeah, I've got bad news. I think the Cancrioth is one of our deception missions. Useful bogeymen. That's all."

Baru's mind was so awhirl and her right arm so shot through with cold sick threads of pain which seemed to wrap up around her throat and jaw and down her tongue that she could barely even muster a lie. "I don't know what you mean," she said weakly.

"Of course you don't." He sighed and took someone's proferred wineglass. "The three of you, Durance and Apparitor and yourself, aren't meant to find the Cancrioth. You're just supposed to rampage around causing diplomatic incidents."

"But the ship—the Prince implied—"

"The Prince, virtue bless them, is eager to blame every possible cause for war on ancient cancer cults. A convenient lie for them, that's all."

But that can't be, Baru thought. Hesychast believes in them, Farrier believes in them, and I have gambled everything on their power . . .

A shout from the deck stopped Baru from any further confusion, panic, or bodily agony: a shout picked up and repeated all across the ship.

"SAILS ON THE PROW! SAILS HO!"

Baru bolted up onto the maindeck. Apparitor was already there. "It's *Sulane*," he said, grimly. "She's circled ahead of us. It's time."

H ELBRIDE'S crew ran up *Cheetah*'s diplomatic flags.

Sulane came at them from the bow, running perpendicular to the wind, tossing slightly in rough surf. She looked very small in the sea, small and outrageously red, like a bloody splinter in the snow: but she grew so quickly as she came. Baru imagined the stabilizers of her hwachas and rocket batteries flexing on their springs, steadying the gunnery crews, keeping their instruments trained on *Helbride*, so rich with paper and canvas and things that burnt.

Apparitor chewed his lower lip into blisters with worry. "We'll be fine," Baru assured him. "It'll work."

"I'm not afraid of *Sulane*," he muttered. "She'll kill us or she won't. There's nothing I can do about it now."

"Then what?"

"Iraji hasn't passed out this often since the last time we did work in the south."

"Is it stress?"

"No," Apparitor said, but he was interrupted by Tau-indi's arrival.

"Your Federal Highness." Apparitor bowed and kissed Tau-indi's hand. "Thank you for coming aboard."

"Your Excellence, I could *not* be more charmed. How is Lindon?"

"Very well," Apparitor said, though he clearly worried otherwise. "Will Xate Yawa be joining us?"

"I'm here," Yawa said, appearing from below in a simple peasant's dress. She looked down at the laman with deep unease. Baru wasn't sure if she disliked lamen, or Oriati, or Princes. Probably, she thought, it was Princes.

The laman seemed to make Apparitor uncomfortable too, or, at least, self-conscious: his eyes skittered over their hips and up their soft proud throat, where they had painstakingly reapplied the golden paint of their station. Baru remembered Apparitor saying, *a man can become a woman, or a woman a man, depending on how they dress and act—but what we hate, in the Mansions, is a liar.*

Who did not carry their childhood prejudices? Even Tain Hu had looked down on the Belthyc people. Even Baru would sneer at a plainsider.

"Firing range in ten seconds," Branne reported.

INS *Sulane* came straight at them.

"Masks on," Apparitor ordered.

Baru reached up and slid the porcelain half-mask down over her head and looked back up again, faced now in white, like bone. Apparitor's banner of hair streamed out from behind a mask marked around the right eye with the silver polestar. Captain Branne's full-face sea mask glistened with oily filters and the weathering of harsh eastern seas. Execarne slid on his dull varnished wood. Yawa's black judge mask shone with faint purple highlights. Together they faced the mutineers.

Tau-indi Bosoka and the Enact-Colonel Osa looked at each other. Baru watched the Prince shiver.

"We're in firing range," Branne said.

Sulane did not launch.

"Keep course," Branne ordered. "They've got the fighting rudder. It's on them to turn off."

Sulane came closer yet. Waves split across her prow like tendons on a scalpel. Baru counted the spears that lined her rails, and the red-masked marines who stared back at her, and the count brought her no comfort.

A ship's girl looked up from her chart of figures. "We're in the fifty-fifty bracket." Any rocket fired from *Sulane* now stood a coin's chance of striking *Helbride's* rigging and dooming them all.

"She's adjusting course again," Branne reported. "Correcting for the wind. She'll ram us in two minutes."

Baru raised the spyglass, and beheld her.

The killing woman stood on *Sulane's* bowsprit, half-crouched, bare-footed, her weight low and swaying as the frigate chopped through the waves. She wore knives across her chest and a bug-eyed mask. The mass of her calves flexed and relaxed with feline ease. The storm crossbow in her arms could have lanced a harpoon into a good-sized whale.

She raised a hand and pointed.

You. I want you.

Baru could have vomited, so sudden and profound was the fear. Would she haul Ulyu Xe out onto the bowsprit and keelhaul her while Baru watched?

Would she drag Baru's parents in a net behind *Sulane* until they came apart for the sharks?

Xate Yawa inhaled hard, and did not speak.

Then *Sulane* began to shout. The officers led the crew and the crew called out across wind and waves. The human mind has an ear for the human voice, and Baru heard clearly:

SAVE YOURSELVES, the mutiny bellowed. *LEAP THE RAIL. SWIM TO US. WE WILL HONOR YOUR SURRENDER.*

"Ah," Yawa clucked. "The amnesty. Very predictable."

"Keep your stations!" Captain Branne roared.

"Don't shout," Yawa murmured. "Show the crew you trust them."

"Captain Branne," Tau-indi said. "I presume you have a signal lantern aboard?"

"Yes, Your Highness."

"Send my compliments to Province Admiral Ormsment at once. Ask after her health, commend her again on the olive oil she sold me in Treatymont, and assure her that I will offer her asylum in the Oriati Mbo."

"You'll *what*?" Svir roared, wheeling on the Prince. "The fuck you'll give her asylum! That woman betrayed her oaths and killed my people!"

"And you killed my neighbor Abd's people," Tau said, "you lured him into war and burned his friends, and I do not know where he has gone. But here I am, saving your life with my flags, just as you saved mine. Listen to me. You must give Ormsment a way out, or she will fight like a wolverine."

"They're navy." It was Iraji, coming up to stand by Apparitor. "They'll never go live in the Mbo. They exist to burn Oriati people."

"I have to believe otherwise," Tau said.

Sulane passed *Helbride* barely two lengths away, turning hard. No rockets ignited. No torpedoes fired. She executed a full turn and came back on *Helbride*'s stern, pacing the clipper.

Suddenly she fired—

—Baru's heart nearly burst in terror—

—but the salvo of white hornets blew up harmlessly all around *Helbride*'s masts. They were only signal fireworks. Cries from aloft as the topgallant crews called out to each other, and the indignant shriek of the ship's beggar gull.

"It worked," Baru breathed. Her plan, Iraji's plan, she must be careful to remember to credit him, had worked. *Cheetah*'s flags kept *Helbride* safe. Ormsment would not make the navy responsible for an act of open aggression against a Prince's ship.

Apparitor sighed hugely and hooked his hands in his belt. "Tell the crew they're free to take turns at the sternrail mooning those bastards. Ormsment can't touch us."

Not until we have to leave the ship, Baru thought. Not until then.

TAU-INDI seized Baru's right shoulder and hissed. "Who is that woman on their prow?"

Who indeed. "That's Tain Shir."

"Tain Shir?" The Prince shuddered. Baru felt it in their fingertips. "Oh no."

"You know her, too?"

"I know Cairdine Farrier, who created her. She was his . . . argument." Tau-indi Bosoka came out of Baru's right-hand darkness and stood before her, huddled like a wet finch, hands cupped before their face, elbows tight together. Baru realized they were resisting the urge to reach out: to Baru, or the Enact-Colonel, someone, anyone. "He used her to provoke war in places where he wished to dictate the terms of peace. And then she . . . there was an expedition sent into the jungle. An expedition intended to uncover the old sciences. She did not return."

Baru knelt to be closer. "What do you know about Farrier?"

"I know that he was once a good man," Tau-indi said, still shivering, "and that he now seeks a single treasure in his wars and expeditions—"

"A secret that will turn you against each other in civil war."

"Yes." A little clever gleam in Tau's eyes. "You *are* his agent, as was rumored."

"I pretend to be," Baru said, with every scrap of belief she could scrounge. "And Tain Shir?"

"Tain Shir led his atrocities. The Invijay were not all warlike, before she led one of their nations to victory over the others. The Invijay horsefighters called her ahuihane, the Bane of Wives, because she would take husbands as her prizes. On their jungle patrols the Jackal soldiers were so afraid of her that they would whisper," Tau swallowed, and went on, bravely but with profound fear, "a ut li-hen, a ut li-hen, ayamma, ayamma. . . ."

Baru knew the Invijay, distantly: Tain Hu spoke of them with contempt. Distant Tu Maia cousins from failed invasions of Oriati Mbo, diminished into nomadic tribes. But she didn't know those words, *a ut li-hen, ayamma. . . .*

"It means," Tau-indi husked, "*it grows in her, the cancer grows.* The Jackals were afraid that she had the old power."

Baru hesitated, caught between the desire to ask—*do you mean the Cancrioth?*—and Execarne's warning. She didn't believe Tau would lie about such things. But then again, Tain Hu probably hadn't believed *Baru* would lie about the freedom of her nation. . . .

She tried a little quip. "Shall I befriend her, then? As you befriended me?"

"No." Tau-indi turned away, quickly, too quickly for their wound; she saw them crease up around the pain of the glass-cut down their back. "She cannot be reached. Death would be a mercy for her. Murder would be justified. Ayamma. The cancer grows."

"You're hurt, Your Highness."

"You cannot help that," Tau said, with terrible dignity. And they left in a rush of bright khanga, without saying good-bye.

Yawa picked her delicate way across coils of rope and canvas to Baru. "You should be careful," she said, "consorting with royalty like that."

"You seem to like Heingyl Ri well enough," Baru said.

"She is *aristocracy,* and a virtuous young woman besides."

"Do you think the Cancrioth's just a Morrow Ministry mirage?"

"No," Yawa said, instantly. "No, Hesychast's shown me things . . . they're real."

"I think Tau just told me how to find them."

"*Did* they," Yawa said, with sudden interest.

"I think Tain Shir met the Cancrioth."

Yawa hissed and pulled Baru into the shadow of a canvas tarp. "What did you say?"

"Tau just told me that Shir led an expedition into the deep jungle. In search of the 'old science.' Apparitor said the same thing. That she never came back."

"That's not possible." Yawa jerked her chin upward, a classical Maia *no,* or, wait, Baru remembered now, it was not *no* but *refusal of an inferior's request*: a very succinct *get out of here.* "I know she went into the jungle, but what drove Tain Shir mad wasn't any cancer."

"She calls you *Auntie,*" Baru said, unthinkingly: her mind was on that dim gallery under Moem, where Tain Shir had promised to follow her forever, and ever, and ever. Oh gods. What if Shir was *actually* immortal? What if she had what Hesychast sought?

Yawa recoiled. Too late Baru realized what she'd implied.

"Little girl," Yawa purred, "I've had enough of your threats. First my brother, now my niece?"

"That's not what I meant—"

"Isn't it? Didn't you just imply that my niece could be taken to Falcrest as proof of the Cancrioth? Didn't you suggest that *I* might be tarred by that association?"

"I didn't mean to imply that—"

"How cruel of you, Baru. Do you think this is what Tain Hu wanted of you?"

"You don't know a *damn* thing about what she wanted—"

"I didn't know her? My dear, I half *raised* her!"

"That didn't stop you from betraying her to Falcrest—"

"Nor you."

"At least I *tried* to save her!"

"Very successfully, I see."

"Fuck you. She came back for *me*."

"And my brother followed her!"

In the sudden silence beneath the wind-whipped canvas, Baru realized that of course Yawa was right. Baru had ensnared them both for Falcrest.

"I think we should be plain with each other," Yawa said. Baru could see her vicious smile only in the tightness around her eyes. "I know you're working to steal Aurdwynn from me. I know you're the one who killed the Priestess in the Lamplight, so you could secure her ledger of secrets. Now you've sent your agents to pry the North away from Heingyl Ri. You want the trade money, yes? Or is it the Stakhi you're after? Is that it? You think you can conspire with their King? Is that your dream, little Baru, to be the next Shiqu Si?"

Baru's suspicions clicked together like teeth.

"*You* stole the Priestess's ledger! Not Iraji, *you* did it, you—you common cutpurse! Give it back, or I'll—"

But she could not make herself threaten Yawa's brother again.

"This is the last time I'll warn you." Yawa summoned the ice and finality of the Judge passing her verdict. "Stay away from Aurdwynn. I spent my whole life gaining power over my home. I will not now surrender it to an islander whelp with delusions of empire."

A STORY ABOUT ASH 3

FEDERATION YEAR 911:
24 YEARS EARLIER

SOMETHING had to be done about the tumor growing in Tau-indi's soul. Something had to kill the botfly-friendship curled up in their heart.

Tau-indi respected Abdumasi and Kindạlana's choice to be together. Oh, did they respect it! And yet Tau-indi hid in empty rooms and plucked unripe fruit and cried sometimes, wishing that they had the courage to say, listen my friends, I don't mind, I'd be glad to know, so why do you have to make it a secret between yourselves?

Why do you have to keep yourselves from me?

One day Mother Tahr made time to go for a walk with Tau-indi. Laman and mother went away from the lake, down the rock gardens on the south slope. Jewel-eyed krakenflies hovered and darted across the streams, hunting tiny nymphs in the water, hunted in turn by frogs and bats. Tahr pushed Tau-indi to name a few of them, but Tau-indi was in no mood for that child game.

"You're not happy," Tahr said, gently.

Tau-indi was silent.

"Is something wrong with Kinda and Abdu?"

Tau-indi had worn calf-wrapped thong sandals and a sharp sari. They felt quite silly and overdressed, walking alongside their mother in her gardening gloves and old khanga wrapped up around her thighs, but they had wanted to seem grown-up. It would be *impossibly* embarrassing to cry in tall sandals and a nice sari.

"There are much bigger things to worry about," Tau-indi said, voice cracking horribly, "than my friends Her Highness and Abdumasi Abd. Don't you think, Mother?"

Tahr touched their chin. Her voice was hard enough to make Tau-indi hurt but it was a good hurt, a respectful kind of hard, she was only giving them the respect they had asked. "You want to be brave? You want to pretend you're okay?"

"We are mbo people," Tau-indi said, spitting all the words with stubborn bravery, "bound together. I'm okay as long as I have my friends."

"Oh, lama, you say that like it *hurts*."

"How can I ask anyone to help me when I can't help anyone?" That was the trap of trim, wasn't it? What if you felt awful, awful, and yet you were unable to ask for help, because you could give nothing in return?

Tahr stopped and made Tau-indi look at her. "You learn principles well," she said, her hands touching Tau-indi's throat, their cheeks. "Okay, brave lama, here's my advice. Trim doesn't work like that. The whole reason we *have* trim is so the helpless can cry out for help, knowing that others are glad to give without return.

"But I can't be the one to help you right now. I am fighting a war of letters, trying to convince the Princes of the Mbo to understand the true danger of Falcrest, and I'm losing. You are all alone. Hush, hush, don't cry, we all have to figure out how to be alone before we can be good for anything else. No one can help you? Then figure out what you have, what you have that nobody else has, and pick it up, and use it."

Tau-indi couldn't keep the bitterness out of their voice. It felt like they had bitter anger in their blood, in their loins, changing their body and the shape of their thoughts. "What is that thing I have, Mother? The thing that will make me useful to others? Kindalana is smarter than me, and Abdumasi more practical."

"You want me to tell you?"

"No," Tau-indi said, thinking. "No, I have an idea."

THEY called the household together and asked to be told everything that anyone knew about their hostages from Falcrest, Cosgrad Torrinde and Cairdine Farrier.

Cosgrad Torrinde lived in a room in the sentry house, where he kept curious habits. He ate grapefruit constantly and started like a child at the sight of insects. He was terrified of compost and nudity. He was very beautiful, everyone agreed, although because his skin was paler than even a Segu man, the slim contrast between his eyes and his skin made him seem ill. He dwelled on ancient medical texts and asked after griots who had witnessed works of surgery. Many attested (with glee) that he had a comically, foolishly huge cock, which he naturally hid out of shame.

As for Cairdine Farrier, they had never met a man so eager to be elsewhere. Not that he hated his guesthouse (he stayed with Padrigan and Kindalana), far from it; rather he was constantly eager to be at the *next* place, to meet the new

people, to think the new thought. When he wasn't skittering around Lake Jaro
on his kayak, which he had built himself, using techniques "taught to him by the
Bastè Ana," he was holding court among the housekeepers or working in
the fields, where he tugged weeds energetically and listened in fascination
to the most ordinary things.

Cosgrad was, it was felt, the cleverer and quicker of the two, but Farrier was
more likable, and he had the art of laughing at Cosgrad, which made Cosgrad
sputter and clench his fists.

Gossip suggested that the two remained implacably at odds.

Tau-indi decided to seek their special purpose in the hostages. If they could
be made happy, that happiness would return to Tau.

So they dressed carefully and painted on the gold paint and green stars of
their station from breast to nose. When honeycomb and raspberry water was
arranged they sent sentries out to request a palaver between Their Highness
Tau-indi Bosoka, Federal Prince, and the two Falcresti hostages.

Cosgrad Torrinde arrived first and threw himself prostrate across the
packed earth floor. "Your Federal Highness! I am humbled, humbled." He was
so young! He'd said he was turning twenty-three, but that he didn't want to
celebrate his birthday, because to celebrate the fact of a birth was royalist.

"Please," Tau-indi said, talking from their stomach, trying desperately to
keep their voice from cracking. "Stand. Why would you bow before us? Don't
you hate royalty in Falcrest?"

"Oh! I don't bow? I wasn't sure, I thought I might, it's how we met Princes
in the books about old Falcrest, which I always loved." He leapt to his feet and
put out his left hand, then, blanching, his right, trying not to grin but grinning
anyway. "I'm so happy to speak to you, Your Highness. I feel that I have *everything* to learn."

Tau-indi felt a little warmth, deep down in their gut, for this poor man. All
his time on Prince Hill he'd been questioned and interviewed and plied for
stories of the far northeast—but what had he been allowed to do for anyone
else?

His trim must be in a terrible snarl.

Tau took the man's hand and smiled through his incredible grip. Oh, he was
strong. "We are here to ask you to be our tutor."

"Oh, no no, there's been a mistake." Cosgrad pumped Tau-indi's hand twice,
up and down. "Didn't Miss Bosoka tell you? I'm the one who needs a tutor,
I need a guide, I'm the one who should be at your door asking for your help!"

Tau-indi smiled generously at the Falcresti man. He had a strange face, didn't he? His pale skin made him seem as if he'd been emptied out, or never filled: awaiting the breath of life, the gust of storm wind out of the east.

"The first thing you should understand about us," they said, "is that we are mbo people, bound together, and that we are always happiest when helping someone else get what they want."

Cairdine Farrier arrived a few minutes later. He begged Tau's forgiveness, for he'd thought there was a directional taboo today, and he'd taken a long route around the lake. "I'm surprised you care," Tau said, quite struck by Farrier's conscientiousness. "The calendar taboos have been rather sliding out of practice these past years."

"I want to learn everything about you," Farrier panted, "and be as good at it as you are! Can't slip up now."

"Hello, Farrier," Cosgrad said, warily.

"Cosgrad," Farrier clapped him on the shoulder. "Have you started talking about squid yet? This man can't go a week without bringing up squid."

Cosgrad blinked three or four times. Tau couldn't tell if he was trying to control himself, or steel himself to fight back. "Tau would like you to be their tutor," he said. "How would you like that, Farrier?"

And he fixed Farrier with a look of such challenge and conviction, such utter *doubt* in the man's good faith, that Tau was instantly fascinated. What did this mean? What did Cosgrad think Farrier would do, or fail to do?

Farrier sighed. "I'm sorry, Tau. Kindalana's already asked me to tutor her, and I simply felt it wouldn't be seemly. If I refused her, then accepted you, how would it look?"

"Why?" Tau asked, utterly bemused. "How could it be unseemly to tutor someone?"

Farrier looked at Cosgrad. His smile was, for the first time, fake. "Some people," he said, "believe that men have impulsive flesh, and that this flesh responds to signals emitted by women. Particularly women in their earliest fertility. I am twenty-two, and Kindalana is nineteen. We're both . . . highly charged. In some people's eyes it's already too much that I stay in her home."

This seemed so immediately ridiculous to Tau-indi that they had to mind their manners and not laugh. Sexual attraction was simply a by-product of the need to exchange joys: like any powerful principle it could be deranged and made terrible, but it had nothing to do with flesh and signals! Even if, dwelling upon it, Kindalana did have a sort of magical effect on Tau lately.

"Farrier was quite the womanizer in school," Cosgrad said, with no trace of jealousy or bitterness, an absence so marked that it was like an eclipse; you can see that something is in the way, concealing the truth. "With no one else around to keep an eye on him, I've got to be sure he doesn't misbehave."

Farrier winked at Tau. "If only he knew, Tau, that my students are the women I *don't* pursue. One has to have principles, eh?"

Tau-indi wanted to ask Kindalana about all this, but the idea of bringing up sex meant they would have to ask Kindalana why she and Abdumasi were being so secretive, and that secret made Tau sick with rage.

N OW Tau-indi, too, went to war. It was a war against their friends.

In the morning and the evening they helped Cosgrad Torrinde catalog insects and plants, telling him about the ratoon rice that had once grown on the monsoon-plains south, and about the new development that had raised the farmers up to better crops. He was *monstrously* curious about everything—and Tau-indi did not use the word *monstrous* idly, because he was also stupidly rude. A field hand came up the hill with a machete wound, rotted and swollen, and Cosgrad insisted furiously that they had to wash it out with boiled water and put maggots in the wound—maggots! As if he'd never heard of botfly or nagana! Insects could never, *ever* be allowed to grow in anyone's flesh.

"What does that mean?" Cosgrad struggled with the phrase Tau had just pronounced. "That didn't sound like Seti-Caho, the words you just said."

"A ut li-en?" Tau-indi shivered. "Yes, it means *to grow in us*, in the old tongue the Cancrioth used. We use those words when we speak of taboo parasites like botfly."

"The Cancrioth, yes, that's what I thought. Who were they?" Cosgrad hovered with his incredibly smooth paper and his charcoal pencil. "In Falcrest, see, there are legends of the Cancrioth—legends and, of course, rag-paper novels. We think of them as raiders, highly degenerate, bred to survive in tropical climes by a partial regression to the animal template. . . ."

"Degenerate, no." Oh, the griots had always been so *oblique* about this topic! It was hard to teach, for fear of tearing a little hole in the mbo with the words, and letting in old power. "The Cancrioth were councilors and philosophers who ruled the continent of Oria before the Mbo. They gathered in Mzilimake, in the southern lands beyond the veldt, where the fish in the water glow with inner light, to study the heat that boils up in the uranium land."

Cosgrad's pencil whirred and jagged. He broke it and threw it aside and snatched another from his breast. "Yes, yes . . . why did they gather there?"

"They wanted to find immortality, down in the hot places where the uranium seeps in pitch. The heat of the hot lands never dwindles: an invisible fire burns in the caves below, and fills the rivers with light. Because the heat never dwindles, it must be immortal. And—ah, Cosgrad, this is *hard*."

"Courage, Prince! Courage!"

"The Cancrioth said," Tau-indi vomited up in a rush, "that the water coming out of the uranium mountains had a special charge, and if prepared and applied properly, that charge could induce cancer, which was a higher form of vitality: for does not cancer grow in living flesh, and displace that flesh? Is it not more energetic and prosperous?

"In cancer was the secret of the new energy which would never die. And they made rituals to grow horns on their flesh, and tumors that spilled from their orifices, and some of them even had horns of tumor that grew beneath their eyes so that they had stalks like *snails*.

"And they made drugs and compounds with the hot water, they played with rabies and disease, and all this drove them into frenzy, saying, a ut li-en, we grow in us, we must grow and fill up the whole world! And for a long time they came very close, they ran rampant across the face of the world, for they were very clever and very fierce. Until the mbo rose up and stopped them."

Cosgrad had cracked his pencil again. His hands were trembling. "Ah," he said, "goodness. How radical, how extreme. They *altered* their flesh? And the changes, were they inherited?"

"I don't want to talk about it anymore," Tau-indi insisted. "It's bad for our trim, to bring this knowledge up into the community."

"Just that one question, Tau, please—these changes induced by their special cancer, did they go into the germ line? Were the Cancrioth able to pass on their mutations?"

"I won't speak of it!" Tau snapped.

Later they asked Farrier, trying to be sly, "Does Falcrest think of my people as . . . tumorous? Do they associate us with cancer and disease?"

"It is a prejudice some hold," Farrier said, tying a ribbon around his latest effort at a proper calligraphic scroll. "Will you help me with this knot? In Falcrest the belief is that all the Oriati live in a sort of humid quilt of jungles and savannas, full of tsetse and malaria and stranger disease. Lions and tigers everywhere, and whales in the rivers. An ignorance I hope to correct." He winked at Tau. "Why? Do you associate yourselves with cancer and disease?"

"No," Tau said, shuddering, "we are proud, most of all, of turning away from that path; just as we remember slavery, and take pride in eradicating it. And if some of us went back to that path, I think the Mbo would have to rise up to stop them, or give up all claim of goodness forever."

* * *

So Cosgrad could be uncomfortable, at times.

But he also told Tau-indi all about Falcrest, and that was a weapon Tau-indi needed. They'd show Abdumasi, with all his money and his griots. They'd show Kindalana, with all her guests and her diligent studies. Tau-indi, too, could bring a great gift to Prince Hill!

On the griot days, the days Prince Hill gathered in the house of Abd to learn about the war, Tau unleashed their new weapon against Abdumasi. "Cosgrad Torrinde tells me," they would say, following one of the griots, explaining why a battle had gone the way it had, "I have learned from Cosgrad to expect this, and that . . . no, it's not like that, it's like *this*, Cosgrad has told me."

Soon the griots came to Tau-indi to learn from *them*.

The epic wanted the names of the enemy, First Fleet, Second Fleet, Third Fleet, frigate and torchship, mainsail and Burn. The comic wanted to mock Cosgrad's manners. The gossip teased Tau-indi about Cosgrad's exotic looks, about his strange spare body that he kept taut as bark rope. *Is it true*, the gossip would ask, *that in Falcrest they worship youth, and that all the old are put to death at fifty?*

Whenever Abdumasi said something hopeful about the course of the war, Tau was there with dreadful intimations of Falcrest's secret strength. Whenever Kindalana tried to explain the policies of the Federal Princes, and the intra-Mbo squabbling that made everything about war complicated, Tau was there to explain how Falcrest would exploit these gaps.

Tau-indi reveled in the storm-cloud power they had obtained. They could put themselves at the center of the affair. They could tell everyone that things were even worse than they knew.

They could spoil the mood.

A principle of spite moved them. Bitterness had been visited upon them by Kindalana and Abdumasi, tangled together in secret, and now they would visit bitterness in return.

"Torrinde's like your pet!" Abdumasi said, completely impressed by Tau-indi's offhand mastery of Falcresti ranks. "Does he follow you around? Can you get him to come swimming with us? Manata, we should start swimming again, all three of us! Summers used to be so good."

Kindalana sniffed and lit a joint in the small fire. "Cosgrad swim? Not a chance. I hear he only bathes in private. Tau couldn't convince him."

"Oh," Abdumasi said, disappointed. "What a waste! Have you *seen* him? He's like one of those bulls whose muscles are too big for their skin! Tau, do you ever," and he lowered his voice to a conspiratorial hush, "I know he's quite a bit older, but do you ever, you know, get to *peek*?"

Tau caught Kindalana's artfully disinterested exhalation. She had looked away as if she didn't care.

Kindalana was jealous! Kindalana didn't want Abdumasi to see Cosgrad Torrinde, or, perhaps, Kindalana wanted Torrinde all for herself. Wasn't she Segu, after all, where men had only recently stopped being treated as chattel labor?

"He's far too old for me," Tau-indi said, trying to sound as airy as Kindalana looked. "Of course, I thought Mother might be interested in him. But she seems to have her eye on someone else. Don't you think, Kinda?"

Abdumasi covered his mouth in shock. They *never* talked about the tension between Padrigan and Tahr.

Kindalana dropped her joint in the dirt and stamped it out. "I've been trying to get closer to Cairdine Farrier," she said, "but he's slippery. I know Cosgrad's a naturalist and a botanist. He's here to study fleshy things. But Farrier, what's he want? Why's he so careful about what he says and does? He talks like a big happy man, but catch him by surprise and he's *scared*. . . ."

"I think Cosgrad's trying to blackmail him!" Tau whispered. "I think Farrier stole Cosgrad's love, and now Cosgrad, out of jealousy, is waiting to catch Farrier in some mistake or scandal . . . you know, secret sex or some such . . ."

Kindalana and Abdu pointedly did not look at each other.

Victory, Tau thought, victory. I have struck a blow.

They did not know at the time that Cosgrad Torrinde was on a mission from a woman named Renascent, a mission to prove his worth for a secret station. Even if Tau had known, they wouldn't have understood.

How could a station be secret? How could you help anyone that way?

THE storm season of 911 passed on into the spring and then the summer of 912. For their next birthday Tau elected to celebrate on the frettes down south, a stepped land where tangled trees grew down the scooped-out edge of the Jomino Mesa and booming waterfalls rainbowed from the high basins down over the mouths of ancient limestone caves.

Tau-indi led the mule procession, riding alongside Cosgrad. The Prince Hill parents, Padrigan and Tahr and Abdi-obdi Abd, followed behind them with their children and groundskeeps and sentries, where Cairdine Farrier told foreign jokes and asked people about money. As Tau led the procession they felt like a gleaming star, like a Prince.

A river cheetah crossed their path twice, carrying her kittens to higher ground. Cosgrad leapt in delight. "You have cats! I thought cats were from the high north. In Falcrest all our cats are very small, and quite disobedient. I was sure they'd come down from the Wintercrests."

Falcrest could hardly be allowed to take credit for cats. "Cats started living with people in Devi-naga Mbo, to eat the sea rats."

"That's the story?"

"That's one story. Another story is that house cats gathered in Mzilimake to make a plan as to how they would walk on two legs and use tools. But they were thirsty from the trip. So they lapped up the water from the sahel next to the jungle. But there were so many cats that they lapped up all the water and made the desert, which is why their tongues are so rough."

Cosgrad laughed in delight. "But that doesn't explain why they became domestic!"

"Of course it does: the desert was very hot, so the cats ran away into our houses, because we had shade."

"Oh," Cosgrad said. "And you're *sure* your house cats didn't come from the north?"

"We have hunting cats, tame leopards, monsoon tigers, sand cats, burrowing cats, river cats, flying cats that leap between trees, house cats, and cheetahs like her. Watch carefully, now, and you might see her run across the water, which they can do if they are very fast. . . ."

Cosgrad waved off a fly. His eyes never left the cheetah. Tau watched the hard muscles of his arm move in delightful ways. "Everything's so complicated here," he said. "So many kinds of cats, so many languages, so many crops, so many stories, so many"—he looked once at Tau-indi, with the same incredible fascination—"kinds of people."

"It's a very rich land, and very old. Everything has found a way to live together. There are difficulties, of course, but they sort themselves out. That's the world."

Cosgrad rubbed his mule behind the ears and made soft assuring noises. "It is the world. I never thought it could be so strange." His voice was soft and fretful. "But it's all so *complicated* . . . so very hard to fit into one theory of the origin and purpose of life. . . ."

They left their mules at a hitching-place and climbed the trail up onto the frettes. Water crashed down from the mesa above, forking waterfalls of mist and thunder, and they moved under the shade of the mangroves in a ring of angry birdsong as the tree life protested their trespass.

"Now, remember," Tau-indi reminded their party, "it's taboo today to gather under the shade of the same tree."

Cairdine Farrier nudged one of his friends, a very bright young woman who worked as a barrister to handle the House Padrigan's unfamiliarity with Lonjaro law, and murmured something. She grinned and nodded. Tau had the deep suspicion they were whispering about the Noble Privilege of Trim.

"Mangroves!" Cosgrad shouted, hurtling off into the brush, waving his arms. "*Mangroves!* How can there be mangroves here! We're inland! Mangroves don't grow here! It's impossible!"

His voice trailed off into the greenery.

Everyone laughed at him. "He's not wrong about the mangroves causing trouble, though," Abdumasi said, "it's actually hard to tell which tree is which. This is a tricky taboo."

"We'll have to split up and explore." Tau liked that—with the group divided, Tau would get a larger share of attention from whoever accompanied them. "That will be my birthday project—the exploration of the frettes! Let's meet up on the mesa-top when the sun gets red, and tell each other what we found."

Tahr Bosoka and Abdi-obdi Abd went off one way, two mothers talking about the war. Abdi-obdi Abd had trade positions in Kutulbha, the Segu capital, but more and more of that port's shipping was going over to military use. Padrigan followed them a little with his eyes on Tahr, until it became clear he was not invited along. Then he and Farrier took the housekeeps and groundskeeps and clerks to picnic in a frog-licker's clearing not far off. You could get *very* high if you licked a frog, or even die: Tau-indi hoped that Padrigan wasn't angry enough to lick the wrong frog.

"Let's go find Cosgrad," Tau-indi suggested.

The three of them tiptoed down spidered roots to stay out of the mud. Kinda and Abdu pushed each other back upright whenever they slipped. And a warm principle struck Tau-indi, something that lived in the sweaty warmth and the birdsong and the sound of their friends' breath behind them.

They wanted to turn around and ask nakedly for everything to be forgiven. Everything since that fight with Kindalana at the lake, where they'd made themself out to be the best Prince, and far above childish things like comfort from a friend.

They were so *happy* here, exploring with their friends. This was what mattered, this togetherness—and it could never be allowed to pass.

"What's Cosgrad after?" Abdumasi asked, as loud and braying as a donkey, puncturing the moment.

Kindalana, of course, had a good answer. "Mangroves need to grow on tidal plains, where water rises and falls. He's confused how they can live here, too."

"He can't have missed the waterfalls, though. They would feed mangroves just as well as tides."

"I think that mangroves need salts, too. So he must be confused, since the waterfalls are freshwater, right? That's interesting." Kindalana bit the web of her hand thoughtfully. "Cosgrad sees things I don't, sometimes. He has a sharp eye."

They found Cosgrad knee-deep in a murmuring stream, staring petrified at a branch. On that branch a tiny tongue-sized frog stared back at him, swelling up into an angry little bladder and saying *robbot, robbot, robbot!*

"Sst!" he hissed, when they got close. "Don't move! The frog is dangerous!"

He looked a marvel. His long coffee-colored hair had gotten loose of its tie to run down his back, and the light through the mangrove canopy burnt his beard stubble in colors of bread and cinnamon. His rolled-up canvas breeches, soaked through, clung to his thighs and loose-laid masculinity. The silk chemise left on him when he'd given up on his jacket had ridden up to bare a wedge of stomach muscle and a thin line of sun-toasted hair that all led the eye down. He stood there, tense and masterfully unmoving, his ridiculous vain body portioned out into ridges and packets of muscle by his ridiculous vain exercises, staring down a frog.

"That one's not actually poisonous," Kindala said. "You don't have to be afraid."

Abdumasi sucked in a huge not-laughing breath.

"Oh." Cosgrad's eyes narrowed warily. The frog ballooned into an outraged ball and said *wart! wart!* "You're completely sure it's safe?"

"Colored in stripes, kills all types . . ." Abdu began.

"Ah. Yes. Colored like sick, only a trick. It doesn't rhyme in Aphalone, see, so I forget it. . . ."

Tau bit their cheek and wished that they could laugh at Cosgrad's silliness. The problem was that Cosgrad was bound to them by trim. They had led their friends here to say, look, Cosgrad is mine, aren't you envious? And now Cosgrad wasn't being impressive at all, except, perhaps, to the lecherous eye.

"The leeches might give you more trouble, though," Kindalana said.

Cosgrad looked down at his proud calves and made a noise of dismay. "What! What are those? Are they slugs? Oh! Oh no! They're *attached* to me! They're going inside me! My blood—they're drinking my *blood*!"

Clearly Cosgrad Torrinde couldn't be left to explore the mangrove forests on his own. "I'll take him back to the picnic," Tau said, grabbing Cosgrad's arm to help him out of the muck. "Catch you two back there? Tell me what you find."

Kindalana considered them with hooded eyes, suspicious or unsure.

"Sure," she said. "Catch you back there."

*　　*　　*

TAU-INDI set Cosgrad on track to the picnic clearing, told him that the leeches would fill up and drop off in a few minutes (he hopped around in panic), asked him to say hello to Padrigan, and then doubled back.

Kinda and Abdu knew Tau-indi loved the wet complexities of the mangrove forest but hated the slippery climb up to the caves behind the waterfalls. So they'd go inside those caves, wouldn't they, to keep secrets from Tau? That was where they'd go.

They'd go to the caves and leave Tau-indi all alone.

Tau-indi trudged along thinking sullenly about days when the bonds between the three of them were roads to move warmth and comfort, not strings of bile and jealousy. Somehow their friendship had been conquered. No more wandering days that tasted like raspberry and honey and sweet lake water, no more days acting like griots or daring captains, no, now they were all three like the dukes of Aurdwynn. Laying siege to each other.

They climbed upslope. The waterfall hammered their face with hot metallic drops. Sunlight sprayed through the roar. Behind the roaring curtain they found—oh, the jealous heart-needle feeling of it—Kindalana's khanga hung on a rock by the mouth. Tau-indi swallowed the urge to pick it up and bring it to her.

Instead they sat by the mouth of the cave and listened to the voices inside. Eavesdropping? Never. They were just coming to be with their friends on their birthday, *their* birthday, and if they accidentally happened to overhear something, well, it was their friends' fault for keeping secrets.

Voices came.

"Thank you," Kindalana said, with plainly sexual relief. "Mm. Thank you. Ah, that's better."

"Good," Abdu said, oddly gruff. There was a long silence.

"Too fast for you?" Kinda said lightly. "Did I come too soon?"

Abdu made an uncertain noise, and then, with some hurt, "I guess I thought we'd stopped."

"I know. I know. It's just . . ."

"You needed a distraction from your little crush?"

Tau-indi's heart thumped. Was it about them? Did Kindalana have a crush on *them*?

"It's not a crush," Kindalana said crossly. "I don't like him. He's ridiculous. He just turns me on. *You* know how it is! There was that harbor authority woman who kept searching your cargos, and you hated her, but you just couldn't stop asking me to play *pay my special toll* like I was her."

Tau-indi didn't want know these things nearly as much as they'd thought.

"It's the clothes that get you." Now it was Abdu's turn to speak with practiced lightness. "He's always so prudish. It makes you curious. You see him getting all sweaty in a silk shirt. You imagine peeling the leeches off his legs, higher and higher, and—oof! Okay, okay!"

Tense silence. Kindalana drew breath a few times. Finally she said, "I'm sorry. This wasn't fair to you."

"You know I can't say no. You're . . ." A rueful laugh. "If there's any trim in the world, some day you'll have a husband whose face could start wars."

"You're a good friend, Abdu, and you deserve better than me."

"There's nothing wrong with you, Kinda."

"There's something wrong with—using you like this. I just need . . . you know. The war's driving me mad. The things I'm learning, every day, about them and about us, who we are as a nation and what we've done to deserve this . . . I feel like I'm overflowing. I need simple things. Things that feel good right now."

"You don't fuck me because you're guilty about the Cancrioth, or about Tahari."

"No. Not that."

"Is it Tau? You're worried about Tau again?"

Yes! Tau-indi's heart shouted. Yes, worry about me, you clotted assholes. Worry about your young friend!

"Tau's furious with us," Kinda said. There was a noise of stones moving. "And I really don't know what to do. My patience with them is running out. I thought . . . when they pushed me at you, down in the lake, I thought it was because they were worried about you. They wanted someone to take care of you, because . . . you know, things are going to change. . . ."

"I know I'm not a Prince. I won't go with the two of you when you come of age. I knew it wasn't going to last."

There was a soft exchange of breath: a kiss. Tau-indi imagined them curled up against each other with mad loving hateful relish. Even listening to them like this, the jealousy wasn't sexual, or as little sexual as anything in Tau-indi's mind this year. No, it was a nobler kind of poison. They'd been friends! They'd been good together, the three of them! Why was this necessary, this closeness between two of them? Why was it required, if there had been nothing wrong with their third?

"What do you think they're angry about now?" Abdumasi asked. "I mean, I can tell they're angry, Tau's not subtle—"

"Not subtle!" Kindalana must have made a face, because Abdu laughed the shocked laugh of someone finally talking about a taboo thing. Tau-indi wanted to roll up into the waterfall and be sucked all the way out to sea. They had *thought* they were subtle . . .

Kindalana sighed. "Tahr and my dad. I think they think it's my fault, somehow. Tau thinks I made it happen, and they're furious with me. It's Farrier who's made them think that way, I expect . . . the way he flinches from me, it's like I walk around naked."

What? No! That wasn't true at all.

"Oh," Abdumasi said. "Your dad and Tahr? Is that a thing?"

"Only since she got back. She's been sleeping with him occasionally."

"I can tell she's different. More . . . intent?"

"She's stopped caring about trim." Kindalana threw a stone. It whistled out past Tau-indi and vanished in the waterfall. "It's not like you and me, I don't think. I get the sense Tahr just doesn't want to put things off anymore."

"What do you mean?"

"Like she thinks time is running out, so she might as well take what she can get."

"Does it bother you? The affair?"

"Apparently it bothers Tau a lot."

"I didn't ask about Tau."

Kindalana's voice moved deeper and pitched sharper. "Well, I'm talking about Tau. Tau's working too hard. Their trim's in a snarl and it's making them miserable."

"Sometimes," Abdumasi said, so softly that Tau almost asked him to raise his voice, "I almost get up the courage to tell them that thing I told you. The thing about their dead twin."

Tau-indi pressed their cheek up against the cold stone.

"Tell me," Kindalana said. Their voice rolled out of the cave like something old and far away. "Tell me like I'm Tau. It's a beautiful thing to hear."

"I want to say, Tau-indi, it's the opposite of what you think. You didn't kill your twin so you could be Prince alone. Something was wrong, over in the place where people live before they're born, and you couldn't both make it through the Door in the East. So your twin sacrificed themself to help you make it into the world. They gave up a chance at life because they knew we'd need you over here, Tau, you in particular.

"And that's why you're the bravest, Tau, that's why you're the only one who's brave enough to talk to Cosgrad and learn all these terrible things. That's why you can keep your house together when your mom's gone and you're sick with snails. That's even why the griots come to you to learn. Because your dead twin gave their life to set your trim. You have a gift we don't.

"You're the only one on Prince Hill who knows how to be alone."

The jungle dripped and murmured with life. Tau-indi clung to the rock so they wouldn't reel off and hit their head and die like a fool for not knowing what to think or how to feel.

From the cave came a murmur and a soft choked sound. "It's okay," Kinda-lana said. "Hush, Abdu, it's okay. Don't cry. It's okay."

"I don't want to lose you," Abdu said. "I don't want to lose Tau."

"Everything's going to change." Their voices were very close together. "We can't stop that. We just have to figure out how to be strong."

"Like Tau."

"Like Tau."

TAU fled. They fell on the way down the wet rock and cracked their left knee and skinned a huge peel off their right side and stumbled on weeping silently and making agonized oh, oh, *oh* faces.

In a tangle of kudzu near the trail they found Cosgrad Torrinde.

He was sitting with his face in his hands, a rock balanced on his left knee, a tiny frog on his right. He'd tried to peel some of the leeches off. His legs were covered in huge red scabs and the tiny black remnants of leech-mouths, still attached.

He looked up at Tau-indi with hopeless frustration, and Tau-indi looked back at him with quavering dismay.

"It's too complicated," he said. He threw a fistful of leech-flesh into the mangroves where it spattered and made the leaves tremble and rain. "Your land, it's impossible to understand. That's why you have a story about everything, down here, because it's the only way to make sense of anything. No laws, no rules; they don't even work! The mangroves grow wherever they please! It's magic! Oriati Mbo runs on magic!"

"You're afraid," Tau-indi said, recognizing, somehow, the dismay in Cosgrad's voice. "What are you afraid of, guest of my house?"

"We're going to lose," Cosgrad said, snatching at the kudzu vines. The frog on his right knee vibrated with indignation. "I'll never understand you, so Farrier will take her favor, Farrier will try his methods, and he'll fail! We're doomed, Tau, the whole work of the revolution is doomed!"

Oh principles. Tau realized that Cosgrad was tripping—he'd licked the tiny frog! He licked the frog to see what would happen! And now he was having frog dreams!

Cosgrad picked up the stone and underhanded it in a tight snapping motion. "We're going to lose!" He began to weep in quiet sighing bursts. "I can't understand you, you're all too old and complicated, I'm too young and simple and Farrier's going to have his way, and he'll fuck it up, and we're going to lose! Back into the silt and the ooze! The end of humanity!"

"Come," Tau murmured, "come, come."

They walked the poor man back to the picnic as he fought with frog dreams. "It'll be all right," Tau whispered to him. "No one will lose. Everyone can win. We'll teach Falcrest the magic of trim, and everything will work out. Falcrest can be made mbo, and filled with delights, and we can even give you all the other kinds of cats."

THE truth was an awful birthday present!

Tau had been all wrong about their friends. Kindalana and Abdumasi hadn't been keeping their trysts secret from Tau—they'd thought Tau *wanted* to be alone, Princely and self-reliant. They thought Tau had pushed them together.

Perhaps now their friendship could be repaired? Perhaps. But the strangeness between them had become a habit, and habits were hardest to fix.

As they all straggled home from that birthday, each of them bugbitten and thirsty and maybe satisfied, depending who, Tau-indi resolved to make another try at reading the Whale Words. A good Prince should read the Whale Words beginning to end, for if Oriati Mbo had a holy text, it must be the Words.

Everything in the world happened in circles, the Whale Worlds told Tau. This was why the world held together. The end of the story told the beginning how to happen, so that the story could go on.

Beware those who would change the ending, O you whose story is the story of rule. For those who wish to master the future also wish to master the past. And in their work to build a tall tower they will undermine the foundations of everything.

THE MAP ENTIRE

J AMAN Ryapost's skull grinned at Baru from its bolted frame.
Suicide upon exaltation.
He had reckoned the costs. He had found himself too deep in debt.

Baru woke from the dream with a shriveled pig's bladder curled in her arms, drained almost entirely of wine. The dregs had run out like sweet afterbirth down her stomach, and she found her mind cold, hard, and hurting like the length of a nail. She rolled out of the hammock, did her exercises, washed her mouth, and decided to spend her odd focus on the most difficult task available.

"Iraji?" she called. "Iraji, I need you."

He was not in his hammock.

She bundled up her parents' letters in her arms and went looking for him. *Helbride*'s sailors were crowded thicker than ever on middeck, their hammocks pitched two or three deep in some places. The Oriati from *Cheetah* had set up their camp on the maindeck, preferring the sun and rain and wind to even the appearance of captivity. Enact-Colonel Osa's sailors were pitching in (literally) with *Helbride*'s work, helping to tar up the hempen ropes.

Baru slipped aft to Apparitor's nook, but Svir was not there: he was probably up on the deck, hopping and swinging up in the ropes like a red clown fish darting through his home anemone. She sighed, and turned to go, and then saw Iraji huddled in the right-hand aft corner of the nook, the same corner where Baru had huddled at the last meeting.

Hello," he sniffled, and tried to smile. "Looking for Svir?"

"For you, actually. . . ." Baru clutched the letters awkwardly. "I wondered if you'd help me . . . go through my parents' letters."

"Do you need an analyst?"

"No, I just . . ." She dithered in the threshold, playing with the canvas curtain. "It's just that I can't, ah, well, it might become difficult for me, and if someone's nearby, I'll be too embarrassed to . . ."

"To grieve."

"Yes."

"So you want me to be with you, so you'll restrain yourself."

"Yes, that's right."

"Well," he said, tremulously, "I'm sorry, I'm not the right person for that just now."

Baru felt like an ass. "Are you all right?"

"No," he snapped, "my ship is full of Oriati!"

Oriati like him. And he had come to Falcrest very young, like Baru. He could never pass as one of the Mbo Oriati, and he would never really be Falcresti: now he had a ship full of both, to make it clear he was neither.

"Let's get together with Apparitor tonight," she suggested, fumbling for some way to help him, some answer to his pleas for a friend, "and play Purge?"

He looked up at her with entirely inexplicable dread.

"Yes," he said, smiling with only his mouth. "Let's."

WITH her dive knife Baru slashed open the letters from her parents. She sorted them by date, waited briefly and pointlessly over a rag in case she wept, and began to read. There would be two hard places, she expected. First, after she defected to the Coyotes: would her parents have dared to write, would they have said, *at last, you are truly our daughter? We are so proud.*

And second—

After Sieroch—when they learned that she'd betrayed the Coyotes—

Fuck it, though! So what if it hurt? Control the pain, Baru, get the information, add it to your plan. Are they all right? You have to *know*! Baru grabbed the top letter, scrabbled at its stuck-together pages, hissed as she cut the tip of her thumb, and at last, with a little print of blood, unfolded it against the deck.

At the top of the letter Mother Pinion had sketched a cormorant, surfacing from a dive, her hooked beak raised to the sun. The low sharp contours of Halae's Reef in the background.

Baru exploded into sobs.

She did not cry. She mastered her furious homesickness. Letter by letter she followed her parents' lives and the patterns of them leapt up to kiss her.

Mother Pinion wrote the body of the letter in shorthanded Urunoki, and Solit then scribbled comments and designs in the margins. Pinion sent drawings she'd taken during her work as a surveyor and message-runner. Solit rather favored diagrams of clever devices he'd encountered or made while working in the Iriad shipyards, where, he reported soberly, he helped the Imperial Republic prepare its brave new fleet, which would protect the seas from "Oriati aggression." Together they intimated small acts of sedition, confided to Baru the traditions they'd kept safe from the brackish Falcrest tide, and hinted at occasional lovers, including a plainsider woman. That shocked Baru: a plainsider? But perhaps the occupation had brought plainside and harborside together—

And there was—

—a *code!*

Baru could *feel* the bumps of information carved into the negative space between words. She couldn't articulate what exactly she'd detected. Were the spaces between the letters somehow systematically arranged? Would the first letters of each line spell out a message? Perhaps if she translated it all into Aphalone . . .

A plainsider lover? *Really?* Plainsiders raided, stole, and trafficked with pirates. Obviously some of that had to be prejudice, certainly the plainsiders believed harborsiders were corrupt, haughty, and tightfisted . . . but a plainsider *lover?*

And with that clue Baru cracked the code.

Every sentence that described her parents acting out of character contained a hint. The code was not cryptographic but steganographic, meaning that it hid the truth behind secret shared meaning, rather than mathematics.

When mother wrote, *Solit and I fought today over who missed Salm more. We tried to hide it from our neighbors, but what's fought in the home quickly spreads*: no, they would *never* fight over who'd missed Salm the most!

They were part of an armed resistance. The fight was growing.

Solit wrote, *The shipyard work is very boring, and sometimes I think I find a new man to my left every third day. It's hard to see others promoted in the favor of our overseers while we work down here to bend Masquerade steel. I guess they say the right things.*

The blacksmith Solit *bored* by the chance to work with steel? Utter nonsense! He was saying that many people had given up, and some had turned traitor, obeying their elders as they had been taught—even when those elders were Falcresti bureaucrats.

"A new man to my left every third day . . ."

Was that a *fact?* Had Taranoke lost more than a third of her native population? Census and Methods would know for certain . . . maybe Solit had gone and looked it up . . .

Baru bit at the silk sutures in her cheek. Cold tears sprang up.

Her parents wrote, *Today was the customary beginning of the Iriad market, although lately we see no Oriati ships. We hope to entice them back once we can remove the protectionist clauses from our treaty of federation. We have learned much from the Masquerade, medicines and shipbuilding, doctrines of discipline and profit, and I hope that Falcrest will soon let us reopen our markets to the Oriati and reap the benefit of free trade with those less fortunate.*

They'd been bargaining with the Oriati. They'd offered what Taranoke had always offered to the Mbo: a port for their traders and explorers. But now Taranoke also knew how to build Masquerade ships and deliver Masquerade inoculations. Taranoke could be an ally to Oriati Mbo in the war to come. . . .

Baru read the rest in a rush, and oh, it moved her to the choking edge of tears that she could still tell *exactly* when her parents broke character—

They wrote,

Of course the Oriati are bitter about losing our market, and not eager to risk such losses again.

They meant, the Oriati remembered the Armada War, and many of them would not dare to fight Falcrest again.

But at least one of their bolder merchants has begun to reach out to Taranoke, seeing new opportunities. We've sampled a few of his wares, and spoken to a few of his factors, and we find his offers enticing. He says that he knows old, old business concerns, long-lasting and quietly powerful. . . .

That was the last letter they'd sent.

The bold merchant they'd mentioned could be no one but Abdumasi Abd. Abdumasi Abd who Baru had destroyed, or, worse, lured into the navy's hands.

She might, by now, have destroyed her parents, too.

When she looked down at herself she found her right hand clasping her left wrist, as if to pin the hand in place.

"N O," Apparitor said, laughing, "you can't see Tain Hu's will."

"It's a bet, Svir, come on"—Baru slapped the boards of his cubby's floor—"let me see if if I win the round!"

"Why are you so interested, anyway? Are you sentimental now? Is that your new game?"

"Xate Yawa stole a palimpsest I need," Baru said, pausing to belch. She had secured a bottle of Grand Purifier with an early victory, and she did not intend to forfeit it till it was empty. "I thought if I had Tain Hu's will I could trade it for the palimpsest."

"You think *she* cares about Tain Hu's will?" Apparitor finally selected a card to play. The Minister of Time. He paid his fee in beans and bought himself an extra turn, making Iraji groan and declare said Minister "fundamentally unsound bullshit."

"I'll stake . . ." Baru thought about her assets. She couldn't think of anything solid. "I'll finish the bottle if I lose, you show me the will if I win."

"At the rate you're going," Apparitor said, "you'll have no stakes left when I win."

"I fold," Iraji said, wiping his tableau of faces and beans. "I hear too much bickering. Would anyone like a brine shot? It soothes the constitution."

He poured a shot of hard whiskey and a shot of diluted canning brine, a foul and compelling combination if you took both shots together: like swilling out your guts. Baru had two before she switched back to The Grand Purifer. Apparitor went on to win, growing more loose-tongued with each drink but not less devastatingly capable, his patter flowing between Aphalone and Stakhi as he took the pot. They played not for money but for chits with the names of nations and great leaders carved upon them. Baru wanted to get Shiqu Si or Iro Mave, but didn't manage.

He won again. He kissed the card for the Empire Admiral and fell back, belching, against his hammock. "So," he said, thickly. "We never finished our conversation."

"Which one?" It felt as if they'd never finished any.

"How *would* one destroy the Imperial Republic?"

Baru giggled, and covered her mouth, quite appalled at herself. "Bankruptcy, I think. The Empire could be rendered insolvent. By disruption of the trade."

"Spoken like an accountant."

"I am discovered," Baru said, holding up her hands in surrender.

Apparitor pawed overhead, knocked over a bundle of maps in bone cylinders, and, pouncing on one, revealed a schema of the Ashen Sea. "That won't work, though, see?" He stabbed, roughly, at Falcrest, and missed, indicating instead the middle of the Mother of Storms. "Falcrest is the heart of the Ashen Sea trade circle. It pumps the blood."

"That's exactly why bankruptcy *would* work—stop the trade, stop the money—"

"Listen, listen." He waved his fingers. "Say Falcrest can't buy any more shit. No more great merchant fleets. No more trade ring. Take away that trade and you, uh, you get a lot of war, because if people can't get what they need, they try to take it—"

"A ut li-en," Iraji whispered, to Baru's horror.

"—and then"—Apparitor flourished over the map, behold—"over the course of forty or fifty years, that's how it happened with the Cheetah Palaces at least, those wars and raids lead to the destruction of most major cities. That's, uh, that's how it goes in a world where people take what they need, instead of trading for it. Then I'd expect plague, as refugees flee the violence, smallpox, measles, buboes, the Kettling. Then isolationism to hold back the plague, and five hundred years of chaos. The Palatine Collapse wiped out all complex interconnected civilization. I mean, it's remarkable, it's brilliant—" He belched articulately. "—in Falcrest we've got the entire known world hostage to our own economy. If we go down, so do they."

"People got along fine without Falcrest's trade," Baru said, skittering around thoughts of Taranoke and her parents. She hurt. The glass cut she'd suffered on *Cheetah* was stitched up with silk through her cheek, her missing fingers still ached and curled, and her period was due to start in a few days: meaning a dull awful heaviness in her stomach.

She drank some more.

"They got along fine on their own," Apparitor said, "but now they're connected, like the Llosydanes, remember the fucking Llosydanes? Stars help them if the trade stops. They'll all die. Everyone will die if the trade stops. Because everyone's connected."

"Quitter." Baru waved her bottle at him. "How would you destroy Falcrest *without* ruining the rest of the world?"

"Oh, I wouldn't." He belched again. "I fully expect this fucking war to spiral out of anyone's control and kill us all."

"How nihilistic."

"Not if you read your history, eh? Seeing as civilizations always collapse, all of them"—his hands moving rapidly left and right, to Falcrest, to the Camou, to the far eastern continent, to the unknown west, left and right—"the Jellyfish Eaters and the Cheetah Palaces and everyone else, and I think it's our turn now: I just want to go. I want to go away."

Baru stared at him. "Go *where*?"

"East," he said, catching Baru's attention with his finger, and pointing east, into her blind right, then west, then east again. A ring glinted on his pointing finger. Quite hypnotic. "East into the unknown. To escape the end of the world."

"The unknown . . ." Baru inhaled, long and slow, staring at the map. The unknown was on her blind side: she couldn't see it, she could only see the known world, the Ashen Sea. Her mind caressed the shapes of money implied by the map. During the Armada War, Falcrest had chewed the fertile northeastern corner off Lonjaro Mbo, and the Tide Column, too, which controlled the trade between the Ashen Sea and the Mothercoast.

Now Oriati Mbo had more people than it could feed, and its ships could no longer move food as freely . . . they *had* to go to war, or starve. . . .

East. West. East. West. Apparitor's finger ticked back and forth.

"Look," he said, "look at this."

Left. Right. Left. Right. Great rings of light began to shine around the re-flections on Apparitor's glossy hair, and the lamps above.

Baru shook her head in confusion and—

She heard a crackle of undead sound, like a fist pushing up through shallow earth. She smelled salt. Tain Hu cried out hoarsely as she wrapped her own death-chains around her and battled the tide. The frigate birds drummed. On Apparitor's shelves the stacks of rag novels glistened in the lamplight, *Antibirth at Convent Clair, Nab Banadab and the Madness of Men, The Death Ship,* im-possible truths from behind the moon's silver mask she would wish she'd never known.

"The map," she choked, having trouble with her tongue. "I can see the *whole map . . .*"

Oh fuck oh joy she could *see!* She could see her whole world again, left and right, Apparitor's entire face, Iraji's two arms opened to catch her as she tot-tered. She had the other half of her world back!

Baru looked right, into the place that had been missing.

And there before her was the Emperor. Bound to the ropes and rigging of the Throne. Lifting one gloved finger to point at her. And with his motion the apparatus of Empire creaked and bent, stirring the people and the ships, send-ing waves of coin and laundry bleach crashing up on distant shores to toss dead crab and pus-bloody corpses onto beaches of soap and ash—

"*WHAT IS MY WILL?*" the Emperor asked. "*TELL ME MY WILL. ARE YOU THE ONE WHO THINKS MY THOUGHTS?*

"*WILL YOU NOW BECOME ME?*"

He reached out to her and pulled on the cord that bound them, a cord that ran from his face like a slithering umbilical across the world until it fastened itself on Baru's right eyeball. Like a strangler vine, it sent tendrils around her eye, inside her mind, fastened to eyelets drilled into the back of her skull.

Baru heard herself roar and rattle. Her jaw clenched.

Iraji held her. The curtains behind him parted—Iscend and Xate Yawa rushed in—Baru stared at them in awe, dumbstruck by the symmetrical wholeness of them, the leftness and the rightness, joined together.

"You idiot," Yawa said, "you fool, you gave her too much."

A seizure. She was having a seizure. She'd been poisoned. Yawa had gone to Apparitor and made a deal, *let's make her have a seizure, and then we can threaten her with medical internment.* Seizures were cause for lobotomy, weren't they?

Oh, Hu. What's gone so wrong with me?

"Hello," the Empire said.

* * *

"HELLO," the room says. Everyone else is gone and Apparitor's cabin is *staring* at her. Why has she never noticed that the room is made of eyes? Eyes in the whorled woodgrain, eyes in the flare of the lamplight, eyes with thick shadowy lashes peering between the books. Eyes in the charts, and their pupils are islands, their irises are currents and storm-tracks. Everything made of eyes.

"Hello yourself," Baru breathes, and she realizes that at last she is speaking directly with the Empire Itself. The fabric of causality which binds all choices back to the Imperial Will: the swarming summation of all those whose lives are bound up in Falcrest, whether in prosperity, or misery, or defiance.

When the Empire's work is done, resistance will be indistinguishable from service. There will be a map of cause and effect, and all causes will lead to one effect. Falcrest's triumph.

Baru looks down and sees herself gowned in taut canvas. Ropes and eyelets draw the canvas shroud tight against her body—no, look at those bloodstains spreading against the fabric. The canvas isn't drawn tight over her skin. The canvas has actually *replaced* her skin. It feels like sail. She is full of wind.

Hundreds of ropes bind her to the stone and steel of the Imperial Throne.

She *is* the Emperor Itself.

She can feel the lobotomy pick in her brain. She can feel the ghost of its presence. It has emptied her of will, so that she might become a perfect vessel for the design of the Empire.

"This," the Empire tells her, "is your destiny. Allow me to be more precise. This is the destiny you chose when you accepted Cairdine Farrier's patronage."

She sits on the Throne: she posesses ultimate power.

She is lobotomized and bound: she has no power at all. She is an emblem and an instrument of hidden forces.

Then Tain Hu cuts her way out of the Empire's eyeball.

Her sword tip pierces the pupil of a woodgrain whorl. Ink jets: the eye screams in the only way an eye can scream, by widening, and Hu slices her way free from within. She wears her leather tabard with its mailed shoulders, her riding jodhpurs, and her long black hair bound up tight above her hawkish nose.

"Your Majesty," she says, sardonically, and bows deep and wide-armed. "I came as soon as I heard."

"Heard what?" Baru says, in a voice made of all her voices, the declaration and the plea, the whisper and the scream.

"That you'd been made Empress, of course," Tain Hu says, and her

hobnailed boots ring on marble as she strides up to the Throne. "I do love to
rescue young women. They are often effusively grateful. I saved Oathsfire's wife
from an ambush once, and when I would not take her money, she looked at me,
like *this,* petulant and hooded, and she said, well, how *shall* I reward you?"

"How?"

"I told Oathsfire that she'd been lost in the woods a while after the rescue."

"But what really happened?"

"I put her up in a cabin, shot a grizzly, and prepared it properly. We ate bear
steaks and amused ourselves on the new rug."

"You rake," Baru complains, and then she feels motion in the ropes that
bind her.

Hemp creaks. Slowly, in painful convulsive jerks, the rigging of the Throne
forces Baru's right arm to raise. A knife is necessary, the Empire decides, so a
knife appears. Ah. No. It is a lobotomy pick.

"Insurrection," Baru groans, trying not to speak, but the ropes are pulling
her tongue and peeling back her lips, "can be understood as a disorder of the
mind, a form of uncleanliness. The purpose of Incrastic thought is very simply
to align individual behavior with the greater good of mankind. Everything we
do works to this end. A hygienic person is easily aligned, because their
purposes—that is, the map which connects their desires to their behaviors, to
their rewards—is cleanly laid out.

"A filthy person, however, has a snarled and confusing map. They cannot
directly link their desires to their behaviors, or their behaviors to their rewards.
They may desire happy friends, but behave in ways that make their friends miserable, and yet their friends, trying to be kind, reward them with advice and
company. They may desire sexual congress, and seek it out indiscriminately,
doing so in a way that does not better the community with healthy, well-tended
children.

"Because human virtue is the only god, the only sin is to detract from this
virtue. Disorder and poor hygiene are therefore mortal sins. But worst of all
the uncleanly are those who promote disorder, for they not only possess perverse behavioral maps, they disturb and rearrange the maps of others. The in-
surrectionist not only *behaves sinfully,* but creates *sinful states.* Knowing that a
sinful state is complex and disordered, we understand that the treatment for
insurrection is to enforce *simplicity.*"

Baru's arm is made to brandish the lobotomy pick.

"Simplicity begins in the mind."

Tain Hu brandishes her cocky, lopsided grin. She has drawn her sword, too, the tip aimed not at Baru but at the throne behind her. Goodness, Baru thinks, that is a *sharp* sword; no real sword was ever so sharp, was it?

"Nice doctrine," Hu drawls. "You sound like my uncle-in-law's sister. Do you have a word for that in Incrastic pedigree? Your aunt's husband's sister? I'm sure you do."

Look out, Hu! Baru wants to scream to her. I have a lobotomy pick! I'm not in control of myself!

But Tain Hu is perfectly aware that Baru is not in control. She seems to take this as a challenge. Her eyes glimmer black and gold, amused. She mounts the steps up to the Throne.

A man steps into her way.

He is Cairdine Farrier's stooge, Governor Cattlson. "You brigand bitch," he says, sulkily, and then he swings his sword at her—a thunderous stroke down from the high arc. But Tain Hu turns the mighty blow so it slides down her own sword and over her shoulder. As she did in the plaza duel, Tain Hu beats him in the head with the back of her sword so he falls. But this time Tain Hu lunges and pierces his heart. An unbelievable yet spectacular geyser of heartblood jets from Cattlson's chest, paints Hu's leather tabard, and glistens on her mail rings.

Cattlson says, with frank irritation, "But I'm *bigger*!"

"I stand for Baru Cormorant," Hu says, and then, winking, "and she lies for me."

Baru feels faintly weak-kneed. The ropes of the Throne creak as they correct her posture. The pick in her right hand waits, cobra-poised, for Tain Hu to come in stabbing range.

"Hu," Baru tries to say, but all she can do is yawn and drool. The Throne does not will her to speak. She never did manage to warn Tain Hu of her own treachery: not until it was too late.

"Hush," Hu says, "hush, it's all right: trust me."

Don't trust *me*, Hu.

"I mean it," Hu says, neither smiling nor winking, but fixing Baru with the plain intensity she often used in field command: a woman who knew death, and trusted it as a companion. "I'm bringing her to you. I know you don't understand why. But you need her. Trust me."

Tossing her sword to her other hand (a trick she would never use in battle) she undoes the steel snaps and thong ties of her tabard. It falls off her. Beneath it, she is sensibly dressed, but not modestly. The dancers in Treatymont had a way of walking, foot crossing over foot, that made their hips sway. Tain Hu doesn't walk like that. She comes up the stairs to the Throne shrugging out of her tabard, padding straight-hipped and barefoot like a curious catamount, absolutely self-possessed.

Baru shivers at this sudden and quite surreal turn toward erotica: she is still bound to this cold Throne, and she still holds her lobotomy pick. Those things do *not* belong in a fantasy of brown and muscled Hu padding up to her with a sword, displaying to Baru the incalculable ways in which her body is (and still remains) the most ferociously arousing thing Baru has ever seen. The cuts and bands of muscle beneath her smooth, dark-scarred body, strength which appears in unexpected places as she looks about and stretches, as if to say, *I am made to do everything well.* The perfect definition of her back, down which Baru has spent minutes running her hands. Baru has seen plenty of breasts, but likes Hu's best, although she would struggle to describe them in particularities: but above this list of specifics Baru likes something about the totality of Hu, an ease and power which Baru did not see in her fellow schoolgirls, or even in the wary adults of post-occupation Iriad. She moves, Baru realizes, a little like Ulyu Xe, with that same unity of purpose. But where Xe is tranquil and reactive, Tain Hu prowls. She pounces. She has the smug mastery of a large cat.

This is what Tain Hu shares with Tain Shir: a sense that she is her own dominion, unmastered by the world.

She steps out of her trousers: she unties her linens and lets them fall. Baru realizes with a shock of horror how this dream or hallucination will end—Tain Hu is going to die naked on her knife. Tain Hu will writhe against Baru in carnal desire and then Baru will stab her and Tain Hu will die in blood—her last moans a poisonous admixture of agony and orgasm.

Sick. Sick. The technique is abominable.

"No," Hu says, in response to her thoughts, "it's not like that. Or—it is, yes, that will happen, because that's how they want it to go, but you taught me how to beat them. Look."

Tain Hu reaches the throne. She flicks her blade here, and there, and cuts away the ropes that bind Baru's right arm. Suddenly she can move again! She tries to hurl away the lobotomy pick in horror—

And Tain Hu closes her fist around the pick, so it can't get away. "No," she says. "Hold that. Make it a knife. Yes. Change it into a knife. Like that."

She snaps the small cords that hold Baru's mask to her skull and flips it off. Without the mask Baru finds her lobotomy wound gone. She can move her eyes where she pleases now.

Tain Hu's golden eyes shine back at her, full of trust and love, and Baru is grieved beyond words that she will betray them.

Tain Hu kisses her, fiercely. She bites blood from Baru's lip and draws away, lingering. "Remember that," she says. "You've been forgetting."

She is close against Baru, and warm. Baru remembers that there is nothing more wonderful than a naked, trusting body in your arms, especially when she is so strong and so at ease.

"Hu," she says, desperately, "I'm losing control. I think I've destroyed my parents. I think Aminata was always Farrier's agent. I ruined, ruined the Llosydanes, all for one stupid name. I don't think I can beat them—"

"Baru." Hu presses the flat of her sword to Baru's lips. "They're too clever for you. As you were too clever for me. How do we beat the clever? They lay out their roads for us to walk down. So how do we escape?"

When the roads belong to the enemy, you do as Tain Hu had done in Aurdwynn. You go into the wilderness instead. As Tain Shir had gone into the jungle, and returned a monster. . . .

"Shir." Hu shivers. "You're in her thrall, Baru, do you know why? Because you're a terribly narcissistic person. And you see in her what you'll become." She cuts Baru's left hand free, impatiently, and with a *what are you doing waiting?* frown she lifts the glove to her breast. "She'll make you worse, if she can. Don't let her. I always tried to make you *better.*"

Softly she sighs under the caress of the glove.

"Do you have to be naked?" Baru protests. "It's—It just seems unseemly."

"I want to be," Hu says, "because you're afraid of enjoying it, aren't you?"

Baru has to admit that's true.

"Listen," Hu says, "listen. There is a difference between acting out their story, and truly obeying their story. Do you know what it is?"

"Please," Baru begs, "please tell me."

But then, as in all good erotic dreams, she wakes up unfulfilled.

THE eyes in the walls closed. The Throne slipped away like an octopus.

Baru woke in a hammock, mostly naked beneath a cotton shift: she deduced instantly that she'd been here a while, and they'd stripped her to keep her clean. "How long," she groaned.

"Only a few hours." Iscend Comprine knelt and grinned fetchingly. "You've been quite a difficult patient."

"Am I going to be lobotomized?"

"Only if it becomes necessary, I'm sure. You've been conscious, but not coherent. Your left side was paralyzed, but you refused to believe it. We had to tie you down to protect you."

To Baru's bemusement, she felt wonderful, as clear and quick as a warm river. She didn't remember exactly how the seizure had begun, or where . . . she'd been trying to make a wager with Apparitor . . . "What happened? Did I drink too much?"

Iscend grimaced and touched her brow. Baru interpreted that as some sort of Clarified distress: she wouldn't signal it unless she wanted Baru to *know* she was in distress. She must be having trouble sorting through competing imperatives.

"It's all right," Baru croaked. "It's all right to tell me. I serve the Throne. If you can help me, you help the whole Imperial Republic."

"Fiend," Iscend said, fondly, "you're trying to turn me away from my master."

"I'm on a mission for your master, remember? Hesychast needs me to find the Cancrioth. All else being equal, it's better if I have more information, not less. What's wrong with me?"

Iscend lowered her head to murmur, "When we tested you in the Elided Keep, we detected two separate responses to the Farrier Process."

"I don't understand."

"We divided your perceptions down your centerline." Baru remembered this. They'd put a helmet on her with a huge bladed nose, separating her vision into two hemispheres, and run Hesychast's word-response test on each side. "We checked your disambiguation responses in each hemisphere. The Farrier Process works by creating subconscious associations which alter behavior; and indeed those associations are strongly present in you. But only if the test stimuli are presented on your *left* side. The right shows very different patterns of association. I believe your seizure was caused by some sort of exchange between the two minds."

"Two minds? What do you mean?"

"I mean," Iscend said, "that we've seen this condition before. In the Metademe we have induced it by cutting central areas of the brain with a length of wire. The two isolated halves of the mind diverge in opinions and habits."

"Like those stories about the Tahari seditionist? Two personalities in one body? With separate handwriting, and separate friends, and even different names?"

"No." Iscend had extraordinarily precise body language. She pinned that thought on a finger and pushed it aside. "That's a peasant myth."

"Why am I different?"

"You are exactly like everyone else. All of us contain these two selves, left and right. But they are usually kept in synchrony, like two diaries written by one woman." She drew a perfect line down Baru's nose. "Your injury has allowed them to diverge."

Her blind half—wasn't blind at all? Was there another Baru, across a mental moat, just outside her awareness?

"Which one am *I*?" Baru whispered.

"I don't know," Iscend said, in fascination. "To which one am I speaking?"

22

BARU IN THE BILGE

I HAD made Dziransi the instrument that would deliver Baru to her humiliation and much-deserved death. If I hadn't fucked it all up aristocratically, and I was confident I hadn't, then the dream-hammer had driven into his brain the conviction that Heingyl Ri must marry his master the Necessary King, and that Baru would be the dowry which bought the marriage.

So Baru would die in the high cold, far from the home she pretended to love. Consumed by the politics of the land (*my* land) that she'd tried to play for her own advance.

Which would all be very cathartic and satisfying, if I could just get her off *Helbride* and deliver her to her doom. There were too many witnesses aboard. Baru's disappearance had to be made secret, an inexplicable and unattributable act of chaos, if Apparitor and I were to avoid Itinerant's retaliation.

She had not yet set up her vendettas to expose our secrets if she ever vanished. We still had a chance. She could be drawn out alone and snapped up in silence.

Since the boy and I had agreed to cooperate on Baru's removal—he providing the seizure which would give us medical pretext to threaten her—I had been working on a way to net Baru alone once she fled *Helbride*. Faham Execarne's Morrow-men would provide clothes for the operation, which was to say insulation from local authorities, boats, money, muscle that could be trusted not to spill before or after. Iscend would be the sharpest tooth in our jaw, as clever as Baru and certainly quicker.

But I was more and more certain that we needed someone at Baru's side. Someone who would lead us to her no matter where her madness and her narcissism brought her.

So in the creaking dark of star watch I left Iraji drowsing in my hammock (Svir had asked me to speak to him about his faints, and I'd exhausted him with talk: nothing else, for ill or weal) and padded through drowsing sailors to the ladder belowdecks.

The woman in the bilge would fit neatly into the gaping hole at Baru's right. The beautiful woman Baru liked to dandle about, exploiting and deceiving, until she could be discarded. It would only be a matter of finally offering her that long-delayed Imperial pardon.

I shivered as the cool wet air touched my bare feet. In my memory Baru slumped on the wall of Svir's cabin, the poison in full bloom, her roar and rattle seized away by the emptiness of convulsion.

She had fallen for the trap exactly as she always did. Arrogant. Proud. Conceited. Oblivious to the maneuvers of those around her, except where she was causing them.

Except—

There were moments, instants of instants, when I felt her watching me, and thought she *knew*—

And as she tipped back into that seizure I might have sworn before an ilykari, if pressed to oath, that I had seen her right eye wink at me.

HELBRIDE crossed into the northern edge of the Kraken Still. These were chaos waters where no gazetteer could predict the winds and no chart would ever save a ship from ruin.

But Captain Branne chose her course well, and the spring luck went their way.

Helbride passed through clear warm channels between volcanic islands, the water choked with thickets and heaps and bladdered mounds of ash-kelp, swarming with crustaceans and long worms. Mutinous *Sulane* stalked them at a careful distance, wary of mines or foulage. As a test of *Helbride*'s legal wards, Apparitor sent a group of wildlife enthusiasts out on a boat with an Oriati clerk. *Sulane* did not respond. Perhaps the Oriati clerk held Ormsment back, or perhaps she feared a trap.

Baru wondered what Tain Shir might be doing. But she did not show herself.

The boat crew returned excited and aghast. The shallows around the nearest atoll were infested with some kind of bristling serpent or enormous underwater centipede, which burrowed invisibly into the silt and lurked until a fish came near. Then the lurkers snapped upward like springs, seized the fish in huge crescent jaws, and bit or battered the unfortunate fellow to death. The clouds of gore attracted small sharks, which the worms ate too, and octopodes, who protected themselves with coconut half-shells tucked beneath their bodies.

Baru would very much like to go see the centipedes and the octopodes. But there was no time. Yawa had already begun to move against her.

Baru stopped by the surgery to scrounge hangover remedies and a hot rock, in anticipation of period cramps. She suspected the surgeon was taking small bribes to allow ship's officers to conduct assignations in the quarantine slots. The *Helbride* officers had been unexpectedly pleased to take *Cheetah*'s crew aboard, and Baru hadn't understood why until she realized the officers could ethically fuck foreign passengers—the Oriati being entirely outside the chain of command.

She'd made a joke. Something about people bringing back diseases from Kyprananoke. And the ship's surgeon told her, levelly, "No one will go ashore at Kyprananoke except Apparitor and Durance's handpicked operatives."

"And me, of course." Baru selected a smooth round hot-rock.

"No," the surgeon said, with the faintest quaver, "you will not go ashore at Kyprananoke. After your seizure, I cannot allow it."

Baru turned slowly, so the man could consider what fury he'd tempted. "On what authority?"

"Mine. I am the ship's surgeon. I rule everything inside a living skin on *Helbride*."

"My service jacket doesn't have a living skin. And it tells me I can tear up your letters of physic and send you down to pump bilge—"

The surgeon crossed his arms. "I examined you myself. I collected signed eyewitness statements, including the testament of a Clarified expert. You're epileptic. You are an agent of the Republic; neither by injury nor by neglect may I allow the Republic to come to harm. You will not leave my ship."

"I have seizures if I'm fucking *poisoned*!" Baru roared.

"There's no way I can know poison was involved."

"You are going to regret this. You are going to regret it so dearly."

"You won't have the *capacity* for regret if you seize again."

"Why is that."

"Because I'll be forced to perform an emergency transorbital."

Baru flinched and dropped the stone. Phantom steel grated in her eye socket—groped up into her brain—her first instinct was to look around, wildly, for the lobotomy pick, and throw it overboard. But just then Xate Yawa swept in, fully masked in purple-black ceramic and a blood-spattered surgical gown. "One of the wounded from *Cheetah* died," she told the surgeon. "I cut him open to try to get at the bleeding, but he was too far gone. The patient in bed six."

She swiveled to Baru. "Ah," she said. "Have you been informed of your medical arrest? I see you have. Very good. Never fear, my dear! We'll see to matters on Kyprananoke."

Baru had been outmaneuvered. She had no riposte ready.

She snarled at Yawa and went in search of weapons.

* * *

Aᴸᴸ the ships are moored on the east side." Apparitor chewed his lip. "Why *east*? Why's no one taken the westward berths?"

"What the fuck did you put in my vodka?" Baru demanded.

"A special preparation of ergot. Oh, fuck me. Do you see what I see?" He offered Baru his spyglass—they were up on *Helbride*'s hummingbird prow, balanced on the fan of ropes.

"Ergot?" Baru snatched the spyglass. "You gave me *cow poison*?"

Ergot was a wheat fungus. Cows would eat ergot sometimes, and go mad— or so Cairdine Farrier said. But now Baru remembered a line in the *Manual of the Somatic Mind* about a drug called ergotic theogen: a fungus grown on the right kind of wheat and then chemically transmuted. It caused various hallucinations, convulsions, psychosis, and (in large doses) gangrene.

"Hesychast uses it to break down resistance in mental patients." Apparitor touched the spyglass and steered her toward the trouble. He seemed almost solicitous; not sorry, but at least sincere. "I added a little vidhara, too. My personal mix! There, look . . . oh, will you look at that?"

The Islands of Obsidian Dreams stretched out before them like the bone shards of a crushed skull. On the southern horizon loomed the ruptured ruin of el-Tsunuqba, the riven god-mountain of the Jellyfish Eaters. Only in ancient art could you see the volcano in its forgotten wholeness, Mount Tsunuq, the Big Tit, a green and gentle cone with fertile slopes and a steaming peak— like a younger and less weathered Taranoke. In those days the houseboats sprawled out from Tsunuq like game tiles scattered across the sea. And at night the jellyfish farms filled the ocean with the green light of a million shining bells.

"There was a school here, in those days," Apparitor said, Baru powerless to hide her interest, though she knew he was distracting her. She had never been taught about Kyprananoke. "The Tiatro Tsun, God's Theater. Her library had books from across the Camou. The Liturges kept their houses there, each with nine secrets carved inside nine wooden rings, and the tenth finger bare, for the secret yet unknown. And the gray-haired Scyphu who ruled the Jellyfish Eaters came to consult them with teas of exum and subum from the jellies of the royal blooms; and all the world admired their wisdom. Or so it was recorded."

On the Day of Thunder Capes, after portentous decades of quakes and smoke, Mount Tsunuq's north face exploded with a blast they heard in Aurdwynn and Segu. The detonation blew the mountain's bowels out across the sea. Imagine a drunken man bent over, belching up his innards: when he comes up all that's left is a sunken starving frame. All that survived of Mount Tsunuq was the southern face, a blackened lip jutting up from the ocean, three thousand nine hundred feet tall. Today they called it el-Tsunuqba.

But the volcano's erupted gore splashed into the sea and made the kypra, a maze of atolls, reefs, and islands. In time life returned. The Jellyfish Eaters had passed into history, and the kypra became Kyprananoke.

"Too bad about the school," Baru said, with true regret. "If we had their library, we could know some of how the world lived before Incrasticism." She could test the truth of claims about the Jellyfish Eaters's downfall: could it be blamed on their way of life, their unsanitary practices?

"Oh, the library survived," Apparitor said, looking at her with that cunning baited smile. "Four of the Liturges fled before the eruption, warned by the jellyfish. They stole as much of the library as they could. Afterwards they made a deal with the gray-haired Scyphu families to reestablish Tiatro Tsun. Kyprananoke kept its archives and great school until not sixty years ago."

"What then?"

"Incrasticism came upon them, of course," Apparitor said, "and the scholars and archives were taken to Falcrest to be joined with our Faculties. Far too precious to be left out here on the little islands, we judged. In exchange we destroyed the compost pits they used to grow their traditional and rather toxic roots, consolidated their freshwater aquifers under government control instead of family rule, and moved them all over to coconut and arrowroot and imported foods. These islands are too young for much good soil, so Falcrest says agriculture must be rationalized. Gave them all horrible tooth problems, the sugar did. Lucky we had dentists, hm?"

"Bastards," Baru muttered, recklessly.

"As ever," Apparitor agreed. "But we were discussing your brain."

Baru had never been anywhere so astonishingly *low*. Even on the plains of Aurdwynn you could always look north and see the high Wintercrests ramping up toward the sky. Here on the kypra there was nothing taller than a tree, except for el-Tsunuqba like a dead hand in the southwest. And if the sea ever rose . . . Baru imagined herself alone on the last spit of rock, with the tide coming in from both sides. The world's margins closing in on her. She shivered, and the shiver brought her back to the memory of seizure, and to Apparitor's poison.

"I don't need my mental resistance broken down," she said.

"But you are the victim of a lifelong program of brainwashing."

"The fuck I am—"

"Be rational!" Apparitor put his fist between them. "Let's count your life. Count the good and bad things that have happened to you. Come on! Make an account! One. Farrier spots you in a marketplace and gets you into the Iriad school, that's good." He put up a finger, to keep a running tally. "Two. Soldiers kidnap your father and destroy your family, that's bad. Did Farrier have anything to do with it? No. Did you ever wonder if he did? I doubt it very much. Three. You make a friend in the school, that's good, but who warns you against her? Farrier. Four. Your friend turns on you, she beats and threatens you for your tribadism, that's bad, Farrier turned out to be right. Do you see his method? *Do you see?*"

Baru's guts revolted: fear for Aminata, fear of Aminata, too much bad wine, too many bad dreams. She gagged and spat into the bow wake.

"You all right?"

"You tell me. You're the one who poisoned me!"

"I poisoned you because Yawa said that might give us a way to threaten you. And *if* we have something to threaten you, we can start to trust you: which is the *only* way we're going to survive this place."

"We've survived plenty," Baru said, though she knew it was sullen.

"Not like Kyprananoke. The Oriati Termite spymasters are here in great force, looking to flip the government to their interests. The archipelago is a chasm full of of intrigue and corruption. And now something far worse has come to play in the shallows. Look! Look at what's waiting for us!"

Baru saw why all the ships at Kyprananoke had put in to the east.

The Kyprananoki built their homes on storm stilts, or as freestanding flotables like very dowdy ships, tangled together by a web of laundrylines and moorings and buoy bridges. In the east the islands roared with shipping— ketches, clippers, dromons, junks, barques, canoes, brigs, brigantines, and outriggers.

But in the west a great stillness. No one moved in the waters or the boardwalks. *Nothing* moved. Except for the dirty red-and-yellow flags that flew like pus-stained rags from every line and rooftop.

"No," Baru breathed. "It can't be."

"If I remember my Oriati flags correctly . . ." Apparitor inhaled. "It must be."

"The Kettling's not real," Baru insisted. "This is an Oriati trick." Diseases killed people by fever, by pus, by worm and buboe and diarrhea. But they did not melt people into dumplings full of green-black blood. Certainly there had never been a Summer of Black Emmenia, when all the pregnant women of Mzilimake Mbo lost their babies and, mostly, their lives. . . .

"If it were anywhere," Apparitor murmured, "wouldn't it be here?"

That made a certain awful sense. The Masquerade had ruled Kyprananoke for a little while, and then abandoned it. What if the archipelago was secretly a

Masquerade honeypot now? A cultivated preserve? Smash the roaches' nest, and you'll only scatter them. Better to leave the pirates one perfect harbor. Better to leave the smugglers one port—where all the Ashen Sea's sicknesses could ride the dirty ships and mingle. . . .

"I suppose," Baru said, quietly, "that this means *no* one's going ashore."

"Not until we've observed the spread of the plague, at least."

"Very wise."

But Baru was already planning how to get onto Kyprananoke alone, and get to Unuxekome Ra, and then to the Cancrioth: how to get the prize all alone.

DO you think I'm your *friend*?" Shao Lune lifted her chin in disdain. "Is that what why you keep coming down here?"

Baru had to admire Shao Lune's bargaining skills. In exchange for the names of *Sulane*'s officers, she'd earned a longer chain, which let her get rid of her bucket and use a bilge pump as a toilet. For a list of Ormsment's supporters in Aurdwynn, she'd bought herself canvas curtains to convert her platform into a kind of pavilion, and oils and perfumes to soak the canvas and cure the bilge stink. Other tips had scored Shao Lune planks and nails, and now Baru found her stripped down to strophium and trousers, hammering her new gains into an expansion of her sleeping platform.

She swore viciously as she worked: Baru dallied on the stairway for a while, listening to Lune's rage. There were two topics Shao Lune would not yet breach. She would not discuss whether Ormsment had other conspirators in the Admiralty (Rear Admiral Samne Maroyad, Censorate Admiral Brilinda Vain, and Province Admiral Ahanna Croftare the primary suspects).

And she never, ever spoke of Tain Shir.

"I came to bring you more soap." Baru underhanded the sac of gut into the bilgewater just outside Lune's reach.

"Cunt," she said, without much enthusiasm.

"Get a little dirty," Baru suggested. "Worth it to get clean, isn't it?"

"Did you come to watch me wash my filth off? Is that your peccadillo?" Shao Lune cast the slack of her chain into the bilge and managed to hook the floating bag.

Baru hopped down from the stairs onto the platform. "Your trick worked. We got a diplomatic seal off *Cheetah*, and it turned *Sulane* away."

"Yes, I could tell you'd found some Oriati by the pervasive floral stink."

"They don't *actually* eat flowers, you know."

"We haven't been burnt to ashcakes, either, which did give me a clue it had worked."

Baru frowned at the planks underfoot, which bounced a little much. "Your engineering's not right. You should be sistering the joists before you cover them—"

Shao Lune began banging at the nails again, wielding a block of hardwood in place of a hammer. "Would you get on with it? Threaten me a little, dangle a reward, and ask me what you need to know."

Baru sat against the post at the center of the platform. "I think I might sell you on Kyprananoke. There are Oriati agents who'd trade secrets for a navy prisoner."

Shao snapped around with a hiss. "Kyprananoke? We're going to *Kyprananoke*?"

Baru nodded.

"You can't leave me there."

"Why ever not?"

"It's absolute anarchy. The Kyprists have taken over now that we've left—they're tyrants!"

"A military junta seizing command?" Baru mocked her with a gasp and a flutter. "I can't *imagine* such a horror!"

"You can't sell me. You need me to testify against Ormsment."

"I don't plan to be rid of Ormsment in a courtroom. . . ."

"I can help you." Shao Lune clasped her hammer block between her hands like a prayer anchor. "You want to use the navy against Parliament? Fine. Let me introduce you to the other merit admirals. Let me convince them to get rid of Ormsment for you."

"I don't want to wait for you to be useful. I want to get something for you *now*."

"We're haggling, then." Shao Lune sat with her legs folded beneath her and her shoulders square, eyes sharp, thinking desperately. It was only that Baru found it so *satisfying* to see the perfectly coiffed and composed officer stripped down to laborer's clothes and toiling in chains. . . .

Her eyes lit. "I can tell you about Xate Yawa. How she's plotting against you."

Perfect. Baru feigned disinterest. "I know all about her medical arrest." She tapped the deck with her right hand, to emphasize the point, I know *all* about medical arrest, and she smashed her finger stumps. Nausea coiled her up.

"She's going to sell you to the Necessary King," Shao Lune said.

The revelation caught Baru strained like a mooring rope between astonishment and groaning misery. Her dead fingers seemed to have grown like cold thread up her arm, across her shoulder, into the back of her head: she clawed at the boards and howled silently.

"How," she gaped, sounding monstrous: how did Shao Lune even *know* about the Necessary King? "How do you know that?"

"I'm *very* capable," Shao Lune purred.

"Tell me how."

"What do I get?"

"You get to come with me." She picked herself up with gritted teeth. "When I go ashore to Kyprananoke. With the Oriati Prince. We're going to hunt for a woman named Unuxekome Ra, who once trafficked with Abdumasi Abd—"

"Abd!" Shao Lune reared up in horror. "He's alive?"

"I hope so. Tau-indi Bosoka thinks so. And I need to know where Abd gets his money."

"But Admiral Ormsment told me he'd been killed at Treatymont . . ." Shao's chains rattled. She was pacing behind Baru's back. "Why would she hide Abd from me?"

"Because she's not as selfish as you," Baru suggested. "If Parliament learns the navy's hiding Abd from them . . ."

"Purge. But I was staff captain in Treatymont! They'll think *I* knew!"

"Better help me find him, hm?" Baru grinned at her. "Unuxekome Ra is our next clue."

Shao Lune considered her with narrow eyes and a full-lipped sneer. "What do you want to know about Yawa?"

"How fine is her control over Iscend?"

"The Clarified is deviating. They always do, when they're away from their home mazes too long. She's begun to use her own command word on herself."

Baru found this delightful. The slave was applying her own chains to gain her freedom. "That's *remarkable*. So you overheard her. You know the word now. Did you use it?"

Shao Lune's sneer broke into a grin, too. She was very pleased with herself. "I gave Iscend the only command she would accept from a prisoner. I demanded to be used as an instrument in her mission."

"And she told you . . ."

"She told me that Xate Yawa plans to trade you to the Necessary King as a dowry. You insulted his honor. He covets your punishment."

"And Iscend must have known you'd tell me. . . ."

"Of course she did," Shao said, and her grin widened into a triumphant self-satisfied smirk. She crouched on the edge of the platform, balanced on her toes and hands. Her eyes gleamed in the lamplight. "Iscend is Clarified, and the Clarified serve the Republic. The Republic must *never* collaborate with royalty."

Ingenious. Iscend Comprine could be made to sabotage Xate Yawa, whenever Xate Yawa's schemes defied the values of the Republic. And if Yawa wanted control of Aurdwynn—she would need a truce or an alliance with the Necessary King.

What better way than to give him a bride?

Not Baru, mind. He'd never trust her as a wife, and anyway she was very unlikely to produce an heir for him: Dziransi had said he was an honorable man who would never rape. But wouldn't the traitor Baru Cormorant make an exceptional dowry? Here, as a gift, take this woman who stole your honor. Show her to your lords to prove that you always get your revenge.

Baru only had one obvious countermove.

What if she could find a *better* dowry? What if she could say to Yawa, *use this man as dowry instead of me*? *I have already made the offer, and I know the King craves his return.*

She could offer Yawa the King's traitor brother Apparitor.

Baru's heart crashed like a mismanaged currency: cheapened, devalued, undercut. Had she really committed herself to this? Would she take Apparitor away from Lindon as Tain Hu had been taken from her? The letter was sent, the arrow was shot . . . why did she always come to her regrets so *late*?

"Say," Shao Lune said, casually, "is there a chance you could get me some rum?"

BARU woke up in chains, mostly naked, violently ill. Her breasts ached and her thighs trembled with carnal exhaustion. She had a hangover so brutal that she resolved at once to vomit, which she achieved by sticking her head over the edge of Shao Lune's platform and throwing up into the bilgewater.

Why was she still on Shao Lune's platform?

Oh dear.

She sniffed a bucket, gargled freshwater, and rolled over. The chains wrapped around her were Shao Lune's; she got free with a little slithering. Shao Lune slept under a rough blanket a few feet away, a lovely assembly of sine curves. In sleep she had an expression of smug victorious delight that made Baru want to throttle her.

Baru staggered around empty-headed and made an account of how much she'd drunk.

An empty vodka bottle floated in the bilge. A sac of Oriati wine, drained into a sad gut heap. A flask that smelled of whiskey discarded on the steps. Baru remembered sitting there, already blissfully smashed on vodka, talking with Shao Lune.

They'd discussed their various solitudes. Baru first: she'd been taken from her home, sent to a distant province, seduced by a glorious woman, compelled to betray and execute that woman for promotion into a world of betrayal and intrigue. Shao had been cruelly unsympathetic, entirely arrogant and dismissive, except that she had *very* consistently tried to one-up Baru in her stories of misery, manipulation, callous betrayal, and lonesomeness. Shao Lune had been persecuted all her life by those who wanted to tear her down for beauty and intelligence, driven into the navy to escape the infuriating ineptitude of her teachers, forced to keep her own council by the jealous and those who would take credit for her work.

That was enough to tell Baru that Shao Lune had been alone with her ambition for most of her life. Feeling an uncomfortable kinship, Baru had begun to tease the prisoner. The prisoner had retaliated, viciously, with aspersions on Baru's intelligence, integrity, and acuity. Baru had liked it so much she got some more rum for Shao Lune. By this point she was so drunk she could perceive Shao's emotions with absolute clarity. It was all so obvious! Why couldn't she understand people so confidently when sober?

Shao wasn't cruel or smug. She was fucking *terrified*. She'd been dragged into Ormsment's mutiny, she'd gambled everything on a *second* mutiny to get back on the winning side, and now she was a captive resource in the internal politics of the Throne.

They began to trade ribald stories. Their first, and their best: the same, for Baru. Shao showed no surprise at Baru's taste for women. She was, if not a proper tribadist, at least unconventional in her desires, and differently than Ulyu Xe and Iraji. Her stories depended not on the beauty or status of her lovers, but on how fraught and dangerous their courtship, and on how ably Shao had manipulated the situation. Privately Baru suspected Shao was a narcissist with a taste for the illegal. She delighted in playing the perfectly reserved and composed Falcrest woman by day—did she, Baru wondered aloud, ever need to lower her guard?

Not lower it, Shao said, with rum-fueled humor. One did not *lower* a fortress's walls. One opened a gate and send out a raiding party to obtain what one required.

What did Shao Lune require, then?

She required Baru to come closer.

That would be quite unwise. Shao Lune was a prisoner, and Baru had standards.

But the prisoner had already hooked Baru's ankle in a loop of chain. Baru ought to defend herself, oughtn't she? Defend yourself, Baru.

Baru thought she was much too drunk for that.

Was she afraid? Was she a coward?

No. She was braver than Lune could possibly know.

She ought to prove it, then. She should say something brave.

Come over here and fuck me, then.

Then Baru was pinned beneath her on the hardwood, cold chains slithering over her skin, Shao Lune's teeth in her lower lip. A long vague interregnum of foreplay. Shao's attentions wrapped Baru in chains and stretched her taut across the platform. Was she afraid, Shao Lune wondered? Didn't she think Shao Lune might drown her in the bilge?

Baru had answered with husky honesty. I'd deserve to drown. I would be glad to rest.

(Had she said that? Fool.)

Shao Lune had looked down at her with irritation and dismay, not amused or entertained by self-pity, but instead obviously turned off. Then she'd berated Baru, excoriated her for wanting to give up. Shao Lune would not be imprisoned and manipulated by a spineless self-pitying slug. Was Baru a spineless self-pitying slug? Did she have no will of her own?

Baru had tried to get up and get at her and that provoked Shao Lune's merciless counterattack. Baru remembered the tremendous relief of having no control. She remembered her release, the climax she couldn't reach with Ulyu Xe. She was pragmatically relieved to have that release, and she ought to be a little gleeful to have scored a Falcrest woman.

But she wasn't proud.

Baru rubbed her aching face. Well. She had made—not a mistake, it hadn't cost her anything, and at least she'd gotten laid. But she'd embarrassed herself. She was glad that she'd let Shao Lune make the advances, so she didn't feel like a filthy rapist. Still, Shao was a prisoner, there was an inequity of power between them. Had Baru considered that carefully enough before she let herself be seduced?

Or was this another principle compromised?

She gathered her clothes and stumbled up to middeck to wash herself in brine and a little precious freshwater. She felt like frozen shit. But no one seemed to care about her condition. The crew had gathered into whispering clots, and everywhere there was talk of plague ashore on Kyprananoke.

BARU glared against the sunlight. Through the canvas crowd of the mooring swarm she could see *Sulane,* red of sail and dark of purpose, moored far enough from them to avoid trickery, close enough to watch.

Ormsment was waiting for them to leave their ship before she struck. Baru would oblige.

At the center of the maindeck the Prince Tau-indi Bosoka held court beneath a canvas awning. Under their mayorage the *Cheetah* crew did *Helbride*'s laundry, arranged for fish and bird-catch, and scrubbed the deck. Tau was, Baru thought, the happiest person on the ship.

Tau met her with level, worried eyes. "Your Excellence. I was told you felt unwell."

"I've been resting," Baru lied. She saw Tau's fine nose wrinkle at the smell of drink on her, and seized by embarrassment she scooped up a smoky candle in a brass cup and held it between them. Candles were terribly expensive: *Cheetah* had carried boxes and boxes of them. "I, ah, Your Federal Highness, I need your help."

"You do. You're very sick."

"This? It's just a hangover."

"The drink is bad medicine, Your Excellence, but it's not the sickness."

Baru squinted against the sunlight. "How would you like to get off this ship and find your friend?"

"I'd like you off this ship, certainly," Tau said, frowning, "for a year's rest in a house that gets no news. But you're right that I want very badly to find Abdu."

"So let's go!"

"You and I?"

"And whoever else you please to bring." Baru spun in place to check for Apparitor or Yawa. Her brain gyroscoped. "I've been placed under medical arrest, they won't let me go ashore. But if you can get me to Kyprananoke, I think *I* can get us to Unuxukome Ra."

"You think she'll know where Abdu has gone?"

"She wrote a letter to her son that was carried by Abdumasi Abd's ships. Maybe she can tell you what Abdumasi planned. Won't it bring you a little closer to him, to know more of what he intended?"

"You learn well." Tau smiled. "But you're asking me to go against an Incrastic doctor's medical opinion. That's a bleeding offense on a ship."

"You're not a Masquerade citizen. They'd never bleed you."

"But you're still asking me to defy my host's wishes. That's terribly rude."

"Your *host*—you mean Apparitor?" Baru clasped indignant hands to her breast. "What about *my* wishes, Your Federal Highness? What right does he have to hold me?"

"Isn't there a terrible plague ashore?"

"Yes, but it's mostly confined to the west side, and we needn't go there—"

"Won't the mutineers on *Sulane* come after you once you leave *Helbride*?"

"Certainly! But if *you're* with me, I keep your diplomatic protections!"

Tau-indi's frown broke into a broad dawning smile. "This sounds like a dismal plan."

Baru huffed. It was her *only* plan. "You're refusing me?"

"Oh, no, I'll get myself and the enact-colonel ready to go at once."

"You will?"

"I think it'll be good for you," Tau said, "and a suture has to begin with one stitch. Also, I have resources on Kyprananoke that you lack."

"What if Apparitor tries to stop us?"

"Why," Tau said, still grinning, "then he's denying my diplomatic right to free movement. And if I am no longer a diplomat, why should my seals fly over *Helbride*?"

Baru had to laugh in appreciation at that. Then she thought of something that might chill Tau's warmth. "I want to bring the prisoner Shao Lune."

"The navy woman? Why?"

Because, Baru's heart muttered, she'll probably die if I leave her here. "She knows Ormsment's tactics. She can help us protect ourselves if *Sulane* sends a party ashore."

"Trim will guard us," Tau said. "But if you wish, I won't deny you. Although I won't be responsible for her care. She is a sailor and a killer, and I cannot be bound to her."

Trim again. But they caught Baru's thoughts on her face, and held up a finger in reproach. "Before you cast me as the magical primitive with one answer for everything, which is to wave my hands and call on my gods, consider our respective positions, please. Consider what I have achieved, and by what means. Has it occurred to you that the Falcresti dismiss my beliefs? That they assume I play lip service to trim to guard more cynical maneuvers?"

"You don't really believe," she said, with surprising disappointment.

"Oh, I do believe, with all my soul! But"—Tau winked—"isn't it funny that my genuine belief is most useful to me because the Falcresti think it's disingenuous?"

That made Baru think of something she'd forgotten. Someone had been telling her, *there is a difference between acting out their story, and truly obeying their story. Do you know what it is?*

Her stomach knotted up before she could push the thought. "I strive to keep an open mind," Baru groaned. "Will you excuse me?"

"Take a bath," Tau-indi suggested.

As Baru bolted aft, she caught the eyes of the Enact-Colonel Osa ayaSegu. She was tying fighting ropes around her fists. As Baru passed, Osa held up a line, taut between her fists, and pulled; Baru heard the creak of fibers at their limit.

Baru lost control. Her stomach revolted. She aimed herself over the rail and gagged up a thin stream of wine-sweet sick. Someone gave her a cup of brine. She swallowed it to gag, threw up again, and washed herself out.

Now the enact-colonel was shaking her head in pity.

"SAILS AWAY NORTH!" cried the masttop girl, a shriek so powerful it roused all the birds off the rigging. "NAVY RED IN THE NORTH!"

"That must be *Scylpetaire*," Captain Branne snapped, shoving past Baru. "*Sulane*'s companion turns up at last—watch girl, what's her name-flag! Shout it down to me!"

"She's *Ascentatic*!"

"*Ascentatic*?" Baru pushed her way through the scrum after the one-eyed captain. "What ship is that?"

Branne stood halfway up the rail, her lips thin and quivering. "*Shit*," she spat. "Bloody shit."

"She's from Annalila Fortress on Isla Cauteria." Apparitor descended from the ropes on Baru's blind side. "If she's come to help Ormsment . . . then Rear Admiral Maroyad is with the mutiny. Which means the mutiny's spread beyond Ormsment's command—"

Branne seized his hand and gripped it hard. He stared numbly at the eastern horizon.

"Lindon," he said, hollow as a new year's hope. "Lindon needs me."

THE signal rockets went up from *Ascentatic*'s prow to cry their questions. Who are you, Juris Ormsment? What are you doing here? Who sent you? Will you ask our help?

Aminata couldn't bear to wait on deck for an answer from *Sulane*. She paced Captain Nullsin's cabin, wanting to go below and interview Ake Sentiamut again, trying not to chew at little dry flaps of skin around her nails. When Nullsin came below she had to swallow the hole in her chest just to get a word out. "Sir? What word from her?"

"*Sulane* sent warning of disease and recommended we stand off." Nullsin grimaced at the hammer that had replaced his missing hand. There was nothing tangible he could strike or fix. "Maybe she just meant to warn us of the plague ashore. Maybe . . ."

Maybe Province Admiral Ormsment was trying to say, *I'm contagious. Learn of what I've done and you'll be tainted. Come any closer and you'll have to choose a side. Stay away, for your own sake.*

"Your orders, sir?"

"Well. I have a clear command from a superior officer to stand off." Nullsin smiled impishly, though he tried to hide it. "But if that were not clearly communicated to one of my juniors, and she took some boats ashore to learn what's really happening here . . ."

"Say no more, sir." Aminata didn't salute, for it wasn't an order. Maybe there was a *little* wink.

But before she gave her orders she went back to her hammock and reread the letter. She had nearly left it on Cauteria, that mysterious convict's plea, but some dutiful instinct against unread mail had made her take it on *Ascentatic*. After the Llosydanes and the vultjagata she'd gone back to it at last, out of desperation to know anything more about Baru. Now she kept it pinned to the planks beneath her hammock with the cormorant quill.

To the Oriati Lieutenant who I know is close to my lord, I write this by the mercy of my captor, who hast permitted me a final inscribtion on the eve of the voyage which I hope will end in my death. Instead of a will I leave to the world this letter.

My lord Baru Cormorant will very soon fight a great war. In this war the sides will be: Her mind and Her heart.

It is true that my lord has accomplished very much with her mind and that this organ often seems to rule her.

However I have learned through close inspection and some provocations and difficulties that my lord also possesses a heart which feels the full range of feelings. It is merely very well concealed and somewhat prickly like an urchin. I believe she thinks of her heart as an unfortunate growth. A sort of emotional hemorrhoid.

It is therefore my final duty to reach out to the woman whose name she most often spoke with respect and ask her to carry on my station as her companion and protector.

Please see to the well-being of my lord even when she will not. Please ensure that she is not alone even when she convinces you that she needs no one (she is lying). Please do not abandon her even when she makes herself wholly intolerable.

She will not betray you. When I am done with her she will have had her fill of betrayal for one life. Thus I will protect you.

I name you,

By my station as Duchess Vultjag,

A knight of Baru Fisher, Queen of Aurdwynn (by acclamation),

And a ranger of the Duchy Vultjag.
And I remain,
My lady's sworn Field-General,
Tain Hu.

Baru, Aminata wondered, Baru, what are you doing? What's happening
here? What became of this woman who thought she was your friend?

A STORY ABOUT ASH 4

THE summer of 912 grew hot.

The termites built their mounds and the crows fished for the termites with sticks.

The griots came up Prince Hill to tell the war.

Cosgrad Torrinde recovered from his frog-licking and developed diarrhea. He was appalled and embarrassed that everyone had to work to filter enough water for him. He would boil his own drinking water on a little pot-fire even after they filtered it, and the housekeeps murmured that this ingratitude and mistrust was making him sick. His room filled up with smoke and steam and damp, which caused mold, and he scrubbed miserably in between bouts of shit. Cairdine Farrier came and visited him now and then, and they muttered together lowly, but inevitably the mutters would rise to shouts and Farrier would leave and Torrinde would crouch miserably over his pot.

Tau-indi couldn't figure out how to go talk to Kindalana and Abdumasi and repair their friendship.

The griots began to soften their proud words. Kindalana noticed the change in the epithets and pointed it out to Tau, as she would point out anything she thought was hidden from others. "The unsurpassed cunning of Eyotana Six-Souls" became merely "the clever words of Eyotana Six-Souls." House Mbunu's captains slipped from "invincible" to "formidable." The skittish, fragile-looking Falcrest frigates were promoted, in metaphor, from water-bugs to makos and barracudas.

Tau didn't need Kinda to explain that this was a bad, bad sign. To the extent that the Mbo had a military, it was made of the brave and the venturesome, and its goal was to intimidate and dazzle so the enemy could be embraced and absorbed. When the heroes lost their shine, they lost that war, too.

Padrigan and Tahr brought their children together to explain that it was time for their Instrumentality, a course of lessons that would make them ready to go anywhere in Oriati Mbo. They would be prepared to visit the archipelagos

of north Segu and the very southern outposts of Zawam Asu, where indige-
nous tribes watched the Mbo's explorers guardedly, and the Mbo's explorers
tried very carefully not to disturb them.

Tau-indi and Kindalana had to spend hours cloistered together, reading or
speaking to griots. Tau liked the griot lessons better: here they were encouraged to talk back, to question, to share their own stories, for griots were the
living texts of Oriati Mbo. But Kindalana excelled at the written word, and
what Tau at first took for brooding was, they realized, an almost trance-like
absorption in the work.

"Everyone is unhappy in the Butterveldt farms," Tau-indi said, after they'd
listened to the griots who'd talked to the griots who'd been to the Butterveldt.
"How can Jaro feed itself without the farms?"

The Butterveldt was the great temperate grassland that divided Falcrest
and the northeast of Lonjaro Mbo. Right down the middle of the Butterveldt
ran the Tide Column, the long narrow waterway that connected the Ashen
Sea to the huge Mother of Storms in the east. Tau-indi imagined the farmers'
unhappiness as a plague of urchins, crawling up out of the Tide Column to eat
their crops and pleasures.

"It's the blight," Kindalana said curtly, her eyes squeezed shut, her hands
tracing shapes in the air. She liked this memorization trick, which Tau-indi secretly suspected she'd learned from Cosgrad: she could associate certain facts
with motions of her arms. "Something's killing the millet and the wheat. Something from Falcrest, the farmers say."

"What can we do?"

"Burn the whole crop." She drew a line from her chin to her throat, like she
was putting on her Prince paint.

"But then we'll starve."

"Yes, Tau, we'll starve. So we'll have to open the treasury and buy excess
crop from Devi-naga and Mzilimake, if they have it. And if we can get ships
through the Tide Column to Devi-naga without Falcrest taking them."

Tau-indi wished Kindalana would stop saying useful things, and say something warm instead. Every day Tau tried to break the chill between them. Every
day Tau failed. "Yes, fine, we can buy grain from the other mbo nations. But
what can we do for the farmers who lost their crop?"

"What?"

"The farmers aren't going to have anything to sell. They deserve help."

"Talk to Abdumasi." She touched her nose, and her ear, like one of Tahr's
chains. "He knows trade. He could figure something out, perhaps."

Tau did not want to go talk to Abdumasi.

* * *

M EASLES!" the ferrymen on the lake reported. "Measles in Jaro!"
Measles ripped through the city people, and cruelly, so cruelly, it
killed their babies first. The morgue bakery ran out of ways to make ash cake,
and so the mothers couldn't burn and eat their infants children properly, which
left the city swarming with wailing sobbing child-souls. Tau and Abdu wanted
to go and call the souls out of the city, but Padrigan and Tahr forbade it. Measles was too dangerous.

And the month after that, as Jaro griots raced to spread the word of the
measles and the names of the dead (this made Cosgrad Torrinde panic, and
beg Tau to stop the griots, lest they carry the disease—but Tau tried to explain that the mbo *knew* disease, that the griots moved too quickly for their
exhalations to pool in one place), a mother-of-worms was found in the cisterns
in the Segu capital Kutulbha.

Nothing revolted Tau more than the mother-of-worms, a great mass of ma-
ture and fecund parasites, gathered in a snarl in the water. Cistern inspectors
found the colony creature squirming in white lashing loops, shedding and peeling off masses of egg to fill up the drinking water.

No mother-of-worms had ever been seen in Segu Mbo. They lived in southern Mzilimake and Devi-naga. But somehow one had made it to Segu, and
worse yet, some merchant in Devi-naga, some cruel and selfish soul who Tau
cursed with balled-up fists, had bought all the wormsbane and hoarded it.
Wormsbane only grew in the jungle that bordered Devi-naga and Mzilimake,
and it was the best treatment for worm infestation in a body: there was no easy
way to get more.

Rumors circulated, of course, that the merchant was a Falcresti agent. Tau
wondered, cynically, if Falcrest had moved the merchant, or if the only motive
was greed. The mbo should prevent such atrocious avarice . . . but the mbo, of
late, seemed thin, like a ragged net.

Ships refused to dock in Kutulbha. If you drank a worm egg it would grow
inside you and crawl out through your foot over agonizing weeks, burning like
a bee sting.

Wracked by famine in Lonjaro and a shipping stoppage in Segu, the mbo
staggered.

And then all the money froze.

Tau-indi couldn't understand it! Everyone still needed everything, the
goods were out there, the money was available, supply and demand existed,
nothing had changed! But all the griots complained that the merchants had
tightened their fists and the families on the road were ungenerous. The hawala

banks stopped conducting transfers across the mbo, preventing merchants from moving their fortunes.

The principles of anxiety and miserliness had snarled up the mbo.

Tau went over to Jaro and talked to the merchants in the bazaar, who had talked to their suppliers, who had talked to the shipping captains, all of whom were slashing their prices, down and down and down, trying to get *anyone* to buy: no one would, not even at ruinous discounts.

"Something must be wrong with our trim," Tau-indi said, baffled. "Why would everyone just . . . stop spending money?"

"It's not trim!" Kindalana shouted, throwing down the knotted string she'd been using to do figures. "You idiot, you *idiot*, don't you learn anything from Cosgrad? It's a deflationary collapse!"

"A—a what?"

"Everyone's uncertain and afraid," Kindalana snapped, her posture perfect, her gestures articulate, every inch the young Prince. "Why would they invest in new business right now, or try to sell their crops abroad, when ships are being taken and ports are being closed? You might lose it all. Better to eat your own food, and keep your goods to yourself, and wait, wait until the world stabilizes. So the ports idle, and the businesses who rely on the ports close down, and the hawala banks stop loaning and sending. The mbo's gold and shell and jade is all locked up in vaults and attics. It's not *moving*. Do you understand?"

Tau did, actually: there was less and less money on the market, so each piece of money was worth more, each golden coin or silver bar could buy *more* things, which made people even *less* willing to risk it on a loan or a shipping expedition. It was like water freezing, a phenomenon Tau had never seen: it grew slow, and thick, and clotted.

"I think," they said, politely, "that the solution is clear. We must make everyone unafraid. We must cheer them up, and make them brave. The griots should be encouraged to tell the ancient epics, and the comedies."

Tau's politesse just enraged Kindalana further. "You," she said, stalking to the door, "think like an old person."

"I think like a Prince."

"Haven't you learned *anything* from him?" Kindalana shouted. "Anything at all? This isn't about trim! We're like an old, old elephant, and Falcrest is running us down, herding us toward the pit!"

"No," Tau said, calmly. "There's no Falcrest, really, nor any Oriati Mbo. Just two groups of people. It's always about the connections between people. That's where we'll make a difference."

Thinking back upon it, Tau realized that Kindalana had taken inspiration from this moment: if not, perhaps, in the way Tau expected.

That night Kindalana drank sorghum malt beer with Cairdine Farrier and told him loud jokes. The bearded man seemed to relax a little. Tau couldn't figure out why Kindalana was acting so crudely, until they realized Kindalana was trying to behave like a commoner, and an adult.

COSGRAD Torrinde's diarrhea cleared. Tau went to visit him, to be sure he was comfortable.

"What should we do," Tau asked him, "if everyone stops spending their money, for fear of risk?"

"Print money," Cosgrad suggested.

"*Print* money?"

"Yes. Use fiat currency. Paper notes that say they can be exchanged, later, for gold or gems or bone. Flood the market with your paper, and expand the supply of money: you must shock the market back into motion, you must lubricate it with, ah"—he searched for words in Seti-Caho—"with lube? Is that the word?"

"No," Tau said, giggling, "that means sex oil. Perhaps fish oil, or olive oil?"

"Oh. But my point stands! You must print fiat money."

"Cosgrad," Tau said, deeply concerned, "that would be lying. You can't trade someone a promise to give them something valuable *later*. You'd be inventing something from nothing. You'd be paying them with *magic*."

And in accord with Tau's fear for Cosgrad's trim, not even a week later Cosgrad developed tetanus.

"Your Federal Highness!" a clerk screamed, running into the sleeping-quarters. "Your Highness, come quick!" Tau-indi leapt out of bed to find Cosgrad curled up and snarling in irritation. He insisted it was just a backache but no, the signs were clear, he had tetanus. Tau-indi made a hasty calculation on the calendar. Tetanus hit hardest when it hit fastest. If Cosgrad had contracted tetanus on Tau's birthday, up in the frettes, then it *should* now be survivable.

"Get frogsweat and weed," Tau-indi ordered the groundskeeps.

"Apple ester," Cosgrad said. He stared balefully at Tau-indi. "If it's tetanus, I want apple ester."

"I don't know what that is."

"Of *course* you don't!" He snarled, and tried to turn over, and screamed.

Tau ordered a chorus to sing around his room to drown out his agony, lest his pain spread. Cosgrad shouted at them with incredible distemper until his jaw locked up.

The griots came to Abdumasi's house to sing about the ongoing war, about the principles of justice, the elephant slow to anger but terrible in its fury. The Oriati Mbo would show no more mercy. Kolosan and Cho-oh Long Oar would sail a thousand ships east to smash Falcrest, smash them so decisively that the fish would lose their taste for the flesh of people and turn to eating seabirds.

Tau watched Abdumasi and Kindalana as the griots sang. They sat together between two raspberry bushes, and Abdumasi settled against Kindalana's side, his head pillowed on her breast. Kindalana stroked his head, but her eyes were far away, and thoughtful.

The men of Prince Hill were all love-struck, and the women of Prince Hill all thoughtful. It was up to Tau, as it had been up to the lamen in ancient and more traditional days, to mediate.

The mbo continued to fray.

Between Prince Hill and the frettes to the south was a great expanse of irrigated rice-field, fed by long canals. The fish that lived in the canals began to die. Birds shed their feathers and flew blindly into rocks. Ants were found presenting themselves on the grass to be eaten by goats, which was an awful omen. Tau-indi imagined principles of death moving under the earth, under the clouds, leaping from man to laman to woman.

Something terrible was happening.

And then Tau-indi was seized by a thought as hard and hateful as tetanus muscle. They remembered their own spite, their desire to possess Cosgrad so as to make their friends jealous. Hadn't they said, in fact, that they were fighting a war against their friends?

Cosgrad Torrinde was bound to the mbo as a hostage, a prisoner volunteered by Falcrest to maintain tenuous diplomacy. Thus trim bound Cosgrad to the very war itself. The large reflected the small.

Tau-indi Bosoka had made Cosgrad a guest of their house, and used Cosgrad in their battle against Kindalana and Abdumasi, a foolish selfish battle.

Without realizing it, Tau-indi had connected the war between Falcrest and Oriati Mbo to their own childish war against their friends.

The logic of trim was irrefutable.

The war could not end until Tau-indi Bosoka made peace.

THEY walked to Kindalana's house. The bees were gone, as was Cairdine Farrier, who'd gone over to Jaro to study the death rites. The raspberry bushes had withered. Tau used the mallet to ring the door, and smiled at the door sentry, and walked up to Kindalana's room, dry-throated, wishing that they could do something with their hands.

"Yes?" she said. She'd been dyeing cloth. Her arms were wet to the elbow. Sweat and motion had pressed her ratty old work shift close against her, but Tau-indi noticed that with distant disinterest compared to the fright and buzz of meeting her eyes. She swallowed very slowly, as if to hide the motion from them: as if to pretend that she did not need to inhale or swallow, she never needed to move anything into herself, only out.

"Do you still want to go together?" Tau-indi asked.

She'd ask a clarifying question now. She'd make Tau-indi say something she already understood, so that she could draw them out.

"What do you mean?" she asked.

"Do you still want to work together to serve the mbo, as Prince companions, the way we used to talk about?"

"Oh." Kindalana wrung the wet from her hands in short snaps of the wrist. "Your mother's going to be here soon. I don't know if it's a good time to talk."

"Do you want help with the dye?"

She looked at Tau-indi with her jaw set and her hands loose at her sides, turning, turning again, as if she could stir up the air between them and knead it out flat and simple.

"I don't understand you," she said.

Tau grinned and shrugged. "Me neither."

"Okay. Come help."

Someone came into the house later to visit Padrigan, and the housekeeps brought the two filtered mint water. Tau-indi and Kindalana both knew who it was, so they talked to each other stiffly and loudly, to warn their parents not to have sex.

When they were done, Kindalana said, "I'm trying to seduce Farrier."

"*What?*" Tau squawked. "Why?"

"Because you're right," Kindalana said, "there's power between people, and I don't think Falcrest understands that power. And Farrier's afraid of his attraction to younger women, to foreign women, and whatever he's afraid of, I need to pursue. Because that's how I'm going to beat them."

Tau imagined "seduction" as a ridiculous theatrical process in which one's clothes "accidentally" fell off. "Kinda," they said, "this doesn't seem like good politics. . . ."

But Kindalana looked back at them with those serious studious eyes. "We're Princes," she said. "The Mbo trusts us to do our jobs. If Falcrest thinks women have special seductive powers, then I'll take advantage of it."

It seemed troublesome and unfair and strange to Tau. But it was also so complicated that they didn't know how to argue.

* * *

COSGRAD Torrinde's tetanus passed. For a while he suffered spasms and babbled. "I have to go," he'd say, trying to charge out through a wall. "I have to go! Renascent told me, she told me, go out and determine by what means matter becomes meat and meat becomes flesh and flesh becomes thought! Determine the mechanism of heredity, so that I may write my law in it! I can't fail her, I can't, I can't, I have to go work!"

"You're not making sense," Tau-indi said, patiently. They'd seen so much of Cosgrad by now that the man's body had lost all mystique and become faintly comical. It was hard to be impressed by a man's cock when you knew it got hard and wibbled while he slept.

He stood there panting and hunched over, grimacing at the wall. "If I don't get the Metademe," he said, out-and-out whining, "they'll give it to Farrier, and all Farrier wants to do is breed *plagues*. Plagues and vile thoughts. He doesn't understand eugenics, or anything else, except flattery and pageant!"

But soon Cosgrad's muscle spasms faded away like a knot coming undone. For a few months Cosgrad was weak and biddable and profoundly apologetic. The only lingering problem was his stiff neck.

His stiff neck didn't go away.

After a while he began to complain that his neck hurt so much he couldn't move his knees.

Tau-indi, sitting with him, wanted to scream in frustration. They knew what would happen now, and they were afraid Cosgrad would die of it.

Meningitis hit Cosgrad harder than anything before. He contorted into shapes like the letters of an underwater alphabet. He fought with dreams. When they gave him frogsweat and everything else they had, the dreams only got worse. He stared at Tau-indi with red-rimmed eyes and hissed, "What are you? How do they make you? Tell me how!"

"Me?"

"Tell me how they made you!"

"I came from my mother and father. . . ."

"And where did they come from! Where, Tau, where! No, I'm sorry, I'm sorry, no one knows that." He lapsed into silence for a moment and then he came up shouting. "They made you special. They made you different. Tell me how!"

Oh. It must be the Falcresti confusion. "No," Tau-indi said patiently, "they didn't make me into a laman. I chose my gender. Didn't you choose to be a man? Or do they say, you have a penis, so you're a man? What about people with both? What about the people who don't want sex and all the other sorts? How do you sort them, if you don't let them choose for themselves?"

"Degeneracy," Cosgrad muttered. "The Oriati have decayed. Too much drift. Not enough competition among you, to keep the breeding healthy . . . but oh so *rich* . . . so much raw material to work with, so much pedigree to study, if only, if only I had the Metademe. . . ."

Tau brought Cosgrad cold water, chilled in the night and stored below-ground. He wept it back out and screamed about a world unbound by law, spectral shapes in the mangrove shadows, bloody leeches clinging to his calves. "Farrier!" he would scream, red-eyed and roaring in his meningitis dream, "Farrier! They are not yours to take!"

On the next month, the gossip and the comic refused to come to Prince Hill to tell the story of the war. There was nothing funny to say. There was no gossip to tell.

The epic came up the hill, trudging and broken, covered in grief ash, with the satirist trailing behind.

At the beginning of the war the epic had named Kolosan and Eyotana Six-Souls, Cho-oh Long Oar and the Man with the Rudder Thumb, the sons and daughters of House Mbunu, and even salt-jeweled Nyoba Dbellu. The epic had bound himself to those stories. He was fated to tell of their thousand-dromon fleet, advancing bravely up the wind, into the skittering Falcrest frigates with their forest of sails and their unquenchable fire.

The ruin of these heroes and hunters, whose lays and sagas now darkened and dripped with unnumbered tears.

The thousand-ship main assault on Falcrest had failed. The fish would not lose their taste for the flesh of people, for no flesh had come into the sea, only wrack and ash. The swarming armadas of the mbo had been tricked and drawn in and then Falcrest's fireships had fenced them in. Everything had burnt.

Already they were calling this defeat the Unspeakable Day.

The satirist got up to mock the dead, the foolish overconfident leaders who had brought more than a hundred thousand sailors and fighters to ruin. Everyone wept silently and clung to each other, trying to be polite and strong: trying to let the satirist do their necessary work.

The satirist fell on their knees. "My brother," they wept, their voice rent, the principles screaming through them, "my brother, my brother. My brother is burning!"

They had no brother. But no one doubted they told the truth.

Padrigan and Tahr embraced each other and wept, she in the place of his missing wife, he in the place of her missing husband. Kindalana went off into the darkness and then came back to the fire with an armful of her fine garments, which she cast into the flame, to burn into ash for mourning. Abdumasi ran to his mother's arms and then looked at Tau-indi trembling with some inexpressible grief.

Tau-indi stood there trying to imagine some way in which this was *not* their doing, the course of the war as selfish and disastrous as their own conduct, the world visiting retaliation on Oriati Mbo for the monstrousness of its young Prince.

Cairdine Farrier whispered, "Tau, Your Highness, there are better ways than war. Please remember, as the news comes bitter, that there are many in Falcrest who would rather trade and teach than fight with you."

"There are many in the Mbo who would trepan themselves before they forgave this loss," Tau said, with more grief than bitterness.

"Perhaps," Farrier said. "Perhaps the Mbo needs to learn how to rid itself of those people. So we may have peace."

The next day a mob sailed across the lake from Jaro to kill Cairdine Farrier and Cosgrad Torrinde.

And in the chaos there came up Prince Hill a sorcerer, her hands and eyes alight with blue-green uranium power, to cast a spell of ruin. She spoke En Elu Aumor, the tongue of the Cancrioth. Abdumasi Abd witnessed her, and Tau-indi, and the two men of Falcrest. And in that spell all their fates were written: three men to seek that power, and one laman to refuse it and all it represented.

But first, before they could go to their fates, they had to survive that day.

23

THE PITHING NEEDLE

THE plan to disappear Baru forever had encountered a complication. Call me a callous old bitch, but I prefer that my pawns be interchangeable. If one falls off his carriage and dies of a broken spleen I damn well want another ready to take his place. The smaller the conspiracy the more its success hinges on particular people, and people make me nervous. I've never known anyone who didn't compromise themselves somehow. My brother married a royal. I betrayed my brother for it. Heingyl Ri took a Falcresti husband. Even Tain Hu trusted the wrong woman, in the end.

There is no unalloyed good in the world of power. Even a healer has to choose whom to save.

Himu help me if Heingyl Ri refused to divorce Bel Latheman. Himu help me if I had to kill Bel. But Ri *had* to be ready to wed the Necessary King. There was only one path between the Falcresti quicksand and the jaws of the Stakhieczi, and I needed access to the Stakhieczi royalty to walk Aurdwynn down that path.

I prayed to Devena that the Necessary King would not be too much like Ri's father for her to ever bear the child.

But before I could see to Heingyl Ri's remarriage, I had to get Baru to the Necessary King. And I'd just lost my best way to do it.

Iscend had a particular technique to prepare her catch, which she called ikejime. I would have called it prissy and obsessive, but the fish were exquisite, and anyway if you insulted Clarified they would make a great effort to correct their wrongs, which I found exhausting. It was hard to explain that sometimes I just needed to excoriate someone.

On the day we sighted Kyprananoke, I came up onto the quarterdeck to enjoy the wind and speak to the charming Mister Execarne. But I paused at the quarterdeck stairway to observe Iscend's fishing. She had magnificent poise. Such grace and strength. If I could trick this avatar of all Falcrest's obsessions, this epitome of youth and incision, then I could beat Hesychast and all the rest as well. I could still save Aurdwynn, and my brother, too.

Iscend's net came up fat with squirming silver, and she dumped the whole load of fish into a tub of water chilled by a brick of *Helbride*'s precious ice, stunning them. One by one she selected her favorites and performed her ikejime. The pithing needle glittered in her fist.

I'd threatened to pith Baru. Apparitor and I had agreed upon that step: poison her into seizure, place a medical arrest upon her, and watch her squirm her way free and flee onto Kyprananoke. She would be driven out of the safety of *Helbride,* where we couldn't move against her without eyewitnesses, and onto the turbulent kypra.

There, in the anarchic eye of the Ashen Sea, she would vanish—whisked away by Iscend, shipped north in captivity, delivered to the Necessary King. Apparitor and I would complete the mission to find the Cancrioth, and that success would earn Hesychast his triumph.

How fitting that an old woman would destroy Baru, mm? She'd been raised by Falcrest, raised to let old women do the work. Let us lay out the smooth road for you, so you may prance down the easy way and trample the dried-up rind on your way to take the credit.

Damn Baru. And damn Iscend for straying.

It happened like this: first she grasped the fish firmly around the gills. Then she drove the needle into the brain behind the eye. If done correctly (and it always was) the fish would fan its fins and then go limp. Iscend returned the dead fish to the ice water, where its flavor would remain succulent until she was ready to cook.

As she completed the first ikejime I saw her mouth move.

She constantly murmured mantras and qualms to herself, but I noticed *this* whisper in particular because it was hesitant. I'd never seen Iscend hesitate before. What could she be saying?

Her fingers flashed. The needle went in. The fish died.

Iscend's lips fumbled with a word. What was it? *Maia,* perhaps? Was she imagining each fish as a person with a gender and a race? Some kind of mnemonic exercise?

Her fingers flashed. The needle went in. The needle came out slick with fishblood.

Iscend whispered *Gaios.*

I clutched the rail in a fit of fury. Not this! Not now! Not here before Kyprananoke, where the dangers would be greatest—where the opportunity had been arranged! For a Clarified to utter one of her own words was an Act of Punishment, instilled since childhood. Iscend had been taught that if she ever said *Gaios* there would be maggots conjured in her bed.

She pierced the fish. The needle glinted in the sun. Gaios.

There was no one here to put maggots in her bed.

I saw the sigh of contentment that swelled her chest.

I FOUND Mister Execarne up on the quarterdeck, slouched in a wicker chair, his long-line trailing into the water and a huge overstuffed cigar blunt clenched in his teeth. "Hello, Yawa," he puffed. "Care to join me?"

I did care. I wanted to sit down with him and have a long idle conversation about nothing in particular. But I hadn't the patience with myself.

"I'd care for you to join me in a little work," I said. "I thought you'd be up and about, scheming to contact your people here. Kyprananoke doesn't agree with you?"

"There's a secret buried here which I wish I didn't know," he said, smiling up at me: but his eyes went to the distant carcass of el-Tsunuqba, looming against the sky. "You managed your share of outbreaks. You know that the necessary measures can be harsh."

"I do . . ." I said, inviting him to go on.

"But here I am, putting my own thoughts before yours. What can I do for you?"

"Iscend's deprogramming herself."

"Shit."

"Quite."

"I *hate* Clarified," he said, matter-of-factly. "I hate your master. I'd see him in the harbor if I could."

He couldn't, though. There had been a time when his Morrow Ministry's secret police had curled Falcrest in their squid arms, every sucker bound to a high minister or a member of Parliament. But that had ended by the Emperor's will, ended in the clatter of Judiciary printing presses. Raven courts drowned the Morrow Ministry's elite by the hundred. Urchins in Falcrest's Caulbasis Down still told stories of gulls with the rolling panicked eyes of long-dead spies, trapped in the animals that ate their flesh.

"So I'll have to bring in more clothing for the job, won't I? Damn." He blew a smoke ring over the rail. "I'm not supposed to have assets on Kyprananoke—Falcrest 'remanded the islands to local authority,' remember? That's why this place is such a festival for the Oriati Termites now—they use these islands as a junction to dispatch their spies. I had to 'kill' a number of agents on 'failed' missions to move them to Kyprananoke, and let me tell you, keeping them contentedly dead takes a *lot* out of my purse. You're asking me to burn this whole operation to grab one woman."

"I'm asking you to help me take Baru off the board. Her master wants an

Oriati civil war, war that will spread across the Ashen Sea and cost my people—
if you care—"

"I do—"

"—absolutely everything."

Execarne offered me the blunt. I took a grateful drag. His long-line twitched;
he began to reel it in, hand over hand, his arms dimpled fetchingly with farmer's
muscle. "Does Hesychast know how you plan to use her?"

"Hesychast just wants the Stakhi fat and well fed. Using Baru as a dowry
fits well. She's lost to the Farrier Process, anyway." She seemed to think that the
grief and disaster she provoked were inevitable, unchangeable. Farrier had
made her well.

"We're playing a dangerous game here, Yawa," Execarne said. I liked it when
he used my name. "Moving against Farrier. He can swing half of Parliament
just by changing the side he wears his cock."

His line jerked enormously. Thank Wydd he used a safe grip, or it would've
cut through his fingers. With a shout of surprise, he let the long-line drop. We
watched in shock as whatever he'd caught, a shark or swordfish, tugged the
line in short sharp jerks, three of them in quick succession, a long slack interval, then five jerks, then seven.

"Well," Execarne sighed, "I'm not going to reel *that* one in." He slashed the
line free. "What were you saying?"

"You were telling me we were in danger, fighting Farrier. And I know."
I wanted to take his arm in mine. And why not? Why not? I did. "But I cannot
let Baru get Aurdwynn. And I cannot let her defraud even one more good
woman to her doom."

She was all counterfeit, our Baru. The hints of yearning? The ill-hidden
grief? Even her preoccupation with "rescuing" Tain Hu's house on Moem? All
scattered like pepper for the hounds. Designed to throw me off the scent.

I'd realized the truth in that fetid cave beneath Moem, as Tain Shir hacked
off Baru's fingers. My mad niece was *right*. There was nothing on this ashen
earth that Baru would ever value above her own power. Not her parents, nor
her lovers, nor her home, nor her very selfhood. Give Baru a choice between
honest death and terrible enduring life and she would choose to endure: even
as some hideous Cancrioth implant, a knot of blackened cracked flesh festering in the skull of another woman.

That was the difference between us: why she had to be removed, and I had
to go on. There were things I knew I wouldn't sacrifice but Baru had no limit.
She'd shown me that herself. She could kill Tain Hu and I couldn't abandon
my brother. She spent people to achieve her power, and then, in a disgusting

aristocratic loop of self-justification, she claimed those people who'd died for her as reason to go on spending: *how can I stop, lest I betray those who gave everything for me?*

She'd killed Tain Hu to grant herself a universal license. A sacrifice that would justify any future atrocity. *That* was why she always appealed to Hu's faith in her, and wielded that faith as a bludgeon against me. Dead Hu could never repudiate or abandon her.

Dead Hu was now Baru's line of unlimited ethical credit.

"I won't leave it to chance," I decided. "Baru can't be given any more opportunities to trick her way free. I'll do the lobotomy as soon as we have her."

"You're going to go ashore with us?"

"I will. We'll let our woman tail Baru when she makes her move." I was not afraid of Kyprananoke. A strange violent city frightened me less than a ship alone on the sea. "Your agents will bring the necessary apparatus when we seize her. Then I'll conduct the surgery. Then she disappears. No one else needs to know."

"Not even Tau?" He clenched up like a fist around a fear much deeper than I had ever seen in him, a fear beyond Parliaments or kidnappings. I had seen its like only in the faces of ilykari who felt they'd lost their way toward the virtue. It was a very nearly eschatological terror, a fear of world's ending. And his eyes flicked, again, to el-Tsunuqba in the distance. Seeing my bafflement he said, as if this explained everything, "I hate lying to Tau."

"Then don't lie. Tell Tau she had to be stopped."

I had another reason to move against Baru now. If I could only show her to Shir, maybe Shir would, in all her madness, recognize that I had avenged Tain Hu.

Maybe I could bring Shir home to her father.

Perhaps then Olake could forgive her, and me.

"It's a shame." Execarne sighed, and settled his cigar again. "She had a fascinatingly disfigured mind."

BARU packed the lies that would protect her. Payo Mu from Aurdwynn, Ravi Sharksfin from Taranoke, Barbitu Plane from Falcrest. Her gorgeous mask and Aminata's faithful boarding saber. And her incryptor, which she kept in a waterproof gut-pouch on her belt. When she left *Helbride,* she would need to carry everything she needed to see this through—whether it stopped with Unuxekome Ra or led all the way to the Cancrioth.

"Baru," Iraji croaked.

Baru whirled right, checking her blindness, but in fact he'd just snuck up the ordinary way, on her left. She completed a near-full orbit to find him in the doorway of the arsenal, bracketed by boarding spears. He'd been crying again.

She shocked herself: without hiding the legends or making any effort to conceal her preparations to leave *Helbride,* she went to him. "Iraji. What is it?"

"I'm afraid," he whispered.

Baru tore the canvas curtain shut behind him, and tacked it to the wall. "Is it Apparitor? Did he hurt you? Is it Yawa?"

"It's *you*," he said, and began to weep again, silently. "Oh, Baru . . ."

She offered him a snifter of vodka, which he refused, and a seat on her hammock, which he accepted. She did not leap to the idea that he was in love with her, or any such ridiculous tosh. She remembered her revelation, on Moem, about hash functions and cartouches. Iraji's grief was a cartouche, a hash of many possible inner states into one hunched, red-eyed distress.

She asked questions that would allow her, tenderly, to update her notion of Iraji's inner state. "You're afraid you've wronged me."

He nodded.

"Because you helped poison me."

He nodded again, shakily, and put his arms around her. She held him wordlessly. She selected her most recent item of evidence on his behavior—she'd asked if he was all right, and he'd said, *No, my ship is full of Oriati!*

She put the two ideas next to each other, Iraji's role in her poisoning and Iraji's distress at all the other Oriati, and searched for connections.

A channel opened.

We need Oriati protection for an Oriati place, he'd said. *We need a bond of trim. . . .*

"You made a bond of trim with me," she said. "And now we have so many other Oriati aboard. Do you believe . . . is trim real for you? Is this place an Oriati place, now?"

He took a big long breath, firmed himself up, and said, "You saved my life. And look how I repaid you. Poison in your bottle."

"I don't hate you," Baru said, quite honestly, "for doing what you had to do."

"But when we poisoned you . . . you were calling out to Tain Hu," Iraji whispered. "You were so hurt."

The wound too raw to probe. She made a riposte, to put him back on the defensive. "Iraji." She took him by the shoulders. "Why are *you* so afraid of having Oriati people aboard? Is it about why you left them? Is it . . . ?"

"I'm afraid I've destroyed the world," he said, in utter earnest. "I'm afraid I've doomed us all to war."

Baru's mind flickered along lines of logic. He'd been born in Oriati Mbo, and he'd fled, but still he believed in their ethos: he had reached out to Baru as a human being, to connect them: he had betrayed Baru in service of his master, but on a ship now full of Oriati, a ship where he felt himself *reconnected* to the great web of the Mbo. . . .

Did he feel he'd passed some principle of betrayal into the whole Mbo?

"Iraji," she said, slapping him on the back, "I think the Mbo can digest you and I."

"Not I," he said, and teetered, his eyes rolling up in his head, his chest spasming, "oh no, oh principles, ayamma, ayamma, *save me*—I have to tell her—let me tell her!"

And Baru grasped the patterns. She knew the boy's doom.

Over dinner at the Elided Keep, Iraji had listened at the door as they spoke of the Cancrioth, and he'd fainted.

On a boat off Moem, Baru had said, *old Duchess Unuxekome can put us on the trail to the Cancrioth.* And Iraji had fainted.

On sinking *Cheetah*, Iraji had asked Tau-indi, what powers frighten you so? And Tau-indi had said, the same powers that attacked my ship, powers they would not name.

And Iraji had fainted.

"You're one of them," Baru whispered. "Aren't you."

He clutched at her and groaned in fear. She went on anyway. "That's why you ran away to Falcrest as a child. That's why you've been conditioned to go into syncope when we speak of them. You're trying to hide your own identity *even from yourself*. . . ."

Iraji slumped against her.

No wonder Apparitor had remained on *Helbride* at Moem. No wonder he hadn't seemed very enthusiastic about hunting the Cancrioth. No wonder at all that Baru had detected a flash of fear in his eyes when she refused to give up the mission.

He already had evidence of the Cancrioth in his hands, and he loved that proof, and he wanted to protect him.

Baru held Iraji's head in her lap and checked his breathing. Slow, serpentine terror licked the edges of her eyeballs. She knew a way to use the boy as a lure. Iraji's secret could lead her to the Cancrioth, and, perhaps, to final victory over Falcrest. . . .

But that would consume the boy. As giving Apparitor to the Necessary King would consume him.

She checked her bandages and the silk stitches in her cheek. She seemed to be holding together.

Then she scooped up Iraji and carried him to the maindeck, where Tau-indi was gathering their party to go ashore.

"Iraji's coming with us," Baru said. "He needs trim to heal him."

Tau-indi knew exactly what she was about. She could see it in their eyes; she could see they had known, since *Cheetah,* that Iraji had a secret, that he had seen the Cancrioth and knew its name. But they did not know, Baru thought, that Iraji was one of them.

"Did he ask to come?"

"He's bound to me," Baru said, trying to grin. "Remember? Didn't we get out of that ship? Aren't we bound together, Tau, you and he and I?"

"If I let you do this," Tau said, with absolute dignity and composure, "you must honor the principles of trim as you travel with me. A time may come when you wish to make one choice, and trim forces the other. Are you prepared for that?"

"Of course," Baru said.

24

IRAJI

"WE must go carefully," the enact-colonel whispered to the ambassador-prince. "Death is in the air."

"I wish," Baru murmured, "that I'd stolen Yawa's gown."

"But you would miss this lovely wind!" Tau cried. "It doesn't smell of plague or death. I should say it smells of . . . ginger."

"It's always the plague you don't smell that gets you," Osa said, straight-faced.

The escape from *Helbride* had been a contest of papers and insinuations. Prince Tau-indi had very deftly used their diplomatic freedoms to extract Baru and her companions from the surgeon's authority. Under a filter mask it was easy to pass off Iraji as one of the Oriati boys, sick and in danger of death, going to the Oriati embassy. The only other complication had been a brief attack by the dancing seagull, which wanted Baru's mask.

But they were safely away, passing through the swarm of moored ships, and now Iraji dozed in Tau-indi's lap. Osa and Baru rowed. Shao Lune brooded in the stern.

Baru caught her eye. "Tell me about Kyprananoke."

"You read the files."

"They lacked your keen insight, Staff Captain."

"If you insist." Shao Lune was unamused. Perhaps, having maneuvered her way out of *Helbride*'s hold, she no longer cared to taunt Baru. That was quite unexpectedly hurtful. "While Falcrest held Kyprananoke we arranged the exile of the old Scyphu families. They inconvenienced our control. But when we withdrew our government, this left no one of any authority except for the barbers we had trained up as surgeons. The rebels fought for revenge on the collaborators, and the collaborators did what was necessary to hold their power. In the end the Kyprists retained control."

"The Kyprists are surgeons?"

"Not all of them." Shao Lune tipped her head back to breathe clean air. "Some are the generals of the old Republican Progress Regiment."

"Secret police," Baru translated.

"Yes." Shao opened one storybook-perfect eye, wet red with exhaustion, still venomously alert. "They have excellent accountants, you know. We used them to prosecute the black market. Kyprananoke was our furthest port before we had Sousward, and in those days we were careful to keep all the trade in our hands."

Shao Lune had probably not been more than a girl, those fifteen years ago. She said *we* as if she'd been there, because she was navy, and the navy had.

"And we left because . . . ?"

"Because it was no more use," Shao said, indifferently. "No cash crops, desultory fishing, no minerals. Your Sousward would serve better as a trade hub and fleet base. Kyprananoke could be left like rotting bait, to draw up the smugglers and pirates."

"And they didn't go back to their old ways?" Baru probed, thinking of home.

"I told you," Shao said, with sudden spiteful interest. "We destroyed everything that kept them together, so that they'd need us more than we needed them. And then we didn't need them at all. So we left. And like the savages they are, they came apart."

In Baru's memory, Cairdine Farrier asked the question again. *What do they have to offer us? What medicine? What sciences? What is worthwhile about their society?*

She hadn't known how to answer that on the Llosydanes. Here she felt that even if she had the correct instruments, she would find that most everything worthwhile had already been lost beyond recall.

But were the Kyprananoki to blame? No.

Hadn't they been pillaged, and wounded, and left to die?

THE kypra had no edge. Dead Mount Tsunuq's molten gore had spattered down in strings and mounds across miles of shallows, and the coral had grown up between the stone into a maze of channels, lagoons, and pocket coves. A good diver (Baru thought of and wished for Xe) could easily bottom and return.

Helbride was the only proper clipper in the mooring swarm on the east side, and therefore any boat from *Helbride* was remarkable, but Baru had hoped that they would get ashore without much attention. She had hoped they would not be marked as a major political event.

She did not get her wish, for they were serenaded by a floating band.

Barber-General Thomis Love's Singing Marshals, forty strong, beat their big drums and blew their trumpets from a barge moored off the promenades of Love-port. A tangle of stalls, shops, boardwalks, and tent pavilions drifted at moor in

Loveport cove. "Rather like your Iriad, isn't it?" Tau said and, seeing Baru's face, detecting some clue she couldn't fathom, "Oh, I'm sorry. You must miss it so."

"I do," Baru admitted.

It *was* like Iriad. Pirate captains haggled over sealed map-cases, privateer mates traded letters of take with Oriati attachés, stilt dancers advertised ratting dogs and birding cats for sale, teamsters hauled bundles of planks to the south quays, taciturn cooks called to customers with bursts of spicy hot-stone steam, acrobats mimed brutal war and vigorous sex on bamboo frameworks, addicts staggered from pole to pole in mumbling trance, rhetorics shouted their retorts from the posts of floating galleria, geometry clubs of old Kyprananoki and Oriati gathered to work on tile puzzles on the ground between big pots of dried beans and raisins and candied corn, pulque-makers and ash-paper sellers moved product in narrow stalls where coins clicked and flipped like game pieces, money everywhere, money and sun-touched flesh, the smell of spices hammered into fresh sizzling fish and the delectable sound of crab legs torn by teeth. Somewhere close by a handball game had drown a raucous crowd.

But there was something wrong. The music—the music was wrong. Baru knew that melody the band played, why, it was—"In Praise of Human Dignity." An Incrastic hymn.

"Good grief," Tau said. "They think we're a Falcresti delegation!"

"So they do. I'll take the lead, then. We're on a goodwill tour, showing how much we're not at war."

"Excellent."

The barber-general waited with his band and retinue, surgeons in white caftans with bandoliers of scalpels, generals with peace-knotted rapiers on their belts and soft orange shoulder-length gloves. The men and some of the women went sensibly bare-chested in the late spring heat, the men shaved sleek, the more heavily built women haltered in nets or cotton strophia. A few of them, men and women and a scattering of lamen, favored khanga; the tradition upon Kyprananoke being that lamen should dress to hide their bodies.

Each and every one of them wore a white ceramic mask.

"Kyprists, of course," Shao murmured to Baru. "They idolize our image."

"Do we still fund the Kyprists covertly? No? Then why do they pay us service?"

"How would *you* hold this place together? Islands full of gava, tunks, jellyfish eaters, three cultures older than the king's mummy? If they could see each other's faces they'd set right back to cannibalism."

"That's nonsense," Baru insisted, "they have common economic interests, they could work together to benefit from the trade—"

Shao Lune laughed. "You think like a schoolgirl."

"Fuck you."

"Tonight, if you're interested," Lune murmured, which made Baru shiver in disgust and desire.

As their whaleboat closed in, the band faltered and fell out of tune. Hurried conferences proceeded between sunken-chested Barber-General Love and his associates, and spyglasses were raised to inspect Baru's boat. Despite three Oriati aboard, the presence of a Falcresti naval officer, a masked technocrat, and a great pile of baggage seemed to satisfy the Kyprists that this was indeed a delegation from Falcrest, and finally they launched back into "In Praise" with fervor. Baru and the enact-colonel threw ropes to the waiting stevedores and helped Tau-indi up onto the boards. Shao Lune muttered obscene things but went about pretending to be Baru's steward: the enact-colonel was already un-loading Tau's luggage.

Baru composed herself, shoulders back, chin down, elbows out, hands in, showing her angles. "One step behind me," she ordered Tau, and together, as the smell of cooked crab got under her tongue, they stepped up onto the pier to greet Barber-General Love's delegation.

He was a fiftysomething man of unexpectedly pale skin, with a narrow chest, stooped shoulders, and no hair except a bristling gray mustache. "Thank you," he said, in a firm clear voice, his hands raised and clasped, the gloves or-ange and silky fine. "Thank you for coming. We are so grateful."

"Thank you for receiving us promptly, Barber-General."

"Everything is prepared. My fellow Generals on the Storm Council have been alerted. My surgeon has a full report on the outbreak and my Superinten-dent of Progress has drawn up a program of raids against the Canaat rebels. As soon as your marines are ashore, we may begin."

The poor bastard. He thought *Helbride* had come from Falcrest to help him destroy his enemies. "Barber-General." Baru coolly offered her hand. "My name is Barbitu Plane, from the Ministry of Purposes. I'm sorry to hear about this Canaat rebellion."

"They don't know what they want." Love shook his head. "They're like children. Less . . . developed."

"You understand, of course, that my first priority must be containment of your epidemic."

"Of course." His sweat smelled like fear. He had a very firm grip but he kept shifting his hand, searching for a better hold. "If the Canaat steal a ship, they'll spread the disease all over. They must be crushed."

"Certainly we must work together." Baru opened an arm for Tau-indi, who slipped in at her side like they were walking together into a dance. "May I present Prince-Ambassador Tau-indi Bosoka, of Lonjaro Mbo."

Barber-General Love looked at his aide-de-camp, a spectacularly competent-looking Oriati woman in a net shirt and long skirtwrap. She looked back at him and said something in el-Psubim, the old tongue that came before Kypra-nanoki. Baru recognized the word for *war*.

"I'm surprised to see you traveling together." Love tilted his head between Baru and Tau. "Given what I've heard of recent, ah, actions in Aurdwynn."

Tau took and kissed his hand. "We are on a tour of mutual solidarity."

"Word from the Llosydanes had it the war was already underway."

"The Llosydanes are a nervous place." Tau laughed easily. "Barbitu and I are on a mission of joint charity, to help ease tensions after the recent unpleasantness."

"Perhaps," Barber-General Love said, with a flat smile, "if the Prince-Ambassador is interested in easing tensions, they could discuss the Canaat with the Oriati embassy."

"I would love to," Tau said, sincerely. "What should I say?"

The aide-de-camp stepped in smoothly, to say what the Barber-General, politically, should not. "The Canaat rebels have Oriati munitions and Oriati money. Strange ships come and go in the west. Are you funding them?"

Tau's golden throat kinked with tension. They looked quickly at Baru, signaling confusion. "I'll look into it at once, I promise. I don't want war here, Governor. No embassy of the Mbo's should ever want war."

"The sudden bankruptcy of the rebels would certainly restore my faith in the Mbo's goodwill." The Barber-General signaled to his aide-de-camp, who snapped her fingers at a portly majordomo overseeing the baggage.

"Ah—that reminds me." Baru dropped her voice, as much to hide her own nerves as to protect her confidence. "I'm tracking an exile from Aurdwynn. One Unuxekome Ra. Do you know her?"

"I don't understand."

"She's a Maia woman, former aristocrat, exiled during the insurrection in 922—"

"I know that." Governor Love wore the marks and medals of an Incrastic citizen on a thin collar, all rendered, in capable miniature, with fine paint and scrimshawed pearl. They stared at Baru as if in echo of his dismay. "Of course

I know of her. How could I not know the leader of our enemy? The war-leader of the Canaat revolt?"

"WHERE am I?" Iraji leapt upright in the bed. "Baru, what's happened?" She shushed him with a hand on his hot cheek. "We're on a houseboat. Moored off Loveport, one of the kypra islands. Tau is here."

"*Helbride*—Svir—are they all right?"

"Everyone's fine." Baru had tried to lay out an outfit he might like, and draw a warm bath from the solar tank. She was really quite nervous whether he'd like that outfit. "I snuck you off *Helbride*."

She watched him uncurl his hands and relax his calves. "Why," he said, when he was firmly in control of himself. "Why did you take me?"

"I knew Svir wouldn't let you go."

"I didn't ask to go." He threw off the thin cotton sheets and rose magnificently. Baru had no sexual response to him but his poise and grace were monumentally striking. She'd undressed him to sleep off his faint, in private, out of respect for whatever modesty he had, which was not apparently very much.

"I need your help," Baru said. That was as specific as she dared be. "About . . . the matter you confessed to me."

He splashed water from the bath on his face. "You know he'll come for me."

"Not once he realizes what we're doing."

"What are we doing?"

"Completing our mission," Baru said, and waited, breathless, for him to faint.

He swayed, sighed, inhaled sharply. "I can't do what you want."

They had to discuss it elliptically, lest his conditioning trigger again. Baru sat on the bed and smoothed out the sheets. "It would be enough," she said, "if you accompanied me while I trailed my coat."

"What good would it do? I'll just look like any other Oriati boy."

"Not if you say the words."

"The words—" The bathtub rattled and sloshed in his grip. "The words. Yes."

He slipped into the tub like a gymnast, arms pommelled on the handles, feet pointed. Wordlessly Baru offered him soap and a razor. He went to work. Baru was fascinated to see him shaving his pubic hair down. "Is that *safe*?"

"Svir likes it."

"How odd."

"If I want to go back to *Helbride,* will you let me?"

"You'll have to sit in a quarantine boat for a while."

"But you won't stop me."

Baru considered the point of her pen. She had the urge to whirl and snatch Iraji's razor from his hands, to throw it out the window into the sea, where it couldn't hurt him: where he couldn't hurt himself. She shut her eyes. She wanted very badly to weep for him.

"I wouldn't stop you," she said.

"Thank you."

Baru knew she had weaknesses as a thinker. She was arrogant, self-centered, and blind to what she disdained. But she believed that she really *was* a savant, in the Incrastic sense: gifted with particular insights, sudden knife-tip revelations, stabbed up from her subconscious. Often enough her deductions struck the truth. Not often enough to be perfectly reliable; not often enough to trust without danger.

But enough, now, to help Iraji tell a little more of his story. "May I ask some questions?"

"I'll put my feet up," he said, and did. His face subsided into a little moon in the bath. "It keeps me from fainting, sometimes. You'll save me if I—but of course you will."

"Of course I will. So. Ah." She picked at the seams of the sheet. "You left them as a child?"

"Yes," the Iraji-moon said. "I was afraid of the . . . I was afraid of them. So I walked into a Masquerade school."

"You knew they'd follow you. So you sought protection. You went where they couldn't ever find you."

"They love me," Iraji whispered. "They *need* me."

"Why?"

"Because I was meant to inherit one of the Lines."

"What does that mean?"

"I mean they would have taken a cut—" He faltered, sank a little below the water, tried again. "A cut from my mother's immortata, and they would have implanted that cut in me. And it would grow in me. Ayamma. I was consecrated for that purpose. A ut li-en."

"Her immortata?"

"Her tumor."

Gods of stone and fire. The "immortata" must indeed be a transmissible cancer, passed from person to person, just like dogface, the cancer which dogs gave each other by biting. This was the inoculation Hesychast sought, the means of splicing behavior from body to body.

But the name, *immortata*—

Baru fell forward on one hand, thunderstruck. Could it truly grant immortality, as she had imagined? Could you put not just disciplines and behaviors but *yourself*, your mind and memory, into a tumor grown of brain-flesh? Could you then cut a piece of that tumor free and regrow yourself in another body? Was that how it was done?

Could you actually live forever?

"Will it help Svir if I be your bait?" Iraji whispered.

Baru howled against the armor of her heart. Would it help Svir? Would it? Not if she told Yawa, *this man would be the perfect dowry for his brother, send him in my place.* Not if she wanted to unite the Stakhieczi and the secret power of the Cancrioth against Falcrest. Svir would be beyond all help then.

Iraji didn't believe Baru was only a callous calculating husk of a woman with no purpose but her own betterment. Baru just wished he could convince her of it, too.

"I don't know," she said, with terribly difficulty. "I—can only promise that it'll help me."

"It will help him," Iraji said. Baru looked up in shock at his tone. He had gathered his knees to his chin: the razor's wooden handle bobbed in the suds before him, the blade depending downward into the foam. He ought to keep it dry, Baru thought. "It will help Svir survive."

"What?"

"They know he's here. And they won't let him leave unless he has something they cherish."

The Cancrioth. He meant the Cancrioth. "They're here? Iraji, you *know* they're here?"

"Of course they are," he said. "Who do you think sank *Cheetah*?"

"A navy ship. A ship with cannon, for false-flag attacks. . . ."

"That's not what the Prince Bosoka thinks."

"Tau's superstitious. . . ."

"The power of my people isn't superstition. I think they unleashed the Kettling here. I think they need to test how it behaves . . . and to warn Falcrest they possess it."

"The Cancrioth released the plague?"

But Iraji had thought of something else. "Baru," he whispered, "if the Prince Bosoka learns what I am . . ."

She went to kneel by his tub. "They'll be kind. They're generous, they understand. They know, already, that you met the Cancrioth."

"No. No." He gripped his skull like a boy with meningitis, curled up in wrack. "They don't know I *am* Cancrioth. Cancrioth aren't people. They're wounds in the mbo, and they have to be stitched up."

"Yes. The wounds have to be stitched shut. The Prince will try to befriend and care for you, to sew you back into trim. As they tried to befriend me."

"No. Not me. The old power is in me, the uranium light . . . I'll be bound up. They'll stitch me shut. Every hole. Mouth and nose and eyes and ears and ass and prick. Shut."

"Out of superstition? No, Iraji, no, nothing so cruel. . . ."

"Superstition? *Superstition?*" A hysterical crack in his voice. "What if I'm full of cancer? What if it leaked out of my body, somehow, into the aquifers, and the children drank it, the children who get sick so easily, and they all woke up one day chanting *ayamma, ayamma, a ut li-en, it grows in us!* They'll bury me in concrete, Baru, they'll bury me alive in wet concrete!"

Baru thought for a moment, but in her heart she already knew the answer. She couldn't bear to expose Iraji to more danger. Not even to find the Cancrioth. Tain Hu had consented to the danger of rebellion, yes. But Iraji had never wanted anything but his happiness with Svir.

"Can you draw?" she asked.

"Yes," he said, warily. "Svir taught me. Why?"

TAU arranged a reception at the Oriati embassy, where they would begin their search for Unuxekome Ra by consulting the embassy's intelligence resources.

But the embassy was also very beautiful, Tau said, and worth visiting just to see. It stood on a busy pavereef named Hara-Vijay, a peculiarity of the kypra, shallow coral rings filled with concrete and rubble and built up into artificial lagoons. The embassy stood on pilings in warm blue water.

The name was a peculiarity, too—Hara-Vijay meant "wheat scout" in the Invijay dialect of Urun—and Tau explained, frankly and apologetically, that this name was the relic of a mania, some decades ago, for the performances of a Lonjaro griot who'd romanticized the Invijay horse-tribes in her work. "We would rename it if we could, but the Kyprananoki have taken to the name, there being few Invijay here to complain."

"Why would they complain?"

"Wheat scouts are sacred. No one likes their sacred names used thoughtlessly."

Baru rolled her eyes. "Are you sure *you* aren't romanticizing the 'sacred traditions' of these 'foreign tribes'?" She didn't believe the Invijay were all born on horseback to a life of raiding, as Falcrest seemed to think, but nor was she ready to accept the Oriati narrative of the Invijay as peaceful matriarchal irrigationists corrupted by Falcrest's machinations. Probably the Invijay were complicated and everchanging, with a history full of grandeur and shame. Like everyone else.

"I've lived with them. Wheat right is very real. The hara-vijay are responsible for tending the plants of the Butterveldt. They can commandeer raiding parties to kill foreign farmers who disrupt the growth, or call war on tribes who threaten the commons."

"You lived with the Invijay?" Baru blinked at the little Prince in surprise. "Out on horseback? Why?"

"We sent a mission to try to understand why the Invijay had turned against us."

"Why?"

"Tain Shir," Tau said.

"Oh."

"Quite. Are you ready? You look very nice."

For the reception Baru had selected a shimmering green silk sherwani and matching gloves, over a blue undercoat and loose blue trousers. Over her polestar mask she had fixed a green-glazed cover from her wardrobe, with a jade inset at the forehead. Her boots were practical, steel-tipped. Tau wore a hip-hugging green khanga and full dermoregalia, nostrils chained to ears, throat scaled in silver over the bright green uranium-stars of Lonjaro Mbo. They were beautiful.

"I think I am," Baru admitted, having run out of things to fuss over.

"You think you're very nice?"

"No," she laughed, "I think I'm ready. But you look beautiful, Tau."

"Thank you!"

She settled her steel folio on her hip. She was also carrying the picture Iraji had made her, and the words that burned in her mind. But she would not admit those to Tau. "You'll let me know when you've contacted the shadow ambassador?"

Tau grinned at her. "I'll let you know *after* we've exchanged our signals. So you don't spy them."

The Oriati kept a proper ambassador for the business of trust, and a shadow ambassador for the work of espionage. The shadow ambassador would discreetly escort Tau and Baru to a private place, where they would share what they knew of the Kyprists, the Canaat, and the plague. Baru had needled Tau about this distinction—wasn't Tau both ambassador and spymaster?—and Tau had replied, quite earnestly, that their espionage work was always conducted in the name of peace, and therefore did no harm to their trim.

"Baru," Tau said, taking her hand. The pleasant citric tang of their soap. "Why did you really bring the boy? Beyond your charming efforts to believe in trim?"

"Eh?" Baru pretended to be distracted by the silver scales on Tau's long arched throat. "Oh. He's a hostage. So Apparitor doesn't trouble me while I work."

"While we look for this woman who might have seen Abdumasi Abd."

"Quite." Not *precisely* a lie. "We'll go to Unuxekome Ra and ask her when she last saw him. Where he was going. Where he kept his records, and his contacts. Whatever we can learn."

"It's very kind of you to hope for his survival, when everyone else thinks he's dead." Tau kissed the back of their hand in gratitude, and placed it, gently, on Baru's shoulder. "But what you learn here could pin the attack on Oriati Mbo. You could make a case for war."

"Please trust me," Baru said, desperately, "I *don't* want war, not unless I can be sure Falcrest will lose it—"

"*We will all lose the war!*" Tau cried.

"All right. All right." Baru didn't know how to soothe them: probably they would not want to be soothed, with the whole world burning in their heart. "Whatever I learn, I'll share with you, all right?"

"Swear on your parents."

"I swear on my parents," Baru said, and then cringed inside and out. She had to stop making bargains without tallying the price.

"You must be careful, now," Tau warned her. "If the Kyprists discover you're talking to the Canaat rebels, they may well kill you."

Baru tried a smile. She'd dared a little makeup, a masculine touch: she thought it put an interesting shine around her eyes in the mask. "Trim will protect me. Won't it?"

"Unless you've lied to me. Then trim will not protect you at all."

"Of course I've lied, Tau. I'm a cryptarch."

"Baru." Tau cupped her masked cheeks. Their upturned face was black and gold and glorious: the honest fear in their eyes as raw and sickly-sweet as oyster. "You must be very careful. There is a terrible power loose on Kyprananoke. Do not provoke it."

Baru felt a thrill of horror. *Of course they're here,* Iraji had whispered, his voice wet with the fluids of his body, particles of grief and fear. *Of course they're here. . . .*

"You're alluding to," she said, rubbing her scalp, "the civil war? Principles of discord?"

"No. I mean the epidemic flags in the west. And the power that might have set that epidemic loose."

"Maybe it's just a seasonal plague—all the winterlocked diseases have been freed up by the spring winds, to gather here by ship—"

"No, Baru." Tau's voice trembled with fear and vulnerable defiant strength. "You know it's not."

BARU had read the Kyprist reports. They were exceptional record-keepers, these Kyprananoki tyrants. In the smokehouses their barber-surgeons performed mass autopsies on the corpses headed for the kilns. Some of the dire diagnosis came from these.

The rest came from another method the Kyprists had learnt from Falcrest.

In the quarantined west of the kypra, index patients suffered in stone cells. Convicts who had been exposed to the living and the dead, to their flesh or blood or breath, to sniff out the plague's vector. One by one, on a fixed schedule, they would be executed and dissected. Had those exposed to dead flesh been infected? Had the men been struck harder? Or the women? Had lovers passed the disease to each other? All in the name of containing and understanding the plague.

The plague.

A hemorrhagic fever of extraordinary latency and mortality . . . first stage indistinguishable from a brief flu . . . second stage after eight to forty weeks* without symptom . . . the skin bruises at the slightest touch, the stool blackens, thirst and headache are most severe . . . blood weeps from the digestive tract . . . hemorrhage spreads to other organs with unpredictable course . . . liver, spleen, and kidneys struck next in more than a third of cases . . . the most rapid and certain deaths occur if bleeding spreads to the brain . . .

A characteristic green-black tint colors the blood . . .

Index patients on Mercipole Isle achieve a Blister Number of 2.9 except in pneumocystic cases** (however see—and here a scribble erased this line of the report).

Mortality in the index population approaches seven in ten.

Survivors experience persistent aches, visual abnormalities, madness . . . infectious reservoirs remain in the eyeballs and semen for weeks after symptopause . . .

Vectors: Tainted blood and flesh. Sexual contact. Airborne transmission, but only in the case of pneumocystic cases** . . .

The effects upon pregnant women are particularly acute. The fever induces massive uterine bleeding and sepsis of the fetus. Total mortality in mothers and unborn children.

*The latency period presents an obvious challenge to the forecast.

**Pneumocystic patients hemorrhage into the lungs. The sputum and vapor emitted by coughing is highly infectious, with a Blister Number of—(another scribble: this line, too, had been destroyed).

"I always wondered," Baru whispered, "why they called it Kettling, in the stories . . ."

Tau seemed to stare through her. They were looking at the imagined suffering, at the dead. Baru was afraid that their warm eyes would suddenly swell with blood. "I would tell you," they said, in a ghostly voice, "but the reason for that name is secret, and although it is pathetically obvious, I vowed not to reveal it."

"You know where it comes from."

"Of course I do. That's why I'm afraid."

"Is it true that the Mbo will unleash the Kettling on anyone who invades your heartlands?"

"I can't tell you."

Baru was about to ask, *did someone release it here, and why?* But just then Shao Lune and the enact-colonel came out onto the houseboat's bow with them.

Shao Lune wore her freshly cleaned and starched uniform, without any pins or insignia. She'd skewered her hair into an intricate braid with two steel picks. Beneath the uniform she'd slipped an item of mountaineering gear, a thick net bodystocking designed to trap insulating air between one's skin and overclothes. Baru would never have thought it could be used as erotica, and about that she was very wrong. The net drew faint lines on Shao's wrists: she had run a slender silver chain across her open collar, and the net sectored her skin beneath.

The suggestion of control and submission did not escape Baru. Nor did the temptation to imagine the contours of the net.

Shao winked. Baru was so distracted that she didn't anticipate the enact-colonel's warning. "They're coming ashore. Now."

"Oh principles," Tau breathed. "She's coming *now*?"

"How many?" Baru snapped, for they must mean Ormsment.

"All the marines." Shao had climbed up the houseboat's mast to get a better view. Baru could tell by the pace of her chest. "Ormsment is with them. I think they're trying to reach the Kyprists before Baru does."

"And Tain Shir?"

Shao spat on the very fine rug. "I didn't see the bitch."

"What about *Ascentatic*?" The other navy ship had exchanged coded rocket volleys with *Sulane,* but there was still no hint as to her purpose.

"She's sent no one we saw." Osa buckled on her knives. "Prince Bosoka, I know you'll refuse, but I must advise—"

"We're not skipping the reception," Baru and Tau said, in more or less the same words, except that Tau added an apology. "We need to reach that embassy. All my resources on Kyprananoke depend on it."

Osa began to rope up her fists. "So be it, then."

"You do know," Shao Lune whispered to Baru, "that Ormsment is—"

"Coming in to attend the reception. Of course."

"Of *course,* she says, of *course* she's attending a diplomatic reception, how sensible, how obvious."

"It *is* obvious. The Kyprists would invite the commander of any Falcresti warships anchored offshore."

"You know what they're afraid of, don't you?"

"Death, I'd think." The Kyprists feared that *Sulane* and *Ascentatic* had come to burn the islands and cauterize the plague. "They want to assure Ormsment they have the plague under control."

Shao smirked. "What if Ormsment tells the Kyprists you're a renegade? What if she demands your head?"

"Why, then my naval attaché will have to tell them who's *really* gone renegade, won't she?"

"What if I don't? What if I let Ormsment take us?"

"Then we'll die together in our formalwear."

Shao studied Baru with narrow-eyed amusement. "And if I'm—"

"Ormsment's deep-cover agent, waiting for the perfect moment to betray me?"

"Exactly."

Baru tugged her toward the gangway by the chain at her throat. "Then I'll raise you both a toast before I die."

THE EMBASSY

S HE took Iraji!"

Apparitor burst into my cabin with his hair in wet ringlets. He caught me halfway into my quarantine gown, still doing up the horrid mantis-skeleton: this made me cross enough to stay silent about the tripwire on my door. He tangled himself up very thoroughly, and after a few hops and an exclamation about my virginity, he fell on his ass.

I looked down at him where he sprawled and selected the drawl of an aristocrat. "I shouldn't worry about Iraji. Baru is always fixing on this man or that as her disposable companion."

"Iraji is not *disposable!*" Apparitor kicked at the wire, and then, with a sudden blank-faced calm, drew his dive knife to slash himself free. "I want him safe. I want him back, Yawa, and if I lose him I'll—"

I sighed heavily. I was in truth already nervous. Himu's fingers worked in my gut: Execarne had arranged his operation for tonight, and if I were not back on *Helbride* by dawn, Baru safely packed away, there was every chance Ormsment and Tain Shir would find me. "What will you do to me, Svir?"

"I don't know." Apparitor groaned. "I think he went with her voluntarily."

"Why would he do that?"

"I'm not going to tell you."

"Then whatever can I do to help you?"

Apparitor hopped to his feet. He smelled so strong of whiskey I thought for an instant I'd stumbled into an operating theater. Ghastly pink round his eyes, the waxing crescent of a grief moon, and he'd chewed his nails past the pale tips of their beds.

"You've got to call it off," he said. "What you're about to do. You can't go ahead with it."

He knew. His crew had probably seen Faham flashing messages ashore in the night.

"I won't call it off."

"You *have* to. Iraji could be hurt."

"You've lost worse than one dear boy to this mission."

"Not him. I won't lose him. Not in this place."

"You've been perfectly willing to risk him before—"

Apparitor's throat had a tantrum. His tendons stood out in such defined rage I thought they would peel his jaw wide open till his cheeks ripped. But above his chin he was blank, blank, calm and green-eyed composure: his teeth did not even click. I swear to Wydd that for one moment all my old street instincts told me he would kill me.

And so I knew I'd found something important.

"Perhaps," I purred, "if you explained *why* he mattered so much to you . . . ?"

He lied to me. He lied a long weepy lie about his broken heart, his burning passion, his fear for his lover Lindon Satamine. How could he survive the loss of his only comfort, dear Iraji? Hadn't I heard their frantic grappling these past nights?

I listened to him and did not believe one word. Their burst of carnal appetite was not desperation but the product of Apparitor's meddling with vidhara, a remarkable aphrodisiac: he and Iraji had been very careful preparing Baru's dose, which required some experimentation.

But at the end of his performance I assured him I would delay the attack.

"Tonight?" Execarne murmured, as I came up onto the quarterdeck.

"Tonight." He was deep into his drugs, red-eyed and slow of tongue. "Will you be sober for it?"

"Not if I can help it," he said. He'd explained to me that he saw the world as a construct produced by the locus of human perceptions. By drugging himself into calm, he claimed, he was smoothing out the world around him, preventing the intrusion of misfortune and chaos. In that respect I thought he was very Oriati, and he certainly did seem to get along well with Prince Tau-indi. "Are there any complications?"

"Nothing of significance."

"I don't like this place," Faham said, and I followed his gaze over the rail, across the bright blue shallows, through a copse of masts to the sprawl of the kypra. I'd never been this far south before. The wind had died with the evening, and in the west the plague-flags hung like snot from the empty houses of the quarantine.

I could read the doom of this place in its law-books. All power here flowed from the single precious aquifer beneath el-Tsunuqba's stony base. The junta of Kyprist governors held that aquifer, and the easterly ports; I thought it *very* convenient that plague had struck the west, where the Canaat movement thrived in the fishing villages and cricket ranches and the shallow farms that eked out cassava and yam and pepper and saltwater rice and bok choi in sea-slime fertilizer and preparations of their own shit.

Their cisterns would run out soon. They would need to come out, through the quarantine, to get more.

And in reply the Kyprists would do exactly what Hasran Cattlson and old Duke Lachta would have done. They would use force to quell the uprising. They would not have enough.

So they would ask the two Masquerade warships at their port to use the Burn.

"I don't like the water situation," I said, as a gentle prompt to make him share *his* fear.

"I don't like . . ." He sighed heavily. "There's something I oughtn't tell you about. But it is wearing a hole in me, Yawa. Maybe soon I'll need to share it."

"I'll be ready to listen," I promised.

A very fat, very greasy, very familiar gull settled on the rail near Faham. "Aw, hello," he clucked, and patted himself for some salt pork. "Do you know who trained this little monster? Apparitor told me."

"Who?"

"One of the prisoners who traveled on this ship. A duchess." Faham fed the creature a crumb from his purse. "She studied birds on her last voyage."

BARU rowed into Hara-Vijay down a broad shallow canal carved out of the coral by the weight of monolithic stones. In the years before the Masquerade thousands of Kyprananoki had worked together to drag those stones, greasing them in fat and kelp to get them sliding, hauling the whale-gut lines, wearing the way smooth by sheer persistence. At low tide the canal could be waded on foot, if you wore tall boots and went slowly. At high tide it flooded with glowing jellies longer than a man, and the birds descended to feed on the jellies, and the jellies devoured each other, and turtles crept from the coral to snap the jellies in their beaks.

"*Oh,*" Osa said, in disgusted fascination. "Look at that!"

She pointed astern to a golden jelly, an obscenely huge flesh-bulb with arms a hundred feet—*a hundred feet?*—yes, Baru checked their length against the mile markers, a hundred feet long. A white petrel had come hovering too low to the water, as petrels did, and the jelly snared it. The shrieking bird disappeared in a slow coil of tentacles as fine as hair.

"You should avert your eyes," Tau said, reproachfully.

"Why?" Baru was queasily fascinated.

"What if you see a cormorant devoured?"

"Will it be an omen?" Shao Lune said, tauntingly. "Will it be a sign of her Excellency's doom?"

Baru felt moved to defend the Prince. "I like cormorants. They dive so well."

"They fly like shit, though," Enact-Colonel Osa said, from the other oar. Baru looked at her in surprise. She shrugged. "I did my finishing study on the flight behaviors of seabirds. Short wings, cormorants. They don't last too long up there."

Tau beamed at Baru and Osa. Baru realized Tau had maneuvered them onto a common subject. "Er," she said, trying, for whatever reason, to please Tau, "perhaps they fold their wings so often, while diving, that the behavior has begun to alter their flesh?"

"That's the Incrastic account, I suppose," Osa muttered.

"And what's yours?"

"Do you care?"

"Osa," Tau said, reproachfully. "Don't be rude." But the moment was gone.

The Oriati embassy compound stood on stilts and pilings in the lagoon, the outbuildings linked by rope bridges and floating walkways, the structures themselves built of concrete and sturdy imported Oriati hardwood fastened together not with metal but black resinous treenails. Great gold-and-jade banners hung flat in the calm. From the open-air pavilions came the delicious smell of hot honey.

The reception was underway, the Oriati having brought in smaller parties to garnish the area with principles of celebration. Tau pointed out a puzzle club from Loveport, a party of children "straight off a syndicate pirate ship, bless their little hearts" playing with the octopi in the rocky aquarium, a group of Oriati writers from Galila, which was a kypra island famous for its studios, gathered in a circle to smoke hash and mumble toward inspiration, and even a local banker in a Falcresti waistcoat throwing her daughter a birthday. The embassy staff themselves had thrown out a silken sheet on the main steps, inviting their visitors to trample on luxury (the joy of their company being worth far more to the properly trimmed household than the fabric itself).

"All is prepared," Tau said, contentedly.

"I'd say." Osa did not like the pre-parties at all. "Everyone's had a chance to case the grounds and slip in their agents."

"An embassy is not a fortress, Osa."

"It *should* be," Osa muttered.

"You would put thorns on dessert cakes if you could, Osa, to keep them from being licked." Tau aimed Baru toward the quays at the north edge of the lagoon. "I expect the Prince-Ambassador will turn out in person to say hello. Dai-so Kolos is an old colleague. Look for the laman with the curiously straightened hair . . ."

But no straight-haired ambassador waited at the quayside.

Their gondola kissed Hara-Vijay's mortared rubble pier, and they came up to meet a small party of Oriati in khangas or death-white uniforms. A lean man in a puffy white blouse stepped forward to salute them with his rapier to his brow.

"Your Federal Highness." He kissed Tau's hand, and then Baru's. "Your Excellence Barbitu Plane. Ladies of the house. I am Scheme-Colonel Masako ayaSegu. I can only offer my poor company in lieu of the ambassador's. May I send ahead for anything? A refreshment? A companion?"

"Guide," Shao whispered to Baru, "not *companion* companion."

"Trust a sailor to think first of whores."

"I wouldn't want the gava girl to grope the wrong hole."

"I don't grope at all."

Tau and the scheme-colonel began to apologize to each other: for being late, for their ill dress, for the condition of the embassy grounds and the state of the weather. Then, when Baru thought it might *finally* be over, they started reassuring each other that everything was quite all right on each point. Baru couldn't take it.

"Where's the Prince-Ambassador?" she demanded.

"With their sincerest apologies, Dai-so Kolos is away on a fact-finding mission."

"What sort of facts?"

The scheme-colonel smiled diplomatically. "They are tabulating the size and number of fish that may be caught from a little yacht. A spontaneous excursion, for their health. Of course the embassy's services remain at your disposal, Your Federal Highness."

Osa let out a very soft sigh of relief, perhaps because the embassy was in the hands of a military man and a fellow ayaSegu. Under a Termite officer (a scheme-colonel would be a Termite, just as Enact-Colonel Osa was a Jackal) surely their security would not be neglected.

"Excuse me," Baru said, loudly and rudely. "Excuse me. Are the embassy's services also at *my* disposal?"

"Yes, Miss Plane, of course."

"I'm looking for someone's parents. He is an Oriati boy. I assume he must therefore have Oriati parents. Where are your eugenic records?"

Tau blinked at her. "What are you doing?"

Baru held her body carefully still despite the urge to jitter in place. "I'm try-ing to track down the birth parents of a boy in my care. I have a portrait, well drawn, and a few snatches of rhyme he remembers. Who could I speak to about this?"

"I'm afraid Oriati Mbo is quite, ah, larger than your esteemed home, Your Excellence, and we do not practice eugenics. Therefore it can be difficult to keep a comprehensive census." Scheme-Colonel Masako offered his left hand, the hand you were taught, as a child, to keep off food and other people. "But I can, of course, bring your portraits and rhymes to our archivists?"

"No!" Baru screwed her eyes up in suspicion. "I've been *entrusted* with these documents. I cannot let them out of my hands."

"Ah. Very Falcresti." Masako glanced at Osa, who glanced at Tau, who was staring at Baru with their brows furrowed. "Is the matter urgent?"

"Not really," Baru admitted, which was to her advantage, because she needed time for word to percolate through the embassy that a Falcresti technocrat was asking questions about a mysterious boy. No—she ought to think of Iraji as a man. She ought to make a practice of it.

Masako bowed. "Then I'll ask around during the reception, and introduce whoever from our staff seems best qualified. Now, if you'll come with me, I'm sure the pineapples are approaching perfectly browned . . ."

"What are you doing?" Tau whispered.

"I'm looking for Iraji's parents," Baru said, which was the truth. She did not have to say those parents were Cancrioth, did she? She had sworn to share what-ever she *learned,* not what she already knew. . . .

On *Cheetah* she'd debated the difference between goodness and playing-at-goodness. She knew which side she was on now.

"You didn't tell me," Tau-indi said.

"It's between me and him."

"I could help."

"He doesn't trust Mbo people. He wants me to handle it."

"That's very sad," Tau said, with genuine hurt.

"The grounds are secure, I think," Osa muttered, "Masako seemed comfort-able, and he didn't show me any secret signs."

"Oh, how I wish it were so." Tau smiled wearily at his escort. "The embassy is thoroughly compromised, and Masako cannot be trusted. Something's gone terribly wrong here."

Osa frowned. "Why do you say that?"

"Because Dai-so Kolos hates fishing. They have ever since they saw me put a barbed swordfish hook through my hand."

* * *

BOLTS of fluttering sailcloth divided the courtyard of the embassy into warm shade and narrow ley lines of sunlight. Oriati griots sang soothing stories, people of wealth and influence schooled and darted in ever-shifting cliques, and even the big security men were armed only with tall glass flutes of wine. Not in an oil portrait in the Exemplaries could Baru have found a finer picture of springtime ease.

"Look at all the tits," Shao muttered. "It's like a bordello revue."

"There's very little breast partialism on Kyprananoke," Tau said, as if Shao's disapproval were born of ignorance, rather than disdain. "It's simply a matter of culture. Rather like your royalist era in Falcrest, when I believe the taboo was instead on bare calves?"

"Don't you speak of our royalty," Shao snapped. "You made them, didn't you?"

Baru rolled her eyes. "Let's split up. Tau, take Osa and go make your hellos."

"Whyever should we?" Tau protested.

"We'll center everyone's attention if we stay together." Also, she needed to begin showing pictures of Iraji and repeating the Cancrioth phonemes. "Shao, with me, if you will."

Baru was relieved to find everyone's Aphalone very good, and more relieved to find Shao Lune kept her fangs folded. They circulated about the pleasant courtyard, making introductions beneath the blooming lilacs and the chatter of little honeyeater birds. Shipping factors from a new local concern (Consolidated Kyprananoke Hulls, Largely Liable) put out feelers about sponsorship from Falcrest, for wasn't it about time that the Republic admitted Taranoke was just too much trouble as a trade port? Several dashing young local women who styled themselves griots and truthtellers confronted Baru about the possibility of civil war.

"War is a bloody business," Baru assured them, "and causes plagues. We're here as friends."

A fat Kyprananoki man in a lovely dashiki dress came at them sidelong, and archly: his body was female and the dress was androgynous, but he made his masculinity plain with paint and carriage. "Ah," he drawled, in a voice smoked by a long hash habit, "the unexpected guest from Falcrest. What a *lovely* gem in your mask. It must be a very subtle symbol of something."

"It represents obscene wealth," Baru deadpanned, taking his hand. "What a wonderful dress."

"Thank you kindly. Would you like to buy it? I'm rat broke." His eyes flickered over Shao Lune. "A net? Are you a fish?"

"I'm Miss Plane's slave," Shao said, sweetly.

The man grimaced. "Slave jokes. How modern." Oriati Mbo had, in its ancient days, entirely annihilated the practice of slavery on the Ashen Sea: one of those things Oriati people liked to shout about when drunk and determined to prove that the Mbo was the greatest nation in the world. "Well, allow me to introduce myself. Ngaio Ngaonic, trade factor for the great nation of Devi-Naga Mbo. As you might expect from a nation on the far end of the Tide Column, and thus subject to Falcrest's tariffs, I have very little trade to oversee here."

"But you're Kyprananoki," Baru said, rather too bluntly, "aren't you?"

"I am! Born and raised! But I won a citizenship and a Devi-Naga name for my work during the Armada War. Shuttled water to a stranded crew for nigh on three months." He winked at Shao Lune. "Begging your pardon for aiding the enemy."

"Granted, of course," Shao said, puzzling over Ngaio's bare chest, until she figured out what Baru had intuited at once. She was, at least, blessedly cosmopolitan, and did not need Ngaio's masculinity explained to her. "We're all of the sea, aren't we?"

"And to the sea we shall return. Tell me," Ngaio pointed with the back of a curled hand, "have you met Tau-indi Bosoka, the laman over there?"

"Yes," Baru said, cautiously, "we traveled with them."

"You poor souls. They're rather a fundamentalist bore, aren't they?"

"Quite," Shao purred, as Baru cried, "Not at all!"

Ngaio laughed. "So I deduce, from your split opinion on Tau-indi Bosoka, that you two must have different stances on the Great Embrace?"

"Oh," Shao Lune said, and laughed a high derisive laugh. "Yes. This is Kindalana's plan? Wherein Oriati Mbo signs an Act of Federation and joins the Imperial Republic?" She laughed harder. "That'll be the day!"

Baru faded away from the conversation for an instant, into a colder place, where she could pass the name *Kindalana* over her memories. She remembered Tau's voice, as *Cheetah* sank beneath them. *When I was a young laman during the Armada War, my two closest friends were Kindalana of Segu and Abdumasi Abd. Now, our great house entertained two hostages from Falcrest named Cairdine Farrier and Cosgrad Torrinde . . .*

"I'm all for joining Falcrest," Ngaio said, touching his heart. "Anything but war. War is a way to kill those who least deserve death, and enrich those who least deserve life. If I might put a word in Falcrest's ear, Miss Plane—"

"Is there an outbreak of Kettling on Kyprananoke?" Baru asked.

"Hush!" Ngaio snapped, and when this got the attention of a passing server,

he took a flute of champagne and beamed. "Do you think the Kyprists want that known? Never mind spoken openly in the Oriati embassy?"

Shao sidled in with a well-timed question. "Do you think the Oriati brought the disease?"

"No," Ngaio said, sadly, "it began out on the west edge, in Canaat territory. The locust farmers had it first. Everyone knows the Canaat are backed by the Mbo, and why would the Mbo poison their own allies? So I think the Oriati didn't bring it."

"But Kettling comes from the Mbo," Shao insisted, "it's in the legends, everyone knows the Summer of Black Emmenia—"

"Five hundred years ago."

"Nonetheless, in the Mbo!" Shao was breathing hard now, which Baru could hardly believe—what had softened her frost? She couldn't care about the welfare of Kyprananoke, so what had pricked her conscience?

Ngaio Ngaonic knew.

"To tell you the truth," he said, pausing for a delicate sip of champagne, "I just assumed Falcrest had released the plague to control the Canaat. Perfectly deniable. Perfectly natural. Your navy must have a few carriers, stashed away somewhere . . . ?"

"We would *not*," Shao Lune hissed. "On Kyprananoke? Are you *mad*? It would get everywhere. Everywhere."

Ngaio took another sip and smiled at her. "So it's not a way to slaughter all the Canaat, and leave no bases for 'pirates' on Kyprananoke before the war? I quite expect those warships that arrived recently to join in the bloodletting. And to read a mournful editorial in *Advance* afterward: 'Can't those savage islanders ever stop murdering each other? If only they'd had proper hygiene.'"

"But we don't *have* the Kettling," Shao said, with matronizing patience. "It's an Oriati disease, do you understand? It is not endemic to Falcrest. Now I ought to go check on the quality of the plumbing, before I drink any of your water."

"You ought to unbutton, too," Ngaio said, critically, "or your breasts are going to shrivel up in sweat like little baby faces."

"That does not happen," Shao snapped, and stalked off.

Baru took the opportunity to unfold her little portrait and ask: "Do you know anyone who might be this boy's mother? He recites this scrap of poetry, *ayamma, ayamma, a ut li-en* . . ."

Ngaio had no idea what she meant. A passing Oriati woman, fully pregnant, handsome in a black eyepatch, stopped to look. "Who's that?"

"A boy," Baru said, for the first of many times, "whose parents I'm trying to locate. Do you know this scrap of poetry? *Ayamma, ayamma, a ut li-en—*"

* * *

B Y the time Governor Love and the Kyprist party arrived for dinner, Baru had flashed the picture of Iraji at every Oriati person she could find, Tau-indi excepted. She would have kept on looking, too. But the Kyprists brought Ormsment as their guest.

Province Admiral Juris Ormsment had dressed for a presentation to the Emperor. The starched dress reds, the black cuff-pins, the short boots that slipped off so easily. Jeweled tiles of her merit fastened like Purge pieces at her neck. On her left hip curved an officer's boarding saber. She chatted easily with Barber-General Thomis Love, who wore a sleeveless waistcoat and an expression of immense relief. Behind them forty Masquerade marines in full battle rig stood at impassive attention, their short lances cocked at parade rest. The poles pushed the barge to a halt one inch from the quay.

"They can't step onto embassy ground," Tau-indi whispered to Baru, "without declaring war. Not so armed, and in such force."

A many-legged thought crawled over Baru's chin. She snatched at it, hissing. Tau held up their hands: "What's wrong?"

"I had a terrible thought—" They huddled under the south pavilion, among the ruined husks of pineapple. Lizards the size of short knives had come out to bicker over the pulp. "What is *Ascentatic* up to? What if they're here to help the Kyprists? What if they decide to strike this embassy, to root out whoever's funding the Canaat?"

"They'd be mad to try it. It'd be an act of war, and Parliament would purge the navy. Every last seat in Parliament wants a chance to install their pick of admirals before the banquet opens." Tau smiled against bitterness. "Your navy will be the first to pick the Mbo's fruit, after all."

Baru squeezed their hand. It was very nice to touch someone without thinking up excuses. "If worse comes to worst, and there's a fight, the embassy has security. . . ."

"There are families here, Baru."

There are families everywhere, Baru thought. That has never stopped anyone: except the people who lose.

Scheme-Colonel Masako stepped out to greet Barber-General Love and the province admiral. There was a general exchange of courtesies and salutes, and then Ormsment and two bodyguards—both tall capable men, neither one plausibly Tain Shir—marched straight up the long boardwalk toward the embassy courtyard. A drummer beat out a few bars of the Whale Words, something about ships: Baru could hum it, but never remember the verse.

"Well," she said, straightening her lapels, "shall we go meet her?"

Tau swallowed. The chains between their nose and ears rustled and chimed. "I know Ormsment. Shall I make introductions?"

"No need. We became acquainted over dinner last year. Where's—" Baru whirled in a thrill of panic. "Where's Shao Lune?"

"I'm here." She stepped out of Baru's rightness, Osa shadowing her at a careful two strides. Shao had picked a dart from one of the steward's trays, the sort used to lance meats: she threw it, offhandedly, at one of the overhead balconies. Someone up there flinched. "I didn't find anyone sneaking in through the plumbing. Maybe Ormsment's given up."

Baru arranged herself. "Let's go find out. Shao, why don't you button up?"

"Why?"

"It's formal, that's all."

Shao Lune stared at her former admiral with petty serpentine hate. The woman who had complicated her career, Baru thought, the woman who had endangered Shao's very favorite thing, which was herself.

"Let her think we're fucking. Let her think I've gone mad. It'll make her sloppy, to see one more of her sailors lost to you."

AMINATA tipped the griot a silver piece. The girl kissed the coin in delight, wished bright bells and soft scars on Aminata, and danced away in glee. Aminata, feeling very bittersweet, sighed.

"She thought we were from the Mbo, didn't she," Lieutenant Faroni whispered. "That's cute. It's like we made her a real griot."

"They don't even have a griot school here," Aminata groused. "I bet she hasn't learned eidesis, even. It's all fake."

"So are we," Gerewho said. And he was right. Aminata's little party had come disguised as Oriati spiritists trying to sell Captain Nullsin's good whiskey, and thereby secured themselves a vantage as the reception kicked off. Aminata's interrogation of Ake Sentiamut and her fellow rebels had left her and Captain Nullsin in a bitter bind. The rebels said Ormsment was a mutineer, on a mad mission of revenge against Baru. But they themselves were rebels, traitors, left behind by Baru's design. Aminata couldn't take their word alone.

She needed a glimpse of how Baru and Ormsment reacted to each other.

When Baru walked in arm in arm with a cruel-looking navy woman, Aminata hired one of the local "griots" to keep an ear on Baru's party and learn the woman's name.

Her name was Shao Lune, the griot reported. Aminata's files said that she was Juris Ormsment's staff captain.

Aminata covered her eyes and groaned in horror.

All the signs seemed to confirm what Aminata had most feared. Baru was building a mutiny inside the navy. A mutiny that would draw in unreliable officers to be purged . . . all part of Cairdine Farrier's grand plan to provoke Oriati civil war and insinuate his agencies into the Mbo. Yes, Ake Sentiamut and her friends insisted that Juris Ormsment was on a mutinous mission to *kill* Baru . . . but here was Baru, dangling Ormsment's staff captain on her arm.

Which made it very hard to believe they weren't in league. Just as Baru's letter to Aminata had suggested: *I intend to recommend you to Province Admiral Ormsment* . . . And who else was with them? Oriati Mbo's ambassador to Falcrest, Tau-indi Bosoka.

Tau-indi whose ship had been lost at sea. Aminata had fished a cabinet full of *Cheetah* dishes out of the water herself. The destruction of a Prince-ship would be a tremendous goad to war. And where better to begin that war than here on Kyprananoke?

There was the question of Tau-indi Bosoka's motive. But they had a long record of contact with Cairdine Farrier. By blackmail or by greed they might be in on Baru's scheme—stoke tensions, draw out the navy's warmonger admirals the way she'd drawn out Aurdwynn's rebel dukes, eradicate them.

King's balls. It was so hard to find a way to deny it now.

AMINATA remembered Rear Admiral Maroyad's orders. *Find Baru Cormorant. Learn who she's working with—every last name. Bring her back here if you can. And if you can't, remove her from play.*

She remembered what sweet well-hung Calcanish had said to her on the Llosydanes:

Beware Baru Cormorant.

But—a stupid silly girlish part of Aminata kept saying—but Baru's your *friend*. Baru was the one who made it. The federati who did her duty, took her exams, and got her post.

And there was the one matter of the letter from Tain Hu, which stirred in Aminata all sorts of horribly naïve and anti-Incrastic sentimentality about honor and friendship and deathless trust.

The evidence against Baru was overwhelming. She was leading a false prowar mutiny just as she'd led a false rebellion in Aurdwynn. Aminata just didn't want it to be true.

She had *Ascentatic*'s double complement of eighty marines waiting on her signal to storm the embassy, arrest Baru and Ormsment, and fight their way back out. It would possibly be enough to start a war: locally, at minimum. Everywhere, in the worst case.

She could with one shot of a flare pistol bring the storm surge of history down on the Ashen Sea. That was her duty. It made her itch.

"Mam?" Faroni whispered. "Are you with us? Ormsment's coming in now."

"You ever look back," Aminata muttered, "and ask yourself, fuck me, what did I do to deserve this?"

"Never, mam," Faroni said, hurriedly: as if she was afraid Aminata would go off on a ramble about the weight of duty. "There's Baru again, and Shao Lune, and the Prince-Ambassador . . . and now that's Thomis Love with Ormsment. Quite a collection, isn't it?"

Gerewho adjusted his sommelier's nose, a grotesque elephantine trunk which was supposed to enhance one's grape-sniffing, so he could speak clearly. "Lieutenant Commander?"

"You say *mam*, Ensign, you don't pronounce my rank."

"Yes, mam, it's just—the mam over there made a sign to me."

"The mam over there?"

"Yes, mam, the—er, that mam." He pointed to the staff captain Shao Lune, who held her gloved hands clasped behind her back as she waited, two steps back from Baru, to be presented to Juris Ormsment.

"The staff captain," Aminata said, "what sign did she make?"

"Well, mam," Gerewho said, "if I'm not mistaken, it was the navy cant for *I'm drowning: throw me a line.*"

Aminata blinked. "And she made this sign at you?"

"She threw a dart at me first, mam."

"A dart?"

"Yes, mam," Gerewho said, holding up a discarded meat skewer, "bounced it off my shoulder."

Shao Lune wanted them to rescue her. Which suggested Baru had her here as a prisoner, right? Maybe even a hostage? A way to control Ormsment? If Aminata could get Shao Lune out, she could be the key to the whole situation. But that would mean exposing herself to Baru.

Beware Baru Cormorant, Calcanish had said.

She will not betray you, Aminata's heart said.

Duty is what you do even when you have no reason to do it, the navy said.

Aminata put a hand on her flare pistol.

26

THE BLACK EMMENIA

THERE had been a moment in the battle at Sieroch when Baru understood everything.

An arrow pierced a shield and Baru *saw* the forces that conspired to kill the man beneath. Not merely the velocity of the arrow and the thickness of the shield; not merely the man's discipline, to keep his shield fixed in place as his brother died beside him; but, also, the lines of causality that crushed down upon this instant and forced it into the pierced-eyeball shape of itself.

She saw the mines that yielded the ore that went to the steel furnaces and then to the smith and the fletcher to make the arrowhead. She saw the old-growth trees cut down for shepherding pasture so that the people could sell wool in the new markets, the old trees replaced by softer younger wood, that softer wood made into the shield.

She saw the ancient collision of Stakhieczi desperate for farmland and Maia desperate for grazing land and the warrior traditions produced by those wars and sustained in the villages by centuries of raiding, traditions which taught the man how to hold his shield in the phalanx, and how to brace against arrows, and how to keep his position and his stance as his brother retched in the mud with an arrow up his armpit.

She saw a man's life calculated by the thrashing manypartite engine whose eternal components were enigmatic and half-glimpsed like the limbs of behemoth kraken surfacing in fog and whose outputs were nothing other than changes in the design of the machine itself: changes that were people, for the machine was of man and yet no man within it could discern its entire shape.

She saw everything. Master these forces and she would be the master of all creation.

Now, as she crossed the courtyard to greet the traitor-admiral, flanked by viper-faced Shao Lune and golden glorious Tau-indi Bosoka and the imperturbable enact-colonel, Baru again felt the inevitability of the forces that converged here.

The Masquerade had conspired to steal the Ashen Sea trade ring from Oriati

Mbo. For that they needed a southwesterly port. So the Masquerade had come for Taranoke, and from Taranoke Baru had gone into the Masquerade. And they had sent her to Aurdwynn, to execute the will of the Throne, and that execution had made an enemy of Juris Ormsment. In the name of her dead, Ormsment mutinied and chased Baru across the face of the world.

But the wake of her mutiny was wide, and if it touched her comrades, she could destroy the very navy she loved.

And so here, as close as she had ever come to her prey, she could not kill.

Baru walked within concentric wards of power. The seal of diplomatic privilege. The Emperor's mark. The force of the embassy guards. The etiquettes of Falcrest which said *you will not begin a bloodbath at a reception: that is neither subtle nor hygienic.*

Barber-General Love laughed unctuously at something Juris had said. No—Baru corrected herself—he wasn't unctuous, she was being unfair: Juris was apparently very funny. Even Thomis Love seemed like a man who might have been decent, if he hadn't become a barber-general. But Baru hated to trust these impressions.

Together the traitor-admiral and the Kyprist governor wandered west around the perimeter of the courtyard, pretending not to see Baru. Thomis had requested a treat for Juris—Scheme-Colonel Masako went ahead to fetch it. Here it was now, wheeled out by a pair of Oriati stewards, a glass-faced cabinet bearing the legend THESE WHISKEYS ARE OF HISTORICAL VALUE, FOR DISPLAY ONLY.

Juris Ormsment smashed the cabinet's glass face with the butt of her knife.

The watching crowd gasped. Juris reached through the wreckage, seized the neck of a bottle of Grendlake City Fire, and raised it, turning, in salute to Baru.

"Agonist," she said, with relish. "That's what they called you at the Elided Keep. What a name."

"Hello again, Juris."

The traitor-admiral reversed her knife. She stabbed the cork, extracted it, and dropped the cork-tipped blade on the grass. "Hello, Your Excellence," she said. "It's been a while since our dinner. A winter and a spring."

"I hope I've impressed you with my *primal vitality.*"

"I did say I was afraid I'd overlooked something about you, didn't I?"

"You spoke of my whole race, actually."

"So I did."

"Miss Plane?" Governor Love blinked in confusion. "Province Admiral, what's happening here?"

"That's not her real name," Juris told him. "She is Baru Cormorant, a renegade and a traitor. And I've come to arrest her."

"Province Admiral!" Masako feigned shock. "This is Oriati ground! Our guests are under the protection of the Mbo!"

"So they are." Juris clapped Thomis Love on the back. "What do you say, Governor? These are your islands. Willing to let the Oriati protect a traitor to Falcrest?"

Thomis Love blanched. "A *traitor*? Her? But she showed me the mark. . . ."

"Excuse me." Tau-indi put up one hand, to draw attention, and with their other they made a motion as if to shield Baru. "This woman is my guest. And I am inclined to take violation of that guest right as an act of war by the navy."

The griots stopped singing.

Baru risked one step closer. Her heart beat loud. She and Ormsment looked eye to eye. Juris's brown skin had darkened toward black beneath the spring sun. Under the red naval mask her even eyes measured Baru carefully. She was very intimidating, in the manner of women who seem unassuming until you consider the decisions they might make to hurt you. Baru swallowed and spoke. "Come home, Juris. You can survive this yet. If it's contained."

"You didn't let *Mannerslate*'s crew survive. Or *Cordsbreath*. Or *Inundore*. Or any of the others."

"They were necessary sacrifices."

"So am I. Necessary to stop you."

"Juris, please, I can offer you asylum." Tau opened his arms. "We had a lovely time in Treatymont, didn't we? You bought me that incredible jar of olive oil. Let me show you my home. There are seas in the south unknown to Falcrest, and we need good sailors to explore them."

"Even you, Tau-indi?" Ormsment's mask tilted sadly. She sagged as if struck in an organ she did not know she still possessed. "Oh, you'll live to regret you ever knew her, Prince."

"I never regret trying to know someone, Juris."

Ormsment took a breath from the whiskey bottle. Baru shivered in dismay at her slow contented smile. Juris Ormsment was savoring her last moments.

"There's a riddle," she said, "about power."

"Is it the one about the ministers and the antidote?" Shao Lune called. "You always tell that one, *mam*."

She slipped out from behind Baru, one arm snaking around Baru's waist, pulling them together hip to hip. Ormsment's fists spasmed in fury. Baru watched something smash against the back of her eyes, like a wave slapping a dam, and wished she could turn this woman, turn her or possess her rather than face her anger.

"Staff Captain. And here I was hoping you hadn't been killed as you bravely resisted interrogation. I overestimated you, I think."

"We reached an accomodation," Shao said, haughtily. "Governor Love, my name is Shao Lune. I am a *loyal* officer of the Imperial Navy."

Thomis Love held up his hands. "I don't understand."

"Juris Ormsment is a mutineer. I helped her plan her revolt, and then, when the moment was right, I joined the Emperor's agents in bringing Ormsment to justice." Her voice rose. "This pretender admiral is a fugitive charged with the highest of crimes. And if you grant her so much as a pipe to piss in then my navy will burn your little rock till it cracks into the sea. Understand?"

"I do not," Governor Love said, calmly. Baru saw the way he clasped his hands in decision. He was a quick thinker, canny under pressure. She would need to win him over. "I understand nothing. I know nothing of a mutiny, and I have only acted to honor my diplomatic obligations. The Kyprists of Kyprananoke are loyal allies of the Emperor and Its Republic. I want that on record, please. You, there, will you record that? Thank you."

Something hammered at Juris Ormsment's bones. A rhythm like a war drum, calling her to violence. Baru could see it, and it made her want to hide.

The traitor-admiral saluted Shao Lune, calmly and elegantly. "Thank you for carrying out your duties, Staff Captain. You've briefed Baru on my riddle. That saves me a little work." Her eyes came back to Baru. "Yes. It's the riddle about the ministers and the antidote. Three ministers taste poison; one lowly secretary has a dose of antidote. Each minister demands the antidote, threatening the secretary with blackmail, sterility, or violence. The riddle is, whose power wins? Which threat compels the secretary to obey? I'm very curious, Baru, for your answer."

Baru *had* actually come up with a very good answer: the only correct answer, she thought, the pithing needle which pierced the riddle and found the truth within.

The entire riddle was an Imperial trap. It put the question of power upon the actors trapped in the poisoned dinner: it set them against each other, these ministers and secretaries, and asked which of them held the "true" power. And so it concealed the agency which had arranged for these ministers to be poisoned in a room with one bottle of antidote. It distracted responsibility from the one who had *arranged* the scenario of the riddle.

Power was not the province of those who made choices. Power was the ability to set the context in which choices were made.

"May I taste the whiskey?" she asked. "I've heard prisoners ask for City Fire as their last request."

Ormsment looked at the priceless bottle in her hand. She thought for a moment. Then she hawked and spat down the neck of the bottle, and the Grendlake City Fire was ruined.

"Fuck you," she said, and offered the bottle.

Tau-indi sighed in disappointment.

"What a waste," Baru said.

"Like the death of good sailors."

"No," Baru said, moved to viciousness, "the whiskey never vowed to die for the Republic—"

Ormsment snapped over her. "Let me answer the riddle. Hush. Quiet. Let me answer that riddle about power. Who has the power here? Well, you've got the Emperor's blessing. You've got your man in command of my navy, you've got Tau here wrapped around your finger, you're well on your way to the war you want so badly. And I'm not willing to order my marines to storm an embassy full of innocents. So I can't touch you.

"But I will not, I *will not*, stand for a world in which my honest sailors are sacrificed in the name of the Emperor's intricacies. Actions must have consequences, do you understand?" She rose up and her voice dropped into her gut, into the low bawling roar of the sea officer crying against the storm, "I came to capture you, Baru Cormorant, and to hold you to account for those you betrayed. I came and I failed. I do not have the power to do it. But actions must have fucking consequences for the world to be good. I must make you face the consequences of what you've done.

"So I have sent *Scylpetaire* to take your parents."

"Oh," Baru said, as the world creased around her, a mark in the page, *before* this moment and *after*.

S HE'D thought that her mother and father would be safe from the Throne, inoculated against threat by Baru's disregard for Tain Hu's life.

But Ormsment had never known Tain Hu.

"I didn't want to do it this way," Ormsment said, her voice sober, her hands at ease, her shoulders set. "I don't threaten innocents for their daughter's guilt. It was Shir who convinced me, I want that known. Shir who was once the Emperor's agent . . . like you."

"I don't . . . I shan't . . ." Baru tried to decline to care. If she could only signal that she would let her parents die rather than surrender herself, then perhaps Ormsment would believe her, and spare her parents. All she had to do was visibly and convincingly not give a fuck.

But you can't, can you?

No more than you could've let me die.

If I hadn't had the courage to volunteer.

"So who now holds the power?" Ormsment bellowed the word, *power,* and the courtyard was silent. "You, or me?"

The power is yours, Baru thought. It is yours. The engine that manufactures all things is driven by the past: by hope and by sorrow, by fear and by rage, by all the passions and calculations of our past it conjures up the mechanisms that drive us forward into the carved channels of our futures.

And you have gone into my past, Admiral, and found the piece of the engine that drove me down this channel.

How can I go to Falcrest to outlaw the death of fathers if it will kill my last father?

"I don't want to hurt your parents." Ormsment stepped up into the ring of empty space between them and the crowd subsided around her. "I think people need to carry their own weight. You and I, we can't cast our sins down on our parents and our crews. So I'd rather we settle this ourselves."

The crowd gasped and murmured. Tau-indi stiffened with a sudden thought. But Baru's eyes were all for Ormsment, who touched her saber. "I challenge you, Agonist. Here and now, on neutral ground."

"A *duel?*" Shao Lune said, with a perverse excitement.

Ormsment nodded but her eyes were all for Baru, who was thinking of her own saber, and how afraid she was to draw it. "To the death. With diplomatic witnesses to attest to Parliament that I acted on my own. No one else dies for us. No great wars begin. We settle this like women."

Baru would die if she went into the ring with Ormsment, Ormsment who had been in real battle. She would be run through. The fear of it made her hands tremble and her spine hurt and the stubs of her missing fingers ache. Run, Baru, her bowels urged her, run, run! But she stood there expressionless and trapped. She *couldn't* duel—there were political reasons, too, of course, very important political reasons—for if Baru signaled any care for her parents here, then the Throne would know that she could be controlled through Salm and Solit. Then they would be snapped up and enslaved.

But what if she turned her back on Ormsment? What if she said, so be it, send your ship to take my parents, give my parents to your nightmare Tain Shir?

They might be maimed. They might be keelhauled to death and their severed limbs would sink but their bloated stub torsos would drift on pockets of corpse-gas. And if they died Baru would never know if she had done them proud. She would never have a chance to tell Pinion she was forever her mother's faithful daughter. She would never tell Solit she was still the greatest thing he had ever made.

But maybe that was how it had to be.

Wasn't that how her story went? Wasn't she supposed to sacrifice everything to see her work complete? Every time she'd met an obstacle in Aurdwynn, she'd been able to sacrifice someone to defeat it. Muire Lo and Nayauru, the dukes and duchesses, Xate Olake, Tain Hu—yes, yes, she couldn't fight, if she died in a duel here she would fail Tain Hu—

> Baru, they're your *parents*.
> They never volunteered as I did.
> You must be brave for them!

Baru couldn't decide. She wanted to scream, to rage and howl, to grip her ribs and tear them wide open so the torment would slump out of her and pool like intestines on the flagstone. She wanted these calculations out of her head forever. Like a ship's mainmast she was only kept from toppling by the two powerful tensions pulling her to each side.

Ormsment waited with her hand on her sword. The crowd was utterly rapt.

And then Baru felt relief. Hideous warm relief, soiled, pathetic, like pissing herself. At last it was over, and there would be no more loss. She could give up. She could close her accounts. If she fought and *died* here she would never have to spend a life again—

"Baru."

Tau-indi's breath warmed her cheek. The little laman had to pull themselves up on their tiptoes by Baru's soldier to whisper in her ear. "Baru, breathe. Listen. We got out of *Cheetah* together, didn't we? We were locked into a dying ship and trim saved us."

"I saved us," Baru croaked.

"You did. Trim is nothing but people. Believe in that trim again, Baru. If you go into this duel to protect your parents, if you are truly and selflessly devoted to saving them—" Tau swallowed, and went on, with warm hope. "—I tell you that you cannot lose."

"Trim isn't real that way," Baru whispered. "Trim won't stop a sword."

"People are real."

"Will Osa stand for me? Is that what you're saying?"

"No!" They laughed as they sighed. "Baru, you *must* face this yourself. Think of all you've achieved these past weeks—"

But what had she achieved, really? Compared to her time in Aurdwynn, where she had ruined currencies and ordered massacres and torn down an entire aristocracy? She'd thrashed and sweated in misery on *Helbride*. She'd upturned the Llosydanes like a cluttered breakfast table looking for the scent of Abdumasi Abd's sponsors. She'd written letters for Ake and the Necessary King, and nabbed Tau off their sinking ship, and cringed from Tain Shir, and fled from a mutiny, and lost two fingers, and suffered a seizure, and hurt, hurt so terribly and so often . . .

She did not have the Cancrioth. She hadn't reached Falcrest. She was no closer to liberating Taranoke. Her grand plan to pitch Falcrest into a war on two fronts was still embryonic.

"I've done nothing," she said, flatly. "I've made nothing."

"You've found people," Tau whispered, with urgency, and trust, and a soft encouragement Baru knew she never deserved. "Yawa and Svir have come to know you, haven't they? You've met me, and Osa, and Iraji, who you clearly care to protect. That lovely diver who was at your side when we met. And I *know* you want your parents safe. I know you care for them."

I do, Baru thought. I want Mother and father Solit to be safe. And I want Ulyu Xe and her companions safe, too. And even Shao Lune, though she looks very excited to watch me die.

"You are bound to Ormsment, now," Tau murmured. "Isn't she here because of you? Because of the pain you caused her? She is no less your companion. You are less alone than you once were, Baru, and that is all of everything. Go forward! You will be safe."

"You want me to *kill* Ormsment?"

"I want you to trust in trim," they said, as they smiled up at her. "No one will die here unless it is deserved. Ormsment refused the peaceful way."

"It's a duel to the death, Tau!"

"It's a duel to the end. If you win, killing her is a *choice*. I told you that I would ask you to face what you could not face, didn't I? And you swore on your parents that you would not lie to me. Now trim has called that oath back on you and given you a chance to prove you are worthy of your parents. This is a test, Baru! A test of your trim! I tell you that if you go against Ormsment now, and if you have in true faith tried to help your parents and all your companions, if you have honest intentions and good hopes, the bonds you have built will protect you and help you see this through. Face what you have done to her, Baru. Acknowledge she is real. It is the only way."

But, Baru thought, Tau, I haven't been honest. I haven't told you what I'm doing with the little portrait of Iraji. I haven't told you the Cancrioth are here. So even if you're right, and this is a test, I will fail, I will invite the most hideous disaster, and you'll know that Ormsment was right.

You will regret ever knowing me.

She hesitated there with Tau's lips up at her ear and her right side turned to Ormsment.

And on that right side,
up on the balcony above the garden,
there was Aminata.
Looking down in anguish, as if all she wanted
was to leap down and come to Baru's aid.
Aminata! It's me!

And from the corner of her eye Baru saw Scheme-Colonel Masako's face. She couldn't name the expression but she recognized it instantly, because she had made it herself so many times. It was the mask of an agent keeping their tenuous calm in the instant before a secret arrangement came to fruition.

On some venal, calculating level Baru must have seen that face and thought, oh, good, the duel will be interrupted, and I'll be spared.

That was the impulse that made her take the first step into the circle.

T HERE was a better world, a world Aminata could not imagine how to find, where she would vault this balcony and land light-footed among the gaudy important people below. And she would call out, "Ormsment! I know you're a traitor!"

Then she would step forward, between her friend Baru and the traitor Juris Ormsment, to offer herself as Baru's fighter in this duel. She would take her old boarding saber (Baru had kept it! She had kept it close! Like the cormorant feather in Aminata's shrine!) from Baru's hands and raise it up to guard. And whether she lived or died, in Falcrest they would hear of what had happened on the embassy island Hara-Vijay, where Lieutenant Commander Aminata dueled the Traitor-Admiral Juris Ormsment in defense of the Emperor's own. And they would all marvel that such gallantry could yet spring from such old soil.

Ake Sentiamut *insisted* that Ormsment was a mutineer.

But—*but*—

What if Juris was about to save the entire navy from purge? What if she'd discovered Baru's scheme?

Aminata's hearts and hands ached to go save Baru. She was *so close.* Just one leap and one shout and they would be together again, and all this uncertainty could be resolved. . . .

But what if throwing in with Baru set Aminata against Samne Maroyad, who trusted her? Against Captain Nullsin, who'd helped her dig out that burnt boy? And his orders were to obey the chain of command until they had proof positive Ormsment was a mutineer.

So Aminata kept her hand on her flare pistol and squeezed her jaw shut, and although she knew she would regret her inaction for the rest of her life, her duty pinned her in place.

"COME on!" Ormsment barked. "They said you were brave at Sieroch. Will you be brave for your parents now?"

As if by an outside will Baru was stepping forward. Her hand was on the hilt of her saber, Aminata's boarding saber, and her mouth moved, her tongue curled, she spoke: and a soaring freedom took her heart. She could not bear the choice as Baru Cormorant. So she made the choice another woman would have made.

She said, without knowing the words until they left her mouth,

"I stand for Tain Hu."

And she drew, and the saber came out with an eager rasp, the blue killing edge as long and lunar as the underwater moon she had hallucinated while she drowned. Enact-Colonel Osa nodded once, in satisfaction and respect. The crowd murmured, and children were drawn away, and Juris Ormsment drew her own saber with hydraulic grace: the rage that animated her pumping itself down her arms, into the blade. She went down to the plow guard, her left foot far out front and her hilt tight against her stomach with the blade tipped up towards Baru's face.

"You didn't order me shot dead," she said, with wary respect. "You didn't beg the embassy for protection. You didn't run."

"I love my parents," Baru said, and that was the truth.

"Come on, then," Ormsment said. Baru looked at her and saw surprise: the surprise of a woman suddenly at peace, after so long she had forgotten how it felt.

Baru put up her saber to the high ox guard, two-handed like a longsword, like Tain Hu's own favorite blade, and waited for the first strike.

And then the dead invaded the courtyard.

"I'M thirsty."

She was a stooped Kyprananoki woman in a black caftan and a hood, and she walked with a cane. Her voice came very weak. If not for the hush she might never have been heard.

"I'm thirsty," she croaked. From the shade of a lilac tree she stumped toward Governor Love. There was something wrong with how she moved, sore and roundabout, as if she had to fold herself away from certain inner pressures.

"What's this?" Scheme-Colonel Masako pointed to her, drawing a general sigh from the audience, who hoped the theater would reach a proper climax with Baru's surrender. "Excuse me, mam, are you with the birthday party—?"

"I'm thirsty," a woman in a broad pregnancy khanga called, and when she stood up Baru saw that she was fat with child and that the child had gone wrong. Black blood streaked her calves and ankles.

Black blood. Oh Himu. Baru stumbled backward from the duel, fumbling to scabbard her sword, turning desperately to find Shao Lune and Tau. There was a moment for Ormsment to sneer and begin to pronounce *coward*, and then—

"*I'm thirsty!*" the pregnant woman screamed, and her scream went raw, and she doubled over a cramp or contraction, the grass beneath her blackening with a fat drop of blood; she was in the middle of a miscarriage, but she kept her face up, glaring at Governor Love, her trembling fists raised. "*I'M THIRSTY!*"

"I should like to leave," Tau whispered, drawing Baru into the crowd. Osa was already pushing people aside.

"We have to go," Baru hissed. "Shao, lead the way, I know you found a way out—"

A man in the crowd of partygoers threw back his white Kyprist mask. His teeth were black. His eyes streamed blood. A chevron cut across his right shoulder marked him—the documents had said—as a Canaat fighter; Pran Canaat meant *the world for people,* but what made everyone shout wasn't the chevron but the blood that poured from his nose and mouth and eyes, a second mask of blood that ran thick like new clot.

"I'M THIRSTY!" he howled, and he clawed two handfuls of blood off his face and lunged for the nearest man. "DRINK ME!"

"*PRAN CANAAT!*" another bleeding throat shouted. "*DOWN WITH KY-PRISM!*"

Ten of them, Baru counted, twelve, fifteen, their caftans opened, their masks removed, the bleeding dead who raised their faces with cries of *I'm thirsty* and *Pran Canaat!* and offered their sickness to share. The courtyard rang with screams. Blood and fluids on the grass. The Scheme-Colonel Masako watched it all with a little smirk of satisfaction. Masako, of course. Masako whose lies had tipped Tau-indi off to something wrong, Masako whose embassy had been accused of funding the Canaat rebels—

He had smuggled these sick rebels into his own house. Why? Why? How could he benefit? Because Barber-General Love was here, and so many other Kyprists.

There was no more time to think.

The woman with the cane fell on Governor Love. Ormsment and her body-guards had flinched away, afraid as only a good Incrastic could be afraid of the plague—and now the woman was on Love, tearing at him, clawing off his mask, spitting, shrieking, and a knife flashed in her right hand—

Thomis Love screamed like a wretched child.

"I'M THIRSTY," the woman screamed, "AND YOU DRINK!"

She disemboweled herself.

Baru would never forget it: the way the woman opened her innards to smear her death across the Barber-General. She bled and slithered on him in rapture—Tain Hu had known this, she had told Baru, *madness is a way to power*—oh Wydd, make her *stop* that ecstatic screaming, as her organs fell thickly over the Kyprist governor—

Love howled. His mouth was full of black blood.

Ormsment blew a wooden whistle and forty *Sulane* marines rushed the embassy.

THEY'RE Canaat." Faroni reached for her weapon. "They're inside the walls."

Aminata saw a man bleeding from the eyes and she knew at once what it had to be. *The bushmeat defense,* the navy files called it, but it would forever be the Black Emmenia to her, for she had heard stories of the green-black blood in the orphanage.

Someone had eaten one of the forbidden meats from the forbidden place. Someone had done it here, on Kyprananoke, and then they had shared the behemoth sacrament of their blood.

"They're *sick*," she said. "Get up. Get out. Now."

And she fired the flare pistol up into the sky, to call *Ascentatic*'s marines.

Faroni jumped onto Gerewho's cupped hands, leapt, caught the eave above, and hauled herself up on top. "You next, mam," Gerewho panted. "Hurry!"

"Wait—I have to find—"

Baru had disappeared in the crowd. Where? Where was Baru? Aminata had to follow her! There was the Oriati ambassador in their bright khanga—running for an archway—there was Baru! But she was headed *into* the embassy! She would be caught inside!

"Fuck," Aminata snarled, because she would never, could never be at peace again unless she got to talk to Baru one more time. Just once, to understand, to know the truth. Did she remember Aminata? Had they really been friends?

But Baru had gone.

She stepped onto Gerewho's hand and pulled herself onto the roof. Her marines swarmed up ladders from the reef behind the embassy to meet her. "Lieutenant!" Aminata called, marking the woman in command. "Take your first company and blast holes in the roof! Get down there and get everyone out! I want diplomatic protections—this is a rescue operation!"

"The courtyard's dirty!" a marine bawled. "Dirty blood in the courtyard!"

"It's Kettling!" someone shouted, to general dismay. "It's the fucking Kettling! They set it loose!"

"Look at their eyes! Their eyes are bleeding!"

The sergeants brayed for discipline.

Aminata had the space of a breath to decide what to do. Without orders she would lose control of the marines. She had no time to lay out the facts. All she knew was that there was live plague in the courtyard below, she was the officer in command, and she had a duty to discharge—

—*but Baru was down there*—

—but it was her duty, her duty to be sure not one splash of dirty blood made the waterline—

"Second company!" She pointed down into black blood hell. "Burn it!"

SULANE'S marines came through the front gate in a blast of sparklers and a wall of pepper smoke. They were carrying the grenades in their fists, and the smoke streamed back across them in the sea wind, parting over their masks, maning them in chemistry.

They hit the crowd with the blunt end of their spears. Ormsment beat her way toward them with a broken whiskey bottle.

"They've blocked the way out!" Baru shouted, over the screams. "We can't get back to the boat!"

"Shit." Osa herded them away from the chaos. "Shit shit shit."

"Tau." Baru grabbed their arm. "Did you find the shadow ambassador?"

"I did, I did, we passed the signals—"

"Do you see her?"

"Yes! Over there, she's calling to us!" They pointed to an archway into the embassy's manor house. A woman beckoned—why, it was the eyepatched pregnant Oriati lady Baru had spoken to earlier. "Osa, get us that way."

Baru caught sight of Ngaio Ngaonic, a napkin wrapped over his face, shoving determinedly through the screams to the woman in the pregnancy khanga, who was miscarrying, publicly and horribly, her child probably long dead inside her, her body sustained by drugs and madness. She screamed in convulsive agony, and came up again, raising her fists, *"KYPRISTS DID THIS!"*

The Black Emmenia, Baru thought, it's the Black Emmenia, and Ngaio knows it's fatal, so why is he going to help her—

But that was what people did when the world went mad. They tried to help.

Someone on the balcony above the madness fired a Falcresti flare pistol. A sputtering blue spark arched up past the seabirds. Baru followed the arc of smoke down to a tall Oriati woman in local clothes who looked exactly like—

Aminata? *Aminata?* It couldn't be!

"Aminata!" Baru shouted, waving. "Aminata, it's me!"

Then she remembered her fear that Aminata was Cairdine Farrier's agent.

"What are you doing?" Shao Lune hissed, pulling down Baru's arm. "Don't draw attention!"

Ormsment's marines beat at the crowd with the long shafts of their lances. It was not enough, there were too many people and they were too desperate to get out, and the black blood was driving them. A sergeant bawled an order, *"Ring smoke! Throw!"* The marines ripped their grenades free and the fuses spewed thin jets of sparks as the smoke went up: smoke, thank Devena, not fire.

A man clung sobbing to a screaming Kyprist surgeon. He was bleeding from empty eye sockets into the surgeon's hair.

Shao Lune pulled Baru. "Stop watching! *Go!*" Osa had actually picked up the Prince-Ambassador. Together they plunged through the crowd toward the archway, where the silhouette of the shadow ambassador beckoned, here, *here.* Something wet splashed on Baru's face. She clawed at herself in silent shock—it was only someone's wine, hurled—a Kyprist staggered past her with a crossbow bolt in his chest, blinking rapidly, as if to clear his head—

Falcresti marines appeared on the rooftops. They wore dark green slashes on their masks: Ascentatics. They're going to burn us, Baru thought. I know that's what they'll do. They're confused, so they'll burn everything.

"Tau," she said, "Tau, I'm sorry." The lilacs were all torn from their branches, swirling underfoot. "Tau, I'm so sorry."

Tau would not look at her.

"In here," the woman in the archway called, and then they were hurrying through into a low stone hall, and the woman lowered a steel portcullis behind them, chaining it shut, sealing them inside, away from the screams and the spreading death.

* * *

INSIDE: stucco walls, a low arched ceiling, soft light, quiet.

Tau-indi wept fiercely and succinctly. Baru tried to imagine what they might be thinking: how they had said the duel was a test of Baru's trim, and what they might conclude from the way that duel had ended. A wound, they would think. A wound in trim . . .

Tau touched their throat, spoke a silent word, and clasped Osa's hand. "What's happening?" they asked, without panic, but with absolute sorrow. "I heard the cries. Canaat rebels, I think. How did they get in?"

"Masako let them in," Osa growled. "That fuck."

"Why?" Tau said, but their flinch away from Baru said they already knew. A wound in trim admitted disaster and tragedy into the human world . . . and when they had called on Baru to prove her trim, what had appeared but the Black Emmenia itself?

The shadow ambassador's pregnancy gave Baru a thrill of protective horror—oh, keep this woman away from the Kettling, lest the Black Emmenia take her, too! She had the classical Oriati brow, slashed by the leather band for her strapping black eyepatch.

She said, by way of hello: "Apparently Scheme-Colonel Masako has decided to support a Canaat coup against the Kyprists. He is using the embassy to pen and reduce the pro-Falcrest leadership."

"Where's Dai-so?" Tau demanded.

"Fishing."

"Dai-so hates fishing—"

"They're on the wrong end of the lines," the shadow ambassador said, grimly.

"Masako killed them?" Tau's tears became a low, unexpected growl. "Dai-so's dead?"

"I'm afraid so. There's been an . . . adjustment here. The Termites wanted to fund the Canaat against the Kyprists, so we'd have a harbor here, on Kyprananoke, when the war began. Dai-so objected, on grounds of trim, and the Termites—I'm sorry. There was nothing I could do."

Tau took a ragged breath. Paused. Blew it out. "Well. I'll see to Masako's trim for that. Will the coup spread?"

"All across the kypra. The Canaat are coming across the quarantine now, storming the east side. It's civil war."

"The Falcresti warships will step in to stop them?"

"I expect so."

"Will they set fire to the infected islands?"

"Without question," the shadow ambassador said.

"We have to stop it." Tau-indi switched to Takhaji, the old tongue, for a short passionate conversation with the shadow ambassador.

"Check your clothes," Shao Lune hissed. "Check everything." She and Baru went over each other for any black blood: there was nothing on them but wine. Baru slumped against her in relief. The woman held her for a moment. It was not a selfless act, nor generous, nor very kind. But it was the warmest Shao had ever been.

"Kettling." Shao drew away. "It's actually Kettling. I thought the Oriati exaggerated it to frighten us. Who would be mad enough to let it out?"

"I thought I saw Aminata," Baru said, stupidly.

"Aminata isiSegu? The Burner of Souls? Maybe Maroyad sent her down from Cauteria, to help handle the Oriati." Shao gave a pop of incredulous laughter. "Even the Burner could probably learn a trick from these savages. King's balls, that woman with the cane. She really disemboweled herself?"

Baru could only nod.

"Savages," Shao Lune repeated.

"No," Baru said, slumping to the ground. "She was dead anyway. She decided what her death would mean."

"She disemboweled herself, Baru."

"She fought with the weapons she had."

A blast echoed down the hall. Hot air blew on Baru's stitched cheek. Tau-indi and the shadow ambassador looked up from their Takhaji conference.

"It's the marines," Osa said. "They're coming in to take prisoners."

Baru thought, I must be taken, I must go back to Aminata, and to Ormsment. I must give myself over and save my parents. I must. She even started to get up.

"Where are you going?" Shao snapped. "Don't be an idiot."

"I have a way out. Please follow me." The shadow ambassador led them toward a very narrow stone staircase. "We'll get out under the reef."

"That's suicide," Shao Lune protested. "You mean for us to swim all that way?"

"We'll be fine," the shadow ambassador said. Baru thought she had the air of a woman who knew more than everyone about what would happen next. "I have a guide."

They plunged down stairs carved into volcanic rock, trampling on each others' heels, swearing, chased all the way by the screams and the big-bell tones of a fire alarm. Shao Lune held up a scrap of cloth and watched it bend. "The fire is drawing up the air."

"Those poor people," Tau whispered. "Those poor people. They came to celebrate."

"Trim, huh?" Osa said, bitterly.

"Have faith, Enact-Colonel," Tau said, but it was the weakest Baru had ever heard them. And they looked at Baru in fear and horror.

Baru thought, with dull guilt: I wished for something to interrupt the duel, didn't I? I wished for it.

They went sideways through a corridor so narrow Baru was afraid the shadow ambassador's pregnancy wouldn't fit, but she was agile enough. Now water lapped at their feet. A black pool opened before them and the passage plunged down into it. There was nowhere else to go.

The shadow ambassador grabbed a rope that trailed down into the blackness and showed Baru how to loop it around her right wrist so she could cling to it. "Like this. It will hurt. You'll be pulled so quickly you'll think you're going to be dashed to your death. But don't let go until you see sunlight above you, understand?"

"No I do not." Baru was not going to get on the rope until she understood. "Why are we tying ourselves to this rope?"

"We have to get all the way under the Hara-Vijay reef, out into the sea."

"So we need to swim *along* the rope, don't we?"

"It's too far to swim to open water."

"Then how—"

The shadow ambassador's one good eye seemed to smile. She had a little cleft in her lip, like the navigator on *Mannerslate* (who Baru had led to die): probably it had been sewn up when she was a child, and she had learned, while healing, not to move her mouth much.

"Thank you for asking after the boy," she said. "It shows you've a good heart."

A ghost licked the length of Baru's spine, a raspy cat tongue of intuition, *something's still wrong.* . . . She stuffed her portrait of Iraji and her incryptor into the gut-pouch in her jacket pocket and tied it shut. Osa and Tau were stowing Tau's jewelry.

"Onto the rope, please," the shadow ambassador said. "We're going to be towed."

A MINATA watched them burn.

She had to watch. She had ordered this. It was her duty and that made it a weight she had to carry forever, these people who she'd watched chattering and flirting and planning their long ambitious lives, burning now, humiliated by the flame, stripped not just of flesh but of their dignity, screaming, screaming.

While she commanded marines on *Lapetiare* she'd led the taking of pirate ships, both true pirates (who mostly surrendered, but were very erratic) and Oriati privateers (who mostly fought, and were very disciplined). In the low compartments and long oar-banks of burning ships she'd fought with grenades and knives. She had definitely stabbed one man enough to kill him: slowly and in agony, she suspected, for it was a gut wound.

So she knew a little about death.

But everyone she'd killed on those ships had been a killer, too.

On Hara-Vijay, she watched her marines butcher families and children. She watched Burn fire lick across the courtyard of the Oriati embassy and claim the screaming Kyprananoki spattered in black blood. The marines on the roof with her seemed to go mad: some of them fell down trembling and refused to shoot. Some of them howled and laughed as they threw grenades. How could you bring yourself to kill children? Apparently you laughed. You laughed at the way their bones bent in the heat. You laughed at yourself because it was so *easy* that it became absurd.

People's knuckles popped in the heat. Their eyes. Their nostrils eroding. Rivulets of simmering fat. One plump Kyprananoki woman in a dashiki dress hauled herself up the trellis at the south wall, got onto the top, and hesitated. She was looking back down—at one of the Canaat, the pregnant woman with black blood on her legs, who was curled raving in the fire—oh, queen's cunt, she wanted to go back and help the pregnant woman—

"Shoot her!" the sergeant snapped.

A crossbow bolt stuck in the woman's rump. She fell southward, off the wall, out of the fire.

"Bring up the piss!" Aminata cried. The shout went down the line to the boats at the reef, where combat engineers hauled up big tubs of piss-soaked sand. But the fire was already under the eaves, up the trellises, among the purple flowers and spreading across the embassy compound. Aminata knew at once that the whole of Hara-Vijay was lost, and she ordered her marines out.

First company pulled some of the embassy's staff clear. Most of the Oriati guards had already gone.

There was no sign of Baru.

By sundown the Canaat had broken quarantine all over the kypra. All around Hara-Vijay people screamed *"I'M THIRSTY!"* and killed the orange-gloved Kyprists in the streets. The Canaat had bombs and grenades and even pistols, stupid, brutal, flashy weapons that fired sprays of broken metal and left hideous wounds. Weapons of terror.

And some of them were bleeding.

Aminata's order to burn the embassy guests had accomplished nothing. Nothing. On the Llosydanes she'd found a little boy in the wreckage of a beer-hall with his head burnt to a stump, and she'd washed that boy, and cast him into the sea, and gone to her shrine to beg Baru for answers.

She'd followed Baru to Kyprananoke. And now *she* was the one burning the children.

Her imagination would not stop chewing at her wounds. She heard Baru's knuckles popping in the heat. Her fierce storm-eyed face screwed up in confusion, an arrogant sort of dismay, *this isn't right, I didn't plan on this,* and then the fire took over her face—tendons shriveling, muscles cooking, the lips seared against the skull and rolled back to reveal a dying rictus, *Aminata, why did you burn me?* her face peeling away to scored bone, eyes empty, black holes asking, *Aminata, why did you burn me, why?*

"Mam?" Faroni whispered. They were on the boat back to *Ascentatic.* "Mam, are you . . . are you all right?"

"I think I just killed my best friend," Aminata said. She looked at her sooty gloves. "And I don't even know if she deserved it."

On *Ascentatic* she went down to the wardroom and put her boot tip against the cormorant feather wedged into the planks.

The gray quill did not bend in fear. It did not turn to look at her.

She could step down and break it in half. She could. Do you hear that, Baru? Are you alive? I am not your friend. I do my duty even when it means burning you. Friends don't do that. I cannot call myself your friend.

What if Baru was alive, and in trouble right now? What if Baru needed Aminata's help? What if Calcanish was lying, and Baru *wasn't* involved in any conspiracy against the navy and the peace?

Thoughts of treason stalked Aminata like starving dogs. She had run from dogs, as an abandoned child in Segu Mbo: the ports were desolate and abandoned after the Armada War, the orphanages unable to meet rent, the dogs of the dead left to wander and rut in the streets. If Baru really was an agent of the Empire, wouldn't Aminata be blameless for joining her?

But then she would be betraying her duty to the navy.

"Fuck," Aminata snarled, and put her head in her hands. Her boot came down, accidentally, and shaved the barbules off the right side of the feather. Aminata knelt and tried to set the feather right. But it would not go back. It would not go back.

That was what she'd told Baru, the last time she'd seen her. *You can't go home. You can't find it again. Even if you go back, it's not there anymore. Someone's always changing someone else.*

Someone's always changing . . .

"Gerewho," Aminata breathed. Why had she just thought of Gerewho?

Because he'd reported that Shao Lune was signaling to him. *I'm drowning: throw me a line. . . .* Which Aminata had interpreted as a plea for rescue from Baru.

But what if Shao Lune wanted to get away from *Ormsment*? What if Shao Lune had seen *Ascentatic* crew and assumed they weren't under Ormsment's control? And that was why she was asking for help?

Why would she expect a lieutenant commander to fall outside a province admiral's command?

Because she knew something, a secret which would invalidate Ormsment's authority. If Aminata could only prove that, she could convince Captain Nullsin to help Baru—

No. Aminata beat at her temples with the heels of her hands. She was rationalizing! She wanted Baru to be innocent—framed—she *hadn't* blown up the transports at Welthony, *hadn't* manipulated Ormsment into that disaster on the Llosydanes, it was all a trick—but that was selfish fantasy. She had to do her duty.

But her duty was to gather *all* the information . . . and Shao Lune might know something . . .

It was a hunch worth checking on, wasn't it?

"Lieutenant Commander Aminata!" a seaman shouted. "*Sulane*'s sending a party! Province Admiral Ormsment's aboard. Says she wants to talk about combining our efforts. Cap'n wants all officers on deck!"

Aminata pulled the broken feather from the planks and tucked it into her collar. It itched against her throat. She swallowed. It tickled her chin a little, like a gentle finger-touch, and she had to smile.

She would find the truth. And if Baru were still alive, somehow she would pick up her friend's trail, wherever it led.

She said aloud what she wished she had cried out to the world as she leapt into the dueling circle. She said it and it felt more right than duty.

"I . . . stand for Baru Cormorant."

BARU surfaced into sunlight and shouts.

The embassy on Hara-Vijay cast a bar of smoke against blue sky. Past the reef, Loveport crackled with signal fireworks: booming fusillades requesting reinforcements from *Sulane,* from *Ascentatic,* from *Helbride,* ordering Kyprist loyalists to the shorelines, to the barricades, to their spears and machetes.

Far in the west, single yellow starbursts burst over dark villages. A Masquerade code. *Quarantine broken.*

The Canaat were coming out to claim their freedom.

Baru desperately wanted know what thing had towed her. Back in the cave a pull like a draft horse had snapped the rope taut and drawn them all down. The tunnel was too dark to see ahead, but there came over Baru a rhythmic wash, the stroke of a huge fin. As if the rope were not being hauled in by a winch or crew but towed by an animal.

As they passed out into sunlight she'd tried to squint through the wash of water and resolve the animal's form. But all she'd seen was a human skull receding before her. And its jaws were stuffed with bone as thick and spongy as marrow.

Osa and Tau treaded water, arms linked, heads together: the Prince was reassuring her of something. Baru spun her blindness round and found a boat waiting: Shao Lune had just popped up gasping at the stern, as if she'd taken the time to swim underneath and inspect the hull. Baru reached up to the boatwale to haul herself up.

Someone seized her hand. The stumps of her missing fingers crushed against wood and she screamed aloud. The hand pressed down, as if to milk the bone from the wounds, and Baru howled, howled.

"Ba-ru!" A face appeared over the boatwale: a grin full of silver and porcelain and lead and the teeth of dead men. "There you fucking are, you shit-stuffed umbilical, you dreg. Come *here.*" Strong hands grabbed her by her lapels and lifted her up to meet a knife, a sharpened hook, a curve that would pierce her throat and seize her arteries and windpipe and pull them out through the wound. The voice was a woman's, heavy Urun accent in the Aphalone, and familiar, so familiar—a storyteller's voice, thick with salt and pitch.

She sounded like her son, minus the joy.

Unuxekome Ra threw Baru down into the bottom of the boat. Her boot came down on Baru's breast and pushed: Baru's breath went out like a bellows.

"Save yourself," Ra said. She let her boot up so Baru could draw a breath, tensed, and pushed. "Lie and save yourself!"

"I have a file—" The boot came up, she drew a breath, spat on Ra's next stomp. "—of your son's deepest secrets!"

"I don't care. Try something else."

"I can give you—Xate Yawa!"

Her broad brown face with the sun behind it, noble face of a duchess, weathered face of a pirate and a grieving exile. When had she learned of her son's death? How fresh was the wound?

"I'll get to Yawa when I get to Yawa." Ra's knife glinted as she stooped. "Anything else?"

Duke Unuxekome had no children. Duke Unuxekome had no siblings. "I'm carrying your son's heir," Baru cried. "I have his child!"

Ra recoiled as if struck physically by the power of blood. Baru got a leg up and kicked her in the cunt. She fell away, knife up, growling—and then Shao Lune tackled Ra, dripping wet and shouting, "That's my *pardon*!"

"Stop it!"

It was the shadow ambassador. She stood in the prow of the boat, wrapped in a dry khanga, her eyepatch dripping briny tears down her cheek. "Ra," she called. "We need them alive. Don't you hurt her."

"Baru. Baru." Ra kicked free of Shao, grunting, narrow-eyed. She pulled herself up by the boat's tiller, false teeth clicking, and she was laughing low and hateful. "My son wrote me a letter about you. He said he wanted to be your husband. He was my only child, did you know that? He was the last Unuxekome."

Baru blindsided her to gain a moment's distance. The boat was a little felucca, two crew aboard beyond Ra. One of them, a Kyprananoki man with his lips slashed off, helped Osa pull Tau-indi aboard. "I need someone to take up strangling me during sex," Tau groaned, "and then I can maybe enjoy all these drownings."

"Ah," the shadow ambassador said, and sighed. "Prince Bosoka. I'm glad you're safely aboard. I am afraid you can go no further as you are, Your Federal Highness. The bonds you bear do not belong here. They must be cut, lest they strangle you."

Tau-indi's head rose. Their eyes fixed on the shadow ambassador. For the first time Baru could remember, there was not the littlest hope in their eyes. Only dread.

"No," they said. "Oh no."

E XECARNE touched my shoulder. "I need to tell you something, Yawa."
The deeper we'd traveled into the kypra's channels the tenser he'd grown. I almost wished he would light another joint, because his twitches and growls of dismay (as if his thoughts were nipping at him) chafed at my own tension. "Now?" I snapped. Our boat had just butted up against Baru's rented houseboat, and Iscend was poised to leap aboard. "Can it wait?"

"I don't know. I don't know if it's still here. I don't know if it'd work."

"I can't follow you, Faham."

He locked eyes with me, though I wore the quarantine mask. He was a strong man, a man of energy and charm, and it horrified me to see him hollow with worry. He said, very precisely, very rapidly, "A contingency was put in place when we occupied Kyprananoke. A way to deny the islands to the Oriati. Or to contain a pandemic disease . . . in the expectation that a plague crossing the Ashen Sea would first be detected here."

"Does this contingency matter right now? At this very instant?"

Now he seemed to stare past me. Later I would realize he was looking at el-Tsunuqba, the ruined mountain with its perilous stone shelves and heaps of ash and obsidian debris teetering above the open arms of the ruptured crater, like a cup with its broken side aimed towards Kyprananoke.

Later, when I knew about the thousands of blasting charges implanted in that mountain face, I would understand what he feared.

He was the Morrow Minister, master of spies. I was the Jurispotence of Aurdwynn, and sanitation and hygiene were my dominion, especially the containment of plague. No wonder he wanted my advice. The choice he faced was appalling.

I think that he shared with Tau-indi Bosoka a profound hope that by reaching out he could somehow bind the horror before it entered our the world.

"No," he said, nodding his head, yes, it does matter right now: but he said no. "I'm sorry."

I would tend to him once we had Baru. "Gaios," I said, "Iscend, go in and bring them out. Gaios."

Execarne waved to his clothier, the man executing the operation. Iscend led the way in, and the Morrow-men followed. They took the houseboat in two smooth minutes.

Baru, Tau, and Osa were gone. Iscend found only Iraji inside.

The boy walked like a heron with a snapped leg. Broken grace. I had my mask on and so I indulged in a terrible habit, I gave him my silent sympathy, the boy looked like he needed it.

Iraji's grief seemed to eat his face like noma.

Of all the diseases I'd treated in Aurdwynn, I think noma was the one I hated most—because it was so common, because it was so simple, because my father had it. Noma is a disease of starving children. It kills nine in ten, mercifully (the mercy is for those who are disgusted by the child, make no mistake, those who speak of *a mercifully dead child* mean that mercy for themselves).

The tenth child survives to live a bitter life.

When a starving child develops noma, the digestive factors in the child's mouth become so desperately voracious that they turn on the flesh of the face.

The mouth eats itself. First ulcers develop, and then, rapidly, a painless rot. It is incurable. Soon the tongue is devoured. Soon after the lips. The flesh of the lower face peels away. In time the bone, too, although not always.

My father suffered noma as a child. He kept a scarf over the hole where his mouth had been. When Olake and I were eight, a whore in our house—she worked in the bed next to ours, behind a curtain, and we learned how to shame her customers if they didn't pay—died of a hideous vulval rot that got into her blood. The rot looked so much like noma that my father took the blame: people said he'd put his hole on hers in the night, people said he'd cast a spell on her.

So the whore's mother came over and stabbed our father in the gut. It took him eight weeks to die. Men scream differently without a tongue.

He was the first man I ever killed. Olake told him what would happen while I brewed the tea, and then I served his cup, and father poured it down his hole and held us till he passed.

Iraji looked like a man who would drink a poison cup. "Oh, child," I said, though I wore the mask and its clockwork voice-changer, though I sounded of gears and death. "What did she do to you? Where has she gone?"

"She went. With Tau and Shao Lune and Osa. She went to them."

"Went to who?"

"I have to go to Baru. I have to take her place."

"Hush, hush, it's all right." Execarne appeared with a cup of coffee and a blanket. As he wrapped Iraji, he glanced sharply at me and made an o-shape with his fingers. We were out of time. Even now Shao Lune would be laying the trail for Execarne's Morrow-men, and we had to pick it up before the jellyfish dye ran too thin.

"She went in my place, do you understand?" Iraji husked. "I have to go to her. I can't let her do this for me."

I sat there in the itchy quarantine gown, and I think its alien weight was the only thing that kept me from throwing everything aside to help Iraji. I wanted to say, oh, child, how well I know this pain. How well I know the need to go to my twin and suffer in his place.

Baru isn't worth it, do you understand? Baru eats people.

Instead I adjusted the ticking voice-changer pressed against my throat and spoke.

"What place of yours did Baru take?"

A TREMENDOUS explosion sounded from the direction of Loveport. An Oriati mine, detonated above water. Baru imagined a police post or Kyprist warship shattered. There were fire bells everywhere now, and from the west, in constant streams and squadrons, came the boats of Canaat fighters crossing to the Kyprist east.

On the little felucca, Unuxekome Ra touched the point of her blade and swallowed. "You're doing it here?" she asked the shadow ambassador. "What if you cut too much?"

"I won't," the pregnant woman said. "The Prince's ties are thick."

What did that mean? Tau's ties of trim were thick? They were going to cut Tau's trim? Who were these people?

Baru scrabbled up to sit. A thrill in her chest. A sound like cavalry in her ears. She wondered for an instant if she were about to seize again, if this sense of everything coming together was a precursor—

"Oh gods of fire," she breathed, staring at the shadow ambassador, who was not, she realized, pregnant at all. "Oh gods of stone and fire."

Baru's plan had worked.

She'd dangled her bait, and the great fish had swallowed. She had shown the picture of Iraji, and mentioned the rhyme he knew, and the shadow ambassador had heard—

"No," Osa breathed, staring at the shadow ambassador. "It can't be . . ."

Beneath her khanga, the Oriati woman's wet dress clung to the curve of her stomach. Her small breasts were not much swollen, Baru judged. She wasn't pregnant.

With her left hand, the child's taboo hand, the shadow ambassador of Hara-Vijay touched the baby-sized tumor that filled her womb. With her right she pointed to Tau-indi Bosoka.

"No," Tau gasped, "no, no no *no,* please don't—"

"I cut you," the shadow ambassador intoned. "I cut you out of trim. Na u vo ai e has ah ath Undionash. I call this power to cut you. Alone you will serve us, Tau-indi Bosoka, alone we will be your masters, to save the nations we both love. Ayamma. A ut li-en."

"*STOP!*" Osa roared.

"Ayamma," the shadow ambassador repeated. "A ut li-en. It is done."

Tau fell weeping onto their knees. Had their hands been cut from their body, Baru would not have pitied them more, or wanted to go to them more terribly.

The shadow ambassador lowered her hand. "Well," she said, shivering now, "that's over with. Ra, take the boat west. We'll lose our tails in the kypra and then go home to *Eternal.* I'll signal our return on the uranium lamp."

"Incredible," Shao Lune breathed, staring at the Oriati. "They think they're doing *magic. . . .*"

Ra laughed as she unstayed the boat's tiller. "You stupid little girl. You think it's all theater? Because you can't understand it, it's not real?"

"It's just superstition."

"Is it?" Ra pointed past her. "Is it just theater? Is that theater, you wretched Falcrest cuge? Is *that* theater?"

A school of ghostly white jellies had surfaced behind them, thousands of them drifting together, their feeding tentacles intermingled—and through that jelly raft there came a blade like the moon.

It was a fin. A tall black dorsal fin, slightly backswept, and on the leading edge it was fitted with a steel cutting surface. And as the creature turned, as Baru realized this same beast had towed her under the reef, the whale's long body breached the surface for a moment.

Behind the fin, a bony tumor ruptured the creature's back. The growth ran down along its spine halfway to the tail. At first Baru thought it was a huge barnacle, or an infection, but no barnacle gleamed that unnatural bone-white color, sun-bleached and sterile: no infection could be so solid. The tumor had erupted from within the beast. A tumor of bone. And although the tumor knobbed and festered with hideous spines and bulbous growths, it wept no pus, the wound was clean, the skin knotted tight with scar tissue around the extrusion, even the contours of the tumor had been streamlined by the flow of water. . . .

The creature rolled lazily to bare its passing flank. A tremendous white eye-shape, blank, empty, gazed on Baru: beneath it was a single black eye, keen, aware. For a moment great teeth glimmered at her in a carnivore yawn.

Embedded in the tail end of that tumor was a grinning human skull. Its lower jaw subsumed into the flesh. Its eyes filled with furry, swollen bone.

The whale blew a gout of water through its blowhole and the blow whistled like no living whale should ever whistle, like thunder piped down a thigh-bone flute, like the mad shriek of an archon folded into the world.

Baru had found the Cancrioth.

ETERNAL

TAIN Shir shoots the maelstrom in the rowboat she took from the men she killed.

The ocean crashes up against the ruin of el-Tsunuqba, the corpse of the old mountain. Jutting obsidian half-smoothed by the sea shatters and bares fresh edges. Craters and crevasses climb skyward to a ruptured, tilted crater. The slope is sheared along flat planes where ancient and devastating forces cracked the stone. It is a landscape indifferent to humanity and if all the shaheens and suzerains of ancient days had carved their works into the flanks an eon ago not one trace would now remain.

She rows the sea below those slopes, where the waves have cut a phantasmagoria of sucking cave mouths and belching geysers. Narrow slit passes open between walls of flood basalt. Whirlpools roar in the labyrinth of debris and through one of these whirlpools Shir makes her transit to the interior of the corpse.

Earlier in the day she leaves *Sulane* at the edge of the kypra and she hails a fishing ketch to make her way south into the settled islands. The fisherman's old Psubim name is Haga el-Anagi and he has not taken an Aphalone name for he speaks to no one but the fish. Shir enjoys his company. If all the works of humanity were exiled from the face of the sea, his life would go on unchanged. He is uncontingent and unmastered.

She goes into the kypra and hunts an Oriati agent to learn where his masters nest. He will not break even when she loops his arm in a wire tourniquet pulleyed to a bucket and lets that bucket fill drip by drip with water from the solar. He dies. She finds the Termite station by inspecting sewer records for a warehouse or shop that produces too much shit.

She parleys with the spymaster there. Freely she admits her purpose which is to locate one Unuxekome Ra. The Oriati spymaster says she will trade Ra's location for information on the Falcresti ships and their intentions. Are they here to prevent the uprising? Are more ships on the way?

No, Shir says. We came for one woman. Ra will lead me to her.

Ra is in el-Tsunuqba, the spymaster says. She goes out there in a little felucca.

Thank you, Tain Shir says.

After she leaves she climbs up to the chimney and gasses the spies.

She does not hesitate in her judgment, for all who participate in the apparatus are complicit in its crimes. Even the least functionary in the lowest ministry. They had a choice to refuse to participate in the devastation of Kyprananoke but they did not. The spymaster would plead that she has a duty to her nation. The spymaster would plead that through small evils she prevents greater disasters. The spymaster would plead, I did not know what they were doing, I did not know who I was working for, how could I anticipate the use of Kettling?

Shir would ask:

Who says you have a duty to a nation? Who says you cannot reject an unjust duty?

Who says you can decide which evil is small enough to tolerate, and which is too great to allow?

Who says you should allow anyone to hold such power over you, the power to use your work for purposes you do not understand?

If the spymaster could be forgiven for helping to arrange the civil war upon Kyprananoke, then Shir could herself be forgiven for what she has done. And she cannot be thus forgiven.

Shir holds her breath, plunges the trigger on a slim grenade, waits for the crystals to crush and mix with the smoking agent, and drops the cyanide bomb down the chimney.

She watches from the roof. No one comes out.

Tain Shir fashions herself an atlatl, the bloodiest weapon in all of human existence, if you reckon the lives it has taken. As the uprising begins she kills a Kyprist and takes his patrol canoe. Paddles east. She moves between two rednesses, evening light in the west and the sooty stain of firelight thick in the east. A group of Canaat rebels hail her. When they see she is a foreigner they demand that she heave to for inspection.

Shir complies. When the biggest man steps between their boats she waits until he has one foot on each side and she embraces him and stabs him in the taint and pushes him back into his boat with a blast grenade under his body.

She takes a pistol and some shot from the boat's carnage. The rocket-powder comes in tiny clever sacs of animal gut which can be stuffed down the oiled barrel. She smiles at the workmanship. Hello again. Cancrioth craft, as she remembers it from the jungle.

She knows where Baru Cormorant will go.

Tain Shir is here to teach a lesson. A lesson about the costs of manipulation, and the hubris of forcing others to pay those costs for you, and the lie that you can serve a master today without also ceding to him all your tomorrows.

She rows south, to scout the teaching ground.

Past the maelstrom the fjord plunges in toward the flooded caldera of the dead mountain. Light kindles all around her. A million worms cling to the shadowed stone cliffs.

And by this light Tain Shir beholds the immense grandeur of the ship that destroyed *Cheetah*.

Four hundred feet of golden-clad hull. A rudder like a door to heaven. Eight masts and their rigging is so vast that it might swaddle a baby sun on the first night of its radiance. Shir computes a crew of at least a thousand. Cannon peer through windows in the huge hull.

There is no nameplate. But great symbols down the flank speak in En Elu Aumor, the sacred tongue of the Pitchblende Dictionary. They say:

Eternal.

On the high rail, a tiny man stands silhouetted against lantern light. Shir sees the long horn of crabbed flesh jutting from the eye socket. The man is onkos. He bears the immortata. The cancer grows.

The Cancrioth has come out of its fastness to walk the world again. And Baru Cormorant will be with them soon. She must be taught. She must know that she will never gain her freedom by insinuating herself with her enslavers. She must learn that she can no longer expend those around her to pay the toll of her passage into power.

Shir will use all of Baru's friends and companions to teach her.

And if Baru fails to learn, then Shir will retrieve from the place where she once hid him the man who she was tasked to capture and vanish on Taranoke fourteen years ago.

Baru's father Salm. The very wheel and shaft of Baru's mission. The man Baru has resolutely believed must be dead. For she has swallowed Cairdine Farrier's protocols of grief, which do not permit any hope of reunion. And she has made death and loss the feet she walks upon.

Tain Shir will break those feet from under Baru and cast her down into the ash of those she treads upon.

Yes. She judges this fine ground for teaching.

BARU
CORMORANT needs us
WILL you
RETURN for her?

ACKNOWLEDGMENTS

Sine qua non: Gillian Conahan, Marco Palmieri, and Jennifer Jackson.

Endless thanks to Rachel Swirsky, Ann Leckie, Kameron Hurley, Max Gladstone, Yoon Ha Lee, Brooke Bolander, Mia Serrano, Alyssa Wong, Amal El-Mohtar, Ilana Myer, and all the others who talked me through this process. I couldn't have done it without you.

Some of the wonders of Baru's world are less fantastic than they seem. The naturally occuring nuclear fission reactors in Mzilimake's hot lands existed on Earth in the past, although long before human history. Baru's brain injuries, while somewhat idiosyncratically presented, are all known to occur in real people, though I make no claim of clinical accuracy. While the specific gender of "lamen" is fictional, many societies around the world have a third gender, and the partible paternity practiced on Taranoke is as real in our world as the matriarchy of the Bastè Ana. Cancer can be transmitted not just clonally between individuals (as in the sad case of Tasmanian devils) but across species—tapeworm to human transmission has been observed. The famous case of Henrietta Lacks, in which a woman's unethically harvested and quite immortal cervical cancer cells provided the necessary human tissue for polio vaccine research, is a striking example of the durability and longevity of cancer cell lines. More than twenty tons of HeLa cancer cells are now thought to exist, spread around the world in a distributed superorganism which has contaminated other cell lines. The Cancrioth's immortata is a similar superorganism, though it has been divided into specialized "breeds" targeting specific areas of the body by the selective amplification of tumors with the desired effects. Readers repulsed by the Cancrioth's practices would be well cautioned to consider that both Oriati Mbo and Falcrest are hardly unbiased observers, and that it is easy to demonize that which offends our own sense of hygiene.

Stranger ways of life exist in Baru's world; we must not be too quick to pass judgment.

Those who fear cliff-hangers may rest assured that the end of Baru's story is written. We must only help her reach it!